The Star Chamber

John Wilkes

"Those who inflict must suffer,
for they see the work of their own hearts,
and this must be our chastisement or recompense."

— Percy Bysshe Shelley
   Julian and Maddalo

Published by Pepperdine Press Books
Order and Distribution Center
Post Office Box 3143
Fayetteville, AR 72702

This book is a work of fiction. Names, characters, places and incidents are either products of the author's imagination or are used fictitiously. Any resemblance to actual events or locales or persons, either living or dead, is entirely coincidental.

ISBN 0-9668643-0-1: $17.98 Softcover

First Edition
First Printing

The Star Chamber

A Novel By
John Wilkes

ABOUT THE AUTHOR

John Wilkes received his A.B. in History from Harvard College, an M.Phil. in Jurisprudence from the University of Oxford, and his J.D. from the University of Texas School of Law. He held judicial clerkships at the Fifth Circuit Court of Appeals and the United States Supreme Court, was selected for the U. S. Department of Justice Honors Program, and served for 13 years as Chief Deputy for the Attorney General of Texas. He was also a Deputy Independent Counsel under Kenneth Burke and an Associate Independent Counsel under George Jeffreys. Wilkes now resides in Tuscaloosa where he is a Visiting Associate Professor at the University of Alabama School of Law.

FOREWARNING

This book is pure political parody. It is fiction. I made it all up. Nothing in it is true, and you are a damn fool if you believe a single word of it.
If you get the notion that it is about real people or real events, then you should consult a physician or get yourself a cold beer.
Same goes for television and newspapers.

John Wilkes
Tuscaloosa, Alabama
January 8, 1997

Chapter One

Election night in Montgomery, and the polls had just closed. The capitol lawn was like a carnival midway, only with more drunks and less decorum. Fifty thousand people, surrounding the capitol and spilling down Dexter Avenue past the new Judicial Building, a scene that reminded me of the March on Washington set to rock music. T-shirt stand hucksters and political button vendors, trying to unload their wares, were discounting them like Confederate bonds. Four giant television screens faced out toward the crowd, and babbling pundits were filling air time with the drone of their own platitudes, saying so much and understanding so little. Not unlike the unmediated reality in 1861.

This was where James Madison Cannon had begun his political career some twenty years ago, and it looked as if it just might be coming to an end here tonight. If so, it was a fitting place for his last hurrah. Even the most ardent Democratic partisans and professional hangers-on were anxiously awaiting the results, fearing defeat at home and across the nation. Their optimism had been battered by the constant political and legal assault of the last four years. Their ranks had been decimated by deaths and indictments. Their enthusiasm had been tempered by personal suffering and financial ruin. Not unlike the harsh reality check of 1865.

I wasn't here four years ago, when Goat Hill was Mount Olympus for an evening, but I had watched on television. I knew it was an entirely different mood tonight. The country was in a different mood.

Cannon had captured the White House in 1992 and thought he was going to be the cheerleader for the American dream. He did have a few quiet policy victories, but the next four years had often been a personal nightmare for both him and his wife. The Washington press corps was the Washington press corps, and the editorial page of the *Wall Street Record* was in the *Twilight Zone*. The Republicans had taken control of both the House and Senate in 1994. Congressional committees held hearings on something different every week, pretending that the nation was facing a constitutional crisis over a newly discovered parking ticket or the firing of some disgruntled bureaucrat. Then there was the never-ending Independent Counsel investigation. And the impeachment resolution. And having the most intimate details of his personal life under the voyeuristic gaze of that three-headed hydra—the Puritans, the Pundits, and the Prosecutors. It couldn't be much fun, yet he had asked for the job. And now he was asking for seconds.

A popular local group of some repute, Little Joe and the BeeJays, rattled the speakers with their version of "The Night They Drove Old Dixie Down." Great tune, but I wondered if it might be an omen for the election outcome. I thought for a moment that I heard someone calling my name, but the band was playing so loud I couldn't tell for sure. I looked around for a familiar face but saw none. Then the music suddenly stopped. Everything stopped.

Feedback screeched from the public address system on the steps. The Fairhope High School band scurried into formation and started playing "Hail to the Chief." What was going on? Was Cannon already here? He'd never been anywhere on time in his life. People stopped talking, and I could sense the crowd flowing toward the area in front of the podium.

I saw the network anchors on the big screen and the capitol on every channel, but I couldn't hear what they were saying. What the hell? Ohio hadn't been called yet. Texas wasn't in. California was still voting. Had someone called the election? Was Cannon conceding defeat? Was he announcing his resignation?

Then Cannon appeared on the steps. Diane and their daughter Cassidy were there with him, displaying their practiced stage smiles as they waved to the throng of supporters and reporters. The crowd whooped it up as if by instinct, but their faces made it clear that no one had a clue what was happening. I damn sure didn't.

The cheering stopped almost immediately when Cannon stepped to the bank of microphones, and cameras clicked like a firing squad as he raised his hands. I was close enough now to see that he had only two sheets of paper in his left hand. That certainly wasn't a typical Cannon speech. Is this how it would end, with a whimper?

Cannon cleared his throat, once again strained from a long campaign. Very deliberately, he placed his hands on the podium and looked out at the crowd. Then he began. "Fortuna's winds are unpredictable. On rare occasions they are the furious whirlwinds that bring together giants like Bryan and Darrow to confront the eternal dialectics of the human condition. More often they are only the gentle breezes, invisible yet chaotic, that blow unnoticed through ordinary lives to silently shuffle our hopes and dreams. Sometimes it is impossible to tell the difference."

Well, that's the damn truth, I thought to myself. As I tried to understand my own experiences of the last three or four years, it was difficult to make sense of it all. Especially so from a perspective larger than my own, since that's the only one I've ever had. The down draft had hit me pretty hard, and I remember the day—March 15, 1993. Until then my life had been somewhat normal. Well, normal by Texas standards, that is. I had a good job as Chief Deputy in the Texas Attorney General's office, clear title to a Ford Bronco, a little house in Hyde Park, tolerable child support payments, access to good bookshops, a wife on the faculty at the University, and enough room on my credit cards to take an occasional trip out of Texas or the country. But, I repeat myself.

I had been working all afternoon on an appeals brief for *Tarleton State University v. Howard*, an interesting case in which some professor was fighting the administration's attempt to censor the links on his homepage. My sympathies were with the professor, as was the law, but our job was to defend the school's position. It was often like that working for the government. Otherwise, though, it was not a particularly memorable day. When we finished work about 7:30, I went to Scholz' Garten for dinner and libations with a couple of the senior staff lawyers who also worked late on a regular basis.

Beth never cooked dinner or expected me home anyway, but that week she had gone to Dallas, working during spring break with a colleague at SMU on an article for some women's studies journal. When I got home about 11 that night, I headed straight for the bathroom to recycle the remains of the evening. Then I stumbled out and realized that something was not quite right—like all the damn furniture was gone, for starters. And most of my books. And the stereo and all my old albums. And, well, it appeared just about everything else worth taking.

Since the thieves had even made off with the phone, I went next door to a friend's house to call the police and report the robbery. Raymond Rodgers opened the door almost as if he were expecting me and didn't seem at all upset as I cussed my way past him to the phone, complaining about being cleaned out. It wasn't that I had anything particularly valuable, just that some of the things were personal. And that I felt violated by someone having been in my house. As I picked up the phone to dial 911, he said, "Slow down, John. I don't think there's any need to get the police involved in this."

"Huh? And why not?" I asked. "That's what we pay 'em for. Surely the boys can take a break from dunkin' donuts and knockin' heads long enough take a report. It's not like I'd expect 'em to actually follow up, but I'll need something for the insurance claim."

"Because you haven't been robbed, at least not in the criminal sense," he said. "Beth is your prime suspect in this case. She had a couple of graduate students loading a Ryder truck when I got home this afternoon, and our local constabulary doesn't have any jurisdiction in Dallas, which is where your furniture and soon-to-be-ex-wife are by now. Sit down, pal, and have a beer."

"Well, hell, I think I will, . . . and you can tell me the rest of this fine tale," I opined, dumbfounded and still holding the phone.

"Oh, it gets better," Raymond said as he handed me a longneck. "I stuck my nose in your business more than I had planned. I made some clever remark about her throwing your sorry ass out, and she proceeded to tell me more than I ever wanted to hear. I wouldn't take it personal, though, if I were you. It was more a dissertation on men in general, but the punch line is that she resigned from the University, is taking a marketing job with a bank in Dallas, and is moving in with some woman, a professor at SMU."

I just sat there on the couch, stunned and speechless, trying to replay my life for the signs I'd missed and emptying the bottle in a vain search for instant clarity. I should have been an expert on divorce by now, but it didn't seem to get any easier to understand. The only common denominator was me, and the only conclusion was that I wasn't very good at being married. Or, maybe, like Hemingway once confessed, I was just a bastard. "Oh . . . . Got any more beer? I can feel a drunk comin' on," I said as I lunged for the refrigerator to hide the stupid look on my face.

The hangover lasted about six months. I worked harder than ever, but it just wasn't very rewarding anymore. I spent too many evenings at the Dry Creek Saloon, trying to numb the pain and drink myself young. During the summer I practically moved in with Amy St. John, a journalism graduate student who was covering state government for the *Texas Observer*. That was amusing for a while; but, after about six weeks of MTV and student angst, I told her I didn't think that was gonna work out. The door knob hit me in the ass, but I kept on going. That fall wasn't much better. I wasted about a month trying to get one of the shiny new Assistant AGs to file my briefs before I realized what a dumb move that was for a guy who was supposed to be managing the legal staff. Besides, I wore boxers, and she had a boyfriend.

I knew I was still a pretty good lawyer, but it was becoming clear that I needed to move on to something else and get my life back on track. I talked with Steven Wolfson, Dean of the UT Law School and one of my old mentors, about a teaching job, because I thought that would be a more stimulating intellectual environment. I had once intended to be a law professor, and I had a respectable resume that included Editor-in-Chief of the *Texas Law Review*, an M. Phil. in Jurisprudence, clerkships with Judge Thornberry and Justice Brennan, and two years with the U. S. Department of Justice Honors Program before coming on board with the state Attorney General in 1981. Wolfson was encouraging, almost enthusiastic I thought, but they didn't have any full-time positions open at the time.

Then the breeze blew again on January 19, 1994. I remember the date because it was my daughter's 14th birthday, and I had just gotten off the phone sending flowers. I looked up from my desk, and Jenny Rudolph, my Administrative Assistant, was standing in the doorway with a strange smirk on her face. "Long distance call holding on line two for General Bubba," she said with a broad smile. Only one person called me that (at least to my face), my old friend Sean O'Rourke.

Sean and I first met as undergraduates in Irv Rein's public speaking class at Harvard, but we really didn't get to be pals until a few years later when I was at Manchester College, Oxford, and he was a Fulbright Scholar at Trinity College, Dublin. We backpacked around Europe that summer and kept in touch after we came back to the states. He had been an Assistant United States Attorney in New York for a few years and then followed his old boss, Kenneth Burke, into private practice at Davis, Martin, Barton and Fish, a big Wall Street firm with over 300 attorneys, bearing the name of John W. Davis, the old patrician who lost a presidential race to Calvin Coolidge and lost *Brown v. Board of Education* to Thurgood Marshall.

I picked up the phone and tried to sound professional. "Office of the Attorney General, John Wilkes speaking," I said, disguising my normal redneck twang.

"General Bubba! I'm glad to know that you're still on the civil list and wasting the taxpayers' money. I was afraid that you might have found honest work by now."

"Not much chance of that," I replied. "Good to hear from you. I've been meaning to call, but I've been too distracted lately to attend to the civility of friendship. What's up with you?"

"Big changes," he said, sounding almost jubilant. "They're going to name Burke as Special Counsel to take over the investigation of Jefferson Savings and the questions about Cannon's financial affairs while he was governor of Alabama. I've been asked to join his legal staff, and it looks like we'll be moving to Birmingham next month."

Since Sean sounded so excited, I did not mention the article in the *New York Times* that morning where Elliot Abrams called the Iran-Contra Independent Counsel "a Frankenstein's monster that refused to die" and John Poindexter bitterly complained about the hypocrisy of the Congressional hearings. "Congratulations are in order, I suppose, assuming that one can be congratulated for moving to Bombingham. At least it beats practicing law, and y'all will get away from all them Yankees for a spell," I quipped, knowing that his wife was not going to be particularly excited about moving to the heart of Dixie.

"I'm really looking forward to it. Burke is a good man, and this promises to be more interesting than what I've been doing here at the firm. How are things with you? Still enjoying your job?"

"Oh, my personal life has gone to hell in a handbasket, but I'm doing okay. I feed on self-pity. As for work, well, I'm still churning it out and pretending to like it, but I've been looking around for something a little less routine. I talked with the law school, but that wasn't an option. I even backslid on my conscience and made a few discreet inquiries to the corporate pimps downtown at the local branch office of Fulbright and Jaworski. Fate saved me from that one, though. It seems that I'm still in the penalty box for having been a little too enthusiastic for Cannon against their old Texas Transplant, Charles William Horton Stuart, in the last election. Such heresy didn't set too well with the oil slicks and River Oaks reactionaries in the Houston office."

Sean laughed, then said, "Sounds to me like you need a change of place, pal. Would you ever consider leaving Texas? Voluntarily, I mean."

"Oh, I don't know. I guess I might, but despite being a professional complainer, I'm really pretty comfortable with things here. At least I always know who the enemy is and where they can be found."

"Listen," he said, "How 'bout I come to Austin this weekend? We can catch up on old times, and I've got a proposition I want you to consider."

"Come on down! I'd love to have you here, and I certainly won't have any problem clearing my social calendar. But what's this about a proposition? You pushing some 12-step program that takes old lawyers and gives them a new start addressing envelopes at home?"

"No, nothing like that, but it's something I'd rather not discuss on the phone. Just book me a room at the Driskill for Saturday night, and I'll let you know what time I'll be arriving as soon as I can get a flight."

"If we're going to be talking about something we can't discuss on the phone, I don't think you want to stay at the Driskill. The place has ears. I'd invite you to stay with me, but I was undecorated by a midnight minimalist last year, and I'm a little shy on furniture. Let me get you a room at the round Holiday Inn down on the lake. It's got a nicer view and a breakfast buffet with good grits and redeye gravy."

"Whatever," Sean said. "I'll see you Saturday."

Sure enough, Friday's paper had a story that the White House had caved in to all the Republican carping and that Kenneth Burke would be named Special Counsel to take over the "Whirlpool" investigation. I didn't know much about him other than that Sean considered him his mentor and had always spoken highly of him. I did recall that he had once chaired the American Bar Association's committee that reviewed federal judicial nominees, and I thought he had been nominated by President Stuart for some fairly high position in the Justice Department.

I met Sean at the airport just after noon on Saturday and took him to the Holiday Inn, a place that held a special memory for me. I happened to be staying there in 1974 on the day that Richard Nixon announced his resignation. I didn't know at the time whether to be overjoyed at his leaving office or depressed that we'd no longer have him to kick around. I still think he got off too easy, but I always smiled when I drove by and recalled being there at that magic moment.

After checking in at the hotel, we drove out to Chuy's on Barton Springs Road for lunch. We got a table in the back corner and began re-telling old war stories and exchanging more recent ones while stuffing ourselves with the Tex-Mex diner fare. Then Sean started to shift the conversation to the future, asking me if I'd figured out what I wanted to do on the job front.

"I still don't have anything definite," I said, "but I've been considering going to work in Lloyd Doggett's campaign. I think he's one of the finest people in politics, in Texas or anywhere else. He was serving in the State Senate when I first moved back, and now he's on the Supreme Court. He has been an outstanding Justice, and we've become pretty good friends during the last few years. No question that he'll be elected to Jake Pickle's House seat. They want me to work issues for the campaign, and that could well lead to a staff position in Washington. Not that I'd want to do that forever, you know, but it would be a good change and a comfortable place to park my butt while I decide on something for the longer term."

Sean paused for just a moment, then said, "I didn't think you were interested in leaving Texas or working with the federal government."

"Well, being on Doggett's staff wouldn't be exactly either of those. It'd be more like a Tejas outpost on the Potomac. I wouldn't have to wear a tie or fill out a time sheet, and the work can't be that hard if Phil Gramm can figure it out. Besides," I said as if I believed it, "if you're lucky enough to have lived in Texas as a young man, then wherever you go for the rest of your life, it stays with you, for Texas is one great big portable barbeque."

Sean ignored that digression then looked straight at me and asked, "Would you consider coming to work on Burke's staff?"

"Yeah, right," I said, knocking back the rest of my Corona.

"No, I'm serious," he said, sounding as if he were. "It's not a long term deal, it's not in Washington, and it might even be interesting."

"Interesting? Hah! I know you have a high opinion of Burke and all, but from what I've seen in the papers, you boys are on a political snipe hunt that's going to make everyone look pretty damn foolish, no offense intended. Whirlpool was a nothing real estate deal that went belly up, and Jefferson Savings was peanuts compared to Sunbelt, not to mention the billion dollar sinkhole of Silverado and Keating's two billion dollar swindle at Lincoln Savings and Loan. As far as I can tell, except for the biggest clump of conspiracy nuts since the Kennedy assassination and the lemon suckers from the last campaign, everyone else thinks it's a real yawner." I then turned toward the waitress and ordered two more beers.

"Oh, give me a break," Sean said. "If you really think that, then you'll be in a position to make that argument to someone besides me and that velvet Elvis over there. Burke's putting together a top quality professional staff, and you'd have more legal contacts and connections there than you would on the House payroll. Birmingham's not Austin, I admit, but you could easily spend weekends in Atlanta, Nashville, or New Orleans. Or Key West. And I'd really enjoy working with you. Besides, and don't take this the wrong way, you really do need to get your shit together and do something else with your life. You've got too much going for you to continue like you've been doing lately."

"Okay, fair enough I guess, but there are two big problems that you seem to be overlooking. First, I'm a yaller dawg democrat. Second, I haven't practiced any criminal law since I was at Justice fifteen years ago," I replied, almost smugly, until I realized how long it had been.

"No, I haven't overlooked that. I've told Burke all about your background, and he's done some checking with several of the local judges and bar association types. He authorized me to fly down here to talk with you about it and see if you'd be interested. He wants to build a bipartisan staff so this operation doesn't look like a political witch hunt, and he doesn't want the team to look like the New York Yankees. We've got a battalion of FBI agents and more than enough seasoned lawyers with criminal trial experience lined up already. He wants you to come on board as Deputy Counsel to manage the office and the legal staff. You've done that for three Attorneys General here, and he said anyone who could work with the likes of Mark White, Jim Mattox, and Dan Morriss should be able to make it work in our shop." Sean slowly put his napkin on the table and asked, "So what do you say? Will you at least think about it?"

I told him that I would, and he didn't mention it again until I was taking him to the airport on Sunday. Sean said he would call back on Wednesday and that he hoped I would say yes.

Chapter Two

After returning from the airport I called and asked Raymond and his wife to have dinner with me. They had witnessed my crazy life for the last 20 years, and I always trusted their judgment and valued their advice. To my surprise, they both urged me to pursue the deal with Burke. Raymond also thought working with Doggett would be a good move, but they agreed that it was time for me to move on to something new. Perhaps they were just tired of playing cameo roles in my pathetic social life, but they even volunteered to help me rent the house and take care of the place until I could sell it. All that made too much sense to sound like something I would do, but it was certainly worth thinking about.

When I got to the office on Monday morning Jenny said that the boss wanted to see me about something as soon as I had a chance. That was a little unusual, because we usually talked on Monday afternoons when I reported on the divisional staff meetings, but I thought it would be a good opportunity to let him know that I was thinking about a career change. I went down the hall to Dan's office, and his secretary told me to go on in, that he was expecting me. Before I had a chance to slide into the subject, Dan said, "I've had a call from Kenneth Burke in New York asking if I thought you were any good and whether I would mind if he offered you a job."

"Well, I had been planning to talk with you about that and life its ownself, but I just heard about the deal this weekend," I said, wanting him to understand that I hadn't initiated the contact and that my interest was not a result of my lack of commitment to working for him. "I've been in this office for 13 years, and I've enjoyed every one of them, but I've been thinking that it's about time that I had another mid-life crisis, and this time one of my own choosing. I thought I might enjoy teaching at the law school and, you know, trying to see if I couldn't turn out at least a couple of bright ones who would want to do something besides sell their neurotic little minds to the highest bidder. I taught Jurisprudence and Legal History there as an adjunct one year and really enjoyed it. I've also been talking with Doggett's people about doing something with the campaign, but that's, like I said, just in the talking stage. Nothing definite, but that could work out."

"I know about all that," he said without a pause. "Lloyd and I had lunch last week, and Wolfson was telling me how they wished they could hire you when I was at the law school's Christmas party. I've sorta been expecting something like this since Beth left, I suppose, but I really think you should talk with Burke. It's the type of experience that doesn't come along every day. You can always work on the Hill anytime you want, and from what Dean Wolfson said they would offer you the first position that came open."

"I guess that answers both of my questions, in a way," I said with considerable relief. "My first concern was, and is, that I didn't want to cause any problems for you by leaving with an election coming up. Someone's going to have to keep this place humming while you're out on the hustings, but, with unaccustomed modesty, I'll admit there are other folks who can do that as well as I could. The other thing is, I think this Whirlpool deal is a real political tar baby that could very well taint anyone who gets anywhere near it. You don't think so, huh?"

Dan leaned forward, looking toward the door, then said in a voice that would not be overheard by anyone in the outer office, "I don't think there's any question that it is political and that it has real potential to be a disaster, but I think Ken Burke has the experience and the good sense to keep it very professional. I also think you might learn something working with him. The guy's been a real player on the legal stage for years, and he's been on the scene long enough to understand the drama of politics without becoming an agent of those who want to make this farce the longest running act in town. I'm certainly not going to push you to do it if you're afraid of being sucked in, but I don't expect they can convert you."

Dan said he would back me on whatever decision I made, and I went back to my office, thanking him for being so supportive but without knowing exactly what I wanted to do. The rest of the day was spent in staff meetings, so there was little time to give it much more thought. During our regular meeting at the end of the day, I waited until after we had finished reviewing the status of the case files and the divisional updates before returning to topic, and then only briefly. I told Dan that I had not made any firm decision about what I would do but that I wanted to start the clock on the 30-day notice for resignations. He flashed a knowing smile and told me that I could count on a strong recommendation whenever I needed one.

As I was leaving Dan's office I stopped by the door and turned back. "Just one question. What exactly did you tell Burke when he asked about me?"

Dan got this mischievous grin on his face. "He asked me if I thought he could count on you to call a spade a spade," he said. "I told him you'd probably call it a goddamn shovel."

On Tuesday I thought seriously about calling Judge Thornberry to get his take on Burke and the job with the Special Counsel. Homer Thornberry knew politics, having served 15 years in Congress before having been appointed to the Fifth Circuit by Lyndon Johnson and having been through an interesting but stillborn Supreme Court nomination of his own. I realized, however, there was no need to do that. I had never known him to speak ill of anyone, and he would have had kind words for Kenneth Burke, waxing philosophical and telling me that it was a choice I had to make for myself. I was already beginning to feel like some hayseed Hamlet, so I didn't need to make that call. I realized it could be a good career move, as much for the time it would afford for reflection and the exploration of options as for the experience.

One option I knew I would never have again if I went to work with Burke, however, was that of a federal appointment worth a pitcher of warm spit. I wasn't at all sure that I would ever be interested in rooting for a place at the federal trough, but taking the job with Burke would put an end to that possibility. Conspiring with a Republican investigation of a Democratic president did not seem a hot career path for any of the party faithful, and I damn sure had no chance of being appointed by a Repug regime. Nor, for that matter, would I ever want to work for the heartless philistines. Finally, I told myself I wouldn't take a federal appointment to anything less than something requiring Senate confirmation; and, with the politics of personal destruction that had come to dominate the process, I did not think I'd want to play "This Is Your Life" on national television. Not with my life, anyway. So, that left me looking at the immediate choice between the Doggett campaign and the Burke deal, and I thought it prudent to wait to hear from Sean before getting back to Doggett's folks.

I spent the day on Wednesday reviewing my own files and trying to get an idea how quickly I could get them closed or at least caught up enough to transfer them to someone else on the staff. It was a reminder of how little substantive legal work I was actually doing, but it also made me realize that I needed to draft a detailed procedural memo on the formal responsibilities and the unwritten nuances of the job. I asked Jenny to hold all my calls except for Sean, and I worked through lunch, not noticing the time until the phone rang just after 4:30.

I picked up on line two, and, without bothering to identify himself, Sean asked, "Well, have you thought about it?" I allowed as to how, yeah, I had and that I'd be interested in knowing more about what they might have in mind.

"Great! That's what I was hoping to hear," he said. "I'm in Birmingham right now. We've been looking at office space all day, and we've just signed a three-year lease for quarters at Chase Corporate Center, a new office park a few miles south of downtown."

"Three years? How convenient. That would be February 1997, right? Does that mean that y'all plan on stretching this thing out until just after the next Inaugural?" I said, not trying to hide the cynicism in my voice. It reminded me of how the Federalists had passed the 1798 Sedition Act to silence their political opponents, setting the expiration on the date of the 1801 Inaugural.

"Oh, don't be such a jerk," Sean shot back. "By taking that term, we were able to get the space for considerably less than anything we could find for a shorter term down here. The government will be able to sublease the space if we finish sooner, and I know Burke doesn't think it will take nearly that long. Just settle down and tell me when you can come to New York and talk with the boss."

I did settle down, and on Sunday I was on a plane for New York. Sean met me at La Guardia and drove me back to their place for dinner. As we crossed the Queensboro Bridge and turned up Third Avenue, I realized again how different this world was from the one I had chosen, and I say that without being judgmental. I remembered coming to the city for the first time in 1966 and being thoroughly overwhelmed. It was the summer after my junior year in high school, and my parents had brought me here to visit the Columbia campus. Morningside Heights was a neighborhood quite unlike ours in the little Texas town of New Boston. Still is.

Sean and Carmen had a comfortable three bedroom flat on East 83rd Street, garage parking for the Volvo, an easy walk to Central Park and the museums, and combined housing and car expenses about four times what I was paying for a lot more space, physical and personal. Just a different perspective, that's all. Carmen showed me to my room, then the three of us went to dinner at a little Italian restaurant in the neighborhood, the perfect atmosphere for unfolding from having flown middle-seat coach.

Afterwards, back at their place with another bottle of merlot, Sean brought me up to speed on everything that had transpired since the announcement and prepared me for my meeting with Burke the next day. I was especially anxious to know more about my potential boss. Burke came with a strong Republican pedigree, but not the fanatic strain of Paddy Buchanan and the Reverend Marion Rabbidson. He was more of an Eisenhower type, and his father had held some minor diplomatic appointment under Eisenhower. He had been appointed U. S. Attorney for the Southern District of New York by Gerald Ford and, having earned high marks as a prosecutor, stayed on through the Carter administration until 1980 when he joined Davis Martin. He billed at $425 an hour, and among his major clients had been Exxon in an oil spill and Babcock & Wilcox in the Three Mile Island accident, so I figured we wouldn't be having too many conversations about the environment.

More intriguing than Burke's clients, I thought, was his commitment to public service and the irony of events in Washington. As Chair of the ABA Standing Committee on the Judiciary from 1984-1987 he had consulted a number of public interest groups regarding nominees and had been seen as instrumental in sinking the nominations of several Reeder ideologues for the federal bench—including Beard's nomination for the Supreme Court, despite the fact that he had personally supported Beard. In 1989, Attorney General Thornburger had asked him to leave his lucrative practice and come to Washington as Deputy Attorney General. Burke answered the call to public service, but the nomination was scuttled before it was ever made. Shurmond, Hatchet, and 12 other right-wing GOP senators, aided and abetted by the Federal Legal Foundation and the National Right to Life Committee, opposed his appointment in retaliation for the Beard defeat. In a public letter to the president, they suggested he drop Burke and nominate someone who would be more supportive of the goals of the 1988 Republican Platform. After finding himself twisting in the wind, Burke sent a letter withdrawing his name from consideration. It sounded somewhat like a Greek tragedy, and I was surprised that he would even consider taking on the Whirlpool investigation after that.

The next morning over coffee I gave Carmen a book I had bought for her, *Crazy in Alabama* by Mark Childress, and she gave me a look that said anyone would have to be crazy to be there in the first place. Sean and I caught a cab to the office downtown and feared not as we rode through the valley of the skyscrapers. Burke lived somewhere out in Connecticut, but he was already at work when we got there about 8:15. I wasn't scheduled to talk with him until ten o'clock, but I got the call shortly after nine and was on my way upstairs to meet the man. Sean led me to Burke's office and made the introduction, then he excused himself to leave us alone. I immediately thought that this guy might have been sent over from central casting to front for the firm. Reminded me of Leland McKenzie on "L. A. Law," only with more self-confidence. He was in his early 60's and, I'm not sure if it was his gray hair or his assured manner, but I could tell immediately that he was in his element. We began with the usual pleasantries, but it was obvious that he had been well briefed. Yes, Sean and I had met at Harvard. Yes, that was an interesting choice for someone from the Texas piney woods, but I thought I had been able to overcome it. Harvard that is. Yes, I enjoyed my clerkships and the time at Main Justice.

I carried on a polite conversation while simultaneously trying to read the room. Large corner office. Green carpet. Dark mahogany desk, positioned to establish distance. Numerous plaques and framed certificates. Diplomas—Yale undergraduate and Michigan law. A round conference table with six leather chairs. Three stacks of files. A low credenza topped with a bust of Abraham Lincoln and granite bookends holding non-fiction—biographies of Theodore Roosevelt and Robert Wagner, Ford's *A Time to Heal,* Cuomo's campaign diaries, one on the firm of Skadden Arps, and, one of my favorites, *Unlikely Heroes.* A well-tailored charcoal wool suit. Silk tie. Starched white shirt. Gold cuff links with some kind of seal that I could not quite make out without being too obvious or appearing inattentive to the conversation.

Burke was every bit the gentleman I'd been led to believe he was, and I did not detect any hint of the zealot in his voice as he outlined his approach to the task before him. It would be a thorough, efficient, no nonsense operation. Most of his work at Davis Martin was already reassigned, because he was taking unpaid leave and thought it would be a gross breach of ethics to have any outside legal work. The transition from Justice to Special Counsel was going smoothly, and he intended to devote his full time and undivided attention to the investigation beginning February 14.

He wanted me to manage the Birmingham office and to help coordinate the investigation with the Washington office. An important part of my job would be to read the political landscape in Alabama and provide an interpretation of Southern political culture for the rest of the staff. I would be involved in all the major decisions, as a part of the management committee, and I would be expected to contribute to the policy discussions and freely voice any reservations or objections that I might have. He said he expected it would take about a year, 18 months at the outside, and he offered a salary of $105,000. What did I think?

Well, I thought that all sounded real interesting and said so.

For me, it would be a raise. Aware that the salary was below the maximum authorized, I also knew that Burke's salary was capped at $107, 000. I repressed a smile as I thought about the significant cut he was taking. Burke made well over a million dollars last year, yet he was willing to give up that income and all private legal work to take on this assignment for $50 an hour. I was not sure whether I was appreciating the irony or admiring the man.

Then Burke leaned forward, reminding me of a closer at a car dealership, and asked if I thought I'd be comfortable under those conditions. I thought for a moment, then said yes. But told him I thought the better question was whether he and the rest of his staff would be comfortable working with an ole Texas boy who was pretty skeptical about the whole mess. He smiled, leaned back, and said that was exactly what he wanted, a Southerner with a Democratic pedigree who wouldn't mind being a bullshit detector. Okay, he didn't say "bullshit detector," but that was what he meant.

"Fair enough by me," I said.

"Is there anything else we need to talk about?" he asked, meaning that he was finished and needed to get back to work on something else. I didn't have any more questions, so I stood up and started to leave. As I reached the door he was already reading a file, and without looking up he said, "My secretary has the personnel forms ready; be sure to sign everything before you leave. I look forward to working with you."

"I'm looking forward to working with you, too. I'll see you on the 14th," I replied. Strolling back down the hall I felt like I'd already done a days work, but it was only 10 o'clock. It took me about 20 minutes to find my way back to Sean's office, only getting off on the wrong floor once and getting lost in the maze of cubicles and offices twice. Sean was out, so I used his office to complete the paperwork and make a few phone calls back home. The most important was to my office, and I was glad that Dan was not in when I called. I asked Jenny to tell him that I had accepted the position with Burke, to place me officially on vacation for the rest of the week, and to schedule meetings with Rita Kirk and Jimmie Neal for tomorrow afternoon.

It was almost noon before Sean returned. Standing in the doorway, he asked, "Well . . . ?"

"Well . . . ," I replied, "looks like we're going south, white boy."

"Great! Now I won't have to learn the language," he said as he put on his jacket. "Come on, there are some people you need to meet. We're having lunch down in the conference room on 32 with the other associates here who will be coming aboard next week."

Cream cheese and cucumber sandwiches were not my idea of lunch, but the other folks at the meeting were all very impressive. Each one had all been hand-picked by Burke from the finest at Davis Martin.

William Bailey, like Sean, was a partner who had worked with Burke in the U. S. Attorney's Office in the late 70s. According to Sean, Bailey was a no-bullshit guy. And he often taught Evidence to cops as an adjunct faculty member at John Jay College. He would be heading the Washington office and handling the investigation of the death of former Deputy White House Counsel Hal Goodall, a long-time friend of President and Mrs. Cannon.

Paul Barefield, a highly regarded criminal trial lawyer in private practice in Ashtabula, Ohio, was not there, but he would meet us in Birmingham. He would be working with Sean on the Jefferson Savings aspect of the investigation. The name sounded familiar. I think I might have met him before, if he was the same guy who had clerked for Skelly Wright on the D.C. Circuit in the late 70's.

Navita James was a former Davis Martin associate now with the U. S. Attorney's Office in Manhattan. And quite a looker. Reminded me of Faye Wattleton with an ivy league law degree. She was assigned to the prosecution of Roby Douglas, a local traffic judge who had already been indicted for defrauding the Small Business Administration in connection with his operation of Financial Management Services. She would be working the case with Nathaniel Norton, on loan from the firm of Grady, Howell, McGill, and Turner in Atlanta. That was good news for me. It meant I wouldn't be the only one on the staff without an accent.

Dale Herbeck, another Davis Martin associate who specialized in property and financial transactions, was to head the investigation of Whirlpool Bluff Estates, the resort development in which the Cannons were partners with the Banaghans. He would be joined in that work by Michael Zuckerman, an Assistant U. S. Attorney from Philadelphia, who would be coming to Birmingham next week.

They each briefed me on the status of their work which, at this point, consisted of little more than having reviewed the existing files and having talked with the previous investigators from the Department of Justice. Two things became very clear. They were an outstanding group of attorneys, and they were all very loyal and committed to Burke. I did my medium "country lawyer" routine, self-effacing but without the slow drawl and folksy language, and told them that I only knew what I had read in the papers but that I was proud to be working with such an outstanding collection of legal talent. And I was. We agreed to meet again at noon next Monday in the Birmingham office, and I took responsibility for booking rooms for everyone and having an agenda waiting for them when they checked in Sunday night.

On the flight back to Austin I reflected on my decision and felt pretty good about it, and I don't think it was entirely because I got an aisle seat this time. Burke did seem to represent the decent aspects of the Republican Party, and I appreciated what I sensed was a professional approach to the task by everyone involved. Hell, I thought it might even be fun.

Chapter Three

Tuesday was a blur. I talked with Dan that morning, and we decided how to reassign my duties in the office. He said I could always have my job back when the investigation was over, and I said thanks, but we both knew that was not going to happen. I had lunch with William Moore, Doggett's campaign manager, and did my best to make sure that the door would still be open after I finished working with the Special Counsel. The afternoon was spent reviewing procedures and files with the staff who would be handling my office management responsibilities and my duties as political liaison with the Ledge and our supporters around the state. The staff really ran itself, and the only immediate blip on the political radar screen was the increasing number of opinion requests that we were getting on school prayer. Seemed some group over in Houston, calling itself the Women's Federation for World Peace, was heading a big petition drive for prayer in the public schools as the solution for all the world's ills, and the only minor thing standing in their way was the Constitution.

Sometime that day I filled out the forms to withdraw my money from the state retirement system and cash in my accumulated vacation days. Thank you, people of the great state of Texas. I didn't have much time to reflect on either my new job or its larger political implications.

That evening I threw a going away party for myself and invited everyone who was still working at five o'clock to have dinner with me at the Pecan Street Cafe. I was glad that I'd just cut a fat hog from the retirement system, because twenty-three folks showed up. After dinner we continued the celebration across the street at Esther's Follies, then knee-walked down Sixth Street to another bar where Duck Soup, one of my favorite local bands, was playing. I was still buying rounds when the last set ended. Our office was an unusual collection of lawyers, and I had truly enjoyed working with them. Having been there so long, I had a hand in hiring all of them, and they had made my job look easy. It was a fine leave taking, but I knew I would miss them.

The rest of the week was anti-climatic in many ways. The good news was that on Wednesday I found someone who was interested in renting my house, and I made them a deal they couldn't refuse. I called the Goodwill Store and made arrangements for them to pick up the only furniture of consequence I had left, a hide-a-bed sofa that had been either too heavy or too ragged for Beth to cart away. The sad news was that I would be away from my two children, so I drove to San Antonio on Thursday and spent the evening with them on the Riverwalk. Appropriate, considering my new job, that we had dessert at a place named The Kangaroo Court. Damn, they were great kids, and I was really going to miss getting to see them so often.

The bad news was that I realized I had not given any thought to finding quarters in Birmingham. I only knew two people in Alabama. I had met Jeanne Jackson at an environmental law conference in Atlanta a few years ago when she was President of the League of Women Voters, and her husband, Mark Lester, was a history professor at Birmingham-Southern College. Although we had not kept in touch on a regular basis, our paths had crossed often enough for me to consider them friends. I called to tell them that I was moving to their fair city and to plead for their help in finding a furnished apartment. They said they would check out what was available, and we made plans to have a late dinner on Sunday evening when I got to town.

On Saturday morning I loaded my clothes, two bookcases, my new computer, and a couple of boxes of books into the back of the Bronco, had breakfast with Raymond and Peggy Rodgers at Cisco's Bakery, and said good bye to Austin. I couldn't help but thinking on all the good times I'd had and special friends I'd made since first coming here for law school twenty years ago. Thoughts rushed through my head in no discernible order. Both of my kids were born here. The time I told Governor Clements to jump up my ass. The counselor from Camp Wimberly who played with my heart. The view of campus from the top of the Charles Whitman Memorial Tower. Meeting John Henry Faulk and hearing Stevie

Ray Vaughn. The LBJ Library and Barbara Jordan's lectures. Half-Price Books. Tex-Mex made right. Willie's Fourth of July Picnic and Brain Fry. The big pink circus tent that was the capitol dome. Views of the sunset on Lake Travis from the patio at The Oasis. Swimming at Hippy Hollow. Good times, mostly. Perhaps I'd be back someday, but that was uncertain right now.

So long Austin city limits. I cut over to Houston and hit I-10, then spent the night in New Orleans, enjoying a wonderful dinner and the charm of the French Quarter during the relative quiet before the craziness of Mardi Gras. As I was having a cup of coffee at Cafe du Monde and thinking about the challenges of my new job, I could see the statue of another president across the street in Jackson Square. I remembered that he had been vilified by the opposition press over a bank deal and that his wife had been a target of their unsavory rumors. Same song different verse right here in Louisiana with Huey Long. It was his fight with Standard Oil that pissed them off, so they said he was stealing money and chasing skirts. When that didn't work, someone shot him. Perhaps that is the price that backcountry southern Democrats must always expect to pay when they champion the common folks against the moneyed interests who think they deserve to own the White House. Or, maybe, it was just time for me to go to bed. Alone.

I stayed around long enough on Sunday to catch the jazz brunch at the Court of Two Sisters and still made it to Birmingham around 8:30 that evening. I had booked reservations for everyone on Burke's staff at the Marriott Courtyard on Montgomery Highway, right next to the Chase Corporate Center where we would be working for the next few months. The whole scene was very suburban, but I figured that it would be convenient until folks found their own place, and we had the government weekly rate.

Mark and Jeanne lived in Homewood, not too far from where I was staying. Mark grilled steaks, and I maintained my reputation by showing up with two bottles of the finest Texas Hill Country vino, straight from the Llano cellars. Actually, it was not too bad. Pretty good for a local winery. Better than my reputation, in fact, although they were polite enough not to remind me of my behavior the last time we had dinner together. The details of that occasion are unimportant, but I will say that I reached Dan Jenkins' Sixth Stage of Drunk.

They were not too polite, however, to question why I had chosen to join Burke's staff. I found myself repeating most of Sean's arguments and falling back on my own rationalization that it was the quickest way out of an intellectual rut that had become my career. No, I didn't think there seemed to be much to investigate. Yes, I thought Burke would be fair. Not much else I could say, really.

After their two boys went to bed, Mark produced a bottle of brandy, and we talked until well after midnight. It was an informative visit for me, because Mark had known Cannon since the late 60s when they worked on Alabama political campaigns together, and I learned that Jeanne had been on his staff in the governor's office about ten years ago. I listened mostly, since I was trying to get a read on the local political environment and to fill in the large blank spaces in my knowledge of Alabama politics. They referred to President and First Lady as Jim and Diane, told delightful stories about Josh Banaghan, and spoke well of the current governor, Jim Bibb Vance. In their view, the whole Whirlpool story was old mud being thrown by long-time Cannon haters in Alabama, being stirred by the Republicans in Congress, and being spread by the national media and right-wing nuts.

On Monday, the staff met in the lobby of the hotel, and everyone was present except Bailey and Sean, who were in Washington with Burke, meeting with Justice Department officials and preparing for a press conference on Tuesday. We walked over to check out our new offices in Building Two of the Chase Corporate Center, a modern edifice of red granite and chrome with dark glass windows. Only a listing on the building directory gave any indication that we were in business. No one had the code for the security lock on the main office door, but, the guard finally saw us on the monitor and let us in. Everything seemed to be on schedule. Supplies were already delivered. Cable and telephone service was already installed, and the Lexis and Westlaw terminals were already on-line. The Government Services Administration had provided furniture and cars. The Office of Personnel Management had agreed to reassign a receptionist and legal secretaries for our staff.

I was pleased to find that my office was located next to Burke's, with a connecting door between the two. That was important, I thought. Not because I wanted to touch the cloth, but it was a prime location, a communication gateway with inherent power on any office map. I would have direct access, and, more importantly, I would know who else did and what was going on at all times. We would also be sharing the same secretary, whom Burke had arranged to have transferred from the U. S. Attorney's Office in Manhattan. It was encouraging as a sign of his confidence in me.

While everyone else was busy moving into their office and organizing their files, I left to explore the city and prepare to do my job, which was, in part, to be smart and know what was going on in Alabama. I remembered that back in my football days at New Boston the first thing I did when we arrived at another school's home stadium was to walk the field, testing the turf and looking for holes, and it felt like I was doing the same thing before a different kind of game. One of the things I knew I would need was a good legal library and a place to work at night. Mark had shared directions to his favorite research retreat, so I heeded his advice and headed toward town on I-65 to the Lakeshore Drive exit for Samford University, a little Baptist school with a cozy campus and red brick Georgian buildings that looked older than they actually were. I found the Cumberland Law School in Robinson Hall, just behind the main library. I introduced myself in the Dean's Office and, thanks to a phone call from Mark, was able to secure library privileges and a study carrel there. It would be a perfect hiding place, and I thought the faculty might prove to be a potential source of good conversation, valuable in itself and an opportunity to learn how to talk like a faculty member at the same time.

I was tempted to spend the rest of the afternoon at the Davis Library reading Alabama history, but I decided to go on into town and visit some first hand. I had never been to Birmingham before, but it was easy enough to find Kelly Ingram Park, the scene of the infamous confrontation between civil rights demonstrators and Bull Connor's police dogs and fire hoses. As I walked across the park on a crisp February day and recalled the televised madness of thirty years ago, it was hard to imagine why it ever happened, but I could feel the terror of times past as I passed through James Drake's "Police Dog Attack" sculpture. The park was now a haven of serenity at the western edge of a modern business backdrop dominated by towering corporate offices, truly was a place of revolution and reconciliation, and Birmingham was now a modern New South city with a black mayor.

Then, at the far corner of the park, I saw the Sixteenth Street Baptist Church. I never thought of myself as particularly religious, but as I crossed Sixth Avenue to the church I knew I was on hallowed ground. The church had been the headquarters for the black community struggling for civil rights against an intransigent white power structure, and it was there, on a long ago Sunday morning in 1963, that a bomb had exploded killing four black children preparing to attend services. A time of insanity. The violent thrashing of a deformed and dying order, unreasoning and uncaring, was still a grotesque memory that evoked both shame and guilt among white Southerners who were unable to repress the trauma of the past.

Interestingly, however, those who had suffered the most seemed to have been energized by the struggle for freedom. Across from the church and facing the park was the new Birmingham Civil Rights Institute, a monument to victory, or at least survival. Walking through the exhibits was an education for me, not only about the past but about how stories get told, who gets to tell them, and how they come to have meaning.

As I returned to the main hall I stopped for a few minutes to collect my thoughts about what I had seen and experienced, then I made a small donation to the collection box near the exit. Picking up a brochure about the foundation that operated the museum, I was quickly jerked back to the present. I noticed that Josh Banaghan and Jefferson Savings had been among the major benefactors in providing the initial funding for the project. On another page was a picture of Mayor Arrington at the dedication ceremony, flanked by President Cannon and Governor Vance helping to cut the ribbon. My first response was an emotional rush, knowing that these were the good guys who had the courage to help the state overcome its darker past and to build the dream of racial harmony. My second reaction was a sinking feeling, fearing that I was about to witness a very different dream, a nightmare that might bring an end to political careers and the vision of progressive social change.

I decided to skip dinner and get to bed early that evening, but there was a message from Mark when I got back to the room. He just found out that Dr. Bill Harrison, their friend on the teaching faculty at the UAB medical center, was leaving for a one year fellowship in Baltimore and was looking for someone to sublet. Sounded good to me, so they came by, and we went to see it. Turned out to be damn near perfect. High ceilings, wood floors, a fireplace, and it was fully furnished, which was a significant improvement over my place back in Austin. It was on the third floor of the old Barnett Apartments on Highland Avenue South, recently yuppified and renamed Hampton Court. A quiet neighborhood, far enough from work yet close to downtown. Caldwell Park was less than a block away, and there was an interesting used book store, the Highland Booksmith, just around the corner. I told Dr. Harrison that I'd take it, and he said I could move in on Saturday.

On Tuesday morning the staff gathered at the office to watch Burke's press conference with Attorney General Otis on C-SPAN. It opened with a prepared statement introducing Burke to the press and the public as the best person for the job. The Attorney General stepped to the podium and said without hesitation, "This morning I am announcing that I have asked Kenneth Burke to serve as Special Prosecutor in the Jefferson Savings-Whirlpool matter. He has accepted. A week ago I said I was looking for someone who would be fair and impartial, who has a reputation for integrity and skill, someone who would be ruggedly independent, and I think Mr. Burke fits that description to a 'T'. He is an excellent prosecutor, having served with distinction as an assistant United States attorney in the Criminal Division and as head of the Special Prosecutions Unit on Organized Crime in the Southern District of New York. He was appointed United States attorney by a Republican president, and his principle, his integrity, and his ability caused the subsequent president to continue him in office. As a prosecutor I had long heard of Kenneth Burke as the epitome of what a prosecutor should be, effective, fair, absolutely vigorous, and a person with a reputation for the highest integrity. He exemplifies public service at its best. I am enormously grateful that he has heeded this call one more time."

Harriet G. Otis was a real piece of work. When she was first appointed, I thought it a good choice. Time had led me to question my judgment. Today she seemed rather scripted, and the press corps tossed the expected questions, shallow and obvious and only marginally relevant. Burke was all business, answering their questions without grandstanding or appearing patronizing, and we all agreed that he did a good job of establishing the tenor for his investigation. Then he was off for further meetings with the Justice Department attorneys who had been working the investigation since November.

Then we switched over to NBC's coverage, because they would always make sure that no government action appeared to be well intentioned. Sure enough, they had a clip from Senate Minority Leader Ira Dolor. "I don't know Ken Burke," Dolor said. "I don't know him at all, but they did comply with our demand. I do know that he leaked some information about Judge Beard and others to liberal groups. I wish they had gotten somebody who wasn't in Walsh's law firm. And the *Wall Street Record* raised some questions that were new to me. Some curious things about defending Clark Clifford. But I think we—my view is to wait and see what kind of staff he puts together. I'm going to try to find two or three Republican senators to be a little watch-dog group to keep an eye on the Whirlpool developments and how it's being conducted by Mr. Burke." You could always count on The Unhappy Warrior to complain about anything, even when he got his way.

Chapter Four

After watching Burke's press conference, I again slipped away and continued my research, going first to the *Birmingham News* and reading the morgue files on Josh Banaghan. And what a read it was. Banaghan had emerged in state politics in 1960, having been elected to the Democratic State Committee and serving as the state co-chair of the Kennedy-Johnson campaign while still an undergraduate at the University of Alabama. He then left school for two years to work in Washington on the staff of Senator Lister B. Hill. The next clipping I found had him chairing the state Young Democrats convention in 1964 and displaying clever parliamentary maneuvers to elect a liberal young lawyer, Boyce Brooks, in a heated contest for state president of the organization over Nelson Grenier, a junior level executive at Alabama Power. Two years later Banaghan was hired as an administrative assistant to run the Birmingham office of Senator John Sparkman, a post he held until 1974. He then earned a masters degree and taught political science at Samford for a couple of years and later served briefly on Governor Cannon's staff as an economic development assistant in 1979.

Banaghan's business career had begun in small real estate developments in the early 1970's, and he asked Cannon to join him as an investor in the Whirlpool Bluff project in 1978. Cannon was then the state Attorney General, but he and Banaghan had become acquainted when Cannon was a college intern in Senator Sparkman's office back in 1968. They purchased 230 acres on the Sipsey Fork of the Black Warrior River just above Smith Lake up in Winston County and planned to sell 5-acre lots for vacation and retirement homes. As far as I could tell from the newspaper clippings, there was nothing fishy about the deal at the time, but it was an investment that would eventually give its name to the present investigation. Too bad they weren't able to get this much free publicity for the project when they were trying to sell lots back then. It might have made some money.

In 1980 Banaghan had acquired a small bank up in Madison County, a few miles outside of Huntsville. Then, in 1982, he ran for Congress, winning the Democratic nomination but losing in the general election to an entrenched incumbent. Right after the election he bought controlling interest in Jefferson State Building and Loan in Birmingham, later changing its name to Jefferson Savings Bank. The institution was relatively small, but it was already in financial difficulty when he took over, saddled with long-term low interest home mortgages while having to pay higher rates for money market certificates of deposit. Banaghan tried to turn it around with a combination of creative marketing and aggressive advertising to increase the deposit base and by creating Jefferson Financial Corporation, a subsidiary that would allow him to use his experience in real estate, to increase the income side of the ledger. It didn't work. In 1986, Jefferson Savings appeared insolvent, and Banaghan was removed as Chairman of the Board. Three years later, with losses at $47 million, the institution was closed.

Most of the stories about Jefferson Savings carried the byline of a financial reporter named Janet Fox, and I discovered that she was now the Business Editor of the *News*. Fortunately, she was in her office, and she agreed to talk with me and provide further background information. We walked over to a place called the Social Grill for coffee, and I soon discovered that Ms Fox was not your ordinary newspaper woman. My impression in her office was that she had leveraged her good looks and a journalism degree into a respectable job but that she would be more suited to the fluffy role of a blonde news reader for one of the local television stations. Turned out that she had an MBA from the Wharton School and had been with *Forbes* magazine before returning home to work for the *News*. And she wasn't wearing a ring. I was very embarrassed that I had been thinking like a Yankee and real glad that, for once, I had been listening instead of running my mouth.

Janet's take on the situation was very informative. She said that Banaghan was a true populist who had tried to run a community bank in a big city. That meant that he ran Jefferson on the "friends and neighbors" plan, just like he had done in politics. The good thing about that approach was that he was able to get things done. He had been instrumental in providing funds to restore and maintain the Alabama Theatre, and he had been on the committee to save the historic Sloss Furnace site. Jefferson had provided a planning grant for the Birmingham Civil Rights Institute before the city became involved. He had been a leader in organizing the downtown historic district, again providing loans for restoration and adaptive reuse of older commercial buildings. In one instance, he made a loan to Jim Bibb Vance to buy out an adult bookstore on Morris Avenue, close it down, and turn the building into law offices. While the big banks were building office towers in Birmingham's financial center at 20th Street and 5th Avenue North, Banaghan restored the John A. Hand Building on the southeast corner of 20th and 1st Avenue North for the home office of Jefferson Savings and its subsidiary, Jefferson Financial. While other institutions were developing subdivisions with entrance gates and golf courses in Mountain Brook, Jefferson Financial went after the more modest markets and tried to provide homes for working class families in transitional neighborhoods and in rural communities.

The downside to Banaghan's philosophy, however, was that he often made investments with his heart, putting money into the romantic instead of the pragmatic, doing much good but seldom doing very well.

There were, Fox thought, three things that had led to Jefferson's eventual collapse. First, the preferential loan rates for historic preservation and energy efficient homes had reduced income. Second, the economic policies of the Reeder years had led to layoffs and high unemployment in local manufacturing industries, so the low and middle income families could not make their mortgage payments. Banaghan had been too slow to foreclose, and, by the time he did, there was no market for resale in those areas. Finally, Banaghan's optimism and his failing mental health had led him to continue seeking high cost deposits and expanding risky developments in search of a big lick when he should have been trying to retrench and cut his losses.

An example of the latter, she said, was the decision to develop a resort community on Dauphin Island, a 12-mile stretch of beach off the Gulf Coast. Banaghan was fascinated with Alabama history, and he had a somewhat romantic notion of the potential for marketing with a historical theme. Pierre LeMoyne, the Sieur d'Iberville, and his brother, Jean Baptiste, the Sieur de Bienville, had claimed the island for France in 1699, and it was once the capital of French Louisiana. He was also impressed by the relic of the island's Civil War history, Fort Gaines, built in 1822 facing Mobile Bay. In response to shelling from the fort in 1864, Union Admiral David Farragut said, "Damn the torpedoes! Full speed ahead!" as he ran the Confederate gauntlet and took Mobile. That was Banaghan's attitude as well, but the results were not the same. Just as the development was getting underway, Hurricane Elena hit the island in September 1985, wiping out the marina, destroying all the homes under construction, and spooking the market for beach front property sales. Jefferson took a $4 million hit above the insurance coverage.

The Federal Home Loan Bank regulators in Atlanta moved in and began an audit of Jefferson in early 1986 and eventually forced his removal. When everything unraveled, Banaghan's problems with his bipolar disorder became more serious, and he was hospitalized for several months following a stroke. He lost everything he had, his wife filed for divorce, and he was charged with several counts of bank fraud but was eventually acquitted after a jury trial in 1990. Some people speculated

that the investigation had been instigated from the office of Congressman Richard Shanker and pursued by political appointees in the Stuart
Administration as a payback for the aggressive campaign that Banaghan
had run against Shanker in the 1982 general election. Janet said she was
skeptical about that theory, but she had no doubts that the current investigation was a political payback by Stuart partisans, being pursued only
to embarrass Cannon with guilt by association.

I sat there silent for a few minutes, thinking that it was a pretty sad
story and wishing that it had turned out differently. All I could say was,
"I didn't know all that." Then, realizing how stupid I must have sounded,
I said, "I really appreciate your helping me with the background of the
whole situation. That all makes a lot more sense and explains the situation better than what I'd seen in the national press coverage, including
The New York Times," foolishly thinking I was paying her a compliment
while recovering my professional persona.

"Well, it certainly makes more sense than does your investigation,"
she replied. "Jefferson's failure accounted for a tiny fraction of the S &
L losses in this state. Nationally, it ranked 195th. Even here in Alabama
there were several much larger, including two here in Birmingham that
were headed by our former Republican governor and a former Republican Congressman. Why don't you reopen those cases while you're at it?
Those guys are still living high, and Banaghan is living in a trailer park
on Social Security disability payments."

"Hey," I said with a wince, "I just started work here yesterday, so
don't be so hard on me. I'm still trying to understand it all myself. And I
happen to be a lifelong Democrat."

"I'm not particularly interested in your politics. I don't let my personal views affect my news judgment," she said convincingly, "and I
don't care whether you're a Democrat or a Republican. This is about
basic fairness and simple human decency."

What I wanted to say was "damn right," but I couldn't very well do
that. So I settled for saying, "I'm really very grateful for your taking the
time to help me with this, and I hope I can get back with you after I learn
more and can ask better questions."

"Doubtful," she said, looking straight at me without blinking.

I wasn't too surprised by that response. "Well, I hope that you'll
reconsider. This has been very helpful, and I'd like to talk with you
again."

"I meant doubtful that you'd be able to ask better questions," she
said, opening her purse and handing me a dollar for her half of the
check.

"No, please, I'll get this," I protested. "I invited you, and you've been most generous with your time. The least I can do is pay for the coffee." But by then she was almost to the door.

"Not everyone can be bought, Mr. Wilkes. Besides, I have a firm policy against accepting gifts from my sources," she said, glancing back with a sly smile that softened the blow of her words.

As we stood on the sidewalk outside, I continued my attempt to restore some civility to the conversation without sounding like I was actually begging to talk with her again. I could take a little more of this abuse if only she would agree to provide a similar assessment of Roby Douglas and his operation of Financial Management Services. Finally, as she tossed her scarf over her shoulder and turned to walk back to her office, she said, "I can get your number. I'll give you a call when you can return the favor."

"Please do. Soon. And it doesn't have to be just business. I'm a long way from Texas, and I'd sure like to see this town with a local guide," I said, wishing immediately that I could grab those words out of the air and stuff them back in my mouth. I quickly flashed a crooked smile as a shield, but I knew it was too late.

"Doubtful," she said once again, but I didn't think it sounded entirely so.

I stood there watching her walk away, then I headed west on Third Avenue for a few blocks, digesting the conversation about Banaghan. At 20th Street I turned left just to take a look at the former Jefferson Savings headquarters. I liked the architecture of the building, tastefully restored to its 1920 appearance. It had character and gave human scale to a downtown area that was in danger of becoming like Atlanta, or Dallas. The Resolution Trust Corporation had acquired the building in 1989 and found a local buyer who converted it to commercial office space. There were no visible signs that it had ever been a bank. Some would say, I guess, that it never was.

It was getting late, but there was not much I could do back at the office, so I continued my exploration of the city. I liked this place. I had to admit that the images in my mind, of polluted air and pervasive racism, were far from the present reality. The steel mills no longer roared, and the racists no longer ruled. And it was fairly certain that the steel industry would not be making a comeback.

Walking back north on 20th Street, I shortly found myself at the heart of the 5th Avenue financial complex Janet had mentioned, four imposing modern bank buildings that represented the city's commercial soul. They were the icons of the present, replacing the statue of Vulcan and making it merely a quaint reminder of the past. It was only 4 o'clock but the sun did not shine on the sidewalks of the intersection. It was cold. Like a banker's heart. I knew why the staid corporate drones who sat in offices on the upper floors of these towers looked down on Banaghan, his institution, and his dreams. It was the Potters sneering at George Bailey, writ large and yet again.

Just a couple of blocks north, life reappeared as the street met Linn Park, and the comfortable sounds of laughter as children played made me realize that the sun was still shining. On the west side of the park was City Hall, and what looked like an art center was across the way on the north. To my right, both literally and figuratively, was the Jefferson County Courthouse, but the most pleasant discovery was the public library tucked away on the southeast corner. I knew it was almost closing time, but I thought I might yet have time to get a card and find a couple of books on Alabama history. Still, I couldn't resist making a wide swing through the park just to walk on the grass and watch folks enjoying themselves.

As I entered the library, I fortuitously found myself in the Southern history room and quickly started scanning the titles for something that could give me some insight to the Alabama political culture. It felt like being home again, since I'd misspent too many hours in library stacks labeled F, E, and JK, but I could not recall having read anything about Alabama. Mindful that I was short on time and could not count on my usual method of serendipity to find what I needed, I retreated to ask one of the librarians for a recommendation.

There were two women at the reference desk, and as I walked toward them I was faced with a dilemma. One had confederate gray hair and looked like she spent her weekends working on genealogy. She was probably a member of the United Daughters of the Confederacy and a certain source of knowledge on state history. The other looked to be in her early 30s, long curly blond hair that suggested she might not scold people for talking and a long dress that was too cute to be worn by someone interested in serious history. The name plates on their desks only reinforced my quandary. Rose B. Johnson was probably descended from General Algernon Sidney Johnson; Melinda Shelton had probably never heard of him. Tough call. So I tried to make eye contact and approached the one who smiled.

"Hi, Melinda," I said. "I've just moved here, and I'm looking for a good history of Alabama, something that might combine social and political history, probably published in the last five or six years. Could you help me find something like that?"

"Sure," she said, walking toward the stacks. "There are a couple of things you might want to read. The best state history is rather dated, Moore's *History of Alabama*, published in 1934."

"Well, is there anything a little more recent. I am particularly interested in something that would cover the last 50 years."

"You might want to take a look at Hamilton's interpretive bicentennial history. I've seen a new history in the University of Alabama Press catalog, but it's not out yet. One of the authors is Leah Atkins, an undergraduate professor of mine, and another is Wayne Flynt, who was one of my professors in graduate school. That sounds like what you'd want."

"Yeah, it does." Obviously my instincts had been right. Melinda knew exactly what I had in mind. And she knew about the state's historiography, too. "I guess I'll have to settle for the bicentennial history."

"Okay, here it is. Oh, and you should also read Dr. Flynt's book, *Poor but Proud*. It's a wonderful study of the poor white culture. Scholarly," she said with a laugh as she pulled it off the shelf, "but it's an easy read."

"Thanks. Now can you tell me where to go to get a library card?"

"I could, but the business office in the East Building is already closed for the day. I can show you where it is, and you can get a card tomorrow morning," she said as we were walking back to the desk.

"Oh. Well, I have to be in Montgomery tomorrow. Is there any way I can get a temporary card or something?"

"Follow me," she said as she got her coat and started toward the exit. "Where did you say you were from?"

"I'm not sure that I did, but I'm from Austin. Sorry I didn't introduce myself. I'm John Wilkes. I just moved here this week to take a new job with the federal government, but I've worked in state government for a long time back in Texas."

"So how did you know my name, Mr. John Wilkes? Are you a spy?"

"Not exactly. It was on your desk plate. You've gotta be more careful. Most of the people who come in here can read, even those of us from Texas."

When we stopped at the circulation desk, Melinda checked out both of the books and handed them to me. "Now don't lose these. And, when you get back from Montgomery, come in and get your own card."

"Yes, ma'am, I promise. And thanks." What a deal. I'm not sure that I would have done that for a stranger, even one as charming as me. Librarians had changed a lot since Eudora Welty was a little girl.

That evening I finished the state history and got a good start on Flynt's book. Poor white folks are pretty much the same all over the South it seems. At least the story he told could very well have been set in east Texas where I grew up with the same kind of people. I thought I'd be able to figure out this place pretty soon. If I hadn't already.

Chapter Five

I was up early on Wednesday and went jogging through the hilly neighborhoods behind the office. God, I hated jogging, but I convinced myself it was easier than giving up beer. And it wasn't real jogging. Loping would be a better description. A Clydesdale paying for the load in the wagon.

After a quick shower, I stopped in the lobby and downed three cups of what was supposed to be coffee. It tasted more like tin, and even those little packets of fake milk couldn't hide it. The styrofoam cups didn't help either. Everything about this ritual reminded me of the sorry side of the suburban New South. Drinking bad coffee from plastic Dixie cups; probably made people vote Republican, too. But, I really needed the caffeine, my current drug of choice.

Before anyone else got to work, I moved my books and bookcases into the office, primarily for decoration and storage. There wouldn't be room for them in my new place, the only drawback to moving into a furnished condo. I called and made an appointment to meet with Michael Osborn, the Special Agent in Charge of the FBI's local office, then I called the Federal Courthouse in Montgomery to see if Circuit Judge John Franklyn would be in his office today.

The FBI visit was a required courtesy call, because we would be working closely with them in our investigation. The call to Judge Franklyn's office was personal. Well, personal in the sense that he had long been one of my personal heroes, and I just wanted to meet him. I really didn't have to go to Montgomery, but I wanted to make the most of this week and get a reality check on the places and people that were still only vague images in my mind.

Everyone else was in by 8:30, and, after a brief staff meeting, I was out the door for another day of field work. The FBI offices were on 8th Avenue North, not too far from the library, so after meeting with Osborn I stopped by to return the books. I first got my borrower's card, then I went upstairs to again thank Melinda for her assistance and to let her know that I had, indeed, returned the books.

Melinda greeted me with a tone of voice somewhere between teasing and relief that the books were back. "Good morning, John Wilkes. I thought you were going to Montgomery today. Were you just practicing lying for your new job with the federal government?"

Ouch. I was glad I hadn't been more specific about what my job was. Her response only reflected a general distrust for the federal government. I was getting a pretty good idea that people in Alabama were fed up with all the negative national media attention to Whirlpool, and the appointment of a Special Counsel could only make matters worse. "I'm on my way right now, but I just wanted to say thanks again for letting me borrow your books. So thanks."

"No problem," she said. "And have a good time in Montgomery."

"I've never been there, but I understand it's a radical place, a hotbed of revolutionaries from Jefferson Davis to Rosa Parks."

"Actually," she said, "it's a very nice place. I go there a couple of times a year to see one of my best friends, and since you're interested in Alabama history I think you'll enjoy it. If you have any free time, be sure to see the Dexter Avenue Baptist Church and the Civil Rights Memorial at the Southern Poverty Law Center."

I had forgotten that the Southern Poverty Law Center was headquartered in Montgomery, but I was very aware of its work. I had once met the director, Morris Dees, when he was in Texas working on a death penalty appeal, and I occasionally sent them a small contribution when their solicitations came early enough in the month. "Your good friend doesn't happen to be named Morris Dees, does he?"

"No, her name is Lindsey Armstrong. She's a communication professor at Huntingdon College, but she does some research and consulting with the Center. If you've ever read their newsletter, you might have seen some of her articles on the rhetoric of the Citizens' Council and the Klan. And if you haven't, you should."

I wasn't quite sure if that last remark was an assessment of the articles or an assumption that I needed to be educated. Whichever, she was probably right. And I did plan to stop by the Center while I was there.

As I started to leave, Melinda said, "Oh, I almost forgot. Thought of another book you might be interested in reading." She handed me a copy of Carl Elliott's *The Cost of Courage*. I knew a little about Elliott's political career and remembered that he had been the first winner of the "Profile in Courage" Award given by the Kennedy family a few years ago. I expressed my gratitude, checked out the book, and was off for the capital.

Montgomery was about an hour and a half south on I-65, and I was surprised by the terrain. It had been dark when I came through last Sunday, so I couldn't see much. I guess I had expected to see vast cotton fields, but it was rolling hills and pine trees, not unlike the country around New Boston where I'd grown up. The radio scanner provided a smorgasbord of the southern mindset—classical music on the NPR affiliate, ads for weed killer and honky tonks and auto parts stores, old time rock 'n' roll, three country stations, and the flatulent fat man, Rush Limbaugh. That stupid sumbitch made me want to puke. As I approached Montgomery, I fumbled around in the floorboard until I found my Hank Williams tape and popped it in as an appropriate tribute to the city's favorite son. Hank wouldn't have had much use for Limbaugh, and neither did I.

Finding the Federal Courthouse would, I assumed, be easy once I got to Montgomery. I took the Clay Street exit, and followed a path toward town as the street name changed from Bibb to Madison. Eventually I saw the capitol, and turned right on Bainbridge to get a better look. Jefferson Davis had taken the oath there in 1861 as President of the Confederate States of America, and the governor's office had been occupied in the past by various stripes of populists and colorful characters such as Big Jim Folsom and George Corley Wallace—and more recently by progressives like James Madison Cannon and Jim Bibb Vance.

As I slowed to look, I noticed the Dexter Avenue Baptist Church just down the hill and turned back in that direction. I had seen pictures of the church before, but I had no idea it was so close to the capitol. Ironic, I thought, that the birthplace of the civil rights movement was only a block from the cradle of the Confederacy. And amazing that fate had brought Martin Luther King, Jr. to town just in time to give voice to Rosa Parks' courageous act of resistance to the old order. This city had been one of the primary battlegrounds for the second American revolution. Police Commissioner Lester B. Sullivan, a kinder-gentler Bull Connor, had tried to play a role in stopping it. Yet, today he is remembered, if at all, for being on the losing end of a lawsuit against *The New York Times* that resulted in even greater freedom to speak truth to power. And here, as a Federal District Judge, John Franklyn had stood tall to enforce the commands of the Constitution against the constrictions of custom. Which reminded me, I needed to find Judge Franklyn's office.

I drove around for a few minutes, thinking I'd be able to see the Federal Courthouse in an obvious location, but no such luck. I did spot the Southern Poverty Law Center, one street over behind the church. It was in an impressive new building, especially so since I had imagined it would be some little storefront operation. And a few blocks away on Washington Avenue, I saw the antebellum brick home that now housed the offices of Bankhead, Sayre & Haardt—Diane Cannon's former law firm. Finally, I gave in, swallowed my male pride, and asked directions. It was only one block away, at the intersection of Church, Lee, and

Court. The John M. Franklyn, Jr. Federal Building had five entrance doors, each with a different Latin inscription above it. Like a character in a Frost poem, I entered under *macte virtute*, leaving *pro bono publico* for a later time.

Judge Franklyn had served on the federal bench since his appointment by Eisenhower in 1955, and at times it had seemed that he was the only white person in Alabama who had ever read the 13th, 14th, and 15th Amendments. He was constantly called upon to conduct practical seminars on the meaning of the Constitution for state and local officials who found themselves in his court during the 1960s. President Carter had elevated him to the Court of Appeals in 1979, and he had recently taken senior status. Franklyn was one of the three great judges of all time from Alabama, the others being, of course, the late Justice Hugo Black of the United States Supreme Court and Judge Arnold Richards of Birmingham, the Chief Judge of the 11th Circuit. Richards was likely to be Cannon's next appointment to the Supreme Court, and everyone whose opinion I respected on such matters thought he would make a great Justice. Or Chief Justice.

I had left a message with Judge Franklyn's clerk that I would be in before noon, and she had indicated that I would probably have a chance to talk with him. When I arrived at his chambers, the secretary asked me to have a seat and said that he would be right out. The judge appeared momentarily, and I introduced myself, explained my present mission, and tried to express my high regard for his career. He was wearing his overcoat, a handsome dark wool herring bone, and had his hat in his hand, obviously on his way out, so I was thankful that I had gotten there in time to meet him. When he asked if I had time for lunch, I quickly recovered and said of course I did.

We walked to the Elite Cafe, nearby on Montgomery Street, and had an enjoyable lunch, although I didn't quite see anything elite about the place. I soon discovered that it was the "E-light" and was one of the state's main political watering holes, especially during the legislative session now in progress. About half the customers stopped and stared like diners in one of those old E. F. Hutton commercials, and there seemed to be considerable interest among the resident political menagerie about the stranger having lunch with The Judge. I had not anticipated such a high profile entrance to the political scene, but it was too late now to do much about it.

Judge Franklyn was interested in my background and how I had come to be working with Burke. Turned out that he was originally from Winston County, which he called "The Free State of Winston" because it had tried to secede from Alabama during "the wahr." He was also familiar with the area around Whirlpool Bluff and said it was a beautiful place that should have done well if interest rates hadn't been so high back then. I steered the conversation back to his career, and he then shared some of the off-record events related to several of the important civil rights cases in which he had been involved. Even as a law student I had always found the stories behind cases to be as fascinating as the legal issues involved, and he was a fine storyteller.

When Judge Franklyn signed the check for lunch, I felt like a kid at an all star game, almost wanting to ask for his autograph. On the way back to the courthouse I did thank him too profusely for his time and told him that I thought Alabama should be proud for having given the nation such outstanding judges as Black, Franklyn, and Richards. He'd of course heard all that before, but I knew that he had not always been appreciated by the local politicians. He downplayed his own role. Said he just happened by chance to be on the bench when events led to some interesting cases that could not have been decided otherwise. He was, he said, especially flattered to be included with Judge Richards, whom he called the finest legal mind and the best judge he had ever known. I should make an effort to meet him during my time in Birmingham, he added, because it would be much easier now than after he was appointed to the Supreme Court.

I took leave of Judge Franklyn outside the courthouse and followed his directions to the State Bank Department on Union, just east of the capitol. Again, this was just a courtesy call to touch base with the director and staff so I'd have faces to put with the names if I had any questions regarding their records on Jefferson Savings. Like all state agencies, the place was staffed with kids just out of college looking for experience for a resume and with older placeholders who'd become as lifeless as the pale green paint on the walls while waiting for their retirement date. Needless to say, I didn't stay long.

Before heading back to Birmingham, I wanted to see the Civil Rights Memorial that Melinda had mentioned, and that would take just a minute. It was a fountain, designed by Maya Lin, outside the Southern Poverty Law Center. Inscribed in the black granite were a quote from King and the names of 40 people who had been killed in the movement between 1955 and 1968. Although I thought I was fairly well informed, I recognized only about half the names. Standing there I felt a kinship with those who had fought for fundamental freedoms, and being in Montgomery made that feeling even more real. I went inside the Center, hoping to find a bookshop and thinking I might also have a chance to say hello to Morris Dees. He was not there, but the receptionist told me that I could get a copy of "Free At Last," one of their publications that told the stories behind the martyrs, from the Teaching Tolerance project. I left one of my new business cards with a note for Dees, then went downstairs to find the tolerance project offices.

Tolerance is a funny concept. It doesn't mean that one has to embrace differences or even respect those with whom we differ; it only means we have to stop being repressive bigots, stop defending our position by trying to punish or destroy those who disagree or are somehow different. That, at least, was what the term originally meant in the religious context, where it was a significant step forward from the theological imperative to kill heretics and infidels. While I'm sure the Teaching Tolerance project aimed to eradicate racism, I think that tolerance might be the best they could hope for. Maybe it's all any of us can hope for, whether the issue is religion, race, politics, or lifestyle. Slack is a wonderful commodity, and there's too damn little of it.

Entering the project offices I immediately sensed an attitude that was refreshing, quite unlike many of the reform projects I'd seen or been involved with where everyone thought they had to take themselves as seriously as they did their work. This group of folks seemed to be enjoying themselves, and the conversations were almost playful. I found a copy of "Free At Last" on the publication shelf and also picked up a couple issues of the KlanWatch newsletter. As I was starting to pay at the register, I was almost struck blind. Working at one of the tables across the room was the most beautiful woman I had ever seen. I mean, not just attractive but . . . alive. She was animated and articulate and . . . well, I don't know, she was just . . . amazing. It was obvious that she commanded the attention of everyone else in the group. And she certainly had mine as well.

Then, after I don't know how long I had been staring, she glanced my way and saw that I was looking at her. She smiled, held eye contact for long enough to make my shoulders tingle, flipped her long brown hair, all the while continuing to carry on a conversation about whatever they were working on at the table. Was she flirting with me, or was I just wanting to think so? Then I heard a distant voice, like a television too loud in an apartment next door, saying, "Sir. Sir. Your change."

"Oh, yeah. Excuse me," I said rather embarrassed. "Just keep it as a donation to the project. I really admire what you folks are doing." I didn't think that $6.35 would make much difference in the battle against racism, but it might keep the sales clerk from thinking I was too weird. "Looks like y'all are busy today," I said, stalling until I could think of something else.

"Oh, we're always busy. Never enough time or money to do everything we'd like," she said.

"Well, I'm an attorney, just moved to Birmingham, but I'd be glad to help out if there's ever anything I can do up that way. Pro bono, of course," I said, shifting the conversation in the direction I thought I needed it to go.

"We really don't have much use for volunteers," she said. "Our work is so very important, and we don't let just anyone work on legal research or litigation. No offense but volunteers really just get in the way and take up space. Unfortunately, however, staff turnover is pretty high, so you might want to send a resume to the employment coordinator in our legal department. Couldn't hurt anything. If you really want to help, though, you could send a check. We always need more money."

"That's what I've heard," I said, but not saying everything I'd heard nor everything I was thinking. For once, I wasn't going to let my mouth betray my mission. "That woman over there in the black sweater looks familiar," I said. Yeah, in my dreams.

"Oh, yes, Dr. Armstrong is our communication consultant. Working on a new public education campaign for Teaching Tolerance this spring," she said.

"Lindsey Armstrong? From Huntingdon College?"

"Yes. Do you know her?"

"Uh, no, but I've read some of her articles. Good stuff. Maybe I've just seen her picture in the newsletter." What a lie, but I thought it was a safe one.

Nope. Not safe. Lindsey overheard her name and saw me looking at her, and she was coming in our direction with a grin as big as Texas.

"What's going on over here? Did I hear someone taking my name in vain," she asked.

"Oh, no, Dr. Armstrong. I was just saying how I thought your essays were some of the most thoughtful I had read." And I was just thinking that I was glad I had been able to speak in a complete sentence while looking at the way she filled that sweater.

"Really? Which ones did you have in mind for such a high compliment?"

Uh oh. She'd already called and raised. What had Melinda said? "Well, I'm afraid I don't recall the specific issues, but the ones on the rhetoric of the Citizens Council were outstanding," I said. Close call; adequate response.

Lindsey smiled and said thanks, but I moved quickly before being asked for more details about articles I hadn't read. "I'm John Wilkes. We haven't met, but we have a mutual acquaintance, Melinda Shelton. I've just moved to Birmingham, and Melinda went out of her way to help me find some books I needed in a hurry. Anyway, when I told her I was going to be in Montgomery today, she mentioned that y'all were friends, but I didn't expect to meet you. Amazing coincidence, huh?"

"Yes, and a pleasant one, too. Melinda and I have been friends since high school. I don't recall her mentioning you, though. How long have you known her?"

"Well, I only met her yesterday. It's not what you would call a long friendship, but, like I said, she was very helpful when she didn't have to be. I just moved to town on Sunday and was trying to find some good books on Alabama history and politics. Since I didn't have a library card, she checked them out on her card and let me take them. And then this morning, she suggested that I should be sure to drop by to see the memorial out front. I don't remember how it came up, but she also told me that you did some consulting here. But, I'm rambling, and you're busy. I'm glad that I had the chance to meet you, and I hope we'll run into each other again. I'd like to hear more about what you're working on here." Yeah, and read ancient Sanskrit love poems while we drink spiced wine and frolic in a hot tub, I thought but did not say.

"Well, I'd like that, too. Let me know if you're going to be in Montgomery again. Or, maybe I'll see you sometime when I'm in Birmingham. My parents still live there, and I always have dinner with Melinda whenever I'm up that way," she said.

Hot damn! I started to give her one of my cards, but I decided against it. Guess I still must have had some reservations about taking this job if I was reluctant to tell strangers what I do. Especially beautiful strangers. I thought about giving her my home phone number, but that would only make me look horny. No doubt, though, she'd seen that look before. Probably wouldn't have stopped me, except I couldn't remember the number. I just made some more small talk and left on a pleasant note. With a big smile.

Chapter Six

On the way back to Birmingham that evening I continued my socialization process by listening to Alabama's "Greatest Hits" tape, but my mind kept replaying the conversation with Lindsey, wishing I'd been more articulate or had been a little more sophisticated in trying to get something going. I'm usually better than that. It was not my greatest hit. A part of me had wanted to say more, but that part of me usually got me in trouble. She did seem somewhat interested, though. Maybe.

The trip to Montgomery had been well worth the time. Getting to visit with Judge Franklyn would have been enough, but the capitol, King's church, and the Southern Poverty Law Center added to that. Melinda was right; it was a nice place. Meeting the woman of my dreams was an additional unexpected surprise. So fine.

The official part of my day, stopping in at the Bank Department, was the least interesting, but while there I did pick up a copy of *Alabama Times*, a weekly tabloid of politics and public affairs that seemed to contain all the political gossip and some good reporting and features. Not quite the *Texas Observer*, but in the same spirit. There was an article by some guy named Ted Schroeder about how Nelson Grenier, a GOP candidate for governor, had played a key role in getting the national press interested in the Whirlpool story to embarrass Cannon, who just happened to have trounced Grenier in a landslide in the 1990 governor's race. Another one by the religion editor, William Brann, was on how Reverend Jay McCarthy and the Christian Citizens Council were going all out to re-elect Lieutenant Governor Jerry Elkay Coughlin, a plump Baptist preacher and the great white hope of the Republican party.

Maybe there was something to this Southern middle name phenomenon, since Jerry Elkay Coughlin and Jim Bibb Vance were both incumbents and looked to be safe bets for the election. Shouldn't push it too far, though, and go for four—like Charles William Horton Stuart. People who never read the *Social Register* would think you didn't know who your daddy was if you had too many names.

It had been a good day. I stopped by the office when I got back to town to see if anyone was up for a beer, but everyone was already gone.

Just as well. I got a burger for dinner and spent the evening in the room reading Elliott's book about his political career. He was one of the good guys.

I forced myself to go jogging again Thursday morning. Even more difficult was the decision to spend the morning in the office, but I knew I'd better be marking my territory. I didn't want to appear to be out of the loop, and I knew how quickly that could happen, especially when a new operation is just getting organized. I dictated notes on my first three days of research and made a few phone calls.

One of the first calls was to Melinda Shelton at the library to get recommendations on state newspaper subscriptions for the office, but I phrased my inquiry vaguely enough that I didn't have to explain where I worked or why I wanted to know. She recommended the Birmingham *News,* the *Black & White*, the Montgomery *Post-Advertiser*, the Montgomery *Examiner*, the *Alabama Insider*, the *Alabama Times*, the Anniston *Star*, and the Tuscaloosa *News,* and I made a note to order them all. Although I hadn't asked, she also gave me a brief dissertation on Alabama journalism and mentioned folks like Jack Nelson, Howell Raines, Emory Jackson, Brandy Ayres, and Paul Hemphill. That little exercise was an old Southern tradition, claiming good writers to compensate for the region's historical image of illiteracy.

The second reason I had called Melinda was to talk about Lindsey, hoping of course that she would pass on my interest, but before I had a chance, she said, "Well, I hear that you met my friend, Lindsey."

Yes! I must have made some kind of impression. Enough, at least, to merit a phone call. "Yeah, I ran into her at the Southern Poverty Law Center, and we had a brief chat."

"She said you were cute. Reminded her of the Nick Nolte character in *Prince of Tides*."

That's good, I thought. I usually reminded myself of the Jack Nicholson character in *Terms of Endearment,* but I was smart enough not to confess that just yet. "I'll take that as a compliment. Pat Conroy is always sympathetic to us good ole boys. Makes our weaknesses appear to be virtues."

Other than the rush from the phone conversation, the rest of the morning was relatively uneventful. I made the rounds at the office and talked with everyone individually, trying to get a sense of where they were with their aspect of the investigation and to learn what I could be doing to make their job easier. I have always had an aversion to staff meetings, even if I chaired them, and I intended to call as few as possible. For some unknown reason otherwise intelligent people feel a need to pontificate, even if it has nothing to do with the task at hand. Maybe such meetings serve some therapeutic function for the compulsive talkers, but I had never developed the talent for suffering through pointless rambling or the ramblers themselves. At least not gladly. And if building team spirit is the point, I'd much rather do that after work over a beer. Then, at least, people would have a good excuse for spouting incoherent nonsense.

My trust in the dedication and integrity of the staff was reaffirmed by the conferences. Everyone was taking responsibility for pursuing the investigation and was farther along at this point than I had anticipated. Talking with Dale Herbeck and Mike Zuckerman, the two guys handling the analysis of Whirlpool Bluff, reminded me why my fieldwork was important. Herbeck kept talking about lot values by making reference to his family's place in the Hamptons, and Zuckerman said he didn't understand why Cannon thought anyone would want to retire to the boonies of northern Alabama. Their comments gave me some insight as to how the American public might view the investment—and the investigation. I also realized that I should be able to speak to those questions from the staff, so I checked the map and decided how I would spend my afternoon. Any excuse would have been adequate to get me out of the office, but this one sounded like it might pass the straight face test.

As I drove north on I-65, the rolling hills that surrounded Birmingham gave way to the more rugged southern foothills of the Appalachian chain. I stopped for gas in Cullman, home base of both the Folsom political family and a former Republican governor of little consequence named Guy Hunt. I then headed west on U.S. 278 and quickly realized that northern Alabama was an hour and a world away from Birmingham. Kudzu alongside the highway, filling the gullies and climbing the utility poles, was one of the first signs that things were different. The Kudzu carpets gave the rural mountain South that same mysterious feeling that W. J. Cash had attributed to the moss-draped trees of the plantation South. An environmental conspiracy if there ever was one.

This part of the state was all-white, mountainous, and mostly covered with a forest of pine and mixed hardwoods. The log cabins and tar papered shacks of the past were gone, replaced now by mobile homes and those Jim Walters finish-it-yourself houses that somehow never got finished. Modernity intruded in the front yard as bass boats and satellite dishes now seemed to outnumber lawn jockeys and tire gardens. Driving past the small farms with chicken houses, the fescue pastures with a few beef cattle, and the occasional groundhog sawmill, I smiled at the contrast between this culture and the streets of downtown Birmingham or the space and technology center that had grown up around Huntsville.

There were two ways to reach the property at Whirlpool Bluff Estates. The quickest way was to take the gravel road north from 278, but I was enjoying the afternoon and had plenty of time, so I decided to go in the back way. Just past Double Springs I cut back north on Alabama 33, continued on past the Southern Homes mobile home factory, and soon reached the bridge over the Sipsey Fork. At the bridge, a narrow dirt road turned south through the woods and paralleled the west bank of the river for about two miles. The country was beautiful. I could understand why there would be a market for weekend cabins and retirement homes here.

Finally I came to the sign at the entrance and turned left onto the private road. The development sat atop a high sandstone bluff overlooking the river. There appeared to be only seven or eight houses on the property, although several additional lots had sold signs and faded orange survey tape indicating some activity. Part of the property had been designated a wildlife management area operated by the state and providing public access to the river. I recalled an article in the files from the *American Speculator* or some other right wing rag that had made the charge that Cannon's property had benefited from the installation of the boat ramp, but, from what I could tell by looking at the pickups and trailers parked there, it was being used by local folks for fishing. The land immediately adjacent to the river was covered by a scenic easement granted in trust to The Nature Conservancy to prevent residential development and ecological intrusion. I hadn't read anything explaining how that was supposed to be a devious act for personal financial gain, but I was sure that some political opponents had or would find that suspicious, too. Somehow. I was confident, though, that Burke would keep our investigation focused on important matters and not let us be diverted by small matters or small minds.

As I looked back up the river from the boat ramp I could see the geological formation that gave Whirlpool Bluff Estates its name. The huge sandstone bluff rising some 60 feet above the river had a concave face, carved by the swirling eddy of the river eons ago. An ancient whirlpool cutting into the stone left a monument that inspired the name for the development. Now, the present political currents had provided a water torture of a different type as torrents of accusations swirled around President Cannon, giving the Whirlpool name of our investigation at least two meanings. Maybe three. I wondered who might get sucked into this political vortex and hoped that I would not be among the victims.

Driving back south toward U.S. 278 I noticed that much of the land for the next couple of miles was posted, and many of the no trespassing signs were corporate markers for a company called Swift-Bowling Land and Timber. Made more sense now why the state had been interested in building the public access ramp on the river at Whirlpool Bluff. Then I saw stark evidence why Banaghan and Cannon had dedicated the scenic easement. An entire hillside had been clear-cut to the edge of the river, leaving only a single post with a Swift-Bowling no trespassing sign, as if anyone would want to trespass on that eroding wasteland. Devastating. I felt more sadness than anger, because I knew too well the political and economic circumstances that led to such environmental foolishness for short-term financial gain. The corporate interests were motivated only by greed, and as Jeanne once said, "they come, they see, they saw, they lay-off, and they're gone." Happened once long ago, and now they were back at it again. The small landowners who were drawn into the process couldn't really be blamed, because they were struggling to survive by almost any available means. Bad choices led to no choices. It was an old story all across the South.

On the highway back to Birmingham I was trying to organize everything I had been doing all week when I saw an exit sign for Arkadelphia. That seemed to ring a bell in the recesses of my mental files, then I remembered that was where Josh Banaghan was now living. I slowed just in time to make the exit and took an unplanned detour for one more piece in the puzzle I was trying to complete. I headed west on Alabama 91, and in less than ten minutes I was in downtown Arkadelphia.

The place consisted of six churches, about a dozen houses, and the commercial district—Swann's Grocery and General Store. I stopped at the store to get a Coke and see if anyone knew where Banaghan lived. Sure they did. Yep. But no one appeared too interested in telling me.

"You a reporter?" one man asked.

Okay. It was clear that an affirmative answer would be the wrong one, but owning up to being a federal prosecutor would be even worse. "No, just curious. I heard he'd moved here." All true so far.

The inquisition stopped, and several of the men started talking about Banaghan. He was a regular customer and a regular guy. Kinda strange, they said, because he was always reading books and giving crackerbarrel reviews. But they liked him just the same. A good story-teller. Not stuck up like most big city bankers. Made a small donation to the rural fire department, but he couldn't join due to his poor health. And they were tired of all the Yankee reporters writing stories about him and disparaging their community. Why, they wanted to know, didn't everyone just leave him alone?

Finally, someone did mention that he lived about a quarter of a mile south on County 35, and after an appropriate delay, I took my leave. Banaghan did not live in a trailer park as Janet Fox had said, but he did live in a mobile home, a white one with brown trim, set among a small pine grove on a slight hill off to the right. I pulled into the driveway, but only to turn around. As much as I wanted to meet him, I knew I couldn't do that here and now. We would meet soon enough, and most likely under less comfortable circumstances. I slowly backed out of the drive and headed for Birmingham.

Seeing Banaghan's trailer put everything in a whole new perspective. The full force of the federal government and a special prosecutor were about to take on a man living out here in obscurity on Social Security disability benefits. Oh, yes, we'd find out if he'd broken any laws ten years ago, and if so we'd indict him. That was our job. How the hell did I get involved in this?

Maybe I shouldn't have taken this job. Maybe I shouldn't have read Carl Elliott's book last night. I saw too many parallels between Banaghan's rise and fall and what had happened to Elliott. Elliott had grown up poor in Gober Ridge, worked his way through law school, fought for the little folks, and served them well in Congress from 1948 to 1964. He was a champion of federal support for education, because he thought it would help poor folks in Alabama, both black and white, get better jobs and better lives. He read books, which was an unusual experience for many politicians in this state. And, when he had finished reading them, he always gave them to school libraries in his district. Then, in his last hurrah, he took on the Wallace machine in the 1966 governor's race. Spent his congressional pension on the campaign, argued that the people must not give in to the forces of hatred and bigotry, lost the race, and ended up broke. And sick. And forgotten. And it didn't seem right.

Chapter Seven

Burke would be arriving on Saturday, and we had a dinner and legal staff meeting scheduled that evening. That made Friday an obligatory office day, and everyone was in scrunch mode. It was somewhat amusing to watch folks adopting a more formal persona and getting into role. There was little discussion, even about our work, and the real kicker was no lunch break. The secretarial staff had it the worst, however, since everyone expected immediate priority to be given to the final typing of their own section of the briefing book. I tried to boost morale by bringing in barbeque sandwiches from Jim 'n Nick's and assuring the staff that everything was on schedule, but my rather laid back manner only made the tension more apparent.

Actually, I was fairly excited that Burke would be here tomorrow. I was looking forward to getting to know him better, watching him work and learning more about his approach to the job ahead of us. I had lots of information, but I also had lots of questions. How would he balance the legal questions with the political pressures? Would it become a disguised witch hunt or just another professional assignment? Would he try to hotdog it with the media or go about his business with quiet deliberation? Just how independent could he be from Justice and Congress? Would we be trying to solve crimes or be pursuing individuals in search of crimes? Would Burke be looking for the truth or primarily for indictments and convictions. Lots of questions. And very important ones as far as I was concerned.

I thought I might have a chance to get a better reading on things that evening, because Sean and Bailey would be arriving soon. I picked them up at the airport that afternoon, and we drove straight to the office. It was like old home week. I was glad Sean was here now, but everyone else seemed equally excited. The atmosphere in the office improved immediately, and the noise level approached that of a bar. People were joking and almost normal again. That was a good sign. I was beginning to think that this bunch was suffering from humor deficit disorder.

That evening we all met for dinner at a place in Five Points called The Mill, and the conversation continued. That gathering was helpful, at least for me, because it was the first time I had the chance to read the group dynamics away from the office. I was pleased, but not surprised, at the quickness of the wit and repartee. Smart folks with smart mouths. The downside was that the Smoky Brown Ale continued to flow until midnight, so I didn't have a chance for any private conversation with Sean that evening.

On Saturday I had to move into my new place, and Sean needed to work in the office. The questions would have to wait, but I would know soon enough. I spent the most of the day exploring my new neighborhood and thoroughly enjoying it. I liked being closer to town, and I much preferred the older homes and big trees to the plastic environment in the bulldozed burbs. And it was a neighborhood for walking. I spent an hour or so at the Highland Booksmith and for 12 bucks picked up used paperback copies of two books, *Scandal* by Suzanne Garment and *Feeding Frenzy* by Larry Sabato. I spent another couple of hours reading in the park and discovered that, for books about politics and the press, both were rather thoughtful and somewhat insightful. An enjoyable way to waste an afternoon.

As I got ready for dinner my mind again turned to Kenneth Burke. He had taken rooms at the Tutwiler Hotel for his stay in Birmingham, and that said a lot about the man. The only good thing I ever heard or knew about the Department of Justice under Reeder was that Attorney General William French Smith had lived at The Jefferson during his tenure in Washington. It was my favorite Washington hotel, and the Tutwiler was downtown Birmingham's version of The Jefferson. It was comfortable, quiet, tasteful.

Our dinner was scheduled there for 7:00 o'clock in the Jemison Boardroom, a private dining room on the ground floor. I arrived a few minutes early with the briefing books and found that it did, indeed, look like a boardroom. An impressive walnut table, maybe 15 feet long, was in the center of the room, looking much like a corporate conference table set with nine places for dinner. There was a working fireplace on one wall. Queen Anne furniture, a brass chandelier, antique maps and prints, and a couple of blue leather wingback chairs with reading lamps finished the decor. I thought I could get used to this.

The polite talk during dinner gave no hint of what was to come. The fact that wine was not served nor made an option indicated that this was not merely a social occasion, but I cheated by ordering Chicken Something that had been marinated in white wine and tarragon. As soon as the table was cleared, Burke walked over and closed the door, walked slowly back to his chair at the head of the table, and placed his briefcase in front of him. Anticipation was an understatement of what I was feeling. All eyes were on Burke as he sat down, paused, and put on his reading glasses.

Burke looked up and around the table as if he were taking roll, then he began. "Please excuse me if I dispense with the usual after dinner pleasantries. I consider this an extremely important assignment. It's important for the country to get this done and get it done as quickly and as thoroughly and as fairly as possible. And when Attorney General Otis asked me to accept this responsibility, I felt an obligation to respond. I'm very grateful to each of you for your commitment and to the Attorney General for the trust and confidence that she has placed in me to carry out this important assignment.

"I'm totally satisfied that we'll have the independence and complete authority to do this job right. I have taken a leave of absence from my law firm so that I can work full time to conduct and finish as expeditiously as possible a complete, thorough, and impartial investigation."

That was good news. I was glad to know that he had kept his word about abstaining from private practice. I knew how much money he made and could make, but I also knew he had to give it up to avoid any possible conflicts of interest and conflicting demands on his time.

Next, Burke detailed the source and scope of our authority. "The scope of our investigation is reflected in Regulation 603.1, entitled 'Jurisdiction of the Independent Counsel.' I drafted this resolution broadly and did so deliberately to give us the total authority to look into all appropriate matters relating to the events that bring us all here this evening.

"The specific language authorizes us to investigate whether any individuals or entities have committed a violation of any federal criminal law relating in any way to President James Madison Cannon's or Mrs. Diane Rankin Cannon's relationships with Jefferson Savings Bank, Whirlpool Bluff Estates, or Financial Management Services.

"In addition to that specific general language, there is further language which gives us the jurisdiction and authority to investigate other allegations or evidence of violation of any federal criminal law by any person or entity developed during our investigation and connected with or arising out of that investigation."

Well, that part did concern me a bit. That was a little too broad, I thought. Special Counsels were supposed to be appointed only for limited investigations of high government officials when it might appear that normal Justice Department employees would have a conflict. Burke might be trusted not to abuse such discretion, but, as a matter of public policy, I didn't care much for that language. In the wrong hands it could be used to authorize a reign of political terror and selective prosecution of political opponents. I resolved right then to make sure that wouldn't happen, at least not without my strenuous objection.

"As some of you know," he continued, "when I was United States Attorney I was a hands-on prosecutor myself. I prosecuted several major cases personally. But I have chosen each of you for your particular strengths and because I have full confidence in your ability and good judgment. This will be a team effort.

"I talked to Director Fimus earlier this week, and he has assured me that the FBI will be at our complete disposal. We're obviously going to try to do our job consistent with the minimum of expense, because I can imagine the justifiable public indignation if our expenses exceeded the amount of the financial losses we are investigating."

Yeah, Fimus would certainly cooperate in almost any investigation of American citizens. No question about that. He had to be one of the worst appointments Cannon had made. Even worse than Otis. It would be a real contest which of them cared less for individual rights and liberties, but I thought Fimus was the more dangerous of the two. Otis was merely a maternalistic scold. Fimus was a government hit man in the ongoing war on the Bill of Rights.

Then Burke touched on a topic of personal interest to everyone there. How long would this take? "My time frame is to finish this as quickly as we can consistent with doing the job right," he said. "It's very difficult, not yet knowing the all the facts, to try to put any time frame on it. I would like to think we can complete our work by the end of the year, but that should not be seen as a firm deadline. My experience in these matters has always been every time you try to put a time limit on something you're always wrong. It always takes longer. So I'm reluctant to do that, other than to tell you that I'm going to start tomorrow and just go flat out until we're through."

"It is my intention," he added, "to make periodic reports to Congress and the American people. I think people will want to know what we find out. And if cases are brought, why they're brought; and if they aren't brought, people deserve to know that we have found no evidence of crimes. Experience has shown that waiting for a final report only increases rumors, speculation, and conspiracy theories."

Another good sign, I thought. What we did not need was a media circus. If we made regular reports on our work, that might keep the press and the pundits subdued. Well, probably not, but at least they'd have to deal with the facts. Good plan. We'd see if it worked.

Burke then did something that surprised me. His voice took on a strange tone, a slight hint of self-righteousness that I had not expected, as he said, "I also think it's pretty obvious that this is not your garden variety case. This is different because it involves a President of the United States, and I think the differences are obvious to everybody in the room. I would certainly expect that before this investigation is over that we would question both the President and the First Lady and that it would be under oath.

"I think the history of these political situations is that it is difficult to conduct this kind of investigation at the same time a Congressional investigation is going on. The decision whether to have hearings obviously is not mine, but I think just looking back at the past, we can all see that that is not an easy relationship. Mr. O'Rourke and Mr. Bailey will have something to say later as to the potential conflicts we may be facing in that regard."

I thought we should probably be more concerned about the potential for political motives in our own shop, but at least he was aware of what might happen on the Hill. He'd faced that before in his career, and he knew that reason was a rare quality in an election year. I glanced around the table and tried to read the faces, but I couldn't get any sense of what the others were thinking. Except for Norton and Bailey, who were skeptical about everything. I liked that.

Then came the pep talk. Burke's voice returned to normal, and he said, "I trust that when we have completed our work you will be able to say, without hesitation, that the public has been served and that you have done your best and learned something in the process. That is all that you should expect from public service, and it is more than enough.

"Thank you. That's all I have to say. Unless there are any questions at this point, I'd like to ask each of you to bring us up to date on the status of your particular aspect of the investigation."

No surprises. Burke would take the assignment seriously. And he hoped to be finished by the end of the year. If so, that would be great timing for trying to sign on with Doggett in January. I sensed, too, that he had little patience for those with a political agenda, especially the grandstanders in Congress who were more concerned with scoring points than in finding answers. Fine by me, but I figured that we would just have to expect that and try to do our job anyway. We were dealing with a political issue that had only recently been made a legal issue. I'd watched the Texas legislature too long to expect much restraint or even basic common sense from 468 folks facing an election next fall.

Mike Zuckerman and Dale Herbeck were seated to Burke's left, and he turned to them to begin the reports with a summary of the Whirlpool Bluff real estate investment. Herbeck's remarks were relatively brief. Despite having the honor of the name for our investigation, he said, he thought it might be one of the first areas we could complete. On the surface it appeared to be a legitimate real estate investment, though it was one that ultimately lost money. So, where's the potential crime in that?

Whirlpool Bluff first became a political issue in March 1992 during the presidential primary campaign when an article by Luis Gerucht appeared in *The New York Times*. It was somewhat ironic how it all got started, and that tale revealed much about how connected and convoluted politics is in Alabama. Josh Banaghan, at the wrong end of one of his bipolar mood swings, had talked to Nelson Grenier, a lawyer and member of the Republican National Committee, about his past business dealings with Cannon and Vance. Although Banaghan and Grenier had been on opposite sides politically for years, they had been business partners in some real estate projects. The essence of Banaghan's anger was that state bank regulators had been instrumental in having him removed from control of Jefferson Savings after his stroke in 1986. The real rub was that Cannon wouldn't step in to help him then and later had tried to distance himself from Banaghan, even after he was acquitted on bank fraud charges in 1990. Grenier, who had challenged Cannon for governor in 1990 and had been beaten like a yard dog, saw this as a chance to vent his hatred and embarrass Cannon. Banaghan's wife had suggested that Josh became more talkative after Grenier had offered to ease his financial pain.

Anyway, Grenier recorded the conversation and then contacted Gerucht, whom he had used in the past for planting stories against his corporate rivals back when he was President of Alabama Power. Banaghan and Grenier then became the prime unnamed sources for Gerucht in a series of articles that sought to raise vague questions but never came close to offering any evidence that the Cannons had done anything wrong.

I remembered reading the articles during the 1992 campaign, and I think that was when I realized that the Old Gray Lady was just as big a whore as any of the tabloids. I mean, it was obvious that they had invested a lot of time and money in pursuing the allegations of sinister financial deals at Whirlpool Bluff, so they felt they had to publish something. It was also obvious that they had found nothing on Governor and Mrs. Cannon. At least no facts. That did not stop them, though, from printing the stories based upon political spite and partisan imaginations. As news stories, no less. Couldn't let facts get in the way of a good rumor that might sell papers. Now it was clear what had actually happened. Although Cannon had refused to intervene to help Banaghan, Gerucht had twisted the tale to imply that Cannon had breached both law and ethics to help his old pal at Jefferson Savings. Amazing. After that, I came to understand that newspapers—all newspapers—should be read skeptically and treated as commercially motivated entertainment. Or pulp fiction.

Dale and Mike were prepared to recommend that two allegations regarding Whirlpool be cleared and closed, and those were the two that seemed most dear to the hearts of the political opposition. The charge about the access road and boat ramp being private financial gain from federal funds was an easy call. The state agency involved had been trying unsuccessfully for years to purchase a right of way for access on that part of the river, and Whirlpool Development let them have it for free. Then there had been several news stories about a "questionable" $30,000 mortgage that Diane Cannon had secured to build a model home on the property. Everyone who had looked at that one, including the FBI financial analysts, agreed that she could have gotten an unsecured loan for twice that amount on her signature at any bank in the state. Those transactions were above board, neither implicated federal criminal law, and both had occurred more than ten years ago.

Among the things they were looking at now was whether the Cannons had appropriately treated interest deductions and capital gains on their tax returns. The corporate records were so incomplete that it was difficult to reconstruct even now. Perhaps the Cannons had miscalculated their deductions, but it did not appear that there was any criminal liability. Besides, we were now well beyond the statute of limitations on income tax fraud. Mike added, however, that they were continuing to investigate whether Banaghan had used federally insured funds from Jefferson Savings or a Small Business Administration loan to meet the debt requirements for the property, and they would be working closely on those questions with the staff assigned to review Jefferson Savings and Roby Douglas's Financial Management Services. The final irony, it seemed, was that any criminal liability in the matter would be related to Banaghan's activity, which was still within the extended 10-year statute of limitations for bank fraud.

When they finished I had a couple of questions, but Burke was running this show and did not seem inclined to open it up for discussion just yet. Probably a good idea. We could have been there all night if he did, and this was supposed to be an overview. He thanked them for keeping it brief and nodded toward Navita James and Nate Norton, indicating that they should proceed with their update on Douglas and his small business investment company known as Financial Management Services. Douglas was one of the primary reasons we were in business, and I looked forward to hearing the details.

Navita had a head start on this one. Her position with the U. S. Attorney's office in Manhattan had allowed her to begin working with the Justice Department while still in New York, and Douglas had already been indicted last fall by the U. S. Attorney here in Alabama. Douglas was a local traffic judge in Montgomery, appointed by Durwood Dilberry, a former Republican governor. He was not a particularly upstanding judge, either, having been investigated by the Alabama Judicial Discipline Commission on numerous occasions. On the side he owned and ran a little loan company called Financial Management Services that was partially funded by the U. S. Small Business Administration. You could get an idea about the operation from the fact that Financial Management had made loans to 57 companies during the 14 years it had been in business, and 13 of the 57 were to phony shell corporations secretly owned or controlled by Douglas himself. The SBA estimated that more than half of the write-offs, more than $1 million, would be from his companies.

After that teaser, Navita's review was methodical and clear. She was all business. Even somewhat dull, I thought, but I tried to pay close attention as she presented her analysis. "Financial Management was incorporated under Alabama state law in 1978 and licensed by SBA in 1979," she began in a monotone. "Mr. Douglas was president, making all decisions relating to its operations until September 15, 1993, when the SBA placed Financial Management into receivership because of capital impairment."

How did these things happen? Was it just like the S & L debacle, a result of new powers without adequate rules? Would it be rude for me to give a big yawn about now? Before I could ask, she explained, "Our recent review of the records shows that SBA conducted 11 cursory examinations of Financial Management during its 14-year existence. When questions were raised about the operations, Mr. Douglas always seemed to lie to the examiners, and his glib explanations often convinced them that he had corrected or eliminated the problems. While SBA finally took action against Financial Management in 1993, its inadequate oversight during the 12 years of lax regulation under previous administrations resulted in a $3.4 million loss to the taxpayers."

Then, getting to the details that I thought would explain what made all this our concern, she concluded, "As president of Financial Management, Mr. Douglas authorized improper transactions includeding sham loans to his own companies, loans to insiders and business associates, and loans for unauthorized purposes. In addition, Mr. Douglas has been indicted by a federal grand jury in Montgomery for allegedly falsifying a $400,000 capital investment in Financial Management and allegedly falsifying the status of certain loans on the company's books."

Just the facts. What Navita did not explain was why a Special Prosecutor was needed to put this piddly-assed little loan shark in the pokey. After all, he and two of his buddies had already been indicted by a federal grand jury based on information developed by the local FBI office and the U. S. Attorney. There was, of course, more to it than that. I was about to add my views and share what I had learned about Douglas, but then I saw that Norton was prepared to do so. From our earlier

conversations and his posture now, I could tell that he was eager to unload. Glad that I had hesitated, because it was an interesting show.

"Let me add a little additional background to what Navita has provided," Nate said. "From her description of Mr. Douglas, you might get
the mistaken impression that he is a small-time con man and self-dealing
crook, but that's not exactly true. He is a major league scumbag. He's
been running scams for years, and he has fooled and used people all
along the way. He was national President of the Jaycees, and he was appointed by President Ford to the U.S. Bicentennial Commission and the
U.S. Council on Inflation. While he was busy losing millions at Financial Management, he feathered his own nest with a big house with a
swimming pool, another house on the lake, and a Mercedes roadster."

Norton then gave us the political background, and it was enlighten-
ing. Even for me. "Douglas and Financial Management might have continued doing business as usual, except for a change in administrations in
January 1993," he said. "The SBA completed a rather thorough examination and referred the report to the FBI. Then, FBI agents entered the
offices at Financial Management Services on July 21 with a search warrant for records and files on questionable loans identified in the examination."

Where was Norton going with this? Did the Cannon administration
target Financial Management for a rigorous examination because Douglas had supported Dilberry and Grenier in their campaigns against Cannon? My inquiring mind wanted to know.

Norton did not elaborate but continued to lay out the chronology.
"Douglas must have been surprised to find that SBA was finally onto his
game. His first lawyer met with the Assistant U. S. Attorney, learned the
facts of their case against Douglas, and almost immediately withdrew
from further representation of Douglas. Then Douglas retained an attorney named Adam Tiler, who, not coincidentally, was the law partner of
Nelson Grenier's 1990 campaign finance chairman. The U. S. Attorney's
Office told Tiler it was prepared to indict Douglas on felony charges at
the September meeting of the grand jury. Tiler then placed calls to the
White House in August and suggested to aides that President Cannon
might have an interest in the investigation, that it could be embarrassing
for the administration. He was hoping that they might foolishly involve
themselves in the matter, but this ploy proved a dead end. The aides
never called back."

"Failing to get any political relief from the White House," Norton
said, "Tiler then tried to force a favorable decision from the new U. S.
Attorney. Mary Beech Gould, recently appointed by Cannon, took over
shortly after Labor Day and met with Tiler on September 7, 1993. At this
meeting Tiler suggested that Douglas could implicate a number of

prominent Democrats in criminal activity, some of whom might be too big for her to prosecute. According to Gould, Tiler provided no names or details, only vague insinuations, and said that Douglas would cooperate if the government would grant him immunity. Gould offered only use immunity so Douglas could proffer his allegations to the FBI, and she told Tiler that she thought that the case against Douglas merited a felony charge. No deal."

It was hard to tell whether Tiler was practicing law or playing political hardball, but it soon became clear what was really going on. Norton saw it all very clearly and proceeded to help everyone else do the same. "A week later, unable to cut a deal for Douglas, Tiler requested that Gould recuse from the case and request a special prosecutor. Nice try, but Gould said there was no apparent basis for recusal and that Tiler and Douglas had offered none. That same week, probably on September 17, Douglas started talking to Nelson Grenier's old buddy Luis Gerucht from *The New York Times*. That put an end to any further negotiations. On September 23, the same day that Douglas was indicted by a federal grand jury in Montgomery, an article appeared in the *Post-Advertiser*, quoting Douglas and first mentioning his charges against Vance and Cannon."

That brought the "ah ha" look to the faces around the table, but Norton just smiled and continued, "At this point things really started to get interesting, so pay attention. In addition to the legal strategy provided by Tiler, Douglas began a series of almost daily meetings and more than 40 telephone conversations with Judge James Boutwell Crommelin. Judge Crommelin, a very colorful character, got his start in politics working for Shurmond and the Dixiecrats in 1948 and was elected to the state senate as a nominal Democrat in the 1950s. Insiders called him 'the Lizard from Lowndes.' Made a reputation for himself as a lawyer for the White Citizens Council fighting school integration and was elected to the state Supreme Court, where he distinguished himself by upholding the state law against teaching evolution, only to be overturned nine-zip by the United States Supreme Court. Crommelin supported Goldwater in 1964, and some years later came out of the closet as a Republican. He was an outspoken critic of Cannon as early as 1976, the year in which Cannon was elected Attorney General and Judge Crommelin lost yet another try for a political comeback."

"Anyway," Norton said as he wrapped it up, "Judge Crommelin put Douglas in contact with Floyd Crump and David Winderig at Critics Unlimited, the right-wing anti-Cannon propaganda factory. They helped Douglas spin and peddle a story that he had been forced into a life of crime by pressure from President Cannon and Governor Vance. News stories to that effect by Gerucht in the *Times* and Jay Fuhrman of the

Washington Sun appeared during the first week in November. That same week David Winderig coached Douglas and helped produce an NBC interview with Douglas in Tiler's office. Consequently, Gould contacted the Department of Justice and announced her recusal from the case on November 8. That's the twisted road that led to appointment of a special counsel and eventually to our being here tonight."

Some of that I already knew, but for the first time I was starting to see a pattern that had eluded me before tonight. Somehow listening to the presentations was different from reading reports, and it allowed my mind enough leisure to pull things together. Two things seemed to emerge here. First, no big surprise, those fanning the political flames and stoking the press reports were Republicans who had long opposed Cannon. They were, it seemed, getting a lot more help from the national media than they'd ever been able to get in the state papers. The local editors and reporters were not so easily seduced by such political fantasies, because they knew the folks involved and their real motives. On both sides.

Second, I was beginning to understand that racism was a part of the mixture fueling the political fires that brought Whirlpool to a boil. What was interesting, I thought, was that Douglas, Grenier, and Crommelin had once been Democrats, back when that party was the bastion of white supremacy. Since the civil rights movement, however, there was little place for the old racist bigots and Ku Kluxers in the Democratic party, so there had been considerable switching to the Republican party in Alabama. Like Charlie Graddick, who had been endorsed by the Klan when he lost in the 1986 gubernatorial primary. Of course, even after he made the switch, he still got beat. Maybe they were forced out by young liberal activists, maybe they didn't like having to associate with black political leaders, or maybe they were more comfortable in a party where their views about race were still embraced. It was a motley collection of haters and baiters. And these new converts appeared to be the most zealous in trying to ruin the careers of folks like Cannon and Vance. They were more like Jeff Sessions and Jeremiah Denton than like John Buchanan or P. W. Crum. That is to say they were meaner and nastier than those who were Republicans because they had been born that way.

Burke had been taking notes during Nate's presentation, but he said nothing yet. I was glad that he seemed interested in working through this as quickly as possible, but I would've liked to have known what he was thinking right now. He just nodded his approval for a job done well, then suggested that we take a short break. I guess he was thinking he'd like to investigate the facilities in the men's room.

Chapter Eight

When we returned to the board room I was hoping that Burke would provide some color commentary on Douglas and Financial Management, but he seemed more interested in listening and learning for the moment. He again thanked Nate Norton and Navita James for their work then looked down the table to his left, indicating that he was ready to proceed wth the report on Josh Banaghan and Jefferson Savings Bank.

Paul Barefield led off with the history of Banaghan's acquisition of Jefferson in 1982 and the regulatory problems that finally resulted in its takeover by the Resolution Trust Corporation in 1989. Banaghan had been removed from management in July 1986, and the Federal Home Loan Bank Board examination showed a capital deficiency of $10.4 million at the end of that year. By the end of 1987, Jefferson had lost $12.1 million, and the state regulators recommended that it be closed immediately. Finally, two years later, federal regulators acted to close the institution in 1989, at which time it was $47.7 million in the hole, ranking 194th in losses among institutions that year. Jefferson Savings was small potatoes, even in Alabama, constituting only 3.3% of the losses in the state. Banaghan was then indicted for bank fraud in 1989 but was acquitted. Barefield's analysis was more detailed but not inconsistent with what Janet Fox had told me about Banaghan and the history of Jefferson Savings.

One thing, however, came as a surprise. I knew that Jefferson had lost over $4 million on the retirement and resort development on Dauphin Island, but I didn't know that one of the investors in the project had been none other than Nelson Grenier. I was even more surprised to learn that, for some unknown reason, Jefferson Savings had paid Mr. Grenier $362,500 for his interest in 1988, allowing him to pocket a handsome profit on his investment while the taxpayers ate the losses. Seems he was one of the very few people ever to make any money from Jefferson Savings.

Our job with regard to Jefferson Savings, Barefield said, was to examine a number of criminal referrals on the institution and affiliated individuals that had been prepared in 1992 and 1993 by investigators from the Atlanta office of the RTC. Specifically, the referrals dealt with questions about Banaghan's relationship with Cannon. Did Cannon and Whirlpool benefit from the misuse of insured funds at Jefferson? Did Banaghan misapply loan funds from Jefferson to pay Cannon's personal loans or campaign debts? Did Cannon or Vance benefit in any way from Banaghan's operation of Jefferson? Did Banaghan misapply Jefferson funds to his personal accounts or related companies? It was standard insider stuff that usually followed the closing of any savings and loan during the 1980s, but this one had come within the province of a special prosecutor because the referrals involved a former business partner of President Cannon.

I noticed Sean getting a file folder from his briefcase, and I was looking forward to what he would have to say about the Jefferson investigation. Not only would he be versed in the details of the paper trail, but he had spent the week with Burke in Washington, working with the investigators from Justice and the Resolution Trust Corporation and talking with the staff of the House and Senate Banking Committees. And he had good political sense.

Sean was as relaxed and professional as always. "First," he said, "I have to tell you that we're going to have some problems here that do not usually present themselves in an investigation. The minority leadership in Congress has a particular interest in these matters, and they have already demanded hearings. I anticipate that the Democrats will agree to that, if only to avoid the stock accusations of a cover-up. Mr. Burke and I have discussed this, and it is our intention to seek an agreement to delay any hearing schedule until we can get our work done and to try to get them to limit the scope so as not to interfere with our investigation. We all saw what happened as a result of the Iran-Contra hearings, and none of us want a repeat of that."

Yeah, we all knew that Ollie North walked and became the hero of the Newt Reich. Congress freely granted immunity to the witnesses, and the courts overturned the convictions obtained by the Independent Counsel. And before he left office, President Stuart granted pardons to everyone else.

"Now, I have no idea how successful we will be with that," he added. "Senator Dolor, the Minority Leader, has threatened to block all major legislation in the Senate unless hearings are scheduled soon, and Gastone Diletto, the Ranking Member of the Senate Banking Committee, is marching in lockstep with Dolor. On the House side, the major problem is Dick Leech, the Ranking Member of the House Banking Committee. I can't quite figure what's going on with him, but he will clearly be the political point man for the opposition in the House. He has already been calling press conferences and leaking RTC documents. These guys have been calling for hearings since November, and I don't know that we can reason with them at this point. We thought that appointment of an Independent Counsel would have satisfied them, but it's obvious what they really want is some serious television face time for themselves."

"Second," Sean continued, "this phase of our investigation was, just like the others, conceived in politics and born in the last campaign, but it is even more bizarre. The Resolution Trust Corporation had pretty much written off the Jefferson Savings case after the 1990 acquittal of Banaghan and two other insiders on bank fraud charges. However, the March 1992 *New York Times* article by Luis Gerucht injected the issue into the presidential campaign. In less than two weeks, Ellende Varken, an investigator in the RTC Atlanta office, managed to get the case reopened, decided it should be top priority, and had herself assigned to conduct the investigation. That was no trouble, considering her political background and the fact that the Stuart appointees running the RTC would not mind finding something to hang on Cannon during the campaign."

So, this was another ball tossed into the air by Grenier through his connection to Gerucht. That guy was driven and determined to get even with Cannon for the thrashing he took in the 1990 election. Or something. I was beginning to get a little tired of this. It seemed that Mark and Jeanne had it right. All of these charges had been instigated or invented by Cannon's enemies in Alabama, then spread by complicit reporters during the 1992 campaign. Failing to keep Cannon from being elected, the Republicans in Congress were determined to keep him from governing by a barrage of hearings and special prosecutors. I gave Sean a look to let him know that I well remembered our conversation in Austin when I had expressed my doubts about this whole deal. I could tell he knew exactly what I was thinking.

Sean quickly looked away and again returned to his notes. "After dropping the scheduled investigations of ten much larger institutions in Alabama, Varken spent much of the summer in Birmingham combing through the Jefferson records. By the end of August, she produced a criminal referral, a report that suggested that Banaghan had been drawing checks between companies he owned and naming the Cannons and Vance, not as targets for criminal prosecution, but as potential witnesses of allegedly illegal activities. Obviously a gratuitous political act, right? Wait; it gets better. It was also during this time, according to sworn testimony, that an unidentified female employee of the RTC was telling people at a cocktail party in Atlanta that the Cannons had been named in a criminal referral related to bank fraud in Alabama."

Continuing to illuminate the political trail, it was also obvious that Sean had done his homework on this. "This information was transmitted on September 1 to the FBI and the Republican United States Attorney in Birmingham. They looked at it and decide that it is not worth pursuing, not even strong enough to open an investigation, much less take to a grand jury. Not only was the report short on proof. Not only had they already lost one case against Banaghan on similar charges. By this time Cannon was the nominee and leading Stuart in the polls, so it would be obvious to everyone except Varken and the press mongers that any such action would be an unfounded and embarrassing attempt at inflicting political damage.

"That might have been the end of it," Sean said, "but that was not to be. Mrs. Varken kept calling the FBI and pushing them to act on the referral. She told the agent in charge that this could change the course of history and implied that he and the U. S. Attorney were afraid to charge Cannon. She also complained that she had passed up the chance for a better job with the administration in Washington to pursue and help with this investigation. Varken, it turned out, was not the only one concerned about Cannon's lead in the polls at that time. Sometime in September, White House Counsel G. Gordon Bray contacted the RTC to inquire about the status of the criminal referral on Jefferson Savings. On September 17, President Stuart's cabinet secretary, a former Treasury Department General Counsel who was now working as White House liaison to the Committee to Re-Elect the President, contacted the Attorney General to see if she could get the details of any criminal referrals that might involve Cannon. In early October copies of the RTC referral were delivered to the Attorney General for his personal review and decision, and later that month the FBI in Birmingham started getting pressure from him to take another look at the allegations.

"On October 19, Tom Davenport, the U. S. Attorney here sent a letter to the Attorney General expressing his resentment of the political pressure from above and refusing to become involved with the matter before the election. One week later the local FBI requested the RTC office in Atlanta to redirect their resources and resume the criminal investigation of the two major Alabama institutions that had lost almost $1.5 billion. The Stuart administration, already facing public criticism for an investigation of Cannon's passport files, backed off and let it drop."

"As you know," Sean went on, "that was *not* the end of the matter. Even after the election Varken kept pushing the referral and demanding action. In February 1993, a career Justice Department lawyer reviewed the file and said it was without merit, and on March 19 the Assistant Attorney General reached the same conclusion. The chief of the Fraud Section and a former chief of the Public Integrity Section at Main Justice, told us that the referral was 'junky' and that it had 'come in halfbaked.' The problem was that no federal crime was alleged.

"However, in May, 1993, Ellende Varken again took up her crusade and started calling the FBI, the U. S. Attorney's office, and the Department of Justice. She quickly discovered that no one was very impressed with her allegations. Nonetheless, she was encouraged by Richard Menteur and Austin Leugen, senior RTC investigators in Atlanta, to continue her pursuit of something implicating the Cannons. Instead of working on the two major failures targeted by the RTC and the FBI, Mrs. Varken came back to Birmingham and spent another three months developing nine additional criminal referrals involving Jefferson Savings. Can you say *zealot*?"

Yeah, and I could say a lot of other things, too. Like witch hunt and abuse of authority by political partisans in regulatory agencies. The FBI and the Republican United States Attorney had both seen Varken's report for what it was, and at least two career attorneys at the Department of Justice had also rejected it as a political crock. It was all I could do from jumping in and asking why no one at the RTC had put a stop to this nonsense, but, before I did, Sean explained that they tried. In fact, it was the efforts of RTC supervisors to provide a reality check that had contributed to our having to deal with the issue.

"Perhaps," Sean said, "some of you are wondering why the RTC didn't exercise a little more responsibility in this matter. They did attempt to do so, but Varken was on a mission and was not about to let anyone get in her way. Varken and her associates completed the additional referrals and on September 24 the Atlanta office legal staff asked to review them before they were submitted to the FBI in Birmingham. There seems to have been good reason for this, considering the unsatisfactory quality of the previous referrals. Varken reluctantly provided the referrals and backup documentation, but on October 4 she filed a complaint with the Inspector General alleging that the review was an attempt to obstruct her investigation. Like the song says, paranoia strikes deep. It was also during this time frame that someone started leaking details of the investigation to the press, but that's another story altogether. If anyone is interested, we can discuss the details of that later. I think we have it narrowed down to two people."

Well, I was interested, but I could certainly wait for the rest of the story. There was no doubt in my mind that Varken was one of the leakers, and I suspected that she had some help from someone in Washington. I didn't know about anyone else in the room, but I was about ready to take a break. I was sitting next to Burke, so I thought about making sure that he would see me checking my watch. Probably not a good idea. I reached for the water pitcher to refill my glass, but it was empty. Sean appeared to be almost finished, so I just sat back and relaxed.

"There was no conspiracy to obstruct the Jefferson investigation," he said, "merely a concern that the referrals not be another batch of unsupported allegations. They were corrected and transmitted to U. S. Attorney Gould on October 8, 1993. While they were being reviewed by her office, Gould received a call from Justice asking her to please give Varken a written decision on the original criminal referral so she would leave them alone. So, Gould sent a letter on October 27, informing the RTC, 'I concur with the opinion of the Department attorneys that there is insufficient information in the referral to sustain any of the allegations made by the investigators or to warrant the initiation of a criminal investigation.' Varken, who by this time had become obsessed with the Cannons, suspected that her new referrals would meet the same fate. Four days later, the details of the investigation and the new allegations against Cannon and Vance appeared in a *Washington Post* article by Danielle Leonard, followed by a series of articles in the *Washington Sun* and the *American Speculator* These hit the press, perhaps not coincidentally, during the same week that the Roby Douglas allegations were first floated in the national media. That's when Gould announced her recusal, and both investigations were assigned to the special counsel."

As Sean closed his file, Bill Bailey, who was seated to my right, leaned over and said, "Hope you're up for a beer. I don't plan to take long."

Burke overheard that remark. I thought I saw a small smile on his lips, just for a second before he suppressed it and said, "Thank you Mr. O'Rourke. Mr. Bailey, will you enlighten us on the status of the Goodall investigation?" I wondered if Burke ever found any of this even slightly amusing. Probably not, but I don't guess it really mattered.

"Some of you are probably asking why we are charged with reopening the investigation of the death of Hal Goodall. Let me assure you that I ask myself that question on a daily basis," Bailey began, with only a slight touch of irony in his voice. "The official answer is because Goodall was the Cannons' attorney for Whirlpool matters. Goodall and Cannon had been childhood friends in Fairhope, and he and the First Lady had been partners in the same law firm in Montgomery. He had handled the negotiations with Banaghan to sell the Cannon's Whirlpool interest in 1992, and he also prepared and filed the tax returns to close out their responsibility for the investment. It seems that the Whirlpool files, as well as some other personal and campaign-related records, were stored in his office at the time of his death, and these files were removed to the White House residence area while the Park Police were still investigating his death."

"Now, it does not appear that removing the files impeded the investigation," he continued. "Nevertheless, that has not stopped the lunatic fringe from inventing some of the strangest conspiracy theories ever hatched by a fevered human brain. You've probably heard some of them or read about them in the *American Speculator* or the *Washington Sun*. These range from clandestine love triangles to secret Swiss bank accounts to international espionage. Stir in murder, then borrow anything else you can find in the *Warren Report*, and you'd qualify as a middling editorial writer for any number of newspapers. Before long some Republican members of Congress were inserting clippings in the *Congressional Record* and calling for hearings and a special prosecutor. There is a veritable scandal factory at work, and most of it seems to be funded by Howard Mellonskoff and his foundations."

Burke straightened in his chair, and it appeared that he was uncomfortable with Bailey's colorful debunking of the issue. Bailey knew far too much about criminal investigations and evidence to tolerate such nonsense. Burke knew that and probably agreed with everything Bailey had said, but he was the one who would be held responsible for the scope and tone of any reports we produced. They exchanged glances, but neither had to say what they were thinking. Sitting between them, I might have been the only one in the room to catch the importance of the unspoken conversation that had just occurred.

Bailey played it straight as he finished his report. "Okay, forget about Mellonskoff and his paid minions. At least for now. I have already reviewed all of the investigative reports with the FBI and the Park Police. And, in case you have any doubts, let me assure you that they were very thorough. At this point, I have absolutely no reason to doubt the official conclusions that Hal Goodall was suffering from severe depression and took his own life. While the pressure of political life in Washington and the harsh personal attacks by the *Wall Street Journal* might have contributed to that, there is no basis for the outrageous rumors that continue to be spread by those with political motives. I hope to have my report finished within two months, then I can go back to my law practice, and Goodall's family can get on with their lives."

I was the last to make my report, and I kept it as brief as possible. I tried to relate what I had learned about the local political culture and fill in the facts that could be discovered only by visiting the scenes of the drama. When I mentioned that I had developed a good source of information in Janet Fox, Burke interrupted. "I forgot to mention it in my opening remarks," he said, "but I cannot caution you strongly enough about the need for confidentiality in this investigation. I don't want to read a word about what we are doing in the newspapers. I have not hired a press liaison, and I am the only person who should be making any comments to the media. And that specifically includes any background or off-the-record information. The first time someone leaks information to the press, I'll have a resignation the next day. We are here to find the facts and do our job. I have never tried my cases in the press, and I do not want this office involved in any way in the partisan political games that are being played out elsewhere. Am I clear about that? Good. Now proceed with what you were saying, Mr. Wilkes."

Damn, I hated being reprimanded. Really hated it. Especially in front of everyone. I agreed with Burke and was glad that was his attitude, yet that didn't make it any easier to accept the fact that my remarks had provoked that lecture. I took a deep breath, but I couldn't remember where I had been headed. "I think I've covered what I had to say. The only thing I might add is that y'all need to get rid of those New York plates on your cars if you plan to be using your private vehicles during the investigation. As you know, we have four cars assigned to the office, but sometimes those government tags make folks forget things. You can get Alabama plates and a driver's license at the Jefferson County Court-house downtown. I've got a little brochure that explains everything, so see me if you decide to do that. I recommend that you do. It'll make your life easier, even for little things like writing checks."

It was back to Burke. He thanked everyone for their work thus far. Said it was outstanding and that he was very pleased. Then, as everyone was leaving the room and heading home, Burke motioned for me to stay. He assured me that he had full confidence in my discretion and did not mean to imply that he thought I would divulge any information about our investigation. I appreciated that, but it didn't make me feel any less embarrassed.

Burke walked toward the elevator in the lobby, and I turned the other way and headed for the bar. I regained my sense of humor and almost laughed when I noticed the portraits of Louis Bourbon and Marie Antoinette hanging in the hall outside the boardroom where we'd been meeting. I hoped that wasn't an omen for the Cannons. The bar was dimly lit, but I saw Sean and Bailey motioning for me to join them at a table. I was in bad need of refreshment, so I passed on the beer and ordered a Black Jack on the rocks.

After some friendly fire about Burke crawling my ass at the meeting, I got a full report on what they had been doing last week in Washington. I was sorry that Bailey was going back on Monday, because I really liked his attitude and appreciated the way he could capture the complexities of politics with a few quick but well chosen words. I liked everyone on the staff, for that matter, and I knew they would do first class work on an otherwise mundane task.

I had been waiting all evening to ask Sean about the well-timed leaks from the RTC, and I did so as soon as we got a second round of drinks. He said there was no doubt that Ellende Varken had been the source of the information, and she certainly had the motivation for doing so. She was a big time Republican. Her father had been a career military officer, and she had the same mindset. Said Cannon was a coward for not serving in the military. Got her start as a secretary at a savings and loan, then ingratiated herself with the regulators by implicating her boss when it went under. She had been a big talker in the coffee shop political conversations at the RTC. She also had some personal issues to work through, coming off a divorce. One of her colleagues recalled her calling Cannon a "lying bastard," back before she was even involved in the investigation of Jefferson. Then, after the election, she had been promoting t-shirts or something that made reference to the First Lady as a bossy bitch. She had been consumed by the chance to tie the Cannons into the Jefferson failure and made some pretty loose charges that required major leaps of logic to implicate them in Banaghan's business transactions. After the U. S. Attorney rejected the first referral, she made sure that word of the investigation would be picked up by the media.

Sean knew that Danielle Leonard of the *Post* had copies of the criminal referrals Varken had prepared. It was, he said, a pretty clever strategy to leak it to the *Post* first. If Jay Fuhrman had scooped the story in the *Sun*, it would be too obvious what was going on, and everyone would see it as just another smear from the GOP's house organ. It was possible, he said, that Varken made the contact with Leonard. Ms Leonard had already written one story back in March 1993 about the son of a Cannon cabinet member defaulting on an apartment complex in Atlanta that he had purchased from the RTC. In that instance it was pretty clear that RTC documents in the Atlanta office had been leaked to Leonard to embarrass the new administration.

There was another possibility, but Sean said he was not yet sure about that one. There was a guy at the RTC in Washington named Stan Korst who might have been involved with leaking the Jefferson referrals to the media. Korst represented himself as a career employee, but these days that meant anyone who had worked for the Republican administrations during the previous 12 years. Korst had been a press secretary at EPA for Ann Buford under Reeder, then he had held a similar job under Stuart at the FDIC before moving to the RTC. One of the things he did, under the guise of informing the RTC staff about press inquiries, was to publish a weekly newsletter called the "Early Bird Report." Everyone called it 'the leak sheet,' because reporters always seemed to get copies and had a road map to any potential problems. He reported inquiries about criminal referrals at Jefferson in late September, after the RTC Washington office had copies but before they were sent by the Atlanta office to the U. S. Attorney in Birmingham. Whether that tipped Leonard or only reflected that the material had already been leaked when Varken thought the regional administrators were trying to sit on her, it was hard to say.

In any event, Sean had a copy of an e-mail message dated October 6, 1993, from Varken to Korst indicating that she had talked with Leonard about the Jefferson referrals. That was two days after Varken had filed her complaint with the Inspector General and two days before the referrals were sent to the U. S. Attorney. Whatever the case, it was clear that the confidential RTC documents had been leaked to the press.

The waitress came by just then to ask if we wanted another round, and that stopped the discussion. We told her that we did, but, as law abiding citizens, we would be unable to drive home unless she wanted to be the designated driver. She laughed, I picked up the tab, and we called it a night. As we were walking out of the bar, I noticed an inscription on a plaque over the door—*Fontes Fortuna Juvet*. I certainly hoped so. It had been quite a day, and I was feeling older than 43.

Chapter Nine

Burke was already at work when I got to the office at 7:45 on Monday. This guy was serious. I had hoped to have a few minutes of quiet time to get organized before the day started, but I was soon disabused of that notion.

"Mr. Wilkes, I need to see you for a few minutes," Burke said as soon as he heard my computer booting. He almost shouted the words. Maybe he was just avoiding the intercom. Maybe he had another lecture for me.

"Be there in a minute," I replied. Of course, there was nothing stopping me from going right then, but I didn't want him to become conditioned to my jumping whenever he barked. I guess I was still a little pissed about being humiliated at the meeting Saturday night. Okay, I'd waited long enough. Long enough for him to get the message and long enough for me to realize it didn't really matter. I opened the door connecting our offices and walked on in with a better attitude.

"Mr. Wilkes, have a seat. First, I realize I owe you an apology," he said. "I did not intend for my remarks about press contacts to be taken as a warning to you, but I know you thought they did. I can assure you when I have some comment about your job performance there'll be no doubt what I am saying. And, furthermore, I would tell you in a private conference, not in a staff meeting. I hope we have an understanding. That's the end of the matter as far as I'm concerned."

I just nodded my agreement, then I sat down across from his desk. He was holding a yellow legal pad, and I could tell there was more to come.

"Second," he continued, "I have the impression that you think this is all just politics."

I waited for a moment then realized that he meant that as a question. "No, I think it's mostly bullshit. Politics is more artful. That's not to say I don't think we'll find some criminal violations. I think we will. In fact, I think we already have with Roby Douglas. I assume that every loan file we have from Financial Management represents at least two defendants. But, yeah, obviously I think it's political. That shouldn't be a surprise to anyone. These things always are, to some degree. What makes this investigation different from the others, in my mind, is that all the allegations are about relatively petty offenses that supposedly happened ten years ago. This is not Watergate or Iran-Contra. It's about penny-ante con jobs, not about the subversion of the constitution. Most of this stuff would be considered of relatively low priority in the caseload of any U. S. Attorney."

Burke didn't seem to disagree. "My concern," he said, "is that you might not be taking this seriously. Even granting your assumptions, which I do not dispute, I believe it's important that we approach this investigation in a professional manner."

"Well, I admit that I'm always skeptical, but that's part of my basic nature. It has nothing to do with the specifics of this investigation," I said. "I don't take all of the charges seriously, but I take my job very seriously, my flippant comments notwithstanding. If you ever think I'm too frank in sharing my assessments, I'm confident that you'll let me know. But I thought one reason I was hired was to give you my honest opinion about the politics of this investigation. If I'm mistaken about that, then this would be a good time for me to, uh, seek a new career opportunity, as they say."

"You're not mistaken. Now let's get on to more important things," he said, almost as if that were what he had wanted to hear. I think he probably expected a little more deference from his staff, but it didn't seem to bother him that I had declined to pucker up and plant one.

Almost without taking a breath, Burke moved quickly to the task. "I want you to take responsibility for getting a special grand jury impaneled. It's not that I don't trust the one already sitting, but we are going to require their undivided attention for the next six months. Next, and before I forget to tell you, your briefing book was fine work, and it has already proven invaluable. I spent Sunday afternoon converting it to a database. We now have a comprehensive list of every person and entity that has been mentioned in any of the investigative files. Please see to it that we have subpoenas ready to issue to every person on the list, requesting any and all documents relating to any of the other persons or entities. I don't give much credence to the newspaper reports of document shredding, but I don't want to take any chances."

Oh, yeah. That would get their attention. The request for a special grand jury would be a matter of public record. Those subpoenas are wonderful things, too. No one would doubt that Mr. Burke had come to town and was in charge of this investigation. I better understood now that he had earned and deserved his reputation as seasoned prosecutor who was here to do his job. The list of people and businesses was seven single-spaced pages, and a quick count indicated that we were going to be serving about 215 subpoenas. And, it went almost without saying, the dust would not have settled on the grand jury headlines before word on the nature, scope, and number of subpoenas would hit the press.

"Will that be all?" I asked, knowing that I had a full plate already.

"No. Tell Ms James and Mr. Norton to be ready to go on Douglas. We can use the sitting grand jury for that, but I want a superseding indictment before the end of the week. Use your own judgment as to which trial judge, but it should probably be a Republican appointee. I don't want to have to hear any more recusal arguments from Mr. Tiler. No doubt the clerk will tell you it's random assignment, but there's random, and there's random. That's all for right now."

I talked with Navita and Nate about getting the subpoenas prepared, and I introduced them to the FBI agents assigned to our office by Special Agent Osborn. We had the exclusive use of seven agents, all of whom had all lived in Birmingham for at least three years, and that experience would serve us well. I planned to assign one agent to work with each of the staff lawyers, but I didn't have that worked out yet. It wouldn't matter for now, because they all would be busy handling subpoenas for the rest of the week.

As I was leaving the office and heading downtown to take care of the grand jury request, I stopped to ask the receptionist to forward my calls to my secretary. She was on the phone and had two calls holding. "I'm sorry, Mr. Burke is not giving any interviews," she said.

When she looked up between calls, I asked, "Reporters keeping you busy?"

"That makes 14 this morning," she said with a tone of resignation. It was only 9:30.

As I was driving into town I felt a little silly about having taken Burke's remarks as a personal rebuke. That's just the way he operated. The more I learned about him, the more I respected him. I liked his approach to this job—giving up his lucrative private practice, putting together such a fine staff, taking a chance on me, ignoring the partisan advantages of the investigation, moving so quickly to get things done, trying to deal with the congressional hacks, avoiding being drawn into the media show, and, especially, the preference for straight talk over small talk. If there had to be a special counsel and a Whirlpool investigation, the country would be well served. They could have done a lot worse than Kenneth Burke.

I smiled as I parked across the street from the Hugo L. Black United States Courthouse. It was deliciously ironic, I thought. Although Black had been reviled by the local segs after the *Brown* decision, his life was, in many ways, a metaphor for the South. Black had been a member of the Klan, but he once explained that the Klan was the liberal wing of the

Alabama Democratic party in those days, the populist voice of the people against the railroads and the planter oligarchy. After being elected to the Senate and exhibiting considerable enthusiasm for the New Deal programs, he was appointed to the Court by Roosevelt in 1937. And once there, his devotion to the Constitution and the Bill of Rights continued to reflect the South of Jefferson and Madison rather than that of Calhoun and Wallace. There were many who resented Black, but the impressive new courthouse would still be standing long after they were dead. Too bad I couldn't say the same about their ideas.

The irony became more personal as I entered the building through the green marble archway that camouflaged a metal detector. A bust of Justice Black dominated the rotunda, surrounded by four quotes on wall panels. The text of the First Amendment and an excerpt from his 1968 Carpenter Lecture extolling his devotion to the Constitution were to be expected, but the other two were not. Or maybe I was now more sensitive to their meaning. The first was from his dissent in *Dennis v. United States*, vainly warning the nation in 1951 against the excesses of the anticommunist witch hunt. The second hit home for me more directly. It was a quote from his opinion in *Chambers v. Florida* proclaiming that the "courts stand against winds that might blow as havens of refuge for those who might otherwise suffer because they are victims of . . . public excitement." I hoped he had it right, then I took the elevator to see about getting a special grand jury for Whirlpool.

Jonathan Corwin was the Senior United States District Judge in the Birmingham division of the Middle District of Alabama, and he had responsibility for impaneling any special grand jury. I didn't know much about him except that he was a Reeder appointee, a graduate of Auburn and the University of Alabama School of Law, still in his early fifties. I knew even less about the other Republican judge in the Birmingham division, Julia Hoffman, who was appointed by Stuart. I figured I would soon get an education in such matters. My ignorance was bi-partisan, since I didn't know much about the Democrats, either. Virginia D. Clifford, Edward Cook, and A. George Gaston were Carter appointees, and James Wilson was Cannon's only appointment to the local bench.

Judge Corwin's office was on the sixth floor. He needed to practice smiling, but he was otherwise quite pleasant. And helpful. We had talked for only a few minutes before he agreed to schedule a hearing on Wednesday to consider our request for the new grand jury. He also introduced me to the Clerk of the Court and provided copies of the Local Rules for our office. I didn't ask directly, but I soon discovered how cases were assigned. The deputy clerk called it a random system, but, in fact, they were assigned by alphabetical rotation—Clifford, Cook, Corwin, Gaston, Hoffman, Wilson. To assure a particular judge, all I would have to do was check the most recent filing to see who was up next then wait until the appropriate time to file an information or indictment.

It was almost lunch time when I finished at the courthouse, so I stopped by the *News* to see if Janet Fox would talk with me again. After Burke's comments, I was glad that she hadn't called me at the office, but I wanted to know more about this Nelson Grenier, whose name kept coming up in all the reports. He seemed to be involved, one way or another, in almost every aspect of our investigation. The current talk was that he was planning to run for governor against Vance, but I was much more interested in learning about his past. Janet would be able to fill in all the blanks.

My lunch plans, however, soon fell flat. Janet no longer worked at the *News*. She'd moved to Washington and taken a job with *USA Today*. I was glad for her, I suppose, but disappointed nonetheless. Once again I resorted to the morgue files, and there was more than enough. Grenier had gone to work for Alabama Power straight out of Troy State. One article had a picture of Grenier and Roby Douglas, when Douglas was president of the Jaycees and Grenier was the Jaycees' Young Executive of the Year. He rose quickly in the management structure under the tutelage of Wilton Smith, but later turned on him, becoming president after a bitter board fight that ended in Smith's resignation. It was a pattern of ruthlessly using people that seemed to repeat itself. Grenier exercised his stock options, pocketed several million dollars, and then left the company to start a law firm in 1989.

Governor Cannon named Grenier chairman of the Board of Industry and Commerce, a plum appointment, and Grenier used that post primarily to promote himself and make personal contacts for private business deals. Then, in another self-serving gesture of ingratitude, Grenier switched to the Republican party and ran against Cannon in 1990. He spent $ 2.6 million in a mean-spirited campaign, including $1.1 million of his own money, and Cannon still beat him like a drum. Grenier licked his wounds as co-chair of the state party after that humiliating defeat, and he was now the state's member of the Republican National Committee. Grenier's 1990 campaign slogan had been "A Better Man for the Job," but one editorial detailing his pathetic efforts to smear Cannon as a liberal was entitled "A Bitter Man for the Jab." It didn't take me long to get the picture, and, apparently, it was the same one the voters had of him.

Things moved quickly that week. On Tuesday, the subpoenas went out. On Wednesday, Judge Corwin granted our request for a special Whirlpool grand jury. On Thursday, the FDIC issued a final report clearing the Bankhead law firm of any conflict of interest in their past representation of Jefferson Savings. On Friday, we filed the superseding indictments of Douglas and the two lawyers who had helped him to defraud the SBA. The case was "randomly" assigned to Judge Corwin and set to be tried in late March.

The papers that week were full of news stories about our work, and the editorial responses covered the spectrum. Jack Gourmand of the *Baltimore Sun* said, "On the face of it, the inquiry being run by independent counsel Kenneth Burke looks like a case of swatting a fly with a sledgehammer. Burke is likely to unravel a big ball of nothing." William Streicher's column in *The New York Times*, on the other hand, said we weren't doing enough to hype the Republican charges against Cannon. He called Burke the "in-house, non-independent, untrusted-by-Republicans counsel on Whirlpool." That was about what I would expect from a former Nixon staffer. Archibald Cox was untrusted-by-Republicans, too.

The next week, however, produced an amazing turn of events. The Republicans in Congress, who for 12 years had fought every attempt to hold the Reeder and Stuart administrations accountable for anything, found a new commitment to the oversight function. Problem was, they were running around like a bunch of blind hogs trying to find an acorn. Representative Clapham, ranking member of the House Government Operations Committee, pulled his nose out of the tabloids long enough to call for hearings on the death of Hal Goodall. It wasn't clear what Goodall's suicide had to do with the work of that committee, but it was a consuming matter in the paranoid fantasies of the publisher and staff of the *Pennsylvania Tribune-Review*. And campaign contributions were a consuming passion for Congressman Clapham.

Congressman Dick Leech, ranking member of the House Banking Committee, had been leaking RTC documents for months. Sean was convinced that Ellende Varken had been spoon-feeding Leech everything in her files since last fall, but now he had found a new source for headlines. Leech released a transcript of the taped conversation between Grenier and Banaghan from 1992, wherein Banaghan blasted both Vance and Cannon. Nothing in the transcript had any connection with the House Banking Committee, but that didn't stop Leech from jumping at a chance to attack Cannon. His new charge was that Cannon had actually made money on the Whirlpool investment and, therefore, should not have taken interest deductions. No one believed that Whirlpool had ever made any money, but Leech was ready to pretend that it did.

The spin was not exactly as Leech had hoped, however, when it became clear where he had gotten the transcript. Earlier that day, Floyd Crump at Critics Unlimited had begun selling copies of the tape to the media. No one was particularly surprised that Nelson Grenier would make sure the tape got out nor that Crump would sell it to any unscrupulous reporter too lazy to exercise independent thought. Leech, though, was slightly embarrassed when it became obvious to everyone that he was fronting for the Critics Unlimited attack machine. Very slightly.

We had put in two hard weeks, and with some results. It was hard to believe that it was only two weeks, but I knew it was Friday. Sean was excited that Carmen would be coming in for the weekend. She had decided to stay in New York so their daughter could finish the school term, and this would be her first trip to Birmingham. I was prepared for a little craziness at the office that afternoon. I've had the good fortune never to have worked anywhere that Friday afternoons weren't special. I was not prepared, however, for this one.

When I returned from lunch, Dana, our receptionist, greeted me with a big "Hey, lover boy." I smiled what was supposed to be that knowing smile and started down the hall, then I noticed a small crowd at my office door. Ignoring the hooting, I soon saw the source of amusement. On my desk was a vase with three red roses. Navita was holding the card to the light, trying to read the message, but she handed it to me and waited with a taunting grin for me to open it. I did. It read, "Clear your schedule, and give me a call," and it was signed "The Queen of Hearts." Everyone wanted to know who was sending me flowers, but I refused to tell, pretending it was a secret but being absolutely clueless myself.

With a bit of deduction and a phone call to the florist, I discovered that the flowers had been ordered from Montgomery. My overactive imagination hoped they were from Lindsey, but there was no way she could know I worked here. Way. I had been in the background of the AP photo of Burke announcing the indictment of Douglas last week. I took the chance and called her office. "Dr. Armstrong? This is the Mad Hatter. I have a warrant for the Queen of Hearts." And, if I was wrong, I could just hang up.

"Well, Mr. Wilkes, that was quick. I'm glad to know that the taxpayers have such a clever detective working for them. You were almost late for a very important date. The Wolfe Tones are playing in Birmingham tomorrow night. Zydeco, on 15th Avenue South, at nine. Be there, or be square."

"Can I bring a date?"

"No. You'll have to leave your wife at home!"

"Uh, actually, I'm between marriages right now. But I sorta had plans to do something with a couple of old friends, Sean and Carmen O'Rourke. They're cool, and I promise they'll behave."

"Then we'll have to work on them. Misbehaving was exactly what I had in mind," she said with high teasing in her voice. "But I do have one serious question, John. I can call you John, can't I? You're not a Republican are you?"

"Nope. Never even voted for one," I said.

"Good. I could never have a relationship with a Republican," she replied with a laugh.

"Oh, are we gonna have a relationship?" I asked, trying to sound more bemused than excited. "I thought you were just helping me with music appreciation."

"Don't get your hopes up, smartass. But, by the way, what kind of music do you like? Or do they have anything in Texas besides Bob Wills and kicker tunes? Kinky Friedman, maybe?"

"Well, I like almost anything except that feedback they call heavy metal, but Jimmy Buffett wrote my life. I would've been a pirate if I hadn't gone to law school. But, maybe the two aren't mutually exclusive." I probably should have said Haydn or Bach to impress her, but I was feeling too playful at the moment.

It turned out to be a wonderful weekend, one that I needed in a lot of ways. Good music, stimulating conversation, and cold beer. Not only was Lindsey beautiful and vivacious, she was so damn smart. I had suspected that. And now I knew for sure.

After a few beers, I was going on about the media spin on Whirlpool, complaining about the vast differences between the facts and the fictions being played out in the press. I was partly serious and partly teasing her about being an accessory before the fact as a communication professor. "It's quite simple," she said. "It is much easier to promote political conflict than to provide public comprehension. Melodrama is an easy formula. You can do it with fewer facts and less analytic effort." Of course, she was right. It wasn't so much a grand conspiracy as it was a combination of lazy reporters and media characteristics. Dynamic lethargy.

"But," I said, "shouldn't they at least get the facts right, even if they don't provide the full story?"

"Sure," she replied, "they should. In a perfect world, assuming there's one objective reality, they'd have an obligation to do that. But don't you think you're a little old to still expect that? Publishers and broadcasters see their first obligation to their stockholders. Headlines and McNews make money. You don't have to have a degree in econometrics to compare the salaries of television news readers with those for beat reporters."

Good point, I guess. But what did she mean by too old? Forty-four wasn't old. Maybe she just meant relative to my idealism. Yeah, that's probably what it was. I could have said she was too damn savvy for a 30-year old assistant professor. Could have. Then Sean and Carmen would've known for sure that I was an idiot, instead of just smiling and thinking I was acting like one.

It was an evening of many insights. I was also impressed that she continued to be coherent after we'd put away six pitchers of Red Mountain Ale. And I really liked the way she touched my arm and looked at me when she was talking. Thought I'd died and gone to heaven.

Glad I was floating on an emotional high, because March proved to be both eventful and ominous. The Senate Banking Committee began hearings, and we issued subpoenas for ten White House aides who had been briefed by Treasury officials regarding the criminal referrals on Jefferson Savings. That got a lot of press, but I didn't think it such a big deal. In my opinion, the agency people had an obligation to keep Cannon informed on the status of the investigation. He wasn't charged with anything, and it didn't appear that his staff interfered in any way. Best I could tell, they were just trying to respond to press inquiries, and someone had already leaked the same information to selected reporters. I told Burke we should be investigating who leaked confidential government documents to the press. And while we were at it, I said, maybe someone should be asking how the Jefferson referrals came to the attention of the White House during the 1992 campaign.

Burke told me we'd do one thing at a time. He went to Washington that week for two reasons. First, he and Bailey would be questioning the White House and Treasury employees before the grand jury there about their conversations regarding the Jefferson Savings referrals. Second, he wanted to try to talk some sense into Senators Dolor and Diletto and Congressmen Leech and Clapham regarding the impact of public hearings on our investigation. I didn't think he would have much luck. We had already sent letters asking them not to interfere by calling witnesses or releasing documents, yet they continued to have press conferences as regularly as most people had bowel movements. Not that there was much difference in content.

Burke met with members of the congressional committees on March 9 then held a press conference to put everyone on notice. It was the first time he'd made any public comment since his appointment, and it seemed very appropriate. C-SPAN carried the news conference, so everyone in the office gathered around to watch.

"Good afternoon. We are concerned about the impact of congressional hearings on the investigations that we are conducting as long as those investigations are in progress. There are really two separate investigations. There's the one that I started out with the end of January, which is looking into the activities in Alabama in the 1980s relating to Jefferson, Whirlpool, and Financial Management, and then one here in

Washington into all of the circumstances relating to the death of Hal Goodall.

"The disclosures in recent days about the meetings between the White House and the Treasury officials led us to initiate an additional investigation into the circumstances surrounding those meetings. And I've told Senators Diletto and Dolor and Congressmen Leech and Clapham that when we are finished with the investigation into the meetings, which I'm quite confident we can be finished with soon, we would have no objection to congressional hearings at that point, so long as something can be done to protect against having the contents of the RTC referrals themselves come out in those hearings.

"But with respect to the underlying investigation, the one that we started with, we are very concerned about the impact of congressional hearings. I've been assured that immunity will not be granted to any witness in any of these investigations. I think Senator Diletto and Congressman Leech also understand the potential problems that congressional hearings could cause for our investigation, even if immunity is not given.

"I don't think we've reached any agreement. I recognize that, in the end, it's not my decision whether congressional hearings will be held or not. That is the decision of the United States Congress. But I'm satisfied that I've had a very fair reception from both Senator Diletto and Congressmen Leech and Clapham in terms of having the opportunity to express the concerns that we have."

Well, it was clear that he hadn't gotten any promises, for whatever that would be worth. At least now, though, if they screwed it up, everyone would know who to blame. Burke was quite good with the press. He assured them that the investigation was moving along quickly, and he refused to discuss or even mention the names of anyone who had received a subpoena.

Sure enough, I was right. Dick Leech issued a press release the very next day listing 40 people he wanted to subpoena as witness before the House Banking Committee. Nothing like releasing a list of names to get press attention at the expense of our investigation and the reputations of the individuals. Even Joe McCarthy didn't name names.

When Burke got back to Birmingham he met with the staff, and we learned that there were three other fires he had been fighting on the hill. While he was asking the Republicans to act responsibly, they were demanding that he expand his investigation. First, they wanted him to look into Diane Cannon's gains on pork belly contracts in the late 70s. He declined, reminding them that even if something was amiss, which he doubted, it was 15 years ago and well beyond any statute of limitations.

Then, Senator Dolor said, Burke shouldn't mind if they held hearings about it.

Second, they wanted him to investigate Assistant Attorney General Randolph Webster. Again, Burke declined. Webster's problem was a civil matter regarding billing disputes between him and the Bankhead law firm. If there were any criminal issues, the local U.S. Attorney could handle it, Burke said, because it was not related to his charge regarding Jefferson, Whirlpool, or Financial Management. Leech's press aide said there was political mileage if one could nab a high ranking Cannon appointee, but Burke said that was not his concern. Senator Diletto indicated that he intended to call Webster as a witness at their hearings. By the end of the next week, Webster had resigned his position at Justice to try to resolve his problems at the Bankhead firm.

"You wouldn't believe the mood on the hill," Burke said. "It's already crazy, and it promises to get worse. We'll just have to do our job and try to ignore the political sideshows. I tried to talk some sense into Senator Diletto, but he just said, 'It's payback time, baby!'"

The meeting started to break up, when Navita asked, "What was the third thing? You said you were fighting three fires."

"Oh, I almost forgot," Burke said. "It wasn't much really. Mark Schine, who heads the Lynch Legal Foundation, is trying to make an issue out of the dismissal of those guys at the White House travel office last year. He's written an op-ed piece in the *Washington Sun*, and he's been talking to some of the older members about it. He still has some pull with a few of them, because he worked for Attorney General Meese. I don't think anyone takes him very seriously, though. Anyway, it's not our problem. Yet."

Chapter Ten

Lewis Grizzard died the following week and too damn soon. I commemorated his career and his passing by rereading a couple of his books and demolishing a 12-pack of PBR. He was a real journalist with a sense of humor and a keen understanding of the English language. But, just as I was beginning to think his might be an honorable profession, William Streicher had another column in the *New York Times* saying that Cannon was afraid of hearings, that Burke was doing his bidding, and that Congress should get on with the show, justice be damned.

The real news that week, however, was that Burke got a conviction when Roby Douglas copped a plea to two felonies and agreed to cooperate with our investigation. The guilty plea was due to some good work by Navita James and Nate Norton. Douglas had refused to plead guilty when U. S. Attorney Gould offered him a single felony count last fall, and we got him on two. He couldn't take the deal quickly enough when he saw the list of charges we could have filed.

The cooperation part of the plea bargain was much less valuable. I sat in on one of the FBI interviews with Douglas, and it was apparent to everyone in the room that he was a classic affidavit man. He'd tell any story and swear to anything we wanted. The guy had been lying so long, he wouldn't know the truth if it bit him on the butt. Even if he could keep his stories straight, I didn't think any jury would ever believe him. However, that didn't stop the *Washington Sun* and the *American Speculator* from repeatedly printing his charges that Cannon and Vance had forced him into a life of crime.

The big news from Washington that week was a long and rambling floor speech by Dick Leech in the House. Good thing for him that the Speech and Debate Clause of Article One protects members from being questioned in any other place for their remarks on the floor. Otherwise, I'm afraid that someone might have ordered a competency hearing for Mr. Leech. He appeared to have hunted up all the stories from the *American Speculator*, the *Washington Sun*, and the other tabloids, borrowed liberally from the Critics Unlimited scandal faxes and the infamous RTC referrals crafted by Ellende Varken, and packed them into a single speech. He was, as charitable people would say, not served well by his staff. He did say one thing that made more sense than he realized, boldly proclaiming, "In a nutshell, Whirlpool is about the arrogance of power, Machiavellian machinations of party politics." I didn't understand then just how right he was.

Gastone Diletto could hardly stand to be upstaged by a mere House member. He started telling anyone who would listen that some White House aides—and maybe even Cannon himself as a co-conspirator—were guilty of no less than obstruction of justice. "Secret meetings. Stonewalling. Abuse of power. Interfering with an independent investigation." Wonder how Diletto was going to explain why he still refused to release the Senate Ethics Committee's report on own his conduct? Or why 25 witnesses took the Fifth the last time he was investigated? Or how $30,000 from Wedtech just happened to end up in his account? But, he didn't have to answer for that, because the press was only interested in making Whirlpool the scandal of the day. I kidded Sean about his born-again Senator, and he opined that the only obstruction Diletto had ever worried about was when someone got between him and a television camera.

As the investigation moved into April, we continued to work diligently and quietly. Too quietly for some columnists and congressmen. An editorial from an Orlando paper, taped to the refrigerator door in the coffee room, read "Whirlpool Prosecutor Burke Is Just A Sham From A Sly Cannon." Seemed to be one of the new themes emerging from the far right fringe press, that Burke was put in place by Otis to whitewash Whirlpool and conduct a cover-up by restricting hearings and refusing to leak details of our progress. One day they wanted us to be bringing indictments and calling press conferences. The next we were supposed to stretch it out through the 1996 election. Burke didn't have any intention of playing either of those games. We had a job to do, and we were doing it. And I had to laugh at myself for now defending Burke's professional approach when I had at first been so suspicious of the whole deal.

The campaign against Cannon was being waged now on every front. His staff was spending almost full time responding to our subpoenas or requests from congressional committees. Whenever Cannon appeared before the press to announce a new domestic policy initiative or discuss meetings with foreign leaders, the press corps only wanted to ask about Whirlpool.

As if that were not enough distraction from the business of government, the *American Speculator* returned to its prurient reporting with a story quoting two former Alabama state troopers saying they had pimped for Cannon when he was governor. And, crawling right down into the gutter, they implied that Diane Cannon and Hal Goodall had been "intimately" involved. What a pathetic excuse for journalism.

Turned out later that the troopers were recruited to go on radio talk shows by Lyman Davison, a former Republican state official, and they were represented by Clifton Smegman, another big Republican who had promoted the story about Cannon's draft record during the last campaign. The troopers, Davidson, Smegman, and the reporter were all getting paid by some guy who was a big contributor to Leroy Reichman's political action committee and had put up $80,000 to finance the rumors. The troopers and their lawyers split $25,000, Republican political consultant Eddie Mahem got $25,000 for helping place the story in magazines and newspapers, and the Speculator reporter was paid $5,000. That connection, though, was never reported by the media.

Then, as a result of being mentioned in the *Speculator* story, a woman by the name of Christine Putnam appeared at a C-PAC klavern in Washington, as the paid guest of Ollie North's Legal Affairs Council, and announced that she intended to file a civil suit for defamation and sexual harassment against Cannon. Strangely, the *American Speculator* was not named as a defendant in the suit. She said she wanted to defend her reputation. And make lots of money. Her lawyer's fee agreement also included a cut of any future book or movie rights she might receive.

Putnam also starred in an outrageous videotape called "The Cannon Chronicles," hawked by the Rev. Dr. Elmer Laud for a $39.95 "gift" to his ministry. The video featured rantings by the usual Congressional outpatients and almost every professional Cannon hater in Alabama, including Judge James Boutwell Crommelin and Carl Weiss, a disturbed little fellow who had been canned when it was learned he was using state telephones and raising money for the Contras on state time. The charges made against Cannon on the tape ranged from drug dealing to murder. The Rev. Dr. Laud was always an honorable man. Weren't they all? Praise the Lord, and send your money to Laud.

One day after work, we were all sitting around in the conference room talking about the level of hatred and meanness that seemed to motivate Cannon's opponents. As usual, the television was tuned to C-SPAN, but we weren't paying much attention until we heard someone mention Whirlpool. Bob Dorkman was taking a break from trying to triple the defense budget to crawl down in the gutter. It was a speech that said as much about him as about the abuse of the special orders period in the House. A thousand points of darkness and a thousand pints of slime.

Dorkman was well into his tirade when we stopped to listen. "Mr. Speaker, I wish people could take a breather and try and absorb all of the material that is absolutely exploding on the front pages of newspapers across the country.

"I am deeply concerned about Benny Arnold, fired White House staffer. His title was usher, whatever that means, at the White House. He still doesn't know what hit him. He can offer only a puzzling account of how he was abruptly fired by Diane Rankin Cannon three weeks ago, and he still doesn't have a clue why. Folks, this is no way to treat a government employee of eight years of honorable service, but out the door he went.

"Well, Mr. Speaker, Diane Rankin Cannon isn't the only one who thinks some people should be fired. I called for the resignation or firing of William Kinsey, the last of the gang of four from the Bankhead law firm, and I notice today our Whip, Mr. Reichman of Georgia, has joined me in that call.

"I also called for the resignation of Paula Thompson. Miss Thompson was over here testifying, and she could not answer a lot of questions about what is going on over there. She said she dearly wanted to answer questions, but the special prosecutor, Mr. Burke, was preventing her from doing that. She is the chief of White House administration. She does not have a security clearance.

"The rumors are starting to fly that some of these people from the flower child generation cannot cut it, all of these idealists of the 1960s who were pro-Hanoi, that they cannot get security clearances.

"I called for Mr. Altgeld's resignation at Treasury, and Vickie Claflin, one of his deputies who was in on some of those meetings.

"And I have called for the troopers to come forward. I know it is tough, but they have to come out and tell the truth before our committees, because one of them said he brought Christine Putnam up to a room in the Madison Hotel where she claims, in a signed affidavit, about the type of things that Anita Hill did not have a shred of, but yet she became the poster woman of feminist groups in the United States, radical groups, and otherwise on no evidence but her word against a distinguished jurist. Now the press is still spiking that story.

"This Whirlpool scandal is a moving story, Mr. Speaker, the *Washington Sun*, the New York tabloids, the *American Speculator*, the *Pennsylvania Tribune-Review* are publishing facts that you can't get in most American newspapers. The mainstream American press has shown little to no appetite for publishing anything about violence and sex. Editors and reporters have to grapple daily with a flood of stories, charges, and rumors of violence, even murders in Alabama. There are a few that can be trusted—Martin Ruddy Rimmer, William Ambrose-Cobbett, James Rivington, Jay Fuhrman, Luis Gerucht, Danielle Leonard, Matthew Sludge.

"The head of security for Mr. Cannon's campaign before the Secret Service took over after the convention, he was murdered in Alabama. It was not on the evening news. He was chased by a car down a road in Montgomery, two bullets were fired and hit the car, and they then pulled up alongside of the car and fired four more and hit him as he careened off to the side of the road, dead or dying, and the car pursuing him obviously pulled over, and somebody got out and gave him the coup de grace. At least seven shots, maybe more, killing the head of security for Mr. Cannon during the campaign.

"Now, let me take a pause here. I believe the *Wall Street Record,* believe the story about the reporter smashed in the head in his hotel room and his papers rifled and some stolen. The *Wall Street Record* believes this, too.

"I mean, what is going on down there in Alabama? The state seems to be a congenitally violent place and full of colorful characters with stories to tell, axes to grind, and secrets of their own.

"I can hear groans from across America, Mr. Speaker, and I know there are a lot of people who say that Bob Dorkman comes off in the well like a Tasmanian devil sometimes, a nutcake, but I have talked to several people on your side One of them told me the President is gone. Don't worry. It will all come out. He is going down. I can promise you that."

Laud's videotapes. The right wing propaganda factories. The unfounded attacks and outrageous speeches in Congress. I hadn't seen anything quite like it in the 30 years I'd been following politics. Nate Norton and Dale Herbeck thought it was a very skillful and very sleazy political attack coordinated by Floyd Crump at Critics Unlimited and funded by money from Mellonskoff to various front groups. Mike Zuckerman argued that it was a rich man's game designed to bankrupt the Cannons with high legal expenses, sending a message to him and providing a lesson to any other middle class Democrat who dared run for president. Sean, who mentioned his recent meetings with Diletto and Leech, said that the Republican leadership didn't have any policy ideas of their own, so they just tried to destroy their opponents with personal attacks. Paul Barefield, only half kidding, said they were all jealous of Cannon because he got more pussy than they did. Navita made a good case that much of it, especially here in Alabama, was grounded in racism and sexism. Cannon, she noted, had always been a vocal supporter of civil rights, and his wife's obvious intelligence threatened insecure men with small minds. I didn't have any unique theory of my own, but I found all of those explanations plausible.

My colleagues were both insightful and entertaining, even when they made Texas jokes at my expense. The thing that impressed me the most, I think, was their professional approach to the investigation. They did their job without becoming zealots or cynics, and they maintained an appropriate perspective on the whole situation, both here in Alabama and in Washington. I wish William Bailey had been there that afternoon. I'd like to have had his take on the question. In the few days he was in Birmingham, I came to have a real appreciation for his ability to get to the heart of public issues. And I'd never known anyone who could so quickly debunk a conspiracy theory with both logical analysis and biting humor.

I'd also like to spend a little more time with Lindsey. We'd talked by phone a few times since she was here last month, but it was time for a road trip. I decided that I needed to go to Montgomery soon to talk with the bank commissioner, and Friday would be a good time to do that. I called Lindsey on Thursday to let her know that I would be in town and invite her to have dinner with me. She was coordinating the annual Southern Letters conference on campus that weekend. But she said she'd love to have dinner, if I would attend some of the readings with her.

"Done deal," I said. Then, hoping it wasn't going to be James Dickey, I asked, "Who's on the program?"

"We opened this afternoon with Anne Rivers Siddons, and this evening Molly Ivins is speaking. Miller Williams will be reading his poetry Friday night. On Saturday, Barry Hannah, Donald Hays, Larry Brown, and Larry King will be reading fiction," she said with justifiable satisfaction.

"Damn, lady, that's quite a line-up," I said, sincerely impressed. "But Larry King doesn't write fiction. He writes truth."

"No, it's not the talk show guy. This is Larry L. King, a writer," she responded in that voice like a teacher correcting a know-it-all student with a wrong answer. "And," she added, " they all write truth."

"Oh, I know the real Larry King. He's an ole Texas boy. And if I could write like him, I'd give up lawyering," I said. "But, you're right, and I sit corrected for confusing facts and truth."

We made plans to meet at six, and Lindsey suggested a place called The Oasis. She then asked if she could bring a friend. Having already been too clever, I still couldn't resist saying, "No, you'll have to leave your husband at home."

"Worse than that, it's a preacher," she quipped. "We're old friends, just friends, and I'd already asked him to go with me to hear Miller Williams reading Friday night."

"Want to bring a chaperone, huh? Think that'll keep me from trying something?"

"Oh, no, I hope you do. I was planning on asking you to marry me, in case you did," she said with a slightly wicked laugh.

The day at the Bank Department was interesting, more so than I had anticipated. I reviewed all the files on Jefferson Savings, and I also had an opportunity to interview the director, Barbara Ann Woodrow. Although she was not particularly excited about my being there, she said she was glad to finally have a chance to talk with someone and get the facts on the table. One of the accusations was that she had given special treatment to Jefferson Savings because Banaghan was a friend of Cannon and because Diane Cannon had briefly represented Jefferson in seeking approval to issue additional stock. She confirmed what I already knew from examining the records. She had tried to close Jefferson three years before the feds finally agreed to do so, and that the stock approval, although never issued, was a routine matter.

Ms Woodrow had been burned and burned bad. Luis Gerucht had falsely implied in a page one story in the *New York Times* that she had acted improperly, and possibly illegally, to protect Banaghan and Jefferson Savings. The sting of the article was that she had been a Cannon pawn protecting the governor's former business partner and that the misconduct was a result of pressure from Diane Cannon. She showed me several memoranda, more than 20 single-spaced pages, that refuted every allegation and provided complete documentation. She had prepared this for Gerucht two weeks before his story appeared in the *Times*, and he ignored it completely because it demolished his position. That was the last time she had talked with a reporter, and she would never do so again.

I also learned something else from talking with Ms Woodrow, something that was sure to make our efforts more difficult. Two weeks ago she had met with two of Congressman Leech's minority staff members from the House Banking Committee, and she said they weren't particularly interested in the facts. Their questions were more like opening arguments, and they didn't even bother to review the documents she offered to provide. More upsetting, she said, was that she was being stalked by the national media. On one occasion, when she was picking her daughter up at school, she had been ambushed in the school parking lot by an NBC news crew accompanied by none other than David Winderig of Critics Unlimited. She was tired of such rude treatment affecting her family.

I didn't blame her, and I knew the effect that kind of behavior would have on other folks in Alabama. Media treatment of everyone as a potential criminal would make them less inclined to talk to anyone. I realized, however, that there was nothing I could do about it and that there was nothing I could say to Ms Woodrow to mitigate the intrusive actions of the press.

Fortunately, the evening was much more pleasant. The Oasis was decorated with a Middle Eastern theme, except they served liquor, for which I was grateful. The preacher Lindsey brought to dinner was an interesting fellow named Francis David Rhett. Like politicians, I guess, preachers had to have three names, especially if the last name was Rhett. He was a Unitarian minister from Camp Hill, and he and Lindsey met while serving on the state ACLU executive committee. I liked him immediately, but I told him I was surprised that the Alabama legislature hadn't banned Unitarians. No, he proudly replied, the Camp Hill congregation had been founded in 1843 and was doing just fine. It was much more likely, he said, that they would try to ban the ACLU, like they had tried to do with the NAACP a few years back.

I enjoyed the reading by Miller Williams, too. I didn't know much about poetry. Well, except for limericks. But Williams made it easy to understand. My favorite was one called "Sir," which he had written for Jimmy Carter after the election in 1980. It was prescient, to say the least. After being defeated, Carter had demonstrated his continuing commitment to public service by building homes for poor people, while Reeder and Stuart were making millions by giving speeches to fat cats, religious cults, and foreign governments.

Afterwards, we said good night to Reverend Rhett. I suggested to Lindsey that we go somewhere and have a drink, but she declined, saying she had to be up early for breakfast with the visiting authors. She asked if I wanted to come along, and I jumped at the chance to meet that crew of outlaws scheduled for tomorrow. Then she asked if I needed a place to stay.

Catching my breath, I sputtered, "Uh, I'm staying at Red Bluff Cottage, a little B and B on Clay Street. But, thanks. I booked it, not wanting to appear presumptuous that you would invite me to stay with you."

"It's a wonderful place. Good choice! Anne and Mark, the couple who own it, are friends of mine," she said. "And besides, I didn't say I was inviting you to spend the night. I just asked if you needed a place to stay."

Oh, shit. Whether she was being serious or just flirtatious, I had really screwed up, one way or the other. Either I was out of practice, or I was out of my league. Probably both. I couldn't think of a cute face-saving comeback, so I leaned back against my truck and looked down at my shoes. "I have to go now. I think I hear my mother calling."

"Okay. See you for breakfast. Seven o'clock at the Madison Hotel," she said, with a quick kiss and enough enthusiasm that I knew everything was okay.

I walked Lindsey to her car and watched her drive away. In a white Porsche 356. Yep, out of my league.

The breakfast was fun. I enjoyed listening to writers talk about their craft. Barry Hannah didn't make it for breakfast, which didn't seem to surprise anyone. Someone said he'd being doing well to make it for the afternoon reading. He did, though. And I had a great time. Bought a bunch of their books, and got them all signed. And, as I was leaving to drive back to Birmingham, Lindsey said, "I hope to see you again. Soon. And next time," she said with a grin, "let me know if you need a place to stay." Oh, yes, she could count on that.

The next two weeks were relatively uneventful at work, reviewing documents and interviewing potential witnesses but no big news. I even found some time to work on an article idea at Samford during the evenings. Then we had a little excitement. The April 29 issue of the *Washington Sun* had an article that our office had secured indictments of two White House staff members. Burke was livid. I'd never seen that side of him before. After he'd satisfied himself that Jay Fuhrman had just invented it and that no one on the staff had been a source for the story, he authorized a press release that afternoon stating that we had no sealed indictments against anyone on Cannon's staff.

We were close to concluding our investigation of the White House-Treasury contacts, but we were still working on the final report. I was impressed that Burke had responded so clearly and quickly. He had managed to ignore most of the wild charges being made in the press, but this time it was different. It was not only a lie, it was one that reflected upon our office and our work. What was true, but what he didn't say, was that it was very unlikely we'd be seeking any indictments regarding those conversations.

I'd made the political argument that agency personnel had a duty to keep the White House informed about any potential problems and failure to do so would be nonfeasance. Furthermore, I said I couldn't blame the staffers who had inquired about the RTC's hiring former U.S. Attorney Ike Parker to conduct yet another investigation of the Cannons and Jefferson Savings. I would've done the same. Parker had been dismissed by Cannon, and he didn't go quietly. He subsequently made numerous public statements that indicated he could not be objective about Cannon. The real key for Burke, though, was Bailey's legal memo indicating that there were no violations of federal statutes or ethics regulations. I assumed that the final prosecution memorandum would reach the same conclusions and advise against any indictments.

State politics started to heat up along with the weather in May. Nelson Grenier announced as the Republican candidate for governor, and three days later, right on cue, the *Washington Sun* had an article quoting Roby Douglas that Governor Vance and his wife had illegally borrowed money from Financial Management Services a few years ago. It also seemed that only certain newspapers were able to get interviews with Douglas after he had entered his guilty plea, and rumors began circulating that our office had him in a witness protection program. Most of us got a big laugh out of that one, but Burke issued a statement flatly denying it. Once again he had acted quickly when the press made a false statement about his investigation, but this time it didn't stop the loonies from printing stories that Douglas was getting death threats and feared for his life. Mark one up for paranoia. A lie can get half way around the world before the truth gets out of bed.

And speaking of lies, Christine Putnam actually packaged hers and filed the lawsuit against Cannon. The whole thing was pretty tawdry. First, Putnam's lawyer tried to shakedown Cannon, suggesting that she would go away if Cannon would give her some money or get her a job in Hollywood.

Then, the Lynch Legal Foundation, headed by former Reeder Justice Department flack Mark Schine, got involved in securing some high priced GOP legal talent to handle Putnam's case and in persuading her not to sue the *American Speculator*, which had published the article. They first approached Porter Andersen of Kirk & Polis, who had worked in the White House Counsel's office under Stuart and had been domestic policy coordinator for the Stuart Campaign in 1992. He declined but tried to recruit Nelson Lund, another of G. Gordon Bray's former White House legal deputies and a regular contributor of op-ed pieces for the *Washington Sun*, the *Weekly Standard*, and the *Wall Street Record*. They finally settled on two other former Stuart appointees, a former assistant U.S. attorney in Virginia and a former attorney with the Justice Department's tax division, to take over the case.

Then, out of the blue, the lawyers got $50,000 in seed money for the suit from one of Mellonskoff's front groups, and Patrick Mahoney of Operation Revenge started the Christine Putnam Legal Expense Fund. What a surprise that no one ever reported that little gambit and exposed the coordinated efforts of the Reeder and Stuart crowd orchestrating the lawsuit.

I was pleasantly surprised one day, however, when I returned a phone call to Dean John Watkins. Three names again, I thought, but this time I was wrong. It was from the Dean of the law school at the University of Alabama. Judge Franklyn had asked him to invite me and my guest to attend the Edgar Gardner Murphy Lecture to be presented this year by Judge Arnold Richards. It would be co-sponsored by the Farrah Law Society and the John Archibald Campbell Moot Court Society and presented on May 17th, the 40th anniversary of the *Brown* decision. I was honored and said I would most certainly attend. I immediately called Lindsey and asked if she had plans for that date. She regretted that she did but said she would call me soon to see when I had time to play. Said she had a surprise she thought I'd like. I could think of several.

Everyone got a big surprise the next week, just before the lecture, when President Cannon named Judge Stanley Bryant to replace Justice Blackmun on the Supreme Court. Everyone in Alabama legal and political circles was extremely disappointed that Judge Richards had been passed over for the appointment. Several newspaper editorials blamed it on the adverse publicity from the Whirlpool investigation, expressing regret that Cannon could not afford to name someone from Alabama.

I wasn't disappointed. I was sick. It made no sense. There was no way to pretend he had made the best choice, but it was one Senator Hruska would approve in a New York minute. Richards' opinions were so far superior to anything the Beantown Bean Counter had written. I once fell asleep on page three trying to read one of Bryant's articles on models of regulatory reform. Bryant would not improve the quality of the Court. He had the mind of O'Connor and the personality of Souter. And Richards' reasoned eloquence could have led the court away from the unrestrained statism of Renchberg and Scalia.

While I had sometimes disagreed with Cannon's policy positions, thought them too cautious, I always had to admit that the final result made this a better country than before. In this case, however, that was simply not true. Cannon looked like a chickenshit. I don't mind losing when we get beat in the elections, but I damn sure hated to lose when we had won. Maybe he would do the right thing next time, but I wouldn't allow myself to get my hopes up again.

The non-appointment dominated the conversation at the law school the night of the lecture, but Judge Richards was most gracious, praising both Cannon and Bryant. The moot court room was a large round building on the south side of the law school complex, and it was packed to capacity for the lecture, which was being taped for the state public television network. Judge Richards' remarks were a poignant tribute to Judge Franklyn and his civil rights decisions, delivered with a style that made me wish even more that he was on the Court.

After the lecture I attended the reception at the President's Mansion honoring Judge Richards. Amusing contrast between the content of the lecture and the scene of the reception. The president's home was an impressive white brick mansion with six ionic columns. Built in 1839, it symbolized the oppressive inequities in the system of the Old South, while Judge Richards represented the struggle for justice in a New South. After standing in line for a drink, I couldn't resist asking for a mint julep. Then I saw Judge Franklyn, who motioned for me to come through the admiring crowd around Judge Richards. A camera flashed as Judge Franklyn introduced me to Judge Richards, and I laughed at myself as I hoped that I would be able to get a copy of the photograph.

Judge Richards introduced me to his wife, Kelley, a striking woman with beautiful red hair who looked to be about 15 years his junior. Now I had even more respect for the Judge and knew he was the kind of man we needed on the Supreme Court. Mrs. Richards smiled and asked, "Where's Lindsey?" I was startled, wondering how she knew about my personal fantasy life. I just looked at her, not saying anything, not sure I had heard her correctly. Then she said, "I saw her taping the lecture, and she promised she would be here." So, that's what Lindsey had planned when I inquired whether she was busy this evening. Words and my own reticence had failed me once again.

Just at that moment, Lindsey appeared, slipped her arm through mine, and said, "I see you've made yourself the center of attention." Well, not exactly. I felt like a turd in the punch bowl. Everyone knew I worked for Burke. Did they associate me with the Whirlpool investigation and Cannon's decision not to appoint Judge Richards to the Court? If so, they were too kind to say so. Lindsey and Kelley Richards were old friends, and they were laughing and talking as I tried to rejoin the conversation. Then, Lindsey took my hand and said she wanted to introduce me to some people. I paid homage to Judge Richards and took my leave.

The room was crowded with everyone who was anyone in the upper echelon of public life in Alabama. Earlier I had tried to figure how I could meet some of them without appearing to be conducting an investigation, but that problem had solved itself. Lindsey introduced me to one after another, and I tried to remember the faces that went with the names I knew. Governor Jim Bibb Vance, impressive but somewhat reserved; Hiram Revels, a black state senator; J. J. Roberts, head of the Alabama Education Association and a prominent Democratic activist; James Burgh, a communication professor known for his free speech work; Skip Cowling, founder of Rutherford and Cowling, the most successful political consulting firm in the South; Charles Mattox, an art instructor; J. Bill Haywood, president of the state AFL-CIO; Lisa Leuchter, the AP bureau chief; Brad Watson, an English professor with a hang-dog look; Liz Coulson, a state supreme court justice; Forrest MacDonald, a history professor whose work I had read; Culpepper Clark, some vice-provost or something with the University, yet Lindsey said he was a great guy.

I also met Dean Watkins who was engaged in a serious conversation with two law students. I thanked him for inviting me, and he said he was pleased that I could attend. Told him I was envious, that I had always wanted to be a law professor, but he said it was way over-rated. He then introduced me to the two students, Graham Streett and Amy McClinton, who were there representing the *Alabama Law Review*. I enjoyed talking with them more than anyone that evening, remembering my own idealism and enthusiasm when I was editor of the law review at Texas. I told them I hoped they would continue to find law fascinating throughout their careers. Said that I still did.

In fact, I had been working on an article in my spare time, dropping that to try to impress Dean Watkins. They wanted to know if it had anything to do with Whirlpool. No, I said, but it involved a constitutional question related to criminal sentencing. They appeared more than politely interested, so I explained I was examining the tension between the Pre-Sentence Investigation Manual that directed federal probation officers to inquire about a defendant's religious background and the holding in *U. S. v. Lemon* that federal judges are not to consider a defendant's religious beliefs in sentencing decisions. My argument was that a citizen's religious views were no business of the government. None. Even asking the question could have a chilling effect on a defendant's First Amendment rights, I thought, and it was an unnecessary intrusion that would not withstand even intermediate scrutiny. And sure, I said, I'd be glad to send it to them when it was finished.

It was one of the most enjoyable evenings I'd had since moving to Alabama three months ago. I only wished I'd more time with talk to some of those I met and to do so under less formal circumstance. Made me realize that the life of a faculty member might be both stimulating and rewarding. At least it looked that way from the outside. Anyway, it was a pleasant experience. Much more so than what was ahead.

Chapter Eleven

Folks in Alabama took their politics seriously, much like they did back in East Texas. The governor's race was shaping up as everyone expected, with Nelson Grenier winning the Republican nomination to challenge Governor Vance. The only big surprise in the June 7th primaries was an upset of sorts in the District 28 state senate race. The Business Council of Alabama pumped nearly $250,000 into the campaign to defeat Danny Corbett, Chairman of the Senate Economic Affairs Committee. Seems that Senator Corbett, when he wasn't hitting on female reporters at the capitol, found time to anger the Big Mules by killing tax breaks for business and taking the side of workers on a bill to reduce workers' compensation benefits. Plutocrats 1, Populists 0.

Our investigation had been moving forward more quickly than anyone had anticipated. We had reviewed all the documents and interviewed everyone who could possibly provide information related to the issues under our jurisdiction. Looked to me as if we were way ahead of schedule. The main thing left, and it was of no minor consequence, was to interview the President and Mrs. Cannon. Burke had wisely scheduled that for last. We would be better prepared to pose our questions, and we would have to do it only once.

President and Mrs. Cannon were off in France for the 50th anniversary celebration of D-Day, and President Cannon was also picking up an honorary doctorate from Oxford while he was "over there." Guess there were some advantages to being elected president. That delayed us briefly, but we finally scheduled the depositions at the White House on June 12.

Burke would be there, along with all of the staff attorneys except me. I could have gone along, but there was no real reason that I should. It was not a social call nor one that required my particular skills. Everyone else had prepared their own set of questions relating to their specific areas of responsibility. The depositions, we hoped, would provide an opportunity to resolve any conflicting statements and to fill in the blanks that could be done only by President and Mrs. Cannon.

Although they were certainly important, I couldn't get very excited about the depositions. Sean offered to give me a call as soon as they were finished, but I told him I could wait until he returned and would read the transcripts as soon as they were typed. I didn't say I had something else to do that would be more exciting than sitting around an empty office by myself waiting for a phone call.

I chose the White Sox over the White House. Mark Lester and I took in a little baseball that day instead. The Birmingham Barons, the AA White Sox farm team, played in Hoover, just a few minutes from the office. And I was interested in seeing their new right fielder, Michael Jordan. I also got to see an old right winger that evening in the stadium parking lot. The Reverend Samuel Parris and a group from the Alabama Family Association were praying and holding signs blasting Diane Cannon for undermining traditional family values. Whatever that meant. It was obvious they'd been reading too many Epistles and not enough of the Gospels.

Mark, ever being the history professor, told me that former Police Commissioner Bull Connor had been the radio announcer for the Barons back in the 20s, and he parlayed the name recognition to win his first election. Funny, it seems that a lot of angry politicians got their start as sports announcers. Dutch Reeder was a sports broadcaster before he went to Hollywood, and the Reverend Jerry Elkay Coughlin was a radio announcer for games at Fairhope High School before he went into preaching and eventually became Lieutenant Governor. And Rush Limbaugh used to work in public relations for the Kansas City Royals, but they didn't let him announce any games. His daddy got him that job after he'd been fired from four different radio stations. Come to think of it, Senator Helmut Duke also had a radio career in North Carolina, but it wasn't sports. Just hate and hot air. Much like his Senate career.

The Barons won the game, but I told Mark I thought Jordan should go back to basketball. I also had some thoughts about where Parris could go, but I let it pass.

Back at the office, things were actually pretty boring that month. Although everyone seemed to have enjoyed the White House tour, the interviews with President and Mrs. Cannon produced no surprises and no indication of any criminal liability. Their testimony was consistent with almost everyone else we had interviewed over the last four months. Except for Roby Douglas, who kept changing his testimony to track Nelson Grenier's political agenda and the strange articles in the *American Speculator*.

There was some controversy on the Hill. The House and Senate both voted to hold hearings on Whirlpool, but the Republicans were miffed because the scope had been restricted so as not to interfere with our investigation. The GOP especially wanted to dance on the grave of Hal Goodall. They were sorry about his unfortunate suicide—sorry that it hadn't been murder. Senator Dolor was angry that the Democrats had limited the oversight hearings, but he vowed that the Republicans would not be stopped. Congressman Leech repeated so many of the conspiracy theories that he almost lost it, once complaining that he was being followed and that his house was being watched. Probably suspected the Trilateral Commission.

There were a few tense moments for Leech when it was revealed that he'd been working with a private investigator hired by the *American Speculator* to dig up, or perhaps manufacture, dirt on Cannon. One of the files included personal data on Randy James, a CNN reporter who had questioned the credibility of Leech's sources and the validity of his charges. When confronted on the issue, Leech's press flak confirmed that the Congressman had information in his possession about the reporter and acknowledged that his staff spoke to the investigator several times.

In a statement released by CNN, Mr. James said, "The fact that Congressman Leech would even have any kind of investigative file on a reporter is outrageous. The fact that they wanted to investigate and discredit a reporter suggests a political agenda." Everyone, I'm sure, was shocked by such a pronouncement.

Burke was pleased that the hearings would be limited; however, he was not pleased that the House committees kept trying to call him as a witness. I could tell that he had little patience for such political sideshows, and he certainly wouldn't participate in them. He was interested only in completing our investigation in a professional manner and a timely fashion. We moved a little closer to completing that task on the 22nd, securing guilty pleas from the two lawyers charged with conspiring with Douglas to inflate the capital of Financial Management Services and bilk the Small Business Administration

One day at lunch that week Burke asked me if I knew Senator Ira Dolor. I wasn't sure what he meant or why he was asking. "I know he's a mean son of a bitch. And he has run some of the dirtiest campaigns I've ever seen. His 1974 campaign ads against Dr. Bill Roy were so sickening that I sent Roy $25, and I was a starving law student at the time. But, I don't think I've ever met the man. Why?"

Burke took a long sip from his coffee cup. "I received a letter from him yesterday. About you. The good senator expressed his opinion that you were too much of a Cannon partisan to be objective and fair in this investigation. He almost demanded that I fire you."

"Well," trying not to sound too defensive or to reveal how much I detested Dolor, I replied, "he's wrong about that. I did send Cannon some money in the last election, but I was for Tom Harkin in the primaries until he dropped out. I made a few speeches for Cannon in Austin, and I admit I voted for him against Stuart. But you knew that already.

And I'm damn glad he won. But, if you think I'm causing any problems for you, I'll resign today, or you can announce that you've fired me. Whichever you want."

"No," Burke said, "I don't have any intention of letting you go. I told him that your personal political opinions were of no concern to me. I just thought there might be some history there that I should know about in case he mentions it again."

"No history. No nothing. I think he's still got a burr up his butt over the last election, and I'm a convenient target. Sorry, though, that he's using me to get at you," I said. Usually by the time a man gets to be three score and ten he's mellowed out a little, but not Dolor. Must've put a splash of Sterno in his Metamucil Cocktail that morning.

There was some good news from Congress that month. They passed new legislation formally authorizing an Office of Independent Counsel, to take effect on July 1. All that meant was that Burke would be appointed by a Special Panel of the Court of Appeals rather than by the Attorney General. Nonetheless, William Streicher had a column in the *New York Times* that week calling for the Court of Appeals to dump Burke as soon as the law was signed. "Sure enough," Streicher wrote, "it has come to pass that Cannon appointee Burke has conspired with Democrats in the see-nothing 103rd Congress to contain the scandal. What a setup: the Democrats' favorite Republican prosecutor provides Democrats in Congress the 'Burke Block' for stonewalling hearings, then the Cannon AG asks the court panel to legitimize the lawyer chosen for her by the White House. The place to stop this stonewalling deal is in the Independent Counsel Panel of the Court of Appeals." Streicher then revealed that he had called Judge Sam Chase, head of the panel, and suggested the same. I almost laughed when I read that. Streicher thinking he could persuade the judge to dump Burke. What a joke.

The big news, from our perspective, came during the last week in June. Bailey had completed his work in Washington, both the investigation of the contacts between White House and Treasury personnel and the report on the death of Hal Goodall. I was responsible for compiling the final draft, and I worked overtime to make sure it would be ready for distribution to the Department of Justice, Congress, and the press on June 30.

The report was very thorough, exactly what I was expecting from Bailey. It convincingly concluded that Hal Goodall had been suffering from depression and had taken his own life. Furthermore, there was absolutely no connection between Goodall's suicide and any of the financial issues related to our investigation. It also cleared the White House and Treasury staff with regard to their contacts and conversations related to the Jefferson Savings referrals, the Financial Management investigation, and the RTC's hiring Ike Parker to investigate the Cannons' relationship with Banaghan and Jefferson Savings. There were no violations of criminal statutes or ethics regulations. None. Burke reviewed the final draft and signed off on it before heading to Washington on the 29th, and the official copies were distributed right on schedule the next morning.

The report had been out about 20 minutes when the phone started ringing at our office that morning, Washington reporters calling for me. I didn't have any idea what was up, but I sure wanted to know before I talked to any of them. I tried to contact Burke and Bailey without success. Then my secretary brought me a note that Janet Fox from *USA Today* was holding, said it was very important. I took the call and congratulated Janet on her new job. She said thanks and asked me not to mentioned that she had called me. She had just seen an advance copy of a speech that Senator Dolor was to make to the Conservative Congressional Caucus at 3:00, and she thought I'd like to know that he mentioned my name. That's all she felt she could say, but it was going to be carried live on C-SPAN.

I announced to the staff that I was about to become a media star and invited them to join me in the conference room. I still had no idea what to expect or why Dolor seemed to be interested in me. Then I got a call from Kenneth Burke. Turned out that Senator Dolor was upset with more than just me. Dolor had demanded a Special Prosecutor to investigate President Cannon, and it wasn't turning out quite like he'd hoped. Burke suggested that I watch the speech and call him as soon as it was over.

We all settled in for another of Dolor's mean-spirited monotones, and that's what we got. Dolor didn't smile. I'm not sure he ever did, though he might have experimented with facial expressions in college. His lips were tight and his brow was furrowed as he began without ceremony. "I have joined today with Senator Shurmond and others, my Republican colleagues on the Senate Judiciary Committee, calling on Attorney General Otis to appoint an independent counsel to investigate allegations that Whirlpool prosecutor Kenneth Burke used his office to assist President Cannon and the Democrats to block our efforts to hold extensive hearings on the Whirlpool matter. Mr. Burke and his staff may have been involved in partisanship and election-year manipulation, trying to influence the 1994 Congressional elections. We have reason to believe that Mr. Burke and certain of his staff members have been engaged in blatantly political, clearly unethical, and perhaps illegal activities in their Whirlpool probe."

Taking a line from the past, Dolor raged on, "I have in my possession a White House news release outlining the Burke Report on the Washington Phase which is dated June 29, yesterday, a day before the

Senate and the press received the report at 10:00 a.m. this morning. We have questions whether or not improper political considerations went into the timing of the report, and whether improper advance coordination and disclosure of the report was made to the White House spin doctors.

"The timing of the report—just before the House and Senate committees are to begin their hearings—also raises the issue of whether politics was a factor in the decision-making process. Was it coordinated by one John Wilkes, the Deputy Counsel, and politically driven by his support for Democrats and President Cannon? It is my opinion that the credibility of Burke's investigation is severely compromised by the employment of Mr. Wilkes, a longtime member of the ACLU and a known Democrat who contributed $2,000 to the Cannon campaign in 1992. Furthermore, Mr. Wilkes is the same John Wilkes, who as Chief Deputy Attorney General of Texas, filed comments against the confirmation of Chief Justice Wilhelm Renchberg during the 1986 Senate hearings and against the confirmation of Associate Justice Chandler Thom in 1991. I have strong reservations over the ability of such an individual to function independently of what would appear to be a strong political bias.

"I have called upon Mr. Burke to fire Mr. Wilkes forthwith, but he seemed both unaware of and unconcerned with Mr. Wilkes' political endeavors—even to the extent such activities clearly compromise the ability of the office to remain free of political influence in the fulfillment of its responsibilities. So, it seems to me, it's time for Kenneth Burke to move on to some other line of work," Dolor said, pausing and looking up to grin as if he thought he had a laugh line.

Getting no audience response, Senator Dolor seemed impatient. He wiped the sweat from his brow and plowed on with his attack. "Also," with the enthusiasm of a metronome, he continued, "I have written a letter to Attorney General Otis demanding a list of all of Kenneth Burke's employees. This information belongs to the public, the taxpayers who have been footing the bill for Mr. Burke's partisan cover-up. We have the names of some of them from news reports, and we've been checking them out. We found out their political leanings, and we checked on their political contributions. Nobody here got any. We already know, as I said, that the man directing the strategy, Deputy Counsel John Wilkes, is a liberal Democrat .

"Now, what about all the others who have been helping Mr. Burke during his taxpayer-funded cover-up? We'll get these names one way or the other, because the American people deserve to know what's going on. We need to check these names against Federal Election Commission records and party affiliations to determine if those employed by Mr. Burke were engaged in partisan politics. Let's see if there is any hanky-panky going on."

The phone rang immediately after Dolor finished his speech. It was Burke. I could hear the frustration in his voice, as he told me not to resign and cautioned me not to say anything to the media. No problem with either of those directives. The evening newscast led with the conclusions of the report. One White House staff person was quoted as hoping that "insensitive rumormongers would leave Goodall's family alone now." Doubtful, as Janet Fox would say.

The second story had a sound bite from Dolor's speech and a reply from Burke. He said there was nothing political about the timing of his report. He was just trying to complete his work and inform the public as quickly as possible. Despite the date on the White House press release, Burke said it must have been in error, because no one outside his office had a copy until this morning. Finally, the part I'd been waiting for, he said he had complete confidence in his staff and saw no evidence that anyone's political views interfered with the investigation. But I wasn't so sure that my politics weren't starting to affect my views about the investigation. The whole damn thing had such a putrid smell of political revenge. Not our work, but everything from the original allegations to the cry for hearings to the outright lies being passed off as news.

Dolor's rant was a one-day story. The next day, as expected, Attorney General Otis filed a motion asking that Burke be appointed under the Independent Counsel Act of 1994.

There were some early warning signs that the Republicans were displeased with Burke and might try to block his appointment. They thought he hadn't been making much of a splash in the press with his own investigation. They wanted headlines, and not the ones that followed his report finding that Goodall's unfortunate death was a suicide unconnected with Whirlpool and clearing Cannon's appointees at the White House and Treasury. I didn't take them very seriously, but Burke was more realistic. He'd been through a similar ordeal before, when he was nominated for the number two post at Justice, and he knew exactly what to expect.

Dolor's blast yesterday, it turned out, had been only the opening salvo of the attack. The next day, Senator Reynolds Rantallion, a former pig farmer from North Carolina, took up the cudgel and attacked Burke from the floor of the Senate. "The highly improper reappointment of Kenneth Burke would create a cloud of doubt and suspicion. I have urged the Special Panel of the U.S. Court of Appeals to appoint a new, truly independent counsel that will enjoy the confidence of those who seek truth and justice."

Taking his text from William Streicher's column in the *New York Times*, Senator Rantallion questioned Burke's integrity. "Mr. Burke collaborated with Mr. Cannon's attorney in the Bank of Credit and

Commerce International case. BCCI has been implicated in various allegations surrounding the Whirlpool affair, including allegations concerning possible illegal drug activities in Phenix City, Alabama, and questionable activities surrounding the Alabama Finance Authority. Given both the appearance of lack of independence and the close relationship between Mr. Burke and the Cannon administration, Mr. Burke should not be appointed independent counsel."

Rantallion was one of those convert Republicans. The mean kind. He had been a protégé of former Governor Frank Porter, who appointed him Secretary of Commerce in North Carolina. It was said to be an act of kindness by Governor Porter, known for his emphasis on education, to appoint a man without a college degree to such an important state job. Rantallion's tenure in that post was marked by petty misfeasance like taking a National Guard helicopter to his beach house 43 times and by more serious malfeasance like rerouting a new state highway to enhance land values for one of his corporations.

In 1990 Rantallion headed the Democrats for Duke when Republican Senator Helmut Duke was challenged by a black Democratic nominee. Two years later he turned on his old mentor, became the Republican nominee, and unseated Senator Porter. In the Senate he lobbied the Agriculture Department for $20 million in subsidies for pork sales. dwarfing the commodity trading profits of Diane Cannon. He had a lot in common with Nelson Grenier—a mean streak, a lack of personal loyalty to friends, and a hatred for James Cannon. I never could understand how North Carolina could elect two senators like Duke and Rantallion.

It was easier to understand how Indiana could send someone like Dan Bardus to the House. Indiana had a long history of sending goobers to Washington, so it was no big surprise when Congressman Bardus jumped in and took the floor to attack Burke on July 12. Nonetheless, he almost outdid himself. Conspiracy nuts are hard to figure. Perhaps Bardus and Leech had been drinking from the same sewer.

Bardus began with an attack on Burke's integrity, then he challenged the report. In the first, he took the party line; in the second, he was way out of line. It was a long and rambling speech, and one that must have embarrassed his constituents. But Congressman Bardus was not at all reluctant to spread the tabloid rumors on the *Congressional Record*. With bulging eyes, he shouted to an almost empty chamber, "Mr. Speaker, I am very concerned about Kenneth Burke. He was connected to the BCCI scandal. He represented the International Paper Co. when land was sold to the Whirlpool Development Corp. I have been given to understand that he is a major stockholder in Systematics. All of these things took place, and yet Attorney General Otis decided to make him the special counsel to investigate her scumbag boss and the Whirl-pool scandal.

"One of the very important aspects of the first report by Mr. Burke, is where he says that there is no connection between the death of Hal Goodall and the Whirlpool scandal. But the fact of the matter is that Mr. Burke is obfuscating the issues and keeping the Congress from getting to the bottom of many of these questions.

"There are glaring differences between the Burke Report and what actually happened out there. There are differences big enough to drive a truck through, and I intend to prove there is a connection between Goodall's death and the Whirlpool affair. In addition, Mr. Goodall was not killed in the manner that the report says he was.

"Mr. Burke said that Mr. Goodall took his own life and that the overwhelming weight of evidence compels this conclusion. I think it is totally inaccurate in many ways. I have been criticized by some Democrats because they thought I was insensitive, particularly regarding the family of Hal Goodall. They say, 'Why can't you leave that family alone?' I say, there are a lot of questions that have not been answered, answers that the people of the United States need to have.

"Most of the glaring problems in the Burke Report are the questions not asked. The FBI found blonde hair on Mr. Goodall's clothes. Who do those hairs belong to? Diane Cannon has blond hair. Carpet fibers were found on Mr. Goodall's clothes. Could identification of this evidence help us to determine where Mr. Goodall spent his last afternoon before he was killed? Do they match the carpets in the CIA headquarters at Langley? All of us who have been watching the trial of O. J. Simpson are aware that the technology exists for all sorts of tests.

"Now, a confidential source called G. Gordon Liddy, because he thought Mr. Liddy was a person that he could trust, and he called Mr. Liddy and he met with Mr. Liddy at his home. After I heard about Mr. Liddy's report on the radio, we started checking into the death of Hal Goodall, and we found a lot of inconsistencies in Mr. Burke's report.

"After we shot a bullet into a watermelon in my backyard, Mr. Liddy set up an appointment for me with the confidential source. He told me that there was an Inslaw computer disk near Mr. Goodall's body, but that was never mentioned in the Burke Report.

"Now, the FBI went out there with 16 experts. Now, why wasn't the bullet that killed Hal Goodall found in that park? My confidential source stated that if a shot had been fired, it would have been heard by the guards across the road at the home of an Arab. Somebody moved the body. Who moved the body? Was it the clandestine Bilderberg Society, the powerful international group that hand-selected Cannon for the presidency. Was it the Mossad? Was it a Pakistani lobbyist?

"Here is another interesting thing. They found a fake suicide note in his briefcase that someone had torn into 27 pieces. There were no fingerprints. How did the fingerprints get off of that?

"These questions have not been asked. Yet they say that Mr. Goodall committed suicide at that location. The fact of the matter is there are more questions to be answered. Mr. Burke needs to be taken to task until he gets those answers."

The press was all too eager to take Burke to task and to repeat the questions invented by Bardus. They found that far more newsworthy than questions about where Bardus got the money for his "investigation." Streicher's column in the *New York Times* wanted to know about bullets and skull fragments. Irving Reed at Bias in Media bought a full-page ad in the *Washington Post* blaming the media for ignoring the Goodall conspiracy theories. Pat Robertson used his television talk show to ask, "Was there a murder of a White House counsel? It looks more and more like that." Floyd Crump at Critics Unlimited faxed hundreds of copies of photographs from the scene leaked by someone in the coroner's office, but even the supermarket tabloids declined to print them.

The most persistent "news" coverage and most vicious editorials could be found in the *Washington Sun*. James Rivington, Jr. had a regular political column usually devoted to bashing Cannon, and the Bardus speech was conveniently recycled for that purpose. After leading into the topic with a couple of jokes about Alabama being the suicide capital of the nation, Rivington turned his morbid wit on Goodall's death and Burke's report, asking, "Where did he do the awful deed? And with whom? The FBI found semen in his shorts and blond human hair and carpet fibers on his clothes, and the coroner found the remains of a robust lunch in his stomach, suggesting that he spent part of the afternoon somewhere else before he stopped off to kill himself. Mr. Burke was not curious to find out why."

President Cannon, asked about the Burke Report during a press conference, clearly resented the Republican response. His face became red and his jaw tightened, then he replied, "This case has been closed. I hope that the rumor mongers and those in the media who circulated these rumors will after all this time leave the Goodall family in peace. They have suffered needlessly from those who make a career and a business of gutter politics."

Of course, Cannon had been pissing in the wind if he truly believed the Burke Report would close the case. On July 13th, Floyd Crump at Critics Unlimited and 10 House members led by Bardus and Dorkman sent letters to Judge Sam Chase asking him to dump Burke and appoint someone more independent, meaning someone who would reopen the Hal Goodall investigation and let them continue their slanders. The

Mellonskoff spigot was wide open for anyone wanting to write about the Goodall conspiracy. The campaign against Burke appeared to be gaining momentum, but I was confident that the Court would not let partisan politics undo six months of hard work merely to appease a bunch of rabid Republican attack dogs.

Burke was concerned that someone had leaked the photographs, but he was otherwise unaffected by the public campaign against him. He called a staff meeting and told us to just keep doing our job. He said he thought we were close to wrapping up the investigation, and he didn't want anyone to be distracted from our primary task. He also declined to give media interviews or call press conferences to defend himself or the progress of our ongoing investigation.

I suggested that it might not be a bad idea to set the record straight. Burke smiled and said, "Politicians give speeches because they think it will get them reelected, and editors print their opinions because they think it will sell newspapers. I didn't take this job to be popular or make money. My job is to conduct an investigation, find the truth, protect the innocent, and prosecute the guilty." If that was good enough for him, it was fine by me. Burke was a good man, and I came to respect him more every day.

Chapter Twelve

The House hearings opened and drew a big yawn. Since there was no crime to expose, the Republicans sought to show that there had been a cover-up of the non-crimes. Dick Leech was supposed to make a big show by calling Ellende Varken as his star witness, but she declined to appear before the committee. Not being able to play that card, he invented a new charge. Cannon, he said, had tipped off Governor Vance about the RTC referrals during a meeting in the Oval Office. Obstruction of justice at the highest level. Another good conspiracy theory fell like a thud when Leech could produce no evidence to support his charge. Turned out that Cannon was not even aware that Vance had been named in the referrals until after the meeting. Leech's attempted character assassination backfired, and he was left whining that he hadn't accused anyone of a crime. Yeah, right.

The Senate Banking Committee hearings started on July 28, and both Dolor and Rantallion tried to score points against Burke. Dolor delivered his attack on the floor of the Senate. Sean and I watched it on C-SPAN, and I thought it made Dolor look like a real loser. Sean pointed out, however, that it had been almost a month since Otis had nominated Burke, and the Court had not yet made his appointment official. He thought that Dolor might be doing some damage.

Ira Dolor read the speech, but it was not particularly well-written, and the delivery was wooden. "As the Whirlpool hearings get underway," he said, "the American people should understand that what they will be watching is a limited and tightly scripted account of only a small piece of the entire Whirlpool puzzle. It is like going to a movie theater, paying $6 for a ticket, and getting to see only one 60-second PG movie preview. That is what this Whirlpool hearing is all about."

Then Dolor began a political attack on Cannon disguised as a litany of complaints about the scope of the hearings. "Will the hearings examine the RTC's internal investigation into Jefferson Savings? No.

"Will the hearings cover the Justice Department's handling of the RTC criminal referrals? No.

"Will the hearings take a look at Mary Beech Gould's delayed recusal from the Jefferson case and the Roby Douglas prosecution? No.

"Will the hearings cover the diversion of SBA funds to the Whirlpool partnership? No.

"Will the hearings examine why White House officials rifled through Hal Goodall's office shortly after his death? No.

"Will the hearings explore the activities of the Alabama Finance Authority? No.

"Will the hearings take a look at whether any of Jefferson's federally-insured funds were used to pay off campaign debts? No.

"And will the hearings examine the Whirlpool transaction itself? You guessed it: The answer, of course, is No."

Then, Dolor turned his wrath on Burke. "Independent counsel Kenneth Burke has been masterful in his role as congressional traffic cop. He has commanded Congress to take a back-seat to his own investigation. To our own discredit, we have willingly gone along with this charade. Mr. Burke is, without a doubt, one of the most powerful bureaucrats ever seen in American history.

"We are not going to go away. We're going to continue to press for full hearings. Maybe this is not a cover-up. Maybe it is a question of which word you use. It is certainly an effort not to reveal anything. The Democrats in Congress are certainly responsible for it, and I think the American voters will know that between now and November."

When the hearings began that afternoon, Reynolds Rantallion used his time for an opening statement to blister Burke's butt. Senator Rantallion's face was red with anger, and the perspiration on his forehead glistened under the television lights. He wasted no time in getting to his point, almost screaming, "Harriet Otis appointed Kenneth Burke to investigate her boss, James Cannon."

Then, in a coordinated attack delivered with the same cadence Dolor had used that morning, Rantallion briefed his complaints against Burke. "Because of Kenneth Burke, we cannot talk about James and Diane Cannon's Whirlpool partnership, and how they benefited from taxpayer-backed money diverted from Jefferson Savings Bank.

"Because of Kenneth Burke we cannot talk about Diane Cannon's influencing a state regulator to keep Jefferson open, despite the fact that it was insolvent and should have been shut down.

"Because of Kenneth Burke we cannot talk about the how that interference cost the American taxpayers over $60 million.

"Because of Kenneth Burke we cannot talk about how a cocaine distributor bankrolled the Cannon campaigns and then got sweetheart bond deals with the state of Alabama."

Having blamed Burke for shutting down the Republican Dog and Pony Show, Rantallion then turned his attack on Burke's independence and integrity. "Now that we have seen his work product, any questions about whether Kenneth Burke can be relied upon to conduct a thorough investigation into the Whirlpool scandal has been answered, and in my opinion the answer is no.

"Kenneth Burke's law firm represented International Paper Company, the company that sold the land to James Cannon's Whirlpool partnership.

"What's more, Kenneth Burke also worked with President Cannon's lawyer in a case involving the Bank of Credit and Commerce International—the scandal plagued $10 billion bank failure that has been implicated in alleged wrongdoing involving the Alabama phase of Whirlpool—which we have been banned by Kenneth Burke from even talking about here today.

"Kenneth Burke would not investigate Diane Cannon's pork belly contracts because he said the statute of limitations on securities fraud had expired. That's no excuse!

"Mr. Burke reaches a number of conclusions in his report, and those conclusions say a lot more about this White House and about Mr. Burke than they do about Hal Goodall."

Except for the blustering of Dolor and Rantallion, the Senate hearings were as futile and pointless as those in the House. White House staffers were hauled to the hill and jerked around for a few hours, but there was no evidence of anything. No crime. No cover-up. Even the *Washington Sun*, house organ for the Repugs and the fringe fanatics, was resigned to admitting in a page one headline, "Republicans Fail to Score at Start of Hearings." That was an interesting and telling metaphor. It was a game. Ruining people's lives and careers was mere sport.

I was ready for the weekend. I hadn't seen Lindsey for several weeks, so I called to see if she would like to play. I left a pitiful message on her answering machine, almost begging for an invitation to Montgomery, but I didn't hear from her until late Saturday afternoon.

Lindsey called from Atlanta, where she was on the road observing the Loyal Opposition bus tour as part of the Center's effort to monitor hate groups. I'd never heard of any group called Loyal Opposition, but she explained that it was Phinehas Randell's latest project. I knew all about Phinehas Randell, the fanatic leader of Operation Revenge. Lindsey said that he had slipped out of Operation Revenge to avoid the civil damages against the group. Now, he spent most of his time on his estate in New York, running something called the Patriarchy Institute. This week, however, he was on a bus tour of Southern state capitols, calling for Congress to impeach President Cannon.

"Sounds like you're having big fun," I laughed. "I hope so, because you missed your chance to see my Bronco parked in your driveway this weekend."

"Maybe not. Tomorrow's rally is in Montgomery. Want to come down and hear what real Americans are saying about Whirlpool? Starts at 1 o'clock at the capitol," she said.

"Sure. Any excuse to see your lovely face again." Then, betraying desperation, I asked, "Will you be back this evening?"

"No. I'm on my way to Pensacola where a doctor and an escort were killed at a clinic yesterday, and I'm on my way there right now. Glad to hear such an eager response, though, but I'll just meet you at the capitol tomorrow afternoon."

I arrived at the capitol shortly before one o'clock. I laughed to my-self as I noticed the card tables set up to distribute literature, because the scene reminded me of the Extension Service booths at the Bowie County Fair when I was a kid. Banners in front of the tables identified the pam-phleteers representing groups such as Defensive Action, the Christian Action Group, the American Coalition of Life Activists, the Ratched Institute, and the American Center for Christian Justice. These God hucksters outnumbered their audience. About 15 men, women and chil-dren were quietly milling around, picking up literature, awaiting the ar-rival of Randell's road show. From the hair styles, I guessed that most had just come from church. Not the Episcopal Church.

There was a fellow wearing a judicial robe and passing out copies of the Ten Commandments, suitable for framing. The folks at the ACCJ table were offering free copies of a special anti-abortion issue of the *Hostus University Law Journal*, so I picked one up and began reading it while I waited for Lindsey. Before I got past the first page, a Catholic priest who said he was from Mobile shoved a copy of *Life Advocate* in my hand and started frothing loudly, "The Supreme Court has declared war on the unborn, and, as in any war, you may kill an aggressor at any time!"

Only the sight of Lindsey coming from the parking lot saved me from the fanatic friar and having to debate the arcane "just war" theories of Thomas Aquinas. Just as she joined me on the steps, a loudspeaker in the distance boomed, "Wake up, America. Full public hearings. Impeach Cannon." I looked in that general direction to see a big silver charter bus coming up Dexter Avenue. On the sides were red, white, and blue signs reading, "Obey God's Law. Impeach Cannon Now!" Randell's traveling circus had come to town.

Phinehas Randell stepped out of the bus, dressed more casually than his supporters, wearing a brown shirt, khaki slacks, and cowboy boots. The brown shirt seemed most appropriate. Following him off the bus were his spokesman, Patrick Maloney, and several other men who began passing out protest signs to the assembled crowd. "Womanizing . . . Troopergate . . . Abortion . . . Adultery .. . Sodomy . . . Obstruction of Justice . . . Travelgate . . . Drug Abuse . . . Christine Putnam . . . Hal Goodall . . . Murder . . . Pork Bellies." The signs were made for television, and the local stations obliged.

Randell, a 35-year old Bible college graduate and former used car salesman, now had his own radio talk show, and he knew how to deliver simple sound bites that were sure to make the evening news or the lead paragraphs. "I am glad to see that the media in Alabama are not like that pack of mules inside the Beltway," he said unto the cameras.

The local press corps was eating it up. The television reporters shouted questions as if Randell's answers would be newsworthy. One made the mistake of asking whether Loyal Opposition was affiliated with the Christian Coalition. He looked at the cameras and said, "The reason we have wicked leaders is because we have a cowardly, irrelevant, compromised church. That is why this nation is going to hell. We cannot sell out the sacred law of heaven for short-term political gain. The country is falling into the grasp of those who reject God's law, but do it with a smile and even go to church on Sunday carrying a big Bible. Too many pastors are mushy wimps. They have no guts. They have no courage. They are worried about bad press."

When asked about Reverend Dr. Elmer Laud, however, Randell was more kind. He praised Laud's "Old Time Gospel Hour" for taking on the Cannon administration, and he distributed free copies of "The Cannon Chronicles" and "Cannon's Circle of Power," two videotapes also being promoted by Dr. Laud.

Randell shook hands with everyone in the small crowd that had assembled to hear him, then he stepped behind the portable podium his staff had set up on the west steps of the capitol. His first words set the tone. "James Cannon is a tyrant. He's a monster. The Bible commands us to expose the wicked. Cannon favors baby killing. He embraces the sodomite agenda and is hostile to biblical morality. America lost its way when it took prayer out of the classroom and put Darwin and condoms in, legalized abortion, and encouraged women to reject their God-given roles as suitable helpers and supporters of their husbands. Cannon and his wife brought with them a whole cadre of sodomites, flag burners, dope smokers, welfare deadbeats, condom pushers, and Third World tree-hugging lesbian whales that beach themselves for publicity.

"There must be full public hearings. Period. The Whirlpool hearings are a joke. Political incest is what it is. Tell Ira Dolor and Leroy Reichman to rally the troops and put these Democrat hirelings on the stand now. We are not Mexicans. We have the right to hear the truth. We have a right to impeach James Cannon."

At that point, some of the folks who had shown up to confront Randell with a counter-demonstration began yelling at him. "You're a liar!" Another shouted, "You're giving Jesus a bad name." An older woman stepped forward and said, "Shame on you for preaching hate. Don't you know what you've caused? You should be praying for those murdered at Pensacola."

Randell looked toward his detractors and said, "We must take back America from the humanists, the liberals, the hedonists, the child-killers, and the homosexuals." Well, three out of five wasn't bad. I had thought he might have been talking about me until he got to the last two.

Then Randell ignored the protesters and turned back to address his audience of true believers. "We must not care what anyone says about us. You must enlist in the Army of God and become the green berets of the movement to save America. We need a cadre of people who are militant, who are fierce, who are unmerciful. In the battle for America's soul, there will be turmoil and disruption. Don't let them scare you by saying it's our fault that a few abortionists got killed. The Cannon administration is still repeating the mistakes of Waco."

Raising his voice, Phinehas Randell closed by saying, "I call upon you now to join with us in the Loyal Opposition and be loyal to God, loyal to His word, and loyal to the Constitution of the United States of America."

Then, Patrick Mahoney moved to the podium and announced, "We are going to be holding demonstrations this afternoon at the Bankhead Law Firm, and this evening in front of Cannon's former church, asking them why they did not excommunicate this man, or censure this man. This man is flagrantly promoting rebellion against God's word. This is the single most un-Christian administration in the history of this country." With that exhortation, Randell and his boys picked up their signs and boarded the bus.

I suggested to Lindsey that we be loyal to a good restaurant somewhere close. The woman had been on the road for five days, following Randell all the way from Raleigh, and treating for lunch was the least I could do for the cause. Besides, I was more interested in what she had to say than in what I had for lunch. We talked through lunch and lots of iced tea. It was 6:30 when I noticed the time. We'd been sitting there four hours, and the dinner shift had already started.

As we walked back to our cars, Lindsey asked, "So, do you need a place to stay tonight?" Big grin.

I felt the blood rushing through my veins. "Wish I could stay. Really. But Burke has called a staff meeting for eight o'clock in the morning, and I'm going to have to get back and put in a few more hours tonight to be ready for that." Damn.

"You sure are playing hard to get," she said with a smile and a wink.

"No. I'm kinda shy. But I'm easy."

"We shall see."

"Well, let's see soon. I think we're about to call in the dogs on this investigation and go home," I said.

"If you don't have any plans for the weekend of the 11th, how about a date. Remember I told you I had a surprise? Well, I've got two tickets for a Jimmy Buffett concert. What do you say, old salt?"

I said yes, of course. Then I drove back to Birmingham listening to "Last Mango in Paris."

Burke had called the staff meeting, only the third one we'd had, to assess the status of our investigation and make some major decisions. We were now down to the lick log. It was time to prepare the Prosecution Memoranda, the formal analyses and recommendations related to potential criminal prosecutions in each area of the investigation. I came in about an hour ahead of time Monday morning to make sure everything was in order. Instead, I spent most of my time bothering folks and telling the story about Phinehas Randell's impeachment crusade. And thinking about the Buffett concert.

The meeting began promptly at eight. Burke was in a good mood, and everyone was prepared. We followed the same order that we had during the initial meeting, except for Bailey, who had already completed his part of the assignment and gone back to Davis Martin. One by one, all of the reports reached the same conclusion. No criminal liability for President Cannon. No criminal liability for Mrs. Cannon. Nate and Navita recommended referral of a few cases connected with illegal loans made by Roby Douglas at Financial Management, but none of them were connected in any way with President or Mrs. Cannon. Sean and Barefield said there was a marginal case against Josh Banaghan at Jefferson, but it was probably precluded by double jeopardy due to his 1990 acquittal. Zuckerman and Herbeck said the only thing they could find regarding Whirlpool Estates was a possible bankruptcy fraud charge against a realtor, but nothing relating to the Cannons.

Burke sat there for a few minutes, his hands together and his finger tips on his lips, looking toward the middle of the conference table. Then, he spoke. "We are all in agreement, then, that there is no evidence of criminal liability on the part of either James Madison Cannon or Diane Rankin Cannon relating in any way to Jefferson Savings Bank, Financial Management Services, or Whirlpool Development Corporation?"

Everyone nodded agreement. Burke paused, then very slowly and deliberately, he said, "I would like to ask each of you to have your final reports prepared by Friday. Mr. Wilkes, you coordinate that effort and prepare a draft of our final report to the Attorney General. I think it is clear that our job is done, and there's no good reason to continue spending our time or the taxpayers' money.

"I'd also like to have your final prosecution memoranda by Friday," he said. "We can transmit those to the United States Attorney for her decision as to whether to prosecute any of the potential cases. I don't see any potential conflict of interest in those cases."

Then, pushing his chair back and standing up, Burke said, "It has been my distinct pleasure to work with each of you. I appreciate your hard work and congratulate you on a job well done. Thank you."

Navita and Mike followed Burke back to his office. I just sat there for a few minutes, reflecting upon all we had done. Glad that we were almost finished. Proud to know that reason could prevail over partisan political pressures for witch hunts. Sean and Nate were still there talking about how Dolor and Leech would take the news. Barefield was leaning back in his chair, not saying anything, just grinning. Dale Herbeck had been trying to figure out how to work the coffee machine, and when he did, he announced, "Drinks are on me!" I accepted his offer and filled my cup. The camaraderie was better than the coffee.

I read the newspapers with detached amusement that week. I think most of the Congressional committee members must have reached the same conclusions about the Whirlpool charges, because now even the Republican members seemed to be trying to find inconsistencies in the testimony. If they couldn't find a crime, maybe they could find enough conflicting statements to suggest a cover-up. It was almost funny. Well, of course, it wasn't funny for the young staffers who had to sit through the harangues and to pay their own legal expenses. Pathetic would be a better word. Grown men—and the Republicans on the committees were all grown white men—making asses of themselves on national television. Even the *Sun* headlined their coverage, "Hearings Boring; Viewers Pick O. J."

And it wasn't funny when Senator Kit Medlar wrote an op-ed piece in the *Washington Sun*, asking "Why is Goodall's death still a mystery?" Maybe because Medlar was too stupid to read the damn report. Maybe he didn't have anything better to do. Or maybe he was carrying water for the Lynch Legal Foundation. Senator Medlar had been executive director of the Lynch Legal Foundation for a few years after the voters had turned him out of the governor's office. Mark Schine, who ran the foundation's Washington operation, had been Ed Meese's paid staff apologist for years. Now he spent his time testifying before committees or filing ethics complaints against Democrats, and he was a regular contributor to the editorial page of the *Washington Sun.* So maybe that was the connection. Or maybe Mellonskoff wanted more bang for his bucks underwriting the Lynch Foundation. Whatever, it was unkind and unnecessary.

The pace of work at the office that week was busier than usual as everyone worked hard to complete the final section reports. I would have the next week to knock out the final draft, then Burke would probably take another week to put his finishing touches to it. If everything went according to schedule, we might be out of work by the end of the month. Early September at the latest.

Driving to work on Friday morning I was in an especially good mood. It had been a very productive week, and I didn't have any commitments for the weekend. Thought I might catch up on some reading. Or maybe I could finish that law review article. That ole Friday mood had infected the office, too. I could tell when the receptionist at the front desk was humming "Sittin' on the dock of the bay."

That all changed with the phone call just after ten. Burke took the call. He didn't say much. Just listened mostly. Then hung up. In a few minutes he walked into my office and sat down. Didn't say anything for almost a minute, but I could tell he had something important to tell me. He started to say something, but paused. Then he looked across my desk and said, "That was Attorney General Otis on the phone. The Special Panel has just entered its order naming George Jeffreys as the Independent Counsel for Whirlpool."

Chapter Thirteen

Burke called everyone into the main conference room shortly before noon and made the announcement. There was no rancor in his words nor in his voice. He said he had already talked with George Jeffreys by telephone, advised him of the status of our work, and pledged his full cooperation in making an orderly transition of the duties of the office. Jeffreys was in New Orleans, attending a Federalist Society convention, but he planned to come to Birmingham on Tuesday to meet with the staff and get a full briefing. Then Burke told everyone to take the rest of the day off and to have a good weekend.

Silence, then astonishment and anger. Those were the two reactions that seemed to grip the staff. Six months invested in the investigation. Two million dollars in expenses. Three convictions. Two interim reports. The final report in draft form. The astonishment was that the Court would cashier Burke at this point, with the final report only a few weeks away. The anger was because the staff, all fiercely loyal to Burke, thought it was a gratuitous personal affront to a good man. I wasn't sure what I was feeling. Numb mostly. Although I sensed that Burke had been a bit surprised by the decision, he was the most calm person in the office. Perhaps the only calm person. Unshaken. Stoic.

The office cleared quickly. Lots of vacant looks as folks left the building and drifted toward their cars in the parking lot. I guess everyone wanted some time alone to try to make sense of the announcement. Or to think about their own plans for the future. Maybe some of them would stay. I doubted it. Most were fortunate to have permanent jobs to which they could return. I didn't. And I realized that I should probably give that some thought. Later, maybe.

I strolled back to my office, pondering whether to continue working on the final report or to start packing. Instead, I just sat at my desk, unable to get excited about either option. I turned off my computer and started to leave, but I noticed the lights were still on in Burke's office. I looked in, and there he was. Reading the *U. S. Attorneys Manual*. I think we were both startled. I tried to think of something appropriate to say, but the best I could manage was, "Wanna get something to eat?"

"Can't right now. You go on." he said. "I need to see whether we are supposed to schedule an audit of the office accounts. This doesn't seem to cover a situation like ours."

Always the professional, making an orderly retreat with dignity and attention to practical details. Reminded me that there was still much I could learn from Burke. I suppose he had the advantage of experience, though, having been savaged once before by the radical elements in his own party. And he knew that he was leaving with his personal integrity intact, despite their unfounded charges and cheap shots. Still, I felt a certain sadness that such a gentleman had fallen victim to the ranting rubes.

I was glad I didn't have any plans for the weekend. I wanted to know more about George Jeffreys and why he had been appointed to replace Burke. Not that I thought he'd ask me to stay on with the investigation. Hell, I'd be the first one he'd fire. I was quite sure Dolor's speech wouldn't be lost on Mr. Jeffreys. But I was curious, in a disinterested way. I grabbed lunch then headed to Samford to spend the afternoon in the library. That night, I came back to the office and spent a couple of hours doing computer searches to see what else I could find. Lots. And very interesting.

Jeffreys was born in Greenville, South Carolina, the son of an Assembly of God preacher. He had been a loyal Republican since high school, when he handed out campaign literature for Richard Nixon in 1960. At Bob Jones he was active in the Goldwater campaign and head of the Young Americans for Decency chapter on campus. That record secured him an internship on the staff of Senator Shurmond during his senior year in college, at the time when Shurmond was leading the fight against the Voting Rights Act. Although Jeffreys staunchly supported Nixon's Vietnam policies, he dodged the draft by claiming a 4-F deferment for psoriasis, a bad case of dandruff that never seemed to bother him again after the war.

After graduating from law school at Wake Forest, Jeffreys clerked for Wilhelm Renchberg at the Supreme Court. It was probably during that time that he became obsessed with wanting to be a Supreme Court Justice. He then had a brief career as a corporate lawyer in private practice at Olin, Bradley, & Scaife, where some of the other associates openly laughed at his ambition by referring to him as "Justice Jeffreys."

When Reeder was elected in 1980, Jeffreys quickly began maneuvering for a job at the Department of Justice. He got an appointment as Assistant Attorney General and was a part of the conservative brat pack that included Bruce Flim and Thad Stevens, two other young professional conservatives at Justice. Every Monday morning they met and engaged in long philosophical discussions about how the Reeder Revolution could allow them to change the direction of the law in such areas as busing and school prayer.

One of Jeffreys' duties at the Department of Justice was helping to recruit and nominate conservative judges for the federal bench. I think that's where I first heard his name. In 1982 he and Bruce Flim were pushing hard to get Ben Toledano appointed in Louisiana, but their boy was rejected when the public became aware of his past political history and racial slurs. Jeffreys also advocated the nomination of Robert Beard for the Court of Appeals, trying to reward Beard for his role as Nixon's Solicitor General.

Advancing his own career was also a high priority, and Jeffreys soon tried to get himself appointed to the Fourth Circuit Court of Appeals, even moving to Virginia in pursuit of his ambition. When that didn't work out, he secured a nomination to the D. C. Circuit, where the Attorney General's recommendation carried more weight than did the local pols. The American Bar Association gave Jeffreys its lowest acceptable rating, because he had almost no trial experience, but his appointment still sailed through Senator Shurmond's Judiciary Committee and the Republican-controlled Senate.

On the appellate bench, Jeffreys' performance was predictable. He voted to let the Diablo Canyon nuclear plant open despite professional concerns about design safety. He joined in an opinion restricting anti-Reeder protest signs near the White House and wrote a 30-page dissent against allowing the NAACP Legal Defense Fund and the Sierra Legal Defense Fund to participate in the federal employee checkoff program. And he struck down the affirmative action plan for the fire department in the District of Columbia. To no one's surprise, Jeffreys and Beard agreed on 93 percent of the cases on which they sat together.

George Jeffreys played the game and tried to please all the right people. Yet, he was never nominated for the Supreme Court by President Reeder. He remained obedient, but he also remained on the Court of Appeals while Scalia, Beard, Ginsberg, and Kennedy got the nominations. Many are called, but few are chosen. Jeffreys wasn't.

When nominated by President Stuart for Solicitor General, a post Jeffreys saw as a sure ticket to the Supreme Court, the confirmation process went smoothly His nomination was supported by the conservative Federal Legal Foundation. One liberal group testified against his confirmation because he had shown himself "insensitive to the rights of minorities" and his opinions reflected a "lack of commitment to the concept of courts as an institution to enforce constitutional guarantees for individuals". Jeffreys quickly took offense at that criticism and haughtily said, "The judiciary should be insulated from these kinds of attacks on the motives and integrity of judges doing their job." Didn't matter much. He was easily confirmed. But his words would come back to haunt him.

As Solicitor General, Jeffreys continued to follow the party line. In *Minnesota v. Hodgson*, he argued that the Supreme Court should overturn *Roe v. Wade*. He wrote the brief against a busing plan for desegregating the public schools in *Board of Education v. Dowell*. He also tried to defend the unconstitutional federal flag burning statute in *U.S. v. Eichman*, and he argued against the Court even hearing an appeal in *Ben-Shalom v. Marsh*, dismissing a woman from the Army Reserves. The most notorious move he made was submitting a brief that undermined the Environmental Protection Agency's position in a case concerning the destruction of wetlands. The conviction was overturned, delighting his old friends at the Federal Legal Foundation, which represented the defendant in the case. Jeffreys now served on their board of directors.

Perhaps his most partisan political action as Solicitor General was the 1990 whitewashing of the investigation of two Justice Department officials who leaked false and damaging information about a Democratic Congressman to CBS News. Although the two political appointees reportedly failed polygraph tests, Jeffreys told Attorney General Thornburger to drop the investigation and not to take any disciplinary actions against those involved. One of those guys, David Rapper, later became the press secretary for Congressman Leech, and shortly thereafter the House Banking Committee became a major source of leaks and false accusations about Cannon's role in Whirlpool.

Jeffreys dutifully served President Stuart, but once again he failed to achieve his life's ambition of a place on the Supreme Court. Twice actually. Jeffreys and his supporters actively sought the appointments both times under Stuart, and each time he was touted as a contender. But it was not to be. Souter and Thom—men he did not think his intellectual equals, men who could not match his service and devotion to the party— were chosen instead. Why, he reportedly asked friends, had Stuart forsaken him?

After Governor Cannon defeated President Stuart in 1992, Jeffreys had difficulty letting go of the trappings of power. For 12 years he had faithfully served his party and his president. He had paid his dues. Then, just as he was about to crown his career, just as he would surely receive the nod for the next opening on the Supreme Court, James Madison Cannon had shattered his dream. And cost him his job as well. Jeffreys held onto the office until the last possible minute. He was finally forced to resign as Solicitor General at noon on January 20, 1993, the very moment President Cannon took the oath of office.

Political connections served Jeffreys well, however, and he was offered a partnership in the Washington office of Kirk and Polis, one of the big conservative law firms. It was the same firm that had found a place for Judge Beard after his failed nomination. A seat on the management committee and an annual income of over $1 million appeared to help Jeffreys overcome his disappointment about his fate, but it didn't keep him from trying to get even. He volunteered his services in the Christine Putnam lawsuit against Cannon.

Jeffreys remained active in Republican party politics, filing an amicus brief for the Republican National Committee in a Fifth Circuit case to help Thornburger beat the outstanding debts from his unsuccessful Senate campaign. Jeffreys had even considered a run for the United States Senate on his own earlier this year. Theories abounded concerning his ultimate decision against making the race. Some said he could read the polls. Others said he was only playing the shill for Oliver North, the eventual Republican nominee, trying to keep others out of the campaign. Some thought he had been bought off with the promise of a future appointment. Whichever, it was just as well, I suppose. A man who had schmoozed his way through life and built a career on appointments to office wouldn't have known the first thing about talking to the common people on the hustings.

Now Jeffreys had been rewarded with another high profile federal job. It was obvious who had made the appointment, a Court of Appeals panel headed by Judge Sam Chase. What I didn't know and couldn't even guess was why they had chosen him. I drew a blank on that and couldn't see any particular rationale other than his political history. He certainly had no experience as a prosecutor. I guess he'd be acceptable to the Republicans on the Hill, those who had been demanding Burke's resignation.

In an article in the *Baltimore Sun*, GOP consultant Eddie Mahem had exulted, "Fiske was one of those Northeast establishment types that has nothing to do with being a Republican. Jeffreys is a real Republican." I feared that he was right. Mahem had been paid $25,000 to place the Troopergate story in the *American Speculator* and the *Los Angeles Times*, so he was an expert witness on real Republicans.

Jeffreys would certainly follow orders from the top. Always had. But, in the past, he'd had a patron. There'd always been someone higher up promoting him. This time, though, I couldn't figure out who was behind his appointment.

As I was heading home, I heard an incoming fax. It was a copy of the order appointing Jeffreys. I didn't let the fact that it was addressed to Burke stop me from taking a long look at it. I almost laughed in disbelief when I got to the key paragraph stating the "official" reason for rejecting

Burke. I could almost smell the bullshit oozing before I read the words. "The Court has determined that appointing Kenneth Burke would not be consistent with the purposes of the Act, which contemplates an apparent as well as an actual independence on the part of the counsel. As Burke was appointed by an officer of the incumbent administration, the Court deems it in the best interest of the appearance of independence that a person not affiliated with the Cannon administration be appointed." So they appointed George Jeffreys.

Then it all became clear. Saturday's papers provided the clue. Senator Reynolds Rantallion appeared to be most excited, and he was quoted as saying, "I applaud the decision to appoint George Jeffreys, a truly Independent Counsel. Now that the 'Burke Block' is over, I urge the Congressional leadership to immediately seek new and expanded hearings in order to get all the facts out on the table for the American people." The "Burke Block" was a phrase taken from Streicher's column in the *New York Times* last month calling for Burke's removal by the Court. Judge Sam Chase's order echoed Rantallion's earlier speech calling Burke's appointment tainted by the appearance of conflict of interest.

Rantallion and Helmut Duke appeared to have been hard at work. They knew they could count on Judge Chase. He was the one who, much to their delight, had overturned Oliver North's felony convictions. One of the rumors about the Senate race in Virginia was that North's friends in Congress had kept Jeffreys out by promising a future federal appointment. Maybe this was it.

Judge Chase had been nominated by Reeder at the request of Senator Duke. Chase was Duke's protégé, having supported his National Congressional Club slush fund for conservative candidates, having been active in the old Reeder front group Citizens for America, having served as a Reeder delegate to the Republican National Convention, and having headed the Mecklenberg County Republican Committee. Chase's confirmation hearings had not been without controversy. Questions were raised about his views toward minorities and an article he had written praising "the long-historied, little-loved descendants of the people who built half the civilized world—the Anglo-Saxons." And, unfortunately, Burke had chaired the ABA committee to review nominations at the time. They couldn't forget that.

There were other connections as well. Jeffreys was a partner at Kirk and Polis, the law firm that had prepared a pro bono brief in *U. S. v. Knox*, a child pornography case, on behalf of Rantallion, Duke, and others who were fronting for the Christian Coalition and the American Family Association. And Jeffreys personally defended the major tobacco companies in North Carolina against claims that smoking caused lung cancer and other health problems.

There were other North Carolina ties from when Jeffreys attended law school there and had been active in Republican circles supporting Nixon's efforts in 1972. Chase, like Jeffreys, had been chair of the campus Young Republicans and the Young Americans for Decency in college. In 1970, two years out of law school, Chase was appointed as an Assistant U. S. Attorney under Richard Nixon. Of course he would name a partisan Republican, one acceptable to Rantallion and Duke. George Jeffreys was their man.

Or, maybe it was all just a coincidence. Right.

Whatever the real reasons for appointing Jeffreys, Cannon's opponents in Congress were overjoyed. Robert Dorkman jubilantly expressed the feelings of the Republican attack machine when he declared, "Today, all the president's men face an uncertain future. Their inability to control events by securing the reappointment of Burke has left them trembling with fear." Now that Burke was out and their man Jeffreys was in, they could go full blast. No more limitations on what they could ask or whom they could call before Congressional committees, because the Democrats could no longer hide behind a cautious bureaucrat like Burke. No more reports clearing Cannon appointees. No more reports deflating their favorite conspiracy theories about the death of Hal Goodall. No political allegations too ridiculous to make on the floor of Congress. And no criminal charges too insignificant to be pursued by their new hand-picked Independent Counsel.

I slept late on Sunday. Maybe I was trying to avoid what I knew I had to do. I felt like I had eaten some forbidden fruit from the tree of political knowledge, and it left an awful taste in my mouth. I called and talked with my kids for over an hour, catching up on their school activities and other things in their lives. That always helped me remember what was important when I found myself in depressing situations. It worked again. So what if the new Whirlpool counsel was about to join the partisan witch hunt? So what if I was about to be unemployed? I could always find work. And for such an ornery old redneck I sure was lucky to have two wonderful children. My real job was to make their lives richer and to make the world a better place for them to live. I remembered that, and it helped.

On Monday, however, I still knew what had to be done. I went to the office early and typed my letter of resignation to Jeffreys. I signed it, put it in a plain envelope, and placed it in the top drawer of my desk. I planned to present it to Jeffreys personally when he came on Tuesday. It was something that appointed employees should always do whenever there was a change in administrations, but there were other important reasons for doing so now. Principles were at stake. Besides, I'd rather do it first, before Jeffreys had the pleasure of firing me and Dolor had the satisfaction of bragging about it.

Things were different at the office that day. Dejected acceptance is as close as I can describe the general mood. A little work. Many phones calls. Much coffee. Everyone gravitated to the conference room sometime after lunch, and we had what looked like an uncalled staff meeting. Group therapy was more accurate. No one planned to stay on with Jeffreys. Paul Barefield was returning to his firm in Ohio, and Nate Norton was going back to Atlanta. Herbeck and Sean both planned to rejoin Davis Martin with Burke, and William Bailey was already there. The U. S. Attorney in Philadelphia had held Zuckerman's slot for him. Navita had good news. She had already lined up a Visiting Professor slot at Columbia for the year.

I was the only joker in the deck, but I had been drawing to inside straights all my life. I said I wasn't sure what I'd do, maybe go to work on the Hill in January. It was too late for me to find anything at a law school, Navita's good fortune notwithstanding. I was pretty much back where I'd been when this position came along, but I didn't think I'd go crawling back to my old job in Austin.

Tuesday came too quickly. As I sat in my office awaiting Burke's meeting with Jeffreys I noticed that the date was August 9th. Twenty years ago today Richard Nixon resigned in disgrace. Ironic that those who revered his memory were now poised to get even, to make President Cannon pay for their decades of shame and humiliation.

Jeffreys arrived as scheduled at 2 p.m. for his private meeting with Burke. Only it turned out not to be so private. Jeffreys showed up with an aide-in-tow whose major contribution looked like it was carrying his briefcase. When they entered Burke's office together, Burke opened my door and asked me to join them. That's when I got my first look at the new Independent Counsel. Just about what I expected. Jeffreys was wearing one of those $800 suits, charcoal gray with light gray pin stripes, a white shirt with enough starch to make it look like it was cut from a canvas revival tent, and a red diagonal striped tie. The knot was tied so tight it was about the size of a dog tick. And a gold tie clasp. I hadn't seen a tie clasp like that since I was in high school.

Jeffreys also seemed to be wearing a permanent plastic smile. His receding hairline made him look older than 47, and his vanity had led him to part his hair ridiculously low on the side to cover the balding on top. Looked pretty silly, I thought. I knew I shouldn't judge people by their looks, but sometimes I couldn't help it. I thought those little strands of hair pulled across his head spoke volumes about Jeffreys' concern with appearances over reality. And that goofy grin of his was so insincere. Maybe it was just the overbite. Looked like he had been weaned on a pickle. Or maybe his mouth was stretched out of shape from sucking up and kissing so much ass during his distinguished career of getting and holding appointed positions. Jeffreys had been a world class butt snorkler for most of his adult life, and it seemed to have left a permanent impression on his face.

Jeffreys glanced at me, toward his boy, then back at Burke. "This is my Administrative Assistant, Mitch Palmer. He has my complete confidence, and he can speak for me," he said.

Burke quickly sized up the young aide then looked back to Jeffreys and said, "This is my Chief Deputy, John Wilkes. He has my complete confidence. We can both speak for ourselves. Please have a seat." I could tell that Burke didn't like Palmer any more than I did. And he didn't appreciate him being there. Or maybe he just didn't like anyone measuring the drapes quite so soon.

The conversation quickly got back on course and went as expected. Burke pledged his full cooperation for a smooth transition. He gave Jeffreys an overview of what we'd done and where we were and provided him with copies of the draft final report as well as copies of the two reports that had been issued in June.

Jeffreys was so obsequious. Said that he had not sought the appointment and that he was as surprised as anyone when the court announced his appointment last Friday. I almost choked on that one. He told Burke what a fine job he thought he had been doing and how he hoped to build on Burke's preliminary work. I saw a slight grimace on Burke's face at the word preliminary, but he said nothing. Jeffreys also said he wanted to put his own team in place, although he hoped the current staff would stay on long enough to get his people up to speed. Burke said he would encourage them to do so, but that it would be up to the individuals involved to make their own decisions.

I sat there, saying nothing but feeling like I was being slimed. Jeffreys had a voice like a preacher, a false tone of concern that hardly masked his self-righteous gloating. And Mitch Palmer reminded me of one of those plastic dogs with bobbing heads that used to grace the rear deck of cars in the late '50s. Whenever Jeffreys said something, Palmer would vigorously nod his head in agreement as if to punctuate the conversation with his nose.

One of the most telling moments in the meeting came near the end when Burke asked if Jeffreys would like to meet with the staff that afternoon. Jeffreys revealed more than he intended when he said, "We'd prefer to meet with the staff members individually, but we'd like to put that off until tomorrow or the next day if possible. Mitch and I had planned to spend the rest of the day reviewing the press clips."

Burke was nonplused by that. "I'm afraid we haven't been maintaining any files of the press coverage. I haven't paid much attention to that. All of our files are work files related to the investigation."

Palmer and Jeffreys looked at each other with exasperation. Then Palmer said, "Well, perhaps I could meet with your press secretary today?"

Again Burke disappointed them. "I don't have a press secretary. Never had a need for one, and can't imagine any circumstances in which I would."

There was a brief uncomfortable silence until Jeffreys said, "I think it would be appropriate if we held a joint press conference tomorrow. We could both benefit from that, I think. And it would be a way of fulfilling our obligation to keep the public informed. I would, of course, express my appreciation for all the work you and your staff have done thus far. And, if you would, please refer to me as Judge Jeffreys. You also might say something like, uh, how you know of my reputation for fairness and honesty and how the transition will not affect the ongoing investigation. What would you think of that?"

"Mr. Jeffreys, I have already pledged my full cooperation and have promised to do whatever necessary to assure a smooth transition. If you want me to participate in a press conference, I'll do that," Burke said. But he didn't say it enthusiastically.

With that, Burke stood up, and the meeting ended. I forced myself to shake hands with Palmer and with Jeffreys, and on my way out the door I handed the envelope with my letter of resignation to Jeffreys. He just looked at it without saying anything and placed it in the inside pocket of his coat.

I started to go back to my office, but I didn't much want to hang around there while Jeffreys and Palmer were in the building, scoping the place like hungry vultures. Instead, I stopped to get Sean, and we went to have a beer at The Mill, our favorite retreat in Birmingham. It had a great curved oak bar that fit my elbows, and our favorite bartender, Sherman Morgan, was always full of stories to take our minds off our work. That night the beer also helped.

Chapter Fourteen

Before the week was out, Jeffreys was getting plenty of press. Most of it bad. Only the *Washington Sun* praised his appointment. The White House didn't say much publicly, but the Democrats in Congress did. Just when I was starting to think I was the only one to see the raw politics behind the appointment, it became obvious to everyone.

Most of the objections were made to the cameras, but Senator Levine took his case to Judge Chase on Thursday. His letter was more restrained than most of the sound bites, but the point was the same. "As primary sponsor of the Independent Counsel Reauthorization Act of 1994," he wrote, "I must express my concern at the appointment of George Jeffreys as independent counsel in the Jefferson Savings matter.

"In 15 years of operation of the independent counsel law, the Court has always taken great care to appoint persons who are sufficiently removed from partisan activity. That is not the case with Mr. Jeffreys. The issue with respect to Mr. Jeffreys is that he lacks the necessary independence essential for public confidence in his judgment.

"Mr. Jeffreys' position as co-chair of a highly partisan Republican congressional campaign in Virginia, his recent participation in a televised debate on the Christine Putnam lawsuit, and his offering to file a brief on her behalf are particularly troubling. While no one questions Mr. Jeffreys' right to engage in highly visible partisan political activities, those activities disqualify him from taking charge of the Jefferson Savings investigation. I urge the Court to ask Mr. Jeffreys to provide a complete accounting of his recent political activities or to resign immediately."

Chase had no inclination to remove Jeffreys, and he quickly declined to do so. He replied that Jeffreys could only be removed by impeachment or by the Attorney General for cause.

Friday's paper had another revelation about Jeffreys' appointment, one that had Democrats raising more than eyebrows. Like their hind legs. Kate Macauley of the *Atlanta Constitution* had broken a story that Senators Rantallion and Duke had a private lunch with Judge Chase in the Senate Dining Room on July 14th. Just happened to be at the same time the Special Panel was considering the appointment of the Independent Counsel and at the same time Streicher, Bardus, Dorkman, and Floyd Crump were waging their campaign against Burke. I didn't find that surprising. It was expected. Did anyone think Judge Chase would have acted without consulting his patrons? That would have been real news.

Judge Chase said he couldn't remember any discussion about Whirlpool, that they were just talking about old friends. Yeah, like their old friend George Jeffreys. Duke refused to talk with reporters. Rantallion said they were discussing goat roping and proctologists. I could believe that. These guys were such assholes they probably had personal proctologists the way other people had personal trainers. But I didn't believe that they met—while Rantallion was leading the fight against Burke, while Duke was indebted to Jeffreys, and while Chase was preparing to make the decision—without discussing the pending appointment of the Independent Counsel for Whirlpool.

The local papers led with the press conference Jeffreys had held outside our offices yesterday. For the most part the story was what Jeffreys had wanted. He got to tell the press that he was in charge and would continue what Burke had started. And Burke, keeping his word, had said his lines about Jeffreys having "a reputation for fairness." The only glitch was the obvious contradiction created when Jeffreys told the press hc was pleased that many of the current staff members would be staying on and continuing their work under his direction. That didn't quite square with the truth, the quotes in the same story from Sean, Barefield, Navita, Nate, Zuckerman, and Herbeck, all indicating that they would be leaving. It was the first of many lies and distortions of truth that Jeffreys would spin to project his image.

Mitch Palmer was one of the last people I wanted to see that day, but he walked into my office, closed the door, and sat down across from my desk. He began making small talk that only bored me. Asked where I went to law school, as if he didn't already know. Told me with an air of smugness that he had attended Dartmouth as an undergraduate and had his law degree from the University of Chicago. Asked how I liked living in Birmingham. I wished he would cut the crap and say what he had come to say. Instead, I had to listen to a phatic windup before he eventually made his pitch.

Finally, he handed me the letter of resignation that I had given Jeffreys on Tuesday. "Judge Jeffreys would like for you to reconsider your decision to resign. We want you to stay on and be a part of our team."

"I don't think I'll be doing that," I said. "And I don't think your boss needs any more bad press. The Democrats are beating on his head enough already without Senator Dolor jumping on, too." I was trying to be helpful. I also tried not to smirk when I noticed that he was wearing a pager on his belt.

"We've already cleared it with Dolor's staff, and it's okay with him," Palmer added, not knowing what a dumb thing that was to say. "Judge Jeffreys knows he is going to have to have some visible Democrats on his staff to counter the perception that he might be too partisan. Frankly, we were encouraged that you were the only staff attorney who wasn't quoted as jumping ship, and we thought maybe your letter was just *pro forma*."

Damn these guys were stupid. Clearing every move with Dolor. Thinking that hiring a few Democrats could disguise the nature of their mission. About as clever as putting earrings on a hog. And what was with this regal mantra of "Judge" Jeffreys? Was that something he demanded from his lackeys, or did they think it would make him sound less like a hatchet man? "No, I wasn't quoted because I don't talk to the press," I told him. "And if I had any interest in working for Mr. Jeffreys, I would have written a letter of application."

Palmer didn't get it. "Well, will you at least stay on until we can get our new staff assembled. You're the only institutional memory we have right now. And then maybe you'll reconsider."

"Look," I said, trying to make it clear for him, "I've got some important business to attend to now. I'm going to a Jimmy Buffett concert tonight. I'm outta here"

"Okay," he chirped, "we can talk again on Monday. Think about it."

Lindsey's phone call saved me from having to whack Palmer with the Dictaphone and hide his body. I wasn't planning to give it another thought. The only thing I was thinking about was trying to get laid.

"Hope you're ready to party" said the voice of the goddess on the line. "I'm at my parents' house now, and I'll come by your office to pick you up. You can be picked up, can't you, Mr. Shy-but-easy? I'll be there at 5 o'clock sharp."

"My how you do go on, ma'am," I said in my best Southern voice. "How about picking me up at home? I want to get into some Levi's." Meaning mine, but leaving the question open.

"Sounds good to me, but you'll have to tell me where you live."

"2620 Highland Avenue South. I'll be the guy on the front steps wearing a big smile."

"See ya there. But remember, 5 o'clock sharp."

I had enough time to get home, shower, and change into comfortable clothes. And Lindsey was there at 5 o'clock sharp, just as she'd said on the phone. I hadn't imagined that she'd be a time freak, but I was learning new things about her every time I saw her. I asked where she'd like to have dinner, and she said she'd already made reservations. It was a surprise, she said.

The whole weekend was a surprise. That became clear as Lindsey took the airport exit and pulled into the long term parking lot. She handed me the tickets, and we boarded a plane for Key West. By 8:30 we were seated for dinner at a quaint little Cuban restaurant on Duval Street. One side of my brain was trying to absorb the history of the island, once home to Jose Marti, John Kennedy, Tennessee Williams, Wallace Stevens, Ernest Hemingway, and Sloppy Joe Russell. The other lobe was struggling in vain to separate feelings of intellectual attraction from glandular impulses.

I tried to pretend that this was a normal date as I read the menu. Told Lindsey that I did this all the time. She just smiled. Hemingway once wrote that Duval street had three poolrooms, five beer joints, five bad restaurants, and one good one. This must have been the good one, and I was feeling much more like one of the haves than the have nots. Had a wonderful dinner of slow-roasted marinated pork with yellow rice, black beans, fried plantains, and key lime pie, finished off with Cuban coffee that had my heart racing. At least something did.

After dinner we strolled down the street to Margaritaville where Buffett was playing that night. The local Parrottheads were out in force, but we still managed to get a table near the stage. The music was great, the lyrics were even better, and I was still in a pleasant state of shock. Feeling like Hemingway's six-toed tomcat, I ordered another pitcher of Margaritas, leaned over toward Lindsey, and asked, "Where have you been all my life?"

"Grade school," she laughed.

Pretty funny. But true. I loved her smart mouth and general irreverence. After the last set, we took a long walk on the beach before calling it a night. And what a night it was. Stayed at a little Queen Anne guest house over on Truman Avenue called, appropriately, The Mermaid and the Alligator. Wicked. I overcame my shyness.

I didn't think about work all weekend, and by the time we got back to Birmingham on Sunday I could hardly think at all. Except about Lindsey. My feelings for her certainly made the idea of staying in Alabama much more appealing. Maybe even if it meant working for Jeffreys.

I told Lindsey all about Jeffreys and my reluctance to stay on, but she made a good argument that I should, if for no other reason than to try to keep them honest. I wondered if anyone could stand in the way of the coming Inquisition, but I knew someone should at least try. I just wasn't sure it should be me. Nor did I know whether I was up to it.

I came in late on Monday. I didn't have anything that had to be done, and I thought my tardiness might discourage Mitch Palmer from another recruiting visit. Nope. Only this time it was Jeffreys and his young shadow, and they wanted me to join them for lunch.

As we approached the car, just for grins, I told Palmer to ride in the back seat because I might get sick. I didn't say why. That also meant that Jeffreys would have to drive, the last time I ever saw him drive the car during the entire time I would work there. Another significant difference between Burke and Jeffreys.

We had barely left the parking lot when Jeffreys said, "Mr. Wilkes, I assume that you have had an opportunity to reconsider your resignation."

"Well, I've reconsidered it. And it still stands," I said, looking out the window. "There's not much more I can contribute to this investigation, 'cause I don't think there's much more to investigate. Obviously you fellows think otherwise, so you should probably find someone who agrees with you. And I'm sure that won't be hard to do."

Jeffreys knew exactly what I meant, but that didn't end the conversation. "I know you have some reservations about me, Mr. Wilkes, but I can assure you that I intend to be very fair in pursuing this investigation. I am not a political person, despite what some newspaper reports might lead you to believe. Nevertheless, I am well aware of the importance of public perceptions. Quite frankly, I need you to stay. Otherwise, it will appear that I have conducted a purge of Burke's entire staff for partisan reasons."

Public perceptions. Appearances. Jeffreys sounded more like a campaign consultant than an independent counsel. In a way, I suppose he was. He probably saw this job as a way to get back on the short list for the Supreme Court the next time there was a Republican in the White House. And what better way to speed that process than to inflict damage on Cannon between now and the 1996 election? I wasn't enjoying this conversation. Made me wish I could pick up a remote control and change channels. The best I could do was to avoid a direct answer, so I returned a question. "I don't think anyone will be fooled by your keeping one person, do you?"

"Perhaps not," he said, ignoring my use of the word fooled. "But I have already made arrangements to hire Tom Sandefur, another Democrat and a Senior Fellow at the Kennedy Center for Ethics at Georgetown. He will be my ethics advisor. And there will be others."

"Oh," I said with more than a slight tone of skepticism, "but why would someone with your reputation need an ethics advisor? I thought Independent Counsels were chosen, in part, for their sense of ethics."

Jeffreys looked at Mitch Palmer in the rear view mirror, pausing for a moment as if he were trying to decide whether to let me in on a big secret. "I intend to continue an active private practice, and I believe people will be more comfortable knowing that I have no conflicts of interest. The Independent Counsel Act does not specifically prohibit my practicing law while serving. To require independent counsels such as me—who have no other prosecutorial matters they can turn to in times of famine—to become full-time government employees would waste the superior legal talents of the outstanding individuals called to serve. But, I think it prudent to rely upon the advice of Professor Sandefur regarding my private legal work. It would provide a protective buffer should anyone question my integrity."

What a sleaze. Jeffreys planned to keep working the big fee cases at Kirk & Polis while drawing his full salary from the government. He was already addicted to the money, and he couldn't let go. Burke did. Burke didn't even consider continuing his private practice. And, even if he had, he wouldn't have needed to waste thousands of taxpayer dollars to hire an apologist for his ethics. These guys were worse than I had imagined.

"Well, not to question your integrity," I said without laughing, "but are you planning to continue working with the Independent Women's Forum on the Christine Putnam suit? I think you've got a real political problem with that one. Especially since they're funded by Mellonskoff."

"That was not a political issue," Jeffreys protested. "The group was founded by the wife of my good friend Thad Stephens, and I was just doing my Christian duty. Read you *Bible*, the Book of Numbers, Chapter 25. But to answer your question, no. I will not be signing any briefs in that case."

Jeffreys pulled into the parking lot at Ollie's, and as we were getting out of the car he said, "My friends tell me this is a famous barbeque place. Have you ever eaten here?"

It was famous alright, but not for the quality of the food. Ollie's had been one of the first places to challenge the Civil Rights Act of 1964 when they refused to seat black customers in the dining room. *Katzenbach v. McClung*, I think was the name of the case. They lost. I wouldn't spend my money in a place with that attitude, but I only said, "No, I've never been here."

"I thought you'd have found this place by now," Jeffreys said. "What's your favorite barbeque restaurant? You do like barbeque, don't you?"

"Yeah, I like it. The best barbeque joint around here is the Golden Rule," I said, hoping he would see the irony. No indication that he did.

Sitting at the table listening to Jeffreys and Palmer discussing their plans to expand the staff to 25 lawyers and completely reorganize the office, I was really torn. I was repulsed by everything about Jeffreys. Yet, realizing what kind of operation they were sure to run, I almost felt compelled to stay. And it was at that moment I decided to start keeping a journal, documenting everything they said and did, in case I ever needed to write a book and let the American people know what really happened. I restrained the seething disgust I was feeling and asked, "What would you have in mind for me? I mean, how do you see me fitting into your plans for the new staff?"

Jeffreys smiled. He had taken the bait. Or maybe I had. He straightened in his chair and said, "I would, of course, want you to be on the Policy Committee, making contributions on all the major decisions regarding the direction of our investigation and any prosecutions. Mitch will be my Administrative Assistant, but I would like to be able to count on your experience as well. I also plan to bring in a new Chief Deputy, you understand, but you would keep your present salary. And I understand that you've been in charge of the computer system, so I hope you'd continue to do that. I don't know anything about computers. I'm pretty intimidated by them."

All the time Jeffreys was talking I had been noticing that the cuffs on that Giorgio Armani suit had crawled half way up to his elbow. He was wearing a short sleeved shirt, and there was a big glob of barbeque sauce on his left arm about three inches above the bright gold Rolex. Snapping back to the conversation, I said, "I don't mind staying on for a while and giving it a shot. Then we can see how it works out."

Jeffreys smiled again, that same phony grin like he thought someone was taking his picture. "I was hoping you'd see it our way. You won't be sorry," he said. "I have to get back to my hotel for another meeting, but I'll drop you and Mitch off at the office so the two of you can get better acquainted and begin developing a working relationship."

I didn't see it their way, I already felt sorry, and I didn't think I'd ever have much of a relationship with Mitch Palmer. The first thing he wanted to talk about when we got back was how soon I might be able to move to another office. He wanted mine, since it adjoined Jeffreys'. I could have my choice of any of the others. Fine. I began moving my stuff across the hall to Sean's old office.

Jeffreys spent most of the week interviewing potential staff in his suite at the Wynfrey, a new plastic and chrome hotel nearby in the Riverchase Galleria. Another reminder of the fundamental character differences between Burke and Jeffreys. Mitch Palmer spent his time being important and rearranging the furniture at the office. He also reclaimed the offices that had been used by the FBI and planned to use those for the expanded staff of lawyers.

It was becoming clear that Jeffreys planned to take full advantage of the unlimited budget available to the Independent Counsel. A normal U. S. Attorney has to make choices about which cases are worth prosecuting, but an Independent Counsel isn't hampered by such fiscal concerns. Expense would be of no concern to him, and no case would be too insignificant to pursue. He knew the Attorney General wouldn't risk the appearance of political interference by questioning whatever he wanted to spend. Or whomever he wanted to investigate.

One of the things that most concerned me was the way Jeffreys was building his staff. As I expected, several of the new lawyers were junior associates from Kirk & Polis in Washington and Olin, Bradley, and Scaife in Los Angeles. More disturbing was the fact that he had issued a call for applicants, sending the announcement to the Federalist Society, selected former U. S. Attorneys who had served under Stuart, and who knows where else. The process produced two kinds of applicants for both the legal positions and those requesting transfer assignments from FBI field offices—climbers who only wanted to advance their careers and others who really wanted to nail Cannon. Much like Jeffreys in both respects.

I was glad when that first week was over and was ready for a quiet weekend. I was awakened about 9:00 on Saturday morning by a call from Alan Horan at Smith and Hardwick, a great little bookshop in Forest Park that had become my local source for new titles. On Melinda's suggestion I had ordered *Political Empiricism*, which was supposed to be an excellent collection of case studies on recent Alabama campaigns, and it had arrived. I drove out to pick it up, then stopped at a little place called Bogue's for brunch on my way back.

Bogue's was a neat place with pale green walls and orange booths that were still more vinyl than duct tape, and I often had breakfast there. I usually sat at the counter, but today I occupied a booth just inside the back door, planning to do some leisurely reading. Andy made a mean Denver omelet, and Tina was a great waitress. And an attractive blonde. She looked especially perky today, wearing cut-offs and a red sweatshirt. I especially liked the way she always touched my shoulder when she asked if I needed anything else, but that was always the extent of our conversations. And the touching.

The restaurant had become crowded while I was there, but I hadn't been paying attention. Just drinking coffee and reading. Then I heard someone in the booth around the corner in the front room talking about Governor Vance and Whirlpool, and I tried to hear the conversation. It was in whispered tones, but I recognized one of the voices. It was Mitch Palmer. I sat still and tried to listen more closely, but I was only picking up every third or fourth sentence. Enough to know that someone was very interested in the direction of our investigation and that Palmer appeared to be sharing information that could only have come from our files.

Tina came by with more coffee, and I silently nodded my thanks. I heard Palmer and his group getting up to leave. It sounded like there were four, maybe five, of them. I waited until they were out the front door before getting up and going to the window to see who was with him. Whoa! It was Mitch Palmer, Nelson Grenier, Cliff Smegman, Jerry Elkay Coughlin, Myles Cooper, the political editor of the *Post-Advertiser*, and some fat guy I didn't recognize. Bogue's was not the kind of place I would have expected to see that bunch. I worried for a moment that Mitch might recognize my Bronco in the back parking lot, but they walked across the street and down Clairmont to an office building on the next corner—the Alabama Republican Party Headquarters.

The other shoe dropped quickly. Sunday's *Post-Advertiser* had a story by Myles Cooper quoting "sources close to the investigation" that Governor Vance was being targeted by the Office of Independent Counsel. On Tuesday, Nelson Grenier opened his media campaign in the governor's race with a barrage of radio ads claiming that Governor Vance was surrounded by the "ethical cloud of Whirlpool." There was certainly an ethical cloud, one leaking like a sieve from our office.

There was action in Washington that week, too. John Altgeld and Vickie Claflin both resigned their positions at the Treasury Department. The Republicans called for Jeffreys to investigate them for inconsistent testimony before the Senate Banking Committee. From a political perspective, I figured they did the right thing. It might not have been fair, but political appointees should resign when they become political liabilities. From a personal perspective, I knew they'd been shafted. They were only doing their jobs, and they now had personal legal fees exceeding their annual salaries. They weren't the first Cannon loyalists to fall on their swords. Nor would they be the last.

It was becoming clear now that the Republicans couldn't find anything on Cannon. The hearings consisted of a bunch of underlings looking bored before the cameras. A few of the young staffers stepped on their dicks by revealing notes and diaries that inflated their own roles to match their salaries. Looked to me like they must have been taking notes to cash in on a book down the line, but self-importance always carried a price. That forced the inquisitors to go to Plan B, trying to catch them in contradictions and pretending that they had discovered a conspiracy to obstruct justice. But no one seemed to know what it was they were supposed to be covering up. And they certainly didn't know anything about justice.

The other political news was a story in the *Washington Sun* quoting "sources familiar with the Jeffreys investigation" that Robert Bruce, one of Cannon's top advisors, was under investigation for past campaign activities here in Alabama. That was news to me. And it wasn't even anything within our charter. Jeffreys was appointed Independent Counsel for Whirlpool-Jefferson Savings, not Independent Counsel to Investigate James Cannon and Everyone He's Ever Met. I could write it off as another unfounded Republican rumor, but I'm sure that Mr. Bruce felt otherwise. It is especially hard on folks when such charges are attributed to unidentified sources, leaving people unable to confront their accusers. To clear their name, they have to prove their innocence. Hard to prove a negative proposition when the next day's headline would read, "Cannon aide denies he is a crook."

By late August Jeffreys had his new team in place in Birmingham. He had replaced the seven local FBI investigators with 26 new ones, all of whom had volunteered, from various jurisdictions around the country. The task of coordinating the gumshoes was taken away from the local Special Agent in Charge and given to a retired army general named Eugene Cavaignac. Hand-picked by Jeffreys, he seemed to have the tenacity and compassion of Inspector Javert.

The legal staff now numbered 24, three times the size Burke thought necessary. Bart Gedney, a former U. S. Attorney from Chattanooga, was named Chief Deputy. James Peck from Chicago and John Hathorne from Salt Lake City both gave up positions as Assistant U. S. Attorneys to work for Jeffreys. He even hired a press secretary, a woman named Jo Gobles from an advertising agency in Fairfax, Virginia. Along with Mitch Palmer and me, those four would constitute the OIC Policy Committee.

Jeffreys convened the first meeting of the Policy Committee on August 29th. After making small talk with everyone, he first recognized Cavaignac, who almost clicked his heels as he left the room. Then he introduced the two new executive secretaries, Phyllis Sanford and Peggy Shipman. Phyllis was from Kansas, and she looked like a professional ex-wife. Her mouth formed a permanent frown. She would be working directly under Jeffreys. Peggy was from Pennsylvania and had worked for Thornburger at Justice. She would be working primarily for Mitch Palmer and Jo Gobles. We were instructed that all confidential correspondence and documents should be handled by either Sanford or Shipman. Otherwise, we were to use the secretarial pool for routine typing.

Jeffreys then proceeded to outline the scope of the investigation and where he saw it going. First, he said, we would reopen and go over every aspect that had been examined by Burke, especially the death of Hal Goodall. Second, he wanted Gedney to get a list of all of Cannon's and

Vance's campaign finance reports since 1974 and a complete list of all appointments to state boards and commissions since 1979. Jeffreys wanted to cross-tab appointments and contributions to get a list of names appearing on both. Third, he wanted to subpoena the bank records of all campaign loans made to Cannon or Vance since 1970. "I want each of you to keep in mind," he said, "the engine driving the demonic machine is very simple to identify dollars, very big dollars. It is the crassest, most greedy, avaricious dimension of the fearsome Democratic political control of Alabama and our great nation."

I kept thinking he was going to mention the leaks to the press during the previous week, but no one seemed concerned about that. Guess I was safe from another lecture on confidentiality. This whole Whirlpool investigation was about to get completely out of hand, and I could see where he was going. Jeffreys was going to follow the money. If the Republicans could dry up the normal sources of campaign finance for Democrats, the Republicans would be in a position to outspend them in future campaigns. And Jeffreys knew that sending FBI agents to investigate every major contributor and every banker friendly to Cannon would discourage repeat offenders from giving money to any Democrat in the future. Checking for contributors who had also been appointed to office was an especially devious move. Just collecting that information would give the press enough to suggest that Cannon and Vance had been bribed and sold appointments to the highest bidder. And I had no doubt that they'd find lots of names on both lists. Politicians are not in the habit of appointing their enemies.

"The public perception is that the genesis of this Whirlpool investigation—and everything that occurs in this investigation—is regarding President Cannon," Jeffreys said with the enthusiasm of a speaker at a Republican camp meeting. "Whether or not the facts of a particular case have any direct connection to President Cannon, I think we can proceed as if it's within our authority. The average voter would probably agree, the press is certainly inclined to foster that impression, and Attorney General Otis is afraid to say no to anything we want."

I thought that pretty presumptuous, but Jeffreys was only warming up.

"Mr. Burke was only on the job for six months, and, I must say, he does not seem to have been especially energetic in examining all possible leads to President James Madison Cannon or First Lady Diane Rankin Cannon. I can assure you that I am prepared to spend the next three years vigorously pursuing this case, wherever it might lead and whomever it might snare. Title 18 of the United States Code is a wonderful document. I want each of you to study it well. And remember, man is conceived in sin and born in corruption. There is always something. I expect you to find it. *Carthago delenda est.*"

Chapter Fifteen

It was clear now. Jeffreys was out to scorch the earth and salt the ashes. His first goal was to destroy the Democratic Party of Alabama and anyone who had ever given it aid and comfort in time of war. The Republicans had failed to capture the state at the ballot box, so now they'd sent a hired assassin. Alabama, of course, wasn't their real concern. Oh, sure, it was a trophy they wanted, but it was mostly a convenient example, one to be contemplated before any upstart Democrat commoner ever again decided to play in the big leagues. Stuart's defeat had been an utter humiliation, both for the old patrician and his minions. He'd been the first of their own denied a second term since Herbert Hoover lost to Roosevelt 60 years ago. To make sure it would never happen again, George Jeffreys had been sent forth with a legion of lawyers to destroy Cannon and his friends. And Carthage, the breeding ground for such low-bred enemies of traditional privilege, from whence they had come.

Jeffreys possessed the moral certainty of Savonarola and the political commitment of Torquemada. There would be no discussion. None. I kept watching for Palmer and Gedney to offer some response, still trying to understand the protocol for the new regime and figuring I'd take my cues from them before I said anything. But Jeffreys made it clear he didn't want any comments or suggestions, much less objections or criticism. Participation in the committee decisions meant taking notes and making sure his orders were carried out. He would be the funeral director, and we would be the gravediggers. Being a member of the OIC Policy Committee was going to be a different experience from what it had been under Burke.

September came quickly. Lindsey had become my best friend, but, then, she was about my only friend since the exodus of everyone who had worked for Burke. Her teaching schedule meant I'd be seeing less of her now. And pounding the pavement to Montgomery on weekends.

As far as I could tell, the local papers now seemed to be ignoring our investigation and covering Alabama's two favorite sports—football and elections. Nelson Grenier was challenging Governor Vance in what promised to be another vicious campaign, apparently the only kind

Grenier knew how to run. The Auburn-Alabama contest promised to be equally hard-fought, although it wouldn't be as dirty.

There might have been some local stories on Whirlpool, but I was now out of that information loop. Mitch Palmer had canceled all of the Alabama newspaper subscriptions except the *News* and the *Post-Advertiser*. I guess that was okay, since I was the only one who had been reading them. Jeffreys was much more concerned with national media coverage. The *Wall Street Record,* the *Washington Sun*, and the *American Speculator* were now required reading, and Jo Gobles distributed a daily compilation of press clippings for the staff.

The national press also seemed to be losing interest in Whirlpool. There was still some grumbling about Jeffreys and the appointment process, but it was of no consequence. Mark Schine, mouthpiece for the Lynch Legal Foundation, and Bruce Flim, a self-promoting pundit who had worked with Jeffreys at Justice, were busy churning out op-ed pieces defending Jeffreys. The *Washington Sun* did its best to keep the story alive, alternating editorial criticism of Cannon with complaints that the legitimate media weren't giving enough attention to the Whirlpool conspiracy theories. Jay Fuhrman, the *Sun's* star reporter, published a series of articles based on self-serving interviews with Roby Douglas, but I didn't quite get the point. Couldn't tell if Fuhrman was trying to reinvent Douglas as a credible witness, trying to implicate Governor Vance before the election, or trying to fill a news hole. Whatever, it was a rehash of old news.

Things started to heat up again when Jeffreys called another Policy Committee meeting one afternoon during the last week of September. Jeffreys was still in control, but the format was different. It seemed at times that everyone except me had already discussed the issues. I was determined that I would not sit silent again. Problem was, I always get rowdy when I'm bored. It gets even worse when I'm pissed.

Jo Gobles was first on the agenda, and her review of the media coverage almost put me to sleep. Almost. The most interesting thing was her announcement that all future references to losses at Jefferson Savings should indicate that "the failure cost taxpayers $65 million," instead of the previous figure of $47 million. I was more than curious about that. The institution was only $1.6 million short when the state banking commissioner had recommended that it be closed in 1987, and I was fairly certain that I understood the regulatory accounting practices that provided the $47 million figure when the RTC finally acted in 1989. No way it could have grown an additional $19 million, even if you added in the costs for all the investigations. "I'm a bit puzzled by that," I said. "Could you explain how you got that $65 million figure?"

Jo looked at Jeffreys before answering. "Well, there are several estimates out there. We can't get an exact handle on them, but the range is from a low of $47 million to a high of about $73 million. We just thought it would be more accurate to place it within the range, and $65 million is the figure that seemed most appropriat," she said, again looking at Jeffreys then back at me.

Mitch Palmer jumped in before I could say anything. "Why don't we use the $73 million figure? That's one of the estimates, right? I've seen some of the focus group data, and most people think $47 million is pretty measly compared with most S & L failures. I believe the $73 million figure would also help protect us from some of the criticism we've been getting on our own expenses."

Geezus! They were doing focus groups on public perceptions about our investigation, and Mitch just suggested that we inflate the numbers for better public relations. Appearances. Perceptions. Magic numbers pulled from the air. I glanced at Jeffreys to see if he was as concerned about that as I was. He was leaning over to Bart Gedney, who had cupped his hand and was whispering something in Jeffreys' ear.

"Let's go with $73 million," Jeffreys said. "I think we've got a consensus on that, and we need to be consistent."

I started to object, but I let it go. I didn't know that it made any difference what figure they used. But it would make a difference in my ability to ever put much faith in anything our office ever said to the press.

The outrage continued, but there was no chance for discussion on the next item. Jeffreys announced that he had approved a request to provide security for Roby Douglas—including housing, transportation, and additional cash for living expenses—until the date of his sentencing. A request from whom, and security from what? We were looking at about $3,000 a month in public funds to pay upkeep on a convicted felon. For what? His testimony? That wouldn't be worth much. To get him to say whatever they wanted? Somebody might be willing to pay for that. I'd even heard rumors that the American Speculator already was. But I doubted anyone would believe a word Douglas said.

I looked across the table at James Peck for some hint of what was up, but he cut his eyes back to Jeffreys and wouldn't look at me. Bart Gedney seemed pleased. He told Jeffreys that a friend of his had a hunting lodge down on Lake Martin where we could keep Douglas until he testified. I wanted to suggest that we should find out who had been paying Douglas' legal fees and living expenses for the last year and tell them to provide security for him. But I could see we again had a consensus. John Hathorne's wink at Jeffreys made that clear.

Following the agenda, Gedney reported that he had completed his computer analysis of the Alabama campaign contribution reports and the list of appointments to state boards. Bart was about 50 years old, a former U. S. Attorney from up in Chattanooga, appointed by Reeder. I had made a few calls to check him out when Jeffreys hired him. One of the things he didn't have listed on his resume was that his twin brother, who had been Hamilton County Treasurer back in the '70s, had served hard time at Brushy Mountain for embezzling public funds. After that, Bart specialized in trying to convict Democratic politicians in Tennessee, perhaps hoping he could convince the public that Democrats were just as crooked as his Republican brother. Maybe that's why he had wanted to come to work for Jeffreys in the Whirlpool investigation. Or maybe it was because he'd been fired one year short of vesting his retirement and wanted to qualify for a lifetime spot at the public spigot.

Whatever his motivation for taking the job, Bart Gedney sounded a little too enthusiastic for me to be comfortable around him. "There were literally hundreds of appointees who appeared on the contribution reports," he said. "I realized that it would be beyond our capacity to prosecute them all, but the FBI has conducted over 150 interviews with some of the major contributors. Based upon the result of those interviews, as well as additional information from confidential sources, I have identified three key targets, very high profile Democrats, that merit our full attention. Judge Jeffreys and I have already discussed this, and he has requested and received authority from Attorney General Otis and Judge Chase to pursue this matter. Specifically, we have been authorized to investigate all aspects of James Cannon's 1990 gubernatorial campaign against Nelson Grenier. The order is presently under seal, so please keep this in strictest confidence."

"The final item we need to address," Jeffreys said, "is the recent retaliation against Mrs. Varken and two of her colleagues in the Atlanta office of the RTC. As you know, Ellende Varken, Richard Menteur, and Austin Leugen were recently placed on two weeks administrative leave by officials of the Resolution Trust Corporation. Allegations have been made that this disciplinary action was taken against them as punishment for their role in the Whirlpool investigation. I find this a serious matter, and I think it is within our mandate to investigate. Mr. Hathorne has been handling this, and I'd like for him to explain what has happen so far."

Hathorne was a chubby fellow with a fuzzy little mustache, probably pushing 60. His career had hit a dead end with the U. S. Attorney's office in Salt Lake City, so he had volunteered for this assignment, hoping he could make a name for himself before retirement. He played his part and read his lines with more dramatic flair than necessary. "The

RTC took this cruel action on August 15th without any warning or explanation," he began. "On that fateful day, after Mr. Leugen and Mr. Menteur arrived at work, they were summoned to an office and told that they'd been placed on administrative leave. They were then escorted out of the building and were told to stay off RTC property. Their offices were locked and sealed. Mrs. Varken, then in the hospital, received a call from another member of the Jefferson investigative team, who advised her that the purge had begun and that she had also been placed on leave."

"The three Jefferson investigators each received an identical one-page memorandum that placed them on Administrative Leave to be effective immediately upon receipt but offered no explanation for the adverse employment action. According to Mrs. Varken," Hathorne added, "none of the three were contacted for interviews or information during their suspension."

"On August 29, Mr. Menteur, Mr. Leugen, and Mrs. Varken were told to return to work, but they still didn't receive any explanation for why they were put on administrative leave. Mr. Menteur and Mrs. Varken through counsel requested that the RTC Inspector General investigate the matter. Before he could begin the investigation," Hathorne said proudly, "I learned of the request and, after discussion with Judge Jeffreys, advised him that any inquiry by the RTC Inspector General into the matter would interfere with our work. Accordingly, the RTC suspended its investigation, and that's where we are now. I recommend that we assume responsibility for this matter."

I was about to unload on Mrs. Varken, but Jeffreys suggested that we take a short break. He said he needed to make a short call to his office, meaning Kirk & Polis. I took that opportunity to go back to my office and get my file on Ellende Varken. When Jeffreys returned he said, "Well, I think we should pursue this matter. Since I hear no objections, Mr. Hathorne, will you take responsibility for the inquiry?"

"I object," I said, wondering how everyone would react but not really caring.

Surprise seemed to outweigh annoyance. Jeffreys slowly opened the file folder he was still holding. Hathorne appeared frustrated; his jowls shimmered and caused ripples across his double chin. Peck's lips were tight but his eyes were still on Jeffreys. Gedney had only a slight frown. Mitch Palmer's mouth was open, almost as wide as his eyes. Jo Gobles kept her head down, looking at her legal pad as if trying to avoid being turned into a pillar of salt.

"And why would you object to that, Mr. Wilkes?" Jeffreys asked in an exceptionally flat tone of voice.

"Two reasons. First," I said, "I see no reason why the RTC Inspector General can't handle the inquiry. It's strictly an internal matter. The only reason we should become involved, in my opinion, is when there is a clear conflict of interest or when there is some evidence that the usual mechanisms have been compromised. I don't see that here. What I see is a sinkhole for our time, and one that has nothing whatsoever to do with our charter."

"Second," I continued, "I think our office would be well served not to react too quickly when Ellende Varken cries wolf. This is a troubled woman, and she's a professional whiner. Her past allegations regarding attempts by RTC management to monitor her work caused this office to waste a lot of valuable time. I'm very familiar with her activities, and I've paid considerable attention to the whole situation since I came to work for this office back in February. She is totally political and completely unethical, and I wouldn't have any confidence in anything she said."

Hathorne was blustering, and his face was red. "This woman has worked on the Jefferson Savings connection from the very start, and there might not even be a Whirlpool investigation if not for her," he stammered.

I almost thanked Hathorne for making my point, but I resisted, instead replying, "That's really interesting, but I don't think it's particularly relevant, John."

"Well, you can say whatever you want about Mrs. Varken's professional qualifications," Hathorne snapped, "but she told me that, at one point, there was some talk about assigning her to work on Jefferson Savings when Burke was here."

"Are you kidding? We almost laughed our asses off when that offer was made," I replied, letting my true feelings override the more formal presentational style I had chosen for dealing with these Mandarins. "The last thing that Burke wanted was responsibility of those three individuals, the Atlanta trio as they were known. I think the RTC wanted to get rid of them, and I can understand why. No one had any confidence in their work. Couldn't be trusted. We kept them at arms length."

"Well, Congressman Leech didn't look at it that way, and I don't think you can question his judgment" Hathorne retorted, as if that were supposed to impress me.

"Dick Leech is so dumb he couldn't pour piss out of a boot if the instructions were written on the heel. He was only taking orders from Leroy Reichman, and I can certainly question his judgment," I responded with no small amount of indignation.

Hathorne and I were playing verbal ping-pong. I could see how much he wanted the assignment, probably thinking he could get as much publicity as Varken. Part of me wanted to give in and let him make an idiot of himself. Yet, I still felt some obligation to protect the integrity of our office.

Hathorne was determined to test my patience. "Mr. Wilkes, I believe your political sympathies are coloring your judgment about this matter," he said.

"If you want to discuss the influence of politics on decisions to conduct an investigation, we can do that," I shot back.

With raised eyebrows and a tone of indignation, Hathorne asked, "Are you questioning my integrity?"

"Not at the moment," I said before I could stop myself. "I was talking about partisan politics, specifically Ellende Varken and some of the other Stuart partisans who leaked information about criminal referrals to the White House and the press before the last election."

"You've made that accusation before, but, as a matter of fact, it is false," Hathorne replied. "I asked G. Curtis Thomas, the RTC Counsel in Atlanta, about that allegation, and he assured me that there were no political appointees involved in the decision to pursue the Jefferson investigation."

"I didn't say political appointees. I said partisan politics. And I wouldn't put too much stock in what Curtis Thomas might say about patronage appointments."

"Mr. Thomas is a career employee, and I have no reason to doubt his word," Hathorne huffed.

"Mr. Thomas might well be a fine lawyer, but I wouldn't call him a career employee," I said. Part of my job under Burke had been to know the players in this game. "He got his job with the FDIC under Reeder, then moved over to the RTC under Stuart. Probably didn't hurt that his grandfather just happened to be a former Republican Congressman from Georgia who had served in the House with Stuart and who had been Reeder's man on the Republican Platform Committee in 1980."

"Be that as it may," Hathorne stammered, "the plain fact is that Mrs. Varken and her colleagues have been punished by the RTC, for no other reason than that their devotion to duty has implicated the President and the First Lady. Can you name a single breach of that duty? No, you can't. They have done nothing wrong."

"Mr. Hathorne," I said, pausing to make sure that wasn't a trick question, "I can name several, ranging from outright lies to the merely unethical, but I will confine myself to the breach of RTC regulations that clearly justify administrative action against Mrs. Varken and her colleagues.

"To take a single instance that even you should be able to understand," I said with a disarming smile, "Ellende Varken leaked confidential RTC information during her now-infamous February 18 meeting with Congressman Dick Leech. The release of this confidential information directly violated RTC policy. A Policy Memorandum issued by the RTC's Director of the Office of Investigations and the RTC's Office of the General Counsel on June 17, 1993 stated, 'All referrals are sensitive and must be handled with appropriate confidentiality and care.' Criminal referrals and their exhibits are confidential documents. No one doubts that.

"Nevertheless, Varken provided Congressman Leech with material she knew to be confidential, such as internal RTC memoranda and correspondence regarding the Jefferson referrals, as well as documents from Jefferson Savings gathered by the RTC during the course of its investigation. Varken also provided Congressman Leech with a summary of her conversation with Elizabeth Gurley, an official from the RTC Washington office, after playing the surreptitious tape recording for him, even though she knew that the conversation contained confidential information.

"Predictably, Congressman Leech then released all of these documents to the media. Thus, Varken's unilateral decision to leak RTC documents to Congressman Leech directly resulted in the public dissemination of confidential information in the middle of our ongoing investigation of Jefferson-related matters. The effect was the same as if she had leaked these documents to a reporter, which is also a very distinct possibility.

"Mrs. Varken fully understood the impropriety in releasing these materials. She knew that there are stringent regulations with regard to public release of government documents. As Varken acknowledged, these restrictions exist because disclosing confidential information to third parties might create a problem for an ongoing investigation. However, Varken chose not to notify her supervisors in advance of her meeting with Congressman Leech, because she knew they wouldn't support her decision to provide him with confidential RTC documents."

Hathorne was exasperated. He had been nervously shifting his considerable weight from cheek to cheek during my attack on Varken's actions. Finally, he could contain himself no longer, and he interrupted by asking, "You don't think we have an obligation to protect government whistle-blowers from retaliation?"

Nice try. I just looked Hathorne in the eye and calmly explained, "Of course we would, if that were the case, but the facts refute any claim that Varken was acting as a 'whistle blower' by disclosing this confidential information to Congressman Leech. None of the people listed as subjects in the referrals were her supervisors nor even federal government employees, so that wouldn't be whistle-blowing. That would be criminal. Leaking confidential information to Congressman Leech was no different from providing the information to the press because the outcome was the same.

"More significantly," I said emphatically, "we were conducting an ongoing investigation regarding transactions that directly related to the confidential information that Varken leaked to Congressman Leech. Instead of providing relevant information to this office, Varken chose to politicize the investigation by disclosing the information to a Republican congressman who promptly released the confidential information to the press.

"The leaking of this information constituted a serious breach of RTC policies, and placing those responsible on administrative leave was entirely appropriate. RTC employees have been fired in the past for more minor infractions like misusing postage stamps. Certainly the leaking of confidential information connected to a criminal referral would be cause for disciplinary action and very likely termination of the employee involved.

"If we are going to involve ourselves in internal RTC matters, perhaps we should be preparing to investigate the actions of Mrs. Varken. This particular infraction, while egregious, is only one of many instances in which Ellende Varken acted inappropriately. The RTC General Counsel indicated that the clandestine taping of Gurley was one of the justifications for placing Varken on administrative leave. Hell, even Congressman Leech said Varken's taping of the conversation without Gurley's consent was inappropriate. Furthermore, there is a memo in the file suggesting that Mrs. Varken removed confidential documents from official files and took them home for use in writing a book, which I understand was another of the reasons for the administrative leave. Do you want me to go on?"

Hathorne had slumped in his chair by that point. He had no response. There was a pregnant silence at the table. Then Jeffreys broke the tension by suggesting that we take a short break while he made another phone call to his office. I wanted to ask if he was billing his time to the government or to Kirk & Polis, but of course I didn't. I got a cup of coffee and came back to the table feeling pretty smug. Everyone else just sat there, not saying a word. Especially not to me.

Jeffreys returned and sat down at the head of the table. I couldn't tell whether he was upset with my remarks or by something that had occurred during his phone conversation, but he was clearly uncomfortable. He began to speak, but he wouldn't look at me. It was almost as if he were talking to someone at the other end of the table when he said, "I appreciate your sharing your observations, Mr. Wilkes. However, I am still inclined to pursue an investigation of potential interference and political retribution by administrative personnel at the RTC. Mr. Hathorne, you will have whatever resources you need. Please check with Phyllis, and let's talk more about this in the morning."

There was another reason why Jeffreys wanted to take charge of the investigation. If we were involved, the Justice Department couldn't investigate the activities of the Stuart White House in trying to leak the referrals before the last election. Jeffreys was providing cover for G. Gordon Bray, the former White House Counsel and son of North Carolina tobacco merchants, and Edie Holiday, the White House-Campaign Liason, who just happened to be married to Jeffreys' personal lawyer. Very convenient.

I started to get up, but Jeffreys had one more item on his agenda. A question, really, the significance of which I failed to grasp at the time. Jeffreys looked at Bart Gedney and asked, "Have you made contact with our inside source?"

Bart nodded without explanation, and the meeting ended. John Hathorne looked at me with a satisfied smirk. I tried not to show what I was thinking or feeling at that moment. I disagreed with everything announced or decided in the meeting. No use worrying about it though. And no reason to hold a grudge against Hathorne for doing exactly what I had expected from him. "Let's go get a beer," I said, trying to disguise my depression and hoping to defuse his sense of personal victory.

"I don't drink," Hathorne said as he turned and waddled down the hall to his office.

Why did that not surprise me? I was, though, beginning to wonder what these folks did for fun. Probably got together and swigged Grapette while discussing Justice Bryant's articles on economic models of regulatory reform. I didn't want to drink alone, but I was missing my old friend Jack Daniels. I almost asked Mitch Palmer, but I was saved by a relapse of good sense. Some other time, maybe, when I had more patience.

October is my favorite month, a time when the brilliant colors and the crisp air conspire to drive off the dog days of the Southern summer. Football and politics, with their own twisted logic, continued to dominate the local papers. They actually had a lot in common. Someone once said that the perfect politician would have the characteristics of a great football coach—smart enough to win and dumb enough to think it was important. Come to think of it, Bear Bryant would have been a good governor, and he would have run unopposed. I always admired the Bear because he integrated the University and made people like it, while Wallace had stood in the door and played the fool.

When it came to playing the fool, it would be hard to beat Endicott Tyburn and the *American Speculator* that month. They made a big splash with the so-called Troopergate story, but it turned out to be a bellybuster. Citing an exclusive interview with two generally discredited state troopers, John Cloud and Jim Clark, the magazine had a cover story that Cannon had used the governor's limousine to bring teenage girls to the Governors' Mansion for parties. One of the troopers confessed to picking up three teenage girls at a junior high school one Friday afternoon in October 1992, just one month before Cannon had been elected president. The other trooper confirmed that they were acting at the request of Governor Cannon, and claimed that the three girls spent the night at the Mansion. The magazine reported that both troopers had passed polygraph tests on their stories. "Shocking" read an editorial by James Rivington in the *Washington Sun*.

Neither the *Speculator* nor the *Sun* printed a retraction; however, E. D. Hornbeck did a follow-up article in the *Alabama Times* the next week. The rest of the story, so to speak. Hornbeck confirmed that three teenage girls had, indeed, been picked up at a junior high by troopers driving the governor's limousine, a black Lincoln, and had spent that Friday night at the Mansion after a party. He also identified the three girls. Cassidy Cannon, the governor's daughter, had invited two of her friends home from school that day, and they had a bunking party that night. Governor Cannon, campaigning for president in Pennsylvania, wasn't even in the state that weekend.

The so-called Troopergate story was another typical example of what I found so disgusting about the media and the way lies are conflated with facts. First, some right-wing organ or a cash-for-trash tabloid pretends to have a big scoop on scandal. Cover story or page one headlines imply some shocking story of corruption. A few facts are then dressed up with quotes from anonymous or nameless "reliable sources."

The original story then takes on a folklore life of its own, spewed across the airwaves by Limbaugh or the Reverend Dr. Elmer Laud. Then the broadsides and the networks, after pretending to wring their hands, report that Matt Sludge or the tabloids printed it. That made it legitimate news.

A few weeks later, after the damage is done, one of the Alabama papers or some independent investigative reporter like Robert Parry or Joe Conason will print the real story, the whole story, pointing out the fabrications and innuendoes in the original version.

Finally, the lie thrives while the truth is ignored, because there is never a retraction. And certainly no mention of the rebuttal article by the networks or the major papers. No mention that, in this instance, the troopers had been represented by Lyman Davidson and Clifton Smegman and paid $20,000 by a major contributor to Leroy Reichamn's GOPAC. No mention of the Mellonskoff money behind the *American Speculator*'s antics. No mention that Eddie Mahem, a GOP consultant, had been paid $25,000 to shop the story. The editors, publishers, news readers, and producers then sit around and scratch their collective asses, wondering why the public is so cynical.

Chapter Sixteen

Something else pretty strange happened a few days later. Nelson Grenier was waging his usual vitriolic media campaign for governor. That wasn't strange. It was the same kind of mean campaign he had run in 1990 when Cannon kicked his butt. What was strange was that Grenier kept telling everyone that Governor Vance was going to be indicted by the Independent Counsel, and he kept making charges and citing documents that could only have come from our files. I kept remembering that morning at Bogue's when I saw Mitch Palmer talking with Grenier, Coughlin, Smegman, and Myles Cooper.

Then one Saturday I went to lunch with Lindsey and Melinda Shelton at Christian's, the restaurant and bar in the Tutwiler Hotel, just around the corner from the library. I had been a regular in the bar when Burke lived there, but I hadn't been back lately. When we walked in, though, the bartender recognized me and said, "Hey, you just missed seeing your boss."

"Burke? What's he doing back in town?" I asked.

"No, that new guy," he replied.

Must be mistaken. I doubted that Jeffreys even knew the Tutwiler existed, and he wouldn't have been in the bar. "You sure?"

"Yeah. He left his briefcase," he said as he brought it over to our table. "You better take it back to him."

It did look like Jeffreys' briefcase. Had the initials G. J. on the top edge. I looked inside, and immediately recognized that it contained some of our case files, at least copies of them. On Governor Vance and Financial Management Services. I quickly closed it without saying anything. Glad that I had happened to be having lunch there that day. That kind of sensitive material shouldn't be left around. The newspapers would have a field day, not only with the contents but with the fact that Jeffreys had been so stupid as to walk off and leave them in a restaurant.

We ordered lunch and were soon lost in the conversation. I was having fun listening to Lindsey and Melinda talking about past episodes in their lives. I was learning things about Lindsey I wouldn't have known otherwise. Then Melinda said, "John, you're probably bored by all this girl talk, huh?"

"No," I laughed, "it's like a free showing of 'A Couple of White Chicks Sittin' Around Talking.' I'm learning all your secrets."

"Oh, that reminds me," Lindsey said. "Can I interest you in seeing a play next Saturday?"

"You can always interest me in playing with you," I replied. Melinda pretended to be embarrassed.

"No, silly, seeing a play. My brother's in the cast of 'The Crucible' at the Alabama Theatre next weekend. Have you ever seen it?"

"Oh, sure. I'm a big fan of Henry Miller," I teased. "Why else would I be out with two beautiful women?"

"You're incorrigible," she said. "I'm glad it's almost Halloween so I can put a sack over your head when I take you out in public. You know it's by Arthur Miller."

"Oh, well, then of course I'd love to go, Marilyn," I replied. I would go anywhere with Lindsey, and I had been intending to see one of the productions at the Alabama Theatre since I moved to town. It was a wonderfully restored monument to the glory days of the stage. The play is the thing, I know, but the viewing environment can be an experience in itself. One reason I didn't much like going to the movies any more was those cramped viewing rooms at every Cinema 20. Not much bigger than a bread box. And paying $8.00 for popcorn and a coke—that was more obscene than anything on the screen.

As we finished lunch and started to leave, I was startled to see Nelson Grenier. He was walking around the dining room, head on a swivel, looking under tables like he had lost something besides his mind or an election. I overheard the waiter ask if he'd like a table for lunch. Grenier mumbled something about meeting someone, then he rushed past us and out the door. Really strange, I thought. Then I thought about the briefcase I was carrying.

I then made a decision that I knew I might regret. I decided to keep the briefcase at my apartment and wait until after the election to return it to Jeffreys.

After seeing "The Crucible" that week, I was even more uncomfortable working for Jeffreys. I didn't know how much longer I could do it. The weekends, however, kept me sane. Well, most of them.

On the Friday before the election, Mitch Palmer came to my office and asked if I could drive Jeffreys to a speaking engagement that weekend. "I could . . . , " I said with an inflection to let him know that I was not interested in doing so. "What's wrong? Is his car in the shop?"

"No," Mitch laughed, "I usually drive him to these deals, but I'm going home to New Jersey for my mother's birthday. Would you? I wouldn't impose on you, but everyone else is already gone."

"Tell ya what, Mitch," I said, "I'll do it, but you'll owe me a beer." I didn't have any plans for Sunday evening, and I was trying to be nice for a change. Even if he was a momma's boy, I felt sorry for anyone who had to spend a weekend in North Jersey. I wouldn't have agreed, however, if I had known what it was. Mitch was going to owe me several beers.

November 6th was "God and Country Day" at Briarwood Bible Church and Christian Academy. The Reverend Jay C. McCarthy was the preacher, and Lindsey told me he'd been holding these events on the first Sunday in November since 1964 -- when he endorsed Barry Goldwater. McCarthy was a real promoter. Used to call himself "The Chaplain of the Crimson Tide" when he had a church over in Tuscaloosa, but he stopped that after the Bear integrated the football team. Since moving to Birmingham in 1968, McCarthy had made it in the world of big time religion. The Briarwood compound—church, school, broadcast studio, health club, acres of parking—covered the entire top of a mountain in Liberty Park. Probably called it that because they wanted folks to park their liberty before entering.

Jeffreys shared the stage that night with Reverend McCarthy, who was wearing his Army Reserve general's uniform, and with Lieutenant Governor Coughlin, who had black patent leather hair and was wearing a big election-year smile. I stood at the back of the auditorium and wished I were somewhere else. Since Jeffreys was the last speaker, there was no chance of slipping out early.

Reverend McCarthy opened with a trumpet blast against the ungodly—primarily the First Couple, whom he blamed for everything from homosexuality to teen pregnancy. At least he was an equal opportunity bigot. Then he asked the audience to bow their heads as he prayed against President Cannon, "Appoint a virtuous man to lead the prosecution against him; let an accuser bring him to trial. When he is tried, let him come forth guilty; let his prayer be counted as sin. May his days be few; may another seize his goods! May his children be fatherless, and his wife a widow! May his children wander about and beg; may they be driven out of the ruins they inhabit! May the creditor seize all that he has; may strangers plunder the fruits of his toil! Let their be none to extend kindness to him, nor any to pity his fatherless children! May his posterity be cut off; may his name be blotted out in the second generation! May the iniquity of his father be remembered before the Lord, and let not the sin of his mother be blotted out!"

Reverend Coughlin gave what sounded like a medley of his standard civic club speech and a couple of recycled sermons. Slippery quips devoid of any thoughtful ideas. The words of his mouth were smoother than butter, but there was a touch of malice in his tone. He was the beau ideal of an Alabama Republican, no doubt, but I suspected his charisma had been enhanced by a little amateur herpetology during his ministerial training.

Jeffreys finally mounted the pulpit about nine o'clock. He was introduced by Beverly Russell, a member of the congregation who boasted that she was also chair of the local Republican Women's Club and an activist in the Alabama Eagle Forum. She had that hard look of a faded beauty queen, made more so by the red suit that was too tight in a few places. Jeffreys must have written the script for her introductory remarks, because Mrs. Russell called him Judge Jeffreys and actually said "a reputation for honesty, integrity, and fairness" three times. Somewhat surprisingly, I still found myself wanting to hear what he had to say. Couldn't help it. I did.

"Thank you very much . It's good to be here," Jeffreys said as he received a standing ovation from the faithful who had packed the house. "I am honored that you've invited me to be here this evening to talk about my faith and about how God has called me to do an important job for our great nation.

"I have been very blessed my entire life. I grew up as a preacher's kid in South Carolina, in Greenville, and came from a very devout Christian home. I worked for the Southwestern Company in Nashville for one summer during my college years at Bob Jones University and sold family Bibles in southern Ohio. It was a wonderful experience, a great growing experience for me.

"I thought very carefully about the ministry, and very prayerfully, but I was guided into an avenue that I felt was my calling, which was public service through law. And that is what I then set my sights on after a lot of consideration, especially as an undergraduate, about going on into the ministry.

"I have taught Sunday School for many, many years. In fact, going back to my college years, when I taught high school Sunday School, and I taught it virtually every age level over the years and look forward to, when the demands on me are a little bit less, to returning.

"I try to make my faith very much a daily part of my life. I try to devote some time each day to a program of Bible reading and prayerful reflection, and then I try to think of my faith as going about my day to day work, constantly mindful that we need to invite Jesus Christ into our lives and try to display Christ in our daily interactions with the people that we rub shoulders with in the mall, the country club, the office, wherever we happen to find ourselves. And that's imperfectly, as we are all imperfect, what I very much try to do. I also have inspiration calendars and the like, and I keep those at the ready, especially when I'm here in Birmingham in my hotel suite away from my family and try to have, how shall I say, as much inspired guidance as I can get, because I need it.

"I was attending a lawyers meeting, the Federalist Society, when the call came from Senator Rantallion telling me of my selection as Independent Counsel. I immediately informed my wife, my bride of 25 years, and my three lovely children, Polly, Esther, and Winston, of my good news. Then I turned to the book of *Psalms* for a quick refreshing read of wisdom literature, because I knew, like Solomon at the age of 18, even though I'm far beyond the age of 18, I needed a lot of wisdom and needed it fast, and still do.

"Because my appointment came my way without my, in any way, directly seeking it, personally applying for it, and the like, I know it was God's will for me to assume this position. If one believes that God is moving in our lives, as I do, I couldn't help but conclude that this is part of God's plan, and I think that part of our basic mission on this earth is to humble ourselves and to accept these things. You know, Jonah tried to run away—not to equate my trying to save America with trying to save the city of Nineveh—but I have always tried to steel myself and to say 'If this is what seems to be the will of a Higher Authority than yours truly, then I should learn to submit myself and accept it.'

"Jonah didn't want to go to Nineveh to preach to them. He didn't want Nineveh to be saved, because these people were the enemies of his nation. And after the city was saved, Jonah was angry that God forgave the people of Nineveh and spared the city from destruction. Jonah cried to God, 'I knew that You would do this. I look like a fool. I told everyone that Nineveh would be destroyed in forty days, and now you have decided to spare these people from destruction. Now I look like a liar.' I can certainly understand why Jonah would feel that way.

"I can honestly say I had never imagined I'd be investigating the President of the United States. It had never occurred to me, and it goes again abundantly to illustrate that God moves in mysterious ways. It's just a reminder of how humbling life is and the responsibilities that God puts before us and that we've got to be humbly mindful to do our duty to the best of our ability and with the appearance of complete honesty and integrity—as fully as we can, imperfect beings as we are. Whether the Lord wishes to use me, as now, in the role of Independent Counsel, or in the future in some other capacity, such as the Supreme Court, I will accept His calling and humbly perform my duty.

"Let me not mince words. As a people, Americans have become highly distrustful and disrespectful of institutions, ranging from the basic social unit of the traditional nuclear family to churches, and in this election season, of government itself. President Cannon and his administration are no exception to this powerful trend, the precipitous decline in trust reposed in institutions as a result of scandals. What explains this trend of distrust and disrespect? Part of the answer, I believe, lies in America's over-emphasis on individual rights and liberties. We even hear this in our contemporary music, such as the country and western song which I hear a lot in Birmingham called 'Independence Day.' In my view, that trend is profoundly disturbing. God willing, I intend to draw the line and change the course of history.

"Now, in view of my present position as Independent Counsel, I do not believe it would be appropriate tonight for me to formally endorse or ask you to vote for Republican candidates. I can, however, ask you to pray and to search your hearts. God will lead you to see which candidates can best further His will on such important issues as school prayer, racial busing, flag burning, pornography, evolution, abortion, illegal aliens, socialized medicine, gay marriages, drug abuse, welfare fraud, cutting capital gains taxes, and a strong national defense.

"I also ask that you keep me in your prayers for the next two years as I continue to perform the work God has called me to do for our great nation. Thank you very much, and God bless you."

Jeffreys brought the house down, or up as it might be, and the audience gave him yet another standing ovation. Then the music came up, and they sang the closing hymn, "Onward, Christian Soldiers.".

The rally closed with a five-minute prayer by Spencer Perceval, the local Republican Congressman, a disciple of the Lord and Leroy Reichman. It was a rambling supplication, and I found it so boring that I picked up a Bible and started reading it, which was something I had not done in a very long time. Perhaps it was providence that caused me to focus on Psalm 17, Verse 10, "They close their hearts to pity; with their mouths they speak arrogantly." Whatever the reason, it certainly seemed applicable. And Jeffreys comparing himself to Jonah had almost triggered my gag reflex. The only similarity I could imagine was that Jeffreys hated the Democrats of Alabama and would be exceedingly displeased if anyone suggested fairness toward Cannon and his friends. And that he, too, looked like a fool.

After the benediction, Jeffreys was surrounded by fans wanting to shake his hand and give him encouragement. Some were asking him to autograph their Bibles, and he obliged without hesitation. I could see we were going to be there for a while, so I started looking for the restroom.

When I returned, Jeffreys and Lieutenant Governor Coughlin were engaged in an earnest discussion about Alabama politics. And there was that fat guy I'd seen at Bogue's. He appeared to be with Coughlin, and he and I stood there like silent valets as Jeffreys and Coughlin were talking politics. I finally introduced myself. He said his name was Chub Campbell, and he was Coughlin's campaign consultant or campaign director or something like that. I couldn't understand exactly what he said, because he was talking with his mouth full. In the time we were standing there, I counted him eating four Goo Goo Clusters. It was easy to keep count, because he dropped the wrappers on the floor.

I turned my attention from the fat boy back to the conversation. I knew that Mitch Palmer and Bart Gedney had been pushing to enlist Coughlin's help in digging for dirt on prominent Democrats, but I also knew Jeffreys too well to think he'd ever do it directly. He'd be afraid someone might get the idea he was motivated by political considerations, and that wouldn't be consistent with the righteous public image he always worked so hard to project. I'll have to give Jeffreys credit for trying, but Coughlin was so damn dumb he never did catch on to what Jeffreys was asking him to do. Like Tar Baby, I said nothing. Just bit my lip and listened as they talked past each other. Chub Campbell opened another Goo Goo Cluster.

"I'm not afraid to take a stand for my beliefs, and I'm here to tell you I'm against those gambling casinos spreading into Alabama. Church bingo is one thing, but we don't need casino gambling in Phenix City," Coughlin declared with an air of moral certainty. "Hunting and fishing have become big industries here, and we're all very pleased by that. That's the kind of activity the state should be promoting. You can do that without any risks, as long as the whacko environmentalists don't try to regulate it to death. You know, those environmentalists worship the things that He made rather than He who made them."

"Yes, I'd say hunting and fishing are bringing many people to Alabama, spending millions of dollars," Jeffreys agreed. "The biggest mistake you can make is thinking your salvation is out there somewhere, when all along it could be right here under your nose."

"That's the truth. Fishing is the only real hobby I have," Lieutenant Governor Coughlin continued. "My idea is that a man should go to church twice a week and go fishing once a week. If they haven't done that, then they're really not ready for the rest of the world."

Jeffreys nodded and said, "Fishing is God's gift. I've been somewhat troubled lately that our investigation hasn't moved faster, and I know I feel like I don't have a good week unless I do can a little serious fishing. All I've been able to catch are the small fry. I'd like to do some more, in deeper water, if you have any suggestions. I wouldn't have to catch anything for it to be a success, you understand. I'd get so much pleasure out of just doing it. But, sometimes you can hook a big fish if someone can tell you where to find them."

"I have seen some of your staff down at Lake Martin quite a bit, and that's a great place to relax and talk with friends. Do a little fishing. Yep, it's as genuine a form of relaxation as anything could do at the most expensive health club in New York City, I tell you, and you might even bring home supper. A bass boat is cheaper than a heart attack, irregardless of what the little woman might think. Right? That's what I always say," Coughlin responded, completely missing the point Jeffreys was trying to make about the investigation.

"Right," Jeffreys said with glazed eyes and an insincere grin.

Coughlin was on a roll and seemed to love talking about fishing. "I had to sell my first boat when I decided to run for the Senate back in 1990, but I really missed that boat," he said. "Then somebody gave me a new one right after I got elected Lieutenant Governor. I was out on a deck overlooking the lake with a bunch of my big contributors one day when a boat approached and made a circle. After a while, the boat came back, and a guy in it held up a sign. I tried to read it as it got closer, and it said 'It's yours, Jerry.' Boy howdy, was I ever surprised? It was a Bass Cat Pantera II with a 150-horse Mercury motor, and it was just the right colors. It was really good looking. I knew who it was from, and you can bet that person's calls always get through to me at the office."

Jeffreys was starting to let his frustration show. He didn't care what kind of gifts Coughlin might have accepted from lobbyists, and he didn't know the first thing about bass boats. His face became flushed, and his words were clipped. "I think it might be more rewarding to be a fisher of men. If you catch my drift," he said with an awkward wink.

"Right you are, Brother Jeffreys. Right you are," Coughlin smiled, nudging him with his elbow. "And you know what they say, 'Give a man a fish, and you can't take it off your taxes; but teach a man to fish, and you can take a day off from work.'"

Reverend McCarthy walked over and stuck out his hand to thank Jeffreys for the wonderful speech. "Maybe that will wake people up," he said. "I don't know how a Christian nation can tolerate Cannon and all these scandals"

Coughlin quickly agreed, "Society has become more tolerant, and that is unfortunate because there are some things we shouldn't tolerate."

McCarthy smiled and patted Coughlin on the back as he told Jeffreys, "He's the most popular politician ever in Alabama. I hope Brother Coughlin makes it to the White House so he can straighten things up."

Coughlin flashed a quick grin and said, "I had best be getting on home now to my little Suger Button and the kids. Keep up the good work. And don't forget to get in some fishing if you have a chance." Then he turned and said, "Come on, Chubby. We need to be getting back to Montgomery. We can stop off at a Wendy's and get a couple of burgers on the way."

Jeffreys had hit another dry hole. As Coughlin and Campbell walked away, I tried not to laugh. But I couldn't resist the opening left by the gaps in their conversation. I turned to Jeffreys with a grin and said, "You know, Jonah landed a lunker."

Jeffreys didn't smile. Just took his leave of McCarthy then turned to me and said, "Come on. Let's get out of here."

I'd already voted absentee in Texas. Lloyd Doggett won, but my vote for Ann Richards wasn't enough to stop Shrub Stuart. When the votes were counted in Alabama Tuesday night, Reverend Coughlin had been reelected, and Governor Vance had beaten Nelson Grenier like a red-headed stepchild. The Big Mules—that old Bourbon coalition of corporations and planters that had moved to the Republican party and joined with the religious bigots—had given it their best shot with one of their own, but Grenier had failed once again. Despite spending tons of money to smear Governor Vance, Grenier's campaign message proved to be about as popular in Alabama as shit-flavored chewing gum. Or George Jeffreys.

The real news was that the Republicans captured Congress, both the House and the Senate. Leroy Reichman would soon be Speaker, and Ira Dolor would become Majority Leader, working together to implement their "Contract on America." And, any doubts that we'd soon see a new round of hearings on Whirlpool were soon dispelled. Dolor, Diletto, Reichman, Leech, and Clapham held a joint press conference and pledged to get to the bottom of things. Looked like to me they'd been there for quite some time. It was a real opportunity to punish Cannon appointees and party activists by breaking them with legal bills, and they knew that the publicity of Show Hearings and money spent on lawyers would mean less enthusiasm for the '96 campaign from those who had brung Cannon to the dance in '92.

There was also a renewed sense of enthusiasm around our office after the election. Jeffreys sent telegrams congratulating Diletto, Leech, and several other new committee chairmen. He also placed a call to Senator Hatchet, the man who had once distinguished himself on national television by pursuing questions about pubic hairs on Coke cans and who now would chair the Judiciary Committee. I heard only one side of the conversation, but Jeffreys fawned shamelessly, obviously hoping that he would be called before Hatchet's committee in the near future to present his own nomination.

The November meeting of the Policy Committee was scheduled for the 16th, and I was surprised to find that I was still a member. Figured that I might have been replaced after my futile confrontation with Hathorne last month. I guess my lack of success trumped my lack of decorum, so they decided to keep me on as the token Democrat to maintain the facade of a nonpartisan investigation. I had mixed emotions about continuing to participate in their charade. Sometimes I felt like a movie critic, knowing that my whining and objections weren't going to change the plot. Still, being on the policy committee was the only way I could know what they were plotting. And, as Cannon remarked after reclaiming the governor's office from Dilberry in 1982, "I've been in, and I've been out. In is better."

Jeffreys did not distribute an agenda in advance, or, if he did, I didn't get a copy. He began the meeting with a little pep talk, saying we would be picking up the pace of the investigation and maintaining higher visibility for the next six months. He asked Jo Gobles not to issue any formal release to that effect but to be sure to get the word to a few friendly reporters. Then he told James Peck to ask Judge Corwin for a delay in sentencing Roby Douglas. Interesting. Very interesting.

Douglas had pleaded guilty last March, and our office had been questioning him for eight months. Surely he'd already told our office and the FBI everything they wanted to know. There were only two possible reasons why Jeffreys could want to delay the sentencing, and neither of them were meant to serve justice. Could have been that they knew Douglas was a liar and were afraid he would lose interest in maintaining his story about Cannon and Vance after the sword of sentencing was no longer hanging over him. The less benign explanation was that they knew Douglas would tell any lie they wanted, so they wanted to keep coaching him until they could use his testimony at trial. Whichever, it was a decision they'd already made. I didn't waste my breath.

"I am pleased to report," Jeffreys announced, "that I have had a series of very productive telephone conversations with Senators Dolor and Diletto and with Congressman Leech. They have promised full cooperation with our investigation, and I anticipate a very close and productive relationship with the leadership of the new Congress. I explained that we would be moving very quickly now, and they have agreed to postpone their hearings until August."

Again, I said nothing. Last spring, Burke had asked the committee chairmen to delay their hearings on certain matters for a few months. The Republicans and their lapdogs in the press immediately accused Burke of conducting a cover-up, the "Burke Block" they called it. It was one of their main arguments in attacking Burke's independence and demanding that he be removed. Now that Jeffreys was in charge, however,

Dolor, Rantallion, Bardus, and the others who had savaged Burke were glad to wait until late next year to hold *any* hearings. I guess I expected the hypocrisy, but I hadn't anticipated the tag-team scenario to maximize publicity for political effect. Jeffreys would have a clear channel until August, when Leech would fire up the House Banking Committee, followed shortly by Diletto's Committee in the Senate. How convenient.

As Jeffreys began to tidy his notes, Bart Gedney stood up and distributed copies of a prosecution memorandum. Mitch Palmer and John Hathorne were smiling as they read it. Hathorne nodded to Gedney and Jeffreys, signaling his pleasure with the prospect of filing charges. They'd been waiting for three months to bring charges against someone. Anyone. I tried be patient until the copies made it to me. When they did, I tried not to overreact.

Gedney's memoranda recommended that we bring felony charges against Randolph Webster, the former Associate Attorney General. As I looked over the memo, there were no surprises. We had discovered the basic facts when Burke was still here, but he didn't think the activities of Webster were related to the Cannons or the central focus of our investigation. But, if they wanted my opinion, they would ask for it. And any references to Burke's position would be immediately dismissed by this bunch.

Gedney looked around the table to make sure that everyone had finished reading the memo, then he said, "I am recommending that we act to file charges against former Associate Attorney General Randolph Webster for mail fraud and income tax evasion related to billings and income in his position as a partner at Bankhead, Sayre, & Haardt. We have discovered numerous instances of excessive charges to clients for legal work and three instances where he purchased personal items for his wife and paid for those using the firm's credit card. By causing the statements to be sent through the United States mail, Mr. Webster committed mail fraud. By failing to report the gifts as income on his tax returns, Mr. Webster evaded income taxes on the personal items he charged and that were paid by his firm."

Jeffreys smiled. Mitch Palmer beamed. Most of the others nodded their heads in solemn agreement. Gedney was so proud of himself. Then Jeffreys said, "You have done a splendid job and made a convincing case, Mr. Gedney. Would anyone like to discuss this further, or are we prepared to vote?"

No one said anything. But everyone was looking at me, including Jeffreys, who said, "Mr. Wilkes, you certainly are quiet today. Is there anything you'd like to add before we vote on Mr. Gedney's motion?"

I hesitated for a moment, deciding whether to even bother, then replied, "I have nothing to add, but I intend to vote against charging Webster."

Gedney was hot. "You're just like Kenneth Burke," he shouted. "I've got an airtight case against one of Cannon's closest friends, his golfing buddy and the third highest ranking member of the Justice Department. And you're opposing it. If you're not going to get with the program, maybe you should pack your bags and get back to Texas where you belong."

"No," Jeffreys interjected, "I think we should allow Mr. Wilkes to explain his views on this." There was the fabled fairness of George Jeffreys, urging me to freely speak my mind when he knew it would have no effect on the ultimate result.

"I have no illusions that what I say will affect the decision to prosecute," I replied calmly, "but I'll be glad to explain my reasons for opposing it. First, I don't think the proposed charges have anything to do with the Cannons, the Banaghans, Whirlpool Estates, Jefferson Savings, or Financial Management. The allegations relate to the private legal practice of Randolph Webster at the time he was a private citizen and before James Cannon became president. Perhaps there is some criminal liability, and I know that we are authorized to prosecute any crimes we might discover during our investigation. However, Mr. Webster has resigned from the Justice Department and is once again a private citizen. There is no longer any potential conflict of interest and no reason that the local United States Attorney can't make the call on this and prosecute if she thinks it appropriate."

"Second," I continued, "I'm not sure, as a practical matter, whether justice would be served by bringing criminal charges against Webster. I think the humiliation of resigning his office and the extensive reporting on Mr. Webster's business activities are punishment enough for whatever he might have done. I understand that he is presently trying to make arrangements to repay his firm and his clients and is in the process of amending his past tax returns. If we bring criminal charges and secure a conviction, he'll lose his law license. In that case, I don't see how he'd be able to make restitution, and we'd only be punishing those to whom he owes money. And his family. The guy has a wife and four kids to support. Maybe I'm wrong, but that's sure how it looks to me."

Bart Gedney glared at me, but he offered no rebuttal. The rest of the group appeared somewhat uneasy, and that was the most I expected. Gedney was a lost cause, but perhaps the others would realize what they were about to do. But they still did it. Gedney, Hathorne, Peck, Palmer, and Gobles voted to prosecute Webster. I was the lone vote against it.

"I endorse your decision to bring felony charges of mail fraud and tax evasion against Randolph Webster," Jeffreys announced, almost sounding as if he were trying to wash his hands of any guilt or responsibility. "When do you plan to take this to the grand jury, Mr. Gedney?"

Bart Gedney was flush with victory, almost bragging when he said, "I don't think we'll need to get an indictment. Webster knows we have the goods on him, and I don't think he's got much fight left in him. I am fairly confident we can get a plea agreement on both counts, so we can handle it by information. At least, that's the impression I've gotten from his attorney."

"That would certainly be nice, but I must say that surprises me," Jeffreys responded gleefully.

"Well," Gedney replied, smiling at Jeffreys, "I remembered something you once said. I hit them with the 'family values' hammer, and it worked like a charm."

I could tell that Mitch had been wanting to say something. He raised his hand like a schoolboy and asked, "Bart, what's a 'family values' hammer?"

Gedney had a grin that was almost evil as he explained what he had done. "It's one of my favorite weapons," he said. "It's when a prosecutor threatens to bring charges against someone's wife or kids. I said we were also looking at the possibility of felony charges against Mrs. Webster on the gifts. Of course, that was total bullshit. We didn't have anything on her, and I'd have had to back off if his lawyers had called my bluff. But the big bastard fell for it. I thought he was going to cry right there in my office. It always works with these Southern boys. They've got this inflated sense of honor that makes them easy marks. They'll go to hell and back to protect their families. Works every time."

With that little lesson in human compassion, the meeting was over. Hathorne offered a hearty congratulation, slapping Gedney on the back. Jo followed them down the hall to get more details for prepping the press. Peck and Jeffreys scurried off to talk about whatever they were always talking about. I was trying to hang back and avoid having another conversation about my position, but Mitch didn't follow the pack.

"I believe I owe you a beer, and you look like you could use one," he said.

"You owe me several," I replied, "and now would be a very good time. Let's go."

I took Mitch to The Mill. He'd never been there, and I hadn't since Sean left. It wasn't quite the same now, but the beer was still cold. I was downing it at my usual pace, and Mitch struggled to keep up. Somewhere in the third pitcher I noticed that he was leaning back and staring at the white oak baskets that covered the ceiling, and he almost fell off the barstool. Would have if I hadn't caught him. Guess I felt sorry for him, because three months ago I'd have let him kiss the floor.

"I really like you, Wilkes," he said with a slight slur in his voice. "Not many people do, but I do. Bart hates your ass, you know. Hathorne does, too."

"Well, that's good to know," I said with a smile. "I'd have to wonder about myself if those guys liked me. Besides, I didn't stay on with Jeffreys to win any popularity contests. If I wanted a friend around here, I'd buy me a dog."

"That's funny! I like the way you always say what you think. You were pretty good in the meeting this afternoon, too," he said, "but you know you didn't have a chance. Judge Jeffreys and Gedney both had scores to settle with Webster. You were good, but it didn't make any difference. It was a done deal. I might have voted with you, if there was any way, but it wasn't going to happen, my friend."

I knew Mitch wouldn't have voted with me. Mitch would always vote with Jeffreys, and that always seemed to be for anything that might hurt the president. It was the beer was talking now. But I did want to know what Mitch meant about Jeffreys and Gedney having a score to settle, and this seemed like an opportune time to ask.

I topped off Mitch's glass with the last of the pitcher. "Well, if I was so good," I asked, "why couldn't I convince them?"

Mitch grinned as he started to speak, and I caught him again as he started listing to starboard. "Payback, my friend," he finally said. "Webster screwed them both when he was at Main Justice."

I didn't mind Mitch calling me his friend if he would keep talking. This was about to get interesting. He was drunk enough to talk and probably drunk enough he wouldn't remember what he said. I knew, though, I'd better get some answers soon, or I'd miss that brief window of opportunity. "How's that? What did he ever do to them?"

"Well, I'm not sure about the details on Bart," Mitch said. "It had something to do with a desegregation deal Webster tried to force on Mississippi, but it was mostly about that Congressman from Tennessee. Bart really wanted to get him. I remember he said, 'I almost had that nigger's ass nailed to the wall, and Webster tried to move the trial to Memphis.' Bart had already blown it once. Got a hung jury. The second time he had an all white jury, and then the damn Justice Department joined the motion to move the trial to Memphis. The motion was denied, but they still weren't able to get a conviction. The guy walked. Bart said he'd never forget what Webster tried to do to him."

Mitch finished off his beer. I was afraid it was about to finish off him. "Hey," Mitch asked, "where's the restroom?"

Not now. No way I was going to let him go before he told me about Jeffreys' grudge. "Someone just went in," I lied. "So, what about Jeffreys?"

"Oh, yeah. Judge Jeffreys said he was ambushed by Webster. It was an ethics deal, so you can imagine how much that hurt him."

Yeah, I knew. Jeffreys would really squeal if he were caught in an ethics violation. Pride was his deadly sin. "What kind of ethics deal?"

"Well, you know that rule about not representing a party in a suit against the government for a year after you leave office? The "revolving door" prohibition? It was a misunderstanding, really. Just before President Stuart left office, the Justice Department issued a ruling revising the criminal conflict-of interest regs on that. So, Judge Jeffreys thought it was okay. He was representing Bell Atlantic in a suit against the government. Thought it was okay. Then the Justice Department, and here's where Webster came in, told him that it was illegal. They didn't bring criminal charges, but they made him withdraw and lose a big fee. Webster was behind it, and Judge Jeffreys was really embarrassed because it reflected on his legal ethics. I don't mean to imply that he's a vengeful person, not like Bart. But that's what it was all about. And you didn't have a chance. And neither does Cannon, now that we've got someone working with us inside the White House."

That last remark really got my attention, but Mitch was not through. With a pronounced slur, he asked, "Wilkes, have you been born again?"

Not feeling up for an extended theological conversation with a drunk Republican, I deflected the inquiry. "No, Mitch, I got it right the first time."

With that, I pointed Mitch toward the restroom and paid the tab. I started to worry about him after about 15 minutes. Found him passed out and hugging the stool. I put him in the truck and woke him up long enough to get directions to his apartment. I don't think Mitch remembered a thing about that conversation. However, I didn't forget. I could see more clearly than ever.

Chapter Seventeen

Bart Gedney was in my office before I had my second cup of coffee. I took a long sip, looking into the cup to avoid acknowledging him, but he insisted on having a conversation. "Wilkes, we're going to be ready to go on the Webster plea on Monday," he blared, wanting to remind me that he had prevailed on the decision to prosecute. "What's the procedure? How can we make sure we get the right judge on this? I don't want one of those damn pansy-ass liberals."

I thought for a moment before answering him. "No way to shop it here," I said with a tone of sincerity and a blank look. "It's totally random. You'll just have to take your chances."

He did, and the case was assigned to James Wilson, the only Cannon appointee in the rotation. That, however, did not stop the show. Mitch made the rounds through the offices on Monday morning and announced that Jeffreys wanted as many of us as possible in the courtroom for the arraignment and plea. That seemed a bit odd, but then I realized what he was doing. It was his own little "court-packing" plan. A chamber full of lawyers from the Office of Independent Counsel would give the impression that this was a major case, instead of a garden variety guilty plea for over-billing clients. I decided I had better things to do with my time and didn't plan to participate. They could get their extras somewhere else. Jeffreys thought otherwise, and Mitch said they wanted me to ride with them.

When we arrived at the courthouse, I saw immediately how staged the whole deal was. Always before I had approached on 4th Avenue and parked in the secure lot behind the building, entering through the rear door. Not this time. Jeffreys had all the cars circle the block and park on 5th Avenue so he could make a grand entrance through the media swarm in front of the building. The main entry was almost blocked by reporters and camera crews on the plaza in front of the building, and it was clear that Jo Gobles had done her job. Jeffreys jumped out quickly and strutted through the crowd on the sidewalk, leading a pack of nine lawyers and five FBI agents through a wall of cameras and rude reporters. I had to admit my amazement and my grudging appreciation for that contrived performance.

We filed through the green marble metal detector and took the elevator up to Courtroom 6A. Once inside, Mitch suggested that we sit in the jury box to the right of the bench. Jeffreys and Gedney took their places at the prosecution's table. The room was packed, probably 30 reporters from all the networks and major papers, but no cameras were allowed. That, however, didn't stop Jeffreys from adjusting his tie and straightening his lapels.

The whole proceeding took only half an hour, and twenty minutes of that was Gedney's unnecessary but extended recitation of the details of every instance in which there had been excessive billing from 1989 through 1992. Randolph Webster's voice was hardly audible as he entered his plea and offered his apologies to his friends and family. I was glad that Judge Wilson had the decency to keep everyone in the courtroom while Webster and his family left through a side door, avoiding the press.

Jeffreys, on the other hand, was not about to avoid the press. He stepped outside the courthouse and immediately obliged the media by holding a brief news conference on the steps. Jeffreys put on his officious face and dropped into his preacher's voice as he made his pronouncement. "Former Associate Attorney General Randolph Webster has accepted responsibility for his criminal activity and has admitted his guilt, and I think that this is a time for all of us to reflect on what is an unfortunate day but nonetheless is a necessary one for our nation. This conviction today is a major victory, one that has penetrated the highest levels of government. I anticipate that Randolph Webster will be a key witness in our continuing probe. Now that he has agreed to cooperate with our office, I am looking forward to his providing important information in our active and ongoing investigation matters relating to President and Mrs. Cannon, both here in Alabama and in Washington."

Jeffreys then distributed copies of the plea agreement and the laundry list Gedney had read in court. After taking a few questions and feigning concern for Webster's personal situation, he thanked the reporters for coming, and we returned to the office.

On the way back, I got my first look at the plea agreement. And a surprise. It contained a gag provision prohibiting Webster from talking to anyone about the circumstances of his plea or "the substance, nature, and scope of his cooperation" with the investigation. That was somewhat unusual. Might even be an unconstitutional condition. Rather than asking Jeffreys about it, though, I decided to wait and give it some more thought. He and Gedney were too busy right then congratulating each other on their performances.

Tuesday's headlines were a source of great joy for Jeffreys, and copies of the news reports and editorials were distributed to the staff before noon. A cursory reading warned me to expect some gloating by Gedney and reminded me that I expected too much from the press. It was a page one story in every paper. The standard take was that Webster's plea was a major development in the investigation and a big scalp for Jeffreys. The fact that the charges had nothing to do with Cannon or Whirlpool was conveniently overlooked. No notice that the activities occurred before Cannon was elected and while Webster was a lawyer in private practice. None of the reporters had talked with Webster, and none quoted him. They all carried quotes from Jeffreys at the news conference, and they all reported the details of the charges as elaborated by Gedney in the courtroom.

Webster was described variously as Cannon's closest friend, as Mrs. Cannon's law partner, and as a high ranking official in Cannon's administration. One editorial in the *Washington Sun* called Webster "the John Dean of Whirlpool," predicting that his cooperation was likely to lead to serious criminal charges against both the President and the First Lady. John Dean? Randolph Webster wasn't even Sugar Boy O'Sheean! That's when it hit me why Jeffreys had wanted the gag provision in the plea agreement. Webster was neutered, rendered unable to contradict the wild editorial speculation or to refute anything our office might say about him. Very clever. Totally political. This wasn't an investigation; it was a campaign.

I'm not big on conspiracy theories, but I admit giving them some thought that week. Dale Cheatham, former head of the White House Travel Office, was indicted for embezzling over $65,000 from the office. Was he called a "Cannon associate" or a "White House aide" in any of the news stories? Nope. Dale Cheatham was said to be a "career employee" with years of experience. Most of it was experience working for Republicans, but that wasn't noted. Many of the same newspapers that had been calling for the resignation of Cannon and the indictment of everyone else in his administration expressed sympathy for Dale Cheatham's unfortunate problems. He was right up there with Ben Arnold, the fired White House usher, in the media's gallery of heroic victims.

There were, of course, significant reasons why the press should have treated the Cheatham indictment differently from the Webster plea. Cheatham wasn't a Cannon appointee. Webster hadn't been giving the press corps sweetheart deals on travel arrangements. Important differences.

Another local story that week received no national media attention. Josh Banaghan was hospitalized again. He'd already had two strokes, and his doctors feared that the stress of the Whirlpool investigation had worsened his condition. They were planning to scrape his arteries, hoping to save what was left of his mind from yet another damaging stroke. From newspaper accounts quoting him—as far as anyone could trust that source—it appeared Banaghan was already too far gone to participate effectively in his own defense. That certainly wasn't going to stop George Jeffreys from seeking to indict him. Maybe providence would be kind and spare him from the ordeal of a trial.

Maybe a little vacation would save me as well. This job was getting pretty distasteful, and I was about to come down with a bad case of the blues. Well, more like the blahs. Seasonal Affective Disorder I think is what they call it now, but it's really just the blahs.

Lucky for me, the cure was close at hand. Lindsey finished the semester on December 17th, and I took two weeks vacation time. Picked her up in Montgomery for a road trip to New Boston to meet my folks. About half way there, I realized that this relationship must be getting serious and decided to slow down and make it a two-day trip. We stopped the first night in Oxford, Mississippi, and spent most of our time at Square Books. Willie Morris happened to be there signing his new book, and we managed to work our way into a crowd that had dinner with him at Proud Larry's. It was an interesting diversion, but I was still nervous the next day, getting more so as we got closer to home. I was too old to be getting nervous. I was also getting too old to be bringing a woman home to meet my parents.

The homecoming was not as uncomfortable as I had anticipated, and the next two days passed quickly. I showed Lindsey all the monuments of my youth—the high school, the local drug store, the main drag, even my favorite parking spot. Then we left for Austin, and I repeated the memory tour of my haunts there. We stayed with Raymond and Peggy. Mostly we stayed in their hot tub, and I thought not once about the other whirlpool.

It was good to be back in Austin, if only for a brief visit. The real reason for the stop was that it was on the way to San Antonio where I was picking up my kids for our annual vacation—this year a Caribbean cruise. It could be wonderful, or it could be a total disaster. Turned out just fine. Lindsey liked them, and they liked her. I loved them all. And I loved the sun and the islands and the rum drinks. And the contraband Cohibas.

Lindsey and I drove back on the same route I had taken on my first trip to Birmingham in February, and we stopped to celebrate New Year's Eve in New Orleans. I stayed at her apartment the next two days to recover, watching the bowl games while she was working on a research project for the Southern Poverty Law Center. I almost felt like a native, cheering for the Tide in the Citrus Bowl. They beat Ohio State 24-17 in a fourth quarter comeback when Sherman Williams ran 50 yards with a flip pass from Jay Barker, scoring the winning touchdown with 42 seconds to play.

I also enjoyed the time away from work to do some reading. Lindsey had given me two books for Christmas, and both were quite interesting Alabama political biographies. *The Judge* by Frank Sikora was my favorite, mostly because I learned more about one of my political heroes. John Hayman's *Bitter Harvest* was a more complex story, and I wasn't quite sure what I thought about it. Guess I should have been trained as a deconstructionist so I could have given it a happy ending and been certain exactly what it meant. But, alas, I remained burdened by logical thinking and the rational paradigm.

The only tense moment in our two weeks together came that evening when I learned that Lindsey was working on a project involving the abuse of the Independent Counsel statutes. I suppose I was too touchy about it, but I thought she should have told me sooner. I was wondering what I might have said about my work or the office that would end up in some report or press release from the Southern Poverty Law Center.

"Very interesting," I said defensively. "Why is the Center interested in that? What does the OIC have to do with poverty or racism?"

Lindsey knew immediately what I was thinking, and she quickly assured me that she had not violated any confidences. "I'm using you, no question about that, but it's only for your body not your mind," she said. "But, to answer your question, the report will focus on how the OIC statute is being abused to advance a racist agenda."

I smiled as an apology for ever doubting that I could trust her. "Well, tell me more. About your research, I mean."

"Primarily, I'm analyzing the process and the motives behind the appointment of the existing Independent Counsels, the ones that have been appointed since Cannon became president," she explained. "The Republican line is that his administration is the most corrupt in recent memory, as evidenced by four separate Independent Counsel investigations. My research suggests an entirely different conclusion can be drawn. Look at who is being investigated. The Republicans have demanded and secured Independent Counsels to investigate an African-American Secretary of Agriculture, an African-American Secretary of Commerce, and an Hispanic Secretary of Housing and Urban Development. They also wanted one to investigate the African-American Secretary of Energy, and they're still trying to get one to investigate an African-American Secretary of Labor. Then think how they treated the Surgeon General. It's a consistent pattern. When you look at the civil rights voting records of the members who have been the most vocal against Cannon, it's even more clear. Ira Dolor and Leroy Reichman have an agenda, and they've pursued it with a vengeance."

She was right, of course. And no one had thought to point out those facts. The press coverage was designed to shout "scandal," not to examine the facts and the baser motives behind the GOP demands for investigations. I didn't find the Democrats without fault either. If Cannon had the balls to stand up and defend his Cabinet appointees and his staff, it might have been different. Or if Harriet Otis would do her job instead of trying so hard to be a television network programming director and Internet snooper. Or if the Democrats in Congress would have done their job and put a stop to the nonsense early on. Tom Foley couldn't even hold his district, much less command his troops in the House.

"Sounds to me like you've taken on quite a project," I admitted with considerable admiration for such a quick analytical mind. "I guess I've been too busy to even notice the big picture. Makes sense to me. With the Whirlpool investigation, though, it's a different story, don't you think? This one's just pure political revenge for the last election."

"Yes. And no," she said. "Cannon has always had overwhelming support in the black community. Some boxes come in at 97 or 98 percent. And, if there is any consistent theme in his political career, it has been an unwavering commitment to racial justice. Now, I like that, and you like that, but not everyone in Alabama shares our views on that issue. The Big Mules and the old bigots hate him. What percentage of the black vote do you think Nelson Grenier got in the last two elections? Why do you think James Boutwell Crommelin hasn't been elected to anything since 1962? You know about James Rivington, the editor of the *Washington Sun*? His daddy was head of the Capital Citizens Council here in Montgomery back when they were trying to stop school integration. John Cross, former Grand Dragon and head of the Republican Campaign Finance Council, same deal. And who do you think started all this crap about Whirlpool?"

"Well, yeah, I know that's how it all got started, but I don't think that's what's driving Jeffreys. I mean, I know he hates Cannon, but I think it's his own personal ambition at work. Cannon's election cost him his job and probably a seat on the Supreme Court," I said, hardly believing that I heard myself defending Jeffreys.

"Think again," she said. "Think real hard. Did Jeffreys write an opinion striking down affirmative action? Did Jeffreys try to block donations to the NAACP Legal Defense Fund? Did Reynolds Rantallion and Helmut Duke hand pick him for this job? Has Jeffreys appointed even one African-American attorney as Associate Counsel? Did you see a single black face in the crowd when he spoke to that God and Country rally at Briarwood? Did he send an army of FBI agents to harass every black minister and every black political leader in this state? What about ruining the career of Bridget Bishop, the black woman who worked as Vice President at Jefferson Savings? Has Jeffreys traded his black robe for a white one? Is a bear Catholic?"

She was right again. Absolutely right. About everything except the harassment. I nodded my agreement but asked, "What do you mean? Maybe there is a pattern of racism, okay, and maybe he is a racist, but we're not investigating black preachers and politicians. Seriously, I wouldn't lie about that."

"Then you've got your head up your yah-yah," she said with a mixture of skepticism and concern. "The Center staff has been on this since late November. They get 10 to 15 calls a week reporting the same thing. It's FBI, and they're working for OIC. You might not know it, but your office is behind it. They're ruthless, John. They're threatening to have the IRS investigate every black minister in the state. They're trying to intimidate every black volunteer who ever gave an elderly person a ride to the polls. They're sending a message that supporting Cannon is a crime punishable by thousands of dollars in legal bills. They don't care who they hurt."

I was stunned. Lindsey wasn't making this up. But I sure didn't know anything about it. "I believe you, but I promise this is the first I've heard about it," I said. "What's the angle? What are they trying to prove?"

"It's all about the 1990 governor's race, when Cannon beat Grenier. They're accusing folks of buying and selling votes, looking at cash payments to everyone who was involved in get-out-the-vote activity. One case I know about, because I've worked with the woman on community projects before. She received $20 for a tank of gas to carry shut-ins to vote. Worked all day, drove all over the county, helping people in and out of the car and waiting for them. Even took some of them to pick up groceries and medicine while they were out. Anyway, they say she's lying because she doesn't have a receipt for a tank of gas she bought three years ago. They've threatened to charge her with felony fraud in a federal election unless she implicates Cannon or Robert Bruce. Guess they'll charge her with being part of a conspiracy to take back the White House from the rightful Great White owners in 1992."

I was outraged, as much by not knowing about it as I was by what they'd been doing. And personally embarrassed because Lindsey knew I had been a dupe. I was sure it was Bart Gedney's operation, but he wouldn't be doing it unless Jeffreys had approved it. And I was sure they would have kept it from me, because they knew I'd do more than vote against it. I was determined now to do everything I could to stop it. Or resign and go public. I don't get loud when I get mad, so I managed to sound calm when I promised Lindsey I'd try to find out more about it.

That conversation was the closest thing to a fight we'd ever had. We kissed and made up. And then we kissed some more.

Returning to work on Tuesday was not a pleasant experience. The overcast sky only served to reminded me how much I preferred the recent laughter in the sun on island beaches. Vacations are supposed to be refreshing, but they can also provide a new perspective. The offices seemed especially cold and sterile now. Thin industrial carpet, metal desks, bare interrogation rooms, blinds always drawn, no plants. The press referred to our bunker as the Bat Cave, and that was one of the few accurate conclusions they had drawn since this investigation began. I was beginning to think of it more as the Cave of the Winds.

I would have to wait to confront Jeffreys about the abuse of my trust and the abuse of his powers. He was still in Washington, preparing to crank up a grand jury to once again rake the ashes of Hal Goodall, yet another abuse of discretion. I told Phyllis that I needed to talk with him when he got back and asked her to schedule me in as soon as possible.

Mitch Palmer was running the office in Jeffreys' absence, or, perhaps I should say, Mitch was running around the office. A slow news week had caused the fourth estate to stretch a bit to find something damaging to say about Cannon, and the recycled scandal of the week was a *Washington Sun* article alleging that Cannon had been involved in a large drug smuggling operation near Phenix City back in the mid-1980s. Phenix City, what an excuse for a town. Brothel annex for the brave men of Fort Benning and birthplace of future draft dodger Phil Gramm. Mitch was all excited and was assigning staff to start taking depositions immediately. Looked to me like he was hoping to find something big to impress Jeffreys.

I'd heard all that before. Some conspiracy nut had written a book making the same charges last summer, and Congressman Bardus had repeated them on the floor of the House, relying on a report compiled by an investigator with the *Speculator*'s Alabama project and the purchased allegations from one of the loquacious state troopers on the payroll of a group cynically called Citizens for Honest Government. Tyburn had a similar screed in the *American Speculator* and even accused Cannon of snorting the merchandise.

Burke looked into it last year, and we discovered that the CIA had been running weapons and ammunition from Fort Benning to supply the Contras. The planes returned loaded with drugs, then the profits bought more guns and supplies for the Contras, avoiding the Boland Amendment restrictions. The operation was based at a small airstrip near Seale, just outside Phenix City on U.S. 431. The CIA had used the place once before, back in 1961, when they got General Doster and the Air National Guard to train pilots for the Bay of Pigs.

Reeder and Stuart probably knew what was going on there, but it had nothing to do with our investigation ten years later. There was no evidence that Governor Cannon had even been aware of it. The only time he went near Phenix City was to campaign, to see his momma, or to pig out on Chicken Comer's barbeque.

I suspected that the renewed interest was coming from a private investigator, one of his old pals now in the employ of the *American Speculator*, that Bart Gedney had been meeting with down at the hunting lodge on Lake Martin.

I felt an obligation to tell Mitch all this and save him from embarrassing himself. However, when I told him I needed to speak with him privately, he said it would just have to wait. He was too busy, said the FBI was bringing in a key witness who had information directly linking Cannon to drug smuggling and money laundering.

Who was I to interfere? They'd just think I was trying to protect Cannon, anyway. I went on back to my office and started going through the mail that had accumulated while I had been on vacation, but in a few minutes Mitch stuck his head in and said, "He's here. Come on if you want to hear this."

I followed Mitch down the hall to one of the interrogation rooms and nearly laughed out loud when I saw his star witness. It was Carl Weiss, a sleazy former state bureaucrat who had been fired for misappropriation and had been unemployed for the last four or five years, living off political blood money from Citizens for Honest Government, the ones who made the video with Reverand Laud. Before that, he had worked in Nelson Grenier's campaign against Cannon and was a political and business associate of Les Bobbitt, the GOP state chairman.

Angry former employees always have a tale they want to tell, and sometimes it can be worth listening. Not this time. Weiss was a bitter man who needed cash and had a tenuous grip on reality. He'd been making the rounds of the fringe talk radio circuit for about six months, but no one took him seriously. I motioned for Mitch to step outside the room so I could warn him, but he shook me off, like a pitcher itching to throw his best fastball.

Weiss was soon into one of the most bizarre performances I'd ever seen. Arching his eyebrows, he launched into a land where no mind has gone before. "I was Special Forces, worked for Oliver North and Bill Casey at the CIA, and I was the only real patriot in Cannon's administration. Found out I was raising money for the Contras, and he wasn't getting his cut. That's the real reason why Cannon had me fired. I was his most trusted aide, and then he turned on me because I wouldn't funnel money into his campaign," Weiss ranted nonstop, broadcasting droplets of saliva as he spoke. "I filed a lawsuit for wrongful termination and named the 237 women I knew he'd had affairs with—Sally Cosworth, Maria Halpin, Nan Britton—all of them. The troopers confirmed it, and Clifton Smegman has a picture that could end the presidency. I'm think I'm being followed. I'm afraid my life is in danger."

Mitch sat there grimacing while Weiss spewed venom and spun his incoherent fantasy. It was a tale told by an idiot, full of sound and fury, signifying nothing. I didn't feel sorry for either of them, but I did have some sympathy for the two FBI agents who were trying to take notes. Mitch took another shot at getting his witness back into the real world. "Maybe you should start at the beginning," he said, hoping that a linear story lurked within the man. "When did you first get to know Governor Cannon?"

"Oh, it was long before he was elected governor," Weiss said. "I ran around with Cannon, Jim Bibb Vance, and Nelson Grenier. The four of us sort of hung out together all the time, talking politics and working deals. Cannon gave me the job at the Alabama Finance Authority, his personal piggy bank to help his rich pals. Then I found out about the drug operation outside of Phenix City. They were all involved, doing cocaine at their toga parties and laundering the money through the AFA bonds. Randolph Webster was the bond counsel, and Don Lancaster sold the bonds. The Jews boys parked the money off-shore with BCCI. The crack dealers were the engine for Cannon's political machine. That's how he always got the nigger vote, you know. It's amazing, isn't it, the way all the little details move in a circle. They were all in on it—Hal Goodall, Diane Cannon, Josh Banaghan, Randolph Webster. Mafia connections, too. Cannon grew up in Phenix City, so he's connected. You don't believe me? The troopers and Mr. Smegman will back me up on this. Just ask them. Or ask Bart Gedney what our private investigator found. He's seen the report from the Alabama Project."

I kept expecting to see Rod Serling step out of the closet and welcome everyone to the Twilight Zone. Mitch was sweating now. The FBI agents had quit taking notes some time ago. I'd heard enough and was starting to leave when a shrill beeping noise broke the silence. I thought it might be a bullshit detector going off, but it was only Mitch's pager. With a look of great relief, Mitch excused himself to take a call. As he walked past me, he murmured under his breath, "It's Judge Jeffreys. What am I going to tell him?"

In a few minutes Mitch was back with two more FBI agents. They escorted Weiss from the room and out the door. Mitch and I were standing there alone in the interrogation room, and I couldn't think of anything to say that wouldn't make him feel worse. I almost suggested that he could count a collar if he wanted to nail Weiss under 18 U.S.C §1001 for lying to the FBI, but I resisted rubbing his nose in it. This office would reserve such charges only for known Democrats. "Well," I finally asked, "what did Jeffreys have to say?"

Mitch kept staring at his shoes to avoid eye contact with me. "He told me to drop it. Said the Phenix City drug operation was a can of worms we didn't want to open." Then, looking up, he said, "Please don't tell Judge Jeffreys about what happened with Weiss. I didn't know he was a psycho. I thought I was doing what Judge Jeffreys would have wanted."

"No reason I would tell him," I said. "But, damn it, you're going to have to start showing some common sense, Mitch. You guys should know by now that these assholes making allegations against Cannon are either bitter political enemies, paid liars, or walking mental cases, or all of the above. And if you keep taking them seriously, you're gonna look pretty damn foolish. Weiss will be back on the radio next week, and there's no telling what he'll be saying then. Can you imagine what would happen if you ever brought charges and put one of those delusional bastards on the stand?"

I was glad that little episode was over. I left the office for a lunch meeting with Carolyn Marvin, the Samford law dean who had been kind enough to let me have a carrel in the law library. It had been a comfortable retreat for writing and for hiding when things got too crazy at the office. I'd tried to show my gratitude by impersonating a law professor and occasionally doing guest lectures. I wasn't sure why she'd invited me to lunch, but I always enjoyed visiting with her. She had such a keen mind and an unusual enthusiasm for arguing ideas.

Dean Marvin was also very direct. Usually. We talked briefly about my interest in an academic career, and I hinted that I would be interested in teaching a seminar next fall. Pro bono, of course, because I thought I'd learn more than the students would. We had not even ordered when she followed that by asking, "Are you happy working for the Independent Counsel?"

That was a very encouraging sign. She wasn't inquiring about my emotional state. That was the primer for talking about a job. I thought about how to phrase it before answering, "I don't regret having made the move. It's been interesting. And challenging. But you know that my real interest is in teaching law. That's what I'd like to do, and I think I'd be good at it."

Her next question took me by surprise. "Would you ever have any interest in being a dean?"

"A dean? I don't know. Never thought about it," I said, trying to answer that for myself as well. "I guess I might like to be James Dean."

Fortunately, she laughed. "We'll have an opening for a new Associate Dean's position next fall. With your academic background and administrative experience, I think you'd be the perfect candidate. I've talked with several of the faculty who know you, and they think so, too."

I still wasn't sure what to say. "I'm flattered, of course, but I've never thought about that. My real interests are in teaching and writing. I've just never thought about deaning, or whatever it's called."

"Well, please keep that in mind, and do think about it," she said, giving us both more time. "And, yes, we'd love for you to teach a seminar next year, whatever your decision about applying for the job."

I decided fairly quickly that I'd pushed enough paper in my life and wouldn't be applying for any dean position. But it was good to know I might be employable, because I didn't know how long Jeffreys and I could tolerate each other.

Chapter Eighteen

That afternoon I got another surprise when I returned to the office. Janet Fox had called to wish me a happy new year, at least that's what the message slip said. When I returned the call, I learned that there was more to it than that. She first wanted to know if Jeffreys had the same rules as Burke did about staff members talking to the press. I said I didn't think so. He seemed to love talking to the media and getting his picture on television and in the papers. Nonetheless, I warned her, I still considered myself bound by the Code of Professional Conduct, the Ethics in Government Act, and the Department of Justice guidelines published as 28 CFR 50.2. That left very little that I might discuss about the ongoing work of our office.

"Thanks a lot," Janet said playfully but sarcastically. "See if I ever tell you anything again."

I did owe her one, and I wanted to be helpful if I could. Besides, I was curious, so I asked, "What would you want to know about the OIC, anyway? I thought you were a financial reporter."

"I am," she said, "but I had an inquiry from a colleague on the national desk. I'd told him that I knew someone who worked for Jeffreys, and he thought I might be able to get you to talk. So, I thought I'd at least ask. It's not really about the investigation, not directly anyway."

"Well, ask away. It's so rare that any political reporters bother with the facts, I wouldn't want to miss the chance to see a miracle," I said, trying not to reveal the true depth of my feelings about the Whirlpool coverage.

"Okay. Is there anyone on your staff in the Alabama office named Alice?"

"Alice? No, I don't think so. No one in the Washington office, either. Why?"

"My colleague, who shall remain nameless, has been receiving packages of Whirlpool documents that appear to be coming from your office, at least they aren't part of what's publicly available. Some of it is obviously grand jury stuff. They always come with a cover memo that suggests implications to be drawn. It's signed 'Alice,' and it's post-marked from Birmingham. Ring any bells now?"

"No," I replied, "but I'd be very interested in knowing what kind of documents, and I'd like to see the memos.

"I don't think I can get copies, but I'll send you a couple of clips from the *Washington Sun*. My colleague thinks the *Sun*, the *Wall Street Record,* and the *American Speculator* are getting the same information, and he says the timing and content of the articles indicates that they're using the stuff." Knowing what I was thinking, Janet said, "We don't like getting scooped, but we do have certain standards of practice here and have to get independent confirmation before we can use anonymous sources."

"I look forward to seeing the articles," I said, "and I'll let you know where I think it might be coming from if I have any ideas." That was only a slight fib, because I had immediately remembered the incident with Jeffreys' briefcase at the Tutwiler and the private investigator that was always coming by to talk with Bart Gedney. "Is that all?"

"Nope, one more thing. What do you know about an organization called the Women's Federation for World Peace?"

"That does sound vaguely familiar," I said, racking the recesses of my brain for memory traces. "Oh, yeah, that's a group in Houston. They were pushing for mandatory school prayer back when I worked in the AG's office. What's that got to do with anything?"

"It's not just in Houston, although they might have a chapter there," Janet explained. "It's headquartered in South Korea. It's not officially affiliated with the Unification Church, but some of the same people are involved. Anyway, they're having a big rally here in Washington next month. Elmer Laud is on the program. James Rivington, managing editor of the *Sun,* will be introducing the keynote speaker, who is none other than Charles William Horton Stuart. Supposed to be paying him $75,000 to $100,000 a speech, and this is only one of 11 he's agreed to do for them."

"Well," I admitted, "I must say I'm surprised to learn about the organization, but, knowing that, I'm not at all surprised by that cast of characters. The Moon and his little stars. What a nest of rascals!"

"Don't say anything you'll regret," Janet replied. "The other reason I was calling was to see if you can confirm that George Jeffreys will be on the program. Word here is that he has been invited. Do you know anything about it?"

"No, but that doesn't mean it's not true. Every day I keep finding out new things about who and what we are doing," I said, remembering how humiliating it was that Lindsey knew more about what we had been investigating than I did. "Jeffreys certainly has connections to all the players, and they've all had plenty to say about the Whirlpool investigation. I'll check his schedule and get back to you if I can find anything of interest."

"One more question. Actually two," Janet said. "Have you ever heard of Adnan Kashogi?"

"I've heard the name," I said. "Isn't he the arms dealer that was somehow tied to the Iran-Contra deal?"

"Right. Have you ever heard Jeffreys mention Kashogi or anything about something called Lubbock AK?"

"No, I haven't. Jeffreys and I don't discuss much of anything besides the investigation. And I'm not always privy to all the discussions about that. What's this about?"

"Maybe nothing," Janet said, but her voice indicated that it was about something. "Just a story I'm working on about 'investments' by certain officials in the Reeder administration."

"Sorry I can't help you on that," I said. "Wish I could. You enjoying life in Washington?"

"Everything's fine. And I got married in November. If you ever get to Washington, please give me a call. I'd like for you to meet my husband, and maybe we can have lunch or something."

"Well, congratulations. And I will let you know if I'm up that way." I was happy for her, but I didn't say I'd like to meet her husband. Lucky guy. But not as lucky as me.

I thought the conversation was over, but then Janet said, "Oh, can I ask you about one more thing?"

"Have I ever denied you anything?"

"Not yet," she laughed. "Do you know anything about the Resolution Trust Corporation's $1 million lawsuit against Kirk & Polis?"

"Nope," I replied, thinking about all the phone calls Jeffreys had been making to his office the day the Policy Committee discussed opening an investigation of RTC officials. "Are you kidding?"

"I wouldn't kid about something that serious," Janet said. "Kirk & Polis represented First America Savings Bank in Denver, and it seems that they have been accused of aiding and abetting some of the criminal activity that led to the failure."

"Very interesting," I said. "When was the suit filed?"

"I believe it was in March of '93, but I'd have to check. Just thought you might have heard Jeffreys mention it."

"No, like I said, we don't talk about much except the investigation."

"Well, I just thought it might have come up. It sounds like the same thing I understand your office is looking into regarding the Bankhead firm's representation of Jefferson Savings," she said. "Would you tell me if you knew something?"

"No comment," I replied, sounding like Jo Gobles. "You know I can't discuss the details of our investigation." Of course, I didn't know anything. But I knew a lot more after our conversation than I did before Janet called.

Later that week Phyllis Sanford told me that Jeffreys would be back in the state on Monday. He planned to be in Montgomery for Lieutenant Governor Coughlin's inauguration and to talk with some people at the Bank Department. He'd be back in Birmingham on Wednesday, or I could meet with him in Montgomery if I thought it couldn't wait. I told her I'd see him in Montgomery. I didn't tell her that I couldn't wait to see Lindsey again. I left on Friday afternoon so I'd be sure to have a better attitude for my meeting with Jeffreys.

I called Jeffreys on Monday morning at the number Phyllis had given me, and it turned out to be the Madison Hotel. It figured that he would be staying there. It was the biggest and most expensive hotel in town, and it had all the warmth and charm of a post office. I dispensed with the usual pleasantries and said, "I need to talk with you about something fairly important. What's your schedule like today?"

"Yes, Phyllis said you'd be calling. I'm attending a luncheon with some local dignitaries at the Capon Club, but I'm free until then," Jeffreys replied. "Would you like to come by here sometime this morning?"

Why did Jeffreys feel he had to boast about his lunch meeting? Local dignitaries? He probably meant Grenier and Coughlin. The Capon Club was on the top floor of one of the downtown bank buildings, and it was the home court of the Alabama Poultry Federation. Jeffreys would feel right at home among the lobbyists, at least until he saw how much free whiskey was flowing. "Sure," I said, "I'll come by about 10 o'clock if that's okay."

"That will be fine," Jeffreys said. "I'm at the Madison. Oh, you already know that. Suite 525."

Jeffreys answered the door already wearing a suit and tie, and he seemed offended that I showed up in Levi's and an old sweater. Probably the boots that got to him. "Well I must say, Mr. Wilkes, you look like that little cowboy statue down there," he said, sounding as if he were auditioning to play the Church Lady.

I stepped over the room service trays and walked into the suite. "Nice digs, George. I'm glad to see the taxpayers are keeping you in the style to which you have become accustomed," I said. Surveying the room and looking out the window toward the Civic Auditorium below, I couldn't repress a smile. There in the middle of Lister Hill Plaza was the Hank Williams statue. Little Cowboy, indeed.

Appearing impatient, Jeffreys quickly asked, "What is it you wish to discuss, pray tell, that's so important it couldn't wait until Wednesday? Phyllis said you seemed upset. I certainly hope it's nothing I've done."

"It's something you haven't done," I said. "Would you mind explaining why we're busting folks for being active in politics? When did it become a federal crime to give someone a ride to vote? And where was I when the Policy Committee decided to do it? Maybe I don't understand how you're making decisions in this investigation. Mind explaining that to me?"

I could see that Jeffreys was irritated. He stammered then said, "I think it's very important, in light of the nature of the office and my professional reputation, to provide through a deliberative process, a careful evaluative process, a judgment that is hopefully sober, that is serious and the product of a professional process."

"Yeah? I don't remember any careful decisions being made to start busting black preachers and members of their congregations whose only offense was to support Cannon in the 1990 governor's race," I said. "I must have missed that professional process."

"I will not stand here and have you question my integrity," Jeffreys whined. "What I have instituted, as I have told you before, is a very careful, elaborate, deliberative process. It's not the judgment of one individual, Mr. Wilkes. It's not up to you to decide. It is the judgment of a group of professionals who've taken an oath of office and who take that oath seriously. You were well aware that our office was looking into past campaign practices, and I do not think Mr. Gedney has any obligation to clear his procedures with you. He is an experienced prosecutor with an outstanding record of securing convictions for political corruption. You can't question success."

"Really? I think I can," I said emphatically. "And I think you should. How many Republicans has he ever indicted? You're absolutely right that Gedney doesn't have to clear anything with me, but we all have an obligation to comply with the commands of the constitution. As I recall, that was part of the oath I took. Did you happen to read the quote from Justice Black when we were at the courthouse last month? Probably not. 'The Constitution is my legal bible. I cherish every word of it, from the first to the last, and I personally deplore even the slightest deviation from its least important commands,' he said so eloquently, and I feel the same way."

I could see that Jeffreys had been paying little attention when he asked, "So, what are you saying?"

"I'm telling you, as plainly as I know how, that I cannot condone and will not be a party to Gedney's draconian tactics. Either you rein him in on this, or I'm out of here. It's your call."

"There is no need to make such threats, and you would be well advised not to overestimate your importance to this office," Jeffreys chided, but he also appeared to understand that I would not go quietly. "That said, I believe I understand your position, and I do not wish for our internal discussions to become the issue. You must remember that there are no civilians in this war for the political soul of our nation, but I will encourage Mr. Gedney to be more circumspect in his pursuit of the facts. Should you still have concerns, we can discuss it further at the Policy Committee next Monday, but I really must be going now. I don't wish to keep my hosts waiting."

Whatever Jeffreys said to Gedney seemed to work. I doubted that my threat to quit had much effect, but I suspect Jeffreys realized that exposure of his tactics would be a public relations disaster and a serious blotch on his precious image. The next Policy Committee meeting, though, only confirmed my feelings about Jeffreys and the entire Whirlpool investigation. It was showtime again. The boys had tasted blood with the Webster plea, and they were becoming addicted to the printer's ink. They wanted headlines, and they had seen how easy it was to get massive national attention with piss ant charges. I knew I'd pushed Jeffreys about as far as I could last week, so I was prepared to keep my anger in check that day. As it turned out, it was more difficult to keep from laughing at them.

Jeffreys came bouncing into the conference a few minutes late, along with James Peck and John Hathorne. They had been huddled in Jeffreys' office all morning, so I assumed that they had been rehearsing their lines for whatever we'd be discussing. Jeffreys opened the meeting with an update on the Washington office activities. The grand jury would be hearing testimony regarding the death of Hal Goodall and White House staff actions in removing and reassigning his files. He also reported that he had several productive meetings with Senator Diletto and Congressman Leech regarding their planned hearings on Whirlpool matters. They were, he said, more than willing to coordinate their work with ours, and he would continue to work out the details on timing.

Then, with a self-satisfied smile, Jeffreys crowed, "We were making major progress with our investigation here, and I want you to know that our efforts are very much appreciated, not only by the American people but also by the decent element in this state as well. I spent several days in Montgomery last week, and I cannot tell you how many people offered encouraging words of support for what we are doing."

Let me guess, I thought to myself. Two? Nelson Grenier and Gerald Elkay Coughlin? Maybe more, since Jeffreys had been given an honorary membership in the Capon Club and had been rubbing elbows with all of the lobbyists and corporate executives who roosted there during the inaugural festivities.

"I want to express my appreciation to each of you for your contribution to moving this investigation forward so quickly," Jeffreys continued, "and I especially want to congratulate Mr. Peck and Mr. Hathorne for their outstanding efforts. Rather than spoil it, I'd like to ask them share the good news."

I could hardly wait. James Peck went first. He appeared so proud of himself when he announced that he had negotiated the first guilty plea related to Jefferson Savings. I thought he must've had Josh Banaghan arrested on the operating table, but that wasn't quite it. Instead, John Cartwright, a local real estate appraiser, had agreed to plead to one felony count of conspiracy for signing some back-dated appraisals for home mortgage loans.

After five months on the case, the only thing Peck had discovered was a batch of misdated appraisals in the residential loan files at Jefferson. None of the appraisals were inflated to support dubious loans, but they had been done after the loans had been approved and placed in the files later. Not what I would call a major crime. Peck had labored mightily and brought forth a mouse.

The reaction at the table startled me. Jeffreys smiled and patted Peck on the shoulder, and everyone else applauded as if we'd solved the crime of the century. Peck beamed. "Thank you," Peck said, "but I couldn't have done it alone. I'm especially indebted to you, Bart. I took a page from your book. The guy has two sons in college, and I told him we'd go easy on him if he would plead guilty. Piece of cake, my man."

Jeffreys seemed worried that he might be missing out on the credit, so he jumped in with claims of his own. "I believe Mr. Cartwright is genuinely contrite and sorrowful. It is a good thing that he recognized his wrong and promptly accepted responsibility for his actions."

I was reluctant to say anything, but something wasn't quite right here. "I'm curious about something," I said. "You're charging Cartwright with conspiracy, right? Who else was in on this conspiracy? And why aren't we filing charges against them as well?"

Both Jeffreys and Peck appeared annoyed. They didn't seem to appreciate any questions, especially that one. The smiles left their faces. Peck reluctantly said, "He conspired with Nick Biddle, the senior loan officer at Jefferson. We plan to grant immunity to Mr. Biddle in exchange for his testimony on other matters."

"Seems to me that you might be charging the wrong man in this case," I replied. "I'm not sure this is even a case that requires prosecution by our office, but, if it is, why are we charging the appraiser who signed the forms and granting immunity to the loan officer who induced him to do it? And if you can get a plea agreement requiring Cartwright to cooperate, why do you need to grant immunity to Mr. Biddle?"

Peck started to reply, but Jeffreys cut him short and said, "Mr. Biddle could be especially useful to us. He also participated in some business transactions involving Diane Cannon and the Bankhead law firm. We believe that he might agree to provide some very important testimony in the future, and filing a felony charge against him could complicate matters. He will cooperate. I think that's all that needs to be said at this point."

I wasn't sure if that meant Biddle would agree to manufacture testimony to fit our needs or if they were afraid that a felony conviction would make him less believable before a jury. I was sure it would be a waste of time to ask for a clarification.

John Hathorne had been waiting patiently on the bench, so Jeffreys turned to him and asked him to share his good news. "You'll all be pleased to know that we are also on the verge of our first felony conviction related to the Whirlpool Estates project. By the end of this week, I expect to file a felony information charging Bill Godwin, a Double Springs real estate agent who sold some of the Whirlpool lots back in the late '70s, with bankruptcy fraud. Mr. Godwin and his wife filed for bankruptcy five years ago, and he failed to list all of his accounts receivable as assets at that time on the forms."

Smiling at Jeffreys, Hathorne said, "We're getting a lot of use out of that old 'family values' hammer of yours. I picked it up and hit Godwin right between the eyes. Told him we were going to indict both him and his wife. The next day, he agreed to plead guilty to two felonies if we wouldn't charge his wife."

More cheering followed Hathorne's report. I didn't applaud, but I didn't raise any objections. I still agreed with Burke's position that these cases were ones that could be handled by the local U. S. Attorney and did not need an Independent Counsel. They had nothing to do with the Cannons or any other federal officials. But Jeffreys wanted to score some points, and he could get the indictments if he wanted. And, of course, he did.

The strategy was also routine practice, even if the tactics weren't. Jeffreys called it his "bottom-up" strategy. Prosecutors always start out with the small fry, get them to enter plea agreements on minor charges, then compel their testimony against bigger fish. In these two cases, however, the defendants weren't even small fry. After two years and three special prosecutors, what they had were minnows.

Once again, though, Jeffreys played the charges for all they were worth and then some. He leaked word to the press, and Tuesday's papers had stories quoting "sources close to the investigation" that indictments were near. On Wednesday, Jeffreys orchestrated another "court packing" drill for the Cartwright plea, and the media fell for it once again. It was the lead story on the network news that evening, and the next day's headlines read, "Cannon Denies Involvement as Jeffreys Scores Conviction in Jefferson Savings Scandal."

To allow the Sunday editorials full attention to the Cartwright conviction yet to maintain the appearance of momentum, Jeffreys scheduled the Godwin plea for the following Monday. They stayed with the same formula that had worked so well to exaggerate the Webster and Cartwright pleas: leaking advance word that something big was about to happen, making a major courtroom production of a minor plea, gagging the defendants to prevent them from talking to the media, holding a press conference outside the courthouse, and getting a free shot to spin the story to make us look good.

Despite such manipulative scheming, I didn't see how anyone could believe a routine bankruptcy plea was going to play in Peoria. Godwin's only connection to Whirlpool was that he had sold some lots there 16 years ago. The charges had nothing to do with Cannon. Those facts, however, did not stop Jeffreys from playing to the press. After the plea, Jeffreys assumed his usual position at the podium that Jo Gobles always set up outside the courthouse. As cameras rolled, he read from prepared statement. "Bill Godwin, a key figure in the complex Whirlpool affair, has pleaded guilty to bankruptcy fraud and agreed to cooperate with the Independent Counsel's ongoing investigation of politics and business in Alabama."

Not wanting to take any chances that the reporters would overlook his accomplishments, Jeffreys pointed out, "Mr. Godwin is the sixth person to plead guilty to felony charges and agree to cooperate with the Whirlpool investigation. The others are John Cartwright, owner of a Birmingham appraisal company; Randolph Webster, a former associate attorney general appointed by President Cannon and a colleague of Diane Cannon at Montgomery's Bankhead law firm; Roby Douglas, a former Birmingham traffic judge and owner of Financial Management Services; and two associates of Judge Douglas who conspired with him to defraud the Small Business Administration."

No one questioned Jeffreys on his claim of credit for six felony convictions. The press would report anything he said and ignore the fact that three of the individuals were indicted by Mary Beech Gould, the local United States Attorney, before there was any special prosecutor or a Whirlpool investigation. But Jeffreys statements would not go unchallenged. He'd been very clever in gagging all the defendants, but he forgot one thing. He couldn't silence their lawyers, who sometimes felt the need to tell the truth.

While Jeffreys was holding forth for his admirers in the press, Eric Emory, Bill Godwin's attorney, walked out of the courthouse and stopped to listen. When Jeffreys had finished his performance, the reporters turned to Emory for a response. Jeffreys looked nervous as the microphones were jerked away from his little podium and thrust toward Emory.

I could tell I liked Emory when he answered the first question. One of the blow-dried boys asked, "Mr. Emory, what can you tell us about Mr. Godwin's plea today?"

"What is it about the plea that you don't understand? You were all there," Emory said. "My client has entered a plea of guilty to concealing some assets during a bankruptcy proceeding six years ago."

"Did you advise Mr. Godwin to plead guilty rather than going to trial?"

"I'd have welcomed the chance to defend my client in court, and not just because I could bill more hours. He was unaware of the technical requirements regarding accounts receivable, but he agreed to plead guilty after the Office of Independent Counsel threatened to bring charges against his wife. That's all I think I should say about his decision."

"Judge Jeffreys called Mr. Godwin is a key player in the Whirlpool investigation. Will he be offering testimony incriminating President Cannon?"

Emory came alive with that question and said, "This doesn't have jack shit to do with President Cannon. As far as I know and my client knows, neither the president nor the first lady have any criminal exposure concerning their involvement in the Whirlpool real estate development. As to what Mr. Jeffreys was talking about when he said Bill Godwin will be cooperating with his investigation, I have no idea what he meant. You'll have to ask him."

With that comment, the gaggle of reporters turned back to Jeffreys. One of them shouted, "Does Godwin have any information that would implicate the Cannons?"

At last, a good question. Jeffreys saw me staring at him, and I continued to do so, wondering if he would stick with the lie. "I'm not going to comment on the importance of his testimony," he said. "The point is that the investigation is active, it's ongoing, it is at a critical juncture, and Mr. Godwin is cooperating. Thank you very much."

Jeffreys hardly said a word as we drove back to the office. Someone had finally called his bluff in public, and he had not handled it well. His lack of trial experience was already evident, but his lack of experience on the hustings was only beginning to show. He had lost a minor media battle, not the war. Superior air power in the form of television news and heavy artillery in the form of newspaper editorials would provide the political cover to protect his weak ground forces. His position was safe for now.

Once again, the networks gave the story prominent play that evening, and the *Washington Sun* proclaimed, "Jeffreys Gets Conviction of Another Key Whirlpool Figure, Testimony Could Link Cannon." The stringers for the *New York Times* and the *Washington Post* provided a similar slant. It was our version all the way. No one noticed that the emperor was naked. There was no mention of the telling exchange between Jeffreys and Emory. I wondered why editors even bothered to assign reporters to cover the pleas and arraignments. Maybe they enjoyed the circus atmosphere we were providing. If facts were unimportant, they could save considerable time and money by reprinting the press releases from our office. Some of them did. The screaming pundits and the ranting editorial columnists, in turn, took their facts from the news columns. The result was nonsense, nonsense upon stilts.

February can be a crazy time in the South, even crazier than usual. Hard to explain, but there's a lot of weirdness in Alabama in February. Always has been, I guess. The Confederate States of America was founded at Montgomery in February 1861. Alabama was now once again up in arms to defend Southern womanhood. An Alabama woman was the reigning Miss America, the social equivalent of an Alabama boy having been elected president. Some national group had criticized her recently for talking too much, and the local community rose to her defense. They'd done the same thing when the pundits said Cannon's speeches were too long. And they were again getting pretty tired of the national media attacking Cannon and everything about their state.

Washington politics became even more bizarre now that the Republicans controlled both the House and the Senate. Leroy Reichman was even farther out on the fringe than before, aided and abetted by the new crop of GOP reactionaries. Ira Dolor announced that he wanted to run for president again. Gastone Diletto got his wish for a Special Committee on Whirlpool and an extra million dollars for committee staff to dig dirt and badger the White House.

Perhaps the major irony was Senator Reynolds Rantallion's call for Jeffreys to investigate whether the Department of Interior had hired Randolph Webster's wife as a ploy to buy his silence. Obstruction of justice, he said it was. Webster had been interviewed by our office 12 times since his plea in December, and he had not provided one ounce of evidence we could use or made a single accusation against President or Mrs. Cannon. It never occurred to Rantallion—or Jeffreys for that matter—that the lack of incriminating information might be because none existed and Webster insisted on telling the truth.

Anyway, I finally had a small victory on the Policy Committee in February. When Jeffreys asked for a motion to open an investigation of Mrs. Webster's hiring, I offered one to open an investigation of Senator Rantallion for hiring of Judge Chase's wife as a receptionist. It would only be fair, I suggested, and it would answer any critics who might think it was a payoff to Judge Chase for naming Jeffreys as Independent Counsel. My motion died for the lack of a second, but no one offered one to investigate the hiring of Webster's wife. It was a short meeting.

My sense of victory was also short. Quite by accident, I later learned that Jeffreys had authorized our Washington office staff to question the Secretary of Interior, White House aides, and Mrs. Webster about the circumstances of the job offer. The investigation came to nothing, like most of the false scents we'd been chasing. The only result had been additional legal bills and a little misery for those questioned and smeared by rumor. That and our office taking the taxpayers for another $20,000 ride down a rat hole.

I'd been in Birmingham now for a year, but it seemed like much longer. What had I accomplished? What had I done to make the world a better place? Not much on either count. In many ways I felt like I was making things worse.

Chapter Nineteen

As the Whirlpool investigation continued into March, the first jonquils of spring provided a bright counterpoint to the drabness that had been winter. In much the same way, weekends with Lindsey had helped overcome the routine ennui of my job. The previous weekend Mark Lester and Jeanne Jackson had joined us in celebrating the opening of the Magic City Brewery, the first brew pub in Birmingham since prohibition. The beer wasn't too bad, and it was good getting to spend some time with old friends. My time with Lindsey was magic, as always.

Even Jeffreys seemed to be enjoying himself whenever he was in Birmingham. Nelson Grenier had given him a membership in the Shoal Creek Country Club, a significant unreported gratuity, and he spent considerable time on the tennis courts there. Otherwise he was occupied making big bucks at Kirk & Polis in Washington, serving on the boards of numerous conservative groups around the country, and teaching a course in Christian Legal Ethics at Hostus University.

Bart Gedney and I had reached an unspoken agreement to stay out of each other's face, but the monthly Policy Committee meeting threatened that truce. The March meeting was devoted almost entirely to Gedney's investigation of the 1990 election. I still got angry every time I thought about it. Jeffreys should never have requested the assignment, Attorney General Otis should have had the courage to just say no, and Judge Chase should never have granted the authority. Guess I shouldn't have been surprised. Jeffreys was on a mission, and Chase had his orders. And Otis didn't have the guts to make a good mess of chittlins.

The investigation of Cannon's last race for governor had nothing to do with our original mandate. It was little more than a political vendetta, undertaken only to satisfy Nelson Grenier, assuage his wounded pride from having his butt kicked at the polls, and reward him for stirring up the Whirlpool mirage as a political issue in the first place. There are certain benefits one receives from being on the Republican National Committee and writing big checks.

The entire Gedney phase of the investigation had been marked by malice. The outrageous harassment of black voters was the only part of the operation that had come to the public attention, but hardly anyone outside Alabama was aware of it. The national media had ignored the story entirely. It was becoming clear, though, that the whole enterprise bordered on selective prosecution. Gedney had pursued it for six months, enlisting six staff attorneys, two paralegals, nine FBI agents, and three IRS agents. Finally, he was ready to reveal what he had found.

Jeffreys made a few housekeeping announcements, then he leaned back and turned the meeting over to Bart Gedney. Standing up as he distributed copies of his report, Gedney said, "This is the most extensive criminal investigation in which I have ever participated. I have been exceedingly thorough, because one does not go after the President of the United States lightly. If you strike the king, you must kill him. You will recall that we began, as Judge Jeffreys directed, by comparing every political appointment with every reported campaign contribution. Obviously, there were too many matches to prosecute them all, so we examined the political background of each donor and narrowed our focus."

The focus was only on Democrats, of course. Always trying to make a connection to Cannon, Gedney explained, "We started with the high profile politicians and party officials. Frank McManus is a former chair of the Democratic State Committee, but, as you know, he now works at the White House. We decided to let Diletto and The Committee deal with him. Dan Rutherford, the political consultant, is also a former Democratic party chairman and a major Cannon contributor. Finally had to give up on him, though. Couldn't find anything. He's so clean his butt squeaks when he walks."

Bart Gedney had shown his hand. He wasn't trying to solve a crime by finding a criminal, he was trying to find a crime with which to charge the president and his friends. That's always a problem any time a special prosecutor is appointed and given unrestricted powers and an unlimited budget. It was especially so when political wannabees like George Jeffreys are appointed.

Continuing his report, Gedney announced with some fanfare, "Today, I am prepared to seek a grand jury indictment against John Reeves on felony charges of failing to file Currency Transaction Reports with the Internal Revenue Service. Mr. Reeves is the former president of the Perry State Bank in Marion, Alabama. He is, of course, only the first domino. He resigned under pressure last year, and now he runs a little convenience store in Marion. He's still pretty bitter about that. We think he'll roll over and implicate the owners of the bank, both of whom are part of the Cannon political machine."

Gedney then revealed the criteria that had led him to select which Democrats he wanted to prosecute. Pausing for effect, he said, "The first target is C. A. Jones, an attorney who was state chairman of the Alabama Democratic Party for six years and who was appointed by Cannon to the state Highway Commission. The other target is Joe Hill, an accountant who is also chairman of the Perry County Democratic Committee and who was appointed by Cannon to the state Bank Board. We plan to show that they conspired to conceal large cash withdrawals and bought their appointments with campaign contributions, in effect bribing Governor Cannon."

"Now, here's where it gets good," Gedney leered. "Robert Bruce, Deputy White House Counsel, was Cannon's campaign treasurer in 1990. He negotiated two very timely campaign loans at the Perry State Bank, allowing last-minute media buys and saving the election for Cannon. Bruce also initiated two large cash withdrawals for so-called election day expenses. Neither of these cash transactions were reported to the IRS. We are prepared to argue that Bruce conspired with Jones and Hill to violate federal law, and we believe that Mr. Reeves can be induced to provide that testimony. At the very least we can get an indictment against one of Cannon's most trusted aides. At best, we might even get Cannon."

Jeffreys was delighted. His cheeks swelled as he tried not to break out in that goofy grin. "Well done, Mr. Gedney. Excellent work. Now we're getting somewhere."

John Hathorne immediately moved to seek the indictments, and it was simultaneously seconded by James Peck and Mitch Palmer. Jeffreys quickly surveyed the table before calling for the vote, then he must have remembered our confrontation in Montgomery. He looked at me and asked, "Is there any discussion before we vote?"

Gedney was still standing with his arms folded across his chest. He sneered in my direction as he quipped, "I'd bet Wilkes will want to speak against it."

"Well, Bart, you'd be wrong once again," I replied. "I'd like to be recorded as voting against any indictments in this case, but I've opposed this aspect of the investigation from the beginning. I believe it's beyond our authority."

Jeffreys bristled at that last remark. "No," he interjected, "I have received specific authorization from Judge Chase to pursue this phase of our work."

"I'm sorry," I said, "I failed to make myself clear. I meant to suggest it was beyond our moral authority."

"Oh, now Wilkes wants to be our conscience," Gedney snapped. "Well, let me tell you something, Wilkes. Conscience is but a word that cowards use, devised by sissy liberals to keep the strong in awe. Judge Chase's order is our conscience, and indictments are our arms."

I ignored Bart's outburst, hoping that would let him know what I thought of his opinion. Only Mitch appeared to have any interest in listening to what I had to say, so I kept it short. "I'm well aware that this motion is going to pass, but I just have a couple of questions. First, I'd be interested in knowing who the victim is here, other than Nelson Grenier. Why would Cannon or the bank try to hide the withdrawal of funds from the IRS? What's the motive? The jury will be interested in that question, too, I imagine. Second, do you really believe these guys had to bribe Cannon for their appointments? They've been friends for twenty years. I don't think you can find a jury in the state that will buy your theory."

No one answered. No one said anything. Gedney glared at me for a moment then turned to Jeffreys and said, "Let's vote."

Jeffreys wasn't smiling now. "The ayes have it," he said rather firmly. "Mr. Wilkes will be recorded as voting in the negative." With that, the meeting was adjourned.

As usual, the rest of the group huddled to savor their victory. I was almost to the door when Bart Gedney shouted, "Hey, Wilkes. Veni, vidi, vici. Or as we say in Tennessee, it's our way or the highway."

"Heus, Podex," I replied, "futue te ipsum et caballum tuum." Gedney just stood there with his mouth open and a blank look on his face, like he was waiting for the Texas translation. I doubt if he ever figured it out, but I really had nothing against the horse he rode in on.

Things did not go according to plan with Reeves. Gedney threatened to indict him, expecting the usual plea bargain, but Reeves proclaimed his innocence and said he'd see us in court. The old "family values" tactic didn't work this time, since Reeves had no children nor could we threaten to charge his wife. It was time to put up or pack up, but Jeffreys and Gedney had little trouble getting the grand jury to indict Reeves. Prosecutors can almost always get an indictment, because the grand jury hears only one side of the story, the one the prosecutor wants them to hear. But, I think this particular group would have issued an indictment against Mother Teresa if Jeffreys had wanted one.

At the arraignment, Reeves appeared physically exhausted, and he entered his "not guilty" plea so softly that it could hardly be heard above the snickering from the press section. Outside the courthouse, Reeves' lawyer, Alferd Packer, had plenty to say. Felony indictments sometimes have that effect. Packer told anyone who would listen, "They've got the wrong man. My client was just the hired help at the bank. They ought to be going after the Democrats, the owners of the bank and the people who withdrew the cash." That was a public proffer and about the clearest pitch I'd ever heard for a deal. Packer had just told Jeffreys to go easy on Reeves and he would be willing to blame others. Packer knew exactly what to do, because his law partner Adam Tiler had played the same game in cutting a deal for Roby Douglas. And Jeffreys understood, because that was exactly what he wanted.

It took over a month to get the details worked out with Reeves and his lawyer. They refused to consider pleading to a felony, and even Gedney finally had to admit that he'd have trouble getting a conviction if we had to go to trial. Then someone suggested that if Reeves could provide testimony damaging to Cannon or Robert Bruce, we might consider reducing the charges to misdemeanors. That seemed to refresh Reeves' memory. Finally, after about six sessions with Gedney and Hathorne to get the story right, Reeves agreed to plead to a couple of misdemeanors. Hardly the stuff of headlines, but Jeffreys would be able to claim another conviction.

Once again, I had to admit my ignorance about politics and the press. I got another lesson in life that week. We all trotted down to the courthouse for the usual court-packing charade, and it was like old home week. Jeffreys conned the media once again, and it mattered not that Reeves had been charged only with misdemeanor counts. Jo Gobles couldn't have written better headlines. "Plea Gives Jeffreys Seventh Conviction; Reeves Expected to Implicate Robert Bruce in Whirlpool Scandal; Democrats Fear Additional Indictments Reaching White House," blared the *Washington Sun*.

The *Washington Post* was just as compliant as the *Washington Sun*. Stephen Latrator's article in the *New York Times* was the most shameless pandering, skipping the details of the plea to proclaim, "An Alabama banker has told Whirlpool prosecutors that Robert Bruce, President Cannon's most trusted aide and now the deputy White House counsel, directed him to illegally conceal cash payments to Mr. Cannon's 1990 campaign for governor, sources involved in the investigation said today." Jeffreys had enlisted yet another lapdog.

By the end of March, Jeffreys' prolonged assault on Alabama was starting to have the desired effect. Senator Howell Heflin announced that he would not run for reelection in 1996. Lieutenant Governor Coughlin let it be known that he was very interested in being the next United States Senator from Alabama, and Gastone Diletto pledged that the Republican Senatorial Campaign Committee would make the Alabama race a high priority. The Democrats would have a difficult time holding the seat as long as the state was under siege by Jeffreys and by Diletto's Senate Whirlpool Committee. They had so poisoned the political environment, it was difficult to imagine any Democrat wanting to run for office. And, as long as every campaign loan, every campaign donor, and every political supporter was subject to the harassment of OIC subpoenas, the Democrats would have an even harder time competing financially with the Republicans.

While I was enjoying my weekends with Lindsey and always learned much from her perspective, there were few other people I could talk to, certainly no one in the office. I was frequently in bad need of a reality check. I was trying to keep my law faculty friendships separate from my work, and I didn't want to get into a situation where I might violate the required confidentiality. Not with colleagues at the law school anyway. I'd met some interesting people since moving to Birmingham, but most of the ones I'd be friends with were active in Democratic politics. Or suspects in Jeffreys' political games. Same thing most of the time.

I missed the regular talks Sean and I had at The Mill. I missed the regular clarity of a couple of beers. And I missed just hanging out with the guys. I called Mark Lester and practically begged him to go get a beer. We ended up at the Savoy listening to some good jazz, but mostly I listened to Mark as he kept me entertained with stories of Alabama history and politics. It was good talking with him, and it was necessary therapy for me. I brought him home early and sober and thanked Jeanne for allowing me to borrow her husband for the evening. She was graceful, and I was grateful.

The Policy Committee met again on April 1st to consider whether to bring charges against anyone who had been involved with loans from Roby Douglas and Financial Management Services. Burke had gone over the same ground last year and decided to refer the files to the local United States Attorney for a decision. He said there was no evidence that the Cannons had any contact with Douglas, despite the questionable accusations made by Douglas in trying to save himself and please his financial benefactors.

Jeffreys took a different view, and he had assigned James Peck and John Hathorne to reopen the investigation. They had identified numerous persons with political connections, and I was curious as to what recommendations they might make regarding prosecutions by our office. I wasn't very excited about giving up a Saturday for a meeting that could have just as well been held on Monday, but I didn't think it would last too long. I didn't have to wait more than a few minutes to find out what was up—or to see the clear pattern driving those decisions.

Jeffreys asked John Hathorne to distribute copies of the prosecution memorandum, and we took a few minutes to review it. James Peck was the lead Associate Counsel on the Financial Management investigation, so he made the oral presentation. "Roby Douglas has been very helpful in fingering those persons who borrowed funds from his company, and we couldn't have developed this case without his testimony," Peck said.

"He identified a number of people in what we like to call the 'political family' in Alabama. Now that you've had a chance to examine our memorandum, I'd like to go over those recommendations briefly to get your advice."

First, Peck said, "Les Bobbitt received loans from Financial Management Services for an entity called Liberty Mortgage, which was purportedly a mortgage-service company. One loan was for $275,000 and another was for $20,000, of which about $14,000 is in default, but neither was used for the mortgage company. Bobbitt also drafted legal opinions to the Small Business Administration to help Douglas in his scheme to secure additional SBA funds. Bobbitt is a former state Republican chairman and national committeeman, and he was an unsuccessful Republican candidate for Congress in 1982. We recommend taking no action against Bobbitt."

That was fine by me. I didn't think we should be prosecuting anyone other than Douglas, so my vote made it unanimous.

Jeffreys winked at Peck and asked him to continue. "Next," Peck said, "Roby Douglas reported that he made a $150,000 loan commitment to a friend by the name of Ken Clayton in 1986, but we can find no further records regarding a loan to Clayton. Douglas bought a little burial insurance company in 1985, Capital Savings Burial Insurance Co., and he named his old friend Clayton to the board of directors. As you know, Douglas is currently under investigation by the Alabama Insurance Department for a fraudulent infusion of $150,000 capital into the insurance company after he depleted the assets. Ken Clayton was the unsuccessful Republican nominee for governor in 1974 and later an unsuccessful candidate for Congress. He was also the state Republican party chairman during the late 1980s and early '90s. We recommend taking no further action against Ken Clayton."

Again, I joined a unanimous vote in support of the recommendation. Jeffreys then announced that he was also working quietly to try to stop the state authorities from prosecuting Douglas for defrauding the state insurance department. I was surprised by that and asked, "Why are we trying to protect Douglas from charges unrelated to our investigation? That wasn't part of our plea agreement with him. He already got relief for the other federal felony counts."

Jeffreys' face became flushed, and his cheeks were bright red when he replied curtly, "Obstruction of justice by intimidating a federal witness."

"Whatever you think," I replied, "but someone might suggest that our office is the one obstructing justice by interfering with a state criminal investigation." That was the end of the conversation, and Jeffreys commanded Peck to proceed with his report.

"Third," Peck continued, "Boyce O'Toole is a Birmingham businessman and was president of a company known as Liquid Assets, Inc. In November 1988 Douglas wired $300,000 into an account that O'Toole controlled, and he wrote checks for $250,000 from it to two men who were convicted of conspiring with Douglas to defraud the SBA. He told our investigators that while he was the purported owner and president of Liquid Assets, Douglas secretly owned and used the firm as a front to drain money illegally from Financial Management Services. O'Toole was an unsuccessful Republican candidate for the state legislature in 1992. We recommend against bringing any charges against Mr. O'Toole."

Once more, we unanimously accepted Peck's recommendation. The process was going much more smoothly than I had anticipated, and I began thinking about a quick trip to Montgomery for dinner with Lindsey.

"The next loan is a bit more interesting," Peck said. "It will give you an insight as to how politics works in Alabama. Municipal Judge Ed Dohemy and his law partner, Richard M. Gamon, were involved in several financial deals with Douglas. In 1986, Douglas admitted making a $60,000 loan commitment to Gamon, and we have evidence regarding a $10,000 loan from Financial Management Services to Gamon's law firm for operating expenses, although the money was used for other purposes."

I was ready to vote again, but Peck wasn't finished. It was a bit more interesting. After a deep breath, Peck added, "Dohemy told us that Douglas, who was appointed to his judgeship by former Republican Governor Durwood Dilberry in 1981, suggested that he divert $2,000 of the proceeds of the SBA loan into Dilberry's unsuccessful 1986 campaign for governor against Cannon. Dohemy took the funds and made contributions to the Dilberry campaign in the name of the law firm's secretary and her daughter. Mr. Gamon has served as the Jefferson County GOP chairman and was an unsuccessful candidate for judge on the Republican ticket. We recommend taking no action against Gamon, his secretary, or her daughter."

I was prepared to vote for that, and I moved to amend the recommendation by including Dohemy. Even this slimeball known locally as 'Fast Eddie' did not deserve to have the OIC on him for something that happened almost 10 years ago. Jeffreys insisted that we go ahead and vote on Peck's original recommendation. We did, and it was accepted.

Then, Peck moved that Ed Dohemy be named an unindicted co-conspirator and granted full immunity from prosecution. Something was up, but I wasn't sure what. Jeffreys finally explained, "If we grant him immunity, Dohemy will testify and corroborate the charges that Douglas has made against Cannon regarding another loan."

I realized then I was mistaken to think Jeffreys might take a reasonable approach to the Financial Management case. He knew that Douglas was a liar, bought and paid for, but Jeffreys seemed bent on pursuing anything that might possibly damage Cannon, regardless of the lack of credible evidence. It appeared that Jeffreys and the boys were going to try to support Douglas' unbelievable testimony with that of his unindicted crony, Fast Eddie Dohemy. I decided to wait until we got to the other loans before objecting, and maybe then I'd have more information. I looked at Jeffreys, raised an eyebrow, and said, "Oh, I see."

Peck reached for another file. I thought I detected a slight change in the tone of his voices as he said, "I would now like to direct your attention to John Jebb, a Birmingham attorney. Mr. Jebb was in charge of Jefferson Savings Bank's real estate operations on Dauphin Island in the early 1980s. In 1986, he borrowed $150,000 from Financial Management Services to open his own real estate firm; however, he used the money to purchase real estate and develop lots adjacent to the Jefferson Savings project on Dauphin Island. This constituted a technical violation of the SBA lending guidelines, and I am recommending that we seek criminal charges. Mr. Jebb was not actively involved in Alabama politics, but he did make a $1,000 contribution to the Cannon for Governor campaign in 1986."

"Wait a minute," I said before Jeffreys could call for a vote. "I don't see how this incident differs from any of those we've already discussed. What makes Mr. Jebb's loan so special that we should become involved? I'd like to offer a substitute motion that the Jebb loan and all of the others be referred to the United States Attorney for a decision. This doesn't have anything to do with President or Mrs. Cannon."

"I think you're missing the big picture, Mr. Wilkes," Jeffreys interjected before I was finished with my objections. "Mr. Jebb's loan is indirectly related to Mr. Banaghan and Jefferson Savings. Surely you recall that was included in the original grant of authority, don't you? You seem to be such a stickler for little details like that."

I quickly flipped through my file folders to find a copy of the original mandate. "Well," I said, "there are a number of details. One I think we should consider is the paragraph that reads, 'To the extent you determine that aspects of these matters which might fall technically within the broad scope of your jurisdiction are not sufficiently related to your mandate to warrant handling by your office, you may refer those aspects back to the Department of Justice for handling.' That's what my motion is intended to do."

My motion died for lack of a second, and I slumped back in my chair to see what else they had on tap for the day. Big picture, my ass. The big picture for Jeffreys was the next election and the improbable dream of a seat on the woolsack. The next two reports made that very clear.

James Peck was on a roll, and he looked directly at me when he said, "I am also recommending that we seek criminal charges against Dr. James Burgh, a professor at the University of Alabama. Dr. Burgh received a $65,000 loan from Financial Management Services in 1986 and violated SBA guidelines by using the proceeds to pay off an existing loan. Mr. Wilkes, you will take note that the existing loan was for a real estate investment in which James Banaghan and Jim Bibb Vance were also involved. I would also point out that Dr. Burgh was a Democratic member of the Alabama House of Representatives in the early 1970s and was one of James Cannon's closest aides, serving on the Alabama Attorney General's staff and in the Governor's Office under Cannon from 1977 until 1980. We think he knows plenty of dirt on Cannon, but he has not been very forthcoming."

I had nothing to say to Peck. I could count votes as well as anyone, and I knew they would prevail. I did not, however, tell them that I had met Burgh and talked briefly with him last year at a reception in Tuscaloosa. Silence can sometimes be a virtue, and I had so few of them I took advantage of that one.

"Hearing no objections," Jeffreys said with an air of satisfaction, "all in favor signify by saying aye, and those opposed by saying no." I was, as always, the lone vote against our office attempting to bring charges.

"Now," Peck preened, "the one you've all been waiting for—Governor Jim Bibb Vance! Vance was an attorney in private practice during the 1980s, and he was also involved in numerous financial ventures. He received a loan from Financial Management Services for purchasing and operating capital for a cable television company, then he used the funds to purchase an additional cable system. In the process, he structured the deal so as to significantly reduce his tax liability, and I'm recommending that we seek felony indictments against Governor Vance for submitting a false loan application and conspiracy to avoid taxes."

After the shouting and applause died down, I indicated I wanted to speak against the motion. The smile disappeared from Jeffreys' face and he asked, "What is it this time, Wilkes?"

That was the first time Jeffreys had addressed me by anything other than Mr. Wilkes. No doubt he now questioned the value of keeping me on the policy committee. I know I questioned whether it was worth it, myself. But that didn't prevent me from trying to slow the prosecutorial juggernaut, even if I couldn't stop it. At least I could hold up the mirror, and they'd have to admit how morally bankrupt they had become.

"Not wanting to bore you with little details," I said, mocking Jeffreys' earlier remarks, "I'd like to point out that this transaction has nothing to do with our original authority, absolutely nothing to do with President or Mrs. Cannon. Hell, Cannon and Vance are political enemies, ran against each other back in 1982. I'd like some explanation of what you think you're doing. Since when has it been illegal to try to reduce one's tax liability? That's the American way. If there is a criminal violation—and I'm not so sure there is in this case—why is it of concern to this office? Vance is not a federal official. Why shouldn't this be referred to the United States Attorney for a decision?"

My questions were met with looks of disgust. After a few seconds, I turned to Mitch and asked, "Can you help me with this one, Mitch?"

Mitch glanced first at Peck, then at Jeffreys, reminding me of a designated runner about to take a lead off the base and looking for a sign. "Well, we are authorized to pursue any other crimes we discover in the course of our investigation, and this is one Roby Douglas brought to our attention. And, frankly, we're going to have to start producing some big political names pretty soon, or it's going to look like we're just down here charging obscure citizens with petty offenses. Since we can't find anything on President Cannon, then . . . ."

Jeffreys stopped Mitch before he could finish the sentence. "Mr. Palmer is quite correct. The Vance transaction is one we discovered during the course of our investigation of Financial Management Services, and we have authority to pursue any charges that might result," Jeffreys said rather curtly.

"Yes," I replied, "Mitch is right. About everything."

Once again, as the meeting was coming to a close, Jeffreys turned to Bart and asked a cryptic question. "Bart, how are things going with our inside source?"

"Just fine," Bart replied. "I've put her in touch with Putnam's lawyers."

I was too tired to begin a new argument about the propriety of our office getting involved with a civil suit outside our jurisdiction. I let that one pass, still oblivious as to the importance of the issue. It seemed unimportant at the time.

The day was already shot, and I didn't go to Montgomery that weekend. I did call Lindsey that evening, hoping her voice and constant enthusiasm would help lift my spirits. It worked again. She also had some wonderful news. Well, it was wonderful for her. She had just been notified of her selection as a White House Fellow for 1995-1996. I was excited for her and managed to disguise how much I would miss her.

I took advantage of the free time on Sunday to write in my journal and to accurately record the conversations and events while they were still fresh in my mind. If I ever decided to publish the true account of what went on inside the Independent Counsel's office, I knew I'd better have it right. The public perceptions and the media spin were so at variance with the truth of Jeffreys' single-minded pursuit of President and Mrs. Cannon, I didn't know if anyone would believe me anyway. But I would know. And I would make sure my kids knew that I had tried to do the right thing.

Lindsey came up to Birmingham on Tuesday with two tickets to a Grateful Dead concert. First time I'd ever been to one, and it was quite an experience. A lot of craziness, but it paled by comparison with the machinations at the office. The only music at OIC was Roby Douglas singing in various keys to whatever tunes Jeffreys and his henchmen were calling on any particular day. It was a work-in-progress, not a finished opera. Every time they'd get a new document that confounded their previous theory, they'd rewrite the scenario and change the plot to account for the conflicting evidence. Sometimes I could only keep up with the shifting tales by reading the next issue of the *American Speculator*.

I admit having a small amount of admiration for their devious minds and their twisted imaginations, but only in degree not in kind. I no longer had any respect for anyone on the Policy Committee. Especially Jeffreys, though I don't think I ever had any respect for him. I saw him for the pious fraud he was from day one. Didn't have much respect left for myself, either.

Chapter Twenty

Good thing for me that Jeffreys wasn't in town much for the rest of the month. He spent much of his time in Washington plotting with Senator Diletto about how to get maximum media coverage for their tandem investigations and conducting another round of interviews with President and Mrs. Cannon, but he spent even more time courting clients and pursuing his private law practice at Kirk & Polis. After missing the first deadline and having to request a 45-day extension, he finally filed his ethics forms listing outside income. More than $1.1 million last year. Mostly from corporate clients, concealing documents and perjured testimony for General Motors in a case of exploding gas tanks and protecting the tobacco industry from official investigations and citizen lawsuits. No wonder he was too busy to file on time. I'd say old Professor Sandefur was earning his keep as an ethics advisor, but perhaps he should be drawing his salary from Kirk & Polis instead of the American people. Ethics advisor! What a joke.

I got another good chuckle when I read that the *Arizona Republican* had just been slapped with a $1 million libel judgment for a political story written by Jay Fuhrman, now the Whirlpool reporter for the *Washington Sun*. His co-conspirators in the press quickly rallied to his defense, and I got an even bigger laugh at their transparent efforts to cover for him—and themselves. The White House press corps almost immediately voted him some dinky award for his attacks on President Cannon and coverage of the Whirlpool story, and the *American Speculator* followed with a similar high honor a few weeks later. I kept waiting for the *Washington Post* to award him the Janet Cooke Prize for Creative Fiction Disguised as News, but I suppose they were saving that distinction for Danielle Leonard's coverage of Whirlpool in the *Post*.

May was a slow news month for the Whirlpool junkies, but there was plenty going on behind the scenes. One Sunday morning Lindsey and I were sitting on my balcony drinking coffee and read the paper when I noticed two very curious classified ad in the *Post-Advertiser*. One read, "Alice, got your memos. Would like to talk. Please call Jay Fuhrman at the *Washington Sun*." My first reaction was to chuckle at the reliable sources and sophisticated techniques employed by the award-winning journalist. The other was equally amusing. "Alice: We got your message, and we would like to hear from you. Call collect. Bruce and Ellen, *Wall Street Record*." Then I remembered my last phone conversation with Janet Fox and made a mental note to call her again about getting copies of the "Alice" memos she had mentioned.

That afternoon Lindsey and I went downtown for the dedication of a new sculpture in Kelly Ingram Park. It was a powerful work by Ronald McDowell, commemorating the courage of the young foot soldiers in the struggle for civil rights in Birmingham. After the ceremony, Lindsey introduced me to Mayor Arrington, and shaking his hand was like a link to history. I tried to say something profound about the sculpture and wanted to ask him about his participation in the events, but I didn't get a chance before others were demanding his attention.

The local resentment toward our investigation, after festering quietly for more than a year, finally surfaced. Governor Vance and his attorneys were the most visible troops in the resistance, publicly challenging Jeffreys and his authority. I could see, too, that Jeffreys was overly sensitive and was deeply offended by anyone questioning his motives or actions.

Buford Boone, one of the lawyers representing Governor Vance, showed up at our offices one morning and asked to speak with Bart Gedney. Mitch Palmer was immediately in my office asking me to sit in on the meeting, and I told him I wouldn't miss it for the world. This, I thought, could be fun. I wasn't wrong. Boone was a lawyer from the old school, and his demeanor was very calm that afternoon as he essentially told Gedney to stick it.

"Governor Vance intends to fight the last two subpoenas we have received from your office," Boone announced. "Mr. Jeffreys appears to be on a fishing expedition, perhaps motivated by his personal financial interests or his political partisanship. Our view on this point is reinforced when we consider Mr. Jeffreys' continuation of a law practice in which he achieves significant financial gain representing tobacco companies that may well consider themselves harmed by the official actions of Governor Vance. We have already provided your office with over 150,000 pages of documents dating back 30 years. Now you have decided to issue additional subpoenas for records from the 1990 campaign, and we think enough is enough."

Bart Gedney was agitated and even more rude than usual. "What is Governor Vance afraid of, Mr. Boone? What is he trying to hide?" His questions seemed all the more infantile because of the contrast with Boone's professional manner.

"Mr. Gedney, I am not here to educate you or to argue with you," Boone explained. "I am here as a matter of professional courtesy to inform you and Mr. Jeffreys that we will not comply with your subpoenas and that we intend to challenge the legal authority of the independent counsel to compel compliance. The only legitimate purpose of the independent counsel's office is to investigate matters related to the executive department that would constitute a conflict for the U.S. attorney. You have yet to indicate even the slightest interest in asking Governor Vance questions about our President, the First Lady, or anyone else in the executive branch of the United States government."

With that, Mr. Boone quietly took his leave, but Bart Gedney continued to shout questions as he followed him down the hall to the front door. It was an embarrassing scene. Gedney was so easily outclassed, I shuddered to think what might happen if we ever got to trial.

The following day, Governor Vance called a news conference in Montgomery and told the capitol press corps that he would not comply with the OIC subpoena. "There comes a point when you really have to draw the line on this sort of thing," Vance said. "I have tried to cooperate with Independent Counsel for the last 18 months, but their political zeal has now exceeded the bounds of both law and decency. The latest subpoena requested any and all records relating to my last two campaigns. I have no doubt that George Jeffreys and Nelson Grenier would like to know how to run a winning campaign, but it is not my job to teach them. Nor will I subject my supporters and contributors to harassment by their prosecution machine. We have reached the point of just saying, 'Wait a minute, what jurisdiction, what authority does George Jeffreys have to constantly harass the people of Alabama?' The answer is none."

Vance's statement stung Jeffreys, probably because he knew it was true. On orders from Jeffreys, Gedney quietly withdrew the subpoenas, avoiding a confrontation with Vance and a court test of the limits of our powers. In addressing the graduating class at Bob Jones University the following week, Jeffreys offered a defense of his motives, protesting, "Not a day goes by that we do not discuss what we are doing, why we are doing it, the impact of what we are doing on others, and who we are going to do it to next." What he didn't say, however, was that he and Gedney often laughed about it when they thought on those things.

In an effort to overcome the loss of face in the showdown with Vance, someone in our office leaked word that Robert Bruce, Deputy White House Counsel, was a target of the grand jury investigation and that an indictment for conspiracy was imminent. So much for Rule 6(e) of the Federal Rules of Criminal Procedure and for the truth. Bruce's attorney, Richmond Fowler, was in our office early the next morning to make his case against indicting his client. I didn't bother to ask Hathorne's permission to attend the meeting. I knew he'd be so concerned with presenting a solid front that he wouldn't ask me to leave.

Fowler opened with a direct refutation of criminal motive, the weakness I'd argued unsuccessfully in the Policy Committee. "My client and I were very concerned by the recent news reports, and I sincerely appreciate your agreeing to hear me on this issue, Mr. Hathorne," Fowler said with that smooth Southern drawl. "We agree with your office that the bank should have filed currency transaction reports, but there is absolutely no reason why Mr. Bruce would have conspired with Mr. Reeves, much less cared whether a report was filed with the I.R.S. The reports are not public documents, and they enjoy the same privacy protection as tax returns. Moreover, the money was used for a legitimate get-out-the-vote campaign, and the Cannon campaign promptly and publicly reported the transactions as required under the Alabama Corrupt Practices Act."

Hathorne was on his own today. It was the first time I'd had a chance to observe him at work without Jeffreys and Gedney to back him up, and he didn't seem as confident as usual. He was less petulant than Gedney, but he still had that irritating tone of condescension that marked the righteous inner circle surrounding Jeffreys. "Be that as it may," Hathorne said, "the fact remains that Mr. Bruce structured the May 25th withdrawal with four checks to avoid the reporting threshold, and Mr. Reeves will testify that your client asked that the transaction not be reported. We believe that the grand jury will find that sufficient to issue an indictment."

Fowler was unperturbed by the posturing. "I assume, of course, that you would allow my client to appear before the grand jury and present his recollection of the events in question," he said.

"Of course," Hathorne replied, " we would expect to have him testify under oath before the grand jury."

I watched with interest as Fowler continued the legal chess match. He was finished taking pawns. Leaning forward and resting his elbows on the conference table, Fowler spoke softly as if he were trying to help Hathorne from embarrassing himself. "If you have examined the history of criminal cases prosecuted under the CTR statute, Mr. Hathorne, you and Mr. Jeffreys know that both the legislative history and the trial record strongly support our position. The CTR law was enacted to detect individuals who try to launder illegal income or to evade taxes. Since 1979, there have been 178 criminal prosecutions for failing to file CTRs. Of these, 163 cases involved evidence of tax evasion or illegal income that the defendant sought to conceal. Of the remainder, only 10 cases in the entire history of the statute involved cash withdrawals, and those also involved questionable cash deposits. In short, the federal government has never charged anyone for legally withdrawing their own money from a bank—and for very good reason. Such a prosecution would serve no valid public policy."

"Well, that's all very interesting, Mr. Fowler, and I am familiar with the facts," Hathorne said unconvincingly. "I will present your arguments to Judge Jeffreys when he and Mr. Gedney return next week, and he will be responsible for the final decision."

"I know Mr. Jeffreys has a reputation for fairness, and that's all my client asks. I do hope you will express my desire that this can all be handled without an unfortunate media circus," Fowler said without any need for emphasis to convey the implicit threat behind his words. Everyone in the room was aware that Fowler had called "check" on the press leaks from our office and was prepared to go public in the same manner that Governor Vance had done earlier.

"I can assure you that no one in this office is responsible for the stories regarding you client's possible indictment," Hathorne protested. Jo Gobles was not in the room at that moment, so, at least technically, it wasn't a lie.

"Of course not, Mr. Hathorne, and I offer you a full apology if I was misunderstood to make such a serious charge of criminal conduct," Fowler said with a charming smile as he belled the cat. "And I trust that Mr. Jeffreys will publicly refute those defamatory rumors at the first opportunity."

Richmond Fowler stood and extended his hand to Hathorne, who had nothing to say. Fowler reached for his hat, nodded to me, and said, "Thank you for your time, gentlemen. I will not keep you any longer."

Later that morning I received an overnight mail package from Janet Fox. I opened it quickly, realizing that she must have been able get a copy of one of the "Alice" memos. That's exactly what it was. The memorandum was dated less than a week ago, and it contained allegations made before the grand jury against Robert Bruce and detailed his role in arranging the cash withdrawals from the Cannon campaign account at the Perry State Bank. Attached were photocopies of the four checks for $7,500 each. My heart sank when I saw the Bates stamps on the checks. The numbers left no doubt that they had come from our investigative files. The only question was whether "Alice" was a member of our staff or an FBI agent assigned to our office. Or maybe Gedney had been talking out of school with his private investigator friend. And then I remembered the briefcase I was keeping at my apartment.

As soon as Jeffreys returned, Hathorne briefed him on the meeting with Fowler. They made one more run at Bruce, calling him before the grand jury and giving it their best shot. Even the grand jury didn't buy

Hathorne's theory, so he and Jeffreys reluctantly had to admit they wouldn't be able to get an indictment. Two days later, Jo Gobles released a statement to the press that our office would not be bringing any charges before May 25th. Left unsaid was that May 25th was the expiration for the five-year statute of limitations. Nor did the statement mention Robert Bruce, but everyone knew. Everyone knew that Jeffreys couldn't make a case, not against Bruce and not against Cannon.

Jeffreys thought he might quietly slink away from the confrontation with Robert Bruce, but that was not to be. The next day on the floor of the Senate, the Democrats took the opportunity to counter-punch. Senator Dolor's staff called to give us advance warning of a speech by Senator Robinson, and the conference room was crowded as most of the staff gathered to hear his remarks on C-SPAN 2.

"Mr. President, for almost two years now, I have been suggesting that the time has come for Special Prosecutor George Jeffreys to shut down his costly, lavish, and unnecessary Whirlpool investigation," said Senator Robinson, who had been one of Cannon's strongest defenders.

"And every time I make this suggestion, I have high hopes it will be the last time I do so. I have high hopes that Mr. Jeffreys will finally face facts: That after almost two years, after billing the taxpayers more than $30 million—$30 million—enough is enough.

"Each time, however, the American people have been disappointed. Because each time, Mr. Jeffreys stumbles upon some other blind alley in which to steer his investigation, and the bill to the taxpayers just keeps getting bigger and bigger and bigger.

"The latest blind alley were the unethical tactics designed to intimidate former Cannon campaign treasurer, Robert Bruce.

"Mr. Jeffreys' agents told Mr. Bruce that unless he testified that President Cannon was involved in violations of the law during the 1990 gubernatorial election, they would see that Mr. Bruce was indicted by the grand jury.

"To Mr. Bruce's credit, he and his attorneys would not buckle in to the special prosecutor's blackmail.

"I do not blame Mr. Jeffreys for the fact that his investigation has ended in failure. Everyone knew that it would from the day he was appointed.

"What I do blame Mr. Jeffreys for is turning this investigation into the 'Eveready rabbit,' it just keeps going and going and going.

"And recent news articles have suggested that it will keep on going, because Mr. Jeffreys has his sights set on indicting President Cannon and the First Lady, no matter how much it costs the taxpayers, no matter that he has no evidence of a crime, and apparently, no matter how ugly the tactics.

"Perhaps he sees this as the only way in which he could justify the massive expenses he has racked up in is cushy hotels and offices. Perhaps he sees this as the only way he can ever get a seat on the Supreme Court.

As soon as Senator Robinson had finished speaking, Bart Gedney turned off the television and walked out of the conference room. There was considerable embarrassed hand-wringing among some of the junior staff, especially those who had signed on because they thought it would advance their careers. The true believers, however, only became more intent on pursuing their goal of getting Cannon. Mitch Palmer was standing nearby, looking at me for some sign of my reaction. I smiled to reassure him and said, "Don't worry, Mitch. The networks won't carry it, and the papers will bury it."

The June meeting of the Policy Committee was not particularly pleasant. May had been a public relations disaster for Jeffreys, having to withdraw the subpoena for Governor Vance's campaign records and having to admit he didn't have a case against Robert Bruce. We were facing additional pressure as a result of the agreement Jeffreys had struck with Senator Diletto and Congressman Leech. Jeffreys had been given more than eight months since the election to develop his case and bring charges. We were now down to our last six weeks before the hearings started, then we'd have to share the publicity spotlight with the Congressional committees. Further complicating matters, Jeffreys had made firm commitments to a number of corporate and political clients for high profile cases in the fall.

Jeffreys ran the meeting like a two-minute drill. Score, score, score was the message that day. The problem was that the defendants were not cooperating with our legal and media strategies. Dr. Burgh and Mr. Jebb were proclaiming their innocence and refusing to enter plea agreements. Governor Vance refused to comply with our subpoenas or even talk with us. Even those who had already entered pleas were not providing the incriminating evidence Jeffreys had hoped for to implicate the Cannons. Jeffreys pleaded with us to turn up the heat and get either pleas or indictments, just get something, as soon as possible. We were, he reminded everyone, spending more than $1 million a month, and we needed scalps soon.

James Peck scored first on the following Monday when John Jebb, the real estate broker, agreed to enter a guilty plea to a single misdemeanor. I did not participate in those discussions, but Mitch told me later that Jebb didn't want to take a chance with a jury on a felony charge. He could plead to a misdemeanor and keep his real estate and law licenses.

Professor Burgh proved to be equally difficult. I made sure I sat in on the Tuesday morning meeting with Burgh and his lawyers. James

Peck and Alva Dukov Philips, the only female attorney on Jeffreys' staff, were running the negotiations for our office. Burgh was represented by two lawyers as well—Tom Erskine, a respected former judge from Tuscaloosa, and Hank Drummond, a highly regarded trial lawyer from Ashland—both of whom were frequently mentioned as likely nominees for federal judgeships. If Peck had told me in advance who was representing Burgh, I might have been able to brief him. As it was, I took a seat away from the table where I could sit back and enjoy the show.

Jeffreys really needed a felony conviction, and Peck began the meeting with that in mind. Erskine and Drummond laughed. Peck kept making threats, but it was obvious he was bluffing. Burgh's lawyers cited a knock-down line of cases including *U. S. v. Sabatino, U. S. v. Bowman,* and *U. S. v. Lentz* that couldn't be ignored. I'd read the FBI 302 summaries from the earlier interviews with Burgh, and there was no way Peck could get a conviction. Erskine said he didn't think we could even get an indictment, and Drummond openly dared Peck to try. Tempers were beginning to flare, and the break for lunch came just in time.

The afternoon session resumed with Peck even more determined. First, he suggested that if Burgh would give them something on Cannon, perhaps his problems would go away. Erskine, without even bothering to consult with Burgh, rather bluntly told Peck that his client didn't have any information damaging to Cannon and wasn't going to manufacture lies.

Peck was more than a little frustrated, and he responded with a move that I had never seen and would never have imagined. He said he intended to file misdemeanor charges against Burgh, which he could do by information without a grand jury indictment. Erskine and Drummond laughed again and thought he was joking. No way he could win, so why bother, they argued.

"I'll find something that fits," Peck threatened.

"Like what? Our client has done nothing wrong," Erskine replied.

"I don't have to tell you anything," Peck snarled. "Under *Bailey v. Richardson*, we can bring charges on secret information, and you'll have a hell of a time defending that!"

Drummond laughed in his face, "Oh, so you admit this is a Star Chamber you're running?"

Peck was visibly angry now. "Laugh if you want, but I'm filing a misdemeanor charge against your client tomorrow morning, and I can do that without the Grand Jury" he said. "You might beat it, but you know damn well that a trial is going to cost you and your client at least $50,000. Or, you can enter into a plea agreement this afternoon, and the maximum fine will be $1,000. Or, the sensible thing, you might wish to reconsider my earlier suggestion to cooperate and provide testimony against the president. Your call, gentlemen."

Family values struck again. Dr. Burgh was looking at putting two kids through college on a professor's salary, and Peck knew that. He also knew that Burgh didn't have the money to defend himself. After a short conference with his lawyers, Dr. Burgh agreed to plead guilty to one misdemeanor count of conspiracy. Peck and Philips were victorious, and Jeffreys was very pleased with their work. That made two plea agreements in two days.

For the first time that afternoon, Peck and Gedney asked me to go celebrate. As much as I wanted a beer, I had to decline. Having to listen to their bragging was not a pleasant thought, and I'd probably lose my lunch.

Jeffreys finally got his media fix that week. The Jebb plea was treated as another notch on the bedpost, and the stories suggested it was evidence that Jeffreys was moving forward. The Burgh story, though, was bigger news with more political potential. Jeffreys got carried away at his news conference and told the press that Dr. Burgh had pleaded guilty to a felony offense with which he had not been charged. But it made for better headlines. The *Washington Sun* played it on page one as "Ex-Cannon Aide Pleads Guilty," and implied that Jeffreys had charged Dr. Burgh with five felonies. The *American Speculator* said the professor was "the second most dangerous man in America" in terms of having damaging information that could bring down President Cannon. Jebb and Burgh were both under gag orders, so there would be no rebuttal.

The two misdemeanor pleas were only the warm-up acts for the main event. The headliner hit on Thursday when Jeffreys announced that the Whirlpool grand jury had indicted Governor Vance on three felony counts related to the 1987 cable television deal. Big news, indeed. Jo Gobles proved again that she was a master at media manipulation. The story was the lead on every network, and Jeffreys loved seeing his face on television.

The newspapers ignored the long history of political tension between Vance and Cannon, calling Governor Vance "Cannon's hand-picked successor in Alabama" and predicting that President Cannon was next. James Rivington's column in the *Washington Sun* gloated that "you could hear the old yellow-dog yelping all the way to Atlanta." Democrats in Alabama were finally getting Jeffreys' message, he said, that "there's no future for politically ambitious young men and women in the Democratic Party in the South."

The next week Jeffreys threw a bone to the conspiracy nuts by announcing that he had hired a nationally-known forensics expert to again review all the files relating to the death of Hal Goodall. That story not only continued to energize the Republican fringe and appease Howard Mellonskoff, but it seemed to intensify with every retelling. Jeffreys was learning how to stoke the political fires, and he enjoyed the response. Either he was getting much better at playing the demagogue, or I had seriously underestimated his darker talents all along. Probably both.

One thing that seriously concerned Jeffreys and Peck, and especially Gedney, was that the Vance case had been easier to hype as a political charge than it would be to try as a legal matter. It had been assigned first to Judge Virginia D. Clifford, but she had recused. It was now in Judge Edward Cook's court. I'd never met Judge Cook, but I knew his reputation. He had a high regard for the constitution and a low tolerance for bullshit, both of which were cause for Jeffreys to be worried about his chances for success.

The Policy Committee convened on June 14th in a special called meeting, and the sole item on the agenda was what to do about the fact that Judge Cook would be presiding in the Vance trial. Jeffreys opened the meeting by asking for ideas, so I tried to be helpful by sharing what I had learned about Judge Cook's public career. He had undergraduate and law degrees from the University of Alabama, and he got his start in politics by managing the campaign and serving on the staff of Governor Jim Folsom. His reputation as a progressive Democrat came from his association with Folsom, his early support for public school integration, and his lasting opposition to George Wallace and James Boutwell Crommelin. Judge Cook had a reputation as an outstanding lawyer in private practice until his appointment by President Carter in 1980. In 15 years on the federal bench, he had earned a reputation for fairness and a commitment to individual rights.

My presentation was based on the research I'd done for Burke last year, but it was not well received. It quickly became apparent that Jeffreys had no interest in information that might be helpful in trying a case in Judge Cook's court. Instead, he wanted dirt on Cook, something he could use to force recusal and get the case reassigned to Corwin or Hoffman.

Mitch Palmer suggested that we might attack Judge Cook as too senile. "The old coot is 77 years old," Mitch said. "Can we get affidavits that he goes to sleep on the bench or is affected by heavy medication? Clifton Smegman or Adam Tiler might be able to help us with that." Mitch's idea fell flat, in part, I suspect, because such an argument would not be welcomed by the Dolor campaign.

Bart Gedney said that his inside source at the White House might check to see if there were any personal correspondence between Judge Cook and the Cannons, and he offered to call Nelson Grenier and Judge Crommelin to see if there were political connections to Governor Vance that we might exploit to argue for recusal. He also promised to get his private investigator buddy on it right away.

John Hathorne agreed with Gedney. "We need to look into Cook's financial connections, too," he said. Maybe Senator Rantallion's staff could take the lead on that and bring some pressure to bear on the judge. I'll get in touch with David Windrig. He could request copies of Cook's financial disclosure reports without that being traced back to us."

James Peck was sitting next to Jeffreys, and he was particularly interested in getting the case before a sympathetic judge. "Perhaps," he said with some hesitation, "we could quietly encourage some editorials and op-ed pieces that raised serious questions about Cook's political connections to Cannon and other prominent Democrats. If we could generate a media firestorm attacking his ability to be impartial, or even the appearance of such, we might get him to recuse. It worked on Burke, so maybe we could do the same thing to Judge Cook."

Jeffreys' face lit up as he listened to Peck's scheme. "Brilliant, simply brilliant, Mr. Peck. I knew there was a reason I hired you," he said, launching into a strange little sermonette on the dangers of a liberal society. "We live in a new age of barbarism, and it is increasingly the order of the day. What drives this new age of barbarism is not unrelated to the Cannon political culture of scandal. We must embrace the same value system in this effort as that undergirding negative advertising in politics. Manipulate, distort and hopefully destroy. And in extreme situations, engage in character assassination. As in the campaign, our opponents in this investigation must be demeaned and demoralized quite seriously in the eyes of the American public."

Peck was proud of himself. "I'll have a conversation with Judge Crommelin to see if he'll take the lead in getting something into the press, if that's okay with Jo." Jo Gobles nodded her approval.

Mitch jumped in again. "I know Myles Cooper, the political editor of the *Post-Advertiser*," he boasted. "I think he'd be glad to give it some play in the local press."

Jeffreys liked it. "I'll contact our friends at the *Wall Street Record* to see if they'll help, and I think I can count on Rivington at the *Sun*. I'm also on the editorial board of the *ABA Journal*, and I think they should be very interested in this. Mr. Gedney, you take care of our friends at the *American Speculator*. Miss Gobles, will you take responsibility for getting the message out to our talk radio supporters?"

Jo smiled enthusiastically and nodded again, still saying nothing. I was the only member of the committee without an assignment and, I thought to myself, the only member with a conscience. I had to keep telling myself that, but it became increasingly difficult to believe it. Every time I deposited my check, my doubts increased.

Governor Vance's arraignment was scheduled for June 22nd, and that morning I arrived at the office earlier than usual. I was having a cup of coffee and casually reading the *Wall Street Record* when I noticed the lead editorial attacking Judge Cook's personal connections to President and Mrs. Cannon and calling upon him to recuse himself from hearing the case. What a strange coincidence. No one would ever know the truth. Jeffreys and Justice worked in mysterious ways, unfortunately never in the same direction.

Jeffreys, Peck, and Gedney showed up at the office that day wearing nearly identical dark suits, white shirts, and red diagonal-striped ties. Hoping that they wouldn't ask me to participate in the court-packing plan that day, I had worn my Elvis tie and a tan suit that looked like I had slept in it. No such luck. We were soon on our way downtown for the regular ritual, but today it would prove to be different. A standing-room-only crowd of almost 100 people filled the courtroom, but this time we were clearly outnumbered by faithful friends and political supporters of Governor Vance.

Peck methodically presented the outline of our case, then sat down with Jeffreys at the prosecution's table. Standing with his wife, Allison, and his attorneys, Buford Boone and Jack Hughes, Governor Vance sounded more like a candidate on the stump than a defendant in the dock. Addressing Judge Cook, he said, "Your honor, I am not guilty of the three counts of the indictment. I welcome the chance for a trial before a truly independent judicial system, so that I can have my innocence publicly proclaimed and get on with the business of helping make Alabama a better place for all of our citizens."

Another difference that day was that the media paid far less attention to Jeffreys and cared little about what he might have to add. This time the defendant was defiant and unbound by any gag provisions in a plea agreement. Governor Vance stood outside the courthouse and comfortably faced the pack of reporters and cameras.

Speaking without notes, Governor Vance immediately took the offensive and defended himself and the home goal. "George Jeffreys has been conducting a trial by media and distorting the facts by leaking selected documents and other information to unwitting members of the press who will print anything he gives them," he said. "I resent the personal attacks on me and my family, I resent his besmirching the reputation of the people and the state of Alabama, and I resent his unfounded allegations against President and Mrs. Cannon. This high-tech lynching by innuendo must be stopped. When he gets to trial, he will have to be held to the truth and the facts in front of a jury and a judge. Thank God we still have an independent judicial system in this country."

The reporters vied with each other to see who could be more rude, shouting questions in hope of a good sound bite from the governor. As if there could be any doubt, one television type thrust a microphone toward the governor and asked, "Are you questioning the integrity of the Independent Counsel in bringing these charges?"

Governor Vance tried to smile, but it looked more like a sneer. "I think this is a very thin-skinned man with a high opinion of his own ethics and integrity. Mr. Jeffreys has a very real conflict of interest in that most of his private clients would benefit financially from my removal from office. Furthermore, he's made no secret of his ambitions for higher appointment by a national Republican administration. He thinks this is his ticket to that higher appointment. Mr. Jeffreys is under enormous pressure from the National Republican Party to win a conviction against any prominent Democrat to discredit the Cannon administration and set himself up for an appointment to the Supreme Court that has so often eluded him in the past."

Just as Governor Vance and his wife were walking away, one of those gaudy stretch limousines, a white Lincoln pimpmobile, pulled alongside the curb in front of the courthouse. Nelson Grenier stepped out and rushed toward the crowd of reporters to offer his unsolicited analysis of the day's big event. "I tried to tell the people during the last campaign," said Grenier. "Jim Bibb Vance has some very real problems. This is not a witch hunt. Judge Jeffreys has been very professional and has done the job he was sent down here to do. I, for one, appreciate what he is doing to rid us of the corrupt anti-business political machine that has gripped our state for the last 25 years."

Jeffreys had finally hooked a big fish, even if he hadn't yet landed one. He hadn't been able to find anything on President or Mrs. Cannon, but at least he had a major player in state politics. He could now go back to Washington for a while and face his friends and benefactors without having to apologize for coming up totally empty-handed.

Jo Gobles' press summary the next day was thicker than the usual post-game roundup. On top of the packet, the place of honor, was a long essay from the *Washington Sun* entitled, "The Life and Times of Judge Edward Cook," contributed by James Boutwell Crommelin. It was one of the most scurrilous and unfounded attacks I had ever seen on a sitting judge, making absurd claims about Judge Cook as the kingmaker behind every politician in the state. There was little truth in the diatribe, but it was a well-aimed missive that would certainly help anyone who might want to suggest "the appearance of bias" at some future date. Yet another coincidence.

After the Vance indictment, the office coasted for a few weeks. Jeffreys was heading back to Washington to help Senator Diletto and Congressman Leech kick off the Whirlpool hearings, then he planned to spend considerable time practicing law and making money while those hearings dominated the news. I was ready for a vacation, myself. Lindsey and I planned to spend a couple of weeks in Maine, making memories before she left for Washington in September.

Only one item of business remained before the 4th of July exodus from the heat of the Birmingham summer. Randolph Webster's sentencing was scheduled for June 28th, and Jeffreys wanted to make sure that he got some hard time. A jail term for the former Associate Attorney General and Cannon confidante would be another feather in his cap, so Jeffreys asked that our office be prepared to fight any request for leniency in sentencing. Bart Gedney and Alva Dukov Philips met that challenge and joined Jeffreys in the courtroom on the day of sentencing.

Court opened with Jeffreys reciting every infraction we had discovered and posturing as if the over-billing was the worst thing since smallpox. Dismissing Webster's long record of public service, Jeffreys asked the judge to impose the maximum sentence under the federal sentencing guidelines. Part of the plea agreement, he argued, was that Webster would cooperate with the OIC investigation, but he had not been particularly helpful. Webster had provided no evidence that could be used to develop a case against the President or the First Lady, and Jeffreys didn't think that was much in the way of "cooperation," which was his code word for giving us something damaging on Cannon. Judge Gaston was very accommodating, rejecting Webster's request for a downward departure from the guidelines and handing down a sentence of 21 months in prison. Jeffreys was doubly pleased. He had sent one of Cannon's friends to prison, and he had found another judge who would bend over backwards to give the Independent Counsel whatever he wanted.

Chapter Twenty One

Independence Day had always been my favorite holiday. As a kid, my father would always read the Declaration of Independence before we could begin the fireworks, and it was a tradition I had continued to observe every year. Even if the ideas were drawn from Locke, Thomas Jefferson understood the power of language and dressed those bold thoughts with rhetorical armor before sending them into the battle for liberty. It was fine reading. I only regreted that politicians and citizens today so seldom embrace the revolutionary spirit of 1776.

I found my own freedom clad in t-shirts and cutoffs for the next two weeks. Lindsey and I flew to Boston and rented a Dodge Caravan for our own maneuvers, which began with dinner at the Union Oyster House and ended with Irish folk songs at the Black Rose. We spent the first night at the Irving House out in Cambridge and the next day revisiting memories from my days on campus. Mostly we prowled old bookshops around Harvard Square, satisfying a shared addiction. I also stopped in at J. Press, another undergraduate shrine, and seized the opportunity to update my work uniform for the first time since I'd left Austin. After that, it was up the coast to Kennebunkport.

We had reservations at The Colony and had planned to stay for a week, but we both became restless after two days. Lindsey had too much energy to stay in one place any longer, and I wasn't comfortable being that close to Stuart's Retreat on Walker's Point. We packed the magic bus and embarked on an eight-day road trip that included way too much lobster, goofing off in Bar Harbor, hiking in Acadia National Park, camping at Telos Lake, a canoe trip on the Allagash River, two days in Quebec, and an unforgettable afternoon romp in the woods somewhere in Somerset County.

On the way back to Boston we made time for a side trip to Salem. Lindsey wanted to visit the House of Seven Gables and Hawthorne's home, and she indulged me by touring the old Custom House and basking in the sun with a cold beer on Pickering Wharf. Samuel Adams, I felt sure, would have been proud to have his name on that Honey Porter. We decided against visiting the Dungeon Museum or the Witch Trial Memorial. I'd be back on the job in Birmingham soon enough.

I experienced considerable difficulty in returning to the office and the politics of the Whirlpool investigation, mostly because the vacation had reminded me how little most people really cared about the whole deal. Such a perspective reaffirmed my faith in the good sense of the American people, but it also caused me to question how much longer I could work for Jeffreys.

The media hounds were still at it, of course. Robert Bauman had another sex story in *Newsweek*, based on the story of a snitch from the Stuart White House staff who had unexplicably been kept on and now said she thought that the president had kissed a co-worker a couple of years ago. Bauman seemed obsessed with writing about Cannon's fondness for women. It was his "bimbo eruptions" story during the '92 campaign that created the issue, and he had been so hard on the Christine Putnam story that he quit the *Washington Post*, when even they wouldn't print his imaginative ramblings. Now he had another tale to boost his career.

Knowing my own fondness for beautiful women and that Lindsey soon would be leaving for Washington only increased my doubts about staying on to fight the losing battle with Jeffreys and his disciples. Maybe I should have applied for that Associate Dean opening at the law school, but it was too late now.

The Senate Whirlpool Committee was ready to open its summer season with hearings on the events surrounding the death of Hal Goodall. The poor guy had been dead two years, but that wasn't going to stop Senator Diletto from trying to score political points by playing to the loonies and reopening the personal trauma for Goodall's family and friends. Diletto had no shame, nor did the other Republican members of the committee. Nor, for that matter, did Jeffreys. "The death of Hal Goodall. I think that's the Rosetta Stone to the whole Cannon Administration," Jeffreys once said, and now he and Gedney had just hired another forensics expert to again review the Goodall files.

To orchestrate the television production, Diletto hired Ray Cahn as the Majority's Chief Counsel and cheap shot artist. Cahn had served as U. S. Attorney in New Jersey under President Stuart, and he was among those without a job after Cannon's election. Like George Jeffreys and Ike Parker, he had considerable enthusiasm for his new assignment.

Senator Rantallion had abandoned any pretense of fairness, putting David Winderig, Floyd Crump's deputy dirt digger from Critics Unlimited, on the public payroll as a special member of his committee staff. Senator Medlar stood ready to ask any questions submitted by the Lynch Legal Foundation. Medlar still owed them for giving him a job after he was defeated early in his career, and Mark Schine was now calling the note and the tune. And, of course, Mellonskoff's money fueled them all.

It was probably no coincidence that the rest of the Republicans on the Whirlpool Committee were all middle-aged white guys. Senator Hatchet was the only one with any real stature in the Senate, and he had seriously damaged that standing by his interminable questioning and lurid fascination with pubic hairs on Coke cans a few years ago. Dean Manion, Parnell Thomas, and Harold Velde would be a reliable chorus to support any conspiracy theories Diletto wished to pursue. Loan documents hidden in pumpkins, a grassy knoll on Lot 13, and the drug operations at the Seale airstrip would keep them awake and assure their attendance. To assure the theatrics, Jeffreys raided our evidence room and gave Goodall's briefcase to Rantallion to use as a prop during the hearings.

The Committee agenda reflected the GOP political strategy. First, they planned to concentrate on the so-called "Washington phase" of the investigation. That would serve to distract the White House staff from attending to the everyday business of government and make it more difficult for Cannon to accomplish his policy goals. Since there had been countless hours of hearings last year and who knows how many depositions of everyone involved, faded memories were not likely to produce any new information. What it might produce, the Republicans hoped, were slightly different answers to similar questions, allowing Diletto to claim that witnesses were changing their stories or were suffering from convenient forgetfulness.

Second, closer to the primary season, the Committee would turn its attention to the "Alabama phase" and try to break the Democratic grip on state politics. If all of Cannon's friends and supporters were shelling out money for legal counsel and spending their time answering interrogatories, they would have little interest in the upcoming Senate race, one that Diletto had already declared a top priority.

Jeffreys was clearly a part of the assault team, and he was going to Washington for a joint press conference with Senator Diletto and Congressman Leech on July 17th to generate media coverage of the hearings. Mitch Palmer, Bart Gedney, James Peck, and Jo Gobles all tagged along to be near the action.

Luckily, I wasn't invited, but I did draw the task of taking them to the airport on Sunday. It was not a pleasant experience. Although we were there in plenty of time, Jeffreys soon became impatient having to stand in line with ordinary citizens. After about 15 minutes, he ordered Mitch to cut to the front of the line and ask the agent if First Class customers could be accommodated more quickly. That was another insight into the man. Not only did he fly in the First Class section, but he wanted special treatment. Mitch returned with bad news, and Jeffreys gave him a scolding look for having failed.

The processing was only a little slower than normal, because the agent was working with a long line of travelers from an earlier flight that had been canceled. Jeffreys pushed his way to the desk, and shoved his ticket across the counter. "I have to be on this flight, and I must be seated in First Class," he demanded.

"I'm sorry sir," the agent replied. I'll be happy to try to help you in a moment, but I'm trying to rebook these passengers. They were here first. I'm sure we'll be able to work something out if you'll just be patient."

Jeffreys was indignant. He was used to having his way. Making sure that everyone could hear, he asked loudly, "Lady, do you have any idea who I am?"

Without the least hesitation, the ticket agent kept smiling as she reached for her microphone. "May I have your attention please?" she said, her voice ringing throughout the terminal. "We have a passenger here at the ticket counter who doesn't know who he is. If someone can help him discover his identity, please come to the Delta ticket counter or pick up a white courtesy phone."

With the folks in line laughing and jeering at him, Jeffreys glared at the agent and furiously shouted, "I could have your job, you know?"

She smiled again and said, "I'm sorry, sir, but I think you're far too rude to handle this job." The other passengers broke into loud applause, and Jeffreys huffed away to the restroom to recover. I was glad that no one recognized him.

On Monday, those of us in the Birmingham office watched the big news conference on C-SPAN. Diletto and Leech had prepared statements, and Jeffreys stood behind them, listening attentively, as they lambasted President Cannon, his administration, and the state of Alabama. Diletto used the word "ethical" three times during his speech, surprising everyone that the word was in his vocabulary.

I was sure Jeffreys must have been feeling neglected as the press directed their questions almost exclusively to points in the statements presented by Diletto and Leech. Finally, someone asked the standard question about whether the hearings would interfere with the ongoing investigation by the Office of Independent Counsel. Jeffreys was ready. He stepped forward to the podium, looked into the cameras, then said, "I do want to say this—Congress has its role to play too in terms of publicity and public education, and, obviously, I wouldn't overlook the potential role that the Congress has, if it sees fit, and thus far it has seen fit, to explore these areas and tell the American public what they think happened."

The press corps started shouting more questions to Diletto, but Jeffreys wasn't through. He enjoyed the attention, and he wasn't leaving the podium until he got some more. Raising his hands to stop the questions, he added, "Let me make it perfectly clear, I did not request a delay in the hearings like Mr. Burke did. We have coordinated our various public actions every step of the way and have shared information that we have uncovered, but they are trying the case in the court of public opinion, and I'm trying it primarily in a court of law. I have, throughout this investigation, tried to maintain a close relationship with the Republican leadership in Congress, recognizing that in our constitutional system, the Congress has its responsibilities, and then I, by virtue of the obligations that have been vested in me and put upon me, have a job to do as well."

Senator Diletto tried to return to the microphones to take more questions, but Jeffreys gripped the podium and ignored the signals from Diletto and Leech that it was their news conference. Pretending to be responding to the original question, Jeffreys finally said, "So, to answer your question, I have some very specific concerns. I've been clear about those concerns, and the relationship with Congress has been very good. Very cordial. Senator Diletto and Congressman Leech are honorable men. I think they're being very mindful that there is a criminal justice process under way and trying to accommodate that consistent with their sense of duty to the Republican par—I mean, to the republic. I know some people have suggested that we are coordinating our activities to make sure we get maximum media coverage and keep the issue in the news, but that wasn't our plan. It's more of a convenient coincidence."

The press conference soon ended, and Jeffreys' 15 minutes of fame would have to satisfy him for the time being. That and the big fees he would be pulling in from private legal practice. His high profile as Independent Counsel for Whirlpool had helped generate numerous clients who would love nothing more than to be rid of President Cannon, and Jeffreys planned to log some serious billable hours while the Congressional committees took their shots at Cannon. We didn't see Jeffreys again for the rest of the month.

Diletto's Whirlpool hearings on Hal Goodall's death were an embarrassment for everyone involved. No news was bad news for the GOP, so Gastone passed the baton back to Congressman Leech's House Banking Committee. Tag-team politics at work. Congressman Leech knew he would have to strike quickly. Congress was nearing the start of the August recess, and his colleagues were preparing to let the taxpayers fund their annual overseas visits to check on vital American interests in exotic places.

Dick Leech was limited by his mind, and he was predictable. His star witness would be Ellende Varken, who had prepared the original RTC criminal referrals on Jefferson Savings Bank three years ago and had been obsessed since then with trying to interest the media in her efforts. Although invited to testify during the Banking Committee hearings last year, she had declined. This time she spent two days before the committee, opening with a very carefully crafted statement that seemed to implicate President and Mrs. Cannon, Governor Vance, Josh Banaghan, Jessie Banaghan, John Jebb, James Burgh, and Bill Godwin, conflating the two named as targets with those she had claimed were potential witnesses and conveniently omitting any mention of Nick Biddle and Sarah Bozartes. While Mrs. Varken went on to claim credit for all of the pleas and indictments secured by the Independent Counsel, not a single one of them was even remotely related to her fanciful criminal referrals.

Congressman Leech controlled the hearings tightly and limited the questions from the Democrats on the committee. The only interesting moment during Varken's testimony came when it was revealed that she was represented by lawyers from the Lynch Legal Foundation—the same front group that advised Christine Putnam in her suit against President Cannon, attacked Cannon's legal defense fund, and criticized the Travel Office firings. Leech did not invite Banaghan, Vance, Jebb, Burgh, or Godwin to testify or respond to Varken's charges, so the press reported Varken's uncontested allegations as gospel. It was a good show, but it was never clear what the hearings had to do with legitimate oversight functions of the committee. No new banking legislation emerged from the committee as a result of the inquiry.

In Alabama, the Senate Whirlpool hearings were ignored, and the House Banking Committee hearings were a joke. Leech got almost no help, even from the hand-picked Republicans on the committee. Perceval, Rowbottom, Burton, Hinshaw, Hastings, Hansen, Swindall, and Lukens—all intellectual, moral, and political lightweights. Again, they were rich white guys with little obvious talent other than accepting campaign contributions, the kind of men who always serve on banking committees and consistently vote for legislation drafted by the industry. They had all rushed to support the Reeder deregulation scheme that led to the savings and loan debacle and massive bailouts, of which Jefferson Savings was only a fly speck.

Commenting on Birmingham's Congressman Spencer Perceval and his contributions to Leech's investigation, local columnist Mark Kelly of the *Black & White* wrote, "As for Perceval, he is repugnantly typical of the shallow, moralistic, corporate-friendly drones so favored by Republican voters; sort of a Dan Quayle Lite, if such can be imagined. This malignant horde teems through the Capitol like a frenzy of bottom-feeders, existing to perpetrate the dirty work of the GOP brain trust. As evidence, one need look no further than Perceval's husbanding of the moribund House investigation of the truckload of local nonsense known as Whirlpool. Ask yourself: If there was really anything to investigate, would they let Spencer Perceval be involved?"

Jeffreys took another hit that week. Just before the Senate adjourned, Senator Robinson took the opportunity to question the way in which Jeffreys had been spending the funds from our unlimited budget. Senator Dolor's office faxed a copy of the speech to Bart Gedney, asking us for information he could use to defend Jeffreys. Since Jeffreys was increasingly busy with his private legal work, Gedney was now assuming greater control of the office and direction of the investigation. He convened the Policy Committee that afternoon and distributed copies of the speech.

Senator Robinson's speech was partisan, attacking Jeffreys and calling for an investigation of our office, but his figures were accurate. As I read it, I could certainly see why Gedney was interested in a rebuttal.

Robinson had told the Senate, "I have criticized Mr. Jeffreys for the $30 million cost of his investigation. I have criticized him for drawing thousands of dollars in unauthorized personal living expenses. I have criticized him for smearing the names of some outstanding public servants. Despite all this, I never thought that one day I would be standing here to suggest that it's time to appoint an independent counsel to investigate the independent counsel."

After detailing some of Jeffreys' embarrassing expenditures on rooms at the Wynfrey, room service meals, and First Class travel, Robinson further complained, "Deadlines have come and gone, and so have millions and millions of your tax dollars. We haven't gotten any other progress reports since Kenneth Burke was replaced, but I hope that before Mr. Jeffreys admits failure and closes his doors he will at least fully disclose the complete expense records of his office. The American people deserve to know how their money was spent—and, in some cases, misspent."

"Any ideas," Gedney asked, "how we might respond to this?."

No one said anything. I wanted to say he could cut back on room service or fold the tent, but I didn't think Bart was seeking practical solutions. As with everything else, he and Jeffreys were interested in manipulating perceptions.

"Well, I plan to give them something to talk about," Hathorne finally replied. "The best defense is a good offense. I am fairly sure we can get the grand jury to issue some more indictments."

"Now we're talking," Gedney said. "Tell us what you have in mind, John."

"Okay," Hathorne continued with glee. "I say we draw attention to Jefferson Savings and go after indictments of the Banaghans and Governor Vance. The press will love it—Cannon's partners and his hand-picked successor indicted! I've offered immunity to Nick Biddle, the former loan officer, and Sarah Bozartes, who also worked there. Gave immunity to Ed Dohemy, too. I thought we'd be able to get some help from Bridget Bishop, the little wench who was the compliance officer at Jefferson, but that one didn't work out. Not much help from Burgh, either. Still, we've already got a felony plea from John Cartwright for conspiring with Biddle, and Biddle has been very "cooperative," you might say. Mrs. Bozartes was named as a target by the RTC, and she has some problems with the IRS. I told her we could make all of her problems go away if she could testify about criminal activities at Jefferson, and she has been very helpful. Ed Dohemy has agreed to support the Douglas testimony. And, of course, Roby Douglas will be our star witness. I've been able to refresh his memory, and he'll be great on the stand."

"I like it," Peck said. Mitch added his consent. Jo Gobles nodded agreement. I waited to see how far they would go.

"Now, here's what I suggest," Hathorne continued. "We can probably get Josh Banaghan on numerous counts. No problem there, as far as getting the indictments at least. We can also get something on Mrs. Banaghan, since she had that big loan from Roby Douglas, the one he'll say Cannon pressured him to make. Governor Vance also had loans from Jefferson and from Roby Douglas. With that paper trail, and with what Douglas is willing to say on the stand, we can present the case that it was all a conspiracy. Once we construct that scenario, we can then charge them all for aiding and abetting Douglas in all his other criminal activity."

The meeting concluded with a plan to launch a counter-offensive. Gedney was energized, and both Peck and Hathorne shared his excitement. Mitch, to the extent he was capable of independent thought without talking to Jeffreys, agreed with their approach. By that point, I knew they didn't care what I had to say, but that didn't stop me from thinking there were some problems with their scheme. Ike Parker's preliminary report to the RTC suggested that neither the facts nor the law were on our side for such sweeping indictments. Of course, working in our favor, we did have an unlimited budget. And it was clear now that neither Judge Chase nor Attorney General Otis had any inclination to put any restrictions on Jeffreys' authority to do whatever he wanted.

Chapter Twenty Two

Bart and Mitch reached Jeffreys by phone in Milwaukee, where he was working on strategy for a trial defending Governor Cheeser's "Landmark Plan" to issue state vouchers for home schooling and religious schools. Jeffreys gave them the go ahead to seek the indictments. He wanted Peck and Hathorne to take the lead, and he suggested that we load it up with as many counts as possible. It was a reliable strategy I'd seen before. Bring a bushel of charges, hoping either that a few will stick or that the jury will feel better about giving you only one or two. And one guilty verdict was all he would need to look good, especially if he could get Governor Vance removed from office.

The grand jury complied, and Jeffreys flew back to Birmingham to announce the indictments -- 19 counts against Josh Banaghan, 11 counts against Governor Vance, and eight counts against Jessie Banaghan. Jeffreys met the media outside the courthouse and once again played the part of the pious prosecutor. As always, it worked, and the next day's headlines were his. "Jeffreys Indicts Alabama Governor and Cannon Whirlpool Partners on 38 Counts of Fraud and Conspiracy; White House Denies Connection to Charges."

The press played the word "indictment" as if it meant "guilty," and most readers probably thought it did. Even more clever was the line about "White House denies connection." The word "denies," in the hands of the media, was a synonym for "lying cover-up." Might as well have asked the White House if the president had an affinity for barnyard animals and said "Cannon denies screwing goat."

All three of the defendants pleaded "not guilty" the following week. Governor Vance dared Jeffreys to prove his charges. Josh Banaghan pleaded poverty and asked the court to appoint counsel to represent him. Jessie Banaghan said she was eager to prove her innocence, and the public defender's office was assigned to represent her. Looked like we were finally going to get a trial. Now we'd have to prove our case instead of leaning on people and forcing misdemeanor pleas from folks who couldn't afford the expense of a trial.

Myles Cooper, political editor of the *Post-Advertiser*, did his best to enlist in the cause and to offer support for Jeffreys. Two front page articles appeared on September 3rd. One was a shameless puff piece on Bart

Gedney entitled, "Vance Prosecutor Gedney Known for Bringing Down Politicians." Bart, of course, loved it. He asked Phyllis Sanford to make copies for him, and she spent most of her morning at the copy machine. The other article was more curious. The headline proclaimed, "Road to Vance Trial Full of Twists for Judge Cook, Political Veteran Handling Whirlpool Case No Stranger to Controversy." It was a more mainstream version of Judge James Boutwell Crommelin's diatribe in the *Washington Sun* last month, but it made the same points for the same purposes. It was designed to paint Judge Cook as some courthouse crony and to suggest that he could not be fair on the bench. Looked to me like someone was conducting a coordinated campaign against Judge Cook.

The reason for all the attention to Judge Cook was that he had been assigned to hear the case of Governor Vance on our first set of indictments, the ones on the cable television loans. Challenging Jeffreys' jurisdiction to prosecute charges unrelated to the original mandate, Buford Boone told the court, "If these three people can be prosecuted, then any person on earth can be investigated under the act." The briefs were in, and we were all expecting a decision on that motion any day. I had tried to bet Mitch a case of beer on the ruling, but even he was too smart to do that. No one in our office thought much of our brief or our chances of winning.

Judge Cook's decision, announced on September 5, kicked our butt. In clear and succinct language he said Jeffreys had exceeded the original mandate and declared, "The subject matter of the indictment at issue here bears no relation whatsoever to the Cannons or Josh Banaghan or their relationship with Jefferson Savings Bank, Whirlpool Development Corporation, or Financial Management Services, Inc."

In fact, using a relatively low standard for what we would have had to demonstrate, Judge Cook said, "To show that one occurrence is 'related' to another, one need only determine that there is a reasonable causal or logical connection between the two, some tenable correlation between events. The relation between the indictment herein and Banaghan or the Cannons falls far short of this test. Not only were the matters contained in the indictment insufficiently related to the Independent Counsel's mandate, they were not related at all."

Jeffreys was short on both facts and theory, said the judge, pointing out something I'd tried to explain to Jeffreys and the Policy Committee. "The Independent Counsel has come forward with no evidence to refute facts, nor has he alleged a connection of any kind between Governor Vance and President Cannon. This is not surprising. The Court takes judicial notice of the fact that these two men were political opponents in the 1982 Democratic primary for governor. That they would have been connected in any type of business venture in the period covered by the indictment would be highly unlikely."

Finally, Judge Cook knocked down the arrogant assertion in our brief that no court could stand in the way of any charges Jeffreys chose to file. Gedney and Peck argued that Jeffreys and the Office of Independent Counsel were above the law, but Cook held otherwise. Reminding Jeffreys that the Constitution still had meaning, Cook rejected our position, saying, "The Independent Counsel also claimed that this court has no power to question his authority or to stop this investigation, even if he were engaged in selective prosecutions and abuse of office. I cannot accept the proposition that a citizen can be put on trial in my court for a loss of his liberty and that no court has the power to determine whether there is jurisdiction to proceed in the matter. Such a precedent would be both novel and dangerous."

One might expect a little praise for an Alabama federal judge willing to uphold the constitution against an attempted breach, but that was not a story of much interest to the nation's newspapers. Instead, the scribes of truth rushed to vindicate Jeffreys and vilify Judge Cook. The *Washington Sun* gave it a double shot. Jay Fuhrman's piece in the so-called "news" section was headlined, "Alabama Judge Cook a Longtime Friend and Confidant of Diane Cannon." Echoing the theme, the editorial in the same issue was entitled, "Judge Cook to the Rescue," and, for good measure, there was another op-ed piece by Crommelin, same song second verse. The *Wall Street Record*, which shared the *Sun's* journalistic standards and political views, and perhaps some its sources, joined the chorus with an editorial headline reading, "Judge Cook Comes Through for Political Pals."

The other broadsides also followed the *Sun's* interpretation. Danielle Leonard's article in the *Post* led by pointing out that Judge Cook was nominated by Carter and concluded with a note that linked Cook, through the late Hal Goodall, to the First Lady. Seems that the *Post* had a copy of a letter from Judge Cook to Goodall, one that Gedney's "inside source" had lifted from White House correspondence files. Stephen Latrator's summary in the *New York Times* dismissed the whole incident, calling it a mere "Bump in the Road for Jeffreys." Only the weekly *Alabama Times* applauded Judge Cook's ruling, but it had few readers outside the state.

Even if the national news and editorial response was uniformly behind Jeffreys, there were other opinions. Senator Robinson, one of Cannon's strongest defenders, took the opportunity to again attack Jeffreys. There was no mention of his speech in the press or even on CNN, but Senator Dolor's staff again faxed us a transcript from the *Congressional Record*. Jeffreys and Gedney were visibly upset by Robinson's continued attack, and they immediately provided copies to the Policy Committee as if we were supposed to share their anger.

I read the speech, but I didn't see anything too unexpected. "There is an old saying that good things come to those who wait," Robinson had told the Senate. "And, yesterday, we finally got some good news. Despite attempts by the *American Speculator* and the Junior Senator from North Carolina to intimidate him by investigating his financial disclosure records, Judge Edward Cook had the courage to say, 'Enough is enough.' The three major indictments obtained by Mr. Jeffreys were overturned yesterday—just as many legal scholars predicted, before this witch hunt began."

Robinson discounted the guilty pleas of which Jeffreys bragged so often, and I suppose Jeffreys worried about what that might do to his reputation. "For two years," Senator Robinson charged, "Mr. Jeffreys and his army of lawyers have threatened and badgered anyone they could get their hands on. Mr. Jeffreys has been able to force a few guilty pleas from defendants, but only because they could not possibly afford the attorneys fees which would have resulted from going to trial to defend themselves."

Jeffreys and Gedney were also chagrined that Senator Robinson kept calling for the Attorney General to put a halt to their investigation, so maybe that's what had them so agitated that day. They failed to appreciate Robinson's attempt at humor when he said, "It has long been obvious to most objective observers that Mr. Jeffreys' operation should be shut down, but he keeps going down every blind alley and pursuing more conspiracy theories than Oliver Stone."

Robinson's harping on the cost of the investigation probably stung as well. Republicans have so long talked about waste in government and blamed it on the Democrats, they hated it when their own profligate spending was questioned. "Mr. Jeffreys is not paying for this senseless and useless investigation. The American people are. We are," Robinson said. "We are still paying for Mr. Jeffreys' elaborate office space in Birmingham. We are still paying for his fancy hotel rooms in Birmingham. We are still paying for his expensive meals down in Birmingham. And we are going to keep on paying for them for a long time. Mr. Jeffreys will not close down shop until he can find something, anything, to implicate President Cannon or the First Lady. But the fact is, he has nothing. Zip. Nada. The taxpayers should demand a refund."

That's probably what burned Jeffreys the most. Two years and $32 million, and he still didn't have diddly-squat on the President or Mrs. Cannon. And Jeffreys knew, unless he could come up with something soon, he'd never be nominated for the Supreme Court.

Apparently Mitch had been brooding for the last week about Judge Cook's decision. He came into my office and asked, "Did you see that article in the *Sun*? It proves what Nelson Grenier said Judge Crommelin told Judge Jeffreys about those Williams fellows. They control Judge Cook."

I had no idea what Mitch was talking about. "Those Williams fellows . . . ," I mused for a moment. "Hank and Tennessee? They've influenced a lot of my thinking, too, Mitch."

Now Mitch was the one who had no idea what I was talking about. "Who? No, Claude and Aubrey, the two brothers who own all the banks. You know. They're the real bosses in Alabama politics. They were the ones responsible for getting Judge Cook appointed, and he goes to have lunch with them once a week at their private dining room in the Williams Building. They tell him what to do. It's all here in this article by Judge Crommelin. Nelson Grenier said so, too. And so did the private investigator that Gedney's been working with. See for yourself," Mitch said, thrusting a folded copy of the *Washington Sun* in my face.

"Mitch, have a seat, my boy," I said, glancing over the op-ed screed. "This doesn't prove anything—except that James Boutwell Crommelin hates President Cannon and that James Rivington would print something like this. Gedney's private dick used to work for the Mississippi Sovereignty Commission, and the guy who owns that hunting lodge on Lake Martin worked in Crommelin's losing campaigns. These guys have been geeing and hawing since the *Brown* decision destroyed their little white haven in 1954."

I could tell that Mitch was puzzled by my response, but it did not dampen his enthusiasm. Mitch so wanted to believe in Jeffreys and that his investigation was a legitimate one. "Maybe it doesn't prove anything, but it reflects the public perception that Judge Cook is too political to be hearing Whirlpool cases. And remember," he said, as if I could ever forget, "Judge Chase said that even the appearance of independence must be maintained. Burke couldn't meet that test, right? I'd say the public perception is that Judge Cook is too close to Cannon. I think we can get him taken off the case."

"Don't they teach you anything besides economic greed up there in Chicago? Maybe Posner and Manion do things differently at the 7th Circuit," I said, "but, unless I'm mistaken, you have to ask a judge to recuse before the decision. I've never heard of anyone raising the issue and trying to get a different judge after an adverse ruling. The 11th Circuit is absolutely clear and consistent on that. You can look it up."

"And as for whether Judge Cook has done anything that might appear to be prejudicial," I added, "you better remember what Jeffreys has said about that before he had an ax to grind."

"What do you mean? Are you accusing Judge Jeffreys of being a hypocrite?"

"I'm not accusing him of anything. That's not my job." Reaching back and finding the file containing a copy of a speech Jeffreys gave in 1991, I said, "Here's what Jeffreys said when he was thinking more clearly, back before the 1992 election. Listen closely, and see if you agree." Then, I read Jeffreys own words, "The judge of the future should be called upon to be an active member of his community outside the courthouse. Indeed, we are seeing lively examples of judges as commentators, judges as authors of Op-Ed pieces, and the like. But, more typically and more quietly, judges are increasingly seen not as berobed individuals leading ascetic, monastic existences, but as persons who are engaged in the life of their communities, active in the pursuit of certain political reforms, while adhering scrupulously to the commands and responsibilities of exemplary judicial conduct."

"I still think we can get him thrown off the case," Mitch replied. "You can ask Ross Anderson and Charles Haden about what happens when a trial judge criticizes Judge Jeffreys or seems inclined to support the other side. He got both of them reversed and removed from hearing the General Motors case he's been working on in South Carolina. We can do the same thing here."

That was the last I heard about the subject for a while, because I took off the last week of September to be with Lindsey before she left for Washington. I enjoyed our time together, but I did not particularly enjoy moving day. As much as she liked her apartment on Felder Avenue, she had decided to give up the lease and put everything in storage in her parents' basement in Birmingham.

I knew Lindsey would have a great time as a White House Fellow, maybe too good a time. Although I know she planned to come back to Montgomery and Huntingdon College, I wondered if she would. I did a lot of wondering that week. Like, whether either of us were up to a long distance relationship. And whether it might be a good time to check with Congressman Doggett about an opening on his staff. And whether I had made a mistake when I extended the lease on my apartment . The only thing I knew for sure was that I would miss Lindsey and our discussions, both serious and playful.

Something else I missed was the October meeting of the Policy Committee, which had not yet been scheduled when I left but had already been held when I returned on the 2nd. I didn't think it was intentional, and I don't think it would have made any difference if I had been there. The only major decision that had been made in my absence was to appeal Judge Cook's ruling on the Vance indictment. I already figured they would do that. What I hadn't anticipated was that Jeffreys would continue to publicly attack Judge Cook's integrity and use media reports of the smear campaign as a basis for trying to remove Cook from the case.

After filing the appeal, Jeffreys held yet another press conference outside the courthouse. It was obvious that the pressure was beginning to get to him, because he was playing to his political constituency and rambling far beyond the case at hand. His statement sounded at first like he was having a flashback to his days in Reeder's Justice Department. "Federal judges, like others who wield power, can behave in ways that are viewed by the people as inappropriate or imperious. For example," Jeffreys said, his face getting red and his eyes slightly bulging, "the great debate that swirls over *Roe v. Wade* is about morality, about competing visions of right and wrong, good and evil, Christian conservatives and godless liberals, and differing moral visions about life. But the larger debate is also about power and the appropriateness of courts making fundamental decisions about political policy in America. Are judges simply abusing their power? Are they usurpers, perhaps pursuing their moral vision of what is right, but in the process destroying the right of the duly appointed Independent Counsel to prosecute whomever he pleases?"

I thought perhaps that Jeffreys was ill. His unscripted remarks to the cameras reminded me of William Jennings Bryan in the highly pathetic scene when he came unwound during the Scopes trial up the road in Dayton, Tennessee, three score and ten years earlier. After he noticed that the reporters were confused, giving each other nudges and funny looks, he suddenly went back to reading the prepared statement. "The record in this case—and information in respected newspapers, ranging from the *American Speculator* to the *Washington Sun* to the *Wall Street Record*—create an unmistakable appearance of bias by Judge Cook. I have today asked the Court of Appeals to reverse Judge Cook's decision and to remove him from this case."

That got the attention of the press, which in turn put a grin on Jeffreys' face. I was stunned. Mitch could be forgiven for not knowing the law and procedural rules, but there was no excuse for Jeffreys' ignorance. Unless it wasn't ignorance, which would be even more egregious. Was he doing this only for publicity? Had he been able to have an *ex parte* discussion and get to some of the judges? Who would be on the panel hearing the appeal?

While I tried to make sense of Jeffreys' latest move, the reporters were shouting the kind of questions he was more interested in answering. One television type asked, "Why do you think Judge Cook is biased?" Another jumped in before Jeffreys could respond and asked, "How is the Vance indictment related to your mandate?"

That was what Jeffreys wanted. He rested his hands on the podium and responded with the prepared answer. "Judge Cook himself said that he would recuse himself if anything came up involving President Cannon or the First Lady, but that is not enough," he said. "The public perception is that everything that occurs in this investigation is related to President Cannon, and everyone knows that Judge Cook has an old man's crush on Diane Cannon. Whether or not we can show the facts of a particular case have any connection to President Cannon or the First Lady, a reasonable observer would still question the impartiality of Judge Cook in matters where this independent counsel is a party."

Jeffreys had delivered his sound bites for the day and was starting to leave when he saw Myles Cooper of the *Post-Advertiser* waving his arm to ask a question. Stopping and moving back to the podium, Jeffreys nodded to Cooper, knowing it would be worth his while to take that question.

"Judge Jeffreys," Cooper asked respectfully, "do you think Judge Cook is part of Alabama's partisan political cabal controlled by the Williams brothers?"

Smiling with satisfaction, Jeffreys winked and replied, "Isn't it obvious?"

The result was another publicity bonanza for Jeffreys. Typical of the insipid news coverage was one headline reading, "Jeffreys Attacks Corruption in Alabama Political Family." In the entire packet of clippings Jo Gobles distributed the next day, not a single article or editorial raised what I thought were the basic and obvious questions about jurisdiction or the procedure for requesting recusal. Only one article, Kate Macauley's story in the *Atlanta Gazette*, even quoted anyone other than Jeffreys. Macauley had asked Judge Cook what he thought about the charges of political bias made by Jeffreys at the press conference, and Cook had replied, "I have no connection with Governor Vance, and the Cannons, in my opinion, are not involved in this matter. I don't know what Mr. Jeffreys is talking about, and I doubt that he does either."

The next day's column by James Rivington in the *Washington Sun* made clear what Jeffreys was talking about—anyone and anything that might stand in his way of trying to get to President and Mrs. Cannon. Perhaps revealing more than he intended about the ultimate motives of Jeffreys and his party, Rivington wrote, "Judge Jeffreys is trying to make sense out of the tangled briars of Alabama politics in pursuit of our generation's most famous his-and-her bank robbers, Bonnie and Clod, and he has asked the Court of Appeals to remove District Judge Edward Cook from further presiding over the criminal proceedings against Gov. Jim Bibb Vance. How could anyone imagine that presiding over litigation in pursuit of the Cannons would not create a conflict of interest?"

With the obvious exception of the usual suspects and hate mongers, however, I didn't think there was a media conspiracy. Not really. The problem, as Lindsey had explained to me once, was that most reporters were generally too lazy to do an objective story. They would always go with photographs and press releases over research and analysis, and they would always take a simple dramatic narrative over a complex mundane one.

Whirlpool coverage also suffered from other factors as well. Reporters seemed to have an investment in confirming the framing scandal narrative first advanced by Luis Gerucht. It was as if one could only get on page one or win a Pulitzer by affirming rather than contradicting that assumption. There was glory to be earned in justifying the collective investment in trying to find something on the President or the First Lady, to scoring a hit and taking someone down.

Comparing the transcripts of the Senate Whirlpool Committee with the news coverage of those hearings illustrated what happened when the lazy factor combined with the framing factor. Stephen Latrator of the *New York Times* and Danielle Leonard of the *Washington Post* would always follow Senator Diletto's daily briefings or press releases for their leads, usually echoing the "troubling questions" and ignoring the obvious answers. When the Democrats on the committee would challenge Diletto's version of events or when witnesses would have responses that undermined the scandal theories, those statements were never reported.

I also sensed a news ethic that was disturbing. I first saw it when I had represented the Texas Attorney General's Office at the White House swearing-in ceremony for Justice Ginsberg. Standing near the back of the room, I could hardly hear the official proceedings that day, because the reporters were making so much noise talking among themselves. They made rude remarks about Justice Ginsberg, Justice Brennan, and everyone else participating in the ceremony. They saw themselves and their personal opinions as far more important than anyone or anything else in the room.

If someone actually said something favorable about President Cannon or wrote a piece suggesting that he had ever acted honorably, the writer would be shunned by the other reporters in the White House press corps, proof that the writer was "in the tank." It would be like someone had farted in church. No one would say anything to them. Their editors would simply be embarrassed and pretend it never happened, and the article would never run. It wouldn't be printed, and it wouldn't be news.

I don't mean to say it's all the fault of the media. It's not. Politicians and the people get pretty much what they deserve. If people didn't buy the stuff that passes for news, the corporate media would sell something else. News is always a commodity, and there's not much of a market for reality. I doubt that readers would pay to read about "Plane Lands Safely" or "Former Football Star Is Kind to Wife." And no one makes people listen to Rush Limbaugh or watch alien autopsies.

Politicians? Well, they pretty much asked for it. If they think the press has invaded their zone of privacy, they have only themselves to blame. The politicians want to tap our phones, screen our e-mail, censor television programs, regulate bedroom affection, penalize workplace humor, prohibit all stimulants, and use the law to enforce their alleged family values. They hardly have grounds for complaint when they are held to their own avowed standards. I just wished everyone would get a life and mind their own business. A little slack would go a long way toward reducing heart disease in this country.

Chapter Twenty Three

There were, that fall, signs of a slight change in the standard media story on Whirlpool. Not that it got real or that there was any vindication of Cannon, but the propensity for finding scandal was also being applied to Jeffreys. The *Nation* ran an article on October 30, examining Jeffreys' paid political activities. Kate Macauley of the *Atlanta Gazette* began asking questions and filing freedom of information requests for OIC expense vouchers. And, I can tell you, Jeffreys didn't like it one damn bit. His reaction made me remember the old proverb that "a scorner loveth not one that reproveth him."

More than once I heard Jeffreys yelling at Jo Gobles about getting the press under control. He also ordered Bart Gedney to delay complying with Macauley's requests as long as legally possible and to give her only the absolute minimum required. Even more troubling was a plan they devised to have Larry Klieghorn of Executive Watch, who had a private lawsuit going against Diane Cannon, subpoena the notes and records of every reporter who wrote anything negative about Jeffreys.

Other than that, things were pretty slow around our office. We did receive the new report from the forensics expert on Hal Goodall's death, confirming what everyone already knew, but Bart Gedney cautioned us against letting it leak just yet. Jeffreys was in Malibu that particular week at some fundraiser for a public policy institute, but he spent most of his time working for his private clients at Kirk & Polis in Washington.

Local politics were even relatively quiet after Mayor Arrington coasted to an easy victory for a fifth term last month. Down in Montgomery, it proved to be a little more interesting when Joe Reed was returned to the City Council and Emory Folmar was reelected as Mayor. However, Auburn beating Alabama was the main story in the local papers.

I took advantage of the lull to combine a little business with a lot of pleasure and flew to Washington to see Lindsey. Absence and abstinence were taking their toll, and I was in bad need of a cure for both. We spent an old-fashioned Thanksgiving down in Williamsburg, then I conveniently scheduled myself to work in our Washington office the following week, anticipating a light schedule, long lunches, and late evenings with Lindsey.

Everything went as planned on Monday. The Office of Independent Counsel had office space across the street from the Justice Department, and I had no trouble finding an empty desk to call my own. Meeting Lindsey for lunch was a little more complicated. I followed her instructions, arrived early, picked up my appointment badge at the west entrance of the Old Executive Office Building, and wandered around the halls looking for her office. After climbing the stairs and taking two trips around the perimeter, I finally asked someone where I might find Room 191 and was led to the Speechwriting Office on one of the interior cross-corridors.

Lindsey greeted me with a big smile and asked, "Did you get lost?"

"Nah," I grinned, "I just wanted to explore the building. Great skylights. This place is fancier than Miss Mona's Chicken Ranch."

Lindsey's office was functional, but the stark yellow walls with painted white trim hardly matched the grandeur of the marble and tile in the Indian Treaty Room up on the fourth floor. She introduced me to everyone in the office, and I behaved myself. I didn't try to remember the names, but I had seen them all before, eager young men and women so proud and so important. Mitch Palmer would have been right at home.

Lindsey had planned to give me a tour of the west wing and take me to lunch in the White House mess; however, I didn't think that was a such good idea. Independent Counsel stock was pretty low in the White House at that time, and with my luck I'd be recognized by either the staff or some reporter. The Red Sage was nearby, and the food was better.

When I returned to my office that afternoon, I could see that things weren't going to work out quite like I had expected. The Congressional Republicans had been demanding that Jeffreys investigate the firing of the White House Travel Office employees a couple of years ago, and Harriet Otis had just dropped that project in our lap. Jeffreys would be delighted with the assignment, because it would give him another reason to send subpoenas to the White House, an excuse to hire some more lawyers, and an opportunity for even more press coverage. Some men grow with responsibility, but Jeffreys just swelled.

I'm afraid I wasn't a very good guest that evening. I tried to be excited and ask Lindsey about her work in the White House Speechwriting Office, but I spent far too much time talking about my own frustration with the Travel Office project. "I don't see what the big deal is," I fumed. "They serve at the pleasure of the President, and he had every right to fire them all on day one. Why would they keep anyone from Stuart's staff is beyond my little Texas bain. There was an election, right? Cannon won, and Stuart lost. What did they expect? And besides, why the hell should the White House be making airline and hotel arrangements for the press, anyway? Let them make their own damn travel arrangements instead of having government employees do it for them."

"The big deal," Lindsey said, "is that seven middle-aged fat white guys got fired from cushy jobs as glorified bellhops for the press. That's the big deal. It was a story, because they'd been taking care of the press corps and had a lot of friends in the media who owed them favors. It became a political issue when the Republicans discovered that the First Lady wanted them fired, and the Lynch Legal Foundation demanded an investigation."

She was right, but, I asked, "So what? It's not a crime to want someone fired. It's not even a crime to fire them. And it wouldn't be a crime to abolish the whole office."

"No, it's not a crime," Lindsey said calmly. "It's an opportunity for a bunch of insecure fat boys in Congress to attack Diane Cannon. They don't like her, and they'll do anything they can to publicly discredit her. Part of it is political revenge, because she worked on the Judiciary Committee staff when they voted out articles of impeachment against Nixon. But it's more than that. Remember Wattenberg's article in the *American Speculator* and Pat Buchanan's speech at the Republican Convention? Congressman Bardus claiming that she was having an affair with Goodall, and Dorkman suggesting she is a lesbian. Size matters, and those boys have very small minds."

"The hardest thing for those troglodytes to deal with," Lindsey said, "is that Diane Cannon presents a strong role model for a lot of women, combining family with a career, and she gives young women ideas about things more important than what they should fix for dinner. It's hard to keep women in their place once they've seen the possibilities and their own potential. So who did Congress hire as chief counsel for their investigation? Barbara Stevens of the so-called Independent Women's Forum, a group that backs Christine Putnam and opposes equal rights! Besides, Diane Cannon's a lot smarter than most of those guys, and they find that especially threatening. I know you find that hard to understand, but, believe me, they do."

Right again, she was. I thought smart was sexy. And it was my bedtime. My only hope was that all middle-aged white guys wouldn't have to suffer for the transgressions of a few. I didn't.

On Wednesday I decided to spend the day checking out the Senate Whirlpool Committee hearings, and it was quite a show. The Hart Senate Office Building, where Diletto's committee was meeting, had considerably less character than the Russell Building, but maybe that was appropriate. The hearing room had the ambiance of a convention trade show— bright lights, television monitors, red drapes on all the tables, and a bunch of guys in suits. That day they were going to be trying once again to sell Ellende Varken's story. Perhaps it would be a rerun, but it was the only thing playing.

Ellende Varken opened her act by reading a long prepared statement, updating her previous testimony before Congressman Leech's committee and portraying herself as a brave soldier in the fight against James Madison Cannon. On and on she droned, telling how she fought against enormous political pressure from above and how she felt vindicated by the subsequent work of Jeffreys and the Office of Independent Counsel. Varken had an easy time until the Democrats on the committee began asking questions that shot huge holes in her story.

When the committee took a break for lunch, Senator Diletto beamed for the cameras, but the unforgiving lights glared off his sweaty dome and the microphones faithfully reproduced his nasal voice. For the first time in months of testimony before his committee, he finally had a witness who had suggested that the Cannons might have some criminal exposure, even if only as "potential witnesses" to something someone else might have done ten years ago. "Mrs. Varken raised some very troubling questions in her testimony before the committee this morning," Diletto said with furrowed brow. "This would never have come to light without her dedication and persistence."

Senator Doddridge assessed the testimony for the Democrats on the committee, and his analysis was starkly different. "Varken's testimony contained numerous inconsistencies and implausible statements," he said. "She testified under oath, for example, that the recorder that secretly taped her entire conversation with Elizabeth Gurley on February 2, 1994, turned on by itself. In explaining this unlikely phenomenon, Varken admitted that the tape recorder was not a voice-activated machine, but testified that the tape recorder was eight years old and didn't always function as expected. The Committee issued a subpoena for that tape recorder, but Varken testified that after the recorder died in mid-February 1994, she purchased a new tape recorder and discarded the old one, which had supposedly taped the conversation with Gurley."

"The evidence, however, contradicts Varken's assertion," Doddridge continued. "Office Depot, the store that sold the new tape recorder to Varken, provided records that incontrovertibly establish that Varken had purchased the new tape recorder on January 17, 1994, immediately after meeting with Congressman Leech and over two weeks prior to the taping of the conversation with Gurley. Thus, Varken's explanation of the old tape recorder turning on by itself, which strained credulity in the first place, is refuted by the fact that she had already purchased the new tape recorder and, by her own admission, had discarded the old recorder when she purchased the new one."

"Second," Doddridge said, "another example of Varken's implausible testimony occurred when she stated under oath that she never attempted to profit from the Jefferson investigation. Varken then conceded that in 1993 she attempted to market versions of copyrighted shirts and coffee mugs bearing the logo 'Presidential B.I.T.C.H.,' which stood for 'Bubba, I've Taken Charge Here.' She said she thought such items would sell well because of the 'political climate'—a political climate she had done much to create. Varken provided her RTC office telephone number to potential investors so that she could pursue this business opportunity while at work on the federal payroll. Mrs. Varken refused to acknowledge the impropriety in conducting personal business affairs in her governmental office or in marketing a product that disparaged people she had identified as witnesses in the course of her investigation."

"Third, and bear with me here," Doddridge said, "Mrs. Varken testified under oath that she did not contact the FBI or the United States Attorneys Office about the 1992 Jefferson referral until December 1992, one month after the Presidential election. Varken testified under oath that she "would have had no reason" to contact the FBI or the United States Attorneys Office in September, October and November 1992 to ask whether the referral would be pursued, whether subpoenas would be issued, or whether a grand jury investigation would be opened."

"As before," Doddridge continued, "Mrs. Varken's sworn statements were directly contradicted by the testimony and contemporaneous notes of FBI Special Agent Herman Tuck. Tuck's testimony, along with that of several other career federal law enforcement officials, established that Varken repeatedly contacted the FBI and the United States Attorney's Office between the referral's submission on September 1, 1992 and the Presidential election two months later. The evidence showed that Varken tried during this critical time period to encourage the opening of a formal FBI or grand jury investigation."

Senator Doddridge then laid out a number of facts that Diletto seemed to ignore. "In fact," Doddridge said emphatically, "Varken began calling almost immediately. Agent Tuck returned one of Varken's calls on September 10, 1992, and told her that the FBI and the United States Attorney's Office had not made a decision about the Jefferson Savings referral and that they were not in a position to provide her with daily status reports. Nevertheless, Varken traveled to Birmingham on September 18, 1992, and dropped in on Tuck at the FBI's Birmingham field office. Tuck, who was away from his office, returned to find Varken there waiting for him and demanding to know how soon they were going to act on her referral. Michael Osborn, the Special Agent in Charge of the FBI's Birmingham field office, testified that the timing of Varken's referral and her comment about altering the course of history caused him and others at the FBI to be concerned about Varken's objectivity and overall professionalism."

"Failing to force the FBI to act as quickly as she wanted," Doddridge said, "Mrs. Varken then turned to the United States Attorney's Office in Birmingham. United States Attorney Tom Davenport testified that he was aware of four or five calls that Varken made to his office between early September and October 16, 1992. Varken's contacts with the FBI and the United States Attorney's Office prior to the Presidential election caused several high-level officials in those agencies to be suspicious of Varken motives. For example, United States Attorney Tom Davenport, a Republican appointed by President Stuart, testified that Varken's unusual sense of urgency to open an investigation of the Cannons before the election made him circumspect about the referral."

"In short," Senator Doddridge concluded, "Mrs. Varken's sworn testimony regarding the tape recorder, her sworn statement about not trying to profit, the evidence that she was conducting a private business from a government office, and her testimony under oath that she did not push the FBI and the United States Attorney to act quickly before the election, all demonstrate the character of the witness. Senator Diletto has been desperately seeking evidence of a crime related to Whirlpool and Jefferson Savings, and I think his witness this morning has provided that. I am certain that Mr. Jeffreys, a man with a reputation for fairness and integrity, will examine this testimony carefully. If he finds evidence that a witness has committed perjury, I am confident that he will seek indictments by the grand jury."

Yeah, right. Fat chance of that. As I rushed to the basement to get a sandwich in the cafeteria, I was glad that I had been there to hear Varken's testimony and Senator Doddridge's summary and analysis. I doubted that the afternoon session would be able to top that, but I looked forward to it just the same.

When the committee was called to order that afternoon, Senator Catherine Sloan began the cross-examination for the Democrats. "I am deeply concerned by the fact that you gratuitously listed the Cannons as witnesses when you had absolutely no evidence that they were aware of the activities that are the basis for the referral. Then you pestered everyone you could find, trying to start some kind of criminal proceedings that would, no doubt, have been leaked to the press just before the 1992 election," she said. "Don't you think there's something here that doesn't pass the smell test?"

"What I think is that the Cannons benefited from Banaghan's activities," Varken snapped. "They think they're so smart, and they should have known what was going on. If the committee really wants to know what the Cannons knew, why not invite the Cannons to testify as I am today and have in the past? Why not ask them directly?"

"I appreciate your advice, Mrs. Varken, but I think your political motivation is the key factor here," replied Senator Sloan. "Weren't you out to save President Stuart's election by trying to smear Governor Cannon with guilt by association?"

"I had no personal bias against Mr. Cannon," Varken replied without answering the question directly.

Then, fending off several attempts by Chairman Diletto and Majority Counsel Cahn to suppress the evidence, Senator Lucilla Sartain produced a copy of a 22-page personal letter Mrs. Varken had written in February 1992. The point was not so much that she had been defrauding the government by using RTC computers and writing long personal letters during office hours. Instead, Senator Sartain confronted Varken with the evidence of her own words. Less than a month before she began her crusade against Cannon, Varken had called Governor Cannon a "lying bastard." Pausing for dramatic effect, Sartain looked directly at Ellende Varken and said, "I don't think that's a compliment. Do you?"

"Frankly, Senator Sartain, that was a cheap shot," Varken protested.

Sartain didn't back off, asking pointedly, "What was a cheap shot? Your characterization of then-Governor Cannon?"

Unable to explain away the inconsistencies in her testimony or refute the evidence produced against her, Varken cracked under the pressure of the questioning. She grew tearful and said she was suffering chest pains. A doctor was called, and Mrs. Varken's blood pressure was reported to be 210 over 110. Varken was helped out of the room by one of her attorneys, never to return. Gastone Diletto suspended the hearings for the day, and he quickly left the room without talking to the press. It had not been a good day for the Republican cause.

Senator Hatchet was the only Republican on the Whirlpool Committee to come to Varken's defense. Discounting the total destruction of Varken's credibility under questioning, Hatchet protested, "The Jefferson Savings examination was not a politically motivated investigation. Whether Ellende Varken hated or liked the Cannons is irrelevant, as are her political views, the personal insults she used in the letter, and her attempt to make money on the T-shirts with the B-word."

Mark Schine of the Lynch Legal Foundation, which was providing legal representation for Ellende Varken, was unable to escape with Diletto and could not avoid the media. He didn't even try to defend the inconsistencies in Varken's testimony, instead attacking the Democrats on the committee. "I expected they would go to any lengths to disparage this witness, but to pull a sentence out of a very lengthy letter like that is absolutely despicable. This is a hit-and-run cheap shot that is beneath contempt," he said.

I found it all slightly amusing, but our office had long ago recognized Varken's game for the political vendetta that it was. I told Lindsey all about the hearings at dinner that evening, and we made jokes about how the media scandal junkies would deal with the unmasking of Leech's key informant and Diletto's star witness. Nothing we had imagined, even after a few glasses of wine, even came close to what actually happened.

I nearly spilled my coffee when I saw Stephen Latrator's article in the *New York Times* the next morning. The headline read, "Senate Hearing Touches on Cannon's Integrity." From the day that Luis Gerucht and Nelson Grenier had invented the original plot during the 1992 campaign, the *New York Times* had followed the procrustean dictum, "All the facts that fit, we print." Consequently, every morning seemed to be the dawn of a new error. Either that, or Mr. Latrator and I had been observing two different committee hearings.

When I arrived at the office shortly before 9 o'clock, the door was still locked. Two cups of coffee later, I came back to find the staff in a state of excitement. Jeffreys, who had been pursuing his private legal business down in North Carolina for most of the last month, was going to be in the Washington office for the rest of the week. Not the OIC office, but his real office over at Kirk & Polis. From what I could gather, he was in town trying to wrap up the investigation of the Resolution Trust Corporation before it went out of business at the end of the year. That day, however, he had scheduled a noon meeting on the Hill with the Congressional committee chairs to discuss coordination of their investigations with ours.

The place was in a state of chaos. Mary Surratt, the office manager, was hastily trying to prepare a briefing packet for Jeffreys, bringing him up to speed on what the office had been doing. The fax machine was humming with memos from Bart Gedney and the Birmingham staff. Marty Dies, who was Jeffreys' administrative assistant for the Washington office, was particularly agitated. He served the same function as Mitch Palmer and would be accompanying Jeffreys to staffing the meeting.

I tried to be helpful. I told Marty that I'd be glad to brief him on what was going on in Birmingham and that I'd be glad to go with him to the meeting if he wanted. Not interested, he said. He had been working with the legislative leadership staff and could handle it. That was more than okay with me. I had plenty of other things I could do, and lunch with that group would be low on the fun scale.

Lunch with Janet Fox, on the other hand, might be considerably more interesting. I called her office at the National Press Building, but I ended up talking to a voice-mail machine. Hated those damn things, but I left my number and an invitation for lunch. Janet's office was midway between my office and the White House, so Lindsey might be able to join us.

With nothing else to do, I got another cup of coffee and made myself at home in front of the television in the conference room. I think it was then that I started to worry about my health. I realized that I might be in danger of ruining my kidneys with too much coffee, straining my eyes with too much C-SPAN, or choking to death on all the bullshit being shoveled out of the Whirlpool Committee hearings.

As I watched as Brian Lamb referee a squabble between a couple of Senators on his morning chat show, Senator Walsh seemed to have a good handle on what Diletto was doing. "This whole thing is a political sham," Walsh charged, "there's no question about it. I'll tell you what. If I can bring 200 FBI agents to New York, Senator Diletto's home state, about 100 IRS agents, agents from the RTC, the FDIC, the SEC, and throughout the whole alphabet of the federal government, I'll guarantee you I could hold a hearing on Senator Diletto and the Republicans, and you'd find some interesting things there. That's what's happened in Alabama. Had Charles Stuart been reelected president of the United States, I wonder if my colleague, Senator Diletto, thinks we would have any Whirlpool hearings? Of course not. That's the issue—that the president of the United States is named James Cannon."

"We've seen in this case," Walsh jibed, "some $30 million having been expended on what I call the Dolor-Diletto Hearings and the George Jeffreys Gong Show. They've subpoenaed now, I think, around 250 or 300 witnesses with depositions and huge legal fees. It would be laughable if it were not so serious and were not breaking so many people financially. I think the Republican National Committee should be paying these legal fees for these poor people, and I think it has truly turned into a sham. Those weren't hearings to find facts. They are totally orchestrated and designed with a bias to do something to James Cannon and find him guilty of something 15 years ago, and it may be guilt by association—dragging all these people through the mud and, truly, breaking them financially. Well, Joe McCarthy also used guilt by association, and I think this is, almost, a McCarthy-like inquisition. It is a disgrace to the Senate and to our judicial system."

I guessed from the tenor of his remarks that Senator Walsh was not running for reelection and would not have to work with Diletto and the Republicans much longer. Several Senators had already announced that they would not be standing for election in 1996, and I could certainly understand why.

Janet finally called back about 11:00. "I'm on the Hill, covering a Senate Finance Committee hearing on monetary policy, but I'd love to do the lunch thing," she said.

"Great," I replied, slightly disappointed that time and distance had conspired to rule out my fantasy of having lunch with two drop-dead beautiful Southern women. My knowledge of Capitol Hill cuisine had faded in the years since I had lived in DC, but I still had a certain fondness for two of my old favorites. "How about the Dubliner? Or, maybe the Hawk and Dove?"

"How about, not," Janet said with a laugh. "You are such a redneck, Wilkes."

She was teasing, but she was right. "Hey, they serve food, too. Not just beer," I protested defensively.

"I know," she said, "but I'm on a short leash today."

"That's an interesting image," I replied, trying to get even for the redneck remark.

"Watch your mouth, boy. And meet me at the Monocle at 12:30. That way we'll have longer to visit before I have to get back to the hearing," she said. "You know where it is, right?"

"The Molecule? Sure, everybody in Texas knows where that is. It was John Tower's second home," I replied in my best East Texas twang. "See ya there."

When I walked into the restaurant, I thought it was my worst nightmare. Janet wasn't there yet, but Jeffreys was, sitting at a long table near the back of the room. Apparently he and the boys had extended their little strategy session, and moved it down the hill for lunch. I guess I had thought they'd be meeting in one of the Senate offices or somewhere. But no. Just my luck.

Janet soon arrived, and we were seated a safe distance away from the little Republican cabal. The group was talking in hushed tones, but they were quite animated. I recognized most of them. Clapham, Bardus, and Leech were there for the House, staffed by Leech's press boy, David Rapper. Senator Diletto and Senator Rantallion were there with Ray Cahn and little David Winderig. Jeffreys was sitting at the head of the table, with Marty Dies on his right, furiously taking notes. Ten stuffed suits. I wouldn't want to have a cold beer or a personal conversation with any of them. The stern looks on their faces reminded me of something an old lawyer back in Texas once told me about picking juries. "Never put anyone on a jury whose mouth puckers smaller than a chicken's asshole," he said. I have used that same standard in picking my friends and drinking buddies, too.

Janet had more interest in what they were talking about than I did. She was always working, which was why she was so good. "So," she asked, "what did Jeffreys say about the settlement? They sure came out of that one smelling like a rose, huh?"

"What settlement? They're not settling anything except who gets to piss on Cannon next."

"No, I meant the settlement with the Resolution Trust Corporation," Janet said.

"I don't think the investigation has been completed yet. At least, Jeffreys hasn't mentioned anything about it."

"Don't play dumb with me. I know why Jeffreys is in town. Kirk & Polis just settled that million dollar professional misconduct lawsuit for pennies on the dollar. The records are sealed, but my sources tell me that they got out for about $350,000."

"I'm afraid you've lost me," I said. "I don't know anything about any lawsuit against Kirk & Polis. I thought you were talking about our investigation of the RTC."

Janet was incredulous. "You mean Jeffreys was conducting an investigation of the RTC at the same time the RTC had a million dollar lawsuit pending against his law firm? That would certainly explain a lot of things!"

No shit. It would explain all those phone calls Jeffreys was making to Kirk & Polis the day the Policy Committee voted to open the investigation. It would also explain why our investigation was taking so long. I didn't think I should say anything, because I'd probably say the wrong thing, but Janet's stare made clear that I wasn't going to get off without a response. The only thing I could come up with was, "Maybe Jeffreys didn't know about the lawsuit."

"Don't bullshit me, John. You know he's on the Management Committee at Kirk & Polis, and that suit was filed long before he was appointed as Independent Counsel. I believe that's something they just might have mentioned—the federal government filing suit against the firm and seeking $1 million for professional misconduct—don't you? Besides, I told you about it the last time we talked on the phone."

I looked down at my salad and chased an elusive piece of lettuce with my fork. "Yeah, I think it's something they might have discussed," I said rather quietly, remembering now that she had mentioned it before.

At that moment, three men walked quickly past us and joined the meeting in progress at Jeffreys' table. I could tell from the way they were greeted and seated that they had been expected. I didn't recognize any of them. But Janet did, and she thought it very interesting. Robin McKale, she said, was Ira Dolor's political director. I knew the name, because Jeffreys had caught hell for sending out a fundraising letter for

McKale's congressional campaign last year. Sam Allen and Adrian Crow were political fixers from Dolor's campaign staff, old friends that he had always been able to count on in a crunch over the years.

Very interesting, indeed, I thought. The only question in my mind was who had invited the Dolor campaign operatives to participate in a meeting that was ostensibly about coordinating official matters. Jeffreys had been on McKale's campaign committee and had been involved with fundraising for that unsuccessful effort even after he took the assignment as Independent Counsel, so that was a possibility. Maybe Leech, but he seemed too dumb. More likely, I suppose, was that Senator Diletto was responsible, assuming that term could ever be applied to him. Diletto was heading Dolor's campaign in New York and was one of the directors of his national campaign. The entire history of the Senate Whirlpool Committee reflected an effort to defeat Cannon and elect Dolor, so perhaps I was being naive to think the political connections between his committee assignments and campaign activities would be distinct. I was still handicapped by the ideas I'd first embraced in a ninth grade civics class, but I was beginning to outgrow all that nonsense. It was a hard lesson.

When Janet and I left the restaurant, the meeting was still going strong. I waved to Jeffreys on my way out. He seemed surprised to see me there, even somewhat embarrassed, but he acknowledged us with a nod. He did not invite us to join the group.

Chapter Twenty Four

There were other reasons why I had come to Washington that week. I stopped by Lloyd Doggett's office and had a long chat with Michael Barker, an old friend of mine and now his Administrative Assistant. I had planned to say hello and remind him that I might still be interested in a staff position if something came open. I didn't have to say that. Nor did I have a chance. Barker and I spent the rest of the afternoon talking about Leroy Reichman's shutdown of the government, Dick Armey's stupid remarks that regularly embarrassed our state, and the various Congressional committees that were searching in vain for something on the Cannons. After work, we continued the conversation at the Hawk and Dove, and I had no fear of being called a redneck for suggesting it. Not by Barker.

The week in Washington and my time with Lindsey ended too soon. Being back in Birmingham only served to remind me that I'd be much happier somewhere else. Not that Alabama was such a bad place to live, but the job was beginning to destroy what remained of my political soul. The Diletto's circus in Washington and Jeffreys' interminable witch hunt here in Alabama were undermining not only Cannon's administration but the very institutions of government and the political fabric of the republic. Good men and women would not enter public service or subject their families to the toxic politics of personal destruction that was becoming the norm. Only the slime would survive.

The December session of the OIC Policy Committee did nothing to revive my hopes. Even the housekeeping announcements were discouraging. Jeffreys began by commending James Peck for the outstanding work he had done and announced that Peck would be leaving the staff next month. No big surprise there. The extra $2,987 a month in tax-free housing and meal allowances we each received expired after 18 months on the job, so I fully expected several members of the staff to be returning to the private sector soon. The surprise, at least to me, was that Peck was going to work for the Chicago office of Jeffreys' law firm, Kirk & Polis. And, I was a bit puzzled when Jeffreys said, "Mr. Peck might well be even more useful to our work in his new position." Whatever that meant.

Then the other shoe dropped. Jeffreys planned to replace Peck with Walt Lecraw. Walt was another former Assistant United States Attorney from Dallas who had lost his job when Cannon was elected. I had never met him, but I knew of his reputation as a mean and spiteful prosecutor in Texas. He referred to grand jurors as "the silent lambs," and he was once quoted as bragging that he could indict a ham sandwich. Most prosecutors could, but few were as inclined to try. Lecraw treated every minor infraction as a major case, and he would fit in well. Gedney and Hathorne were especially laudatory of his abilities, confirming everything I already suspected when Gedney said, "Walt knows how to make people squirm, to make witnesses realize they have to tell us what we want to know."

The rest of the agenda that day was devoted to reviewing the testimony of Diane Rankin Cannon. She had given depositions and answered interrogatories from four different federal agencies looking at various aspects of the Whirlpool-Jefferson investigation over several years. In addition, Burke had interviewed her once, and Jeffreys had done so twice. Over and over, she had answered question after question. Sometimes the same questions again and again. Jeffreys and Gedney had long since given up on finding anything substantive on either the President or the First Lady. The goal now was to find any possible contradictions in the answers provided in the thousands of pages of transcripts. Even a failure to remember some detail of events 10 to 15 years ago, Gedney suggested, might be used as the basis for some charge. False information to a federal agency. Perjury. Obstruction of justice. Getting an indictment on any of these, even without a snowball's chance of a conviction, was the goal. The 1996 election was only 11 months away. Time and success—and any hope of Jeffreys being nominated for the Supreme Court—were slipping away.

As the meeting came to a close, I asked a question that had been burning in my mind since my lunch with Janet Fox. Not the one about who invited the Dolor campaign staff to plot Whirlpool publicity strategy with Jeffreys and Diletto. I didn't really give a rat's ass about that. Trying to sound merely curious, I asked, "Uh, where are we on that investigation of the Resolution Trust Corporation folks? Any indication of improper activities or obstruction of justice?"

It was another of those E. F. Hutton freeze-frame moments. Gedney and Hathorne both looked at each other. James Peck sat back down. Jeffreys just stood there for a moment saying nothing but looking down at his stack of files. "Um, we made a decision on that last Friday," Jeffreys said. "I guess you were still in Washington. Sorry I failed to inform you about that. Nothing there. We've closed the investigation. Unless you think there's a reason to reopen it?"

"Nope. That's sorta what I figured," I replied, choking on the implications. It would have been a waste of time to confront Jeffreys with the information about the sweetheart settlement of the suit against Kirk & Polis. He'd probably deny he even knew about it.

We wouldn't even report that we had closed our investigation of the RTC matter without charging anyone. What the public would never know was that Jeffreys also had another motivation for taking on the RTC investigation. He had successfully prevented the Justice Department from investigating the involvement of the Stuart administration in trying to leak the criminal referrals to the media before the last election.

Other matters were not going very well for Jeffreys that month. Editorial writers were beginning to question the ethics of his private legal practice. Even the Republican partisans were starting to raise questions about Jeffreys' conduct of the Whirlpool investigation. Why was he taking so long? When was he going to bring charges against President Cannon? It had been more than two years since the first appointment of a special prosecutor, and no one had yet identified a single crime—not even a misdemeanor—with which James or Diane Cannon could be charged. Rumors would surface on a daily basis that major indictments were coming soon, then disappointment would settle in when nothing happened.

Jeffreys became more irritable. He was overly sensitive, sulking and pouting over the slightest remark about his integrity, or lack thereof. He also seemed to resent having to spend time with the Whirlpool investigation, because several of his high dollar cases were coming to trial. Rather than doing anything to eliminate the obvious ethical conflicts, Jeffreys decided to launch a public relations campaign to defend his conduct. Every time he was in Birmingham, he wanted to give a speech to a civic group or have some other controlled opportunity for positive personal spin.

I was giving speeches, too, but for different reasons and on different topics. On December 15th, I was invited to give the keynote for a Bill of Rights Celebration at the Beulah Baptist Church in Montgomery. Lindsey had given them my name, so I agreed to do it. It was a chance, I thought, to talk about the real Baptist tradition favoring freedom of religion, and I loaded it up with high praise for the contributions of Roger Williams, Isaac Backus, and John Leland. And, I might add, I didn't pass up the chance to take a shot at some of the contemporary television Baptists who had abandoned that proud heritage and would destroy the wall of separation between church and state.

My speech was well received. And so was I, considering I was the only blue-eyed person in the room that evening. The only unfortunate consequence of my giving the speech was that Jeffreys had caught me in the office working on my remarks that Saturday morning. Most of the staff had already left for Christmas vacation, and Jeffreys insisted that I accompany him to a speaking engagement Sunday evening.

I wasn't sure whether Jeffreys wanted the company, wanted to appear more important by having an attendant, or wanted to rub my nose in his performance, but I agreed to go. He even made me drive. His talk was at the Cathedral of the Cross, a big suburban Assembly of God church with full broadcast facilities. Jeffreys liked that. The crowd was smaller than the one for the God and Country speech I heard last year, but that didn't matter. Television mattered.

At first I thought the minister's opening remarks must have disappointed Jeffreys. It was sincere enough, but the fire was gone. In its stead was a combination of smooth and slick and syrup. Television apparently had the same impact on preachers as it has had on politicians and other con artists. I longed for the days when oratory was an outdoor art, when audiences were active participants in the communication experience. Television had killed public speaking and storytelling, making us passive voyeurs in a mass media morass.

Wilkenson O. Bellengabler III, however, introduced Jeffreys with all the fervor his grandfather had mustered on behalf of Shurmond's Dixiecrats in 1948. He followed the publicity bio Jo Gobles always sent out in advance and added a rousing drum roll from the neo-Confederate hymnbook. Hate can be a powerful tonic. Bellengabler had the fire, but it was one that gave heat instead of light. I winced, then I smiled as I remembered the introduction and the response I had received the night before. I felt like I had been at a political rally. But, then, it was. And this was. Just that my experience was with a very different kind of politics than that of Jeffreys and his crowd.

When Jeffreys began speaking, I realized that he hadn't been disappointed at all by that introduction. He began by looking past the crowd to the cameras, and he continued by speaking with that same preacher's voice he always used for television, sounding exactly like the pious fakers on the 700 Club. "I appreciate that fine introduction and your hospitality and the opportunity to share with you some of my thoughts about the Whirlpool investigation. You know, the liberal media have not done a very good job of covering our work, so there are some misconceptions about what we have been doing here in Alabama and in Washington."

"Some have criticized me for being too slow and trying to time indictments to affect the elections in 1996," Jeffreys said, with only a slight bit of self-pity. "I'd have to take issue with the first point, the idea that my investigation is taking too long. Investigations of a complicated nature end up taking a while because of the very demanding aspects of getting all the facts. You know, balancing the check book for the family is always an effort. You get all these bills in that your wife has charged and so forth. Imagine trying to reconstruct the records of a savings and loan company or a failed real estate company with many different land purchasers and so on. It's a big job."

"So a typical independent counsel investigation has gone on for some considerable time, some for as long as seven years," he added, trying to make partisan sound palatable. "Indictments must be brought in a timely fashion, and sometimes they might come just before an election. Now, I don't anticipate that here, but I think it's important for everyone to understand the historical context. I would have liked to have seen this completely wrapped up before an election year. It is not wise, it is not prudent, it is not sound for a prosecutor to be returning an indictment, say, two weeks or a month before a primary or before a general election. Will the critical issues be addressed, will the facts be out far in advance of the election? My prediction is that they will."

"Now, about Kenneth Burke," Jeffreys said, although no one had asked. "I guess the Eleventh Commandment, to paraphrase my friend, President Reeder, the Eleventh Commandment, I suppose, of independent counsels should be 'don't criticize another independent counsel appointed as Burke was by the Attorney General.' Why is complete independence from the executive branch so necessary? The idea, basically, is mistrust and suspicion of power. Just as no one should be the judge in his own case, we should not, as a matter of law, trust anyone appointed by President Cannon or Attorney General Otis to investigate the President or other high ranking officers of the executive branch. We take a page from Lord Acton: 'Power tends to corrupt, and absolute power corrupts absolutely.'

"But, without reflecting on Burke's compromised appointment, what I did was to say that, in light of the duties that have been vested in me by Judge Sam Chase, my job was to take another look at everything and to carry on and to do the most thorough investigation that I can. So, I have certainly tried to build upon the preliminary work that Burke and his colleagues had done, but to go on from there, recognizing that, frankly, they had only been on the job for about six months," he said, as if a U. S. Attorney would ever take that long on a case.

"We have tried to be exactingly thorough, leaving no pebble unturned," Jeffreys bragged upon himself. "We view our mission as to get at the truth, to find out the facts, and that means that you have to, at times, use some pretty harsh measures in the process in order to get to the very bottom of these complicated activities, many of which occurred more than 15 years ago. We will do whatever it takes. Whatever it takes. And I think that's one aspect that people need to keep in mind."

"I have been on the job now for about 16 months," Jeffreys said, warming up to singing his own praises, "and in that time there have been several indictments and guilty pleas here in Alabama, even if they don't relate directly to President and Mrs. Cannon or Whirlpool. We're looking ahead to a major trial, God willing, early in the year against Jim Bibb Vance and Josh Banaghan and Jessie Banaghan."

Then Jeffreys started rambling, almost incoherently. I couldn't tell where he was going when he said, "Frankly, if everyone would come forward, give us all their records from the past 15 years, and simply tell us whatever we want to know, we could wind this up. But individuals still have some rights, and unfortunately that's our system, and we have to live with that system for the time being. Individuals have the right to say, 'No, I'm innocent on all these charges, and I will see you in court.' So, I have been looking ahead to the first big trial of the principals involved in the Jefferson Savings failure. But again, it comes on the heels of these various and sundry guilty pleas we have managed to get from a number of people along the way. Don't forget that."

"Some doubtless are getting tired of hearing about Whirlpool," Jeffreys said, realizing that lots of folks were getting tired of hearing him drone on, "but I think overall the American people would very much like to know the truth. 'You shall know the truth, and the truth shall set you free.' I think they want to know what we find, not something that White House flacks and Democrat spin-doctors come up with. And then the country could come to the judgment day next November and then move on to other things."

"Judge Chase said I had the authority to investigate anything even remotely related to President Cannon, so I want to say it's quite wrong to think I have in any way exceeded my authority," he said, revealing what was really bothering him most, that anyone would question him. "In fact, that criticism has been rejected by United States District Judge A. George Gaston here in Birmingham, a very fine judge. And grand jurors from the Northern District of Alabama, 23 good and honest citizens, have evaluated the evidence we presented to them and have agreed with me that these charges should be brought against Governor Vance, against Mr. and Mrs. Banaghan."

Jeffreys could tell that even this crowd wasn't buying his version. "Now, okay, in a separate case, another indictment against Governor Vance was dismissed by Edward Cook, a different Federal Judge here in Birmingham, and he held that we were outside our jurisdiction. Now, that judge is a Democrat, and there are some pretty convincing newspaper editorials in the *Wall Street Record* and articles by Judge James Boutwell Crommelin in the *Washington Sun* showing that Judge Cook is biased."

"We have appealed Judge Cook's ruling, and, God willing, I will be arguing that appeal soon before the United States Court of Appeals in Atlanta," Jeffreys boasted. Then he added something that came as a complete surprise to me. "The appeals panel for Whirlpool matters is made up of unbiased judges, headed by my old friend Gordo Bowner from North Carolina, and I have an idea we can count on a more favorable ruling. We might even be able to get Judge Cook removed from the case," he said with a touch of superiority.

"It is a heavy responsibility that has been put upon me," Jeffreys said with all the empathy of an undertaker, "and I accept that and recognize that the job really does have to be done in a certain way. It has to appear to be done professionally, rather than politically. It has to be done with the appearance of some respect for people who are caught up in the investigation as suspects, and targets, or simply as witnesses. But yes, it's got to be done just right, regardless of the consequences to anyone."

After a little more self-justification, Jeffreys continued, "I've been blessed to be in public life for long enough to know that criticism comes with the territory and that your job as a public servant is carrying on the work of the people who appointed you, is to call them the way you see them, call balls and strikes, be as thorough as you can be, and then, guess what, yes, you're going to get criticized all the way around."

Jeffreys then started whining as he complained, "Some have even been so reckless as to question my ethics and integrity, and sometimes that does hurt me. I have worked hard to demonstrate my personal rectitude and to cultivate the appearance of fairness, and these attacks have probably undermined my public reputation. I refuse to answer these personal attacks, mostly from Democrats, I might add. Instead, I find comfort in my faith in God and, especially, in the Book of Job and the 35th Psalm."

Finally, he wrapped it up, right on the 28-minute signal from the camera operator. "I ask that you keep me in your prayers. May the Lord's will be done, on earth, as it is in heaven. Thank you very much, and God bless you."

The reaction was much more restrained than that after his speech at Briarwood. I couldn't tell if the audience was awed or bored, but there was only a smattering of applause when Jeffreys finished. He seemed not to mind, for he knew the speech would show three times on the local cable system, and copies would be made available by our office to the commercial networks in time for the late news.

Receiving far less attention than Jeffreys' speech was the final report prepared by Ike Parker for the Resolution Trust Corporation. Although the taxpayers shelled out $3 million for Parker's investigation, not a nickel was spent on a press conference to announce the final conclusions. Not even a news release. Parker must have been disheartened by his own findings, and the press had little interest in a report that failed to confirm their sanctioned storyline.

Our office received a copy of the Parker Report on December 18th. As I reviewed it, I realized why it didn't make network news. It wasn't only that reporters would have had to find a copy and actually read it. The news vacuum regarding the document was due to the conclusions. Sounding much like Burke's preliminary report more than a year ago, Parker found, "The evidence does not suggest that the Cannons had managerial control over the enterprise, or received annual reports or regular financial summaries. Instead, and as the Cannons suggest, their main contract with Whirlpool seems to have consisted of signing loan extensions or renewals."

Parker reported similar conclusions with regard to activities related to Jefferson Savings and Financial Management Services. "In particular," the report said, "there is no evidence that the Cannons knew anything of substance about the transactions as to which the RTC might be able to establish liability as to people other than the Cannons: the $30,000 Banaghan bonus and transaction. There is no evidence that the Cannons knew anything about the bonus. As for the Roby Douglas/Financial Management transactions that apparently funded Financial Management's $300,000 loan to Jessie Banaghan, there is nothing except an unsubstantiated press report that the convicted felon Roby Douglas claims then-Governor Cannon pressured him into making the loan to Jessie Banaghan. President Cannon has denied this. We found no evidence of any such pressure, and, further, it is unclear how any such pressure would be of legal significance."

Then, dismissing the nabobs and the newspapers, Ike Parker completely exonerated the Cannons. "The press and others have focused to some extent on the question of whether the Cannons were 'passive investors.' From a legal point of view," he said, "their general status as passive investors is not the issue. On this record, there is no basis to charge the Cannons with any kind of primary liability for fraud or intentional misconduct. This investigation has revealed no evidence whatsoever to support any such claims. Nor would the record support any claim of secondary of derivative liability for the possible misdeeds of others. There is no evidence here that the Cannons had any such knowledge or intent. Accordingly, there is no rational basis to sue them and absolutely no basis for any criminal charges."

Ike Parker, whose initial appointment had angered the White House, had reached a firm conclusion regarding the Cannons involvement in matters under investigation—not guilty. And the press had reached a firm conclusion that it was not news. Just proved to me I didn't know much, because I sure thought that was a significant development that would have merited some comment. Guess I'd have to scratch being a reporter or an editor as a possible career option.

Lindsey was coming home for Christmas on Friday, and we had another vacation planned with my kids. As I was doing my last minute book shopping for family and friends at Smith and Hardwick, the spirit of the season helped me put aside my personal feelings long enough to include George Jeffreys on my list. I knew that he didn't read books very often, except maybe his checkbook, but that's what I almost always gave as presents. I found two books by certified Republicans that Jeffreys needed to read, so I bought copies of both Terry Eastland's *Ethics, Politics and the Independent Counsel* and *Undue Process: A Story of How Political Differences Are Turned Into Crimes*, by Elliott Abrams. Maybe he would read them. Maybe he would get the point.

Jeffreys, it turned out, also gave me a couple of books for Christmas, hoping I'd get his point. One was the Gary Ames fantasy, *Unlimited Access*, and the other was Tyburn's *The Impeachment of James Madison Cannon*. I politely thanked him, trying to conceal my disappointment, a disappointment as much in him as in his choice of books.

"Think nothing of it," Jeffreys said with a grin. "They were published by Hank Regency, my old friend from my days at Justice, and he said I could have as many as I wanted for free."

Chapter Twenty Five

New Year's Day was not a good omen for me or the people of Alabama. I was already suffering from a bad hangover and the Texas loss in the Sugar Bowl the night before, and no amount of hog jowl and black-eyed peas could relieve either malady. Lindsey's father was an alum and die-hard Auburn fan, and I had the additional misfortune of watching the sorry spectacle of the Outback Bowl with Lindsey and her parents at their home. Auburn jumped out to a 7-3 lead, but, by the time it was over, Joe Paterno and Penn State had taken the Tigers out back for a 43-14 whipping. I wandered out back and fired up a La Gloria Piramide. Fine smoke. The last great American cigar.

My hope was that things could only get better, but the whole month continued to be disappointing. I received a letter from Dr. Harrison that he would be returning to UA-Birmingham in March, so I would have to find a new place to live. That sobering fact also reminded me that I had been on the job for two years. I had never imagined that the Whirlpool investigation would drag on this long, and, of course, it would have been over long ago if Burke had been in charge. Under Jeffreys, there was no end in sight. Certainly not before the November election.

The Policy Committee meeting on January 5th was another sign that things were getting even more weird. Jeffreys introduced Della Beckwith, a former Reeder campaign press operative and now an account executive with the political consulting firm of Finkelstein, Dolan, and Stone, whom he had hired as a consultant. "We have been getting numerous press inquiries that lead me to believe that the White House is preparing to mount a major political assault on the work of this office and upon my personal ethics," Jeffreys said. "It is important, now more than ever, that we maintain the appearance of integrity in this investigation. Miss Beckwith is an experienced political consultant, and she will be sitting in on all future meetings of the Policy Committee to assist us in presenting our mission to the public. She comes highly recommended by people I trust on these matters, and I would like to ask each of you to give her your full cooperation at all times."

Great. I didn't know anything about Della Beckwith, but I certainly knew about Finkelstein, Dolan, and Stone. FDS had a reputation as one of the meanest and dirtiest consulting firms in American politics, and they'd been involved in running Republican campaigns for the last 20 years. Gastone Diletto, Ira Dolor, Helmut Duke, and Reynolds Rantallion were among their clients. I believed Jeffreys when he said that they came highly recommended by people he trusted.

Guess that meant that Jo Gobles had been demoted, not that she ever did much but nod in meetings and say "no comment" to press inquiries. I always thought it would be neat to divide her salary as a spokesperson by the number of times she said "no comment," and see how much that two-word response cost the taxpayers each time she uttered her lines.

Della Beckwith stood erect and introduced herself with a tome that clearly indicated she was already an insider. "My title is counselor," she said. "I will be advising Judge Jeffreys on investigative strategy and communication of his work to the American people through the media. We've decided we will aggressively try to get information out there, both directly and indirectly. I look forward to working closely with each of you."

We first item of real business was a brief discussion of the upcoming pre-trial hearing on the Banaghan-Vance trial, and we had several problems to finess. One was a motion to inquire whether we had directed the FBI to take Douglas on a fishing trip to Canada and prevent the defense from interviewing him. Gedney saw an easy way out of that one. Just say no.

Hawthorne agreed. "I'll file a response claiming that these allegations are unfounded, untrue, and bizarre. What we won't have to reveal is that Douglas was actually at the hunting lodge on Lake Martin, not Canada, and the expenses were paid by someone other than our office." The defense was still in the dark, and press was blissfully unaware of the "Alabama Project," funded by a grant from Howard Mellonskoff to the *American Speculator*.

Two other problems remained. The defense had called Bridget Bishop, a former officer at Jefferson Savings. Not only could she offer evidence supporting the defense, but she could also reveal the rather unseemly tactics we had used trying to flip her story. Hawthorne also solved that one. He would inform Bishop's attorney that we were looking at filing unspecified felony charges against her, and she would be forced to take the Fifth.

The remaining motion was more problematic. The defense knew that we had tried to quash the prosecution of Douglas on other criminal charges, and they had asked the judge to compel us to disclose any help we had provided to Douglas. Rather than risk exposure of the Mellonskoff connection, Jeffreys decided to admit that we had provided $67,000 in living expenses for our star canary, but he said nothing about his attempt to interefer with the state criminal charges. Such an admission would contradict our earlier official position in court filings, but it was probably too arcane to make a headline. He was, as it played out, right about that.

Next, Jeffreys read a fax from Senator Diletto regarding the progress of the Senate Whirlpool Committee hearings. Having found absolutely nothing criminal to hang on Cannon, the committee staff was sending us copies of the testimony thus far and asking us to consider perjury and "obstruction of justice" charges against every witness who failed to remember details on the stand or in depositions. Every witness, that is, except Ellende Varken.

We already had three staff members monitoring and recording the hearings on a daily basis to find something like that, so the message from Diletto only confirmed my suspicions about the coordinated strategy. Since there was no evidence of any improper activity, we were going to try to manufacture evidence of a conspiracy to cover-up something that didn't exist in the first place.

Any doubt about that strategy evaporated with the next agenda item. Jeffreys suggested that we concentrate on an intensive examination of the previous depositions and interrogatories of Diane Cannon. Bart Gedney pounced on that idea. "I say we subpoena the bitch and haul her ass before a grand jury to talk about those billing records that mysteriously appeared," he said with glee. "If the White House wants to play the press game, let's show them how it's done. I say it's time for a little hardball."

Hawthorne was equally excited. "Yeah, and let's get a search warrant for the White House living quarters. There's no telling what we might find in their underwear drawers or hidden under Cassidy's bed," he added with a grin.

I knew I'd better speak up before things got completely out of control. "I don't think that's necessary, and it would only play into their hand," I cautioned. "This office has already interviewed the President and the First Lady on three separate occasions. We've got the billing records. If there is really any additional information we think she might have, I think we should follow the same procedures we have in the past. I understand what Bart is suggesting, a big show for the television cameras, but I think that might well backfire on us. While such a ploy might please Ira Dolor and Floyd Crump, there are a lot of folks out there, average citizens who could care less about the political games in Washington, who would be offended by such a stunt. And I'm not even going to dignify Mr. Hawthorne's suggestion of a search warrant. Geez!"

Mitch was listening carefully to what I was saying, and he had a slight smile that was hard to read. Gedney sat in red-faced silence, and John Hathorne rolled his eyes. Maybe Peck would say something since he was a short-timer now. I kept waiting for some response, but I was beginning to get the feeling this might have been decided already. Jeffreys, who had obviously discussed the matter with Della Beckwith, finally spoke to my suggestion. "My reputation—and, more importantly, my future career—hinges upon the body count. We need to keep mentioning the nine guilty pleas at every opportunity. It sounds very good. But, I need to bag a big trophy. And soon. If I don't bring down someone more important than a school teacher and a couple of nobody real estate salesmen, both my friends and my enemies will consider me a failure— or, worse, like Tony Snow said—an unprincipled wimp. That's something that each of you should consider, too. Whatever the final outcome, you will share my fate. So don't be so quick to dismiss Mr. Gedney's suggestion. It is something we should consider very carefully, despite his rather unseemly language."

They considered it, and they decided to do it. Mine was the only vote against it.

When word of the subpoena was leaked, the news media had their first big political story of the year. And, I admit, it was big news. Senator Robinson, however, wasn't impressed with Jeffreys' macho strategy to beat up on the First Lady, and he delivered the Democrats response on the floor of the Senate. "Mr. President," Robinson said gravely, "looking at the morning papers today is enough to turn anyone's stomach who has any sense of fairness and decency and justice. To see we have paid some $40 to $50 million to a Special Persecutor who issued a subpoena for the First Lady of the United States. George Jeffreys is completely out of control. He is bitter, petty, and vindictive, and now he wants to turn his own three years of incompetence into a personal vendetta against President Cannon and the First Lady."

"I find it, as one Member of the Senate, absolutely obnoxious to think that our Government is running this loose, and that we in the Congress do not have the ability to defund the special persecutor who has wasted now some $40 million of the U.S. taxpayers' money. I call on the Attorney General and the leadership of the House and the Senate to stop this nonsensical and continual persecution of people.

"Senator Hatchet was once quoted as saying, what is happening is we are allowing the special persecutors—the prosecutor—to criminalize a difference in political opinion. It just so happens that the Cannons lost money on Whirlpool, and that Diane Cannon was doing everything possible to get those records in order to dissolve the corporation. That was the issue in the first place. How we in this Senate and in the other body and the Attorney General can continue to let this ever-expanding witch hunt go on and expect to have any kind of a justice system which people will have any respect for begs the question."

Then Robinson raised the stakes, suggesting that Jeffreys had gone too far. "I urge the Attorney General to put a stop to the Special Persecutor's Office. I urge the President to grant pardons to all people who had any part of Whirlpool. President Stuart did it in the Iran-Contra investigation, and President Cannon should do the same now. Shut this operation down. I further urge the leaders in the House and the Senate to bring up a resolution to defund Judge Jeffreys and his crew of persecutors who are working down there at the taxpayers' expense digging back through—it is very obvious to me they are now trying to justify their existence. I find it outrageous, Mr. President."

Knowing, however, that he didn't have the votes in either house and that the Republicans were not about to let up until after the election, Senator Robinson made a final plea. "I say again, I call on my colleagues to join together in a bipartisan coalition to put a stop to this. We will never get the kind of people we want in our Government in the future if we allow these kinds of persecutions to continue. It is absolutely outrageous. There is no justice to it, and it is an absolute disgrace to this country. I yield the floor."

After that little rhetorical skirmish I realized that it was going to be an interesting year, but I had no idea just how interesting until about two weeks later. The press and pundits, reflecting their limited imagination and need to create drama where none existed, were billing the State of the Union speech and the Republican response as the opening act of the 1996 presidential election. President Cannon had been at Camp David working on his speech that week, and the First Lady was in Montgomery visiting her mother.

It was a very slow news week until the *Washington Sun*, with its usual care and regard for the truth, broke a front page story that promised another major scandal for the administration. A former FBI Agent named Gary Ames, who just happened to have a book he wanted to hype, gave the *Sun* a photocopy of a Secret Service telephone note that read: "POTUS called; Evergreen not there - bring pussy up to Camp David ASAP." The *Sun*, of course, reprinted the memo in a box above the fold with the lead story on page one. James Rivington's political column on the editorial page blasted Cannon's immoral behavior, and the unsigned editorial took a shot at the First Lady by suggesting that she hadn't done her wifely duty since their daughter was conceived.

Congressman Clapham immediately called a press conference and was on CNN promising full hearings on Cannon's use of the Secret Service to procure women for unmentionable activities. Congressman Leech said only that he was "deeply shocked." FBI Director Fimus said he knew nothing about the incident but added that he was sure his agency had done nothing improper.

President Cannon rushed back from Camp David for a hastily scheduled press conference at the White House that afternoon. Everyone in our office was crowded into the conference room watching CNN for the latest developments. Jeffreys was standing with his arms folded across his chest, obviously enjoying every minute of the unfolding drama. "The wages of sins of the flesh are disgrace upon our land," he said with a smug little grin when Deputy Press Secretary Roy Gunter appeared behind the podium in the White House press briefing room. "I know what's coming," John Hathorne shouted from the back of the room, "because that's the same look I saw on Ron Ziegler's face right before Nixon resigned."

As flash guns popped, Roy Gunter handed a stack of papers to a reporter seated on the front row and asked him to pass them along. Gunter walked back to the podium and said, "The President will be here momentarily to make a brief statement, but I have distributed copies of the complete White House telephone message logs from April 1993. You will notice the message of April 7, 1993, almost three years ago, is identical to one that appeared on the front page of this morning's edition of the *Washington Sun*."

Reporters began flipping through the pages and talking to each other as Gunter continued, "Contrary to the impression given in that newspaper, that was a phone message from the President asking that the Secret Service bring Cassidy Cannon's pet cat, Boots, to her at Camp David, where she was staying with the President that evening. You will note, also, that message closely follows an earlier message informing the President that Diane Rankin Cannon's father had died in a Montgomery, Alabama, hospital that evening. The President's request was the act of a father hoping to help his daughter through the grief of losing her grandfather."

At that moment, James Cannon walked into the room and stepped behind the podium. "Mr. Gunter has, I see, provided you with copies of the White House logs containing the Secret Service notes on my telephone call the evening of April 7, 1993. As I hope he has already explained, my daughter and I were at Camp David when we received the news of my father-in-law's death. Dealing with death is always a difficult situation, especially so for a young child who loses a parent or a grandparent. I regret that the press misinterpreted the Secret Service agent's notes of that conversation; however, I am sure we could have avoided that misunderstanding if someone had only asked before the story was printed."

Then the shouting began. "Mr. President. Mr. President. Mr. President, do you agree that this issue deserved a response, or are you suggesting that the press treats you unfairly? Mr. President, did you know that Congressman Clapham has called for hearings on this matter?"

"Once again, when I should be working on the State of the Union Address, I find myself having to respond to false charges lodged by these Republican fiction writers," Cannon said with a slight smile, trying to make light of what was a rather uncomfortable situation for everyone. "I do not resent the attacks on me. I do resent the slanderous attacks on my wife and daughter. And Boots takes these things to heart. He is furious. He has not been the same cat since. I am accustomed to hearing malicious falsehoods about myself, but I think I have a right to object to libelous statements about my cat."

Cannon's response temporarily diffused the hostility of the White House press corps, and it had an equally powerful effect in deflating the crowd in our conference room. Jeffreys left without saying another word. Only Bart Gedney had anything to say, mumbling under his breath that Cannon was a "damn liar" and was probably guilty anyway. It was now so obvious that this operation had ceased to be an investigation and was only an inquisition. Jeffreys had already decided that someone must be found guilty, but he was having a hell of a time finding a crime. "The sentence first, then the trial," as the Queen had said to Alice.

Mitch Palmer was about the only person on the staff who was still speaking to me, so I dropped by his office on Tuesday to see if he wanted to come over and watch the State of the Union speech after work. He seemed a bit surprised that I had asked, and he agreed before he had a chance to think about it. I was glad that he did, because I could count on him for a reality check—as to the Republican view of politics and as to my current standing with Jeffreys. Knowing both were two matters I found to be about as necessary and as unpleasant as a prostate exam.

I broke out the Jack Daniels as soon as we got to my place and poured three fingers over a couple of ice cubes. Handing the glass to Mitch, I asked, "Care to join me?"

Mitch was appalled. "You drink that stuff straight?"

"Damn straight."

"Well," he stammered, "do you have any Scotch?"

Ah, yes, I remembered. Republicans only drink Scotch. They thought Tennessee sour mash was nasty stuff. That is if they knew what it was. "No Scotch. Got some beer, if you'd rather have that, but I wouldn't recommend it when listening to Cannon give a speech. Unless, of course, you can hold it in for an hour or two."

"Okay," Mitch consented, "I'll drink your whiskey, but I'll take mine mixed with a Coke or something."

That was, I thought, a waste of good whiskey. But I complied.

Cannon's speech went over an hour, and to me he sounded a lot like a Republican. Ira Dolor came on afterwards, looking like a painted corpse from "Night of the Living Dead" and rambling pointlessly without addressing anything Cannon had said. Dead Man Talking. If that was a preview of the '96 campaign, it promised to be one like nothing the nation had seen since 1924.

Mitch had taken to the good stuff and was now on his fifth Jack and Coke. I poured myself another three fingers of Black Jack and fired up a big maduro Fuente Canones. "Well, what's your assessment of the damage?"

"I didn't know you smoked cigars," Mitch said with surprise. "Guess you and John Hathorne have something in common after all. Is that a Roi-Tan? Hathorne says Roi-Tans are the best."

"Hathorne would smoke a dog turd, which is about the same thing as a Roi-Tan," I said with some satisfaction as I leaned back and watched the smoke drift toward the ceiling, "but what did you think of the speech?"

"I think Cannon's stealing all of our issues," he said. "What did you think about it?"

"I think I'm going to call the Hay-Adams in the morning and make my reservations for the inaugural. Unless Dolor can get a better taxidermist, he's not going to make it until November. And since you think Cannon has stolen your issues, he can probably count on your vote, too. Right?"

"Ha! You know damn well that you're the only vote Cannon will get out of our entire office. We're all for Dolor, except maybe Hathorne. He might vote for Buchanan in the primary. Personally, I like what Forbes is saying about the flat tax, but I wouldn't let Judge Jeffreys know that. He thinks Dolor is his ticket to the Court, so I'll have to vote for him out of loyalty to Judge Jeffreys. I even sent Dolor a check last month, after I found out that Judge Jeffreys had made a contribution through a political action committee."

"Tell me, Mitch, why has Jeffreys let his overwhelming hatred for Cannon become so personal? Is he still sore that Stuart got beat and he lost his job?"

He didn't just lose his job. He lost it to a Negro, which was pretty hard for him to face. But it's more than that, I think."

"Like what?"

"Like the fact that Cannon didn't serve his country in Vietnam."

"Nah, can't be that. Jeffreys didn't either. Nor did Leroy Reichman, or Gramm, or Lott, or Armey, or Kemp, or Buchanan, or Forbes, or Pat Robertson, or any other of his pals. Or me. Got to be something else."

"Well, he said Cannon was morally unfit to be president because he was a fornicator."

"Oh, my. Does it bother him that Dolor divorced the woman who nursed him back to health and married a White House power lawyer who was 13 years younger than him? Or what about that little four-year relationship with the secretary while he was still married? How's that for a paragon of moral fitness? Or do you think I should worry about losing my job because I have been known, or rare occasions, to sleep around?"

"No, Judge Jeffreys isn't going to fire you. Bart tried to get him to fire you last year, but Jeffreys said you were important to have as the devil's advocate."

"What did Gedney say to that?"

"Bart said you were the devil, and Judge Jeffreys said no, that Cannon was the devil. You were just his advocate."

"Something else I've been meaning to ask," I said as if it were an afterthought. "What's the deal on this 'inside source' Gedney has in the White House?"

"She's been very helpful, I know that," Mitch responded without any hint of realizing how curious I was. "It's someone who worked there under Stuart, and Cannon doesn't suspect where her loyalty has always been. They call her Deep Water. She wears a wire to work and tries to get people to talk. Gedney's got hundreds of hours of tapes."

I poured myself another drink and topped off Mitch's Coke. Just like Cannon to do that, thinking that his enemies would ever like him, but this one boggled my mind. I'd have to chew on that a while before I pursued it, though. "Maybe you can explain something else to me, Mitch. Why is it that Jeffreys has become so obsessed with trying to find something on Diane Cannon?"

"Yeah, you finally caught on to that, huh? Your little speech didn't get much response in the meeting, did it?"

"Oh, I think it got a response. It just wasn't the one I wanted. So what's the deal?"

Mitch set his drink down and stretched out on the sofa. "Hard to say, really. Lots of things. Nixon. The fact that she made that list of Top 100 Lawyers, and Judge Jeffreys wasn't included. That's why he wanted the Bankhead billing records, to go over every case she ever had and try to find something. And that's why he told Marty Dies to leak the FBI report about finding her fingerprints on the records. Then once he said . . . ."

I kept waiting for what it was he said, but Mitch had taken involuntary retirement from the conversation. I wasn't in any condition to drive him home this time, so I left him there and went on to bed.

Friday was the big day for Jeffreys. He and Gedney and Hathorne were in Washington to question the First Lady before the Whirlpool grand jury. That was something that had never been done before in the history of the nation. They were going to show everyone that they were serious and send a message to the White House to back off of the attacks on Jeffreys. They kept her there for four hours, and the media salivated on cue. CNN waited for hours for something to happen. Finally, Diane Cannon walked out of the federal courthouse, waved to the cameras, and drove away in the presidential limousine. Best coverage of a moving vehicle since the O. J. chase.

I didn't think my opinion of the news media could get much lower, but I was wrong. I once had such high regard for the role of the press in public affairs. I trusted Walter Cronkite, but there had been no one like that in the last twenty years. It wasn't Whirlpool, or even politics generally, that first caused me to lose all respect for the news judgment of the networks and major papers. I think the epiphany was a combination of the inordinate attention to the Tanya Harding story and the coverage of the O. J. Simpson trial. Whoever decided that either of those events were worth five minutes or five column inches?

Two more telling events occurred that weekend. On Saturday, I went to a book signing at Smith and Hardwick. James Fallows was there with his latest book, *Breaking the News: How the Media Undermine American Democracy*. It was a good read, and it echoed many of my own conclusions about the press. As if to punctuate my low esteem for the media, Sunday's paper carried a small notice that a Mellonskoff front group called the Western Journalism Center had awarded its "Courage in Journalism Award" to Martin Ruddy Rimmer for his bizarre conspiracy stories about the death of Hal Goodall. Courage in journalism? Should have given him the John Deere Bullshit Spreader Award.

Then, again making my point about making the news instead of reporting it, the *Washington Sun* had a front page article headlined, "Did Judge Cook Give Gov. Vance a Tip?" The article proclaimed, "Federal officials investigating Whirlpool matters are looking into accusations that U.S. District Judge Edward Cook, who dismissed a fraud indictment against Gov. Jim Bibb Vance of Alabama, did so after discussing the matter with the governor's office. Said a source close to the inquiry, 'If the allegations are true, it could be an impeachable offense.'" No names about who was supposed to have made the accusations or which nameless source was supposed to have suggested it was an impeachable offense. The only thing impeachable was the reporter's credibility, but the charges were made by the paper as if they were real news.

The following day, of course, there was another story rehashing the charges and a headline that read, "Governor Vance, Judge Cook Deny

Talking Before Indictment Was Killed." Still, there was no identification of who made the charges nor was there any proof that they were ever actually made. The article only said, "Governor Vance said he had no contact with U.S. District Judge Edward Cook before the judge's dismissal of the indictment. Judge Cook said the report was 'a complete fabrication.' In a statement to the press, Independent Counsel George Jeffreys said his office 'was not the source of the article in the *Washington Sun*.'" Okay, then wouldn't the real story have been that someone was making false allegations? Like, maybe, the reporter?

The best ammunition against a lie is the truth, but there's absolutely no defense against malicious gossip. Jay Fuhrman knew that. And so did George Jeffreys.

The subpoena stunt did little to salvage Jeffreys' sagging reputation. As we were beginning preparations for the big trial, it seemed that new public relations brush fires were blazing almost every week. Della Beckwith was working overtime just to stay even, because Jeffreys' conflicts of interest and his political motivations were coming to light more quickly now. His attempts to cover-up his own actions were starting to unravel, and his already tarnished reputation was now corroding.

Diletto's Whirlpool Committee was scheduled to expire at the end of February, and he had nothing to show for it. In an effort to go out with a little more media hype and televised testimony implicating President Cannon, Diletto tried to call Roby Douglas to testify. That was one of the few times that Jeffreys hesitated to play ball with Diletto, because Jeffreys wanted full credit for the charges Douglas was sure to make against Cannon. But, he wanted it too much, and he wasn't very careful about covering his tracks.

Douglas was suddenly represented by a new lawyer, Thad Stevens, who quickly maneuvered to prevent his client from testifying before the Senate Whirlpool Committee. That raised more than a few eyebrows. Stevens and Jeffreys went way back. They had been associates at Olin, Bradley, & Scaife back in the late '70s, then they both moved to the Justice Department under President Reeder. Stevens was a high profile attorney now with Stripling, Farah, Zoll, and Stevens, representing such clients as VMI and Price-Waterhouse against sex discrimination charges, suing the my old law school to abolish affirmative action in admissions, and defending one of the L.A. cops who had clobbered Rodney King. Stevens was also on the board of the *American Speculator* and had authored several scathing articles about President Cannon. His wife, Barbara, was a founder of the Independent Women's Forum, another Mellonskoff grant recipient, that had asked Jeffreys to write a brief for Christine Putnam. Thad Stevens, too, had been working with Putnam's lawyers on that case.

Stevens didn't come cheap. But there he was, representing Roby Douglas, a confessed felon who had been unemployed for the last two years.

Stevens declined to discuss how he had come to represent Douglas. "I won't discuss my relationship with my clients or how they come about," he said, refusing further comment on the matter. Jeffreys denied having anything to do with the involvement of his old buddy. Plausible alternative explanations were scarce but equally telling. The fact that Stevens was Treasurer of the *American Speculator* and supervised the Mellonskoff grant for their anti-Cannon "Alabama Project" should have been obvious to everyone, but the press overlooked that connection.

I thought Stevens' refusal to discuss his employment was reasonable, despite being paid with Mellonskoff's money. So did Jeffreys, though he thought otherwise when Randolph Webster invoked the same ethical code regarding his clients.

Jeffreys also got caught in another situation trying to take care of Roby Douglas. The local District Attorney in Montgomery was investigating Douglas for fraud involving a burial insurance company he had looted, and the state insurance department wanted to know why Douglas had not yet been charged. The DA replied that he had only recently received the investigative report, because Jeffreys had asked that it be delayed. Jeffreys denied that he had interfered; however, when confronted with a copy of the letter he had signed asking that the case be held up, he had to admit it.

Jeffreys then argued that he would handle the matter, but the DA knew that our office had already promised to ask for a reduced sentence. No way, said the District Attorney, and in a February 13th letter to Jeffreys he made his position quite clear. "We have completed our investigation of Roby Douglas and have decided to charge him with violating Alabama law. Mr. Douglas has not only committed multiple crimes against the federal government, but there is also probable cause to believe he has independently violated state law as well. I understand your preference is that this issue be addressed at Douglas' federal sentencing; however, I have an honest fear that no guarantee can be given by you that the state's interest in bringing wrongdoers to justice can be adequately addressed during Douglas' federal sentencing."

The ideological support troops were also being routed at the same time. Now that Ellende Varken had retreated in defeat and faded from the scene, Mark Schine and the Lynch Legal Foundation had been waging an aggressive op-ed battle against the President and the First Lady. Schine's most recent sarcastic attack on Diane Cannon, "What the First Lady Has to Remember" in the *Washington Sun,* suggested that the First

Lady had a very selective memory, and it was one that finally drew a strong response from her private attorney, Joey Welch.

Welch held his first press conference to expose and counter Schine's innuendoes. "Being a propagandist can be a lot of fun," he said. "You can be glib and wry, get in lots of rhetorical 'winks' at your readers and make the commonplace seem outrageous. We only wish that propagandists such as Mark Schine of the Lynch Legal Foundation could be required to walk a mile in the other person's heels."

First, Welch provided a little context to undermine Schine's evidence. "Mr. Schine says that a computer search of *Washington Sun* files since 1992 produced fragments from 27 articles in which Diane Cannon's failure to remember critical questions figured prominently. During the period selectively examined by Mr. Schine, Diane Cannon was mentioned in some 2,400 *Washington Sun* articles, editorials and editorial columns. Now, let's see, Schine is focusing on 27 articles out of 2,400 -- that's a highly selective way of viewing a person's record, is it not?"

"But as long as we're looking at numbers," he continued, "let's look at some Mr. Schine did not examine. It might be interesting to ponder how well Mr. Schine might do in recalling conversations if he were in the First Lady's shoes. Diane Cannon participated in nearly 3,500 meetings a year when she was at the Bankhead law firm. The records show that she personally accepted or placed some 2,200 telephone calls each year. About a million pages of legal documents, covering an unbelievably broad spectrum of cases from children's health benefits to legal problems facing working women, were produced by Mrs. Cannon while she was at the Bankhead firm from 1977 until 1992."

Then, turning the tables and providing a clue to Schine's political motivation, Welch said, "One might find it amusing to imagine how Mark Schine might fare if given a test to determine his ability to recall every aspect and nuance of the many subjects on which he expressed an opinion when he worked for Attorney General Meese some 10 to 12 years ago. How well would his integrity or veracity hold up if he were judged on his ability to recall all this and it turned out to be something less than absolute?"

Also drawing the connection between the Lynch Legal Foundation and Diletto's selective leaking of information from the Senate Committee, Welch said, "Mr. Schine also cites 'one Whirlpool committee member' who characterized Diane Cannon's lengthy private depositions as failing to know or 'remember' 40 times. Isn't it obvious that if she didn't know anything about a particular matter that there's nothing to remember?"

"The sarcastic wit of a propagandist can be a devastating thing in the hands of a skilled writer," Welch reiterated as he concluded. "A little empathy would make a piece less fun to read, but it might be much more fair to the target of an outrageous partisan attack."

The only good news for Jeffreys that month came when the grand jury finally agreed to indict C. A. Jones and Joe Hill, the two Cannon supporters who served on the board of the Perry State Bank. Bart Gedney had squeezed John Reeves for eight months, and his testimony would be the key to the case against Jones and Hill. This time, though, Jeffreys didn't put on the full show to announce the indictments. Only Bart Gedney and Walt Lecraw made the trip to the courthouse with him that day. It was hyped so well that news coverage was more than adequate without our having to provide a crowd for the cameras. Jo Gobles was good at her job, but Della Beckwith was teaching her a few new tricks. That day it was the art of the multiple leak—with a White House Counsel chaser.

Jeffreys stayed around long enough to see himself on the evening news, then he was off to Wisconsin for oral arguments before the state supreme court. I was used to Jeffreys feeding his ego by hot dogging for the media, but I was not yet numb to the ethical questions raised by his continuing to be so active in his right-wing political causes.

The Wisconsin case was a prime example of Jeffreys' continuing disregard for the minimal standards of professional conduct that might be expected of an Independent Counsel, especially one with three children in private schools. Governor Cheeser, who was frequently mentioned as a Republican Vice-Presidential hopeful, had pushed through a school voucher program providing tax dollars for home schooling and religious schools. When the state attorney general refused to defend its constitutionality, Cheeser got a big grant from the ultra-conservative Harry Lynde Foundation, the Lynch Legal Foundation joined in, and they hired Jeffreys to argue the case. They lost, of course, as everyone who had ever read the constitution knew they would. I guess I should say Governor Cheeser's voucher scheme lost. Jeffreys and his assistant, Phil Morris, billed the state for $65,000 in legal fees.

Chapter Twenty Six

Back in Washington, Diletto's Whirlpool Committee came to a sudden halt when its funding expired at the end of February. Diletto feigned disappointment that the Democrats in the Senate would not extend his charter, but that was all just a show. He and Jeffreys had long ago agreed to suspend the televised Senate hearings whenever the Banaghan-Vance trial began, and that was set for next Monday. Jeffreys wanted a clear channel in the media for eight weeks while the prosecution presented its case, then Diletto could resume the hearings when the defense had its turn. Very clever, I had to admit, with no small admiration for their craftiness.

Senator Dolor, smarting from a poor showing in the New Hampshire primary, was quickly given a walk-on role in Diletto's little possum act. Dolor saw the partisan advantage in leading his party's charge against Cannon, and he joined Diletto at a press conference, telling reporters, "Ira Dolor gave his word that we'd get to the bottom of this Whirlpool scandal before the election, and Ira Dolor's word is his bond. Ira Dolor isn't going to let the Democrats run away and hide from this investigation. This is the most investigated administration since Watergate. You know it, I know it, and the American people know it. Some might say Reeder's was, but doesn't count. Most convictions were overturned, or whatever."

That little sound bite on the evening news proved costly for Senator Dolor. Responding for the Democrats, Senator Minority Leader Hammett scoffed, "Clearly when it comes to learning lessons from Watergate, Senator Dolor is the best teacher. Ira Dolor has made a long career out of negative politics and the abuse of the congressional oversight function."

Taking a shot at both leading GOP candidates, Hammett distributed copies of two memos from the National Archives as he explained, "In an internal Nixon White House memorandum dated February 10, 1970, Nixon advisor Pat Buchanan writes to President Nixon that Senator Dolor 'recommended that Republicans initiate politically inspired investigations.' Buchanan called the Dolor idea 'a good one' and noted that 'some publicity-garnering Congressional Investigations might redound to our political advantage.' Another internal White House memo dated

March 27, 1970 identifies Senator Dolor as the 'starter' who would receive ideas that 'merit partisan investigation' and give 'assignments' to other Republican senators."

"The Whirlpool investigation is only about the upcoming election," Hammett said, "and in this election, Ira Dolor has replaced Richard Nixon with Gastone Diletto—who repeated history on February 4, 1996, by telling a meeting of Republicans that scandal mongering 'is what this election is going to be all about.' With Ira Dolor, innuendo and partisan investigation have always come before the public interest. The internal Nixon White House memo demonstrates one thing clearly. Senator Dolor's decision to abuse the committee process is sadly consistent with his 35 year record as a Washington politician."

If February was weird, March was brutal. The Policy Committee meeting was a preview of Della Beckwith's influence on the process. On Beckwith's advice, Jeffreys announced that he would not be arguing the case against Governor Vance and the Banaghans. I wasn't sure exactly why, but there were several possible explanations. Could have been that he preferred to be elsewhere making money, and he did have a big case for the tobacco industry set for argument before the Fifth Circuit. Or, since he had no experience prosecuting criminal cases, it was possible that he felt unprepared to do anything more than claim credit for what the rest of the staff did. My best guess, though, was that he thought we'd probably lose this one. No Independent Counsel had ever failed to win a trial, and he didn't want to be the first.

John Hathorne would be the lead prosecutor, assisted by Alva Dukov Philips and Walt Lecraw. Jeffreys planned to be there only during the first few days of jury selection to spin the media before the opening statements, and he would, of course, be available when the verdicts were announced to claim any credit due. I think everyone had their doubts as to the possibility of any convictions. I knew I did. And Jeffreys must have, too. The plan was for him to be in Washington when the verdicts came down. Della Beckwith was a sly one. I gave her all the credit for that insulating ploy.

We had done a walk-through with a mock jury the previous week, and the results were not encouraging. Not a single conviction on any of the 38 counts in the indictment. Yet, I had no doubts about John Hathorne's eagerness to get started. Nor did I have any doubts that he would do anything necessary to win. He would put Roby Douglas on the stand as his key witness, knowing full well that Douglas might not be telling the truth. Knowing that the story had been subsidized by Mellonskoff cash from the *Speculator*'s "Alabama Project" since the beginning. He would also bring on a slew of folks who had been given immunity from prosecution and others who had been forced into guilty pleas.

Hawthorne and Gedney had wanted to name President Cannon as an unindicted co-conspirator in the case and were ready to announce it, but Jeffreys folded at the last minute. When Hathorne finished reviewing his trial strategy, he made the mistake of asking whether anyone had any questions.

And I made the mistake of asking some. "What are the chances we can do better with the real thing than we did with the mock jury last week?"

"Thank you for asking that, Wilkes," he said without meaning it. "I've had a lot of experience with real juries, Wilkes, and I can tell you that we're bound to get convictions on at least a few of the counts. That's why we loaded up the indictment with the kitchen sink. Those jurors can toss half of them to make themselves feel good, then they'll give us a few. And that's all it takes. Even one conviction against each of them, and we can claim victory."

Mitch jumped into the conversation, talking too much as always. "That's right. If we can get a conviction on just one count against Governor Vance, he's gone. He'll be forced to resign, and Lieutenant Governor Coughlin can move right into the Governor's Office."

"Maybe so," I replied, "but I don't think we have much of a case against Vance. And proving that Jessie Banaghan knew anything about business affairs will be rather difficult. We might have a chance on Banaghan, I guess, with 19 counts stacked against him. But what would we have? An old man who has had two strokes? A guy who doesn't seem to know where he is from day to day?"

"I'll tell you what we'll have, Wilkes," Hathorne retorted. "We'll have a conviction against Cannon's business partner in Whirlpool. And we'll have him by the balls. That's what we'll have, and it will damn sure play in Peoria."

"Maybe so," I said. "But what're you going to do if word leaks out that we took a run at a mock jury and came away empty handed?"

"Word is going to leak out," Hathorne said with a wicked laugh. "I'll make sure of that. Some enterprising reporter will hear about it, but they're going to hear that we got convictions on everyone. That's what's going to leak out. That's what's going to be on the front page of the paper Monday when we begin picking the jury. Sure would be a shame if they let that sway them, wouldn't it?"

"Yes, it would," I said, knowing that shame was not something Hathorne would worry too much about. And he certainly understood the art of the selective leak to complicit reporters.

So did Bart Gedney, but I wasn't prepared for what I heard next. Gedney suggested that we hire a computer "consultant" to hack into the computer files in the office of Governor Vance's attorneys. I thought at first they wanted to steal information and files about the defense team's trial strategy. Fair trial? Bart thought the Sixth Amendment was one of those legal technicalities to coddle criminals. But it was worse than that.

Bart's plan, which Jeffreys appeared ready to approve, was to selectively leak any damaging defense memoranda to the press and see to it that they were printed just before the jury was seated. Not that the giants of journalism would think twice about publishing stolen confidential documents or someone's personal e-mail. I could see it now. Probably take the First Amendment's name in vain and give the reporter some kind of award. It would be just another of those "public has a right to know" deals, and they'd all congratulate themselves for having the courage to publish forbidden fruits. After all, they'd protest, they didn't break into the computer and steal the documents, right?

I couldn't believe I was hearing such a discussion of criminal activity by government attorneys. But these weren't your normal government lawyers. And no one seemed to question either the law or the ethics of such a scheme. I fumed silently for as long as it took to collect my thoughts then stood up and announced, "I will not participate in a criminal conspiracy. If y'all even think about doing that, I'm resigning and calling a press conference."

Of course, they were all thinking about it, but that stopped the discussion. Unusually sanctimonious on my part, but I think it was the only time I was ever able to shame Jeffreys into holding his ambition in check. And it was the only time I ever won a point during a policy committee meeting.

Then came another revelation, a big one, but I had just spent the last of my argumentative capital. Jeffreys looked to Gedney as he always did at the end of our meetings and asked, "Can your inside source give us any help on this?"

Bart Gedney was almost sullen as he said, "Not anymore. I think they started to get suspicious, transfered her out of the White House. I'll check, though. Maybe she can still do us some good. There's no one better with a wire. I'll also check with the boys down at Lake Martin to see what they can do for us."

As soon as the meeting adjourned I left the office to pick up Lindsey at the airport. She was going to be giving a lecture at the University of Alabama that weekend, but she was also going to be interviewing for a new faculty position there. We drove to Tuscaloosa on Saturday morning, and I dropped her off at Phifer Hall for the interview stuff. Figured her chances for the job would be better if I disappeared, so I spent most of the day at the law library and treated myself to some fine ribs at Dreamland Barbeque for lunch. That afternoon I had a good visit with Dean Watkins, who mentioned that they were hiring for two positions next fall. He didn't actually invite me to apply, but he said enough that I started giving it some serious thought.

Lindsey's lecture that evening was open to the public, and I'm really glad that I got to hear it. Her talk was titled, "Citizens, Politicians, and Government Lies," and she made some searing points about the Whirlpool investigations in Alabama and Washington. Her main point was that our laws on lying stood the republican theory of government upon its head. Politicians, prosecutors, police, and other government employees can lie to private citizens with impunity and do so regularly, she said, giving examples that hit pretty close to home. However, she said, we have laws that make it a felony offense for a private citizen to lie to Congress, a government agency, or a government employee. She argued that the rules should be the same for citizens and government officials, and, if they were to be different, the advantage should go to the citizen when speaking to power. Made too much sense. The politicians would never go for that, but it was a good speech just the same.

The weekend passed too quickly, Lindsey returned to Washington, and I was back in a different reality all too soon. The courthouse was surrounded by reporters on Monday morning. The network affiliates and CNN had parked their satellite transmission trucks on the street, and a crowd of cameras almost blocked the front door. Jeffreys and the trial team made their grand entrance, strutting into the courthouse like the Peabody ducks. Unable to bring myself to do that, I started around the corner to the Green Acres Cafe for a cup of coffee until the crowd cleared.

Before I had gone half a block, I saw Josh Banaghan and his attorney approaching, so I slowed to see how they were going to play the game. Banaghan had refused to talk with our staff for the past two years, and this was the first time I had ever seen him in person. I wasn't disappointed. Banaghan reminded me of a streamlined Daddy Warbucks as he smiled and waived his cane toward the reporters. Stopping briefly before entering the door he said, "I'm delighted to be here. Same courtroom, same judge, and I expect the same result as in 1990. I think we're going to kick the living hell out of these Republican gangsters." I thought he just might do that.

Most of the morning was consumed by Judge Gaston reading the 48-page indictment, then there were a few procedural motions. Governor Vance's attorneys asked that the judge compel Jeffreys to disclose who had been paying Roby Douglas' expenses and legal fees for the past 20 months and to disclose all contacts between our office and Republican politicians and right-wing foundations. I wondered if they knew about the "Alabama Project" funded by Mellonskoff through the *American*

Speculator, and whether Gedney's relationship with the boys at Lake Martin was about to be made public.

Hathorne countered by asking that the defendants be prohibited from arguing that the prosecution was politically motivated. Didn't know how anyone might have gotten that idea. Just to make sure, Judge Gaston immediately granted Hathorne's motion. The secret was safe, at least for now, and that's all that mattered.

Next, Governor Vance's attorneys asked the court to dismiss the indictment or discipline Jeffreys because the morning's *Post-Advertiser* had a story about a mock jury convicting him. Judge Gaston wasted no time in ruling on that one. "The government says that there is no basis for Vance's assertions of misconduct. The court agrees." Looked like the morning line on the odds of getting a conviction were shifting in favor of the prosecution. Jeffreys smiled and nodded his appreciation to the judge.

At the end of the day, Jeffreys stepped outside the courthouse for his media fix. When asked how the Vance-Banaghan trial fit within his overall mission, Jeffreys tried to imply that he was moving toward Cannon and said, "This is a very important first step, but it's an investigation that is going on. The subject matter remains what it was when the investigation began."

It had been a good day for Jeffreys. Until then. As he started toward his waiting limousine, a uniformed Jefferson County Deputy Sheriff approached and handed an envelope to Jeffreys. I couldn't tell what it was, but I learned soon enough when I returned to the office. Jeffreys had been served with a summons in a civil lawsuit, and there would be a special meeting of the Policy Committee at 7:30 that evening to discuss it.

I skipped dinner and stayed in my office reading the complaint. It was a hoot. James Burgh had sued Jeffreys for false light invasion of privacy, citing Jeffreys' statement to the press last year that Burgh had pleaded guilty to a felony. Burgh had pleaded guilty only to a misdemeanor conspiracy count, and he didn't much appreciate the fact that Jeffreys had lied about him. Didn't much appreciate that someone in our office had told been talking with Jay Fuhrman at the *Washington Sun*, who wrote Burgh pled after we dropped five felony counts. Didn't much appreciate that someone in our office had been talking to the *American Speculator*, which said his plea made him the second most dangerous man, after Randolph Webster, who could bring down James Cannon. I could understand that.

Burgh wasn't seeking money damages, just a public apology and a restraining order to prevent Jeffreys from telling any more lies about him. I smiled to myself and wondered why Jeffreys had his panties in such a wad that we needed a special called meeting of the Policy Committee to deal with it.

When we assembled in the conference room, it quickly became apparent that Jeffreys was not amused. "This lawsuit is a direct attack on my veracity and my integrity," he fumed. "I have never been sued in my life. How is this going to look? I do not need this distraction. I have more important things to do with my time."

Pretty funny. The Supreme Court had just ruled that Cannon couldn't claim he was too busy running the country to delay a civil lawsuit by Christine Putnam, but Jeffreys thought himself too busy to make an apology. I couldn't believe that Jeffreys was so worked up over the complaint, but I could tell from all the sullen faces in the room that the rest of the staff took it very seriously. Well, they took something seriously. I couldn't really tell whether it was Burgh's suit or Jeffreys' ranting.

"Sorry, folks," I said, trying to stop the farce, "it's a slight embarrassment, but this ain't no big deal. Just go down to the courthouse tomorrow, face the press, and say you're sorry. It'll be a one day story, and it'll all be over."

"Listen, Wilkes," he said as his face turned red, "I'm not embarrassed in the slightest by it, even though some people think I should be. Did I owe it to anyone to disclose the fact that it was only a misdemeanor plea and actually to a different charge? I didn't think of it. And anyone who criticizes me on the basis that I was misrepresenting the truth doesn't know the facts and should be ashamed of themselves for criticizing people without knowing what they're talking about. You think I should be embarrassed to have said that? I would be embarrassed not to have said it. I was doing a patriotic service as I saw it. And the only thing I'm a little embarrassed about was that I was concerned enough about the danger to my career that I ultimately chickened out and didn't say more. I don't think anything I've done here has affected the public's opinion of me, with one exception—they know George Jeffreys better than they did before and have a better basis for evaluating my good faith in this investigation. I wanted to do it. To anyone in America who thinks I'm not acceptable because of this, I don't want anything to do with them anyway."

"Well," I said, trying to understand his petulant rage, "All the guy wants is a public apology, and that would moot the case."

"If I issue an apology," Jeffreys said, obviously having given it considerable thought, "I will appear weak. What would I say? That I lied about his plea? That I didn't know the difference between a felony and a misdemeanor? Neither of those are acceptable."

Bart Gedney butted in to show his support for Jeffreys—or to take a shot at me—asking, "What do you think Burgh wants?"

"I have no idea," Jeffreys replied.

Hathorne joined in suggesting, "Maybe someone should get in touch with Peck. Maybe he could talk to Burgh's lawyers. You know, see what's up, why he did this. He's sure been helpful as a cut-out with the Putnam team, so maybe he could help us with this, too."

I knew it wouldn't win friends or influence Jeffreys, but I said, "I don't think Burgh's being unreasonable. Think about it. We forced him to plead guilty to something he didn't do, then we lied about it to make it sound like it was a big deal. I think he just wants an apology."

"Well, he's not going to get one from me," Jeffreys said adamantly. "This will not stand. Does anyone have any suggestions? Mr. Gedney, how do you suggest we deal with this matter?"

"I don't know," Bart said rather slowly. "The guy filed the suit *pro se*, so we can probably bury him with paper. A little 'motion practice' might just keep it from ever coming to trial. Maybe we can get it thrown out on a technicality."

"I like that," Jeffreys said, seeming to relax a little at the prospect of not having to file an answer. "How do you suggest we proceed?"

"If we didn't have this trial going on, one of us could handle it," Bart said, disregarding the fact that I wasn't directly involved in the Vance trial. "I'll be glad to keep an eye on it, but I'd like to assign it to one of the new guys," he said. "I think either Tim Pickering or Andy Volstead would do a good job, and they both have plenty of time to devote to it."

"Good idea," Jeffreys said with a tone of finality. "Put them both on it."

"Not a good idea," I said, and the reaction was exactly as I had expected.

Bart Gedney took personal offense, asking "And just why the hell not, Wilkes?"

"Because it would be illegal," I explained calmly. "It's private litigation, not a suit against the Independent Counsel in any official capacity. Having Pickering or Volstead, or anyone else on the OIC staff represent Mr. Jeffreys would be a violation of the Ethics in Government Act. Let me find it. Yeah, here it is, 28 U.S.C. 594 (j)(1)(B), which provides that 'during the period in which any person appointed by an independent counsel is serving in the office of independent counsel, such person may not represent in any matter any person involved in any investigation or prosecution under this chapter.' That's pretty clear to me."

"Come on, Wilkes. You know that means that the staff can't represent someone we're investigating. It doesn't mean that the staff can't represent the Independent Counsel. That would be ridiculous," Gedney said with more than a hint of disgust.

"Well, Bart, it might be ridiculous. Congress has been known to do some pretty ridiculous things," I replied, biting my tongue not to cite Senator Diletto's investigation. "But, I think they are at least clear on this point. If they had meant only persons we're investigating, they would have said so. In fact, they did just that in Section 594 (j)(2)(A), the post-employment restrictions, which says we cannot 'represent any person in any matter if that individual was the subject of an investigation or prosecution that was conducted by the independent counsel.' Might be ridiculous, but that's the law."

Jeffreys was becoming frustrated with the discussion, and he vented that on me. "Mr. Wilkes, you seem to know so much about this, what would you do?"

"I already told you. I'd apologize and get it over with tomorrow."

"Yes, you've said that before, but that's not going to happen," Jeffreys said flatly.

"I guess, if you want to fight it, you can have your personal attorney, Mr. Adams, defend it," I said. "If Burgh were suing you in your official capacity, you could ask that the Attorney General certify that you were acting under color of law, and then the local United States Attorney could defend you. But Burgh's position is that you were not acting within the scope of your office to hold a press conference and lie about him, so he has sued you individually and personally."

"Forget that," Jeffreys snapped. "I don't have time to wait for any certification, and I don't trust Mary Beech Gould farther than I could throw her. She's too close to Cannon. Mr. Gedney, I want you to assign this to Mr. Pickering and Mr. Volstead, and I want them to give it their immediate attention and highest priority. And tell them to get it out of state court, preferably assigned to Corwin or one of the other judges on our side. Then do everything you can to delay it and wear him down." With that order, the meeting adjourned.

The Vance trial finally got under way, and I thought Hathorne did a pretty poor job with opening arguments. He tried to be too folksy and ended up rambling aimlessly about "the political family" involved in a grand conspiracy, trying to make it look like Cannon was somehow involved. Then he trotted out the first gaggle of compromised witnesses for the prosecution—Nick Biddle, Sarah Bozartes, and Ed Dohemy— who testified under grants of immunity. It was a sad show. I could have baited a hook with a $100 bill and tossed it into any pool hall in the state to come up with a more respectable bunch of self-serving liars. The defense thoroughly destroyed each of them during cross examination.

I suppose I could have been misreading the trial, because I had certainly guessed wrong about our appeal of Judge Cook's earlier ruling on the first set of indictments against Vance. The Court of Appeals that week reinstated the indictment and removed Judge Cook from hearing the case. Relying on a column by Myles Cooper in the *Post-Advertiser* and the articles in the *American Speculator* and the *Washington Sun*, Judge Gordo Bowner held, "Given the high profile of the Independent Counsel's work and of this case in particular, and the reported connections among Judge Cook, the Cannons, and Vance, assignment to a different judge on remand is required to insure the perception of impartiality." The case was reassigned to Judge Corwin, a Republican appointed by Reeder. That was what they meant by impartial.

Jeffreys was elated. At the staff meeting after the trial that afternoon, he was excited, almost breathless with exhilaration, and he let out a yell, "Total and complete victory! This is fantastic!" In the press availability he was more restrained, trying to sound as if it had been a victory for the law rather than personal revenge. "Judges, in short, do not get to choose what cases they will decide," he said with a taunting tone.

Jeffreys was probably as surprised as anyone, because the Court of Appeals either got it wrong or made new law. In *Fountain v. Filson*, the Supreme Court clearly said an appeals court can't introduce new arguments and evidence, because the parties wouldn't have an opportunity to respond and contest the *ex parte* surprise. Jeffreys knew that very well. As an appeals judge in *Ramirez v. Weinberger*, he had tried that tactic to apologize for the Reeder administration's illegal acts in Central America. The Court practically laughed at him for such a lame attempt. But now he was laughing.

Judge Cook wistfully noted that he was the first judge in Anglo-American legal history to be removed for bias on account of newspaper editorials. No one thought there was an appearance of bias on the part of Judge L. Gordo Bowner, a former director of the Lynch Legal Foundation, who had been appointed by President Reeder at the urging of Senator Helmut Duke and who continued to attend junkets funded by the big tobacco companies. And no one knew we'd engineered the smear campaign in the press.

Judge James Wilson, appointed to the district bench by Cannon, had plenty to say about both the Independent Counsel and the articles that were used to remove Judge Cook from the case. "Disqualification of an honorable trial judge is a most serious matter and should never be based upon hearsay, hearsay on hearsay, and triple hearsay contained in media reports," he told the Associated Press. "This op-ed piece cited by Mr. Jeffreys was authored by a thoroughly discredited, save-your-Confederate-money-boys, die-hard segregationist, Judge James Boutwell

Crommelin and other trash fabricated by the *American Speculator*'s Alabama Project, all funded by Howard Mellonskoff and other wingnuts. The appeals panel would have no way of knowing that, since no record was made in the trial court, and the Independent Counsel defamed Judge Cook with scurrilous allegations made of whole cloth. Throughout the long struggle for civil rights in our state, Judge Cook risked his law practice and even his personal safety to fight the forces of segregation. Now those same forces are still hard at work, no longer hiding under their sheets but using smear tactics in the tabloid press to ruin his reputation on the bench."

Even without Judge Wilson's vociferous objections, the euphoria would have been short-lived. Three days later the *New York Observer* and *The Nation* began a series of articles detailing Jeffreys' conflicts of interest, and numerous editorials called for Jeffreys to resign. The *Los Angles Times* had a damning article that revealed how Gedney and Hathorne had badgered and abused Bridget Bishop, causing her to lose her job and threatening to charge her with a felony to get her to provide testimony against Vance and Banaghan. The *New Yorker* followed with an extensive litany of ethical lapses by Jeffreys, ranging from his representation of International Paper to the squeeze play against the RTC in the Kirk & Polis lawsuit. Even the *New York Times* joined in the call for Jeffreys to resign, but the *Washington Post* remained silent on the ethics issue, still grateful for a big favor when Jeffreys saved them millions in a libel case a few years ago.

On the advice of Della Beckwith, Jeffreys stonewalled the press and refused even to acknowledge the criticism. I felt sorry for Jo Gobles, who always sounded like she was taking the Fifth Amendment with her 'no comment' responses.

Jeffreys did make the network news once that month, and I nearly fell out of my chair when I saw him talking to the cameras in front of the courthouse. Then I recognized that it was the courthouse in New Orleans. Jeffreys had been arguing a case before the Fifth Circuit in defense of the purveyors of carcinogens. He didn't have much time for Whirlpool, but defending big tobacco companies with deep pockets was a different matter entirely. Jeffreys once told me that he always said a prayer or repeated a Bible verse to help him when he was in court to argue a big case. I couldn't keep from wondering what kind of prayer he might have offered for the cigarette makers that day—must have been Proverbs 12:15—and how it might have been received.

Jeffreys did, however, make time to stop in Birmingham for Roby Douglas' sentencing hearing. He praised Douglas for his ongoing cooperation, called him a model witness, and pleaded for the minimum sentence. Jeffreys sounded like he was nominating Douglas for choir boy, but everyone knew he was only trying to enhance the questionable credibility of his star witness. Roby Douglas was represented at the hearing by both Adam Tiler and Alferd Packer. Very interesting. Judge Corwin quickly granted our office's request for a light sentence, giving Douglas only 28 months in the slammer.

The April meeting of the Policy Committee was one of the most interesting yet. Jeffreys was unable to attend due to the demands of his private practice, so Bart Gedney was running the show. Tom Sandefur was there, too, the first time he'd attended one of our meetings in Birmingham. I looked forward to hearing what he might have to say.

We began with the usual update on recent activities. Pickering and Volstead were doing a good job with the Burgh lawsuit, filing numerous motions and, thus far, avoiding having to answer the complaint. They now had the case move to federal court and assigned to Judge Jonathan Corwin, one of our three reliable friends on the local bench.

Bart Gedney announced that Jeffreys had recently hired yet another new Associate Independent Counsel in the Washington office. Tony Comstock, a former Assistant U. S. Attorney and most recently a partner with the firm of Stoner, Rockwell, and Terminiello, would be in charge of the White House Travel Office investigation. Now that someone had suggested Diane Cannon wanted those guys fired, Jeffreys thought it was important enough to assign additional staff and make a special effort to find something illegal, even though Congress had been through the whole deal and found nothing.

The extent of Gedney's influence on Jeffreys and the overall investigation was also apparent when he announced that one of his buddies, former Tennessee prosecutor Oscar Paparazzi, had been hired to continue picking the scabs of the Hal Goodall inquiry. Gedney saw the look of utter disgust on my face and said, "Questions remain, Wilkes. Was it suicide, or was it murder? And in either case, we need to know why." What a maggot. What we needed was to have the decency to release the report that was completed months ago and let people get on with their lives. But both Gedney and I knew that Howard Mellonskoff would not like that.

John Hathorne gave an update on the Vance-Banaghan trial. Things had not been going very well so far, but he was all excited that Roby Douglas would be called to the stand next week. "Douglas has been relaxing down at the hunting lodge. He's rested and refreshed and ready to go," Hathorne said. "We've been going over his story everyday after the trial, and I think he'll do a credible job. He'll testify under oath that Cannon pressured him to make an illegal loan that is at the heart of our conspiracy theory. I think we can spin it to look like $50,000 of the money went to Whirlpool and benefited the Cannons. We'll get plenty of press on that, especially from Stricher and the *New York Times*. They're already primed for that."

Finally, Gedney turned to Della Beckwith and asked her for an overview of the public relations strategy. What he should have said was a damage report, because the tide of public opinion was starting to turn against Jeffreys. The stonewalling had not made the ethical questions disappear. In fact, they were getting worse.

Della Beckwith stood up and slowly circled the table while she talked. "As you all know, Judge Jeffreys been getting some pretty bad press on the character issue," she began. "We had thought that having Tom Sandefur serve as a buffer on the ethical questions would keep that from happening, but now, it seems, Professor Sandefur has also become a target of these scurrilous attacks."

Holding a file of press clippings and stopping behind Sandefur's chair for a moment, Beckwith looked rougher than I had ever seen her. Maybe it was the beige suit, or the glasses, but she looked pretty hard. Then, after a slight pause, she continued to deliver the bad news. "Last Friday, the *Alabama Examiner* had an editorial calling for Judge Jeffreys to resign which also said, 'Professor Tom Sandefur is right about the stench, but wrong about the propriety. He has become the Alfred E. Neuman of ethics counselors. He doesn't worry about anything.' The *Boston Globe* was equally unkind to Professor Sandefur and his role," she said as she held a copy of the article. "One columnist wrote, 'Forget George Jeffreys for a moment. The guy who needs to take a hike—for the public interest's sake as well as his own—is Thomas Sandefur. Not only has Sandefur been a disaster as far as the public interest is concerned, the very idea behind his position is a disaster.' In view of this recent turn of events, I have asked Professor Sandefur to discuss this ethical quagmire in which we now find ourselves."

"First," Sandefur began, "I'll just say this to the *Alabama Examiner*. I testify all over the country as an expert on legal ethics. I don't recall a single time when any judge of a federal court or a state court ever asked me: 'What does the *Alabama Examiner* think?' And as for the *Boston Globe*, well, they endorsed George McGovern, so what do they know?"

"But let me speak to the larger issue," he continued. "This is somewhat unique. Judge Jeffreys felt when he was appointed, fairly or unfairly, there was quite a bit of criticism because he was a partisan Republican. There was some concern, at the White House and other places, that he may not be objective. My personal belief is he didn't need me, but he was thinking of public perception and image problems. He thought it was proper, to preserve public confidence, to bring someone like me in. He felt he needed somebody to assure the public that his decisions are being made on the basis of the right judgments."

Sandefur then began trimming his remarks to protect himself, admitting, "I'm not sure that I know all of his private clients. The relationship isn't one in which, like coming to Mommy, he has to ask me, 'Can I do this? Can I do that?' He has to bring to my attention any situation that he feels could possibly be considered a problem. I would think as a lawyer with his reputation for integrity—and he does have that reputation—that he doesn't have to come to me initially. His first screen is his own conscience."

There were some who questioned whether Jeffreys had a conscience, and Sandefur knew that he had some taint on his own. Trying to put the best face on his own role, he said, "Now, I know the press is making a big deal about my being paid $3,200 a week to be on call. And one Democrat Congressman suggested that I was taking tax dollars to provide cover for Judge Jeffreys to continue his lucrative representation of the tobacco industry and certain foundations with political axes to grind. He actually should be very grateful that I am in this position, making sure that this prosecution is conducted fairly and objectively without any political overtones to it. Who knows what might happen if I weren't doing that? And I've only been paid a little over $150,000 so far. That is practically *pro bono* work for me. People of my stature charge way more than that," Sandefur said with a laugh.

Becoming more somber, Sandefur then concluded his little soliloquy. "Let me just say this. I have seen no case that Judge Jeffreys is working on, at this point in time, that's a conflict with the Whirlpool investigation. If I had my own preferences, I'd hope he'd be a full-time Independent Counsel because of questions reasonable people ask. I have discussed with him that he should take heed. He is concerned, but he doesn't think he's doing anything wrong. Everything that's happening is happening according to the letter of the law. What he's doing is proper, but, as I have said, it does have an odor to it. I can understand how responsible reporters and reasonable people could question George's judgment, and I have been telling him recently that he cannot ignore the issues that have been raised by responsible papers."

I was not particularly impressed by that explanation, and I was feeling a little ornery. I got Sandefur's attention and asked, "So, in your unbiased expert opinion, Jeffreys has done nothing improper?"

Sandefur immediately began to crawdad on his statement. "I didn't mean to use the word 'proper.' 'Proper' is a weasel word. I think what I tried to say—and maybe I misstated—is everything he's doing is 'legal' and 'lawful'—not necessarily 'proper.' It is essentially the same thing, I admit. I'm not trying to split hairs. All I'm saying is, I am expressing myself as an independent person. I'm not saying I would do the same thing he would do. I'm not giving George Jeffreys my reputation. I'm giving him my expertise. I'm not passing on his judgment. I don't think I have the right to. If I were a private independent professor, I could speak freely my mind. I may be somewhat constrained, because when I speak I can't speak as Tom Sandefur, private citizen. I am speaking as Tom Sandefur in the role of hired ethics counsel to George Jeffreys and the office. Therefore, I don't have a right to express judgments which I could have as an independent person. I don't even know why it's relevant."

"Well, "I said, "that's a mighty long answer to such a short question. Don't you think it'd be better if he worked here full time and let a few of those private clients go until we wrap this up?"

Della Beckwith answered that one. "His legal practice is a long-standing commitment, and he honors his commitments to his private clients, as well as to his wife. Case closed." Obviously she didn't particularly appreciate my question, and she certainly didn't want me asking any more. I couldn't tell if that "wife" remark was because I was divorced or because she'd been spending so much time with that shrill media flack for Christine Putnam.

Looking at Sandefur, Beckwith then asked, "What would you think about going public with a stronger defense of Judge Jeffreys and his conduct? I'm sure we could arrange a couple of interviews with friendly reporters."

Sandefur was obviously uncomfortable with that suggestion. "I don't want to do an interview," he protested. "It isn't that I haven't been available for interviews. I have. And it's not because there's anything to hide. I don't want to be in a situation where they're asking me a lot of questions and I'm not commenting, and the story makes me look like a criminal who's pleading the Fifth Amendment. I just feel that there's enough controversy out in the press about these issues that I don't want to add to it. I think it's important that there be no further distractions. I think Judge Jeffreys has become very exposed as a result of these issues, and he has so much important work to do. It's distracting his work to always—even when he has to read about what I may be saying—it distracts his work and necessitates more phone calls and things like that, and I really don't want to be distracting anymore."

Beckwith found that answer unacceptable, especially from a guy we were paying $3,200 a week. Her eyes narrowed even more than usual when she said, "We can discuss this further after the meeting, Tom."

Chapter Twenty Seven

The courtroom was packed with members of the national press when John Hathorne called Roby Douglas to the stand . This was the guy who had started the whole thing, and this was the moment for which everyone had been waiting. The press was ready and eager to hear Jeffreys' star witness make his wild allegations under oath against President Cannon and, only incidentally, against Vance and the Banaghans. The whole show was like something from David Letterman's stupid dog tricks, with Hathorne feeding questions and Douglas fetching and performing as he had been trained in more than 60 interviews with our staff and no telling how many more with the *American Speculator*.

The cross-examination, though, was a total disaster. Douglas admitted time after time that he was a liar. Yes, he had lied to the FBI. Yes, he had lied for years to the Small Business Administration. Yes, he had even lied to Judge Corwin at his sentencing last week. No question that Douglas would tell any lie, anytime, to anyone. The only real questions were whether Hathorne should be sanctioned by the court for putting on suspect testimony from such a tainted witness and how much money Douglas had been paid to tell this story.

Riding the coattails of the national media attention to the trial, *Blood Sucker* made it to the top of the *New York Times* bestseller list that week. I'm sure the author thought it would get him another Pullet Surprise, but it would have to be for fiction. Jeffreys told Mitch that it was his favorite book on Whirlpool, so Mitch bought enough copies for everyone on the Policy Committee. From the title, I thought it might be a book about Jeffreys. And it was clear that he'd had some contact with the author, judging from the bold libel that he'd convicted Burgh on two felonies. It turned out, though, to be just another sloppy example of the fanciful tomes in the growing "Cannon fodder" genre. After reading it, I thought the title aptly described the author and his marketing strategy. And our investigation.

Mitch was surprised when I returned my copy the next day. Actually, I threw it on his desk, prompting him to ask, "You didn't think much of the book, huh?"

"No, Mitch, I didn't. But, as Dorothy Parker might say, it's not a book to be tossed aside lightly. It should be thrown with great force. Into the dumpster."

Mitch was clearly disappointed with my assessment. Instead of trying to defend the author or the book, an impossible task in my not so humble opinion, he asked, "Who is Dorothy Parker?"

I laughed to myself as I remembered Mitch boasting about his credentials from Dartmouth and Chicago Law, but I didn't have the time to compensate for the gaps in his education. "An old friend of mine," I replied, "who had a bad habit of telling the truth."

Truth telling did not come as easily for George Jeffreys, but it was becoming increasingly clear that he was going to have to say something. Tom Sandefur had refused to take the heat, and the stonewalling strategy had failed. Della Beckwith finally convinced Jeffreys that he must go public and defend himself against the ethical questions regarding his private practice.

Trying to milk maximum advantage on both ends, Jeffreys decided to wait until the media had finished reporting and repeating the charges made by Roby Douglas during the trial in Birmingham. The venue was carefully chosen, a conference in Anaheim sponsored by the National Legal Center for the Private Interest, and he arranged to have himself introduced by his old friend, former Congressman William Dingleberry. Dingleberry had been a rabid fruitcake in Congress, and he was still active in many right-wing causes. His visible role in various anti-Cannon groups made him a curious choice for someone wanting to appear "independent," but I was not about to tell them how to run a PR campaign.

Delivering the keynote address to a very supportive audience, Jeffreys announced, "I have no plans to resign. I have no political conflicts. Public perceptions of our investigation are of great significance, and that fact demands special care from those members of the media responsible for reporting on them. The inaccuracies about me are serious and unfortunate. I have given no speeches or written any op-eds or the like with respect to President Cannon. I've in fact extricated myself entirely from the political process, except for a few campaign contributions to Republican political action committees. I am seeking to discharge my obligations, and I want to give every assurance that the Whirlpool investigation is one of my priorities."

Ignoring the distinction between what the law allowed and what was right, Jeffreys proudly boasted, "I fully intend to continue my private legal practice, however, and I will continue to charge my usual fees. That is not against the law. That is what I do in my private practice capacity. My reputation is such that I am often asked to take on novel and challenging legal issues, including constitutional questions. My ethics counselor is the legendary Professor Tom Sandefur, Senior Fellow at the Kennedy Center for Ethics at Georgetown University, and he has affirmed that it's all completely legal."

Having shirked his own responsibility and having laid the blame on Sandefur, Jeffreys then scraped the ethical problems from the bottom of his shoes. "As for the defense of the tobacco industry against health claims, the brief for the Republican National Committee on campaign debts, the work for the Automobile Manufacturers Association opposing pollution standards, the defense of General Motors in the South Carolina case, the Hughes Aircraft litigation against the government, the International Paper challenge to environmental regs, my representing the Lynde Foundation, arguing for the private school vouchers scheme, and the RTC suit against my law firm, Professor Sandefur looked closely at those issues, and he came to the conclusion that I should in fact participate—well, that there was no reason for me not to participate. And I don't think that reasonable observers should be of the view that there is any prejudicial effect on our ongoing investigation of President and Mrs. Cannon."

Very few people bought the defense offered by Jeffreys, but he was confident in the righteousness of his own position. Even the Republican Establishment was disappointed, and former Attorney General Elliot Richardson was quoted as saying, "It is the people who are the most confident about their integrity that tend to be the most careless about appearances." Jeffreys went back to stonewalling and to practicing law. As for his remarks about the Whirlpool investigation being a priority, however, it was not high enough on his agenda for him to participate in the taking of Cannon's videotaped testimony for the trial.

Maybe Jeffreys was still trying to distance himself from the spectacle, or maybe he was too ashamed to face Cannon again in person. I was ashamed, too. We sent five lawyers to the White House to take President Cannon's testimony. Well, John Hathorne badgered him for four hours that day. The other four just stood around with their thumbs up their butts. At least they got a few days off and a vacation in Washington at the taxpayers' expense.

After directing the courtroom drama for nine weeks, John Hathorne rested the prosecution's case against Governor Vance and the Banaghans on May 6th. The following day, Judge Gaston held under Rule 29 that we had not presented enough evidence for the jury even to consider eight of the counts. He dismissed the four conspiracy counts against Jessie Banaghan and four felony counts against Governor Vance. Twenty percent of our case had been lost before the defense presented even one witness or a single document.

Hathorne was not at all dismayed. Back at the office that evening he said, "We knew those were pretty weak all along. The good news is that he didn't throw out some of the other counts that we expected him to dismiss. And even if we don't get any convictions, just think of how much we've cost Vance in legal fees to defend himself." Then with a laugh, he said, "My conservative estimate is that his lawyers have been costing him over $5,000 a day. That's one reason I was in no hurry to conclude our case." The money was, in my opinion, the least of the damage that we had inflicted on people during the last two and a half years. The human suffering of disrupted lives and families and careers could not be measured in dollars alone.

When the defense began to present its case, Josh Banaghan was the first witness called to the stand. For two years he had been saying he wanted the chance to take on the Independent Counsel, and the time had finally come. But things were different now. The nine week trial had taken a serious toll on Banaghan's already poor health. Twice last month he had to be helped from the courtroom after collapsing, and he had missed several days of the trial when he was hospitalized briefly. His doctors had cautioned him against testifying, saying that the strain might well be fatal.

Banaghan ignored the professional advice and decided to take his chances instead of his medication. Just like he had always done in business and politics. At first, as he denied every charge one by one, Banaghan appeared to be doing well. Then he attacked Roby Douglas, the convicted felon, as a liar and a cheat. When John Hathorne began the cross-examination the next day, Banaghan responded with contempt. "Johnny, that's so simple I'd think even a Republican could understand that," he said in reply to one question.

Then, the exchange moved quickly from farce to tragedy. Banaghan appeared to be fading in and out of consciousness, not always following the questioning by an overly hostile John Hathorne. Once Banaghan looked at a document and claimed that Gastone Diletto must have forged his signature. His grip on reality was tenuous at best. Later, he couldn't respond at all. Banaghan sat silently in the witness chair for what seemed like several minutes, his weakened mind and sickly body reminding me of the dying Colonel Kurtz in *Apocalypse Now*. Giving no quarter in his dark heart, John Hathorne continued to verbally pound on Banaghan. He was getting nothing from a stroke-ravaged mind and a memory now gone. On redirect questioning, Banaghan turned to the jury and sadly said, "If you believe that any crime was committed, please charge that to me and not to my wife." Then, broken and abused, he was dismissed from the stand. His attorney helped him into a wheelchair and out of the room.

The following day, Banaghan's attorney called James Madison Cannon for the defense. In videotaped testimony that lasted more than an hour, President Cannon carefully refuted every charge that Roby Douglas had made against him in the press. The only surprise in the testimony, even after careful editing, was how childish John Hathorne appeared in questioning the president and how foolish Cannon had made him look.

Following Cannon's testimony, Josh Banaghan's lawyer abruptly rested his case. Then, in a dramatic move that left everyone gasping and reporters rushing to the phone banks, the attorneys for Jessie Banaghan and Jim Bibb Vance also rested their case without taking the stand or calling a single witness.

Closing arguments took three days and were not particularly impressive on either side. The defense lawyers spent most of their time elaborating the obvious fact that Roby Douglas was a practiced liar who had been coached by the Independent Counsel, but they had been prevented by the judge from mentioning that he had also been paid for by right wing zealots out to destroy Cannon.

The defense attorneys also relied upon the credibility of the president's testimony, forcing Hathorne to reluctantly reverse his earlier position and confess, "This case has absolutely nothing to do with President Cannon. The President of the United States is not on trial. Why? First and foremost, he is not on trial because there was never even any suggestion that he ever did anything improper. There's been no allegations of criminal wrongdoing on the part of the President, even by Roby Douglas. The President didn't take out any loans. He didn't lie to any investigators. The President did nothing wrong."

I know those words came hard for John Hathorne. I still remembered how much he and Bart Gedney had wanted to name Cannon as an unindicted co-conspirator and how disappointed they had been when Jeffreys lacked the confidence to approve that move. I was certain that Hathorne remembered that, too. The only questions I had were two that could not be answered easily. Did Hathorne argue to name Cannon as a co-conspirator, knowing that he had no involvement? Or, was Hathorne now lying to the Court, believing that Cannon was actually a co-conspirator? I would never know for sure.

Hathorne probably scored a few points with the jury when he finally admitted, "You might look at Roby Douglas and say his testimony is obviously incredible. You can't believe him. He's a notorious liar, he's a con man, he's a cheat, he's a thief, he was a federally licensed loan shark." Hathorne had to throw his star witness to the dogs, but he asked the jurors to focus on the documents. We had introduced over 900 documents as prosecution exhibits. Most of them were irrelevant to the theory of the case, but Hathorne was hoping that the jury would be either overwhelmed or impressed by the volume and think he'd made a strong case.

Judge Gaston gave the jury their instructions, and they retired to begin consideration of their verdict. Back at the office, Hathorne was less than optimistic that afternoon. "I gave it my best shot," he said wearily. "I doubt that they will find for us on Mrs. Banaghan or Governor Vance, but I think we might get a conviction on Josh Banaghan. That ought to be enough to silence the critics. We only need one."

As time passed, though, Hathorne became more hopeful. After six days of jury deliberations without a verdict, Hathorne told Jeffreys to be expecting good news. Della Beckwith began polishing Draft B, the remarks Jeffreys should make if we were successful in getting convictions. Then, after eight days, the jury reached a verdict. I was watching on television at the office as Bob Franken announced their decision. Jessie Banaghan, guilty. Josh Banaghan, guilty. Governor Vance, guilty on two counts and not guilty on five.

John Hathorne could hardly contain himself as he gloated to the press, "This case was about crime, not politics. And I think the verdicts reflect that. It's nice. It gives you a warm feeling when the jury accepts your interpretation of some of the evidence."

Hathorne should have stopped there, but that was too much to expect. He couldn't pass up the chance to tout himself and take a political swipe at Cannon. "As for the credibility of President Cannon's testimony," he said with a sneer, "that's going to be up to the political pundits. I represent the United States on matters of crime and not on interpretation as far as political damage. It is not my position to exonerate the president. I'm sure there are going to be a lot of people who are going to have an opinion about it, but I will just say that I would not have put Roby Douglas on the stand if I didn't believe that he was telling the truth. I did not actually call Mr. Douglas a notorious liar during the course of my closing argument. As far as the interpretation that anyone else wants to put on it, that's their business. But as far as the effect of the verdict on the president's chances for reelection, again, that's for the pundits to make that comment and not for me."

Congressman Dick Leech had no such reservations. He seemed to ignore what John Hathorne had said in closing arguments and continued to spin innuendoes like he had done in the past. Too clever to make a direct charge, he slipped his points to the press like he was slopping an Iowa sow. "Care must be taken not to accept at face value any assertion that the verdict in Birmingham has nothing to do with President Cannon," he said. "Careful examination of the trial record upon which the jury's decision was based suggests otherwise."

Shortly thereafter, Jeffreys sought another 15 minutes of fame by calling a press conference at the Washington office to claim credit for the convictions. He beamed as he faced the cameras and sanctimoniously said, "We obviously are gratified by the verdict, and we are very proud of our trial team. So it is a tribute to Judge Gaston and a tribute to me and my very able trial team. This was a complicated case."

"Our compliments are for the 12 jurors who sat dutifully, understanding that this was not just a testimonial case, and that it required close attention to their solemn obligation and their solemn oaths. And they lived up to those obligations today and when they prayerfully sought divine assistance in their deliberations," Jeffreys proclaimed.

Then, revealing that the ethics charges still pricked him, Jeffreys said, "At a time when our system of government is under criticism, when participants in the system find themselves under assault—I was pleased that the jurors could set aside whatever was happening in the public domain and do their duty as God gives them the light to see their duty and to act on that duty. They went about their work with integrity and pride. And when they read that statement in Birmingham today, I, too, felt that same pride."

Jeffreys was obviously emboldened by the verdicts, and he sent a signal to his political backers that he was still hard after Cannon, concluding his remarks by warning, "Now we move forward. There is, in fact, an on-going investigation with respect to the Washington phase. We have an active grand jury investigation underway, and we are taking it a step at a time, getting closer and closer. We're obviously encouraged by the action of the jury today. I'm not going to get into any characterization of President Cannon. I'm not going to get into personal issues at all. We are continuing, and we have another trial in Birmingham beginning June 17th, God willing."

Adequately prepared, the pundits then flocked to the studios to provide their instant analysis, and the reporters went about ambushing the jurors in hopes of getting an angle or a dangle to stretch the story into a tale of woe for the White House. Problem was, that story had no legs. The foreman of the jury said, "The president's credibility was never an issue. I had no reason to doubt what he said." Another jury member confirmed that view, saying, "I felt like President Cannon was a credible witness. I felt like he was telling the truth." One juror seemed annoyed, explaining to a reporter, "The president didn't really have anything to do with this case." One woman juror was even more blunt, responding, "Our verdict was absolutely not meant to be any kind of statement on the President, and it is silly for anyone to think that. It's demeaning for you to even ask such a ridiculous question."

Disappointed by those answers, the press kept looking for at least one juror to say something they could use as a peg on which to hang the Hathorne-Jeffreys implications. A CNN crew caught the last juror leaving the courthouse by a side door, but they paid a price for the live coverage when the fellow stopped, starred into the camera, and said, "President Cannon was magnificent in his presentation. He cleared up a lot of things for us. He just added to the lack of credibility for Roby Douglas, one of the greatest con men whom I've ever seen. Even John Hathorne, in his closing statements, was backing off from Douglas. The deciding factor was the paper trail. Everyone knows, though, that it was all politically motivated. George Jeffreys really wanted to do something to embarrass the State of Alabama. He couldn't get the President, so he did the next best thing and got the Governor. And Roby Douglas perjured himself and invoked the President's name for one reason—to please Jeffreys and save his butt. We all thought that way."

The best jury story the press could find that afternoon was that Josh Banaghan's performance had helped the prosecution more than did that of Roby Douglas. One of the jurors said, "Josh Banaghan messed himself up real bad when he got on the stand. I think the best thing would have been for him to stay in bed." Another agreed. "I thought Banaghan killed himself and hurt the others," he said. "There would have been different verdicts all around if Banaghan had kept his mouth shut. They should have just put President Cannon on and quit."

While the media were trying to create a false drama, a very real one played out in Montgomery late that afternoon. Governor Vance called a press conference at the capitol, and the local affiliates covered it live for the networks. Maybe Vance would take the opportunity to say what he had been thinking for the past three months while his life was on trial. Perhaps the public was about to get a view of the other side, a glimpse into the life of one of those dangerous criminals Jeffreys and Diletto had been railing about for the last two years.

Governor Vance stood with his wife by his side. The Alabama press corps seemed almost respectful in comparison to the shouting hordes that had been reporting the trial for the national media. "First," Governor Vance began calmly, "I want to say thank you for those thousands of individuals who have offered support for me and my family. We deeply appreciate that, and it has been very, very meaningful to us."

"Second," he continued, "to the people of Alabama, I owe a special debt. I cannot adequately express my sense of humility and my appreciation for your patience during these past months. You stayed your judgment. You always seemed to understand what was happening. You trusted me to continue to do my job. I am very proud of the accomplishments which we have achieved together over the past several years."

Then Vance startled everyone in the room. "Although I know I am innocent of all charges made," he said, "I must accept the verdict of the jury while I appeal. However, I cannot, and should not, expect the people of our state to bear any part of that burden. Therefore, my resignation will be effective on July 15th.""

As soon as the shock subsided, Vance concluded his comments with more class than that displayed by Jeffreys, Hathorne, and Leech combined that day. "I believe I have served our people well, honestly, and energetically as their governor. As I have said so many times to the people of our state, I truly love this job and am proud of the work that we have done together. I have tried to honestly identify the challenges we face and the choices we will have to make if Alabama is to be a better place for all of our citizens to live and raise their children. I thank you for allowing me the high honor of serving you as your governor." With that, he took his leave.

The rest of the staff was elated. They stayed glued to the television, flipping channels and seeking any sign of approbation for Jeffreys or jubilation for the verdicts, but I'd seen enough. As I started to leave the room, Mitch asked, "Where are you going, Wilkes? Aren't you going to join us for the victory celebration over at Bart's place?"

"Victory? The government only wins when justice is done its citizens in court, and I don't think anyone won today," I replied, wishing immediately that I had said something else. And wishing that I were somewhere else. "I think I'll just go get a beer and then call it a day."

John Hathorne walked in just as I said that, and I caught the full force of his contempt. "You're drinking quite a lot these days, aren't you, Wilkes? Maybe you should stick to soda pop for a change. It might improve your attitude."

I definitely had an attitude, and I thought about popping him. But, I let it pass and just tweaked his sense of propriety. "Hey. Twenty-four beers in a case; twenty-four hours in a day. Circumstantial evidence? I think not, Counselor." And with that, I took my leave.

I stopped at The Mill on my way home, seeking cold beer to counter the cold reality of how much I hated my job. It didn't work. I pulled up to the bar and ordered a Smoky Mountain Brown Ale. Sherman Morgan was not his usually friendly self. He gave me a look that was colder than the beer, and said, "I guess you boys are real proud of yourselves now?"

I wasn't proud about anything, but I was at a loss as to how to respond. "No," I said, looking into my beer, "I don't think anyone can be proud about what happened today."

"Well," Sherman said, cutting me no slack, "now that Jeffreys has got himself the scalp of a governor, maybe y'all will get your carpetbag asses out of town and go back to helping your rich Republican clients steal from the widow women and orphans."

"Shit, Sherman, give me a break. I'm not a Yankee, and I didn't have anything to do with the trial."

"Yeah, well, you're as much a part of this damn witch hunt as your boss, so don't try to tell me you're not. You've been taking their blood money for over two years. Ain't nobody holding a gun to your head, is they? You're one of *them* now. At least your buddy Sean had the sense to leave when Jeffreys took over. Doesn't it bother you at all what you've done to this state, what you've done to people's lives?"

"Yes. It bothers me a lot," I said, finishing my beer. Sherman just stared at me, and I knew he was right. I threw a five on the bar and left without offering a defense. I had none.

Jeffreys was back in Birmingham on Monday, and he was on a roll. The Policy Committee meeting was what I expected. Jeffreys was congratulating everyone on the trial, and Hathorne kept retelling war stories that enhanced his own role. They were especially excited that Jerry Elkay Coughlin was going to be governor, but they all wanted to speculate as to whether he would stay in the Senate race now. Why was I not surprised that the topic was politics? Wasn't it always, in one form or another? Della Beckwith's prediction that the convictions would put an end to the White House spin that Whirlpool was just a political vendetta did nothing to change my mind.

Jeffreys announced that he had hired two new staff attorneys to open a new angle on the investigation. Bruce Adolph and Mike Ellick would be in charge of something called "Operation Trip Wire." I seemed to be the only one in the dark about this, but I was too depressed to give it much thought. Gedney was rather excited by the prospect and welcomed the announcement. "Oh, these guys are good," he said. "Just what we need for that. They both have records as experienced prosecutors, and they *know* how to get a witness to *cooperate*." Walt Lecraw agreed, "That's their history. That's why we brought them on board."

Hawthorne nodded knowingly. "Chapman's Friend is now in Deep Water, and it's going down to the wire," he said cryptically, bringing a smile to Jeffreys' face. What that meant beat the hell out of me. Sounded like a tip from a track tout on a long shot, but neither of them appreciated the equestrian equities. Guess it was just another example of the inside baseball that confirmed I was now far out of the loop.

The only legal matters discussed were equally political, and Bart Gedney was responsible for both. He presented a two-step plan to retake the offensive. First, he announced that we had just received the FBI report on the Bankhead billing records and that Diane Cannon's fingerprints were all over them. Well, on two of the 108 pages. I didn't immediately recognize why that was worth reporting. I quipped that the FBI might find Bart's fingerprints on his own billing records, but everyone ignored my comment and the obvious implications of its insignificance. Bart said he intended to share the report with Diletto's committee, but he handed copies of the report to Della Beckwith and Jo Gobles, which I found quite odd. Unless, of course, he wanted the information to make its way to the press.

Second, Bart said he planned to name Robert Bruce, the White House Deputy Counsel, as an unindicted co-conspirator in the upcoming Jones-Hill trial before Judge Hoffman. I was astounded and said so. "If we had anything on Bruce," I argued, "we should have tried to indict him. This looks like a cheap shot to accuse him without giving him an opportunity to defend himself. Our case already looks like a gratuitous effort to harass Cannon, and this will only make it even more obvious."

"Perhaps you should leave trial strategy to the professionals, Wilkes. You've done nothing but whine since day one," Gedney said, as if his scolding would change the facts. "I know what I'm doing here, and Judge Jeffreys and I have already discussed this. Naming Bruce as an unindicted co-conspirator will allow us to use John Reeves' testimony about conversations he had with Mr. Bruce regarding the currency transaction reports."

"Well, if you and George have already made this decision, there's little need for me to say anything," I replied with resignation. I knew, however, that they were about to screw up real bad, because I had helped draft the opinion in *United States v. Briggs*, a 1975 5th Circuit case that frowned on such abuse of the judicial process. And naming people as unindicted co-conspirators was specifically cautioned against in the Department of Justice Policy Manual.

"Oh, no, Mr. Wilkes, we value your contribution," Jeffreys said with that syrupy voice that I detested. "Please speak up if you have anything worthwhile to add."

"Think I'll pass," I replied. Gedney smiled with satisfaction.

Jeffreys smiled, too. It was that same smarmy 700 Club smile of the righteous. Then he instructed Walt LeCraw to subpoena the personal bank and credit card records of every defendant and every witness we had interviewed regarding the President or the First Lady. "We need to monitor the income of these people, especially those who have defended the Cannons," Jeffreys announced. "Look for any unusual deposits, consulting fees, trust funds for their children's education, and the like. If anyone is trying to influence them, we need to know that. Keep the pressure on them by all available means, so let's turn up the heat and see if it improves their memory. We don't want anyone to get too comfortable."

That was George Jeffreys' idea of how to deal with witnesses, except, of course, for Roby Douglas and the troopers who had been paid for their testimony.

As the meeting was ending, Jeffreys reminded everyone that Bart Gedney and Walt Lecraw would be heading the prosecution team for the trial of Jones and Hill on charges stemming from Cannon's 1990 gubernatorial campaign. He would not be in the courtroom for this one either, but he still had the gall to say, "Once more into the breach, dear friends." John Hathorne laughed as he added his own battle cry, "Confusion to our enemies!" Meeting adjourned.

I went back to my office and just sat there for a while, doing nothing really and not wanting to do anything. To amuse myself, as much as anything else, I decided to run a Nexis check on the two new lawyers everyone seemed so pleased would be running Operation Whatever. What I found left me sick.

Mike Ellick was an Assistant U.S. Attorney with a history. One example involved a woman who refused to testify against her husband in a federal corruption case he prosecuted. During the trial, U.S. District Judge Robert Takasugi criticized the government for withholding key evidence helpful to the defense, noting, "We haven't achieved a fair trial." The man was acquitted.

Ellick's staff then went after the woman, wiring a police informant to secretly tape her admitting to an extramarital affair in an effort to prove perjury and force her to "cooperate" as a witness. "I wouldn't regard that as sleazy," Ellick told a reporter. When he couldn't make the perjury charge, the couple was then indicted for filing a false income tax form.

The tax charges so angered a federal judge that the case was almost immediately dismissed, holding that "the government's intent was callous, coercive and vindictive," that it "used threats, deceit and harassment techniques," and that it violated the due process clause of the Constitution. After more than five years of constant harassment, the 13 felony counts against the man were finally dropped. He pled guilty to a single misdemeanor and was fined $50.

Bruce Adolph was no better. Maybe worse. As a district attorney, he had once prosecuted the wrong prisoner on a murder charge. Being white, Adolph said he couldn't tell the difference between the men until it was called to his attention by a spectator during the second day of the trial. After the case was thrown out, Adolph defended his actions by saying, "We apologized to him. We felt we owed him that much."

Even more disturbing, however, was a civil rights suit against Adolph that cost the taxpayers $50,000. A local citizen charged that Adolph had him arrested on a false misdemeanor charge, refused to allow him to contact an attorney during his investigation, and tried to force him to give false testimony in an unrelated investigation of his employer. After the jury verdict against Adolph, the local newspaper called him "a prosecutor so determined to get a conviction that he was willing to disregard the U.S. Constitution and the Bill of Rights." A federal judge upheld the jury, saying, "Taking into consideration the seriousness of the affront to the plaintiff's constitutional rights by one charged with a duty to uphold and enforce the law, the court cannot say that a verdict of $2,500 in compensatory and $47,500 in punitive damages shocks its conscience."

The voters agreed and retired Adolph at the next election, but he soon found work in the U.S. Attorney's Office under President Stuart. And now he had come to help Jeffreys nail the president. The most recent news item was an interview with the *Miami Herald* just a few days earlier when news leaked that Jeffreys had offered him a job. Asked what he'd be doing for Jeffreys, Adolph said, "Like any other investigation, we'll do a proactive investigation, what's often referred to as 'stings.' Somebody walks into the office with information, we'll ask them if they would consider wearing a wire and recapture those conversations."

Now I knew where they were going and why Jeffreys had called it Operation Trip Wire. I stared at the monitor and quitely began to fume. Then I realized the time for that had passed. I started to walk into Jeffreys' office, but I heard him and Gedney laughing about the FBI report finding Diane Cannon's fingerprints. Jeffreys' secretary was about to stop me from going in, so I told her I needed to talk with him and asked her to give me a buzz when he was free. That gave me a few minutes to cool off, and it also gave me time to find the file with my original letter of resignation I had given Jeffreys when he was first appointed. It looked fine, so I changed the date, ran another copy, and signed it.

Phyllis Sanford called and said Jeffreys could see me. As I passed her desk, she said, "He only has a few minutes."

"This won't take long," I replied without stopping.

Jeffreys was seated formally behind his desk, positioned like a pontiff granting an audience. "Yes, Mr. Wilkes, what is it?"

"Just wanted to give you my letter of resignation," I said as I handed it to him.

He appeared somewhat surprised but not necessarily disappointed. I suspected that he had wanted me gone but had refrained from firing me because I provided a false patina of bipartisanship for his operation. "Please, sit down," he ordered. "Are you upset by something I've said or done?"

"I'm upset with everything you've said and done," I said, still standing. "And I'm upset with myself for having been a part of it."

"Well, if you really feel that way, Mr. Wilkes, perhaps you should resign," he replied.

"I just did," I said flatly as I turned to leave.

"Wait. Wait a minute," he said, more begging than commanding as he got up and followed me to the door. "What are you going to do?"

"I have no idea," I said. And I didn't. I had heard nothing from the law school since my interview with the faculty in Tuscaloosa last month, so I figured that wasn't going to happen. I had enough in savings to make it for a while. Or I could go back to Austin and volunteer in Doggett's campaign. He wasn't in any real trouble, but the Republicans were running a candidate with the same name in the race, the wife of Long John Doggett, he of Justice Thom hearing infamy. Pausing for a moment, I said, "I think I might write a book about Whirlpool."

"Oh, I think that might be unethical," Jeffreys said with a hint of concern, or even slight fear, in his voice.

"What would you know about that?" It had been a lob I couldn't pass up.

"No one can question my ethical compass, Mr. Wilkes," Jeffreys retorted emphatically. "Beside, you know full well that Thomas Sandefur has signed off on everything I have done, both in this investigation and in my private practice."

"I know full well that Sandefur has covered your ass, just as I would expect him to do for what we're are paying him," I said, realizing that the shoe fit too well. "And so have I, I suppose, but I just stopped. You'll have to find someone else who needs the money more than he needs his dignity."

Jeffreys let that one slide, because he had a greater concern. "If you do write a book, you can't disclose any confidential information. You are still bound by the Rules of Professional Conduct." Then Jeffreys seemed to take another approach, one that actually concerned me a bit. "You can write whatever you want, but you're wasting your time, Mr. Wilkes."

"Oh, and why's that?"

"You don't get it do you? Ken Burke told me you understood politics, but now I see you don't understand the first thing about what's happening here."

"Oh, I know exactly what's happening here," I said with some doubt, "and I intend to help the American people see it for what it is."

"Yeah. Then go ahead and see how far you get," Jeffreys said with a sneering laugh.

"Maybe no one will publish it, I don't know, but someone needs to write about it, to tell the truth about what's been going on here. You've gagged everyone involved, so the victims can't tell their side of the story, even when you lie about them. You've played the press quite well, I'll give you that, and your lapdogs in the media have performed to the tune of Howard Mellonskoff, Floyd Crump, and the Republican National Committee. Perhaps I'll write fiction, since that seems appropriate to explain how you've handled this whole damn investigation from the day you walked in here. You took a few facts and twisted them to make a big lie. I think I might just write fiction to get at the truth," I said, feeling very good about having done so. And feeling quite certain now that I would write a book.

"I want you to have your office cleared out by 5 o'clock," Jeffreys said with a tremble in his voice. I guess that meant he wasn't going to ask me to reconsider.

"No problem," I said, and he didn't try to stop me that time.

As I was leaving the building with the last box from my office, Jeffreys and Gedney were having a deep conversation in the middle of the hallway. Neither bothered to move aside, making it difficult for me to get past them. Then, as I was almost to the front reception area, Jeffreys practically snarled as he said, "Good riddance, Bubba."

Chapter Twenty Eight

I felt a sense of great relief as I drove out of the parking lot. Almost joy. Jeffreys' reaction was pretty much what I had expected. Well, except for the "Bubba" comment. I wanted to tell Sherman Morgan what I'd done and thank him for helping me understand that I had to do it. Instead, I went home, fixed a pot of tea, and dreamed of being back at Oxford.

Ironically, watching the evening news, I discovered that I had something in common with Ira Dolor. Earlier that day he had announced his resignation from the Senate to pursue his campaign for the presidency. His wife, the former Nixon White House lawyer, was smarter and more realistic. She only took a year's leave of absence from her job as executive director of the Keating Foundation.

That evening I took a little more care when writing in my journal, trying to see if I had the stomach and the skills for the book I wanted to write. Should I really try my hand at fiction, or should it be one of those "tell all" insider accounts? Maybe combine the two as "faction"? Should it be detached or personal? Not having written anything in years, except briefs and law review articles, I wasn't sure that I could write a book. Then I remembered that someone once said, "The great thing is to see and hear and understand and write when there is something that you know and not before and not too damn much afterwards." Yet, I still struggled with questions of style and form to avoid putting the words on paper. Then I wrestled with my conscience, not about exposing what Jeffreys was doing but about what I had done. How did I let myself get sucked into this gawd awful mess? How could I explain that?

I scrawled "Whirlpool" at the top of the page, slowly underlined it a few times as I summonsed the Muse, then began, "Call me Bubba. Some years ago—never mind how long precisely—having little money tied up in real estate and nothing particular to interest me in Texas, I thought I would head out and see some other part of the country. It is a way I have of chasing off the black dog of depression. Whenever I find myself growing grim about the mouth; whenever it is a cold, blustery February in my soul; whenever I find myself involuntarily pausing near female colleagues at work and bringing up the rear of every staff meeting; and especially whenever my hypos get such an upper hand of me, that it requires a strong will to prevent me from deliberately going to a bar and

methodically whipping some redneck's ass—then, I account it high time
to hit the road as soon as I can. This is my substitute for the hemlock tea
of Socrates. With a philosophical flourish Cato threw himself upon his
sword; I quietly take to the blue highways. There is nothing surprising in
this. I think most guys, some time or other, have very nearly the same
feelings toward the freedom of the open road."

Pretty self-indulgent and more than a little obtuse, I thought, as I
read over that first paragraph. I kept losing my focus and thinking about
everything that had happened at work that day. Maybe I would do better
after I'd had some sleep and could sort out what I wanted to say. Or decide if I had anything worth saying.

The phone rang too early the next morning, and I squinted to see the
clock as I answered it. Who would be calling me at six o'clock? I had
long ago declared that there was only one six o'clock in my life, and it
wasn't in the morning. My first thought was that something might have
happened to my kids or to one of my parents. It was Lindsey, and she
almost screamed into the phone, "Have you seen the papers this morning?" I hadn't, of course, and I thought Jeffreys might have announced
that he had fired me. I was almost relieved when she said, "Listen to this.
Front page of the *Washington Sun*. 'FBI finds First Lady's Fingerprints
on Recently Rediscovered S&L Papers.' Did you bastards leak that?"

"Well, that's not quite right. Her fingerprints were on the Bankhead
billing records, not S&L papers," I said, realizing as I began to wake up
that it didn't matter. The damage had been done, and that's what Lindsey
was calling about. "I'm not too surprised. I should have known that's
what would happen. Jeffreys is really frustrated, and he always leaks
something when he gets down in the polls or down in the mouth."

"You mean you knew about this and you didn't do anything to stop
it," she said with disbelief.

"I don't think there was any way to stop it. Certainly not now. I
don't work there anymore. I quit yesterday."

After explaining my new unemployed status and rehabilitating myself with Lindsey, I made a pot of coffee. Double French Roast and Mo-
cha Java, a deadly brew sure to do the trick. Then I went jogging and
found it much more pleasant than I remembered. Much better than I ever
felt working for Jeffreys. I took a shower and plopped down to watch a
little CNN, where I saw Joey Welch, the Cannons' personal attorney,
talking about the latest fuel for the fires of scandal.

I missed the opening, but as I began paying attention, Welch said,
"Information selectively leaked by the Independent Counsel to the press
resulted in the predictable headlines this morning. It was also obvious, I
would think, that Diane Cannon's fingerprints would be on her billing
records. They were, after all, her records, and she has admitted examin-

ing them when trying to answer press inquiries during the 1992 campaign. It would have been news if her prints were not on the documents."

Then, rubbing the opposition's nose in their own words, Welch continued, "As Mark Schine once said, it matters not whether one likes or dislikes a particular individual under investigation. The issue is what kind of a justice system we can all live with and the American people can support. A system that sentences an individual's character and reputation to death by prosecutorial leaks and innuendo is a system foreign to the principles of government established by our Founding Fathers."

Turning his anger on the source of the leak, Welch brought a smile to my face when he said, "I regret that Mr. Jeffreys has chosen to try his cases in the newspapers. If he knew anything about the rule of law, he would know that such actions are clearly prohibited by the Policy Statement of the United States Department of Justice, 28 CFR 50.2, and that his strategy of selected leaks regarding the investigation has been held by the 11th Circuit, in the 1992 case of *Nadler v. Mann*, to be entirely outside the scope of a federal prosecutor's duties. I would remind him, too, that Rule 6(e) of the Federal Rules of Criminal Procedure prohibit such leaks."

Next in line, Welch had something to say about Diletto, who, apparently, had been on earlier in the program. "Senator Diletto's Whirlpool hearings have been even more outrageous. People have had their character attacked and their reputations ruined by unsubstantiated hearsay from politically motivated opponents, and they have not been afforded even the bare constitutional minimum of being allowed to confront their accusers and defend their honor."

"It is only a matter of time," Welch warned, "before other public officials, perhaps more in tune with the political preferences of Dick Leech, William Clapham, Gastone Diletto, and Ira Dolor, find themselves caught in the whirlpool of injustice created in large measure by George Jeffreys and his unethical and unprecedented pronouncements. His leaking of information and public speculation about the innocence or guilt of someone he is investigating is nothing less than indecent and cruel. If he is allowed to continue unchecked, we shall all bear the burden of his substantial transgressions."

I fixed myself another cup of coffee and came back to flip channels to see if Jeffreys might have been interviewed and whether he would abandon his sly 'no comment' strategy. Instead, I was rather surprised to find Tom Sandefur giving a speech at the National Press Club luncheon. "I had planned to talk with you today about 'The Lessons of Watergate,' but this morning I concluded that no lessons have been learned from that political nightmare," he said. My guess was that Jeffreys had called

Sandefur and told him to get busy defending him and the need for the ongoing investigation.

I couldn't wait to watch him do the dance. "When I was first hired," Sandefur explained, "I didn't believe that Mr. Jeffreys was part of a political conspiracy by the Republicans against the Cannons. I said if I did believe that, I wouldn't be there. I told him repeatedly, however, that my tenure could end at a moment's notice if I ever thought otherwise or if my advice on ethical conduct and fairness was not followed. George Jeffreys sacrificed a lot of independence by bringing in someone like me, because he knew that if they did something that I thought was wrong, I'd quit."

Yeah, right, I thought, but it soon became obvious that Jeffreys wasn't grinding his organ this time. "There is no relationship between Whirlpool and any of the major scandals in our time that have required the appointment of an independent counsel," Sandefur said. "I don't believe this is a major scandal, involving a President, that called for an independent counsel. The only relationship between Whirlpool and Watergate is the that both words begin with W. I said that on Nightline before I was appointed as ethics counsel to George Jeffreys, and I haven't changed my opinion."

Damn, this was getting good. I almost wished I were watching it at the office with Jeffreys and his henchmen. "There may have been fraud in the Banaghan case," Sandefur said, "but if James Cannon was not President, would anybody have looked into it? No. This is the same kind of mismanagement that took place with regard to many much larger savings and loans. This is nothing compared to what went on in the industry, in hundreds of institutions, all over the country during the 1980s"

Then Sandefur completely jumped the traces and said, "They have absolutely no evidence that President Cannon was involved in any way. The fabricated testimony about the alleged pressure by the President was not only 'hearsay' that ordinarily would be inadmissible, but it was totally irrelevant. None of what was said by Douglas about any conversations he allegedly had with the President had any relevance to the charges against Vance and Banaghan. It was done to smear the President on an irrelevant issue."

A little ass-covering should be allowed in such instances, and Sandefur took his share. "If I hadn't been there, and I wouldn't have had the opportunity to rein them in and set limits, who knows what abuses may have occurred? I once prevailed upon Mr. Jeffreys to correct a false report that Governor Vance had sought a plea bargain. Mr. Jeffreys had wanted to make no comment on the story, thereby leaving the impression that it was accurate. I said to him, 'You owe it to Governor Vance and the public to tell the truth.' This time, however, my warning was totally ignored."

Good shot, Tom, I wanted to say. I could tell stories like that all day. Continuing in his own defense, Sandefur said, "I know that what's happened over this recent period has affected Mr. Jeffreys, but I had assumed I would be in a position to deal with that. Take, for example, the issue of the Federal Legal Foundation. I raised the question of appearances, of his serving on an advisory board that was packed with Republican political operatives and that had been so critical of Kenneth Burke. He said he was unaware of all that, just like the RTC suit. I told him he should think about it, because there could be an inference of partisanship, but he hasn't been thinking about it. Somehow it looks now like I was fronting for him, and I wasn't. That's the part I'm not very comfortable with. I was there to advise him on professional ethical rules. I didn't set myself up as his ultimate moral judge."

Concluding his remarks and knocking them dead, Sandefur unloaded, "My own view—which I can finally express, because I am hereby publicly tendering my resignation—is that George Jeffreys deserved to be criticized for having some very bad judgment. But that doesn't mean he has done anything legally wrong. I have been telling him for weeks that he cannot ignore the ethical issues that have been raised. His only response was that he understood the criticism. Perhaps he did understand the criticism, but the recent leaking of information to the press demonstrates that he understands neither the ethical nor the legal dimensions of his own professional conduct."

I had to laugh. Bart Gedney's strategic leaking of the files had backfired. Sure, he got the media response he had hoped for, making it seem that the First Lady's fingerprints were incriminating evidence. But that was an expensive move for Jeffreys. It brought both my resignation in private and Tom Sandefur's in public. There were now no Democrats on the payroll, and the investigation was openly exposed for the partisan operation it had always been. If Jeffreys was an Independent Counsel, then Rush Limbaugh was an Independent Journalist. The American people were not dumb enough to believe that. Not for very long.

Congressman Clapham rushed to divert attention from Sandefur's dismissive remarks about the Whirlpool investigation. He issued a press release announcing that his oversight committee had discovered the White House Security Office was reviewing FBI files on people with access to the White House. The White House said they had been using an outdated list of pass holders provided by the Secret Service, and the Secret Service denied it was at fault. Director Fimus, as was his practice, denied FBI culpability and blamed the White House. Clapham ragged on the fact that no one would admit hiring the fellow who had been responsible. That was not a crime, but I also wondered who would have hired such an incompetent dork to work there. I also found it a bit strange that Clapham's committee hired Thad Stevens' wife as the GOP's chief counsel for the investigation.

Clapham asked the FBI to retrieve the files and see whether Diane Cannon's fingerprints were on any of them. When the FBI reported that the First Lady's prints were not to be found, there was no press release from Clapham nor any coverage of that fact by the media, despite so much attention to the original story. The guideline for press coverage of Whirlpool seemed to be, "Good news was no news."

I soon got bored in Birmingham and went to Washington to spend a week with Lindsey, just in time to see Diletto demonstrate that he also knew how to play the game. He had been working furiously to get some attention for his discredited Whirlpool investigation, knowing that he was on deadline and needed to make a splash in the press before Jeffreys took over and started the second trial in Birmingham. Over the weekend before the final Senate Whirlpool Committee report was to be publicly released, someone on Diletto's staff leaked the Republican portions to the press. Of course, that was news, and the Republican version was given prime billing in the Sunday papers. "Leaked Panel Report Blasts First Lady, Diletto Recommends Charges on Conflicting Testimony," was the headline.

The next day, after Lindsey went to work, I amused myself by attending the back-to-back news conferences held by the Majority and Minority members of the Whirlpool Committee. I arrived late because I thought it was in the Whirlpool hearing room in the Hart Senate Office Building, but I discovered it was being held next door in the Dirksen Building. Senator Diletto was already holding forth and was almost finished when I got there. "Today we have issued the final report of the Whirlpool Committee," he said as I found a seat at the back of the room. "After 14 months of work, we have discovered a very troubling and continuing pattern of the abuse of power. And each time an abuse was revealed, the White House delivered excuses, memory lapses, and changed stories. Time and time again, the White House seemed unable to give the American people the truth, so we are referring certain matters to the Independent Counsel."

"Throughout our hearings," Diletto continued in that grating nasal voice, "this disturbing pattern was seen again and again. We have witnessed a pattern of deception and arrogance. The facts speak for themselves, and reasonable people can make conclusions going back to the mysterious death of Hal Goodall. The committee also concluded that Mrs. Cannon is more likely than anyone else to have had copies of her billing records. Most roads lead from the first lady and back to her. You can see it yourself. Make no mistake about it."

That was it? All Diletto had was a handful of nothing wrapped in speculative conspiracy theories. The Whirlpool Committee had met for more than 300 hours, taking 10,729 pages of hearing testimony from 159 witnesses in 51 hearings, and took more than 35,000 pages of deposition testimony from 245 persons. The White House produced more than 15,000 pages of documents, and the Cannon's attorney, Joey Welch, has produced another 30,000 pages. And that was all he had. Ray Cahn made Barney Fife look like Sherlock Holmes. Diletto didn't have a smoking gun. Hell, he didn't have a warm butter knife.

Of course, no one was really too surprised. The Independent Counsel hadn't found anything either, and we'd spent $35 million and change. Diletto had only squandered about $1.4 million. Besides, the Republicans didn't need to find any evidence of wrongdoing. They had already accomplished their real goals, which were to distract the work of the administration, to make public service unattractive for Democrats, and to keep the media in the game by making accusations. They didn't need evidence for that. They only needed to be on television.

The Republican gaggle trooped out, and in came the Democrats for their reply. Senator Bonhomme, the ranking member, was the lead-off hitter. "The central question that faced the Whirlpool Committee," he said rather formally, "was whether James Madison Cannon misused the powers of the Presidency? The answer is a clear and unequivocal no. A secondary question was whether Mr. Cannon used his official position in Alabama improperly to provide favored treatment to business associates. In its exhaustive review of accusations from political enemies extending back to 1974, the Committee examined in excruciating detail a number of matters in Alabama. Again, the clear conclusion is that then-Governor Cannon did not abuse his office."

Next, Bonhomme came to the defense of the First Lady, though I doubted that she needed anyone to speak for her. "Having failed to tarnish the President," he said, "the Committee turned its attention to Mrs. Cannon's private law practice in Alabama more than ten years ago. The Committee launched a massive hunt for some way in which to contradict statements made by Mrs. Cannon during the last four years. Again, there was no evidence to suggest that Mrs. Cannon engaged in any improper, much less illegal, conduct."

Then, mocking the Republicans as wasteful big spenders, Bonhomme recounted the enormous cost of the publicly financed campaign against the Cannons. "Direct costs to taxpayers now exceed $41,849,795 as of last month, including: $400,000 from the Senate Banking Committee hearings; $1,400,000 for the Whirlpool Committee hearings;

$3,800,000 for the Resolution Trust Corporation investigation by Ike Parker; and $36,249,795 by the Independent Counsel. Costs of the various Whirlpool inquiries in the House and agency work to comply with inquiries amount to tens of millions more. And we have no idea how many millions were spent on private lawyers to represent innocent individuals questioned by Congress and the Independent Counsel," he added.

Senator Doddridge followed quickly by illuminating the convoluted Republican deconstruction of the testimony. "There are three fact situations here," he argued, "all of which put honest people in a Catch 22.. You get a witness that says, 'Well, I don't recall.' The Republicans say that the witness is being disingenuous. If you have witnesses with conflicting testimony, the allegation is, 'Someone's lying.' And if you have witnesses that have consistent statements, it's a conspiracy. This is ridiculous. You're trapped no matter what you say. You're either disingenuous, lying, or conspiring. And that's just foolishness."

Senator Sartain was pissed, specifically about the Republican attacks on the First Lady. "The venom, the venom with which the Republican majority focused its attack on Diane Rankin Cannon is surprising and disturbing, even in the context of this investigation," she said with disgust. "Is it important to the American people whether Mrs. Cannon has total recall and a photographic memory of every memo, phone call, and detail of every case she handled in her private law practice in Montgomery more than a decade ago? I think not, yet every failure of recollection is treated as a lie."

Senator Sloan also had harsh words for Senator Diletto and his chief counsel, Ray Cahn. She blasted them both as she said, "I am particularly offended by the hard edge of the partisan, political, vindictive nature of the Republican attacks on Diane Rankin Cannon and the women who were associated with the First Lady. The fact of the matter is that she was singled out for special abuse by this committee. I think it is very frightening that a woman who has to work for her family will be subjected to this kind of abuse at the hands of a politically motivated inquisition."

The concluding remarks were offered by Senator Walsh, who allowed as to how, "The American people in their essential fairness understand that what we have seen for the past two years has been a legislative travesty, a partisan political witch hunt. None of us in Washington are unmindful of the fact that leaking is a part of this process. But never before in the history the Senate has there been such a cynical, calculated, and systematic attempt to leak information with the primary purposes to embarrass the President or the First Lady and to distract this Administration from a policy agenda with which the Republicans disagree."

"The Senate Whirlpool Committee's sole purpose over the past two years," Walsh charged, "was to seek political gain, to exploit any advantage, to seek political revenge against President Cannon for having defeated former President Stuart. Unfortunately, from the Republicans' perspective, after all of these hearings, there is no evidence of any wrongdoing by the President of the United States or the First Lady."

The klieg lights went dark and the room was soon empty. Diletto's two-year television series had come to an end without issue, and he pulled the plug because of poor audience ratings. While his final report held very little of value, what he had failed to do was of more importance in understanding the truth about Whirlpool. He didn't have testimony under oath from Roby Douglas, Nick Biddle, Ed Dohemy, Carl Weiss, Cliff Smegman, Lyman Davison, Christine Putnam, the two state troopers, or anyone else who had been making wild charges against the President or the First Lady. No one in the press seemed to notice that, but I knew why. I knew exactly why. They'd be about as believable as Ellende Varken—if they would have dared make their purchased accusations under oath instead of to reporters and talk radio hosts.

It was also worth noting, I thought, that Diletto didn't call Bill Godwin, John Jebb, James Burgh, or any of the other Whirlpool targets as witnesses. They might have had a chance to defend themselves, and it would show what a piddling bunch of plea agreements Jeffreys had managed to get. All his bragging about getting nine guilty pleas and three convictions would be exposed to the withering light of reality and put in the proper perspective. The public would then question what any of that had to do with President Cannon, and they would want to know why Jeffreys had foolishly invested $3 million per victim on what were essentially parking ticket misdemeanors.

There was one other witness Diletto was afraid to call before the Whirlpool committee—Diane Cannon. She responded to his charges in answering audience questions after a speech to a Children's Defense Fund conference that afternoon. I was in Lloyd Doggett's office at the time, paying my respects to Michael Barker and kissing his ass for a job, so we caught the last part of it together on C-SPAN.

The First Lady looked good, and she was good. Someone asked her why the Republican committee members seemed so intent on attacking her. Sparing everyone the psychological explanations about sexual inadequacies, she said, "They say, 'Oh, she's so smart, how could she not know?' The simple answer is there's never been anything wrong about Whirlpool. You see, the very question they ask assumes that there was something wrong about what we did. We said in 1992, when this all started, we didn't do anything wrong. We were passive investors. We lost money. And the questions kept coming, so the RTC hired a national law firm who had access to far more documents than we did because they had subpoena power, and they spent $4 million, and they concluded that what we said four years ago was true. You're always guilty until you can prove yourself innocent in this atmosphere. So we've been forced to spend over $2.3 million on legal bills, wiped out our family savings, trying to prove it. And neither of us has even been charged with any crime. Just wild accusations in the press made by my husband's political opponents or some poor egomaniac trying to sell a half-baked book. I don't know what else we can do."

The next question was one I had often asked myself, would the Whirlpool investigations ever stop? "I don't doubt that there are those who will say that the Independent Counsel investigations and these Congressional hearings should go on," she acknowledged without obvious rancor. "I just would like to ask them, go on where? We've been going on four years, and every time there's an investigation of any sort, what my husband and I have been saying proves to be true. So, I don't have any doubt that this is politically inspired and that it will go on regardless of the facts. It has a life of its own. Since there's nothing there, it ought to finally be put to rest, just as Roby Douglas' lies were put to rest. But every time I think that's the case, it seems to get a new burst of energy from somewhere. Senator Diletto's unkind remarks about me are just the latest blast from the bellows."

Did she think Diletto used the hearings to help Ira Dolor's campaign, as the Democrats on the committee had said, or were there other political motivations at work? That was a real tough one, but the First Lady treated it like a serious question. "I don't know everyone who is working to keep these false accusations alive," she said, avoiding the obvious answer about Diletto and Dolor. "I just know, as someone who's been caught up in it, that there are several people who have opposed my husband and his policies for years, who have been deeply involved in stirring all this up—Nelson Grenier, Clifton Smegman, and Carl Weiss to name a few. Then there are the professional haters who are trying to get rich in the scandal industry by writing books, selling lies, and feeding on the destruction of people's lives."

Did she agree with what the President had said in a recent speech, that the politics of personal destruction had replaced honest policy differences in Washington? "It's very sad. I mean, not only on a personal level, but it's sad what it has done to our institutions of government," she replied. "Politics used to be fun, you know, getting to know each other, having debates or disagreements over issues, but treating each other with civility and respect. Today we are living in an evidence-free slander zone, where people feel they can say anything about those of us in public life."

The final question was from a woman who asked how the investigations had personally affected the First Family. "We'll survive it," she said with a smile. "We're not worried about ourselves, but it's a commentary on the times. What's important is dealing with the problems people have in this country—keeping their jobs, finding health care, reforming welfare, keeping the environment clean—the things that are on people's minds that they want their government to address. Instead, Congress has all these partisan hearings that take so much time while practically ignoring action on saving Medicare or improving education, things that will really affect people and their families. I just don't think that makes for good government or accomplishes anything worthwhile. The American people deserve better."

I saw excerpts from the news conferences on television when I got back to Lindsey's that evening, including the full Republican dress review, and I didn't change my mind about the essential nature of the hearings. There was also a short clip of President Cannon responding to some reporter's question about why polls showed the public believed all the charges made against him during the Whirlpool hearings. What a question. What exactly were the charges? Who—besides Gastone Diletto, Reynolds Rantallion, and Ray Cahn—had made any charges against Cannon? Not one single witness under oath. Cannon's reply was too measured, I thought. I wanted him to fight back, take names, and kick ass. Instead, he took a presidential stance and said, "I believe, in the end, the American people will get it right. They usually do. I trust them."

Chapter Twenty Nine

The political tag team strategy continued on course as Senator Diletto turned his attention to helping the Dolor campaign in more traditional ways, and Jeffreys sent Bart Gedney and Walt Lecraw into the legal ring against C. A. Jones and Joe Hill, the two country bankers indicted for financial transactions related to Cannon's 1990 campaign for governor. Not content to merely charge a couple of Cannon supporters in Alabama, Jeffreys had decided to name White House Deputy Counsel Robert Bruce as an unindicted co-conspirator. That, of course, brought the headline Jeffrey's had been looking for since he took the job: "Whirl-pool Scandal Surges Closer to Oval Office."

Coming back from Washington I was on the same flight with Robert Bruce. I recognized his picture from the papers, and I assumed that the two men with him were his Washington attorneys. The press corps was waiting for them in the baggage claim area at the Birmingham airport, and one of the lawyers gave them a sound bite that should have made Jeffreys gulp.

To the amusement of the other passengers looking on as they waited for their luggage, one of Bruce's attorney unloaded, "The decision by George Jeffreys to name Robert Bruce as an unindicted co-conspirator in this trial smacks of politics. Whether instituted for political reasons, overzealousness, or plain old bad judgment, this persecution, as characterized by the prosecutor's afternoon press conferences—a practice frowned upon in virtually all federal districts—appears calculated specifically to injure Mr. Bruce because of his proximity to President Cannon. To say otherwise defies reality. For two years, Mr. Bruce has been a target of this witch hunt. There was no credible evidence linking him with any illegal act, which is why he was not indicted. The decision to name him an unindicted co-conspirator brands him a criminal without allowing him the opportunity to defend himself. It was not only cruel, it was an abdication of the Independent Prosecutor's responsibilities."

He was right on that. They did it because they were pissed off they couldn't find anything on Cannon. I knew how those guys thought. They just decided if Robert Bruce wouldn't say what they wanted and play their game, then to hell with him. If this destroyed his career and his professional reputation, then too bad.

If Bruce's attorney had pulled his punches to protect the interests of his client, Senator Robinson had no such reservations on that account. Robinson had become the Administration's mouthpiece on Whirlpool, and his speech in the Senate the next day gave a good indication of what Robert Bruce would like to have said at the airport. "For the past two years," Robinson told C-SPAN viewers and a few of his colleagues in an otherwise empty chamber, "Mr. Jeffreys has wasted a fortune in taxpayer dollars in a desperate attempt to validate his witch hunt. What have the American taxpayers received for their money? Nothing, except a bill from Mr. Jeffreys for $40 million. And what have the people of Alabama received from their daily torture sessions as a result of this modern Robespierre's Reign of Terror? Nothing except personal misery, a bad name for their state, and a full employment act for local lawyers."

"Oh yes," he said, "Mr. Jeffreys' crowd browbeat a few people into guilty pleas, threatening to ruin them financially if they didn't roll over. But, when it comes to White House officials, Mr. Jeffreys' batting average is zero. And with the naming of Mr. Bruce as an unindicted co-conspirator, his credibility is now at zero as well."

"Still," Robinson continued, "Mr. Jeffreys and his highly paid assassins saw Mr. Bruce as a way to get at their ultimate target—President Cannon. They leaked that Mr. Bruce was a target and threatened to indict him. To his credit, Mr. Bruce refused to buckle under to this blackmail. George Jeffreys couldn't get an indictment, so he named Mr. Bruce as an unindicted co-conspirator. Shame, shame."

I liked the "shame" part, and I also enjoyed the thrust of his closing remarks as he said, "Many states have laws which stipulate that if someone brings a frivolous law suit, then they have to pay the legal fees and court costs of all parties involved. When it comes to the Jeffreys investigation, frivolous is too kind, but the analogy is right. So perhaps it's high time for the taxpayers to hand him a bill for a change. The President and the First Lady have not been accused of any crime, but their legal bills have now reached $2.7 million. Their net worth has plunged from about $600,000 to zero since they took office. Mr. Jeffreys' latest financial disclosure report reveals that he had raked in $950,000 on the side last year from his private legal practice. Although he cleverly found a legal loophole around having to disclose who his clients were, we all know. Let Mr. Jeffreys pay for the Cannons' enormous legal fees out of his own deep pocket lined with tobacco money. It is time to close down this operation and hold Mr. Jeffreys personally accountable for his spiteful actions."

Being "temporarily between opportunities," as us unemployed types liked to say, I decided to sit in on the trial for a few days and see how

Bart Gedney performed before a jury. I sat on the back row, trying not to be noticed, but Mitch saw me and came back to sit by me.

Gedney was questioning Dorothy Tilly, a former teller, now retired from the bank, getting her to identify the cash withdrawal slips for the record. Mrs. Tilly was very composed, wearing a pink suit and her silver hair having just been "done" for her appearance on the stand. It was all routine stuff. Until the cross-examination. One of the defense lawyers, I think it was the guy representing Jones, asked her whether she thought the prosecutors had done a thorough investigation.

"I think so," Mrs. Tilly said in a soft voice. "Although they recognized that not all of us had any financial authority, for the next 20 months we all became part of a full-blown federal investigation with Mr. Bruce as their main target. For myself, it involved FBI agents interviewing my neighbors, two grand jury appearances, two Independent Counsel meetings, four FBI interviews, and one meeting with the IRS, along with legal fees of over $65,000 out of my retirement funds. I'm a grandmother, a widow. I've always tried to be a good citizen. In all my 66 years, I've never broken any law, and now my grandchildren think I'm a criminal. So, it's more than just my life savings that they robbed. He who steals my purse steals trash, but they stole my good name."

On redirect, Gedney asked Mrs. Tilly why she hadn't ever said anything if she felt so mistreated by the Office of Independent Counsel, but his shot missed its mark. "Over time," she explained with her voice slightly quivering, "where first I had been intimidated, it turned to complete frustration as you gentlemen had free reign with the media in putting out your story while we were completely muzzled by your tactics. The FBI presented my attorney with a letter that stated that I was not a subject or target of the investigation, which meant that anything I said could be used against me."

Pretty damning testimony for the Jeffreys supporters in what was already a bad news day. The morning paper had carried a story that Jones and Hill had been acquitted in two mock trials conducted by the Independent Counsel last month. Jo Gobles was quoted in the story as flatly denying that the office had conducted any such "mock trials, focus groups, or the like." I knew they had. Everyone knew. During one of the court recesses I asked Mitch if Jeffreys had authorized the official lie. "It wasn't a lie," he insisted. "The mock trials were conducted by Jury Associates, Inc., under a contract arrangement. So, we didn't actually conduct them. Jo was telling the truth." Right.

"What else do you guys have up your sleeve there days? Any new delevopments?" I knew Mitch was wanting to talk about something, and that gave him an opening.

"Well, we received a tip that Governor Cannon had authorized the burial of Negro soldiers in the National Guard cemetary in 1979, ignoring a clear prohibition against that in the restrictive covenant on the property. So Bart is working on something about failing to take care that the laws are faithfully executed. That's the most recent project," Mitch confided with an insider's pride.

"None of my business anymore, Mitch, but I think you fellows would be a joke if you tried that one. Not to mention Rule 11 sanctions. Be careful," I cautioned.

The government's star witness, John Reeves, was scheduled for the next day, but I had to miss it. Dean Watkins called from the law school with bad news and good news. They had offered the tenure track position to another candidate, but they had an opening for a one-year Visiting Associate Professor position that he wanted to discuss with me. I told him I'd meet him for lunch, and I drove to Tuscaloosa full of anticipation. The deal was, it seemed, one of their regular faculty members had a Fulbright at the University of Bologna, and they wanted someone to teach the introductory course in Civil Procedure and a second-year course in Professional Responsibility. Neither of those would have been my first choice for classes, but I was operating with a short lever and jumped at the chance. My rationalization was that it would be a challenge; however, it could have been because it would mean another year with Lindsey, who had already landed a job there. No need, though, to study that question too hard right now.

The next day I was back at the courthouse. Between the morning paper and Mitch's report, I surmised that the Reeves testimony had been a wash. He apparently told his story as expected—blaming a conspiracy among Jones, Hill, and Bruce for his not filing the currency transaction report on the cash withdrawals by the campaign. Even Mitch, though, thought Gedney had failed to establish any motive for such a scenario, and the defense cross-examination painted Reeves as damaged goods. The more likely explanation was that he forgot to file it and later concocted the conspiracy story when he got squeezed by the Independent Counsel to implicate Cannon's staff and friends. Reeves had also admitted that he was angry at Jones and Hill when he left the bank, which also raised questions about his motives for testifying as he did.

To counter the defense suggestion that Reeves had been scripted by the Independent Counsel, Bart Gedney called Gordon Hancock, one of Reeves' friends, to prove that Reeves had mentioned potential criminal activity at the bank before he began talking to the prosecutors. Again, Gedney got more than he wanted. When asked about an earlier conversation with Reeves, Hancock testified "I remember after he'd had that big blowup and quit the bank, he was pretty mad at them. He said, 'The right information in the right hands—like Nelson Grenier—could bring them down.' I didn't think anything about it at the time. I mean, I'd heard him call Mr. Jones 'Boss Hogg' before, but I thought he was just blowing off steam and all."

Hancock's testimony didn't help much with the jury. It only reinforced the notion that Reeves was making the charges to get even with Jones and Hill, and the fact that he would consider talking to Nelson Grenier instead of banking authorities suggested that the whole thing was about politics. Deciding to quit before he dug a deeper hole for himself, Bart Gedney rested the case for the government.

The defense opened by calling Rowland Watts, another friend of Reeves, to undermine the prosecution's version of events and their key witness. Watts did just that when he told the jury, "I was surprised when he pled guilty to them two misdemeanors, 'cause he'd done told me before that he was innocent. When I asked him about it, he said, 'Rowland, buddy, when those sons of bitches get hold of you, you're just about willing to do anything to save yourself. You'll tell them anything they want to hear. A man's gotta do what a man's gotta do, ya know. I'm just a little fish in the pond. They're after the big fish. I'm just a small fry.' They'd worn him down to the point where he'd admit anything. I guess I might've done the same thing if it was me."

Not wanting to make the same mistake that Governor Vance and the Banaghans had, C. A. Jones and Joe Hill took the stand in their own defense, denying the charges one by one. Gedney's cross-examination was pitiful. At one point, trying to find some crime, any crime, he was yelling at Jones, "You come in here and tell this jury you spent $100 on a cookout and don't have any receipts, any backup? How much did you spend on hamburgers? How much on sauce? How much on paper napkins?" Even the jury was embarrassed for Gedney after that pathetic performance.

Then the defense played the videotaped testimony by President Cannon, who also supported their testimony but said nothing particularly new or unexpected. He pretty convincingly knocked down the prosecution's charge that Jones and Hill had purchased state appointments with campaign contributions, but that was like shooting fish in a barrel. The defense also called Robert Bruce as a witness, and despite a rather vicious cross-examination by Walt Lecraw, Bruce finally got to tell his side of the story and blast the Independent Counsel.

Closing arguments took a full day, but the jury was out only 45 minutes before returning their verdict. They found Jones and Hill not guilty on all counts.

The defendants were all smiles, and they seemed even happier to finally be able to discuss their ordeal with the press. I followed the crowd outside to hear what they had to say. Joe Hill and his family stood together as he expressed his relief that it was over. "It was not easy for me or my family," he said. "We were subjected to the most intense intrusions and harassment you can imagine. We couldn't believe what was happening when they served a subpoena on our son at the high school, trying to force him to talk about us and what my wife and I might have said at the dinner table. We were sustained during those very difficult times by our faith and the many friends and neighbors who stood by our side. I never had any doubt that we would be able to prove our innocence, and the jury's verdict reaffirms my faith in the people, if not in the Independent Counsel and his abuse of power."

C. A. Jones was less reserved in expressing his feelings about what the Independent Counsel had done and what it meant. "With the presidential election virtually over before the campaigns even begin, maybe Jeffreys and his political operatives will decide to pack it in," he said with a grin. "George Jeffreys now holds the record for trials lost by an Independent Counsel, so the only mischief left for his team is more humiliating courtroom defeats. If Mr. Jeffreys has succeeded in anything, it is in giving the Independent Counsel Act a bad name."

Robert Bruce also had a chance to say something, and his comments were even more biting. I didn't blame him for being bitter; he certainly had every right to be. "Forget about the $850,000 in legal fees this cost me," he said almost as if he could. "I don't think anybody realizes what this political witch hunt has done to our families. I can deal with it. But for my wife and children, it's been hell. How would George Jeffreys like it if his kids had to read in the newspaper that their dad was an unindicted co-conspirator?"

The jury began filtering out of the courthouse, and most tried to avoid the press. Not all were so fortunate. Willa Alexander, one of the women jurors, was the first one trapped by the cameras. I didn't catch the question, but I could tell she was annoyed. "Reeves? He never looked at us. He only kept looking at the prosecutors, like he was saying to them, 'Tell me what to say.' I'm glad it's over," she said with some relief. "I really think it was a waste of time and money. I'd hate to see the government waste any more money on this Whirlpool thing."

J. Daniel Ames, another juror, confirmed Alexander's opinion of Reeves and his testimony for the prosecution. "We just didn't believe Reeves," he said without hesitation, sounding as if he were glad to be asked. "We felt that he was already in trouble because he forgot to do the paperwork, and he said what he said because they told him to. We thought Mr. Jones and Mr. Hill were good family men. They weren't trying to deceive anybody, and they certainly weren't trying to hurt their bank. There was no reason for them to do what they were accused of doing. It didn't make any sense. Robert Bruce didn't care either. Made no difference to him.'"

I thought the best response of the day came from H. L. Mitchell, an old farmer from Talladega, who bluntly said, "They just wanted to make President Cannon look bad, that's all. I've never been a big fan of the Dope from Fairhope, but I sure thought he was telling the truth about Jones and Hill. He said he'd appointed them because they'd been friends and supporters for over 20 years. What's wrong with that? Those government prosecutors acted like they thought he should appoint people he didn't know or something. Biggest bunch of bullshit I'd ever heard. It was a pretty flimsy case. If they're going to spend my tax dollars, they need to get stronger evidence. That Reeves fellow kept changing his testimony. He was going to do whatever he could to cover his butt, because he didn't want to go to jail. That's the way I saw it."

John Henry McCray, a younger man from Bessemer, also had some unkind words for the Independent Counsel. "Those federal prosecutors were too quick to turn people's lives upside-down. They aren't responsible for any of their actions, and they don't care who they hurt. And Reeves was a proven liar, and once a liar always a liar. Nobody believed him."

All this time, Jeffreys had been hiding out at the office, not expecting the jury to come back with a verdict so quickly. It was almost twenty minutes before he arrived at the courthouse to join Bart Gedney and Walt Lecraw to face the press. When he did, he was obviously very defensive about his prize prosecutors getting their butts kicked. There was none of that pompous gloating or praise for the jury that had marked his victory when Vance and the Banaghans were convicted.

Awkwardly washing his hands and reading from a hastily drafted statement, Jeffreys said, "A grand jury returned an indictment against these bankers leading to their trial. I have no apologies for that. Although it was an integral part of our work, it was not at the core of our task, which is to determine whether James Madison Cannon or Diane Rankin Cannon committed any crimes. Our overall investigation has continued to move forward on a variety of fronts as this trial unfolded. The difficulty in this investigation has been getting at the truth as promptly as I would like. I believe there is more than we've been able to find thus far. If people would just trust us and be more forthcoming and more cooperative, the investigation could be over much sooner."

Blinking in the afternoon sun, Jeffreys finished the prepared statement then went on without notes, sounding like he had just smoked his first joint and was trying to deny that it affected him. "Yes, questions go unanswered. Puzzle unsolved. Enigma remains. But some puzzles remain unsolved because we walk away from them too quickly. President Cannon's connections to Whirlpool are too significant, too numerous, and too sustained to dismiss so easily. Nor will it do, as those hostile to this investigation would prefer to do, to simply say good riddance to the Independent Counsel and those nagging questions. It would be unfair and insensitive to dismiss an entire two years of legal work by a highly dedicated Independent Counsel, based upon the outcome of this one trial. And I resent the continuing partisan attacks on my integrity. I have always had the respect and admiration of my former judicial colleagues and many others who cut across philosophical lines."

It was at that moment, I now think, that Jeffreys must have cracked. He still managed that silly trademark grin, but something in his eyes gave it away. Frustration from being unable to find anything on the Cannons and humiliation from being the first Independent Counsel to ever lose a jury trial were more than he could handle. There was a wild look in his eyes, as if some repressed Freudian terror was about to bubble to the surface. Those who didn't know him might have missed it, but I had an ominous feeling that the hunter was haunted, transformed, possessed, obsessed, and dangerous. Just how far he would go to get Cannon was not yet clear, but from that point on none of the old rules would apply.

At the time, I was only slightly embarrassed for Jeffreys, and that was easily overcome by my knowledge of his real motives and the very real effects of his actions on innocent people. I soon learned that I was not alone in that opinion and that Jeffreys had again overestimated his own reputation. One of his former judicial colleagues was on CNN that evening, making that quite clear.

Judge Albert Michaels, appearing on Counterpoint, said, "The allegations against Robert Bruce brought into sharp focus how far George Jeffreys has strayed from appropriate limits on his duty and discretion in the Whirlpool investigation. Even after it became clear that there was no case against Mr. Bruce, Jeffreys proceeded to implicate him anyway. Because an unindicted co-conspirator does not face charges in court, he does not have the opportunity to defend his actions or his name. Nevertheless, Bruce was marked with a label that carries heavy personal and professional symbolism for his reputation and political symbolism for the president. Jeffreys and Deputy Prosecutor Bart Gedney must have foreseen the newspaper headlines their actions would generate. It is hard to find any nonpolitical reason. Mr. Bruce's real crime, in Jeffreys' eyes, was that he was a friend and close advisor to President Cannon."

In what was either a strange coincidence or a record for legislative responsiveness, the House Subcommittee on Crime, held a hearing on July 1st to consider a bill to reform the Independent Counsel Act and limit the powers of those appointed. The legislation was introduced by Jay Gomer, an undistinguished Republican member from Louisiana, and co-sponsored by nine of his GOP colleagues. Lindsey called to tell me about it, and I stayed up late that night to watch the taped replay on C-SPAN. Glad I did, because it was an exciting show.

It was also a sure sign that the tide was turning against Jeffreys when Representative Gomer opened the hearings by pointedly asking, "What benefits have we received from all this? How many convictions? Has it been worth it? It has only whetted the appetite of an element in our society which feeds on scandal and destroyed lives. It sends a message to our young people that they should opt out of public service lest they be attacked and destroyed financially, personally, politically, and even spiritually."

"This is a bad law and it needs to be changed," said the next witness, Joseph Desipio, a former special prosecutor who echoed Gomer's remarks. "I don't believe in feasting on the bodies of public officials and their families. It discourages good people from coming into public service. I don't know how we can expect anyone to serve. I'll tell you, I wouldn't take an appointment in the executive branch at triple the salary."

Former Senator Rudman told the Committee that the Independent Counsel Act was "a basis for tyranny in this country in that one person, given authority without any accountability can make people's lives miserable beyond belief and come up with absolutely nothing."

George Mason, a former Justice Department official in the Kennedy administration, was especially blunt, telling the committee, "The law was and is nothing short of an abomination. It's plain to me these investigations are political."

Even Jeffreys' old friend and colleague, Thad Stevens, appeared and testified from experience that "the damage to targets of independent counsel investigations is invariably immense, even where there is no indictment. They incur enormous costs. Their lives are disrupted for long periods. No one survives an investigation without some serious scars."

Another of Jeffreys old pals from Justice was equally critical of the process. Bruce Flim said, "There may be greater law enforcement deformities than independent counsels, but if there are, they do not readily come to mind. Independent counsels embroil the federal judiciary in partisan politics because the highly charged appointments are made by a panel of three judges who owe their jobs largely to political loyalties.

"Once appointed," Flim explained, "independent counsels characteristically become engines of despotism, not beacons of justice. Unconstrained by budgetary ceilings, they search for any stain on a target's life. It is not a matter of discovering a crime and seeking the culprit, but rather a matter of selecting an individual and then trolling the criminal code in hopes of stumbling on a violation. And, intoxicated with unaccountable power, independent counsels are wont to pronounce guilt without trial.

"Finally, targets of independent counsels are doomed to impoverishment in marshaling their defenses and are often professionally excommunicated even if they are ultimately exonerated. Let's return to law enforcement the old-fashioned way," Flim implored the Committee.

Speaking for himself as well as his profession, Anthony Raines told the committee, "Reporters love this stuff because a special prosecutor investigation is the closest thing our culture has to a contest between a hungry lion and a skinny peasant. Usually, the prey doesn't stand a chance. Independent counsels have powers enjoyed by no other lawyers in America. Special prosecutors don't have to develop any evidence before kicking off an inquiry. A plausible-sounding rumor will do. They may look into every nook and cranny of a person's past and prosecute peccadilloes that previously would have been ignored."

Next, a representative from the Tradition Foundation joined in the critique, noting, "When political disputes heat up, Congress always threatens executive officials with an independent counsel. That procedure usurps executive branch functions and violates fundamental rights of the accused. Even more fundamentally, in practice the independent counsel statute has little to do with real ethical violations. Instead, it is used to criminalize disputes between the President and Congress."

Next, I was surprised to see Navita James, my friend from Burke's staff. She had recently published an historical critique of the Independent Counsel Act in the *American Criminal Law Review*, and her testimony reflected the title of the article—"Bad Law, Bad Policy."

Two former special prosecutors even joined in criticizing the abuse of the process under George Jeffreys. Archibald Cox, of Watergate fame, said, "The law should be revised to narrow the number of people who can be investigated, limit the types of crimes, and limit the duration of the investigations to one year." Lawrence Walsh, the Iran-Contra prosecutor, agreed and added, "It should be only for the rare instance such as the misuse of federal power. I don't think it should apply to something a federal official did before he took office or for something personal." More prophetic words were never spoken.

Justice Antonin Scalia, who had served with Jeffreys on the Court of Appeals, also questioned the constitutionality and noted the ridiculous consequences of the present statute, saying, "Congress has taken the prosecutorial power not by legal means but through political ones. Under this new system, an administration must either keep helplessly investigating itself in one case after another or see itself portrayed as a bunch of crooks and obstructers of justice."

Robert Beard, yet another former judicial colleague of Jeffreys, also presented strong arguments against the Independent Counsel Act. "In addition to everything else that's wrong with it," he said, "the institution of the independent counsel damages lives and reputations in ways that few regular prosecutors ever could or would. The human as well as the institutional costs are enormous."

Furthermore, Beard added, "The Independent Counsel will bring prosecutions that no regular prosecutor would bring and that never should be brought. He has an unlimited budget to investigate one person or a small group of persons. The job, moreover, offers the chance to become a national figure, but only if scalps are taken. The independent counsel statute, therefore, has built into it the certainty of pain and injustice to many innocent people."

Most telling, Beard said, "The main problem is that the independent counsel is accountable to no one. Any regular prosecutor, accountable to a superior, would undoubtedly be called on the carpet, and probably discharged, for what looks remarkably like a partisan attempt to influence the outcome of a presidential election. The present independent counsel law, however, has achieved its main objective: undermining the legitimacy and efficiency of the executive branch."

Jeffreys was asked to testify on the bill, but he declined. The Chair read a terse, one-line telegram from Jeffreys which said, "I will not apologize for doing my duty faithfully and aggressively."

Of course, Jeffreys probably knew he didn't have to defend himself. Even though the new legislation to severely limit the power and funding for independent counsels was voted out of the subcommittee, Speaker Reichman let it be known that he would refuse to schedule a vote on the bill before Congress adjourned. Jeffreys was safe. For now.

Chapter Thirty

Following the 4th of July holiday, something rather unexpected happened. The Senate took up consideration of a bill to reimburse Robert Bruce for his legal expenses. That the Majority Leader would even allow the bill on the Senate calendar was a reflection of the emerging shift in public sentiment about Jeffreys' motives and his performance. Lindsey was home for a long weekend, and we watched the floor debate together. Well, we watched most of it, anyway. On the floor.

Senator Dreyfus, the principal sponsor, opened the debate with an attack on Jeffreys but soon slid into rather partisan, if indirect, allegations against some of his colleagues. "This bill is to pay the legal expenses of Robert Bruce," he began. "I don't know how we can right the wrongs that have been committed, but at least there is precedent to pay the legal expenses for innocent people who have been wronged by the government."

The next point could be expected, as Dreyfus claimed, "George Jeffreys unleashed the full power of the FBI and the IRS to harass American citizens. As if that were not enough, he also used his access to the media to conduct a public smear campaign with leaks, innuendoes, and falsehoods against numerous innocent people. The net effect of this harassment took a real toll on real people and their families. These innocent people had their reputations, their dignity, and their psychological well-being assaulted by an irresponsible Independent Counsel, a man who to this very day refuses to accept responsibility for his actions."

Going behind the curtain, where Senators are usually reluctant to peek, Dreyfus made a couple of points that strained the bipartisan support for his bill when he said, "Whirlpool is the story of an arrogant Independent Counsel trampling the rights of private citizens and dedicated public servants. The purpose behind this abuse is so cronies of the Republican presidential candidate might someday grab the spoils of office for themselves, perhaps anticipating a future Supreme Court or Cabinet appointment, by a political strategy that began within a matter of days of a new President being sworn into office in 1993."

"Nothing is politically right that is morally wrong. All the strategies to save the Dolor campaign from embarrassment will only make the final defeat bigger and worse. It is inevitable. It is predictable. It will happen." Then seeing that he had offended several members across the aisle, Dreyfus tried to repair the breach, concluding, "I urge my colleagues on the other side to save Senator Dolor any more embarrassment. Stop the shenanigans. Work with us to do what little we can to repair what was unjustly done to Robert Bruce."

Senator Hatchet responded for the Republicans, trying to ignore the impropriety of the preceding speaker and returning to the merits of the bill, saying, "Mr. President, as everybody knows, Robert Bruce was unjustly persecuted. This is very, very important legislation. It will establish a decent resolution to what really has been awful. There was no reason to name Mr. Bruce as an unindicted co-conspirator. There was no reason to brutalize him the way he was brutalized. And there is no reason for us not to resolve this matter in an honorable, compassionate, reasonable, honest, and decent way. That is what this is all about."

Surprised at not being called down for the opening remarks by Senator Dreyfus, Senator Hampton spoke next for the Democrats and tried to push the envelope a bit by telling his colleagues, "I agree that we should right this wrong, but we are overlooking a number of other individuals who have been wronged. Can we then try to right this wrong for many, many people who were hauled before the Diletto Committee and before Jeffreys' grand juries here and in Birmingham?"

"For example," he noted, "the secretary to Mrs. Cannon at the White House. Today, she is not a target, she does not expect to be indicted, and there is no one standing at the gate with shackles to take her off to jail. But today she owes over $200,000 in legal bills. This is not someone who makes a lot of money. This is someone who, basically, was doing her job, along with many other people who work at the White House and who have been called before the Diletto Committee and the grand juries."

Senator Hatchet was back on his feet, trying to bring the debate back to the original purpose of the bill and tempering the partisan moves by Dreyfus and Hampton. "My colleague knows if I think there is an injustice, I don't care about the politics," Hatchet said. Then, he explained, "This is special legislation, because Mr. Bruce was singled out for an unjust persecution. I don't think anybody denies his reputation was besmirched and tarnished by inappropriate action."

Trying to show good faith, Hatchet concluded by admitting, "Frankly, without an Independent Counsel, this travesty would never have occurred. Everybody knows who brought this about. Robert Bruce went down the drain financially and reputationwise because of people down at the OIC did not care who they tramped on. And frankly, this will not reimburse Mr. Bruce for everything. It can never restore his dignity."

Senator Hampton was not deterred, asking Hatchet, "Is there any reason why we cannot amend this bill? The Diletto Committee required depositions from 245 individuals and public testimony from 159 individuals, so I propose a fund to compensate individuals for legal expenses incurred responding to subpoenas by the Committee."

With that, Senator Hatchet reverted to his old self for a moment and exposed the limits of his compassion. "Of course, we cannot allow that," he shouted. "They are not going to be reimbursed for their attorney fees for that. This Robert Bruce bill does not cover congressional hearings. Frankly, though, I feel for people who are called before congressional hearings. I do. I wish we never had to call anybody, except to enlighten us and help us pass better legislation. I also think independent counsel are used far too often. I personally do not like it. I personally think it is wrong."

At that point, something came up, and Lindsey and I took a short break from watching the debate. When we returned, the session had ended. Only when reading the next morning's paper did we discover that the bill had been recommitted to the Judiciary Committee. I knew enough about the legislative process to know that the bill would not be reconsidered anytime soon. Certainly not before the election.

Lindsey returned to Washington the following day, and I drove over to Tuscaloosa to see what was available in the way of rental property for the fall semester. I knew I didn't want to live in an apartment complex with a bunch of wild undergraduates. Not that I would mind the noise and the parties, but my Bronco and I would both be reminded how old and rusty we were, having to face those shiny BMWs in the lot and those hard bodies around the pool. I found a great three bedroom Georgian cottage at 45 North Britton, near the university, and signed a year's lease. If Lindsey wasn't interested in sharing quarters, something we had avoided discussing while she was home, I could just say I needed a study and a guest bedroom.

Jeffreys, it seemed, was becoming even more interested in sex than I was. After two years of looking in vain for evidence of criminal activity, he had now turned his attention to Cannon's private life. Bob Bernstein reported in the *Washington Post* that Jeffreys had ordered the FBI to interview all former female staff members who had worked for Governor Cannon and all the women mentioned in the lawsuit filed by Carl Weiss during the 1990 campaign.

One former state trooper told Bernstein, "In the past, I thought they were trying to get to the bottom of Whirlpool. This last time, I was left with the impression that they wanted to show he was a womanizer. All they wanted to talk about was women, if I knew certain women, if I thought he was having affairs with them."

Jeffreys claimed he was using "well-accepted law-enforcement methods" to see if Cannon disclosed any Whirlpool financial secrets during pillow talk. Right. All this had started soon after Jeffreys lost the case against Jones and Hill. Within a week of that defeat, he had gone to a meeting of the Texas Bar Association and helped recruit an old college chum from Bob Jones University to take over the Christine Putnam lawsuit. Looked to me like he was using tax dollars to help his old friend conduct discovery. And the public was about to discover something about George Jeffreys. Something I had seen in his eyes after the trial.

The public revulsion to the matter was expressed by the editor of *U.S. News & World Report*, who asked, "What is the matter with George Jeffreys? He continues to undermine public confidence not only in his objectivity but in his common sense as well. Such trolling in the prurient pool of rumor is morally repugnant and has nothing to do with a serious investigation. Jeffreys is confused by his animus. It is not seemly for an independent prosecutor to spin the media so as to smear the object of his attack. It is obscene for him to abuse his power and fail to observe the minimum standards of decency required when investigating any person. There is an aroma around Jeffreys—the aroma of a desperate man. He should now wrap up or quit—for the sake of law, of justice, and of fair play."

Other than that, there hadn't been much news out of the Independent Counsel's office since the trial. I figured Jeffreys was sulking and licking his wounds, and everyone else was licking his boots to keep their jobs. Political news on the state front, though, was a growth industry that month. Governor Vance resigned on July 15th, and the Reverend Jerry Elkay Coughlin took the oath of office and became Reverend Governor Coughlin. Mitch Palmer called to say the office had plenty of extra tickets for the inaugural ball, if I wanted to go down to Montgomery. I thanked him kindly and declined, not wanting to be reminded that the honors were bestowed not by a vote of the people but ripped untimely from a jury.

Governor Coughlin, nonetheless, acted as if he had some kind of mandate. In the first week, he ordered the purge of all loyal Democrats not protected by civil service, including Robert Bruce's wife from a cabinet position, a black state agency head, and almost everyone else he could fire, down to and including the assistant gardener at the Governor's Mansion. Nothing wrong with that, I suppose, but, all in all, it made the White House Travel Office shuffle look like child's play.

Coughlin's new chief of staff was Myles Cooper, the political editor of the *Post-Advertiser* who had filled the front page of the paper with prejudicial stories about Judge Cook after his ruling and Governor Vance during jury selection for his trial. And to assure continued favorable coverage, Coughlin also hired Luther Summers, the son of the paper's editorial page editor, as his top policy assistant. Nelson Grenier's nephew was named head of the state Public Utility Regulatory Commission. And Lucian Koch, the black agency director, was quickly replaced by Homer Glasscock, a big Republican contributor who was one of Coughlin's buddies from the Jaycees.

The new policy directions for state government were equally visible during the first 10 days of the new administration. Coughlin issued an executive order banning gay marriages in Alabama, not that there was any evidence of an impending outbreak of such unions, and he targeted hetrosexual hormones as well, ordering the state Health Department to suspend condom distribution in the public schools and to offer seminars in abstinence. He moved up the execution date for a death row inmate, hoping to have the chance to throw the switch before the next election.

The next announcement from the new governor was a plan to revise the curriculum of the Governor's Summer School for Honor Students, dumping the humanism modules and substituting ones that stressed "traditional Christian family values" and changing the venue from Birmingham-Southern College to the campus of Sand Mountain Christian Academy. Not only were Governor Coughlin and his apparatchiks trying to purge the liberals, they also wanted to get rid of the liberal arts. Luther Summers took full credit for the changes, and his daddy defended the plan on the editorial page of the *Post-Advertiser*.

The new Governor continued to give his "inspirational speeches" around the state, and he was the keynote speaker at the Alabama Family Council's Workshop on Public Policy Lobbying. One of the anti-smoking advocates at the workshop was reported to have asked Governor Coughlin whether the state would join in the class action lawsuit to recover Medicaid expenses from the big tobacco companies. After a yuk-yuk laugh, Coughlin spoke words to warm George Jeffreys' cold heart when he was quoted in the paper as saying, "No, that kind of lawsuit makes about as much sense as me suing the ice cream companies because I'm fat!"

Other policy directives coming out of the governor's office had implications for the budget. Coughlin refused to allow the state to pay $430 for an abortion for a 15-year old raped by her step-father, putting at risk not only the girl's life but the state's billion dollar Medicaid budget as well. He also recommended a 10 percent cut in the state higher education budget to offset a proposed reduction in the corporate income tax.

Perhaps Coughlin's most interesting fiscal affair was to freeze the budget for the state Ethics Commission. Now, you'd think, with all the fanciful Republican talk about Cannon's ethics, that they'd be eager to beef up ethics enforcement in Alabama. Not so. Seems that the Ethics Commission busted Reverend Coughlin two years ago for using campaign funds to take his wife on a vacation to Hawaii. Coughlin said he had gone there to speak on behalf of Republican candidates, but he had some trouble explaining receipts from the Don Ho Show and the Island Liposuction Clinic. Made Randolph Webster look like a piker.

And that was all just in the first 10 days. No doubt Jeffreys was pleased with what he had wrought, even if he thought he could have done it himself in seven.

Although the Jeffreys legal campaign now had the Alabama capitol safely in Republican hands, the big prize still eluded him. But, even during the August recess, the battle continued in Washington. Congressman Clapham called another of his regular press conferences to personally attack the First Lady and berate the White House for being so slow in giving his Oversight Committee the contents of yet another file cabinet his staff wanted to tote up the Hill. I was too busy trying to outline lectures for the courses I would be teaching in a few weeks, so I didn't follow the flap closely enough to know exactly what it was he wanted this time.

I did happen to catch part of an interview with Diane Cannon as I was flipping channels a few days later. Even the morning talk show producers were catching on that the Republicans had given up on finding anything on the President and had taken to beating up on his wife, either a replay of the GOP's 1992 convention or a preview of the upcoming 1996 gathering of the clan.

The young woman co-hosting the show, might have been the *Today Show*, I don't remember, furrowed her brow to affect concern and asked, "You've said before that you've become used to these personal attacks, but how does Cassidy feel when she hears these awful things being said about her parents?"

"We've always tried to make sure Cassidy could have a normal life," Diane Cannon replied, "but we've also tried to equip her for dealing with criticism of her parents. That's been hard for her. When Cassidy was about 11, we knew that Nelson Grenier would run a very negative, nasty campaign for governor. So James and I decided that it would be only fair to discuss those things with her first, so she wouldn't be surprised to hear people saying things on television or pick up things like that from other children at school. So, one night at the dinner table, we told her that in elections people say untrue things about each other that are not very nice, sometimes even hateful. I remember her eyes getting wide and welling up with tears, like 'why would anybody do that?' Because, of course, she'd always known us as loving parents who cared so much about her."

"I remember once, when she saw Gastone Diletto on television making some wild charges about me during his Whirlpool hearings, Cassidy asked, 'What's wrong with that stupid man? That's not true! Why is he telling those lies?' We'd always taught her that, you know, people should tell the truth and that politics was about helping people. And I said, 'Honey, that's what's going to happen until the next election. There's nothing we can do about that.' But sometimes, I think politicians forget that vicious lies can damage families, especially the young children who are hurt for no reason other than political spite."

It looked like the local Republican leadership, at least, was beginning to understand the political backlash from their tactics. Fearing the obligatory Cannon-bashing that would be the central theme at the Republican National Convention, all the Alabama Mullahs declined to participate as speakers or even go as delegates to the wake in San Diego. The only Alabama celebrity in attendance was Portia Sue Coughlin, the new first lady, and the press jumped on her like a hen on a June bug. Mostly it was smiles and shibboleths. Mrs. Coughlin refused to discuss national politics or to mention the Cannons by name, limiting her remarks to her role as the new First Lady of Alabama. That was enough, though, because her presence served to remind everyone that Governor Vance had been vanquished.

I was particularly interested to read an extended interview in the *Atlanta Gazette* by Kate Macauley. Kate was, I had learned, one of Lindsey's old college friends from Emory, and she had made her reputation as a journalist by concentrating on the role of women in politics, especially Southern women and their deft maneuvers to exercise power without appearing to do so. It was a cultural art form as old as the South, and Kate Macauley's articles often laid bare the skills of those artists hiding their lights under hoop skirts.

Macauley's piece on Portia Sue Coughlin was a fine example of her craft, and Mrs. Coughlin was not at all reticent in discussing her assent to the governor's mansion. "When Jerry Elkay ran for the Senate last time," she confided, "it wiped out our family savings. But, the Lord provided for us, and now we have plenty of money and are very, very comfortable. I would never have imagined that the Lord would have wanted us to have our own airplane, but that proved to be a real bonus. Also, Jerry Elkay was fortunate to receive a lot of invitations to give inspirational speeches, which also helped our finances. I think that's one reason he wanted to be governor, since there's some rule against Senators giving speeches like that."

"Anyway," she continued, "I've always pictured Jerry Elkay doing big and mighty things, but it didn't dawn on me that I might ever get to be the First Lady of Alabama. I'm not into titles, though. I don't need a title to enjoy life, but for people to do constantly for me is a big, big advantage. You know, as a Lieutenant Governor's wife or even as United States Senator's wife, you don't have someone to cook all your meals, clean up after you, or drive you around whenever you want to go shopping."

In responding to Kate's question about how one prepares for the role of First Lady, Mrs. Coughlin said, "Jerry Elkay's always been so smooth on television, while my calling in church work was operating the cameras behind the scene during the broadcast of his services. Now I feel like Lurleen Wallace, living in this big brick mansion, and I like being in the limelight. As a minister's wife I've been on that pedestal, shaking hands with people, raising money, sometimes having to smile when I don't feel like it. You live in a fishbowl, and it's hard to get used to people saying ugly, untrue things about you. I want the people of Alabama to be pleased with Jerry Elkay, and I don't want to do anything to embarrass him or my state. Now, I'm not saying some previous First Ladies have done that, mind you."

Although there was nothing about it in the national papers, Jeffreys also attended the Republican National Convention. When Mitch called to tell me about it, I suggested that was perhaps a little too political for a so-called Independent Counsel. Oh no, Mitch had explained, Jeffreys was not going to be on the convention floor. He was only there to attend a reception sponsored by former staff members and appointees for President Stuart. Strictly non-partisan. I wasn't really interested in what Jeffreys had to say about President Stuart. Or anything else, for that matter, but I watched it on C-SPAN as an excuse to take a break from packing for the move to Tuscaloosa.

Jeffreys was one of several who offered a toast to their fallen general. He raised a glass of iced tea and said, "President Stuart stood for things, he was clear and admirably consistent in those stands, and he didn't try to aggrandize himself, or play to the bleachers, the press, or for that matter, anyone else. He was a very able man, and he was no equivocator when it came to the nation's problems. Solid moorings kept him in port, safely in harbor, not to be beaten about by waves out in the open sea. He didn't need to grow into the job. He was full grown when he arrived at the White House in 1989. And Mrs. Stuart was a fine woman and the very model of a First Lady, supporting her husband as a helpmate rather than selfishly pursuing her own career and the like. She had too much dignity to meddle in policy matters."

Senator Dolor just happened to have been invited to that non-partisan event, but I wasn't quite sure what he said. Standing on the risers at one end of the ballroom, perhaps addled by his recent stage-diving exhibition, Dolor's timing was a bit off, and his remarks didn't quite fit the occasion. President Stuart seemed to grimace as Dolor said, "My wife, like Mrs. Stuart, does an outstanding job. But when I'm elected, she won't be in charge of health care. Don't worry about it. Or in charge of anything else. I didn't say that. It did sort of go through my mind. But she may have a little blood bank in the White House. But that's all right. We need it. It doesn't cost you anything. These days, it's not all you give at the White House—your blood. You have to give your file. I keep wondering if mine's down there. Or my dog. I got a dog named Leader. I'm not certain they've got a file on Leader. He's a schnauzer. I think he's been cleared. We've had him checked by the vet but not by the FBI or the White House. He may be suspect, but in any event, we'll get into that later. Animal rights or something of that kind. But this is a very serious election, and I'm tired of people lying about my record or whatever."

Maybe that had been a trial balloon for Dolor's acceptance speech scheduled for the 15th. He was lucky that the major media didn't report his remarks at the Stuart reception, but the party bosses suspected more sinister forces were at work to draw attention away from Dolor's big moment on the podium in the main hall. The White House Counsel had finally released the batch of documents Congressman Clapham had been wanting for months, and Clapham was now angry that they did.

Congressman Clapham hastily called a news conference in San Diego, intent on making his point even if doing so diluted the news coverage of Dolor's excellent adventure that evening. "Good afternoon," Clapham began. "I want to state at the outset that I would certainly not be holding a press conference today, except for the fact that the White House just released 2,000 pages of documents to the media and to my office. Why now? Why today? I think it's a cynical political ploy. The deadline was not until tomorrow, which would certainly have gotten more media attention—so I have to question the motivation for their release on the same day that Senator Dolor will formally accept the Republican nomination for president. I welcome your questions."

"Do you think someone might question your motivation for setting the deadline on the day following Senator Dolor's acceptance speech?"

"Uh, no," Clapham sputtered, "I don't think so. Next question."

"Is there something specific in the documents released today, anything, that you can point to and say, 'Here, this is wrongdoing.'?"

"No," Clapham admitted. "There's no smoking gun, if that's what you're asking me."

"Since the White House has delivered all the documents you requested, is the threat of a contempt citation now out?"

Clapham's boldness was fading as he replied, "I think that a contempt citation would be moot. Yes?"

"So are you accusing the White House counsel with obstruction of justice?"

"No," Clapham said apologetically, "I'm not accusing him of obstructing justice. One more question. Yes, sir?"

"Do you sense the same zeal among journalists to get to the bottom of Whirlpool as you saw with Watergate, Iran-Contra and the other Republican scandals?"

"Well, I think the media has been with us all along," Clapham said with a smile. "And I would say that, by and large, I don't object to the coverage. Thank you all very much."

It was difficult to tell whether Clapham had been thanking the press for their coverage of Whirlpool or for attending his press conference. Didn't really matter, and perhaps there was no distinction to be made. Unfortunately for both Dolor and Clapham, and by implication Leech and Diletto, the Tradition Foundation's report entitled "Reforming the Imperial Congress," was released the same day, further diverting news coverage from Dolor's speech while undermining the facade presented by his congressional valets.

The Tradition Foundation was not exactly a hotbed of Cannon apologists, yet the report was a scathing indictment of recent events in Washington. The executive summary damned them all, suggesting, "Congress's chief problem is the neglect of legislative duties in favor of efforts to secure reelection and expand individual power. Congress must stop addressing issues in a one-sided, prosecutorial fashion. A large part of the time, Congress is not even pretending to legislate. While Congress defends oversight as necessary, often the reason is pure pettiness. In addition, committee hearings increasingly are the vehicles for publicity seeking, producing little in the way of new policies or legislation, but they frequently manage to get Congressmen on the evening news."

Trying to finish packing and cramming all my stuff in the Bronco, I didn't stay turned for Dolor's speech, and I can't tell that I have suffered any lasting harm from missing it. I did think about it, though, along with what I had seen and read about the convention over the last few days. In fact, the first thing I unpacked when I got to my new house in Tuscaloosa was the computer. I felt only slightly guilty for ignoring the demands of my new day job and setting aside Civil Procedure to begin my book about the very uncivil procedures of George Jeffreys. While it was still fresh in my mind, I wanted to capture my impressions about the intersection of the Whirlpool investigation and the Republican convention.

I stared at the blank screen for a couple of minutes, then began, "Already several fatalities had attended the Republicans' futile chase to recapture the elusive White House. Buchanan, Forbes, Lugar, Alexander, Gramm, Dorkman. All capsized under a wave of public disapprobation. Judge, then, to what pitches of inflamed, distracted fury the minds of the more desperate hunters were impelled, when amid the chips of chewed campaigns, and the sinking limbs of torn candidates, they emerged from the direful wrath of their own primaries to face the serene, exasperating smile of an incumbent president with a 20-point lead in the polls. The party was trying desperately to keep the sinking campaign afloat, the planks from their last platform and the aged ideas of their feeble captain both whirling in the eddies of public opinion. Then George Jeffreys, seizing the lines from Diletto's failed hearings and lashing himself to the mast, slashed at the First Lady, blindly seeking to wound the president's campaign by leaking confidential reports from the FBI."

Oh, well. I could see I was going to have to work on my writing style. That was a bit too . . . something. Cynical? Stilted? Melodramatic. I had a couple of beers and returned to the task of unpacking. I dreaded what was ahead. Not the fact that Lindsey would be moving in, just the prospect of having to move her furniture on Sunday. But, I would think about that tomorrow.

Chapter Thirty One

My first day on the law faculty at the University of Alabama was James Cannon's birthday, but that wasn't a state holiday. And I certainly wasn't invited to any party. Actually, though, I was very excited about teaching, more excited than I'd been about anything in a long time. Well, I mean about any job. I shared an office with Vernon Sims, an emeritus professor who still taught an occasional seminar in labor law. At Alabama, I guessed that meant strike breaking and union busting, but I soon learned that his sympathies were distinctly with the workers. Maybe that's why Dean Watkins put us in the same office, to segregate us from the general population. Well, probably not, but I did think that might have something to do with us being assigned an inside office without a window.

The first week of classes went well, and the students were brighter than I had expected, even if most of them were more interested in making money than in seeking justice. My goal was to find one or two really bright ones and convert them. I just wasn't sure I'd still recognize Justice after working for the Independent Counsel for over two years, nor was I sure she still lived in this country.

I tried to put Whirlpool out of my mind, but there was no way to keep it out of the news that week. Governor Vance was given two years probation, and Jessie Banaghan was sentenced to two years in prison. Josh Banaghan's sentencing was postponed, because he was now cooperating with Jeffreys' investigation of the Cannons. The worm had been turned. That was even bigger news, and I was sad for everyone involved.

Kate Macauley called on Thursday to tell Lindsey she was in Birmingham doing a piece on Jessie Banaghan, and she invited us to meet her for dinner on Friday. As I suspected, dinner actually meant drinks, and we ended up going to Louie's to hear Iris DeMent performing. I briefly wondered whether Iris was related to the federal judge down in Montgomery, but when she belted out "Wasteland of the Free," I doubted it. Great voice, though, reminding me of Lucinda Williams. I soaked in the music while Kate and Lindsey talked through the first set.

Although she was a journalist, I enjoyed talking with Kate. She was spunky, and I could see why she and Lindsey were such good friends. And, although I had worked for Jeffreys, she seemed to forgive me. She told us all the details of her interview with Jessie Banaghan, and that made for an interesting story. It was her first interview for a series she was planning on "The Women of Whirlpool." I kidded her that the title sounded more like a *Playboy* pictorial, and I was relieved when she laughed. Never know about such attempts at humor these days.

"I'd like to get an interview with Diane Cannon, but I haven't had any luck with that so far," she said.

I mused quietly on that for a second before saying, "I don't understand why anyone would want to talk with you—not you, particularly, but the press. After all the hell Meredith Roberts was put through and what your paper and the networks did to Richard Jewell, I can't say as how I'd blame them."

"That wasn't me," Kate said defensively. "But, don't you think some people might see being interviewed as a chance to tell their side of the story?"

"I think some people would much rather be left the hell alone. You guys rip off a piece of their soul, and they have no control how it's going to be served up to the public. At least that's how it looks to me," I said, not meaning to sound as rude as I'm sure it did.

"Well," Kate replied, "I try to let them speak for themselves. You saw the piece I did on Portia Sue Coughlin, and I interviewed Harriet Otis last year. That's my only Whirlpool connection in Washington."

I snorted at that one.

"You laughed. Why?"

"Me? Laugh at the Honorable Attorney General of the United States? Not me. There's nothing funny about Harriet Otis as far as I'm concerned."

Kate cocked her eye and said, "You think she's a patsy, don't you?"

"Yeah, she's a patsy—Patsy D. Cline to stand up to political heat from the Republicans in Congress. The buck doesn't stop with Harriet Otis; it doesn't even slow down there."

Lindsey stepped in before I could say what I really thought. "Kate, you said earlier that the Josh Banaghan case reminded you of someone else you had written about in Alabama. Tell John about that. I think he'd find it interesting."

Kate obliged and said, "Banaghan's story reminds me of Melba Till Allen, who was elected state auditor in 1966 and treasurer in 1974. Big Democrat. A crusader against corruption, she was given credit for helping pass the state's first ethics law in 1973, then in 1978 she was the first public official convicted under it. She was found guilty on two felony counts for putting $700,000 in state deposits in a south Alabama bank in exchange for a $50,000 loan and failing to disclosure that little detail. Mebla Till was sentenced to six months but spent only 30 days in the Montgomery County Jail. Served the rest as a bookkeeper in some retirement home."

"She claimed that organized crime figures arranged the loan and set her up with phony evidence as a payback for having conducted a too-thorough audit of the state docks, or, depending on who she was talking to, to keep her out of the governor's race," Kate said with a skeptical smile.

"Last time I saw her was back in '87, and she was serving up good vittles at The Little Red Hen—kind of a Mom's Downhome Guilt Trip Cafe where she could be Lady of the Manor and make her martyrdom into a living—down on Alabama 143, about two miles south of Marbury in Autauga County. She was always a big talker and had that country-singer, big-hair, big-bosomed, big-ego persona and appearance to the end. A Born-Again Christian, too, since her conviction, and she tried to make a political comeback in an unsuccessful bid for lieutenant governor in 1986. I heard she was writing a book that was supposed to name names, but she died before it was ever published."

"The big difference between Melba Till and Josh Banaghan," Kate surmised, "was that she didn't cave in and kiss ass to try to save herself. I was surprised when I heard Banaghan was cooperating with Jeffreys. And his comment about Brutus, or was it Judas? What do you make of that?"

"If you were looking at 84 years in a federal pen and thought you might cut a better deal," I said finishing my fourth beer, "would you lay down for Jeffreys? It's all about Cannon, of course, and Banaghan repeatedly testified under oath that the Cannons didn't know diddly-squat about the Whirlpool finances. But, watching those guys at OIC work, I soon came to understand that witnesses have a way of changing their minds. Facing the unlimited resources of a relentless special prosecutor, nearly anyone will eventually decide to cooperate. People are put under enormous pressure to lie—either about their own guilt or someone else's—to avoid having their lives destroyed by expensive trials on bogus charges. That's how Jeffreys got those nine guilty pleas he's always bragging about."

Pausing until the waitress left and starting another beer, I said, "Now, after a trial, things work a little differently. In this case, knowing Banaghan's weakness for young women, Jeffreys sent Alva Dukov Phillips up to Arkadelphia to pay a call on Banaghan, take him out to lunch, and flirt with him. I heard she took him a copy of *Bloodsucker* and asked him to autograph it for her. Then, a few days later, they say Jeffreys had one of his lapdog reporters from ABC call Banaghan to say that Jeffreys would welcome him with open arms and could cut him a deal on sentencing if he would flip and give them something on President Cannon or the First Lady."

"Anyway," I continued, "with that inducement, Banaghan said he'd be willing to talk with them, so Gedney formally let Banaghan's attorney know that they might recommend a reduced sentence if his client would provide certain information. But, they're the ones who'll decide whether they're getting full "cooperation." So, if Banaghan doesn't say what they want to hear, they'll say he wasn't being forthcoming. Like they did with Randolph Webster when he wouldn't lie. Then they'd remind him of what can happen to a man in prison, which has a way of making one's memory rather malleable. Nothing scares Banaghan more than the thought of dying in some prison. In the end, he won't be able resist their insistence on their version of what happened, and he'll tell the grand jury whatever Jeffreys wants him to say about the Cannons. And make no mistake, he's one of the best southern storytellers who ever graced a front porch."

"They've still got themselves quite a problem though," I added as I heard myself dropping into that repressed East Texas accent. "John Hathorne had Banaghan on the stand for six hours during cross-examination, calling him a liar, time and time again. So, if Banaghan becomes a prosecution witness and sings a different song, who will believe him? And Hathorne already has some problems of his own from letting Roby Douglas testify in the Vance trial. I don't think he'd risk it again with Banaghan, but Gedney might front for Jeffreys on this one. Beyond that, Banaghan's a very sick man. His mind's gone. He'd have trouble remembering which lies he was supposed to tell. And, if they send him to prison, it will be the same as a death sentence. He'll be dead in a year. But they don't care, as long as he's useful to them right now."

"I don't know, maybe I'm wrong," I admitted. "Maybe Banaghan is just playing with them. He's shown himself to be quite a joker."

"But," I added with certainty, "I do know Jeffreys and what he's capable of doing. Ambition will invariably trump integrity. Every time he starts that pious crowing about his reputation and integrity, it reminds me of what Ralph Waldo Emerson once said of someone, 'The louder he talked of his honor, the faster we counted the spoons.' Only difference is George Jeffreys doesn't stop with the spoons. He'll steal their dignity, destroy their families, and ruin their lives."

I could tell Kate was wanting to take her notepad out of her purse, so I backed off for a moment. I didn't need to be quoted saying something like that during my first week at a new job. Or ever, for that matter.

But, Kate wanted more. "So is this whole deal just white boys against white boys? Well, and their families," she added. "I know you probably still can't talk about some things, but could you suggest any women here I might interview or who you think would have a good story that needs to be told? Anyone besides Jessie Banaghan?"

I thought for a moment, then asked, "You ever hear of a woman named Bridget Bishop? Bet you haven't. I don't think I've even mentioned this to Lindsey, and I've only seen one story on it. Well, Bridget Bishop has never even met James Cannon, but her story is just one example of how Jeffreys has so arrogantly abused his power to ruin people's lives here in Alabama. Whirlpool might be big sport for journalists and politicians, but Bridget Bishop is a tragic victim of their insatiable power game. And no one gives a damn."

"Bridget grew up in a poor black family in rural Alabama, graduated from Alabama State University with an accounting degree, worked eight years as a federal bank examiner, then her supervisors recommended her for a position at Jefferson Savings in 1984. An admirable start on fulfilling her dreams," I said. "Now, at that time remember, Jefferson had the best record in the state on minority loans and a history of investing in the predominantly black neighborhoods in Birmingham. After Banaghan resigned in 1986, Bridget served as interim executive officer at the request of the Federal Home Loan Bank Board. When they finally closed Jefferson in 1990, she helped them wrap it up then went to work for the RTC on other foreclosures."

"She's a single mom with two children, but she was doing just fine, had plenty of consulting work with banks and thrifts, until August 1994, immediately after Jeffreys was appointed," I said, trying not to let my anger spoil the telling. "Her RTC work all of a sudden dried up. When she asked one of her clients why, she was told, 'I don't think it's good business for us to work with you, anymore.' Well, turns out someone from OIC had leaked her name to the *Wall Street Record* as a target of Jeffreys' investigation, and of course they printed it."

I finished my beer and ordered another round for everyone to kill the pain. "Several months go by, nothing, and then two FBI agents show up in December informing her that she was a 'subject' of Jeffreys' investigation. The letter read something like, 'United States of America v. Bridget Bishop. This office is aware of substantial evidence that you knowingly participated in a scheme in February 1986 to create and backdate a number of appraisals for the Jefferson loan files with intent to deceive the Federal Home Loan Bank Board.' Remember, this is several months after it's been in the goddamn *Wall Street Record*," I added with emphasis.

"Anyway, Jeffreys and Hathorne, and I think James Peck was in on it, call her in and tell her they have evidence so strong there's no way she could beat the charges. Told her she should make it easier on herself and her family by pleading guilty to a felony that could land her in jail for five years. They didn't even let her explain, never gave her an opportunity to deny it. But she stood up to them and refused to plead. Said they'd cost her her job and wiped out her savings, and the only things she had left were her family and a clear conscience. I remember after she left, Hathorne was laughing about the fact she was working at a fast food place to support her kids. In a mocking voice he said, 'She said she spent her days crying and praying, and I told her it beat picking peas and making license plates.' That's standard for Hathorne."

"Jeffreys let her twist in the wind for four months then brought her in again, trying to bluff her into pleading guilty to a misdemeanor, but she still maintained her innocence. When Jeffreys realized that his intimidation tactics weren't going to work, he finally sent a letter last December, after badgering her for more than a year, admitting we didn't have sufficient evidence to prosecute her for any criminal offense," I said, as both Kate and Lindsey looked relieved.

"But that wasn't the end of it," I added. "This April, when she was called to testify as a defense witness in the Vance trial, John Hathorne announced that they had reopened her case. Her lawyer then had to advise her to exercise her 5th Amendment rights against answering any questions. You want to talk about intimidating a witness and obstruction of justice? There was no case against Bridget Bishop. None. Some have suggested that Hathorne improperly threatened her to keep her from giving testimony that would clear the defendants. I don't know for sure, but I'm damn sure glad I don't work there anymore."

"I'll try to talk with her, but, you're right, I can understand why she'd rather be left alone," Kate said. "Aren't there any stories with happy endings in this whole deal?"

Smiling across the table at Lindsey, I said, "Yeah, I got the girl. And you've already interviewed the governor's wife—she seemed happy. I don't know, you might try getting an interview with our new Adjutant General, the first woman to hold such a post. General Rosenthal, or Major General to be more precise. Smart as a whip and mean as a snake. I hear she makes grown men cry. I haven't seen any feature stories about her appointment in the national press, but that's the only thing Coughlin's done since he took office that wasn't completely goobernatorial."

Kate was now busy writing notes to herself. She looked up and asked, "Is there anyone in the Independent Counsel's office that I could talk to about what they're doing now, where the investigation is going?"

"Probably. The place will leak like a sieve if you'll print what they want and refrain from writing anything critical about them. I once heard Gedney tell a reporter that he'd have to check with Jeffreys and get approval before disclosing any non-public information. He personally directs the leaks. But you'd better be careful. Jeffreys got one reporter fired from the *ABA Journal* for an article that failed to praise him enough," I said with considerable caution and disdain. "Walt Lecraw would be a good place to start, since he seems to be Jeffreys' main conduit these days for innuendo and story lines, probably even some of the grand jury stuff. But I'm afraid I can't help you much there. The only person who still speaks to me, actually the only person who ever talked to me, is Mitch Palmer, Jeffreys' administrative assistant. "

"I usually have pretty good luck getting information from men, if you wouldn't mind making an introduction," she said, and I didn't doubt that for a minute. "Tell me about this Mitch Palmer. What's he like?"

"Sort of a nerd. Very loyal to Jeffreys. Talks a lot when he's drunk. Lindsey's met him, and she can probably be more objective than I can," I said.

Lindsey had a mischievous smile. While looking in Kate's direction, she asked me, "Why don't you see if you can get Kate a date with Mitch? That would be a hoot."

"I thought y'all were friends," I responded before realizing what Lindsey was suggesting. "But, yeah, I could give him a call and see."

Kate was obviously on duty, handing me her cell phone and asking, "How about right now?"

I dialed Mitch's number, knowing he'd probably be at home on Friday night. "Mitch? John Wilkes here. I need a favor, old buddy. Lindsey has a friend in town, and we need to fix her up for tomorrow night. I know you've probably already got big plans, but you were the first person I thought of. How about it?"

Mitch was so predictable. His only question was, "Does she have big hooters?"

"Would I do you wrong? I should probably tell you though, she's a reporter with the *Atlanta Gazette*. Is that a problem?"

"Not for me," Mitch replied. "Jo Gobles dated that guy who's a reporter for the *Wall Street Record*. Does she have big hooters?"

"Great," I said, avoiding Mitch's main question only to mess with him. "What time are you free?"

"I'm going to the state convention, but that should be over by 6:30," Mitch replied. "Will that work? Or we could all go to the convention, but I doubt you'd have any interest in that."

After a short table conference, I said, "I've never been to a Republican convention, but I'm always up for a new experience. We'll meet you there around noon, maybe get lunch together. See you then."

I turned to Kate and said, "It worked. You must be careful what you wish for, young lady."

Lindsey smiled knowingly at me and said, "I'll drink to that."

Kate, already scheming, raised her glass and said, "Cold beer for friends; cold steel for enemies!"

I excused myself to make room for more beer and returned to find Kate waiting with a list of questions. "Kate wants you to background her on Jeffreys," Lindsey said.

"I don't think I'm drunk enough to do that," I mumbled, trying to deflect the invitation and hoping to hear the last set. "I have the right to remain silent. Anything I say can and will be misquoted and used against me. I have the right to another beer. If I cannot afford one, Lindsey will buy it for me," I said with a disarming smile to Kate and a sidewise wink at Lindsey.

Kate wasn't going to let me dodge quite that artfully, though, and she started by asking, "What one word would you use to describe George Jeffreys?"

"You couldn't print it in a family newspaper, so I think I'll take a pass on that one."

"So," Kate continued, "why do you think people here seem to take an immediate dislike to Jeffreys?"

"Saves time."

She laughed, but that didn't end the interview. "What would you say is driving him to act as he has in this investigation?"

"That's an easy one. Or used to be," I said. "Two words—Supreme Court."

"What do you think he thinks about when he's not working at the OIC or practicing law?"

"Supreme Court," I said again.

"No, really," Kate said, "I'm being serious."

"So was I. I mean, this is a guy who once organized a celebration of William Howard Taft Day at the Justice Department, hoping President Stuart would be reminded that Taft, a former Solicitor General, was later appointed to the Supreme Court! That's what he thinks about every waking minute, I shit you not. Well, that and worrying that Cannon might be gettin' some. Right after Jeffreys was appointed, he showed up at the office and didn't know how to configure his e-mail account on our secure computer system at the office, so he asked me to help him set it up. Guess what he chose as a password—SCT1997. That's all he thinks about, and he blames Cannon for his not being there already. That fact has consumed him, and that's why he's been so ruthless. And he ain't going to stop until he gets even," I explained, just as Iris DeMent returned to the stage and saved me from further questions.

We met Mitch at noon the next day, as promised, and the Republican State Convention was a spectacle to behold. All the party regulars were out in force that weekend at the Hugh Morris Convention Center. Governor Jerry Elkay Coughlin, Senator Richard Shanker, Congressman Tim Bakker, Congressman Spencer Perceval, and National Committeeman Nelson Grenier. Probably hadn't been such a gathering of the unimaginative since the United Conservative Coalition met in the old Jeff Davis Hotel down in Montgomery back in the 60s. A huge banner behind the stage proclaimed the theme, "When Stars Fell On Alabama."

State Senator Cobb Davis, a candidate for Congress from the 4th District, gave the Keynote Address. He had gotten some bad press last month when he lost a legislative battle to have the Confederate flag flown over the capitol. He was still a loser, but he now had a more friendly audience for his message.

"The Confederate flag represents less government, less taxes, and more power to the states," Davis shouted to roaring applause. "Because of the liberal news media and television and Hollywood, you know, it's being perceived as a racial issue, but it's not a racial issue. I am not a racist. Slavery was the best thing ever to happen to those African foreigners, who were uncivilized and given to voodoo, cannibalism and witchcraft until the Christian plantation owners benevolently saved them in Jesus' name. I'm sure that those converted black Southerners are most grateful today. The incidence of drug abuse, rape, broken homes, and murder are a hundred times greater today in the housing projects than they ever were on the slave plantations in the Old South."

I thought I was in a time warp, and it was interesting to listen to the reactions as Kate interviewed the delegates after the speech. Chairman Ed Pettus tried to clarify the party's official position, explaining, "You know, we're not for slavery." Delegate Will Hays was less apologetic, saying, "Thank God, Senator Davis had the courage to take a stand for decency and traditional moral values. The left-wing liberal media and radical groups distort everything we're trying to do." Another Delegate, Walter McCarren, took a stronger stand. "Senator Davis certainly has my vote concerning the Negroes and other foreigners," he said. "What we are doing now is just like back when we owned slaves—taking care of them—but we aren't getting anything in return for our investment now, and that's a shame." Kate finally found a woman delegate and started to ask a question, but the woman's husband grabbed her by the arm and led her away.

After the convention, it was obvious that Mitch had been planning the evening. He suggested that we go to dinner at Cucos, his idea of good Mexican food, then catch a movie. I can't recall anything about the food that evening, and I'm not sure we ever ordered. But we had Margaritas. Lots of Margaritas. Mitch kept ordering pitchers, because it was part of his plan to get in Kate's pants, and Kate kept ordering them, because it was part of her scheme to get Mitch to spill OIC secrets. Lindsey and I went slow, so we could watch the hilarious scene being played out before us.

I played with Mitch, asking him what they were working on now. He leaned over so Kate wouldn't hear and whispered, "Latest issue is the downing of TWA 800. Someone tipped Jeffreys that the Navy was responsible. A missle brought it down, and we think it was on direct orders from the Commander-in-Chief. Seems there were two Alabama troopers on board, heading to Paris to sell their story to *Le Monde*, and Cannon didn't want those facts to get out. The smoking gun, if we can prove it."

"And a lot of smoke blown up someone's ass," I said as I motioned for another pitcher of Margaritas.

Sometime that evening a consensus must have developed that everyone was having too much fun to go see a movie. When Lindsey and I left at 11:30, Mitch was ordering yet another pitcher.

It was almost noon when Kate showed up at our place on Sunday, and I fixed a big breakfast, something in which I took great pride. Spanish omelets and Chile Sandoval, made from an old New Mexico recipe I'd gotten from a friend in Texas. Kate regaled us with stories about the rest of her evening with Mitch. I was not at all surprised when she told us how Mitch had been hot-dogging and tried to impress her by giving a her a private midnight tour of the OIC offices. One of the interesting things she learned from Mitch was that he monitored usenet groups for information about Cannon and Whirlpool, and that he often planted false rumors about the President and the First Lady, posting under a series of fake names with different accounts, on the alt.conspiracy.whirlpool newsgroup.

Nor was I surprised when Kate told us that Mitch had passed out in his office, shortly after they had arrived there. But I was surprised, and somewhat concerned, when she mentioned that Jeffreys' computer password was still SCT1997. Kate said it in passing, almost casually, before she and Lindsey began talking about something else. She didn't say how she discovered that, and I didn't ask. Phrases like "download" and "file transfer protocol" were flashing through my mind, and I really didn't want to know anything about it.

I excused myself from the conversation and went jogging around the campus, thinking how foolish I had been to tell a reporter anything. Even Kate. I should have known better.

My mind flashed back to another incident I couldn't forget. I remembered the argument I'd had with Bart Gedney about his plan to breach the secutity of the defense counsel's computer system shortly before the Banaghan-Vance trial. I was horrified but not surprised by Bart's seeming contempt for the law and Jeffreys' disregard legal ethics at the time, and it was still unsettling now. Stopping that nefarious scheme was one of the few battles I won during my time on the policy committee. At least as far as I know, I won it.

Jogging seemed to clear or cloud my mind regarding Kate's comment and my guilt. Soon I was able to convince myself that it wasn't my fault, that I hadn't knowingly aided and abetted the possible breach of confidential information on a government computer system. By the time I got back to the house, I had completely absolved myself. But I was glad that Kate had already gone when I returned. I wouldn't have to think about it again.

I had overdosed on politics that weekend and hadn't fully recovered when the Democrats met in Chicago to elaborate the obvious and nominate James Cannon for a second term in the White House. I avoided the televised Chicago bull and worked late at the office every night that week, trying to stay at least one day ahcad of my students. I enjoyed teaching, but it required far more preparation than I had anticipated, my previous classroom experience having been weekly seminars.

I wasn't completely successful, however, in avoiding news of the Democratic National Convention that week. Both the national and the local press were all twittering about Chub Campbell having been arrested down at the Chicago stockyards and charged with putting some illegal moves on one of the sheep. Chub's story was that he was just taking a leak; but, it was his word against the cop's, and the sheep refused to talk. The networks and the national broadsheets fretted maybe 20 seconds before deciding that "the public had a right to know" and went with the story. It played again the next day, that time as the lead story, after the police searched Chub's hotel room and found a Cannon Staff Convention Floor Pass and a diary.

I remembered meeting Chub once when Jeffreys was giving a speech, but my only clear recollection was that he had a hankering for Goo Goo Clusters. He was there with Jerry Elkay Coughlin, doing double duty as his driver and political consultant. He had also been at the meeting with Mitch, Smegman, Grenier, Caughlin, and Cooper at Bogue's the day I overheard them plotting against Vance. The major papers now pictured him as one of Cannon's key campaign advisors, but that strained credulity. Buried in the stories, usually after the jump to an inside page, were reports that Chub Campbell was a Republican consultant who had done polling for Senator Helmut Duke, Senator Reynolds Rantallion, and Governor Coughlin.

It was all too cute, and it smacked of a set up. What was Chub doing with Cannon Staff credentials for the convention? How did a photographer for the *National Examiner* just happen to be present when he was arrested? And, wasn't it a strange coincidence that the story broke on the same day that President Cannon was supposed to give his acceptance speech to the convention? Had payback written all over it.

Governor Coughlin, responding to a reporter for the *Alabama Times*, said that he was praying for Chub and his family. A White House press aide admitted during a daily press briefing that President Cannon knew Chub Campbell and regretted the embarrassing situation in which Chub now found himself. But Cannon knew everyone who was involved on either side in Alabama politics, and he'd been pilloried a few times in the tabloids himself.

Cannon's admission was enough for Jeffreys, though, and he immediately issued a subpoena for Chub's diary. Nothing his most vocal opponents could have done would have exposed the depths to which Jeffreys would stoop to smear Cannon as did that subpoena. Or so I thought. The next day's edition of the *Washington Sun* had a story quoting "sources close to the investigation" that the diary contained a suggestion that Diane Cannon had requested the FBI background files on hundreds of Republicans. Turned out, as I later learned from Mitch, that the suggestion had been made by Senator Rantallion during a fundraising event at which Chub was present, and Chub had noted it in his diary for a book he planned to write. But that particular fact was never leaked to the press.

Lindsey and I were watching one of those Sunday morning talk shows that weekend, and Diane Cannon was the guest that day. The discussion was mostly about her recent book, and I was reading the paper instead of paying attention to the television. Lindsey nudged me when the host asked a question about Chub's diary being subpoenaed and the report that the First Lady's name appeared in it. Something like that. I was still paying more attention to the nudge than to the television.

"I'm going to write another book someday, but I can't keep a diary. It would get subpoenaed. I can't write anything down," Diane Cannon said with a laugh. "I have tons of schedules and all that stuff, but, you know, there's been a real crimp put in the historical record by these absurd investigations. I don't even want to say, 'I had dinner last night with whomever,' because, if I were to write that in a diary, the person I had dinner with is likely to get hauled before some committee or grand jury somewhere. It's a question of realism—and whether someone should have to suffer for the crime of being my friend."

"Of course," the First Lady said, "Mr. Jeffreys would love to get his hands on my diary, if I kept one, so he could go after everyone I mentioned, persecute every friend of mine, everyone I've ever had a conversation with. 'What did she really say at church camp on June 18, 1962?' Who can remember those small things said between friends that are now insignificant unless someone wants to use them try to make a phony case against somebody? It's pathetic."

Backing off a bit, she elaborated, "I honestly wish if people had political differences, they wouldn't try to destroy somebody personally. I have watched it for four years, people dragged into this matter, having to hire lawyers, running up legal fees, with no good reason. And I regret that deeply."

Then she explained, finally getting to the crux of the Republican complaint, "Since my husband declared for the Presidency back in '91, there have been an enormous number of attacks and assaults on him coming from all directions. When he became President, there were many in this town and elsewhere who didn't think he should have won and didn't think that he had any right to be here. So, we have had to live with this extraordinary atmosphere of suspicion and false accusations, and, unfortunately, I think it's better not to keep a journal or a diary, regardless of the value such an account might have for future historians."

It was only a couple of days after that when Jessie Banaghan got thrown in the slammer for refusing to testify before Jeffreys' grand jury. She told Judge Hoffman that Jeffreys and John Hathorne wanted her to lie about President and Mrs. Cannon, and she was afraid they'd charge her with perjury if she didn't say what they wanted to hear. Her attorney confirmed that the Independent Counsel had contacted him and promised a reduced sentence if she would implicate the Cannons. Hathorne denied that the conversation ever occurred and, even if it did, he had made no such promise. No one believed him, but the judge still sent Jessie Banaghan to jail for contempt of court until she agreed to testify.

After the hearing, Jessie Banaghan's lawyer told the press, "She's a political prisoner. If James Cannon hadn't been elected president, this never would have happened. From the beginning it's been absolutely clear that the prosecution of Jessie Banaghan was only a means for Jeffreys to get to James and Diane Cannon. Because she didn't succumb to their pressure to lie to the grand jury, because she wouldn't roll over and do their bidding, the full weight of the Independent Counsel came crushing down on her, and that is outrageous. If a government can send you to jail because you won't lie for them, then the right to remain silent is no longer a right, it's a mere privilege bestowed by those in power."

Jessie Banaghan was led from the courthouse in handcuffs, but she smiled and held her head high. Facing a mob of reporters and a battalion of cameras as she entered the county jail a few blocks away, she said defiantly, "My mother refused to cooperate with the Nazis in Belgium during World War Two, and I will not do so in Birmingham today. If you convicted everyone in Alabama who stands in contempt George Jeffreys, the state would be one giant penitentiary. The whole country has contempt for George Jeffreys. The people are saying, 'Enough is enough.'"

Jesse Banaghan's mother, standing by her in tears, said, "I still want to believe in justice and freedom, and I still believe that it is worth fighting for. I'm proud of Jessie. We would ask that our friends pray for us and that she will be able to rejoin her family. The only thing I have to say to George Jeffreys is that he will have to stand judgment for his actions in a higher court. And he will have search his own conscience. Thank you. God bless you."

Mrs. Banaghan's brother was a bit more direct. "She has nothing to hide. She doesn't want immunity. She wants to talk to the American people and tell them what she knows. She's already told them that the president knew nothing about the $300,000 loan. Jessie will under oath without immunity stand up in a court of law or before Congress and testify to everything she knows. But, she does not believe in this sham investigation. George Jeffreys is a liar, and he suborned perjury from her in this investigation. She will have nothing to do with George Jeffreys— ever. The guy's a Nazi."

It was evident that Jeffreys understood the Nazi analogy, and he responded rather defensively when asked about Mrs. Banaghan's comments, sounding wounded as he asked, "Everyone must comply with a lawfully issued subpoena to testify, for no one is above the law. What could possibly explain this type of distrust and disrespect? I can only assume that it is the culture of scandal that seems to pervade the state of Alabama, the culture of lies represented by President Cannon and his friends in high places. Furthermore, let me set the record straight, we did not promise Jessie Banaghan a reduced sentence if she would provide testimony damaging to President or Mrs. Cannon. The Independent Counsel can only make sentencing recommendations, and we have no authority to guarantee any specific sentence. Sentencing decisions are entirely up to the judge. So, she is not being truthful."

Seemed that truth was in short supply all around. And so was reason. The next day, for good measure, Jeffreys got his grand jury to indict Jessie Banaghan for criminal contempt and obstruction of justice.

Chapter Thirty Two

I'd heard enough about Whirlpool to last a lifetime, so I made a vow to myself not to read a newspaper or watch television that weekend. Lindsey and I were going to Montgomery to see Sweet Honey in the Rock. They were performing at the Carolyn Blount Theatre, Red Blount's multi-million dollar monument to social respectability, and Lee Hays, a performing arts professor at Huntingdon, had sent four free tickets. But, even then, I discovered how difficult it was to escape from the pall of Whirlpool in Alabama.

Lindsey had invited her old friend and new colleague, James Burgh, and his wife to go with us. I had considerable respect for Burgh and his work, but I thought it might be uncomfortable for him to be around—or even to be seen in public with—someone who had worked for Jeffreys. And, I was probably feeling some guilt about what our office had done to him. Lindsey assured me that he wouldn't have accepted our invitation if he had any reservations, and, as it turned out, she was right. As usual.

Burgh and I ended up talking a lot about Whirlpool on the way to Montgomery, but especially on the way home that night. I've always believed that if you have to eat shit, you should take big bites, so I just blurted out early on how damn sorry I was about what Jeffreys had done to him, and how I regretted ever working for the bastard. Burgh said he didn't blame anyone except Jeffreys.

Not only had Jeffreys forced Burgh to plead guilty to a misdemeanor he didn't commit, he then called a press conference and said Burgh had pleaded guilty to a felony offense with which he was never charged. Since Jeffreys had Burgh under a gag order, he couldn't say anything to publicly refute the lie, but he had the balls to file a civil lawsuit asking Jeffreys to apologize. I remembered that, but I was curious about why he had later dropped the suit before it came to trial. So I asked him.

"A couple of reasons," Burgh replied. "First, I wasn't seeking money damages, all I wanted was an apology and for him to quit lying about me. Instead of admitting what he'd done and saying he was sorry,

Jeffreys assigned several members of his staff to work on the case and tried to claim he was, by virtue of his position, immune from any liability and couldn't be sued for defamation. I thought that was not only arrogant but also hypocritical, considering the brief he'd offered to write in Christine Putnam's suit against Cannon. Anyway, I concluded that even if I won and the court ordered him to apologize, it wouldn't be sincere."

"Second," Burgh said, "I was handling the case *pro se*, and he had at least two government lawyers from the OIC working on the case. They decided to play motion practice, and I was having difficulty responding to the flurry of paper while trying to teach a full load of classes and pursue my research program. And Judge Corwin was granting their motions for delay before I even filed a response. Then, of course, I still hadn't been sentenced at that time. They kept delaying the date for over a year, holding that sword over my head, and I thought there was a strong likelihood for prosecutorial vindictiveness if I continued to pursue the case. So, I withdrew the suit. Jeffreys will just have to live with his conscience, I guess, if he has one."

I didn't blame Burgh for dropping the suit, and I could understand why he had been upset about what Jeffreys had done to him and his family. And not just the lies about his own involvement. During the Vance trial last spring, John Hathorne kept trying to portray Burgh as part of a nefarious "political family" that, he told the jury, was involved in a great diabolical conspiracy. Burgh hadn't been involved in politics, at all, since he'd worked for Cannon some 16 years ago. He was a college professor, just doing his job and minding his own business. But that didn't stop Jeffreys and Hathorne from smearing his reputation by trying to stretch old facts to fit their fictitious theories. Not if it would help them to destroy President Cannon.

I had been curious about something and felt now would be a good point to ask, "Do you ever talk with Cannon or anyone at the White House these days?"

"No," Burgh replied without elaboration.

"Why? The selfish son of a bitch won't take your calls?"

"Don't know if he would or not, but that's not the reason," he explained. "If my number showed up on the phone or fax logs, even a call slip, George Jeffreys would start squealing that there was a conspiracy to obstruct justice. I mean, look what they tried to make of the White House meeting between Cannon and Vance way back when. Or the hysterical claims that White House staffers were trying to buy Randolph Webster's silence when they tried to help an old friend find work. No, no one can even take the chance of being investigated and wooled around for talking to Cannon. Wouldn't be fair to him, either. I haven't been able to call or talk with him about anything, even about our kids, since they came after me. Wouldn't be worth it. Jeffreys and his boys have put an end to a lot of personal friendships."

We had a great time in Montgomery that evening, and I enjoyed getting to know Burgh and his wife. I also learned a lot from talking with him about his research on free speech theory, which was an interest we shared. I hoped that we'd have a chance to talk and do something together again soon, but I was surprised that it would be quite so soon.

James Burgh came by our house on Saturday afternoon. He'd tried to forget about Whirlpool and get his life back, but our conversation the previous night had caused him to give it some more thought. He asked if I would represent him in pursuing criminal charges against Jeffreys and others at the Office of Independent Counsel. I was curious, to say the least, but I told him up front that I couldn't do that. Not that I had any personal objections or didn't think it should be done, but I was prohibited for three years under the Ethics in Government Act—the Independent Counsel statute—from representing anyone who had been investigated or prosecuted by the Independent Counsel.

"Well," Burgh asked, "I thought maybe that had been repealed. Since it hasn't, doesn't another section of that same statute prohibit anyone who works for the Independent Counsel from representing Jeffreys?"

"Yes," I replied, "and I made that argument when your lawsuit against Jeffreys was discussed by the Policy Committee. Which raises another issue, I suppose. I might be called as a witness if you decide to pursue what I think you've got in mind."

"I appreciate that, and I'm glad to know that at least one person in that office cared about the law," Burgh said. "Could you, then, discuss some hypothetical issues without violating any laws or ethical standards?"

"I don't know why not. Isn't that how faculty colleagues learn, by discussing hypos with each other and arguing about the practical implications of the law?"

"Okay," he said, "now you said that the Ethics in Government Act prohibits employees of the Independent Counsel from representing anyone involved in any way in the investigation, right?"

"That's the way I read the statute."

"And 18 U.S.C. 371 is the conspiracy statute, with which I am intimately familiar," Burgh said sardonically. "So, if some hypothetical group of people discussed violating the Ethics in Government Act, they might be engaged in a conspiracy to violate the law?"

"That's correct," I answered, "but only if one of them actually performs an overt act to further the conspiracy."

Burgh smiled and asked, "Would that be a felony or a misdemeanor?"

"Depends on what the penalty is for the law they conspired to violate. The Ethics in Government Act isn't a criminal statute, and the maximum penalty there would probably be removal from office," I said. "However, knowingly conspiring to violate any federal law is a crime, and there is case law holding that conspiracy to misappropriate the time and duties of a government employee for illegal activity constitutes felony fraud to deprive the United States of the faithful services of its employees. Hypothetically speaking, of course."

"Hypothetically," Burgh asked, "do you think George Jeffreys was familiar with the Ethics in Government Act, under which he presumes to exercise authority?"

"Mr. Jeffreys is a very learned lawyer, I've heard him say so many times, and I would think he's intimately familiar with every section of the United States Code, just as he has presumed that every citizen of Alabama should have been from birth," I replied.

"Now, hypothetically speaking," Burgh continued, "would filing a motion be an overt act in furtherance of a conspiracy to violate the Ethics in Government Act, if it were done in the course of representing a covered person?"

"It would," I answered.

"And, would sending a copy of that motion to the opposing party, by placing it or causing it to be placed in the United States mail, constitute felony mail fraud under 18 U.S.C 1341?"

I was enjoying this hypothetical discussion and said, "Yes, depending on the specific facts, each separate use of the mails to further a scheme to defraud the United States could constitute a separate felony offense under the mail fraud statutes."

"And, continuing our hypo, would placing a telephone call to someone in, say, Chicago, and participating in a conference call to discuss the strategy for handling the case constitute felony wire fraud under 18 U.S.C. 1343?"

"Long question, but same answer," I said, appreciating Burgh's familiarity with the applicable statutes. "Yes, depending on the specific facts of the situation, it could be."

"Let me change the direction a bit," Burgh said. "Are lawyers, employed by the federal government on a full-time basis, prohibited from representing private clients outside the scope of their duties?"

"If you are talking about Jeffreys," I said, "technically, he's not a full-time employee. Just draws a full-time salary. But, hypothetically, all the other attorneys in the office are full-time and would be prohibited from private practice under, I believe it's 28 CFR 45.735-9."

"Okay, now let me ask this," Burgh said. "If Jeffreys were sued in his official capacity, the Attorney General would have to certify that, and then the Justice Department would represent him in an civil action. But, if he were sued for actions outside the scope of his official duties, he would have to get a private attorney. So, my question is, was he ever certified by the Attorney General as acting under color of office when he held that press conference and lied about me?"

"You're right about the process, and the answer to your question is, no," I replied.

"Are there any specific rules or regulations that would prohibit a public official from ordering his or her employees to perform personal services for the private benefit of the official? I mean," Burgh said, "like things ranging from shining their shoes to providing free legal representation."

"I'd have to look it up, but, sure, there are lots of regs on misuse of official position," I said. "I think it's 5 CFR 2635.701, or something close, that specifically states a public official shall not use or permit the use of his Government position in a manner that is intended to coerce or induce a subordinate to provide any benefit, financial or otherwise, to himself. I only remember the cite because I'm going to cover that in my lecture next week."

"What about the unauthorized use of things like paper, supplies, computers, photocopies, secretarial services, legal databases? I assume those would be covered, too," Burgh said.

"Yeah," I replied, "different section on misuse of government property. I think it's 5 CFR 2635.704 that says a federal employee has a duty to protect and conserve government property and shall not use it, or allow its use, for other than authorized purposes."

"And, as I understand it," he said, "anyone who is involved in a conspiracy, however remotely, is considered to be responsible for any act done by someone else in furtherance of the conspiracy?"

"You should know that, if anyone does," I said with a more than a little appreciation of the irony of the situation.

James Burgh paused as if he were considering the implications of what he was about to say. Then, he asked, "That might include criminal exposure for George Jeffreys as well as Tim Pickering and Andy Volstead, the two lawyers who represented Jeffreys, right? And anyone else who agreed to or participated in the scheme, right? Still speaking, hypothetically, you understand."

"Again, depending on the specific facts, that could be the case," I said. "Hypothetically, Bart Gedney might have assigned Pickering and Volstead on orders from Jeffreys, and John Hathorne might have participated in some of the discussions regarding representation of Jeffreys in some hypothetical case. And James Peck might have participated in the discussions, too."

"So, hypothetically," Burgh asked, having obviously thought through whether he was up for another fight, "where would one start to get someone to enforce the law in such a situation?"

"Well, if you're talking about a hypothetical Independent Counsel," I said, "you'd need to file a formal complaint with the Office of Professional Responsibility at Justice, even if Otis would be afraid to bring charges and would probably shirk her responsibility to remove an Independent Counsel for good cause. You might consider sending a copy to the DC Bar's Committee on Professional Conduct, if you want to get his law license."

"If someone wanted to do that," Burgh asked, "who would you recommend they hire to represent them? Specifically, do you know a good attorney who wouldn't have a conflict, and who wouldn't be afraid to stand up to the political pressure."

"I assume we're no longer talking hypotheticals now. What about Hank Drummond or Judge Erskine? They represented you before, and they're two of the finest lawyers I've ever seen."

"Because they are both likely to be considered for federal judgeships, and I wouldn't ask them to do anything that might jeopardize their confirmation," Burgh explained rather pragmatically.

I understood his concern. And I smiled when I realized what effect such a complaint could have on Jeffreys' chances of ever being confirmed for anything. "What about Bill Baxter with Baxter, Talos, and Knight over in Birmingham? Do you know him? I think he'd have the balls to do it, and he'd probably enjoy it after what the Republicans did to him the last time he ran for office."

"The former Attorney General? Great suggestion," Burgh said as he got up to leave, "and thanks for your valuable time and advice."

"Nothing to thank me for," I said. "I always enjoy discussing such interesting . . . hypos. Thanks for stopping by. And good luck."

Burgh opened the door of his car, then turned around with one more question. "John, if you were me, what would you do?"

"I can't give you any legal advice," I reminded him, "but if it were me, and Jeffreys had done to me what he's done to you? I wouldn't have to think twice about it. I'd cry havoc and let slip the dogs of war."

Talking hypos is always fun, but sometimes those discussions can have real consequences. I was reminded of that the following Monday after I heard an interview with President Cannon on NPR. The reporter asked him if he had considered granting pardons to people convicted in the Whirlpool investigation as President Stuart had done in 1992 for those investigated or charged by the Iran-Contra Independent Counsel.

Cannon gave what I thought was an appropriate answer, saying no one had asked for a pardon, that he hadn't thought about that, and that he hadn't given it any consideration whatsoever. All pardons, he added, had to go though a rather involved application and evaluation process, and he would not make any exceptions or presume to decide them in advance based on personal or political concerns.

That sounded fairly routine to me. I guess he could have said "no" or "no comment," instead of saying he hadn't even considered it and overexplaining it like he always did everything else. But I never imagined that the Republicans and their media lackeys could somehow think that was a wrong answer. I really was removed from political reality, and that boringly innocuous answer served to illustrate how just how far.

The Republicans went ballistic, and said by not flatly ruling out pardons he had been dangling them before potential witnesses. Geezus. If he had said he flatly ruled out the possibility of any pardons, then they'd have probably charged him with willfully violating the established procedures for reviewing pardon requests. They had an angle to screw him regardless of how he answered any question that any reporter might ask.

Same way with how Congressman Clapham was treating the deal about the FBI records. If the White House conducted an internal investigation to discover how it happened, then they were obstructing justice by interfering with an investigation by Congress or the Independent Counsel. If they didn't conduct an internal investigation, then they could be said to be callous to ethical questions in the White House, or their uninformed responses to questions about it would be portrayed as stonewalling. Damnedest thing I'd ever seen. And I still didn't understand what the big deal was about the FBI files in the first place. There is nothing wrong with the White House requesting files or information from any executive agency. Clapham's committee staff was doing that everyday. And there was no suggestion that the White House had ever misused or abused the information in any of the files. I just didn't get it.

But, oh, what a work is the mind of a Congressman. More than 150 of them signed a letter the next day demanding that the President promise to grant no pardons to anyone convicted or investigated by George Jeffreys. Former Judge Beard, on television hyping his latest book, said Cannon was flirting with obstruction of justice by talking about pardons for potential witnesses against the President and the First Lady.

Congressman Dorkman took the floor in the House and announced that he was introducing a Resolution of Impeachment against President Cannon. Ranting, as was his usual style of discussion, Dorkman told his House colleagues, "I want to find out about jury tampering, telegraphing messages through media interviews, and tampering with witnesses that are at this moment going before the grand jury in Birmingham. I want gavel-to-gavel hearings on national television. I'm going to make sure that President Cannon will get his day in court, and he will have his day in court, because I am filing impeachment papers. I have had lawyers working on them for about 5 or 6 months, and this is the crowning issue, this is the straw on the camel's back, telegraphing pardon messages to people. It is unbelievable. It is a high crime!"

I walked out of the room and left Lindsey to watch the rest of Dorkman's C-SPAN tirade alone. I went to my study and wrote a check for $1,000 to Loretta Sanchez for Congress, knowing she didn't have much of a chance to defeat Dorkman but knowing it would make me feel better. It was the only campaign contribution I made to any candidate that year. I had taken the pledge and sworn off politics, but Dorkman's speech had caused me to backslide. I was personally embarrassed that Dorkman was a member of the United States Congress. I mean, what if intelligent aliens were monitoring television signals from earth and saw Dorkman? Or what if impressionable young children might mistake that for responsible behavior?

With a little help from his friends in high places, specifically the Speaker's Office, the Dorkman was able to bring up his resolution for consideration during a House Judiciary Committee hearing two days later. You can imagine his surprise, when Bruce Flim, reactionary Republican crusader and old friend of George Jeffreys, appeared as the first witness on the panel and said, "It is more important than ever in the politically-fueled Whirlpool investigation that President Cannon retain the discretion to pardon to correct the injustice of prosecutorial overreaching and to mitigate this Whirlpool madness of twisting political feuds into crimes."

Photographers hustled to get on the floor in front of the witness table, and reporters were trying to write down every word Flim uttered, as he continued, "The high-octane, gold-plated Whirlpool investigation pursued by Independent Counsel George Jeffreys with more fury than the Furies pursued Orestes has already yielded several unjust verdicts of guilt or indictments for conduct that has customarily been addressed in a political forum."

Then came the real kick in the butt, when Flim startled the Republican members by suggesting, "No one should be surprised that Jessie Banaghan prefers jail over answering questions from George Jeffreys. Mrs. Banaghan merely is exercising a choice afforded her under U.S. law. And considering Jeffreys' prosecutorial excesses, her choice is understandable."

Flim's closing remarks were equally interesting, and he concluded, "The transparent partisan dueling over Whirlpool only invites more prosecutorial zealotry. President Cannon should pardon persons convicted or indicted for Whirlpool crimes who would have been left undisturbed by ordinary evidentiary and prosecutorial standards. As Justice Robert Jackson warned more than 50 years ago, the greatest threat to liberty posed by unchained prosecutors like George Jeffreys is that instead of discovering a crime and searching for the culprit, they identify politically vulnerable targets and then scour the law codes to pin offenses on them."

The Chairman dismissed the panel of witnesses and adjourned the committee hearing for the rest of the day. Dorkman's impeachment resolution was never mentioned nor considered again. Jeffreys must have felt betrayed by Flim's testimony and the impact it had in squelching the move to impeach President Cannon. It soon became apparent, however, that losing the battle had not ended the war. Jeffreys had other options available, and he would try them all.

Only three days later, Sunday's *Washington Sun* had a front page story based on information from a confidential FDIC Inspector General's report, and the headline read like an indictment of the First Lady. The report did not specifically accuse Diane Cannon of any illegal acts, but it suggested that Jefferson Savings had later deceive federal bank examiners by using a document Mrs. Cannon had drafted.

FDIC spokesman Stan Korst told NBC News that Inspector General Liz Lamar was livid that the confidential report had been leaked within 24 hours of its completion. Only four copies of the report existed, and one of them was still on Inspector General Lamar's desk. The Senate and House banking committees, chaired respectively by Gastone Diletto and Dick Leech, had been provided with one copy each. The fourth copy had been delivered to the Independent Counsel's Office in Washington. My money was on Jeffreys as the source, but I would have added a fifth suspect. Stan Korst was the former RTC Communication Director under President Stuart, and he was still in that position when the Jefferson Savings criminal referrals were leaked in 1993.

Both the conclusions of the FDIC report and the process by which it became news were the main topic on CNN's Counterpoint program that evening. The running dogs of the radical right were baying at the fox, and Endicott Tyburn led the pack. Trying to appear clever, he predicted, "Jeffreys may well bring charges against the beardless Nixon, Diane Milhous Cannon. We know that, when she's not at the hairdresser, she spends most of her working hours defending her wimpy husband and other children. But those who have kept up with Whirlpool also know that she has been accused of bank fraud, obstruction of justice, and firing Dale Cheatham. Now we learn that she was intimately involved in drafting documents used for criminal purposes. Her cover is up."

Others had a different view of the incident, including Harvard law professor Allen Clausewitz, who responded to Tyburn by addressing the more fundamental corruption of the political process. "Mr. Jeffreys is a Republican prosecutor out to gain political advantage for his party. How else," he asked, "can one explain the leaks from 'sources close to the Whirlpool investigation' on an almost daily basis? The FDIC report is just the most recent in a continuing torrent of leaks emanating from George Jeffreys' office, all calculated to embarrass the White House and none permissible under the rules governing confidentiality of ongoing investigations. Mr. Jeffreys cannot deny personal responsibility for these leaks. Nothing leaks from an office like that without the boss's tacit consent, and, if there is any doubt that these leaks are orchestrated from the top, just contrast the hemorrhaging since Jeffreys took over with the strict confidentiality that characterized the same office under Kenneth Burke."

The pretense that the Whirlpool investigation was a legal matter was no longer necessary it seemed. Everyone now knew it was only raw politics, and the campaign had adopted the available means of persuasion. Rumors, organized letters to the editor, op-ed columns, direct mail, videotapes, web pages, speeches by principals and surrogates, appearances on the talk show circuit, bumper strips, buttons, partisan biographies, and everything else except paid 30-second spots, which I expected to see at any moment. One new approach was employed by the Jeffreys campaign that I had never seen before—endorsements, announcements, and testimonials by convicted felons disguised as news stories in the party's house organ.

The *Wall Street Record* published an exclusive interview with Roby Douglas. Based on his continuing cooperation with Jeffreys and his campaign staff, as well as recent appearances before the grand jury in Birmingham, Douglas announced, "Diane Cannon is going to be indicted after the election. It's a certainty." Then, Douglas witnessed for Jeffreys and proclaimed, "I have great admiration for Judge Jeffreys and am proud to be helping him. The most important thing to Judge Jeffreys is the rule of law, and he has his eye on history." Charley McCarthy couldn't have said it better.

Jeffreys was as sly as ever in his practiced response to the Douglas infomercial. Repeatedly using the Royal We, as had become his style, Jeffreys said, "We are duty-bound and have no alternative but to follow Department of Justice policies and practices on indictments, taking the election into account as we go about our work. The timing is something we must evaluate carefully as we move our investigations forward as rapidly as possible, but I do not anticipate announcing any indictments of the President or the First Lady before the November 5th election. Beyond that," he added, "I have no comment on Mr. Douglas' remarks." Nor was one necessary. Della Beckwith had written the perfect sound bite, full of strategic ambiguity, and Jeffreys had delivered the punch lines as scripted.

President Cannon and his supporters, however, had plenty to say. Buck Etienne, the Ragin' Cajun political consultant who had orchestrated Cannon's 1992 campaign, charged that Jeffreys was "a disappointed loser, an insecure little prick who still hated Cannon for winning and firing his sorry Republican ass. His latest partisan stunt, using a convicted felon to spread his lies and vouch for his reputation, was something even Tricky Dick wouldn't stoop to. I think I'll start taking out newspaper ads and placing television spots to expose his slimy political operation."

The Republican response was immediate. Congressman Bob Swill called upon Attorney General Otis to appoint yet another special prosecutor to investigate Etienne. His letter to Otis said, "Buck Etienne has gone beyond his right to voice and disseminate his opinion, and the First Amendment does not protect him in this case. It is clear from his pronouncements that Mr. Etienne seeks to influence ongoing judicial proceedings by impugning the integrity of George Jeffreys. He is explicitly targeting a statutorily authorized prosecutor for personal attack so as to impair his ability to conduct an ongoing investigation. I will not stand by and silently witness a brazen and systematic effort to undermine Judge Jeffreys' reputation. Judge Jeffreys is extremely sensitive to such negative comments, and his investigation could be damaged by public criticism designed to derail the ability of the Independent Counsel to perform his job. That's obstruction of justice."

Buck Etienne was not impressed, nor was he intimidated by Swill's threat. "That's bullshit," he said. "How can it be that Jeffreys can attack the President, he can attack the First Lady, he can attack the Democratic National Committee, he can attack the whole damn state of Alabama, he can attack anything he wants, but it's inappropriate for me to suggest that George Jeffreys is a Republican? It's the truth, and everybody knows it. Jeffreys is a big cry baby, and I'm tired of his constant whining. He's just gonna have to deal with it, because I haven't even started telling the truth about him."

When a reporter asked the President whether he agreed with Etienne's caustic assessment that Jeffreys was nothing more than a partisan political operative, the President went from campaign mode to closing argument, asking the court of public opinion, "Isn't it obvious? There's been a very long and well-financed campaign to attack me personally. I'd say it's time for Mr. Jeffreys to file a campaign finance report on his taxpayer-funded inquisition, make a full confession, plead guilty to playing politics, and make restitution for his crimes."

Well, I'd say that my faith in both the political process and the judicial process, to the extent that they were ever separate, was now long gone. Any remaining vestige of hope disappeared the next day, when George Jeffreys escalated his personal war against the Cannons. Prohibited by Justice Department policies from announcing any indictments so close to an election, Jeffreys had publicly bemoaned that fact to insinuate that he already had sufficient evidence and would have charged the First Lady. Then stung by public criticism, he allowed one of his cooperating felons to assert as much, and he refused to deny it. Now, reluctant to personally make charges and answer questions, he chose to leak an Interim Report from the Office of Independent Counsel.

The official Interim Report was back-dated to August 9th, making it appear to be a report to Congress on his two years as Independent Counsel, but internal evidence indicated that much of it had been written within the last few days. Copies of the confidential report were delivered to Attorney General Otis, Judge Chase, Senator Diletto, and Congressman Leech, and selected portions of it were leaked and made the news the following day. The opening sentence, quoted verbatim by several papers, telegraphed the entire tone of the document, declaring, "The Office of Independent Counsel has been conducting an ongoing investigation of several scandals involving President James Madison Cannon, who long ago broke his promise to run the most ethical administration in history."

Nowhere in the entire report was there any indication of criminal actions by the Cannons regarding the original matters that had led to the appointment of an Independent Counsel, but the bombshell came in a paragraph on page 37. It read, "Based upon the inconsistency between the testimony of Roby Douglas and that of James Madison Cannon during a federal criminal trial in April, 1996, as well as the inconsistency between the written responses of Diane Rankin Cannon to several federal agencies and the subsequent grand jury testimony of Josh Banaghan, we conclude that false statements were made under oath and that such statements constitute a violation of federal criminal statutes."

The *Washington Sun* headline announced, "President and First Lady Lied, Report Concludes." Only Kate Macauley seemed to have caught the absence of a conclusion, or even any indication of suspicion, as to whose testimony might have been false, and she put that very question to Jeffreys. Her story in the *Atlanta Gazette* quoted Jo Gobles' sinister non-answer that the investigation was "active and ongoing. We do not comment on the record about grand jury matters or whether we have already obtained sealed indictments of the President and the First Lady."

The following day, I found in our mailbox what looked like an official notice for jury duty. On closer inspection, I saw that it was a fake "citizen summons" mailed out by some group called the Coalition of Politically Active Christians. They requested a $1,000 donation, for which the they would send me a leftover copy of that old videotape, "The Cannon Chronicles," that was promoted by Reverend Dr. Elmer Laud on television last year. I usually throw such crap in the trash, but I'm glad I didn't this time.

An enclosed letter from former GOP Congressman Bill Dingleberry made it obvious that the leak of the Interim Report must have been a co-ordinated effort by Jeffreys, involving knowledge and advanced planning by others besides Diletto and Leech. The campaign was now cranked up, and they were taking it on the road. Alleging that President Cannon was guilty of perjury and a host of other felonies, Dingleberry's letter urged immediate political action. "It's up to God-fearing Americans like you to demand an indictment from Special Prosecutor George Jeffreys and the Congress! Only if James Cannon is indicted—which will in turn lead to his impeachment—is there hope for a return to justice in America."

Chapter Thirty Three

Senator Reynolds Rantallion must have received one of those letters from Bill Dingleberry, too, or perhaps he had an advance copy. Rantallion introduced a Senate Resolution requesting that the Office of Independent Counsel bring perjury charges against James Madison Cannon and Diane Rankin Cannon. The leadership referred the Resolution to the Judiciary Committee, and Senator Hatchet called an emergency meeting of his committee that afternoon. Hatchet and the Republicans on the committee approved a motion for immediate consideration, prohibiting any debate, and the measure was reported out on a straight party-line vote.

So much for the world's greatest deliberative body. Moreover, so much for all the institutions of our great republic. So much for civic virtue. And common sense. Jeffreys could find no real crime with which to charge the President or the First Lady, so he had turned to fabricating a crime from the answers he didn't like. Unable to get an impeachment Resolution out of the House committee and unlikely to persuade the electorate to rid them of Cannon, the Republicans in the Senate were now considering a Resolution asking Jeffreys to file those petty charges. And the media, unable to find anything of interest to report about the boring presidential campaign, went wild with anticipation of how this more interesting, but essentially meaningless, political contest might all play out.

The evening news was almost exclusively about the day's events in Washington, and, no doubt, *Nightline* would be devoted to the same topic. Lindsey insisted that we watch *Alabama Week in Review*, the state educational television network's version of *Washington Week in Review*. The program was produced each week in the College of Communication's studio on campus, and she'd been told it would be a particularly lively session that evening. It was.

Paul Summers, the editorial page editor of the *Post-Advertiser*, always had something negative to say about anything, especially about James Cannon. He'd been ragging on Cannon for years, without effect, and Summers' frustration with his own political impotence made his remarks even more acerbic. "There is no question that George Jeffreys should bring charges against the Cannons," Summers screeched. "I've been telling people that for years. How can anyone in the Senate read Jeffreys' report and not see that? Where is the groundswell of public support for the Rantallion Resolution? I wonder what people can be thinking, or if they're thinking at all. Where is the outrage in America? Where is the outrage in Alabama?"

Bill Baxter, the former state Attorney General and the lawyer I had recommended to James Burgh, was also on the panel. I knew him only by reputation, and I was interested in hearing his take on the situation. "Leaking a report accusing someone of wrongdoing is a chickenshit thing to do," he said more quickly than the producer could bleep the expletive. "Either you indict them and give them an opportunity to defend themselves, or you leave them the hell alone. That said, most good U.S. Attorneys will decline to bring perjury charges unless the defendant's purpose was to conceal a serious underlying crime, not merely to avoid some minor political and personal embarrassment. It matters not whether the Senate passes Rantallion's ridiculous Resolution. That's meaningless. But if Jeffreys does bring a prosecution, it had better be a gut cinch—or he can bend over and kiss what's left of his already shredded reputation good-bye."

Matt Lyon, editor of the *Anniston Star*, proved once again that local newspapers have a better understanding of human nature and life its ownself than do the national and statewide pundits. Providing the program with what I thought was a more realistic perspective, he said, "I think we'll see more than a nasty report from Judge Jeffreys, and I think we've not heard the last of this, because he is angry, and he showed his anger when he accused the President and the First Lady of perjury, which was a bit of a reach. In my opinion, Judge Jeffreys has crossed the line. I just want to say this, too. Think about all of these people, both up in Washington and here in Alabama, who have been put through the tortures of the damned. Many have been bankrupted. They've all have had their reputations, their integrity, their honor tainted and besmirched, and all because they chose a life of public service or merely were friends with the Cannons."

The best line of the show came from Mack Bartley, editor of the *Alabama Times*. Bartley hadn't said much during the discussion, but when the moderator asked for his evaluation of the Jeffreys Report, he grunted, "Truth is to Jeffreys as salt to a slug."

On Saturday, Lindsey and I took a break and drove down to Montgomery for the Alabama Highland Games. She was fascinated with learning more about her Scottish heritage and the history of the border Clan Armstrong. I was just glad to hear some bagpipe tunes. It rained during most of the day, and the field was covered with mud—a fitting metaphor for politics—but anything would have been better than worrying about Whirlpool.

The White House, though, was taking the latest developments more seriously. Diane Cannon was back on one of those Sunday morning public affairs shows, sounding rather defensive as she said, "I've said and continue to say that I will cooperate in any way possible to resolve this matter. I'm not surprised about the Rantallion Resolution, given all the accusations and allegations that are swirling around the past few days. There is no substance to these allegations. And I guess, ultimately, I have faith in my husband and in myself, but particularly in the American people. As people hear the truth and as they sort out fact from fantasy, I think it will become clear that these charges are largely from people seeking reduced sentences or those hoping for some political advantage. So, I will just keep talking with the American people, and, ultimately, I hope we'll be able to get back to talking about, you know, questions like 'What's best for our children?' When the headlines fade, those questions will still be with us."

If Diane Cannon had been watching television rather than appearing on it, she might have found some comfort in the remarks of Judge Robert Beard on *Commentary*, where he declared, "Jeffreys' fury is not hard to understand. Having set out to uncover a conspiracy and prosecute real crimes, his office has ended up with a record that ranges from poor to disastrous, prosecuting people for petty misdemeanors. Jeffreys tries to make it appear that he's been successful, repeatedly claiming nine guilty pleas and three convictions, but most people know the truth about what he did."

Judge Beard showed more compassion on that issue than I had ever seen from him, explaining, "If these charges were political, one might ask, why would anyone plead guilty? The answer is to avoid another two years of agony for them, their families, and their children and an estimated $1 million in legal fees that would have left them in debt. It was a tragic choice but an eminently sensible decision for each of them."

Then, Judge Beard addressed the latest developments, saying, "Jeffreys and his staff seem now to feel if they can add a President or First Lady to their game bag, at least something might be retrieved. Angered at the escape of his prey, Jeffreys leaked a report that virtually accused the Cannons of perjury. These are remarks that would be highly inappropriate, and perhaps punishable by disbarment under the code of professional conduct, if made by a regular prosecutor. They are even more so when flung out by an Independent Counsel."

Finally, Beard pointed out something that Diane Cannon should have said, noting, "The answers in the Cannons' testimony and depositions were not prepared in advance; they were spontaneous responses to hostile questioning. Then vindictive prosecutors scrutinized every nuance to see if any sentence could be contradicted. Following that, they chose to squeeze testimony from two convicted felons and use that as a basis for making highly dubious accusations against the Cannons. Subsequently, that information was leaked to unauthorized persons in the media. Now, I understand, some of the confidential FBI files from the Independent Counsel's investigation have been leaked. In this entire process, Jeffreys has behaved in ways more morally questionable than did any of his victims."

The talk shows were just talk without resolution of the issues, whereas the Senate was talking about a different kind of Resolution. The scheduled recess was postponed, so Senator Rantallion took the floor and spent three hours venting his spleen and arguing for adoption of his Resolution requesting that the Independent Counsel file charges of perjury against James Madison Cannon and Diane Rankin Cannon.

Following Rantallion's twisted tirade, Senator Diletto was recognized, and he spent over an hour recapping the conclusions of the Senate Whirlpool Committee and telling those in the chamber that "questions remained." He was short on both arguments and audience, but the thrust was that the Resolution should be adopted. Diletto also took pains to deny that anyone on his staff had leaked the confidential files to the media, something Senator Rantallion had neglected to do. After watching Rantallion and Diletto, I thought Elvis might have been onto a good idea when he shot all those TV sets, and I had a better understanding of why someone would want to do that. Yet, I continued to watch the debates on C-SPAN every day after work.

On Wednesday, the Democrats finally had an opportunity to respond, and that responsibility fell primarily to Senator Hammett, the Minority Leader. "I'll take just a few moments, because I know other members have been waiting to speak," Hammett said when he was recognized by the presiding officer. "First, I want to indicate that it's still my hope that we can find a bipartisan majority in this Senate against the Resolution. I've spoken to President Cannon this afternoon—and as I've said many times before—President Cannon is willing to meet any senator, any time, any place, to discuss the facts about Whirlpool. So, I want to urge my colleagues to see if we can't find a way to resolve this issue. It's important."

"Mr. President," Hammett said, hoping to defuse some of the inflammatory remarks from the previous day, "Senator Rantallion and Senator Diletto made several statements yesterday with regard to the Independent Counsel's FBI reports which I feel deserve further explanation. Let me tell you why."

"Many of us are still trying to make a judgment," Hammett suggested, hoping that were true. "Some have already made a judgment based on what they think they've found in the FBI 302 reports. We are constrained by the rules from making any reference to those leaked reports, even maybe how we got them, though we all know that. And it seems to me, we can't have a full and complete discussion, unless we can talk about the witnesses and their credibility. But anybody can come out here and quote something out of the report or refer to it and say, 'I've made up my mind based on what I saw in the report,' which is hardly fair."

Hammett was clearly frustrated as he told his colleagues, "I've asked the Parliamentarian how far we can go in discussing the report. Names can't be cited from the report. Can't use references identifying persons by other characterizations, such as criminal history or contradictions with previous sworn testimony. Can't refer to the number of anonymous letters, phone calls, and fax transmissions cited in the report. However, information which has been published in the media is no longer under the injunction of Rule 29 and would no longer appear to be confidential. So, if I read an article, say from the *Washington Sun*, and that article included information contained in the Independent Counsel's report or the FBI reports, I could read the entire article in the record. And we can thank Senator Rantallion's aide, David Winderig, for that particular convenience."

"Well, I don't fault the Chair, I think he's correct," Hammett said as he began his attempted defense, "but I do fault the process, which I think is clearly unfair to President Cannon, and would be unfair to anybody else, president or not. And what many of us are trying to do, because we understand the importance of fairness to the President, we have read the report. Some may have read parts of it. And there are undecided senators on both sides of the aisle who are looking for information, facts."

"Now, President Cannon can't see the Independent Counsel's FBI reports," Hammett complained. "I guess he can go through the Freedom of Information Act, but that'd be 30 days or more. And so we can state our conclusions, based on what we've seen in the report, and the parts that were printed in the *Washington Sun*. No one has cross-examined the people who've given statements to the FBI. No one has tested their veracity, tested their credibility. They were simply interviewed under circumstances that none of us can refer to. And no one on the other side of the aisle has questioned David Winderig about whether he was responsible for giving the files to the media."

It was becoming clear that Hammett was going to take more time than the few minutes he had promised, as he asked his colleagues, "Has the President been fairly treated? Nameless accusers. Somebody makes a call or sends a fax, and the FBI writes up the report, and some Senator reads it and decides to vote against the President on that basis. Anonymous telephone calls and letters, testimony from convicted felons, and all the rest, including anonymous Senate staffers shoveling this stuff to the press and the right-wing groups from whence they came."

"But if I understand the Senate," Hammett said, trying to undo the damage caused by the leaked reports, "there isn't a single person in this chamber who doesn't want everyone to have their fair shot. We may totally disagree with them. Whatever. But the one thing that we've always prided ourselves in was fairness, due process. And due process applies not just to the courts, but applies to individual rights in any event in America. And President Cannon is entitled to due process, just as we would like to be entitled to fairness and due process."

Hammett then tried to undermine Rantallion's earlier attack, asking, "How can we be fair under the circumstances? I said publicly how many convicted felons have been interviewed, and I've learned now I shouldn't say that. And other senators on both sides, have picked out words. Yesterday, one senator was referring to 'a conversation at the State Capitol,' obviously referring to the report, and it makes it very difficult to have a full and complete debate, unless we go into a closed session. And that's an option suggested by the Senator from Maryland, Senator Bonhomme."

"There are other ways to get at the truth," Hammett declared, knowing that the Democrats needed to do something dramatic to counter the damage caused by the leaked reports and the media salivation. "Therefore, I am considering asking unanimous consent—won't do it today—that this body give President Cannon the opportunity to answer the charges against him in a closed session. The request would be that James Cannon be allowed to come to this chamber and to stand in this well and to answer his critics face-to-face, charge-by-charge, rumor-by-rumor, and fact-by-fact, and to state his case to those Senators who are truly undecided on both sides of the aisle."

"But just let me indicate that if we owe President Cannon anything, whatever may happen in the end, we owe him a right to say, 'I've had my day in court.' Oh, yes, I know he's been questioned by the Independent Counsel, and some members have read that testimony from the leaked reports. And I think so far we've had a pretty high-level, objective debate. We've had . . . ," Hammett was saying as he was interrupted by several colleagues who guffawed at the tenor of the debate. "Obviously, some people have different views. That's what a debate's all about."

Disconcerted by the remarks of some in his audience and sensing that he was losing their attention, Senator Hammett concluded, "So, I would just say that those of us who are committed to President Cannon's vindication because we believe, having read the FBI report, we can reach only one conclusion, unless we're going to have a double standard for the president and a higher standard than has ever been imposed on any one in history, that we ought to consider some way to do this. But I would hope that, however we finally vote, whatever the final outcome may be, that we can all walk out of here with our heads high and say that we gave President Cannon every opportunity to demonstrate his honesty. What we want to make in the process is a fair judgment."

As much as I was inclined to agree with Senator Hammett, I was nearly exhausted from listening to his defense. I realize that one in his position must try to reframe the grounds of the argument, but I thought he might have done so much more clearly and much more quickly. Maybe Senators are so slow that they have to have things explained more fully. Or, maybe Senators just like to hear themselves talk.

Thursday's debate on the Resolution was a little more spirited, as Hammett and Rantallion sparred a few rounds. When I tuned in to watch, Hammett was trying to challenge Rantallion, but he was too much of a gentleman to really score any points against the North Carolina Nabob. Hammett interrupted, "Will the Senator—will the Senator yield?"

Rantallion must have needed to rest his jaw for a moment, because he replied, "I'd yield for a question. In all fairness, considering how few people are in here, I don't think anybody is going to call the rule on us."

Hammett was upset with something Rantallion had said earlier, and he interjected more than a question, when he said, "I don't think I've ever made any reference to any Republican president or colleague with some characterization. But I happened to be on the floor when the reference was made to President Cannon about 'Mr. Perjury.' It was demeaning. There's no evidence. Nobody has presented any proof that President Cannon has committed perjury, but that was stated by the Senator from North Carolina as a fact. We can all make spectacular statements. The Senator from North Carolina walked in on Tuesday and took about 10 words out of the report—liar, perjury on the witness stand, pressured someone, attended meeting—made a nice statement—it made a nice headline. It was taken out of the Independent Counsel's report. And the obvious reference was that it was President Cannon. And you made reference to President Cannon in that way, without any proof, taking some convicted felon's unverified statement. Now, where is the fairness in all of this? Who's going to be next? Maybe next time it'll be a Republican."

Rantallion was unfazed, asking, "Where's the question in all that?"

"You want questions? Where's the fairness? Where's the press demanding rights for President Cannon? What about due process? Has he had notice? Has he had a right to confront his accusers or to cross-examine a witness? Has he had a fair and impartial tribunal? Where is the due process guaranteed by the Constitution? That should keep you busy for a while," answered Hammett.

Rantallion dismissed the whole lot and said, "Come on, man. Let's cut the . . . .

But before Rantallion had completed his admonition, Hammett shot back, "I'm not backing off from what I've said. I've never said anything to characterize any president. But there's such a thing as fairness, and when somebody wants to ride roughshod over a man who's given years of honorable public service to his state and country, I'm going to defend him. And if that offends the Senator from North Carolina or a certain member of his staff, I regret it."

"Well," Senator, Rantallion replied, "I'll say it again, because that's in the record—'liar.' If I stated it some other way, I did not intend to. But that is a fair statement."

Senator Hammett was beginning to pick nits, which probably meant he knew his arguments against the Resolution were futile. "Well," he complained, "I think the Senator from North Carolina said, 'This is a fact. He's a known liar.' That's not a fact. That's his opinion."

"On the facts," Rantallion retorted, as scattered laughter could be heard throughout the Senate chamber.

"No, it's not a fact," Hammett again insisted. "and there are no facts in the record to support it. That might be your opinion. What I want to do is go back and check the record before I fully respond to the Senator from North Carolina, because I think it's been cleaned up a little since that outburst on the floor. And you were having a lot of fun just kicking our friend all over the place. And he is our friend! It wasn't some stranger you were kicking around."

Hammett was letting his anger show as he faced Rantallion across the aisle and said, "Now you may have gotten a lot of kick out of it, taking the words 'liar' and 'perjury' right out of the report, and then coming in and saying he's a known perjurer, liar. That's only an opinion. And, you know, we're still trying to figure out some way to get the truth on the record. And I say to my friend from North Carolina , I'd be glad to discuss with it with him privately or personally, or maybe you want to go out and make that statement where you're not protected, off the Senate floor."

"I have," Rantallion boasted.

"Go out in public and call him a liar," Hammett dared in return.

"I will," Rantallion promised.

"Go right ahead," Hammett said, not being able to think of a better response.

"I'll make talks all over North Carolina and justify my vote," Rantallion said, his patience growing short. "I'd be delighted to do so. Don't worry about that. Now, if I can get the floor back, Mr. President."

Hammett wasn't through, and he tried to continue the colloquy by saying, "Well, I want to just say to the Senator from South Carolina—"

Rantallion feigned offense, cutting Hammett short by insisting, "I'm the Senator from North Carolina, so get it right."

"I stand corrected," Hammett said without deference, "and I offer my sincere apology to the people of South Carolina."

At that point, the Chair interceded and said, "The Senator from North Carolina has the floor."

Having nothing to lose, Hammett ignored the ruling. "That's only your opinion."

"Oh, no! Oh, no! I'm saying right now as a matter of record: 'liar.' And I mean it," Rantallion objected. "Because I have seen those words from different witnesses, totally unrelated, all coming together. And I said, just so it's not 10 years ago back in the '80s, bring it right on up, from 1992 right on up until today. And I will point out in the record as facts that both he and his wife are liars and all of those other words that were used. And I did use it off the floor, and I have the record right here and the particular news conference. So I've stated that. I've got the record to substantiate it."

Senator Rantallion yielded the floor and made a show of striding out of the chamber, but Senator Hammett continued to complain, "We just had more expressions right out of the Independent Counsel's FBI file from the Senator from North Carolina, repeating words that have already been spoken on this floor, maybe that's fair game once they're in the public domain. And I think everyone knows those words are in the public domain because, first, someone in the Independent Counsel's office, and I'm not accusing George Jeffreys personally, someone in the Independent Counsel's office leaked those confidential FBI files to some Senator. Second, and I will name names here, second, because David Winderig, Senator Rantallion's top staff investigator on Whirlpool matters, leaked those confidential records to Floyd Crump, his former employer at Critics Unlimited, and to the *Washington Sun*, which immediately printed them."

"But," Hammett argued, "if we want go out and just assassinate somebody's character, we can do it right here on the floor, and we'd all be protected—doesn't make any difference who it is, but this happens to be someone who is President of the United States. I'd like to know what we're trying to do to James Cannon? What has he ever done to us to deserve this kind of treatment? Deserve that kind of statement on the Senate floor—perjury? That may be the opinion of two convicted felons down in Alabama and a Senator from North Carolina, but it's not supported by the evidence. And how far is it going to go if this debate gets bitter? So far, it's been fairly tame."

Laughter broke out after Hammett's last remark, but he continued seriously, saying. "We want to convince Senators on this floor that President Cannon has been completely truthful. Now, if you don't like James Cannon, that's one thing. But we're not going to sell President Cannon short, because we know him. But taking something out of some report, some convicted felon, and saying, 'Oh, I believe that because I don't want him to be President of the United States.' We can do better than that."

The real question was whether Senator Hammett could do better in lining up enough votes to defeat the Resolution, but it was clear that he hadn't done it yet. "Insofar as that Rantallion Resolution is concerned, obviously, those of us who oppose it are still trying to determine how we can achieve a majority against it. We believe that the mood is changing, and I'm seriously considering—and I've given the Majority Leader a copy of the unanimous consent request and a copy of the motion—to invite President Cannon into this chamber to let him state his case and submit to questions."

Part of the difficulty faced by the Democrats defending Cannon was that they didn't know what was going to hit them next. "I must say," Senator Hammett complained, "I'm a little disturbed when I hear today that David Winderig, of Senator Rantallion's staff, is still out investigating President Cannon. Now, I don't understand it. Either we have a record, or we don't have a record. I mean, when does this investigation stop? We're told it's not personal. But when do we stop investigating President Cannon? Who are the investigators besides Mr. Winderig? Are they there to try to help President Cannon? I doubt it. Are they trying to find evidence that would support President Cannon's position? I doubt it. But what kind of evidence are these investigators looking for down in Alabama? They're still trying to put that last nail in his coffin. Is that fair? What's the purpose of it? This man has been investigated by the Republicans more than anyone in history, and they're still investigating him today."

"So I would hope that we could invite President Cannon to the chamber. I think he's entitled to speak for himself. And I know some who say it won't make any difference. Well, the President will know the difference, and his family will know the difference. In our hearts, we're going to know the difference, if he was treated unfairly. I reserve the balance," Hammett said as he yielded the floor.

Senator Blott, the Majority Leader, spoke next and suggested that Senator Hammett might want to back off his complaints about the closed files. "With respect to the Independent Counsel's files, first, it ought to be clear that what we're talking about here is not just the Independent Counsel's report, there are also investigative records containing a great deal of information that is directly relevant to this Resolution," Blott said. "And so, if there is to be release of any information that is not now public, it ought to include everything. We ought not to be saying here that we just want the Independent Counsel's report out, but not the full investigative record. If we're going to have full disclosure, then we ought to have full disclosure.'

"The second point," Blott continued, "is that the FBI files are officially the property of the Executive Branch. I don't know how some senator came to have possession of them, but I don't think we can release them. If this is made public, a lot of innocent people will be embarrassed in this case. So, I think we have to evaluate carefully how we handle that."

Senator Doddridge wasn't going to let that threat deter the Democrats, and he did his best to undercut the impact of the information in the files. "I talked with an FBI investigator for Judge Walsh, the Iran-Contra Special Counsel, and he explained the standard practices in such investigations," Doddridge said. "He said, 'We take down everything people tell us, and we put it all in a file. If you'd interviewed as many government witnesses as I have over the years, you might have a little different opinion of what those 302s are worth.' The FBI didn't make any judgments or draw any conclusions about the President or the First Lady. And I think that's significant, because he felt, just watching on C-SPAN yesterday, that we were getting carried away with all this 'Independent Counsel report' business. They put every little bit of information they could find in that file, even statements from convicted felons seeking reduced sentences, and the file is up in S-407. We have to make our own judgment whether to believe that information."

Senator Rantallion was back on the floor, and he knew that the credibility of the files were essential to his case against the Cannons. "Maybe the FBI files are just summaries of interviews and copies of documents," Rantallion said, "but, the Office of Independent Counsel, based on those files, concluded it had probable cause to think serious crimes had been committed. Judge Jeffreys has requested authority from the Attorney General to pursue perjury charges against James and Diane Cannon. That's in the Independent Counsel's Report up in S-407, too. And it's in the newspapers."

Senator Bonhomme didn't let that pass uncontested. Having been tested as a member of the Whirlpool committee, Bonhomme knew how the game was played, and he said, "I think what has happened here is pitiful. Two people, and I personally believe two good people, the President and the First Lady, have been very seriously damaged because of activities of George Jeffreys and someone in the Senate, who breached the confidentiality of the Independent Counsel's files and blew this story open in the middle of an election campaign."

With more emotion in his voice than usual, Senator Bonhomme continued, "This whole report is based on the allegations of two convicted felons who changed their previous sworn testimony on something that was alleged to have happened 10 years ago. Someone made a decision that it would be politically advantageous to leak unsubstantiated unilateral declarations like that to end the political career of an otherwise very fine man. I think at least one Senator, maybe more, and their staffs are involved. I don't know who they are, maybe Mr. Winderig was not involved, and that's why I think we need a real investigation of this, perhaps even another Independent Counsel."

Not directly accusing Senator Diletto for the leak, Bonhomme made his point indirectly, when he said, "FBI reports in the Independent Counsel files—and let's talk a little bit about that. That's important stuff. The reason the Independent Council uses the FBI is because they have usually done a very credible job. I don't know of any area where they didn't do a credible job, with the possible exception of the Wedtech and H.U.D. kickback matter involving a Senator, where the allegations were coming every time you turned around, and they missed some. But these files often contain accusations by nuts, by people who are unstable. They contain accusations by political enemies. In this case, they contain accusations by two felons who were seeking reduced sentences and were being coached by the Independent Counsel. And if we release the reports, of course, there are plenty of reporters who will publish them as though they're the gospel truth."

Senator Doddridge momentarily broke the Senate's code of silence when he picked up on Bonhomme's argument and said, "Well, I think there's a larger question, too. No one seems to know how Senator Dil—a certain Senator and his staff came to have the Independent Counsel report and the FBI files, or who authorized Mr. Winderig to leak them to the *Sun*. But, I would hope that when we conclude here, regardless of the outcome, that everybody can say President Cannon was accorded fair treatment. That's the least he can expect. Surely, the Republican members can recall the words of Senator Dolor, during the Tower nomination debate a few years ago, asking for the same thing when he was Minority Leader."

The Democrats must have been winning some votes, because Senator Blott returned to the floor and said, "If I may simply say one thing—there is much disagreement on this Resolution, but I think there is a growing agreement that it has gone on long enough. And it is my hope that we will be able to bring this matter to a conclusion as soon as there has been a full debate, and certainly this week. And it is my hope that we can now bring it to a conclusion. We are supposed to be in recess, and members need to be in their home states."

"I don't want to create any impression of unfairness," Blott protested to avoid the charge. "I don't want to prevent any Senator from having the fullest opportunity to express his or her opinions, but at some point, as we all know, the debate is over and delay begins. I don't think we've reached that point yet. We've listened, we've debated, we've evaluated, we've discussed, we've read, and I believe the time has come to vote, and I hope we will do so soon."

Senator Hammett was recognized again, and he returned to a topic he had been discussing earlier. "I think it's fair to say that our side was not consulted about the continuing investigation by Senator Rantallion's staff, a unilateral investigation. And I guess they're going to investigate until the last vote is cast. Maybe Mr. Winderig will run in right before the vote, and Senator Rantallion will say, 'Hold it, I've got something. I just got it over the transom from Floyd Crump—or the *American Speculator*. We'll go out and investigate that.' They were down at the Madison Hotel, I think, in Montgomery or somewhere, checking out who knows what, and I understand it came out quite well. Who knows what else they're checking out?"

"Point of personal privilege," shouted Senator Rantallion, demanding to be recognized. "Mr. Winderig is not a member of my staff, and I'd appreciate it if the Minority Leader would stop insinuating that I had anything to do with the leaking of the FBI files to the media."

"If I'm mistaken, I will apologize," Hammett said, "but I am quite certain I saw Mr. Winderig handing documents to the Senator from North Carolina during his speech on Tuesday, and I have received information today that he is down in Alabama trying to dig up more dirt. "

"He is not a member of my staff," Rantallion insisted.

"Oh," Hammett asked, "since when?"

"Since yesterday," Rantallion replied, yielding the floor and leaving the chamber before anyone could ask him another question. What he hadn't said, and what did not become public knowledge for several weeks, was that David Winderig had only been reassigned. He was still on the public payroll and would be back in the news again later for leaking documents from a House committee. Winderig no longer worked for Rantallion, though. He was now in the employ of Congressman Bardus on the House Government Operations and Oversight Committee.

"Be that as it may, we are asking for fairness, and my point is that the right to confront and cross-examine, impartial tribunal, all the things that make up due process, I think ought to be accorded to the President,"

Hammett reiterated. "This wasn't supposed to be a trial, but it's sort of been a trial by leak and innuendo, and I think we've had enough. But we want a vote. That was part of RBN's coverage. 'Democrats delay the vote.' We're not delaying the vote. We've got to overcome all these leaks that were going out early on, garbage after garbage dumped on President Cannon by the Independent Counsel."

Then, raising the stakes in the drama, Senator Hammett said, "We want to do what we can to make certain that the President has a chance to make his case to the Senate. I move, therefore, that the Rules be suspended and that President James Madison Cannon be invited to address the Senate and answer questions in closed session tomorrow, Friday, at 10:00 a.m."

The quorum bells started ringing. To my surprise, and I think everyone's, the Senate adopted Hammett's motion for a closed session to hear and question President Cannon. Had all the members been present, it might have been closer, but the motion passed 63-10. Senator Blott, wanting to give the appearance of fairness, did not try to block the motion, so it passed rather handily. The only votes against it came from Diletto (R-NY), Rantallion (R-NC), Duke (R-NC), Fossor (R-ID), Shurmond (R-SC), Surrepo (R-PA), Medlar (R-MO), Shanker (R-AL), Hatchet (R-UT), and Frenezul (R-OK). Senator Hammett and the Democrats were pleased, but they knew too well that the vote on their motion did not reflect the tally on the Resolution.

Chapter Thirty Four

President Cannon immediately canceled his scheduled campaign events and flew back to Washington to prepare for his appearance before the Senate. All of the pundits were busy punditting each other, predicting what the President would say and how his appearance would affect the vote on the Resolution. As if they had a clue or anyone cared what they thought. Then after President Cannon spent five hours before the Senate behind closed doors, it took all of 15 minutes before Senate staffers began leaking details and another 10 minutes before Senators were available for sound bites on the evening news. The viewers learned that Senator Hammett thought the President did a wonderful job, and Senator Rantallion thought the President failed to change a single vote.

The best thing about the closed session on Friday, as far as most Senators were concerned, was that they had two days to either test the wind among their constituents or to hold news conferences. Most did both.

Senator Bonhomme met the press in the Senate Radio-TV Gallery on Saturday and told reporters, "I have never seen more vivid, stronger, or more honest testimony given in this body in the 15 years, almost 15 years I've been here. And I tell you, I think people all over America would have been impressed by it. The fact of the matter is they believe the President. And they believe the First Lady. Anybody who believes in this country and believes in our system of jurisprudence will give President and Mrs. Cannon the benefit of the doubt. But there's a lot more proof for them than that.

"Furthermore," Bonhomme said, revealing one reason he spoke so boldly, "I think that the American people are rallying behind them and that public opinion in this country is very favorable to President and Mrs. Cannon. In my state, for instance, here in my Washington office on Thursday, we received around 500 calls. On Friday 1,000. Eight-five percent of them were pro-Cannon.

"If President Cannon survives the vote on this Resolution and is re-elected," Senator Bonhomme predicted, "I believe that he's going to be an even better president, and this experience, though hurtful and scarring, I think will help him to be concerned about the downtrodden; those who are defamed and have to listen to ridiculous accusations about members of their family; those who have their privacy invaded or their rights violated; those who are unfairly treated by the press and by the government. Having been smeared himself, I think he's going to be even more concerned. Which one of you would like to have unsubstantiated unilateral allegations said about you? How would you like to go through that?"

Then, Senator Bonhomme snapped a verbal chalk line and gave the press his road map to the real scandal. "I'm not saying that George Jeffreys gave the confidential documents to a certain Senator. I'm not saying that Chairman Diletto let his duties as head of the Dolor Presidential Campaign influence his conduct of the Whirlpool investigation. I'm not saying that Congressman Leech released any confidential files. Okay, I might say that about Mr. Leech. And because it's now public knowledge I don't have to suggest that, just because the main flunky from Critics Unlimited was on Senator Rantallion's staff, that he could be the source of the leaks. But, the plain fact of the matter is that these right-wing groups have been receiving confidential documents and reports and sending faxes to every newspaper that would print them, ever since Ellende Varken began her campaign of false charges back in 1992."

"I hope somehow we do get to the truth of how and why this happened," Senator Bonhomme said, sounding as if he had just explained it. "What happened is just too cute, too slick, too contrived—an organized smear campaign. Of course, this latest charge will not be the last one. I've seen these people try and smear President and Mrs. Cannon for the last five years. But I don't think they've succeeded here. I think there's an overwhelming case in favor of President Cannon and the First Lady. I don't think there's a jury in this land that would find them guilty of anything."

Appearing on *Face the Nation* that Sunday, Senator Doddridge elaborated on many of those same themes. When introduced by the host, he said, "I would say good morning but—last week, I made a prediction that nothing good was going to come of this. That at the end of the whole process people were going to be hurt, Senators were going to be uncertain, and that it was probably a mistake to invite the President to appear before the Senate. I still think people have been hurt by this process, but I think that the good thing that's happening is that the American people are speaking out, not just about the Rantallion Resolution, because a Senate debate does not bring this kind of outpouring of public sentiment. The American people are speaking out about an abusive system, about an Independent Counsel process that has gone wrong. And the American people alone can cure this system by speaking out."

"A number of polls reported in the media suggest that by margins of about two to one," Doddridge said, "the American people are inclined to believe President Cannon and the First Lady over their accusers. In my own office I can tell you that our calls are running about 75 percent in favor of the Cannons, but what is interesting is that so many people are talking about what's gone wrong with the system. And the fact that this is the kind of situation that our country can't tolerate any longer. No political agenda warrants what we have seen for the last four years. No political agenda, however laudatory, justifies the personal destruction of two fine human beings."

"What has happened right from the beginning, from January 20, 1993, is that the various interest groups, together with disappointed Stuart partisans, set about attempting to damage President Cannon, and when the system itself did not accommodate their lies, when the Independent Counsel came up empty, they then leaked it to the media and created the public circus atmosphere that we've seen for more than a week. What we've seen for the last few days is absolutely wrong. But only the American people can fix it. And that is why it is so important for people in this country, no matter how they think we should vote on the Rantallion Resolution, to be speaking out. And they should be speaking out very loudly on November 5th."

"Now, of course, I'm biased about what's been going on for the past few days in the Senate," Doddridge admitted. "But I think President Cannon is an enormously strong person who has endured what no one should ever endure. Can you imagine yourself being held up to what he's been held up to? Can you put yourself in his place and try to imagine it? He has been asked, well, why don't you just resign? He could have gotten out and ended it, but he went forward with it, and he went forward with it for a very specific reason—he and the First Lady are innocent."

"I have spent a lot of time with President Cannon over the last two years," he said, "and I want to tell you about a change in a human being. Earlier in the year, the President was very concerned about his political future and about the personal pain caused to his family and friends by the Whirlpool hearings and the Independent Counsel. And then President Cannon made a decision, and the decision was he really didn't care whether he was re-elected or not. That he was very happy with what he had been able to accomplish, and he wanted his family to enjoy their life together. During his meeting with the Senate, President Cannon was speaking as a person who, in his own mind, didn't care how this came out. And it was a wonderfully cleansing kind of thing, an inspiring kind of thing, for him to finally be able to personally refute all the lies."

At that point, several of the panelists began asking, "Do you think the Senate believed the President? Did he overcome these latest allegations? Will his appearance before the Senate make any difference in the Senate's vote on the Rantallion Resolution?"

Senator Doddridge replied, "For the five hours he was before the Senate in closed session, President Cannon's testimony was absolutely consistent. That cannot be said of the statements of his accusers. I believe President Cannon. I have no idea where the votes are, but I think we have a good chance to defeat the Resolution."

"Senator, you criticized the process. What did you mean by that?"

"Well," Doddridge explained again, "this was a process that's now gone on for something like four or five years, which I think is too long. This is a process in which, beginning on day one, the right-wing interest groups began having daily strategy meetings about how to get President Cannon. Howard Mellonskoff's foundations poured millions of dollars into the *American Speculator* and other right wing groups. They assigned teams of investigators to go out and find what they could and make up the rest, so it was an inquisition right from the beginning. The abuse of the oversight process in Congress was tragic. And the press, well, I won't comment on the role of the press in this whole shameful process. You can read the facts about that in Gene Lyon's book, *Fools for Scandal.*"

"So, you are saying that we should have laws against interest groups expressing their opinions on public officials or issues of public concern or the press reporting those opinions?"

"No, just a second," Doddridge said. "This was a Senate out of control. Where the Republican staff suddenly has a complete set of the confidential investigative files from the so-called Independent Counsel. Where those files are then leaked by Mr. Winderig to political interest groups and certain members of the press. Where interest group activity was drummed up and finally culminated in this travesty that the country has lived through now for the past week. And I think that's wrong. And I think that has to be corrected."

"Now I'm not sure that I could codify precisely how it should be corrected," he added, "but what I am suggesting is that what is at issue is fundamental fairness. And that this process is not fair. That this process is truly a witchhunt, and it's a witchhunt conducted by people who, in order to further their political careers and ideological agenda, are willing to destroy people. The antidote to it is less a new code of behavior than it is the voice of the people. The American people have to look at what has happened and decide themselves whether it's right or wrong. And if they decide it's wrong, they should say so, they should speak out. That is the cure for the sickness."

"Senator, are you suggesting that the problem could be eliminated with stronger criminal laws applying to members and their staff for talking to the press?"

"That is obviously a ridiculous suggestion," Doddridge replied as if he were talking to a bunch of idiots. "I am suggesting that the Independent Counsel Act is a travesty. I am suggesting that the oversight process has gone crazy. I'm suggesting that the whole process of making up dirt and leaking information to the press has become the way we do things around here because people have concluded that it works. And the time has come for the American people to weigh in by simply stating how they feel about this and casting their votes in the upcoming election. I think that the best thing that could happen for our country right now, is for this whole seedy thing to blow up in the faces of those who perpetrated it."

"Senator, how can you expect the voters or the Senate to make an informed decision when their is so much conflicting evidence and conflicting testimony?"

Somewhat more thoughtfully, Doddridge answered, "As I said last Tuesday, when it's all over, people are still going to be debating who did what. I think that the evidence is very strongly in favor of President Cannon and the First Lady. Their testimony was consistent, that of Roby Douglas and Josh Banaghan was not. A document is going to be released tomorrow, which indicates the misstatements of truth in the testimony of Roby Douglas and Josh Banaghan. And all of the inconsistent behavior—the lies to federal agencies, the cozy financial relationship with Cannon's enemies, the collaboration with partisan interest groups, the leaks to certain members of the media, the very unusual relationship with the so-called Independent Counsel. All of these things make the case for President and Mrs. Cannon on the facts."

"Where there is a factual dispute," he added, "obviously we should try to figure out what actually happened. We used to have such a process around here. The perversion of the process isn't so much that the staffers and interest groups are combing through the country looking for dirt, although I think that is perverse. But when they invent lies and peddle those to the media outside of the process that we have for resolving it, that's wrong. Many FBI reports contain allegations of something that, if true, would possibly constitute a reason for impeachment or referring charges. The job of a prosecutor or a legislative committee is supposed to be to make its best judgment on the facts, but the prosecutorial tone and the leaking, that was something that I think was particularly offensive and wrong. When the judgment is made, and then the appeal is the inflammatory process of leaks, that is unconscionable. And apparently it's the way things are now done as a matter of course. I mean it's been done in this instance."

"Senator, the vote on the Resolution could go either way at this point. If the President is absolved, you yourself said a week ago he was deeply hurt. Do you think he would be emotionally ready to continue in office even if he is re-elected."

"I'm really glad you asked that question," Senator Doddridge said enthusiastically, "because let me say this about President Cannon. The one thing, as he said in his testimony, that he has come out of this ordeal with is an even greater sensitivity, and he already had a great one, for people who are hurt by unfounded rumors in the press, for people who are abused in one way or another by the government, and a greater appreciation for constitutional rights of the people. We created a bill of rights and a legal system to protect those who are charged with crimes. Our system presumes people innocent. All kinds of processes we develop in our country to protect people, and they are incorporated in our Constitution. Those processes meant nothing in the case of President Cannon and the First Lady. In the case of President Cannon, anything went. Any law, any rule, any decency could be broken in order to accomplish the personal destruction of President Cannon and the First Lady in furtherance of a narrow partisan political agenda. So what has happened is that President Cannon is probably the most sensitive person right now in America about the importance in our system for protecting those who have been accused. And I think that is going to bring yet another gift to the nation during his second term."

"Senator, could you tell us how you see the upcoming floor vote? Some have expressed concern about the possibility of some last minute revelations on the floor, that some additional charges might be made about something else."

"Oh, I predicted it last week," Doddridge exclaimed. "That's the way these people operate. Hold on to your hat. I've heard that Mr. Jeffreys is planning a public campaign of some kind. I am sure that Critics United and the Lynch Legal Foundation, and these other groups are out doing their thing. And their function, remember, is basically twofold. One, make up lies; two, spread lies. I'm sure they will be doing that over the next 24 hours or so. No doubt about it. Get ready for some more surprises."

The Republicans had equal time on the other networks, and their assessment of the situation was a negative mirror image of the view presented by Doddridge, moderated only slightly by the public opinion polls that seemed to show considerable support for the President. The Sunday gabfests were intended to generate additional public pressure on Senators, but the real action was going to be in the Senate, where the vote was scheduled for Monday afternoon. I finished my class in time to get home and watch the final debate, not knowing exactly what to expect.

Senator Hatchet closed the debate for the Republicans, and he seemed confident that the Rantallion Resolution would pass. "The vote we are about to cast brings to an end a difficult and unpleasant chapter in the history of the Senate's responsibility," Hatchet said. "When the tally is announced, there will be no winners, other than our system of government and our Constitution. There will be no celebrations, no back-slapping, no cries of victory."

"If the Senate adopts this Resolution," he told his colleagues, "there will be deep personal disappointment for the President and the First Lady. For those who have supported them with such loyalty and conviction, there will be profound sorrow. And for those of us who reluctantly came to support this Resolution, there will be the lasting knowledge that we came to a different conclusion from that reached by our colleagues, for whom we have such respect and high regard."

"When the tally is announced, I do not believe the result will accurately reflect the struggle so many members underwent in arriving at their vote," Hatchet noted in an effort to protect those in his party who would defy the opinion polls. "The decision has been very difficult for senators on both sides of the aisle."

Trying to sound magnanimous, Hatchet warned, "I would hope that those across this land who watched these proceedings or followed them would not be swayed by simplistic characterizations of the outcome. Anyone who watched as Senator after Senator spoke, and listened to the care with which those speeches have been delivered, knows that these were deeply personal convictions. Nor, despite reports and rhetoric to the contrary, is this a referendum on the Cannon administration. It is about the rule of law."

"This is a unique case, a unique situation," he declared, not sounding entirely insincere. "I do not believe we'll have another investigation with this number of allegations and this degree of controversy in my lifetime. With the passage of time, there will be an opportunity for calm reflections on the lessons of this experience. But that must wait until the sound and fury of this wrenching struggle have subsided."

Then, in closing, he generously said, "President and Mrs. Cannon have made important contributions to building a better America. Regardless of the outcome of this vote, they will, I am sure, make many, many more."

When Senator Hatchet yielded the floor, Senator Hammett rose to close for the Democrats supporting the Cannons and opposing the Rantallion Resolution. But before Hammett could begin his remarks, Senator Diletto grabbed his microphone and demanded recognition. The Vice

President, in the chair prepared for the unlikely event of a tie vote, accommodated the insistent Diletto and said with resignation, "The Chair recognizes the Senator from New York."

"Mr. President," Diletto said, "I have certain information to put in the record relating to a *Wall Street Record* editorial. I ask unanimous consent that this matter be put in the record."

"Without objection, so ordered. The Chair recognizes the Minority Leader."

Senator Hammett sounded rather solemn as he began, "Today, I am standing with my President, and I'm standing proudly with him. He is still the right man for the job. And let me first save all of the pundits a lot of time. Make no mistake about it, James Cannon hasn't lost. We all should have demonstrated the kind of courage that James Cannon and his family showed during this ordeal."

I could tell Hammett didn't think he had the votes. "We have witnessed an oversight process gone reckless," he said. "We have seen the Senate become a pipeline for gossip and smear—a peddler of rumors and leaks, a partisan hotbed of character assassination. What have we come to here? What happened to decency? What happened to justice and fair play? We're Senators here, not snoops. And I think the United States Senate is a few moments away from setting a dangerous precedent. What we do today will directly affect tomorrow, and I believe what we're about to do is bad news for the United States Senate."

Making one last run at the process, Hammett said, "An historic precedent, included in our constitutional debates and reaffirmed in the *Federalist Papers*, is that the President of the United States can only be removed by the process of impeachment. And the last time I checked, James Cannon was President of the United States, and there has been no Resolution for his impeachment. He won the election in 1992, and he is still in office, much to the dismay of the Independent Counsel and the other right-wing hate mongers in this country."

"Oh yes, the Senate has a role, a critical role," Hammett conceded. "It has the opportunity to vote on his proposals and to monitor the implementation of policies and expenditures. I know that role, because I frequently voted against the legislation offered by President Stuart, and I voted to hold hearings on the actions of his administration. And, as the former Republican Leader once said, 'Everything that goes around, comes around in the Senate.' Sooner or later you're going to find something you said when you were trying to make the opposite argument."

Hammett mimicked Hatchet's sop to those who might have struggled with their vote, when he said, "I happen to believe the case against President Cannon and the First Lady is very thin. I think it's unfortunate. The fact is that a number of Senators, Senators whom I respect on both sides of the aisle, have expressed concerns, which I believe are genuine, even though I do not share them."

"James Cannon walked the extra mile and then some," Hammett declared. "But what did it get him? It looks like from the start he's been walking the gang plank. The press, the right-wing interest groups, the Republicans in Congress, the American people have been watching James Cannon every waking moment since he first announced for president. We had Senators saying he hadn't proven his case beyond a reasonable doubt. Since when did that become the standard of evidence for an American citizen? Reasonable doubt of what? Some leak or innuendo, he has to disprove?"

"So I said, 'Let President Cannon have his day in court. Bring him into this Senate. Let him answer his critics and the charges made by a couple of convicted felons. Let him ask some Senators where the leaks came from. And let him make his statement.' We met in closed session for five hours, and I think President Cannon fully refuted every charge and every innuendo made against both him and the First Lady. Some of the Senators who were his most vocal critics on the Whirlpool Committee sat mute, but I am certain they still intend to vote against him now," Hammett noted.

Then, restating the case he had made last week on the floor, Hammett said, "We spent precious little time during the past four years on the deficit, Medicare, Medicaid, Social Security, health care reform, crime prevention, job creation, Americorps, tax relief for the middle class, student loans, or anything else of real significance to the American people. Rather, votes have been decided by tabloid versions of President Cannon's personal life and events that allegedly transpired before he became President. Faceless people known only as 'he/she' or 'T-13' have woven fanciful talks of pressure, real estate deals, campaign contributions, bank loans, women, and other outrageous conspiracy theories. Two convicted felons changed their previous testimony and made charges against the President in hope that the Independent Counsel would ask that their sentences be reduced. A judge who's not a judge has hurled a nonexistent conversation onto the front pages. Nonexistent. A former political opponent with lots of money and a lapdog scribe for the *New York Times* have played this game for six years. And a fired state employee who couldn't stand up to a polygraph. They all made the evening news. Never saw the retraction."

His anger now showing, Senator Hammett must have known he was winning no new votes when he said, "And one could only guess at who dug up this motley crew of witnesses, why and how their bizarre tales landed on the front pages. But two things are certain: First, a continuing series of leaks has savaged the reputation and family of, and finally the public's confidence in, President James Madison Cannon. Second, James Madison Cannon and Diane Rankin Cannon broke no laws, rules, or regulations with regard to conflict of interest or anything else. Speaker after speaker has affirmed this point, although some have left the false implication that they may have lied under oath, based on contradictions with testimony from a couple of convicted felons. Shame!"

"You each had an opportunity to personally examine the Independent Counsel's report that somehow wound up in the hands of a Senator and in the press. It's not a vacuum up there. But we must take care not to divulge any confidential information, even now, as we face this historic and unprecedented vote," he argued again, but with less passion.

"So I'm obviously disappointed," Hammett admitted, knowing that he would continue to have to work with the Republican majority, regardless of the outcome of the vote on the Rantallion Resolution. "I agree with others who've spoken. We have other work to do, and we'll get it done. This is not going to leave a permanent scar. And I agree there shouldn't be any cheering and clapping and applauding after this vote. After what we've done to this good man and his wife, maybe we ought to hang our heads, whatever the vote."

"And I know we've had some spirited debate," Hammett said with some resignation. "And I want to thank members on both sides. And I want to thank President Cannon. I talked to him a couple of times today. He knows this is politics, and he can count votes. He knows that there are more Republicans than Democrats. That's not much solace, but I guess, having been in politics for 22 years, he can understand that. Some never wanted James Cannon to be President, and they think they're finally going to get their wish. I think it's unfortunate."

"And so I just say to my colleagues," Hammett said before closing, "I think we're making a mistake even considering this Resolution. We did our best. And I want to thank particularly those Republican Senators who will vote to support the President, because I know the pressure was terrific daily, minute by minute, on the other side to line up everybody against President Cannon. I know it takes a lot of courage."

Finally, sounding like he was giving a funeral eulogy for a fallen comrade, Hammett concluded his remarks with high emotion and said, "So we might pass this Resolution asking that James Cannon and Diane Cannon be charged with perjury. It will be the end of his chances for re-election. They will be gone. America will have lost two fine public servants. The President will have won, because he stood by his word and his family."

Quorum bells could be heard ringing, and Senators milled about the floor, talking in small groups, nervously trying to predict the imminent outcome of their deliberations or to avoid thinking about it. Then the roll call began, with only 91 Senators in the chamber, the rest concluding that they would be better served campaigning in their home states or, perhaps, just taking a walk. Despite the battle of words that had polarized the debate, the most persuasive evidence came from the polling data. When the final vote was tallied, the Rantallion Resolution failed by a vote of 44 ayes and 47 noes.

Chapter Thirty Five

The failure of Dorkman's Impeachment Resolution in the House and the Rantallion Resolution in the Senate were a reflection of the public opinion polls and a fair indication that the Whirlpool investigation was finished. Little noted at the time but equally telling was the fact that the Birmingham grand jury had expired without issuing any additional indictments.

Yet, George Jeffreys was not going to be denied. Awaiting the outcome of the Senate vote, he had been huddled all week with Della Beckwith at the offices of Finkelstein, Dolan, and Stone. He would take his case to the public, Justice Department policies against discussing ongoing investigations notwithstanding. He knew that Harriet Otis was afraid to call his hand, and if someone else tried, he would always have Judge Bowner in Atlanta and Judge Chase in DC to ratify his excuses.

The first indication of the aggressive public relations campaign that was to follow was a press release from FDS detailing a series of speeches Jeffreys would be giving during the next week—the American Tobacco Advertisers Association in Raleigh, the Amway Distributors' Convention in Salt Lake City, and Hostus University in Virginia Beach. That same day *Newsweek* reported that Jeffreys had granted an exclusive interview, giving reporter Robert Bauman "extraordinary access, sitting for a three-hour interview, and allowing a photographer to take behind-the-scenes pictures, raising his profile and drawing attention to his pursuit of the Cannons." Then there was the cover picture on *The New York Times Magazine*, with Jeffreys, Gedney, Hathorne, and LeCraw standing in front of the federal courthouse, hands on their hips and smiling like the Four Horsemen of the Apocalypse.

No one was paying any attention to the election campaign, as Dolor rambled aimlessly without effect and Cannon spoke glibly without risk. The President's once-daunting 20-point lead had withered to only seven points as a result of the leaked report from the Independent Counsel and the abrasive debate on the Rantallion Resolution, but Dolor could not seize the momentum, and Peabody had been written off as a jug-eared joke. If Cannon was to be stopped, the Republicans' only hope was for

George Jeffreys to assume the mantle as Field Marshal of the Fifth Column.

Only three days after the Senate vote on the Rantallion Resolution, Jeffreys was scheduled to make a major speech to the American Tobacco Advertising Association in Raleigh, North Carolina. There was plenty of advance hype in the press, and both CNN and C-SPAN planned to carry it live. I had decided to ignore it, but Lindsey asked me to tape it for her to use in one of her classes. At least that's what she said. She was going to be in Montgomery that day for the presentation of the first Lurleen B. Wallace Award of Courage to Vivian Malone Jones. It was an historic event, and an ironic one, because the award would be presented by George Wallace, the man who had stood in the schoolhouse door to prevent Ms Jones from attending the University of Alabama, and the two had never previously met.

Anyway, I never had been able to figure out how to program a damn VCR to record at a certain time, so I just watched the speech as I recorded it. I was glad C-SPAN was covering it, because they always started broadcasting early, and the camera caught Mr. Butts, the guy who dressed up like a big cigarette and usually stalked Ira Dolor's campaign appearances, trying to crash the speech. He was summarily put out.

The other nice thing about C-SPAN coverage was that they also broadcast the introductions, instead of having the news readers chattering about what they had to say. Jeffreys was introduced by some vice president of the American Tobacco Advertisers Association, and his remarks must have been written, or at least approved in advance, by Jeffreys or Della Beckwith. "The Republican agenda has already given our friends control of Congress," he beamed. "and it will soon capture the hearts and minds of the people in this nation, thanks in part to the diligent work of George Jeffreys. But before introducing our honored guest today, let me say a word to the President of the United States, who has talked a lot recently about building a bridge to the 21st Century. With all due respect, Mr. President, if you get to build that bridge, you had better remember that George Jeffreys will be the troll under that bridge, and it will soon be washed away in a whirlpool of scandal and indictments."

Real cute. That's about what I would've expected from the mind of someone whose day job was promoting Joe Camel.

Jeffreys giggled at the remark and smiled proudly as the host read from an extensive resume Jeffreys had provided. After savoring a standing ovation, Jeffreys expressed his appreciation for the generous introduction, even though he had written most of it, then launched into his prepared text.

"I want to begin by talking about something that we don't hear much about these days—integrity. Old-fashioned integrity is important,"

Jeffreys said, as if he'd even know what it was. "Public integrity, business integrity, and spousal integrity. The Framers of our Constitution were realists about man's sinful nature, and they knew that men are not angels. They knew that the common people, confused by the vagaries of opinion and interest that corrupt democratic governments, might elect undeserving scoundrels who put politics above personal honor and private property. If the average citizens lack sufficient wisdom for self-government, then virtuous men of greater integrity must restrain them from ruining this nation. That remains as true in 1996 as it was in 1798."

"It is no less essential in business," he declared, and I thought I saw some in the audience shifting uncomfortably at that. "Our free enterprise system of capitalism does not require that participants be angelic, but the basic moral values are crucial. Those of you in the tobacco advertising industry know how these traits play out day to day. You know that words count. Promises matter. Terms in contracts have meaning. If a cigarette manufacturer pledges to pay his workers the minimum wage, that's a commitment. His word is his bond. In short, integrity—old-fashioned honesty—is vitally important."

"This brings me to my topic for today," Jeffreys said with much fanfare, "Whirlpool—A Perspective from Birmingham and Washington. Each of you have a right to advertise tobacco products, and that is at the core of our First Amendment values. The people have a right to know everything about their public officials, and it is my duty to help them understand the issues. The details of the various matters that have been labeled 'Whirlpool' have some Byzantine twists and turns. At heart, though, it's not difficult. I propose to offer a brief summary, one that I hope won't make you woozy."

Perhaps hoping for more extensive coverage or just offering a pat on the back, he said, "The Whirlpool story has its roots in the 1992 presidential campaign, when an enterprising *New York Times* reporter raised questions about Whirlpool Development Corporation, a real estate partnership. The Cannon campaign commissioned a report which found no wrongdoing and concluded that the Cannons had, in fact, lost money on the deal. Whirlpool, as a public issue, essentially disappeared after James Cannon very narrowly defeated President Stuart. Then, the United States Attorney in Birmingham indicted Roby Douglas in an unrelated matter, and Mr. Douglas began making statements to the media. In October 1993, word leaked to the press that President and Mrs. Cannon had been named in a criminal referral drafted by Ellende Varken, an outstanding investigator with the Resolution Trust Corporation."

"With congressional and media interest renewed in Whirlpool," he added, "the Attorney General appointed a career employee from the Department of Justice to handle the prosecution of Roby Douglas. After repeated demands by Roby Douglas, Senator Diletto, Congressman Leech, and other concerned Republicans, Attorney General Harriet G. Otis finally appointed an Independent Counsel in early 1994. She appointed Kenneth Burke. Later, I was appointed to the position by Judge Chase, a North Carolina native, and I might say I owe that appointment to the two very fine United States Senators from this state, longtime friends of mine and longtime supporters of the tobacco industry."

After prolonged applause from the audience, Jeffreys continued, "Whirlpool is now about several related things. Let me be more specific. Whirlpool is about Jessie Banaghan. We convicted this woman before a jury of her peers after a three-month trial. Since the trial, Ms. Banaghan has refused to testify before our grand jury in Birmingham. She is now in handcuffs and leg irons, incarcerated for refusing to tell us what we want to know, and I can promise you that she will remain so until she agrees to cooperate. She was more than willing to spill her story to the author of *Blood Sucker*, so what is she hiding from us? Some would suggest she is trying to protect President Cannon."

Following more applause, the litany began, "Whirlpool is about Randolph Webster, the former Associate Attorney General of the United States. Mr. Webster is in prison for overbilling clients of the Bankhead Law Firm in Montgomery. I had hoped he would cooperate with my investigation, but he has given us absolutely nothing that we can use against the Cannons. We are now considering additional charges against Mr. Webster when he is released from prison, and that might well refresh his memory and loosen his tongue. Whirlpool is about Jim Bibb Vance, the disgraced former governor of Alabama who borrowed money for one purpose and used it for another. He has not been at all helpful. Whirlpool is about Bill Godwin, a real estate agent who admitted hiding assets in a bankruptcy proceeding and pleaded guilty. Whirlpool is about $50,000 from a fraudulent loan that benefited the Whirlpool Development Corporation, owned by the Cannons. Whirlpool is about Roby Douglas, a respected former judge who, to his credit, admitted his past mistakes and has cooperated fully with our investigation."

I dashed to the kitchen to get a beer, but I don't think I missed anything in that selective line-up. I didn't hear Jeffreys mention Josh Banaghan's name or the fact that he had been convicted on 18 felony counts. Or that he might now be cooperating with the Independent Counsel. Perhaps that was inadvertent, or maybe he just didn't want to say anything that might make Banaghan a less valuable witness.

"It would have been very helpful, frankly, if every person with relevant information had simply come forward and told us everything we wanted to know. We did not meet with that to the extent that I would have liked," he complained. "People still have, as you know, certain constitutional rights, and there is nothing we can do about those technicalities."

"But Whirlpool is not solely about events in Alabama. It is also about questions—and I must be careful to stress that they are still only questions at this point—about the integrity of the Cannon administration in Washington. It is about whether they deceived federal investigators. It is about the White House Travel office firings of those seven dedicated career employees. It is, in short," Jeffreys declared, sounding more like Ira Dolor, "about public trust and how the Cannons have abused that trust."

Then, because you could tell it was bothering him and not because anyone in that audience would have cared, Jeffreys asked, "Why was it thought wise and prudent to appoint an Independent Counsel and transfer these investigations outside the Justice Department? Was it done as a political payback for Watergate and Iran-Contra and all the other prosecutions during Republican administrations? Of course not. Was it done because Dick Leech and Gastone Diletto wanted to embarrass and distract this president? No, they could do that with hearings."

"The simple answer," he said, answering his own phony question, "is that the Attorney General could not be trusted to conduct this investigation. The pressures, the divided loyalty, were too much for Harriet Otis, and the public would never feel entirely easy about the vigor and thoroughness with which it was pursued. In short, if the subject of the investigation is the President or his wife, you must seek an outsider with experience and integrity, such as myself, who is not interested in currying favor with those in high office. Nine million dollars is a small price to pay for an Independent Counsel with impeccable integrity."

Jeffreys then took a moment to downplay all the revelations about his conflicts, but he avoided dealing with them, instead attacking anyone who would dare question his motives. "When I was first appointed Independent Counsel, the commentary was very favorable," he said, overstating the situation by a considerable degree. "As the indictments and convictions have mounted there have been unfounded accusations of a partisan agenda. President Cannon was on television a few days ago, saying that I was out to get him. As history teaches us—and as the lawyers on my staff, like Bart Gedney, John Hathorne, and Walt Lecraw who have investigated and prosecuted corrupt public officials before, will tell you—attacks and accusations on the prosecutor are routine in these political corruption cases."

Next, revealing what sounded like insecurity about having no criminal trial experience, Jeffreys touted the help. "I have a highly motivated legal team, having recruited the best and the brightest, mostly former government lawyers from U.S. Attorney's offices during the Stuart administration," he said, failing to mention the fact that many of them held grudges for losing their jobs when Cannon took office, as did Jeffreys. "I have also employed investigators from the FBI and the IRS. These are not spin doctors. They are battle-tested public servants, men of integrity like retired General Eugene Cavaignac.

"In addition," he said, trying to pretend that his public support went beyond the right-wing scandal machine but not doing so very well, "we have been helped considerably by ordinary American citizens. Almost every day we receive fax documents and suggestions from interested groups, private investigators, and individuals all across the nation, people like Floyd Crump and Carl Weiss. And my staff regularly monitors internet messages and usenet groups for additional leads. Of course, we always hold ourselves to the highest ethical standards as we are unearthing the facts and analyzing the law. I will leave to others—to congressional investigating committees and journalists—the task of making other public judgments about Whirlpool."

Acknowledging that he had been rather slow in completing the investigation and attempting to shift fault away from the time he spent in his extensive private practice, Jeffreys said, "I earnestly wish I could give you a final report on our investigation today. I do not particularly enjoy life in Birmingham, and I would have rather been home with my wife and our three children. But we are not yet at that stage. I can tell you that we are making very substantial progress on all fronts. Although the grand jury in Birmingham has completed its work, we still have an active grand jury inquiry underway in Washington. The investigation is at a critical juncture now, and we are proceeding as expeditiously as possible."

"Many of you have asked me that burning question," he said, though I doubted that anyone had to ask, if in fact they did, "whether the President or First Lady will be indicted after the election. The recent Senate Resolution, requesting that I file charges for false testimony, failed to pass by only a few votes. I would point out, however, that the Independent Counsel is not bound by anything the United States Senate might recommend. I can still, within the letter of the Independent Counsel Act, file any charges I want against anyone I choose. However, it would be imprudent for me to announce now, before the election, whether we will seek or may have already secured sealed indictments of the President and the First Lady. I can only say that we have made very substantial progress on all parts of our investigation, and we are moving ahead very, very quickly."

"Thank you, and God bless you," Jeffreys said, as the audience again jumped up and clapped on cue.

Following the speech, Jeffreys took only one question, which I suspected had been carefully planted by Della Beckwith. The shill tossed the underhanded lob right into the strike zone, asking, "Are you at all troubled by the White House's campaign to raise questions about your independence or integrity?"

"As I said earlier," Jeffreys replied gleefully, "my experience is, people who don't have anything to hide aren't out there attacking you. When I hear that sort of thing, it just makes me work that much harder."

What a performance. The audience probably fell for it, and Jeffreys might even have believed it himself. I didn't. Not for a minute. I thought Jeffreys was a deluded tumblebug who saw himself as Sisyphus. The people of Alabama knew better, too, and most thought he was about to get rolled up in a work of his own creation.

Although the *Washington Sun* and the *Wall Street Record* lavished praise upon Jeffreys and reprinted the full text of his speech, that was to be expected. He could have read from the *Federal Register* and they would have compared it to Pericles' Funeral Oration. And favorable coverage in those papers reached only the true believers who already hated the President and the First Lady. It was merely preaching to the saved and did nothing to win converts to the cause.

I realized that Jeffreys had laid an egg, however, when I caught a segment of *The McLaffer Group* the next day. Some associate editor from *The American Speculator*, launched into Jeffreys rather forcefully, getting my attention when he argued, "The least that one can say about Jeffreys' unethical behavior is that simple good manners require that if he can't prove his case in court he ought to remain silent. But silence is not for the righteous, especially when they command the unlimited powers of Special Prosecutorhood. Unable to secure an indictment by the grand jury or to demonstrate guilt in a court of law, Jeffreys proclaimed it to the nation. To this very day, Jeffreys still pontificates about a vast conspiracy to cover up God knows what, even though he has never proved a shred of this Queeg-like worldview."

John McLaffer was taken aback by that response as well, and he asked his guest why he would say something like that about the man the *Speculator* had written about so glowingly in the past. I was wondering the same thing.

"Despite his distinguished past," the fellow told McLaffer, "George Jeffreys has acted cruelly and wickedly, he has ignored traditional standards of propriety and fairness, and he has spoken in a way no prosecutor ever should. His human failings have been accentuated by the arrogance of his power and the temptation to see himself as the avenging angel of Whirlpool."

Saturday's *Alabama Times* was equally unkind, but that, too, was to be expected. They'd long ago had a buttload of Jeffreys and his witch hunt, but the most damning article in that issue was a reprint of a piece from *Newsday* by Murray Kempton, who was certainly no fan of President Cannon. He cut to the chase, and it must have cut Jeffreys to the quick, all the more so because it was so true.

"Malice may have its excuses, but acting upon it has none at all," Kempton wrote. "You cannot be a gentleman without resisting that worst of all temptations of the flesh, which is hatred for another human being. The most serious defect of hard posturers, left and right, is the assurance of one's own rectitude that too often progresses to mistaking the noxious smokes of hatred for the purifying fires of justice. The embarrassments of hating anyone ought to have already been enough of a burden for Jeffreys to persuade him that they could only weigh heavier if he set himself up as qualified to judge this president. The protracted pursuit of Whirlpool has made it ever more patent that President Cannon's sins are too pallid to be usefully blackened, however ill the will Jeffreys might bring to the job."

Then, *CBS News* announced the results of its latest poll. Only 34 percent of the American public had any confidence in Jeffreys. Most saw his operation for what it was, a publicly-funded witch hunt by a disappointed Republican office-seeker.

Listening to Jeffreys' first stump speech and seeing the unanticipated reaction to it had inadvertently rekindled my interest in my book project. Of course, I hadn't dissuaded Lindsey from thinking it had been a great sacrifice to record the speech for her, hoping I might trade that sympathy for romantic attention. Not that it was ever necessary. Quite the contrary. Most weekends I had to go jogging just to get some rest.

That Sunday, though, I took my breaks in my study, trying to knock out a few pages that would capture my thinking about why Jeffreys had become so obsessed with Cannon and my reaction to his latest futile attempt to bring down the President. I was still searching for a voice and working to find a style that was readable without being dumbed down to the level of newspaper prose and commentary. Thought I might call it "All the Right Men."

There were many ways to tell this story. Jeffreys had been telling a different one for more than two years. But I wanted to begin with the basics, to show why Jeffreys had been so driven, so obsessive. It needed to be told, so I began by writing, "George Jeffreys had once pinned all his hopes and ambitions on the favor of Charles William Horton Stuart. Small reason was there to doubt, then, that ever since that fateful and unfortunate election in 1992, Jeffreys had cherished a wild vindictiveness against President Cannon, all the more felt now because in his frantic morbidness he at last came to blame Cannon for all his political exasperations. The President stood before him as the monomaniac incarnation of all those malicious agencies which some privileged men feel eating deep in them, until they are left living on with half a heart and half a soul."

Recalling Jeffreys opening remarks in the Raleigh speech, I played with his haughty concept of a privileged class of "betters" who thought they had authority to brake the sovereign exuberance of the people. I pictured Jeffreys as pompous John Adams, distrusting the rabble, and wrote, "Vox populi, that intangible malignity, the spirit of democracy, which has from the beginning under Jefferson and Madison championed the common people against those who would enslave their minds, extract their sweat, and control their private lives; to whose dominion even the Christian Coalition sometimes pretended homage; to which even Senator Dolor mouthed praise during the campaign; Jeffreys did not fall down and worship that sovereign beast. Deliriously transferring its idea to the abhorred occupant of the White House, making the president more than he really was, he pitted himself against Cannon, head-to-head."

The Muse was with me, I thought, so I kept writing, trying to fathom what still motivated Jeffreys after two years without success. "All that most maddens and torments; all that stirs up the passions of politics; all truth with malice in it; all the subtle demonisms of life and thought; all evil, to the obsessed Jeffreys, were visibly personified, and made practically assailable in James Madison Cannon. He piled upon the president's head the sum of all the general rage and hate felt by the party of privileged whiteness, from Mark Hanna down to Nelson Grenier; and then, as if his mouth had been a mortar, he burst his fevered brain's shell upon the man who had dashed his dreams of a seat on the Supreme Court."

I was feeling pretty smug about my efforts at writing. I knew I still got carried away by my own feelings about Jeffreys, and that showed, but I was not at all unpleased with the results of my labor. It was still too melodramatic, I thought, but I could overcome that with more discipline. In terms of drama, however, it was nothing compared with what was happening to Jeffreys in the real world.

Lindsey came in at that moment, and I had been wanting to get her perspective on something Jeffreys had said about my writing a book. "Jeffreys once told me he really didn't care what I wrote. Said I didn't understand politics, and I'd be wasting my time. What do you think? Be honest."

Not sparing my feelings, she replied, "He's probably right about that."

"Oh, hell, now you're on his side," I whined. "And I think I understand politics better than Jeffreys or anyone on his staff."

"No argument there. You understand politics, but I think you're overlooking the reality of the media and the publishing business in this country."

"How so?"

"It doesn't matter how well you write or whether you are right," she explained. "The book trade is a business, pure and simple, and if it won't sell, no one will be interested. Except for Hank Regency, but they wouldn't publish anything that undermined George Jeffreys. The so-called news media have proven that what sells is charges against Cannon, and the wilder the better. So, unless you're planning on confirming their story, you won't get very far. They won't be interested in anything else. The same corporate giants that own the networks and the major papers also own the publishing houses. No reflection on your book, but that's the reality."

She was right, of course. But this time I would not be deterred by logic. Like Henry Miller once said, writing might be a prelude to living, and I damn sure wanted to have a real life again.

On Monday, Charles William Horton Stuart proved himself capable of providing a point of light in his own rather dreary life. He'd spent most of his time, since the thrashing he took from Cannon in 1992, getting even richer by giving speeches and raking in enormous honoraria—usually $100,000 a pop—from very questionable foreign sources. And the speeches themselves were not that good, nothing like Peggy Noonan could crank out on a good day. Recently he had made a few talks for Ira Dolor, but they were rather uninspiring, even when compared with Dolor's depressing drivel. That day, however, he had something to say that caused people to listen—and think.

News reports broke about noon, with rumors that former President Stuart would be making a prime time telecast from Houston. NPR first reported the story and surmised that it would be a strong endorsement of Ira Dolor. I guess I assumed that's what it would be, but I remember thinking that Dolor must be more desperate and his consultants dumber than I realized. By the time the evening news came on, the story line was that Stuart would address issues surrounding the Whirlpool investigation, and the pundits predicted that Stuart would reveal evidence linking Cannon with the CIA drug shipments and arms deals at the Seale airstrip outside Phenix City. My money was against that, partly because it never happened but especially so because the pundits were pretending to be so certain.

Stuart came on at 8 o'clock, and he was seated behind a desk in his private office. Not as nice as the Oval Office, yet impressive enough to suggest authority. "For more than 30 years in public service," he said solemnly, "I tried to follow three precepts: honor, decency, and fairness. I know, from all those years of service, that the American people believe in fairness and fair play. In urging President Cannon to take this action today, I am doing what I believe honor, decency, and fairness require."

Maybe he was going to call on Cannon to resign? Whatever it was, he had my attention, as he looked straight into the camera and said, "For more than 3 years now, the American people have invested enormous resources into what has become the most thoroughly investigated matter of its kind in our history. Those private citizens and public servants subjected to constant investigation have already paid a price—in depleted savings, lost careers, anguished families—grossly disproportionate to any misdeeds or errors of judgment they may have committed."

Whoa, Charley! I was still trying to digest that last line, but Stuart had just begun. "The relentless hearings and questionable prosecutions of the individuals involved represent what I believe is a profoundly troubling development in the political and legal climate of our country: the criminalization of policy differences." Then, his argument emerged as he said, "These differences should be addressed in the political arena, without the Damocles sword of criminality hanging over the heads of some of the combatants. The proper target is the President, not his subordinates; the proper forum is the voting booth, not the courtroom."

Then, he said it, "President Cannon should direct the Attorney General to immediately remove George Jeffreys and terminate the Independent Counsel for Whirlpool. Some may argue that such action will prevent full disclosure of some new key fact to the American people. That is not true. This matter has been investigated exhaustively. The Resolution Trust Corporation, the Federal Deposit Insurance Corporation, the Small Business Administration, the General Accounting Office, the House Banking Committee, the House Government Operations and Oversight Committee, the Senate Banking Committee, the Senate Whirlpool Committee, a United States Attorney, a Special Counsel, and two Independent Counsels have looked into every possible aspect of this matter. They have interviewed more than 500 people and reviewed more than 900,000 pages of material. Lengthy committee hearings were held and broadcast on national television to millions of Americans. And as I have noted, the Independent Counsel investigation has gone on for more than 3 years, and it has cost more than $35 million."

Stuart's closing remarks, conceding the upcoming election, were anticlimactic, overshadowed by the massive blow he had already dealt to Jeffreys. It would hardly be noticed that he closed by saying, "In recent years, the use of criminal processes in policy disputes has become all too common. It is my hope that the statement I am making today will encourage the leadership of my own political party to restore these disputes to the battleground where they properly belong. The American people have elected and, despite everything my party has been able to do during the past four years, appear ready to reelect James Madison Cannon as President of the United States. We should accept and respect their decision. Enough is enough."

As you can imagine, no one talked about anything else on Tuesday. Even my students seemed interested in politics and public affairs that day. Either that, or they were unprepared and were trying to divert my attention so I wouldn't call on them in class. The most interesting conversation I had that day was when Bill Baxter called to thank me for referring James Burgh and to tell me he was filing the complaint that day with the Office of Government Ethics, the Attorney General, and the DC Bar's Committee on Professional Conduct. I allowed as to how I was glad and gave him my home number, just in case he needed to interview a potential witness. Baxter said he'd rather do that over a glass of whiskey, and I promised to accommodate him.

I called James Burgh at home that evening to check his pulse and to tell him he was my new hero. We talked for a while, and he thanked me for being willing to discuss the legal issues when he was trying to decide whether to do it. I'll never forget something he said that night; it sticks in my mind even now. We were talking about President Stuart's televised speech and musing about the whole Whirlpool fiasco from the time it was first raised in the *New York Times*. He said, "This movie's not gonna have a happy ending, and there are no heroes." And I knew he was right.

The following day, Jeffreys was at Salt Lake City to give a speech to the Amway Distributors convention. The speech itself was not open to the public or the press, but Jeffreys was joined by Senator Hatchet after the speech for a noon news conference carried live on CNN. Neither of them mentioned Burgh's complaint, but the tenor of their remarks made it clear that it was, along with other recent events, on their minds.

Senator Hatchet fired the first shot as he opened by saying, "I call upon President Cannon to call off his attack dogs trying to impugn the integrity of George Jeffreys. President Cannon should prohibit people from questioning the Independent Counsel's integrity. Anyone who has been around Washington certainly knows that Judge Jeffreys is a man of impeccable character, integrity, and judgment, and his actions as Independent Counsel have been nothing but professional, fair, and impartial. Nevertheless, we are about to witness a rising tide of name-calling and diversionary attacks on Judge Jeffreys' integrity from Democratic Party operatives, White House officials, the President's political advisers and associates, and even some of the people he has investigated. And, I think the press should ask, if the President and his Administration have done nothing wrong, then why are their apologists pre-emptively smearing Judge Jeffreys?"

"Now, let me clarify," Hatchet added cautiously, "I have no idea what the Independent Counsel's plans are. I have no idea whether there will be any future indictments or a recommendation that the House of Representatives begin impeachment proceedings. But I do know that Judge Jeffreys, by virtue of his office, is not in a position to defend himself against President Cannon's relentless attack dogs. Let Judge Jeffreys do his work free from this partisan sniping, whose sole purpose is to divert attention from the substance of matters he is investigating, and then let the chips fall where they may."

Jeffreys stepped forward and placed his notes on the lectern. "I must tell you that, speaking personally, I find all the affronts to my reputation and this widespread motive-impugning criticism a very distasteful aspect of my public life. It's one thing to dispute a man's conclusions or policies, such as his preference for private religious schools or his belief that a public school district need not comply fully with a desegregation order. However," he protested, "it's a different order of magnitude, when they presume that my actions must necessarily stem from some improper motive such as personal animosity, party affiliation, political ambition, representation of private clients, and the like. This constant questioning of my integrity will only lead to a further coarsening of the political dialogue, a lessening of proper respect for authority, and the further eating away of the people's moral values in this country."

Then, I saw that smarmy smile spread across his face, and I knew Jeffreys was about to tell everyone about his reputation for rectitude and integrity. I almost changed channels, but I wanted to hear the questions that would follow. "Independent Counsels are by law above scrutiny by the courts or the president, and those restraints should be equally applicable to their criticism of my actions in the public sphere. I can hold myself to the highest professional and ethical standards very well without any help from James Madison Cannon, thank you. So, in examining my official conduct, it would be wise and prudent for him to fashion his comments in a manner that comports with the values of civility, decency, and human dignity."

There were surprisingly few reporters there from outside Utah and very few questions from the reporters who were there. Perhaps that was why Jeffreys had chosen Salt Lake City as his venue. One local newspaper reporter asked Senator Hatchet if he were trying to send a threatening message to the White House. Hatchet did, indeed, and he said, "I think they know I mean what I say. Now that it appears the President will be unconstrained by the need to face the American people during his second term, especially careful scrutiny of judicial nominees will be imperative. It also appears that I will remain Chairman of the Senate Judiciary Committee, and I tell you today that I plan to stand firm and exercise the advise and consent power to insure that President Cannon does not pack the judiciary with left-wing liberal activists who will make mincemeat of our Constitution and laws. We'll sit on his nominations and delay all confirmation hearings as long as he remains in office."

That outburst led another reporter to ask Jeffreys the obligatory question about how he saw his chances for a future appointment to the Supreme Court. Avoiding the obvious answer by making reference to a snowball, he replied, "The federal judiciary, in a word, is a scarce resource, and must be viewed precisely that way. And thus, I engage not in a romantic search for the lost Golden Age under President Stuart, but must look forward to how the future can be faced—faced not only with a stiff upper lip but, more positively, with real anticipation of good things to come. I felt very honored even to have been considered for the Court by President Stuart. I have a basic philosophy of life, that God moves in the way He will move, and that is a source of great assurance to me. It really is, even if it means that my dreams remain unfulfilled for the time being. But my concern, which remains, notwithstanding the ability and dedication of several able Justices on the Court, is that the values of the past, and thus the professional rewards and personal satisfactions available to me, will decline."

"Mr. Jeffreys," asked another reporter, "you said in a recent speech that your probe had only cost the taxpayers $9 million. The General Accounting Office report put that figure at $53 million, which exceeds the total losses at Jefferson Savings and Financial-Management combined. How do you explain that wide discrepancy between your statement and the official report?"

"Well, I'm not certain those figures are correct. I will have to recheck my records to make sure I didn't misspeak myself. Nevertheless, I still stand by the statement I made, which was that nine million dollars is a small price to pay for an Independent Counsel with integrity. That is still a true statement, regardless if the actual figure is more than that."

I had watched the news conference, so I had to laugh when I read the article about Jeffreys' remarks in the paper. Under the headline "Jeffreys Objects to Attacks on His Integrity," the reporter wrote, "Yesterday's press conference was his second defensive outing this week, fueling speculation that Jeffreys might be on the verge of seeking indictments in the Whirlpool investigation. Rumors have been rampant in Washington recently that grand jury indictments are in the offing, including one of First Lady Diane Cannon."

Attributions to "speculation" and "rumors" are always handy when journalists are fabricating conclusions that have no basis in fact. That is one of the ways reporters do their job to make up some "news" and to help the ignorant reader understand what that news really means. "Where there's smoke, let's blow smoke," seemed to be the journalistic standard. The real story, which I thought would be obvious to anyone with a lick of sense, was that Jeffreys was trying to build a firewall against his own possible indictment. That was, as he had alleged in the Raleigh speech a few days earlier, a common tactic to be expected from public officials charged with criminal acts or abuse of the public trust. But, of course, that irony escaped the press and the pundits.

As I fliped the channels, I did find a bit of humor, though nothing unexpected. Attorney General Otis, on "Fox News Sunday," said, "At this point, I have seen no evidence that would justify disciplining or dismissing Judge Jeffreys. To date, I've pretty much given him everything he's wanted. We have ruled in his favor on all of the ethics complaints against him, and I've had, I think, very cordial relationships with him." Yep, no question about that.

Chapter Thirty Six

Lindsey had maintained her ties with many of the friends she'd met through the Southern Poverty Law Center, and I was glad she had. That connection allowed me to learn more about the state's civil rights history and to meet interesting people, many of whom had fascinating stories to tell. It also meant road trips. On Sunday afternoon we drove down to Selma for a meeting at Brown Chapel AME Church. Lindsey was going to see some of her old friends who had been active in the Montgomery Improvement Association, and I was just going along because I was interested in seeing the church. It had been King's headquarters before the March to Montgomery in 1965, and the meeting was for the announcement of a federal grant making the march route a National Historical Trail. Probably just a coincidence that the announcement came so close to the election.

Both Cannon and Dolor were in Alabama the following week, and their events spoke volumes about their campaigns. Dolor held a rally at the state capitol, attended by about 500 die-hard Republicans from the stone age. According to the newspaper, Mayor Folmar was the there, along with Jeremiah Denton, and they even rolled out George Wallace and propped him up on the stage. Dolor frantically thumped the tub for constitutional amendments on flag desecration, school prayer, and abortion. He also called Cannon a liberal, probably 20 times, but that still didn't make it true—no matter how much Dolor and I both wished it were so. He told an even bigger lie when he jumped on the "liberal mainstream media" and blamed the *New York Times* for being pro-Cannon. Hell, if it hadn't been for the *New York Times* starting the Whirlpool fable, Cannon would have had a 30-point lead in the polls.

Later that week, my friend Mark Lester called and said he had two extra tickets for the Cannon rally at Birmingham-Southern, so Lindsey and I drove over and attended the festivities, along with Mark and Jeanne and 40,000 of Cannon's friends and local supporters packed into the main quadrangle. Cannon appeared more confident and less enthusiastic than when I heard him speak in Austin four years ago. His speech was that same old "Bridge to the 21st Century" song he'd been singing since the convention, but it was still well-received by the home crowd. I thought the best line of the day was one delivered by Senator Howell Heflin, who declared the election a done deal and said, "The pachyderms have raised their snouts, and what can now be heard are the groans of anticipated defeat."

The presidential campaign was virtually over, but George Jeffreys' campaign was not. He was scheduled to give his third public speech at Hostus University. This time, I not only planned to watch the speech, but I planned to have my Professional Responsibility students watch it as an in-class assignment. The Hostus speech was not without controversy, though. Buck Etienne, as promised, had purchased a full page advertisement in the *Washington Post* criticizing Jeffreys for giving political speeches about an ongoing investigation and, especially, choosing to do so at a university headed by the Reverend Marion Rabbidson, one of Cannon's most outspoken critics.

Jeffreys dismissed the criticism and defended his decision, as he did whenever he was criticized for anything. "I am a highly respected figure in the American legal community, and I see nothing improper about my discussing legal issues in a forum sponsored by the American Center for Christian Justice," he said. "The recent affront to my professional reputation is just another attempt to question my integrity, coming from one of President Cannon's attack dogs. It is very destructive, and it is not in the best interest of the country. Such is to be expected, however, in cases where one seeks to vigorously expose and exterminate corruption by public officials. The question you should be asking, I would suggest, is whether Mr. Etienne was authorized by the White House to purchase that advertisement besmirching my reputation."

Contacted by the *Post* for a response as to whether the White House had approved his attack on Jeffreys, Etienne responded, "First, I'm not in the permission-seeking business. Second, I'm doing this on my own, because I know George Jeffreys is a partisan Republican political hack, and because, frankly, no one that I know has any faith at all in his objectivity. When the American people see who he is and what he's doing, they're not going to have any faith in him either."

That exchange did not stop Jeffreys from giving the speech, but it did significantly alter the dynamics of what he had hoped would be another friendly situation where he could polish his tarnished reputation and build public support among the conservative religious audiences. To target that message, the only television coverage of the speech at Hostus was provided exclusively by the school's Religious Broadcasting Network. That strategy failed to consider that the advertisement had alerted the Washington press corps about the speech, and this time Jeffreys was unfortunately trapped giving his speech within easy driving distance for reporters who had some experience at asking questions.

There was apparently some discussion about closing the speech to the press, but that option was eventually rejected. Jeffreys was introduced by Hostus President Rabbidson, who squinted his eyes and read the standard puff piece reciting Jeffreys credentials, then told the audience, "Judge Jeffreys has promised not to mention the name of Jessie Banaghan." That brought a big laugh from the audience, that nervous laugh of infantile fraternity boys and repressed bondage aficionados, because they were delighted that Jeffreys had her handcuffed and incarcerated. Jeffreys was their hero now, for he had shown he knew how to keep Mrs. Banaghan in her place.

Jeffreys had discarded his prepared speech after the advertisement flap, electing instead to deliver a rather boring basket of nonsense about the future of the Supreme Court in American life. He made a few remarks about the danger of appointing "liberal federal judges," but he stopped short of offering himself as the conservative alternative. Jeffreys didn't even joke about that subject anymore, knowing that he would never be nominated as long as Cannon was President.

The more interesting part of the broadcast was the news conference held immediately afterwards. Jeffreys faced the press from behind a podium on a special set in the RBN studio, the one designed to resemble the White House briefing room. It was the first time he had dared to take questions in an open format where he wasn't controlling the situation. I couldn't believe that Della Beckwith would have allowed Jeffreys to take such a risk, but his hubris blinded him from recognizing the political danger just as it had kept him from examining his own political motives driving the investigation from the day he had been appointed.

There appeared to be about 20 reporters waiting when Jeffreys arrived. They all stood up when he walked onto the set and remained standing until he positioned himself behind the podium. The first question concerned the decision to deliver a public speech at Hostus University. A reporter with Scripps-Howard asked, "Judge Jeffreys, as you know, Buck Etienne has criticized you for choosing to give a speech at a conservative religious school headed by a former Republican presidential candidate and vocal critic of President Cannon. Do you think you made an error in judgment in doing so?"

Jeffreys had expected that one, and he was prepared for it. "I have no apology for accepting the gracious invitation from this fine Christian institution, and I would not presume to question whether Mr. Etienne was motivated by religious prejudice. I know he is a Catholic, as are many of his people, but I do not believe he would have me avoid sharing my views about the role of law with Reverend Rabbidson and those in the evangelical community. It is, moreover, very appropriate for me to be engaged in a public information and educational campaign, at a time when the American people are focused on the kind of future they want for our nation, and to participate in that dialogue with the American Center for Christian Justice in what I hope would be an appropriate way."

Drew Turner from *The Legal Brief* popped the next question, one that Jeffreys had not expected. "Mr. Jeffreys, a number of state and federal prosecutors have expressed their concern over the past few months about the conduct of your office, suggesting that you should remember that high profile investigations are not exempt from the strict rules under which prosecutors must operate. Increasingly, leaks, comments, and actions taken by your office have created the perception that political and other motivations might be playing a role in guiding your office's investigation. The Office of Public Integrity has also said that leaks, comments about the evidence, and disclosures concerning the deliberations of pending grand jury proceedings have no place in a fair-minded prosecutor's arsenal. The way in which an investigation of this type is conducted says a great deal about the integrity of those responsible for it. Do you plan to repudiate the apparent leaks and improper disclosures, and what are you doing to ensure your office adheres to the highest standards of ethics and professionalism?"

That one hit a nerve, and Jeffreys tried to slide by without answering the question. "Mr. Turner," he said as his jaw tightened and his face became red, "I am aware of the growing public concern regarding public disclosures about our investigation, particularly regarding statements made by reporters in recent news articles. We fully share the concern that improper disclosures may reflect on the integrity of a criminal investigation, and we are well aware of the ethical and professional obligations of prosecutors in that regard. We have attempted to conduct our investigation in accordance with the highest ethical and professional standards, for which I have always been known."

Turner, a former deputy prosecutor and now a damn good legal reporter, was used to guilty witnesses squirming, and he wasn't about to let Jeffreys get by with that evasion. "Let me try to be more clear, Mr. Jeffreys, and please answer the question with using the royal we. What about the constant stream of leaks from your office?"

Whether caused by the television lights or the intensity of the questions, perspiration was now beginning to appear on Jeffreys' upper lip. "Well, Mr. Turner, as a former prosecutor, you should be aware of the hazards of assuming that unquoted, unsourced, and unattributed comments by a member of the media accurately reflect actual statements we made to that reporter. Moreover, certain reporters often use vague terms to puff their unnamed sources, who in fact are not part of the investigation under discussion. Some reporters will even quote an official from my office and then surround the quotation with the reporter's own analysis and extrapolations, thereby suggesting that the quoted source also made the unquoted assertions. Indeed, even reporters friendly to our office have been known to get their quotations wrong. I see no need to apologize to anyone, because our conduct has been above reproach."

After that second slick non-answer about the leaks, the decorum quickly declined. Reporters began shouting for recognition. They each had at least one question they wanted to ask, and they knew that the news conference would last only 15 minutes. Questions were served and answers were returned as if it were a ping-pong match in the Hostus Student Center game room. And it was a game, but Jeffreys was outmatched.

"Do you plan to seek indictments of the President or the First Lady any time soon?"

"That issue is sufficiently sensitive that I don't think I should be speculating. But I will say, our investigation is at a crucial juncture, and we are moving forward very quickly on several fronts," Jeffreys replied with a wink.

"President Cannon recently suggested that you were 'out to get' him and the First Lady. Is that true?"

"No comment."

"Are you concerned that President Cannon might order the Attorney General to remove you as Independent Counsel?"

"Independent counsels are not, in their day-to-day operations, answerable to the Attorney General. Of necessity, an Independent Counsel exercises a great deal of discretion, of judgment. That's why I was chosen, for my good judgment. I can honestly tell you that Attorney General Otis will do nothing to impede this investigation. If she even considers it, she should recall the political consequences that ensued when Richard Nixon ordered his Attorney General to fire Archibald Cox. I can assure her that any such move would bring a firestorm greater than the one she created at Waco."

"How much longer do you anticipate your investigation continuing?

"Until we get the truth. I wish people would be more open and honest. Just tell us who was involved in the these financial dealings and give us the facts about the real estate investments. If they've done nothing illegal and have nothing to hide, then why aren't they being more forthcoming? The American people have a right to know these things about people who hold positions of public trust."

"Then, would you be willing to disclose the details of your involvement in an investment known as Lubbock AK?"

"No, I will not. That was a legitimate investment in which I was a partner more than 10 years ago. I did nothing wrong. In fact, I lost money on the deal. It has nothing to do with my fitness to serve as Independent Counsel nor with my conduct since I was appointed."

"If you lost money on the investment, why didn't you deduct the $20,000 loss on your income taxes? And how do you explain that all of the public records seem to have disappeared?"

"I told you that I don't intend to discuss that matter. You're asking questions that seem to imply I might have done something wrong, and I cannot prove a negative. And, if I answered your questions about Lubbock AK, you'd just start in on something else."

"Last year, your required financial disclosure report was filed late. Was there some reason that it wasn't submitted by the legal deadline for such ethics forms?"

"I was very busy at the time, and I was granted a special extension. I violated no laws."

"Do you think it created an appearance of conflict that you received substantial income last year from the conservative Harry Lynde Foundation that also bankrolls several conservative groups actively opposed to President Cannon?"

"No. Next question."

"Are you aware that the Harry Lynde Foundation provided the funding for the Hostus Legal Policy Institute which hosted your presentation today?"

"Since Mr. Lynde and I serve on the Board of the Friends of Hostus, I was aware of the foundation's financial support for this fine Christian institution. I do not, however, recall discussing the matter directly with him."

"Is it true that you've discussed with Mr. Howard Mellonskoff the possibility of funding a Deanship for you at Hostus?"

"Well, first of all, let me say that, with respect to the particular individual who you have named, I have never met him, I have never talked directly to him, I have had no arrangement—implicit or explicit—with him personally. I am aware of the commentary with respect to the relationship, and individuals will come their own conclusions about that."

"Have you had any discussions in that regard with anyone associated with Mr. Mellonskoff or his foundations?"

"No comment."

"Mr. Jeffreys, the financial disclosure report that you filed this year indicated that you earned approximately $950,000 in income from various sources, but you failed to list the entities and clients you represented. Is there some reason you concealed that information on the ethics forms this year? Did any of your undisclosed clients create a conflict of interest?"

"We determined that the law did not require someone in my position to reveal his outside clients or other sources of income. I have no conflicts of interest. Next question."

"Is it true that the Government Accounting Office determined that you submitted false reimbursement claims for housing costs in the amount of $9,926 last year?"

"I want to make it perfectly clear that I have reimbursed the federal government for that over-billing. I did not intentionally submit false claims. I was just unaware of the law. I thought it would be legal to claim the full amount, even though I did not actually stay there. I am not a crook. Next question."

"Court documents suggest that you failed to file the required oath stating that you did not purchase or otherwise improperly secure your appointment as Independent Counsel until more than a year after the required date. Can you explain the reason for that? Were you unaware of the oath requirement, or was there some other reason?"

"No comment."

"Did you trade on your position as Independent Counsel by auctioning a tennis game to secure contributions to a private foundation in Virginia?"

"There was nothing illegal about what I did."

"Do you think it was improper, while serving as Independent Counsel investigating President Cannon, for you to have made a political contribution to Senator Dolor's campaign?"

"No, it was not improper. It is an exercise of civic virtue to make financial contributions to political action committees, and the amount of the contribution was legal under existing law."

"Would you comment on the allegations in the complaint allegedly filed by James Burgh against you and several members of your staff?"

"That investigation is active and ongoing, and I cannot comment on any matters that might be before a grand jury."

"Then, are you saying that you have been called before a grand jury?"

"I said, 'No comment.'"

"Are you concerned that the allegations in the complaint might provide 'good cause' for your removal?"

"The only person who can remove me from office is the Attorney General, and, as I said, I have no fear of that happening."

"Did you play any role in finding a new legal team for Christine Putnam, a firm headed by one of your former college classmates?"

Jeffreys stuttered a moment, started to say something, paused, then replied, "That question has been asked and answered."

"What about the situation where you were investigating the Resolution Trust Corporation officials at the same time they had a million dollar lawsuit pending against your law firm?"

"I can confirm that I was on the firm's executive committee at the time the RTC's lawsuit was filed against Kirk & Polis; however, I don't recall, at this point in time, having had any knowledge of that. And there is no credible evidence that my OIC investigation influenced the favorable settlement terms my law firm received."

"It seems like you have developed a convenient lapse of memory about several important events that could call into question your ethical fitness for a position of public trust."

"That's not a question. You're being argumentative."

"Excuse me. Do you think that you have developed a convenient lapse of memory that could call into question your ethical fitness for a position of public trust?"

"That will be all for today, gentlemen," Jeffreys said with a forced smile as he excused himself from further interrogation and hastily walked off the set. He was already late for a reception in his honor at the Ratched Institute.

After watching that news conference, I knew that my class in Professional Responsibility would have plenty to discuss for the next week, and I even considered using Jeffreys' predicament as the hypo for my final exam. It seemed to present interesting questions about numerous sections of the Code of Professional Responsibility. It also presented numerous questions about the criminal code, but I wasn't teaching that course this semester. Jeffreys would have to answer those questions in another forum.

I was interested to see how the speech would be handled on the evening news that night, but the networks, as usual, didn't provide much real news. ABC had nothing about the speech, and CBS only had a brief comment that Jeffreys had delivered his third public speech in 10 days. It was the third story on NBC. They had video from the formal presentation, but nothing from the news conference. A later news cycle on CNN did show a few of the questions from the press conference, followed by Buck Etienne, who quipped, "Told ya so!" The newspapers the next day were equally predictable, with the *Washington Sun* reprinting the text of the speech and ignoring the questions raised at the news conference. The *New York Times* and the *Washington Post* reporters, neither of whom had attended the event, rewrote wire stories elaborating on Della Beckwith's spoon-fed summary of the formal remarks.

Despite the rhetorical carpet-bombing, the fall offensive had fallen flat. Congress seemed paralyzed by the polls showing Cannon headed toward an easy victory, and they had retreated from both calls to arms sounded by Dorkman and Rantallion. The grand jury in Birmingham expired without issue, adding further insult and humiliation to Jeffreys' defeat in the trial of Jones and Hill. The latest surveys showed the public was either bored with the whole deal or somewhat annoyed that Jeffreys was still wasting taxpayer dollars tilting at nonexistent windmills. The counterattack by Buck Etienne and other administration snipers had taken a further toll on George Jeffreys' reputation and his psyche. A seat on the Supreme Court was no longer a possibility. His future as a cigarette lawyer might even be in doubt. Jeffreys was now damaged goods through every fault of his own.

Frustration must have seized the entire staff as they began boxing up the records from the Birmingham office and heading to Washington. I had a call from Mitch wanting to know if we could have a beer sometime. He was resolved to staying behind to maintain the skeleton staff in preparing a draft report on the Alabama phase of the investigation, Mitch came over to Tuscaloosa on Tuesday, and we went to the Houndstooth after my class. I could tell that something was bothering him, but I couldn't resist a few digs about what a bust the operation had been.

"So, Mitch," I said between bites of a greasy hamburger, "looks like George and the boys are sneaking out of town and leaving you here to take the fall."

"I wouldn't say that," Mitch protested. "It's just that our work here is finished."

"I know you wouldn't say it," I replied without sounding too brutal, "but it still looks like a strategic retreat to me. Not a single indictment related to Whirlpool and nothing on the President or the First Lady, which, as I recall, was why Jeffreys was appointed in the first place. Forty million dollars down a rat hole. Not a single indictment even related to the Cannons. And no indictments of anyone for anything in well over a year. I'd say the work here was finished all right. Was a long time ago."

Stung by my comments, Mitch's response revealed more than he intended. "To say that this whole thing was a dry hole is really preposterous," he bristled. "Judge Jeffreys was in a position where he was damned if he did and damned if he didn't. We made the judgment, which in my view is a reasonable one, that there wasn't enough evidence to put the country through a trial of the First Lady of the United States, and now he's attacked because the whole thing was a waste of time. On the other hand, if we had brought the indictment, he would have been called the most venal prosecutor in the history of the statute."

"Maybe both of those conclusions are right, and he's double damned," I said with a smile, trying to get Mitch to lighten up a bit.

"No, we're at a critical juncture, and the investigation is moving forward. Judge Jeffreys plans to continue with the grand jury in Washington," Mitch insisted, repeating the standard dodge that Jeffreys had been using for the last two years. "We're doubling the office space and adding several new staff attorneys. This is strictly confidential, but we've been working on an entirely new prong of the investigation. You'll see soon enough. And, for your information, there's going to be another indictment today!"

I pushed Mitch for more information without success. Iced tea was not the verbal laxative that beer had proven to be in the past. I didn't need to wait long, though, to discover the answer to my questions. The evening news revealed the depth of the desperation that had engulfed Jeffreys and his prime allies in Congress, laying bare their coordinated assault on both the constitution and their political enemies.

Apparently at the same time we were having lunch, Congressman Bardus had called a press conference and released doctored transcripts of Randolph Webster's phone conversations with his wife—conversations that were recorded while Webster was in prison, provided under subpoena to George Jeffreys, who then provided copies of the tapes to Bardus .

Congressman Henry, the ranking Democrat on the Bardus committee, was outraged at the stunt. "If those tapes had been released by George Jeffreys, he would have not only been removed as special prosecutor, he would have been disbarred. The privacy of all American citizens was at stake, not just Randolph Webster. And the idea that any of these tapes should have been made public is highly offensive. But what was even worse was that Congressman Bardus released a transcript that was edited by his chief investigator, David Windrig, in order to give a false impression that was incriminating. And what was left out were statements that were exculpatory."

Speaker Reichman was upset that the doctoring of the Webster tapes, in which key words were changed to appear sinister and evidence of innocence deleted, had exposed the already obvious political agenda of Winderig and Bardus. The committee's chief counsel and three other Republican staff members who had opposed releasing the transcripts resigned, citing Winderig's "unrelenting, unethical, self-promoting actions." Congressman Shay, an outspoken Republican, admitted, "This controversy calls into question our entire investigation. It reduces our credibility when these kinds of tactics become public."

During a news conference at the White House that morning, President Cannon also said, "Chairman Bardus and Mr. Windrig decided they were above that law. It was clearly a violation of Mr. Webster's privacy and that of his family. I think virtually everyone in America believes it was wrong to release the tapes and to intentionally create a false impression of what the whole record indicated. But, unfortunately, that has been the pattern of this entire investigation."

Within less than an hour after Cannon's remarks, the plot had become even more tangled, and I learned then why Mitch had been so excited. Della Beckwith announced that Jeffreys had indicted Randolph Webster on ten counts of failing to pay his taxes while he was in prison.

In addition to Webster, for good measure and to turn up the heat to force his "cooperation" with the OIC, Jeffreys had also brought charges against Webster's wife and two of his closest friends. According to the new indictment, the Websters had used about 20 credit cards and spent $95,000 on school tuition for their children, $20,000 for telephone bills, $29,000 on his debt to the Bankhead Law Firm, but only $30,000 to the IRS.

On of the most poignant scenes on the news that night was Randolph Webster and his family coming home from work Trying to make their way through the media gaggle into their house, Webster stopped to face the cameras and pleaded, "This is all just a game for you, but this is our life. If you'll allow me to get my family into our house, I'll come back out and answer your questions. Okay?"

For the clever and cynical reporters stalking their prey, it was just fun and games. But for the people involved, like Randolph Webster, it meant George Jeffreys continuing to interrupt and ruin your life; it meant crushing legal fees; it meant reporters hounding you and blocking the door of your car and home; it meant continued public ridicule and fraudulent charges; it was a tragedy never envisioned by the framers of the Bill of Rights.

When Webster again emerged from his home, he paused on the front steps while the reporters and the cameras rushed to form a wall around him. Resolutely he said, "Obviously, George Jeffreys thinks that by indicting my wife and my dearest friends, he can force me to lie about the President and the First lady. I will not do so. And my wife would not want me to do so. I want you to know he can indict my dog; he can indict my cat, but I'm not going to lie about the President, and I'm not going to lie about the First Lady. I think I have said 100 times, maybe a thousand times now, I know of no wrongdoing by the Cannons. My wife and I are innocent of the charges that have been brought today. We will fight these charges, and I personally will fight any injustice or any attempt by George Jeffreys to get me to lie about the President and the First Lady."

Following that scene, the network cut away to the offices of Webster's attorney, who said, "Mr. Webster confessed, he has been punished, his family has been brought to financial ruin, and now as he tries to pick himself off his knees, George Jeffreys has tried to shove him back down and prosecute him for failing to pay the huge tax bill that he still owes as a result of the earlier prosecution. Working as a counselor at a half-way house for $9,000 a year, you can understand why it might take Mr. Webster some time to reduce that debt."

Asking the obvious, one enterprising reporter shouted, "Do you think this is a vendetta? Were you expecting this indictment?"

"Yes, to both of your questions," the lawyer replied, "For two years Randolph Webster has been investigated by Mr. Jeffreys for many different things, looking for some way to prosecute him again. At the end of it all, they have reached out beyond the limits of their jurisdiction and brought a very rare tax charge that would not be brought against any ordinary citizen by the United States Department of Justice."

Amid the burst of questions, another asked, "Was your client paid hush money to protect the Cannons?"

"Absolutely not," the lawyer replied. "George Jeffreys has pursued that false theory and tried to find evidence of hush money, and there just isn't any. So he has been reduced to this, trying to force my client to give false evidence against the President and the First Lady."

Pushing the limits of patience, another reporter shouted, "But what about all the consulting contracts your client received from friends of the President?"

That one made it impossible for Webster's attorney to resist the obvious response. Without mentioning either Howard Mellonskoff or the tobacco industry, he said, "If the source of job offers can prove undue influence, then George Jeffreys is in deep trouble, and he should resign before he is indicted."

The next story was breaking news. David Windrig had been summarily fired from the staff of the Bardus committee, and Bardus had been forced to write a letter to House Republicans apologizing. "I am sickened that anyone would think that I would purposefully release false and misleading information. We were just rushing the release to coincide with the indictments," he had written. Perhaps but unlikely, I thought, yet that only raised another serious question. How did Bardus and Windrig know that Webster was going to be indicted today? Had Jeffreys once again leaked secret grand jury information?

The phone rang and brought another surprise. Some producer at CNN had tracked me down, and she said Greta Van Susteren wanted me to appear as a guest tomorrow on "Burden of Proof" to discuss the Bardus tapes and the Webster indictments. After weighing the potential costs and benefits, I agreed, explaining that I wouldn't be able to comment on or disclose anything confidential I had learned while working for Jeffreys. They seemed excited, nonetheless, because it would be the first time that a former OIC staffer had agreed to discuss the investigation on air. Probably should have discussed it with Lindsey before agreeing, and usually I would have. I would have to take enough grief anyway, because she knew I had a crush on Greta. Not a crush really, I always said, just that attraction to smart women with smart mouths. The only downside for me was that I would be patched in from the studio on campus, meaning that I wouldn't get to be in the same room with Greta.

I was at the studio early the next day. It was a bit strange talking to a camera and seeing myself appear on the monitor on the set. But it seemed to work. I didn't pay much attention to what the "former federal prosecutors" were saying. Everyone knew that was the term used to identify lawyers who had worked for a U.S. Attorney under Reeder or Stuart, that is to say a Jeffreys apologist. And they always had one of those guys who used to be on the payroll of the Republican National Committee trying to pass himself as a legal expert.

Greta was in her usual fine form, putting everything in proper perspective. "Most of Webster's conversations with his wife and children were personal, dealing with such subjects as their distress at being separated. Some are conversations with his lawyer," she prefaced before asking, "When you take out the portions of the transcripts that were doctored by Congressman Bardus and Mr. Windrig, is there any evidence of criminal activity?"

Paul Beluga, one of the Cannon advisors, handled that one. "Well I've been told that George Jeffreys has had these same tapes for a number of months now. So you can rest assured that of all the things that Jeffreys can be accused of, reasonable judgment and discretion in prosecuting is not one of them. So if there was any criminality in these tapes, believe me, that would have been reflected in the indictments that he handed down yesterday against Mr. Webster and his wife and others."

That prompted Jerry Spencer, a defense attorney, to jump in and add, "You have to wonder whether there wasn't some kind of little tootsie-two going on between the so called independent counsel and Dan Bardus, so that these tapes were released. In the final analysis, the question is not whether it's legal or not, but whether it's right or wrong. It hurts me as I listen here to a man and wife talking to each other, the husband in jail, in the penitentiary, imagine this, talking to his wife, and it's all being recorded with the idea that it's going to be privileged. And now Bardus releases it. So I think it's very, very wrong."

I realized I was in fine company as F. Lee Bailey agreed, "I think what Representative Bardus has done is tawdry and should be universally condemned. It was cheap and it was political. And I'm sorry to see the conversation with this husband and this wife on the air. And I don't think it amounts to a hill of beans."

Richard Cohen, of the *Washington Post*, was even more direct. "There's no excuse for the way he has trampled on citizens' civil liberties. Webster's menu recommendations to his wife come to us courtesy of the *Wall Street Record*. Bardus leaked it, and he gave another Webster transcript to the *American Speculator*. Bardus has announced his intention to make them all public. But what committee staffers have been reading is in no way incriminating, just the sort of personal matters between family members that is no business of yours or mine. George Jeffreys' abuse of prosecutorial power is now being matched by Bardus' reckless and tasteless behavior. These two guys ought to go after each other."

"Yeah," Spencer said, as if to second or third the point, "and now people across the country are beginning to say, 'you mean to tell me that they can do this? That they can put this squeeze and this twist on people, and they can use all of these tactics against us?' The recordings of a husband and a wife and a—and a lawyer and his client—all of these things the people of this country are now realizing can be done against them, and it's frightening."

Even the regular Republican defenders had nothing to say in defense of Bardus or Windrig, so that subject was pretty much exhausted as we approached the first break. Just before we went to commercial, Greta cued a tape of Dan Bardus defending his actions and protesting, "It's not illegal, anything I've done. Now I want to tell you, if something comes out that you think Danny shouldn't have done, I will own up to it. If this comes out, I'll be honest."

When we returned, Greta turned the conversation to the indictments of Webster, his wife, and his friends. "I'll tell you, I have gone through this indictment and, frankly, it's not as serious as it appears. Some of the things that he's charged with are, for instance, mail fraud. What the mail fraud is, is that the government of the District of Columbia sent a notice of intent to file a lien to him in the mail, and then he didn't make the tax payment. That's a mail fraud count, and there are five mail fraud counts in the case that look pretty weak to me." Turning to one of the other guests, she asked, "How in the world can this be mail fraud? Explain that."

That was the first time I'd ever seen Roy Black without an answer. He turned to a former IRS Commissioner who was also on the panel and posed his own question, "Is there a crime? Is it wrong, if you have a tax bill, that you first pay your Visa card and don't pay the IRS until you get some more money?"

Even the IRS seemed to think Jeffreys had gone overboard with the indictments. Commissioner Cohen responded in a flat accountant's tone, "Well, it's very unusual to indict a person, convict them, send them to jail, and then do it again. You start with that. The case involves, basically, a statement that he couldn't pay all of the back tax he owed. It's not a tax evasion case, as such. This is simply that he's being accused that he paid others instead of the IRS. If you see two or three cases of that a year, it would be unusual. It's a rarely-brought charge. If you sent everybody in the world to prison for doing what he is alleged to have done, you'd have no room for real criminals."

Though I hadn't been asked my opinion, that was fine by me. I was enjoying the show. Then came my big moment. Greta asked, "Professor Wilkes, you're a former member of George Jeffreys' staff, can you explain why he brought these indictments?"

"Well, Greta," I said, cringing a bit at being identified on national television as a former member of Jeffreys' staff, "I must qualify my remarks by disclosing that I had no role in the decision to bring these charges against Randolph Webster. As far as I am aware, that was never discussed while I worked for the OIC. But, that said, I think you have to go beyond the legal issues in the matter. It's obvious that someone found an obscure and seldom used criminal statute, then brought the indictments against Mr. Webster, his wife, and two of his friends. And it is equally obvious that the real objective is not to convict these people but to force Mr. Webster to provide something damaging to the President or the First Lady. I don't think that's going to happen, because, without betraying any confidential information, I don't believe Mr. Webster has any such knowledge."

I was about to explain further, but one of the "former federal prosecutors" interrupted, "Randolph Webster's plea agreement on the earlier charges required him to cooperate with Judge Jeffreys' investigation, and he hasn't done so. Perhaps this will loosen his tongue. While it might be unusual, Judge Jeffreys is following standard practice of federal prosecutors with recalcitrant witnesses."

"First," I responded, "Mr. Webster did cooperate with the investigation. He just didn't say what Jeffreys wanted him to say. Second, his plea agreement only required him to be truthful, not to confirm every screwball theory put forward by the OIC or the professional Cannon haters. And third, I disagree that it is standard practice. It comes mighty close to tampering with and intimidation of witnesses, and you know you'd be saying that if the U.S. Attorney tried to indict any of the witnesses that have testified for Jeffreys." Made me glad I wasn't on the set right then.

Greta stepped in to diffuse the situation with her usual grace. "Professor Wilkes, can you give us any insight into the process by which the charging decisions are made by the Independent Counsel? George Jeffreys has frequently said it is a deliberative process, not just his decision alone. What can you tell us about that?"

'Well," I said, trying to think how to sound tactful, "most of the major decisions are made by the Policy Committee, which meets at least once a month, sometimes more often. Besides Jeffreys, that includes his two media folks and several lawyers. Now, I don't have any direct knowledge, but I'd guess that Walt Lecraw, Mike Ellick, and Bart Gedney were the key participants in this decision."

"And why is that?" Greta knew she was throwing a lob with that one, and I was ready for it.

"Well," I said again, realizing that I needed to stop saying "well" so often, "you have to look at their history, their legal records. When Mike Ellick failed to get a wife to testify against her husband and lost a case out in California, he used income tax charges against them. The judge dismissed those charges as vindictive, of course, but it's not a lesson easily learned.

There was no interruption this time, so I continued, "Walt Lecraw, in a case down in Texas where I used to work, indicted a Congressman's wife to pressure him to plea. Didn't work, and she was eventually acquitted on all counts. In another related political case he lost down there against the Jaffes, friends of Speaker Wright, he indicted a man who refused to wear a wire to help him entrap Congressman Gonzales. After the guy was acquitted on all counts, Federal District Judge Lucius Bunton was so incensed that he told Lecraw to tell his bosses at Justice to stop wasting the courts' time with their 'witch hunts' and not to bring any more 'rinky dink' cases like that. So, Lecraw left Texas and went to work for Jeffreys."

The light was still on, and no one seemed interested in stopping me. "Then there's Bart Gedney. The theory behind this case is not unlike that Gedney tried in *U.S. v. Adams*, a case that reached the Sixth Circuit back in 1989. Alayne Adams had filed a sex discrimination case against the EEOC. When she wouldn't settle, Gedney tried to get her for perjury when she referred to a worksheet as a Form C. The perjury conviction was reversed, because the court said the government hadn't met the burden of showing that it was a material fact. And they also said there had only been five indictments for perjury in the past ten years, and none of them had been for anything in a civil suit."

"Then Gedney indicted her and her husband for tax evasion. They were convicted, but the appeals court overturned the convictions because of governmental vindictiveness and the prosecutor's actual retaliatory motivation. In a stern rebuke to Bart Gedney, Judge Nelson said, 'It is not only the inexperienced and the overly ambitious who may be tempted to misuse the prosecutorial power, although they are certainly subject to that temptation. There are times when the judgment of even the most highly qualified and virtuous of prosecutors—perhaps especially they—will yield to an excess of zeal. One thinks of the Massachusetts men who, in an age not so very far removed from our own, prosecuted witches.'"

Fortunately, I had rambled on so long that there was no time for rebuttal. Greta had cut me lots of slack on time, and I was somewhat relieved when, the moment I finished my last sentence, I heard her say, "That's all the time we have for this—for today. Thanks to our guests, and thank you for watching."

I unhooked my microphone and drove back to the law school for my office hours. I don't think anyone on the faculty ever knew that I'd been on the show. At least they never mentioned it. But I was glad that Jeffreys, Ellick, Lecraw, and Gedney would know. Jo Gobles would have the transcript of my remarks on their desk as soon as it was posted on the CNN website. Brought a slight smile to my face as I imagined them reading it.

Those boys never learn, though. Less than a week later, a federal judge dismissed all counts of the indictments against Webster, his wife, and his two friends. I'm sure they were surprised, because Jeffreys had arrogantly argued that Webster did not have standing to challenge his authority and that the judge could not review the referral by Judge Chase. Wrong on both counts. The order said Jeffreys had ignored the statutory requirement that the Attorney General approve his expansion of authority to investigate Webster on tax charges and that Judge Chase and the special division had exceeded the statutory and constitutional limits on their authority by referring the case to Jeffreys. Really dumb on Jeffreys' part, because Harriet Otis would have approved anything he wanted.

Even more telling, though, was the judge's finding that the subpoena served on Webster was the quintessential fishing expedition. While still in prison, Webster had received a subpoena for all his tax and business records back to 1992. He asserted his Fifth Amendment rights, Jeffreys granted use immunity, and Webster turned over more than 13,000 pages of documents. Then Jeffreys searched the records to try to find some obscure tax violation. The indictment had been based on materials provided under the grant of immunity and was void. The whole thing was thrown out, because Jeffreys had violated basic constitutional rights. There was never any need for the judge to address the question of vindictive prosecution. But everyone knew.

Chapter Thirty Seven

After the disastrous public relations campaign that ended with the brutal news conference at Hostus University and the desperate indictment of Randolph Webster that ended with a scathing dismissal of all charges, the general consensus was that Jeffreys was finished. However, he was not to be underestimated, regardless of how difficult I thought that might be.

At first I didn't see the connection, but a pattern soon emerged that was all too familiar and all too convenient to be confused with mere co-incidence. Only a little reflection was needed to see that it had been brewing for several months—even while I had been on the Policy Com-mittee, blinded by my own discomfort and failing to see what was hap-pening at the time. Now, though, it was clear.

The Christine Putnam lawsuit had been dormant for more than two years. It had once been one of the favorite fantasies of the right-wing junta, back in early 1994. Cliff Smegman had arranged to give Putnam the initial publicity, using paid testimony from the troopers and com-plicit reporters at the *American Speculator* and the *L.A. Times* who were willing to print the allegations or manufacture a few quotes to improve the story. Smegman also orchestrated Putnam's coming out party at a big wing-nut convention and arranged an exclusive series of interviews with Robert Bauman, a reporter who already had exhibited an obsession with Cannon's sex life during the last campaign. Mellonskoff money and Lynch Legal Foundation advice brought out the big guns. Two lawyers who had worked in the White House Counsel's Office under Stuart were instrumental in helping Christine Putnam hire two new lawyers, who just happened to have worked for the Justice Department under Stuart.

The trial court had ruled that the lawsuit would have to wait until Cannon left office, causing many of Putnam's backers to lose interest. Putnam was quoted as saying, "Whichever way it went, it smelled like money." There was a certain odor about the whole thing, but it wasn't money. It was part of a larger effort to get Cannon.

Jeffreys had worked with Putnam's lawyers on a brief arguing against that position, but, after his appointment as Independent Counsel, he'd passed that job to Dudley Pelley, a New York cigarette lawyer. Last week, the Supreme Court ruled that a sitting president could be sued while in office, opining that such litigation would take little time and hardly be a distraction from official duties.

The ball was now back in play, and the head cheerleader was a journalist named Stuart Sellers, who published a long essay in the *American Lawyer*. I didn't know much about Sellers, but I'd seen him meeting with Jeffreys a few times at the office when I still worked there.

Seller offered a circular argument, much like those I had come to expect from Jeffreys, demanding that Cannon had to prove his innocence. As a public official, Cannon could hardly sue for libel on this one or any of the others in the right-wing volley. Then, when he refused to dignify it with a reply, they declared him guilty. "Putnam's evidence is highly persuasive," Sellers asserted, though there was no evidence other than her word. "So, too, is the absence of evidence where one might expect to find it. President Cannon has carefully avoided making any statement whatever—sworn or unsworn—about what, if anything, happened between him and Christine Putnam. He has never personally, publicly denied that. All this amounts to clear and convincing proof of Putnam's allegation."

Then one particular paragraph caught my attention. It telegraphed a strategy that could well have come from Jeffreys. Without attribution to either Jeffreys or his old friend Bob Benson, who now represented Putnam, Sellers revealed, "Putnam's lawyers have visions of putting the president between the rock of damaging admissions and the hard place of possible perjury; of troopers testifying; of loading the record with rumors and leaking their filings; of grilling alleged former lovers of the president; of compelling a physical examination of the president and getting his medical records; of forcing him to answer questions about every woman he'd ever met."

Bob Benson's law firm had only represented Christine Putnam for a few weeks. Her previous lawyers, the boys from Stuart's Justice Department, withdrew after she rejected a settlement offer from Cannon's insurance companies. According to court records, Putnam and her political advisors decided that the lawyers didn't deserve a third of the money and certainly didn't deserve a cut of future book royalties.

When Jeffreys gave that speech at Hostus, he also attended a reception in his honor at the Ratched Institute, a religious outfit that often litigated for school prayer. Shortly thereafter, the Ratched Institute announced that they would bankroll Christine Putnam's lawsuit against Cannon. Benson's firm was chosen to represent her, probably because two of his partners had previously worked at the Ratched Institute. Other than that connection, it was a strange choice. Their previous practice was best known for its defense of the Texas sodomy law and a suit against a local women's clinic.

Although the Benson firm took the case on a contingency fee basis, the money was already flowing freely for Putnam. Patrick Moroney of Operation Revenge and the Christian Defense League announced a fund drive, and Christine Putnam signed a fundraising agreement with some outfit that guaranteed her $100,000 to spend as she wished. Got herself a make-over and a Mercedes. The Ratched Institute coughed up about $200,000, mostly for a couple of private investigators to peek in keyholes and chase old rumors about Cannon, which they hoped to recoup with their own fund drive. Problem was, it backfired. Ratched lost so many of their regular contributors that they had a $1.5 million drop in pledges, laid off seven staff members, and had to close their Washington office.

The article also provided another motivation for those who were so enthusiastic in publicizing the Christine Putnam case—a chance to attack the liberal women's organizations and to undermine the political legitimacy of those in the pro-choice movement. Displaying the resentment that had been festering among Republican partisans since 1991, Sellers asserted, "I'm all but convinced that whatever Cannon did was worse than anything Justice Chandler Thom was even accused of doing." There it was. Seizing on the opportunity to charge NOW and other groups with hypocrisy for failing to support Christine Putnam in her suit against Cannon, the right-wing attack machine could also question their commitment on other social issues.

Two days later, the issue was joined on Larry King Live, and all the players were there to show their cards. The program opened with a film clip of a press conference by the political director of the Ratched Institute who was shown saying, "I think it's very disheartening to see the National Organization for Women willing to sacrifice women's rights on the altar of what now seems to be a political agenda,"

That brought a counter from Pat Schroeder, one of the guests in the studio, who replied, "Well, let's think about that. I think one of the problems a lot of women have, including me, is it looks like it's men's power games between who's going to have power—and there is no greater power than destroying a president—they're kind of using women as pawns."

Stuart Sellers wasn't going to let that obvious point go unchallenged. Repeating the theme of his article, he fired back, "The evidence supporting Christine Putnam's allegations of predatory, if not depraved, behavior by James Cannon is far stronger than the evidence supporting allegations of far less serious conduct by Justice Chandler Thom. Meanwhile, not a single one of the feminist groups that clamored first for a Senate hearing and then for Chandler Thom's head, has lifted a finger on behalf of Christine Putnam. And most striking, in my view, is the hypocrisy, ignorance, and class bias of feminists and liberals—who spurn Putnam's allegations as unworthy of belief and legally frivolous.

The discussion heated up from there, as Patricia Ireland jumped in. "Christine Putnam picked her forum, and she picked her friends," she countered. "NOW will not be rushed to judgment in this case by what may well be right-wing attempts to undermine us. Christine Putnam has surrounded herself with a phalanx of politically motivated lawyers and spokespeople who are opponents of the women's rights movement. Whether she is part of them or just a pawn, we may never know. We are also disinclined to work with the disreputable right-wing organizations and individuals who advance her cause, who themselves have a long-standing political interest in undermining our movement to strengthen women's rights and weakening the laws that protect those rights."

This promised to be better than mud wrestling. Bay Buchanan, in a red dress, didn't even wait for King to introduce her. She immediately replied, "Conservatives wouldn't even have had to even show up at the doorstep of Christine Putnam if the women had done what they say they always will do, and that is to support the woman and take her side, give her proper representation, give her her day in court. They haven't done that. They were not to be found. Christine Putnam does not fall into that profile that the feminists enjoy most. She's not a career woman, she's not the big Ivy League-educated attorney as was Anita Hill, she comes from working people, high school graduate only, secretarial position, very, very pleased to have a new job making $10,000 a year, whereas Anita Hill was the professor from a university. I think there's a real elite element now to the women's movement, and it no longer represents women across this country whatsoever. In fact, they are frauds and hypocrites."

Deborah Katz didn't take the bait. When King asked her to comment on Buchanan's argument, she again turned it on the conservative backers of Putnam's suit. "I think that it's about politics; it's not about their concern for the issue of sexual harassment or women in the workplace. They've never been in the trenches in litigating these cases, they've never been champions of this particular issue. They've routinely gone to the courts and tried to erode the legal protections, and I would say that's extremely hypocritical. Whenever you look at someone bringing a case you have to look at the motives that the person may have. And anytime somebody raises a sexual harassment claim, that doesn't mean that the person should get uncritical support. You know they aren't doing it because they're for women. They view this as a clever attack, some sort of perverse plot to turn back the clock for women by taking sexual harassment law to its illogical extreme."

Responding from a live feed out of Dallas, one of Putnam's lawyers sneered, "That reminds me of what my torts professor at Baylor once said. The best way to get a bad law changed is to enforce it."

King seemed almost at a loss for words, a very unusual occurrence, but he quickly recovered and tried to regain control of the program. Hoping to get closure on the ranting, he introduced Richard Goldstein, a writer for *The Village Voice,* and asked, "Richard, what's your take on all of this?"

Goldstein only added to the rhetorical conflagration when he responded, saying, "What's most remarkable about this litigation is its feminist subplot in the production Republicans are calling The Crisis of Feminism. Republicans are playing the gender card as only the party of the angry white male can. Feminists have never been able to stoke a sex panic with anything like the agility of right-wingers, who may be so adroit at manipulating sexual dread because they spend so much energy managing it in themselves. Indeed, this right-wing sex scandal is a meta-event that transcends ordinary reasoning."

A commercial break ended the argument. The first segment had been over-produced, and the confrontational exchanges were more heated than King seemed comfortable moderating. When the show resumed, he took a bit more control by directing the questioning and calling on a couple of guests who had not participated earlier.

"We'd like to hear now from the woman who is running one of the three legal expense funds for Christine Putnam," King said. "Katie Moroney is with the Christian Defense Coalition and the Christine Putnam Expense Fund. Her husband, Reverend Patrick Moroney was an officer in Operation Revenge, and he has recently completed the Impeachment '96 bus tour. Welcome, Katie. Do you have any response to what our other guests have said tonight?"

"Well," she said, "I still think it's essentially very important that somebody stand up for this woman. Since the liberal women's groups wouldn't even talk with Christine, we felt someone should support her in this terrible case."

Turning to Deborah Ellis of the NOW Legal and Educational Fund, King asked, "What about the accusation that NOW wouldn't even talk with Christine Putnam or her lawyers?"

"Not true," replied Ms Ellis. "I called her lawyer and sent him NOW's packet of information about sexual harassment laws. We never heard from him again, nor have we heard from Putnam's new lawyers. I would give advice to her lawyers if they called me and asked for advice. But, no one has called and asked."

King looked surprised by that and asked, "Is that true, Katie?"

Hedging uncomfortably, Katie Moroney explained, "We did ask the National Organization for Women immediately to get on board before it ever went public and said, 'Would you please just hear this woman? Have a conference call, and let's just talk about this issue.' And, when the conference call was set up, Christine never came. She was out shopping for a dress. I said, 'Christine, what happened?' She said she didn't have many dress clothes with her. She said, 'I needed to go out.' She never received a call. In fact, she said she never probably knew nothing about the phone call."

"Uh huh," King mused. "NOW says this recent fervor in support of women is a cynical ploy to undermine the women's movement. What about that? Did you speak up for Anita Hill?"

"No," Moroney said without elaboration.

"Well, maybe you could explain something else for our viewers," King continued undeterred. "What does Christine Putnam need the money for now, once her suit is filed?"

"Simply her legal fees, from the attorneys," Moroney said. "The money is directly deposited into this bank account. No one will ever know who the donors are. Completely anonymous. Christine never sees the money. She will take no money for anything. She's already said that if they do receive any punitive damages, they will give it to charity."

Not willing to let that fiction pass, King then said, "I thought the Ratched Institute had agreed to pay all the costs of the lawsuit. How much are the lawyers charging? I mean, didn't they take this on a contingency basis?"

"I'm not aware of what they are charging," Moroney answered without answering.

King smiled slightly as he said, "Yeah. If this lawsuit isn't about money, then why did Christine Putnam refuse the substantial settlement offered by the President's insurance company?"

Before Moroney could deflect that one, I heard Lindsey's car pull into the driveway. I quickly grabbed the remote and turned off the television. After two years of a C-SPAN diet, I now seemed to be watching much more television. Not yet game shows of sitcoms, mostly talk shows, but I was still embarrassed. Well, except for Greta and 'Burden of Proof,' but I told myself that was work related. I quickly dashed for my study and began thumbing a civil procedure casebook.

Even the news shows were now becoming like soap operas, though. Despite a gag order on the parties, imposed by Julie Hoffman, the trial judge in the case, Putnam's lawyers were loading up their filings with every rumor their investigators could chase down and a few others that seemed to be the product of their imagination. The Putnam legal team and George Jeffreys seemed to be on the same track now, conducting tandem discovery regarding Cannon's amorous behavior during his days as governor of Alabama. But they were not alone.

Robert Bauman of *Newsweek* was the investigation's chief hand-maiden. He'd always been interested in the stories about Cannon. Not the Whirlpool stuff so much as the tales of other women. He'd been there for all of them. When he still worked for the *Washington Post,* he led the national press in giving play to the lawsuit Carl Weiss had filed against Cannon during the 1990 gubernatorial race. It wasn't like that took a lot of investigative reporting, since copies were readily available at Nelson Grenier's campaign headquarters. During the presidential campaign, he was always in search of "bimbo eruptions," a term he made famous. Then he had the exclusive interview with Christine Putnam. He spent months trying to make the Putnam lawsuit into a national story and quit the *Post* when the editors didn't give it the play he thought it deserved.

Now at *Newsweek,* Bauman had found more support, as the magazine flirted with tabloid journalism trying to catch up with *Time* in advertising and circulation. Bauman ran with a story about a former flight attendant named Carrie Phillips who claimed that Cannon had "groped" her during a meeting in the Oval Office in 1993. Not a crime, but titillating enough that *Newsweek* wanted to make it news. Based on Bauman's article, all the networks and wire services spread the allegation around the world in 24 hours. Cannon's denial, said the press, only proved that he was lying.

Like most of the gossip now passing as news, there was a problem with the story. It fell apart within the week. The *Richmond Times-Dispatch* published a sworn deposition by Carrie Phillips when she was a defendant in a Virginia lawsuit, in which she told a very different story and denied that she had even talked to Cannon. Turned out that she also had some serious financial problems, including a $300,000 lien by the IRS on her condo. She had been shopping her story for several weeks, offering both a book publisher and one of the tabloids an exclusive for $300,000. Neither were interested. Bauman was never asked whether *Newsweek* had paid Phillips for the scoop.

Bauman defended his article by saying he had confirmed Carrie Phillips' version of events with two sources—the highest standard in journalism. He'd also claimed two sources on his Christine Putnam stories, but both the troopers and Cliff Smegman had taken money from GOP operatives. His first "source" was a friend of Carrie Phillips who said Phillips asked her to lie to Bauman and confirm the story. She called Bauman later and told him it was a lie, but he still published the story.

Bauman's second "source" was even less believable. Edna Merkin, a secretary who had worked in the Stuart White House and stayed on a few months under Cannon before being summarily transferred, told Bauman that Phillips mentioned the incident on the day it happened. Merkin, though, had long been an outspoken critic of Cannon and the White House staff, having been one of Gastone Diletto's favorite witnesses on the death of Hal Goodall and reportedly having been the anonymous White House source for the recent anti-Cannon book, *Jiving Jimmy II*. Merkin had also tried unsuccessfully to hustle her own book manuscript about Cannon, including a chapter entitled, "The President's Women." Hardly credible to begin with, but later even she had written to *Newsweek* expressing doubts about the Phillips story.

There were, of course, other possible explanations for the story Carrie Phillips was now telling. Her husband had committed suicide as a result of their financial troubles, and her emotional state at the time could have been a factor. When two of her creditors sought payment from the life insurance policy, she called one of their lawyers in the middle of the night and blamed him for her husband's death. A warrant was issued for her arrest on charges of harassment. That was about the same time, according to news reports, that she had asked Cannon to nominate her as a United States Ambassador, so perhaps reality was an elusive thing. Some doctor on one of the talk shows theorized that Phillips' perceptions might have been affected by a combination of Prozac and Valium, citing studies that have shown a combination of the drugs caused seratonin syndrome hallucinations, including sexual fantasies.

Besides Christine Putnam, Carrie Phillips, and Edna Merkin, it seemed that lots of folks were looking to get rich by making accusations about the president's sex life. Maria Halpin, a former classmate of Cannon, wrote a book implying that she and Cannon had an affair in high school. Although she had retained Mildred Gillars, a book agent well connected with conservative publishing houses and the anti-Cannon network, none found the story of interest nor of much literary value. Not even Hank Regency. Halpin finally printed it herself, then went on Marion Rabbidson's religious television channel to hype the book and to confess she had been in therapy for sexual addiction. When book sales still didn't take off, she sued Cannon for interfering with her business opportunities.

Even Robert Bauman, the sex-story addict, had failed to show much interest in Maria Halpin's tale. That, of course, did not stop George Jeffreys from sending investigators to talk with her. Nor did it stop Christine Putnam's lawyers from taking her deposition and leaking it to the press. That was their standard practice by now—and to be expected in litigation motivated by politics instead of justice. One particularly outrageous leaked document was an unsworn affidavit from an Alabama lawyer alleging that Cannon had raped some woman at a conference. The woman publicly denied it, but that didn't stop the Benson firm. They filed it in a court drop box on Saturday, while the judge was out of town on a Florida vacation, and it was the topic of the day on Fox News Sunday. Good headlines, too, even if it weren't true. What didn't get reported, though, was more revealing. The affidavit detailed how the attorney had made some secret tape recordings and turned them over to Nelson Grenier, who quickly moved to set up an exclusive interview with one of his contacts at the *L.A. Times*. Probably the same reporter Smegman had employed to spread the troopers paid accusations.

Judge Hoffman had allowed the Putnam team to ignore her gag order with impunity and to make her look quite silly. Barbie Bergen-Belsen, Putnam's publicist, was now a regular on the cable news programs, calling Cannon "that little slimeball." The tabloid filings were appearing in the news on a regular basis, and she did nothing to stop them. Guess she was saving her enforcement energy to keep Jessie Banaghan in jail and couldn't spare any harsh words for Putnam's lawyers thumbing their noses at the court.

It had been an amazing week, but things were getting, as Alice said, "curiouser and curiouser." Until now, the coordination and collaboration between Jeffreys investigation and Christine Putnam's legal strategy had been limited to mere speculation. Perhaps it was only a coincidence that Bob Benson's Dallas law firm took on Christine Putnam as a client shortly after Jeffreys had attended a Texas Bar Association convention, Perhaps it was only a coincidence that Jeffreys had unleashed the FBI to interview a number of women in Alabama at the same time Benson's firm had hired private detectives to do the same thing. Perhaps it was a coincidence that the Ratched Institute had agreed to finance Putnam's lawsuit shortly after Jeffreys had given a speech at Hostus University. Perhaps.

Speculation became a thing of the past, however, when someone at the Chicago office of Kirk & Polis faxed a copy of an affidavit in the Putnam case to the *Chicago Tribune* several days before it was filed in Judge Hoffman's court. The *Tribune* reported that Kirk & Polis had confirmed the authenticity of the fax, and Buck Etienne was on television that evening, hammering away and saying, "I think what happened is Jeffreys has pissed away probably $45 million 'investigating the president.' He came up with nothing. Nada. So now he gets in the middle of a sex investigation. I think there's real evidence that needs to be looked into, whether there's collusion between Mr. Jeffreys' office and the attorneys in the Christine Putnam case. I think there's a lot of suspicious evidence. And I hope that somebody investigates this."

"We are not working in collaboration with the lawyers for Christine Putnam," came the official response from Walt Lecraw. "Judge Jeffreys has had no substantive communications directly with them at all."

A spokesman for Kirk & Polis also denied that the firm was involved in the Putnam case, and Bob Benson said it was "ridiculous" to think there was some conspiracy between him and Jeffreys just because they had known each other in college.

There would, of course, be no investigation of Jeffreys and his contacts with the Putnam legal team. The Justice Department was prohibited from supervising Jeffreys, even if Harriet Otis had been so inclined. Judge Chase could do so, but there was no chance in hell that would happen. The major media, those who bothered to report anything about the fax, accepted the official, but telling, denial from Walt Lecraw.

Maybe Jeffreys would offer to investigate himself, but Cannon's legal defense team was not waiting for that charade. Cannon's attorney issued a subpoena to Kirk & Polis for all records relating to the Christine Putnam case. The spokesman for Kirk & Polis, who had previously denied any involvement in the case, now fought the subpoena, citing attorney-client privilege. Then, Jeffreys was forced to show his hand. He filed a motion with Judge Hoffman under Rule 403 of the Federal Rules of Criminal Procedure to quash the subpoena to his law firm, claiming that it would interfere with his criminal investigation.

That move puzzled even his defenders, as the *New York Times* acknowledged, "The Putnam case and Judge Jeffreys' Whirlpool investigation are separate matters, although it has often been difficult to tell how separate." The *New York Daily News* was less mystified, and one columnist explained, "Suddenly Jeffreys is on the receiving end of an investigation, and he does not like that at all. He could be required to reveal documents that show that he had indeed colluded with the Putnam case. This inquiry gave Cannon a wedge to pry the lid off this interlocking network of his most dangerous foes."

Jeffreys denied that he was trying to protect himself or his law firm, few were fooled about his real motivation. Any contact between Jeffreys' staff and Putnam's attorneys—including using a cut-out through one of the attorneys at Kirk & Polis—would be against Justice Department rules. If an attorney at Kirk & Polis was doing something that amounted to legal work for Putnam, that created a problem for Jeffreys. The acts of Jeffreys' partner in the practice of law were still Jeffreys' acts, by virtue of their partnership.

Most of the speculation about the work done by Kirk & Polis was focused on Porter Andersen, one of Jeffreys' partners in the Chicago office. Andersen was a former Special Assistant to President Stuart, and he had been an official with the Stuart campaign during the last election.

He married a White House intern from Chicago and moved back there after Cannon won the election. Andersen had been involved in the Putnam case from the get-go, helping the *American Speculator* and the Lynch Legal Foundation recruit Washington attorneys for Christine Putnam. There was another possibility that everyone seemed to be overlooking. James Peck had joined the Chicago office of Kirk & Polis after leaving the OIC staff, but he had maintained a close relationship with Jeffreys and others in the office. I wondered why no one ever made that connection.

The question was never answered, though, because Judge Hoffman quashed the subpoena, ruling that "the evidence, although relevant, may be excluded if its probative value is substantially outweighed by considerations of undue delay, waste of time, or needless presentation of cumulative evidence. This weighing process," she held, "compels the conclusion that evidence concerning Kirk & Polis should be excluded from the trial of the Putnam matter."

So the question of who at Kirk & Polis was working on the Putnam case remained unanswered, as did the question of what possible relevance the Putnam case had to Jeffreys' authority in the Whirlpool investigation.

Chapter Thirty Eight

George Jeffreys was fortunate in one sense, because the stories about his legal and ethical problems were always limited to a single news cycle. James Cannon, on the other hand, had been living under a cloud of rumor and innuendo for four years. Even now, when it was obvious to everyone that Jeffreys had hit a dry hole on every bogus charge he had sought to investigate—the Cannons' Whirlpool investment, the suspensions at the Resolution Trust Corporation, the First Lady's role in the Travel Office cleaning, the sad death of Hal Goodall, the FBI file fiasco, charges of hush money to Randolph Webster—he refused to admit failure, close up shop, and issue a final report.

In the entire time since he had been appointed, the only report Jeffreys had filed was that on the Goodall suicide. Mitch had told me during lunch last week that the draft reports on all of the other authorized investigations had been written months ago, and he had only the one on the dismissed Webster indictments to complete before leaving Birmingham. Although Mitch had seemed excited about some new goose chase in the DC office, that was hardly an excuse for Jeffreys to sit on the final reports on the other prongs of the investigation. It didn't make any sense. Then I read Chris Kelly's article in *The Allodium*.

The essay was titled "Why Jeffreys Can't Quit," and it captured exactly what Jeffreys had been doing for the past two years. "When you can't find evidence of guilt, the next best option is to prolong the investigation," Kelly explained. "Not only does it postpone the embarrassing admission that your targets are in fact innocent, it lets you keep a cloud over their heads as observers speculate that you must be on the trail of something big. Just keep saying that you are at a 'critical juncture' in the investigation. Even better, you can help this impression along with selective leaks of 'evidence' that would never stand up in a real court. Have an uncorroborated story from a dubious source? Who cares? There's no such thing as cross-examination in the grand jury room. And you can edit, slant, or even falsify that story to your hearts content, then leak it to a few pet reporters—who'll be so grateful for the 'scoop' that they won't question a word you say."

As soon as I got home that afternoon, I called Mitch to ride his ass about the delay in the final reports and confront him with Chris Kelly's argument, which I appropriated and passed off as my own. Mitch did not deny that there might have been some truth to that assessment of the strategy, but he said the problem now was that Jeffreys was trying to hire someone to write the final draft and put the OIC's arguments in readable and convincing form. In other words, spin.

Jeffreys, Mitch said, had wanted either Stuart Sellers or Robert Bauman to write the final drafts, but both of them were reluctant to give up their lucrative new roles as political commentators on the cable news shows. There had been some discussion of either Danielle Leonard at the *Post* or Luis Gerucht at the *Times*, but everyone thought they were too valuable where they were. Jeffreys had also ruled out, for reasons of appearance, Martin Ruddy Rimm and William Ambrose-Cobbett. There had even been some talk about hiring David Windrig, but the leading candidates right now were Stephanie Glass of *The New Republic* and Patrick Smith of the *Boston Globe*, both of whom were available. "Judge Jeffreys wants a genuinely moral conservative, someone religious but not an ideologue, to polish the reports," Mitch confided, adding, "Whatever happens, though, none of the reports will be filed before the election."

The presidential campaign continued, but there was little enthusiasm, even among the candidates. The polls showed voters generally happy with the economy, and President Cannon maintained a lead that was slipping yet still comfortable. Taking a break from the hustings, Cannon was scheduled to give a deposition in the Christine Putnam lawsuit on Wednesday. The media appeared more excited about that than about anything he had said during the campaign or, for that matter, anything he had accomplished during his tenure in office.

The only real interest I had in the president's deposition was the certain knowledge that, even though it was under seal, Putnam's lawyers would leak a copy to the press in an attempt to embarrass Cannon, and I'd have something to talk about in my Professional Responsibility class. I did remember, though, Stuart Sellers' article and his insider's view that Putnam's lawyers had "visions of putting the president between the rock of damaging admissions and the hard place of possible perjury." I thought it more likely that they had visions of dodging Rule 11 sanctions for their own frivolous filings, getting a transcript of the president's sealed deposition to the media, and escaping once more without a contempt citation from Judge Hoffman.

The evening news made much of the fact that a president had never been deposed as a defendant in a civil suit. The clips were of the presidential limousine arriving for the event, but little else was needed to support the speculations of the television reporter. Later that evening the cable channels included a segment showing Christine Putnam and her phalanx of lawyers laughing and toasting at dinner in some local restaurant, looking almost as if they were celebrating the signing of a book contract. The only surprising thing, as far as I was concerned, was that none of the networks yet had an expedited copy of the transcript of the deposition.

By the next morning, however, that had changed. I was on my first cup of coffee and still skimming the paper, paying only scant attention to the television, when I heard some guy almost yelling, "He lied! He lied!" I looked up to see William Krystalnacht, the editor of the *Weekly Standard*, talking about Cannon's testimony and basing his learned analysis on something he'd seen in the *Dredge Report*, an Internet gossip sheet of ill repute.

"Nonsense. Nonsense upon stilts," I smirked to Lindsey as I left for school.

Then all hell broke loose. By the time I had finished my class at noon, *Newsweek* had hit the stands with a story by Robert Bauman that Cannon had been intimately involved with Daphne de Clerambault, a 24-year-old former White House intern, and had denied it under oath during his deposition in the Putnam case. At the same moment Cannon was giving his deposition, George Jeffreys and the FBI had taped de Clerambault talking to a wired informant, a con woman who had been working simultaneously with Jeffreys' office and Putnam's lawyers, and moved in to ambush the young woman during lunch.

According to the *Newsweek* article, Jeffreys and his lawyers had confronted Ms de Clerambault with 20 hours of surreptitiously recorded phone conversations in which she talked about an affair with the President, held her in a hotel room and interrogated her for 10 hours without an attorney present, and threatened her with 20 years in prison for filing a false affidavit denying a relationship with the president. They apparently told her she could save herself by wearing a wire and entrapping President Cannon and Vernon Montaigne, the president's close friend and unofficial advisor.

Everyone at the law school was talking about the story that afternoon, particularly Ms de Clerambault's taped claims that she had "earned her Presidential Knee Pads." Already people were cracking jokes about the Oral Office, referring to Cannon as the Head of State, and saying perhaps the young woman had misunderstood when Cannon offered her a position on his staff. Of course, no one bothered to question whether the story was true.

It was breaking news, but it also sounded like breaking laws. What was Jeffreys doing taping a witness in a civil suit unrelated to Whirlpool and without authorization from the Attorney General and the court? How could Jeffreys have known what Daphne de Clerambault might have said in an affidavit that was under court seal? Why did Jeffreys deny Miss de Clerambault the right to speak with her attorney? Was Jeffreys guilty of intimidating and tampering with a witness in a civil suit? Was that obstruction of justice? And how did Robert Bauman know so much about the sting operation and the contents of the taped conversations?

When I got home that afternoon Lindsey was watching the news on television. Sam Donaldson furrowed his brow as he said ominously , "The President will be out of office in a matter of weeks, if not days." She flipped over to CNN where Wolfe Blitzer was panting, "Top advisers have discussed various scenarios, including resignation!" This was the kind of story that made them salivate. Bagging a president was big game, one for which a generation of reporters had been wishing and waiting.

Breathlessly, Blitzer put on his solemn face and told Bernard Shaw, "Well, over here at the White House, there is a desperate mood among some of the president's closest associates, obviously very worried. This is obviously the most serious crisis that has affected his presidency. Even a former White House chief of staff is now musing openly about the possibility that the Vice President may have to take over, saying, 'This is a difficult moment for the nation. I worry about his ability to lead the country.'"

Over on ABC, Gary Stuphanonvelopes, a former Cannon friend now getting fat with a book contract and a pundit's position, was raising the possibility of impeachment. Like a rat looking to get off the ship, he said, "I don't think a president is loyal to his people if he either knowingly asks them to lie or asks them to say things which he realizes are not very credible, asks them to take him on his word without giving them reasons to take him at his word. And I think that is the trap that Cannon has set right now. I believe the President has a huge problem. Judge Jeffreys has a real passion about this case now, and I think he's deeply offended."

Even Chub Campbell had rehabilitated his reputation and was being taken seriously, at least seriously enough to fill network air time. "I don't really know, but let's assume, okay, that his sexual relationship with the First Lady is not all it's supposed to be," he said with a sheepish grin. "The public for the most part is quite forgiving of adultery, but voters take a far dimmer view of perjury."

When asked what the president might think of his off-color analysis and the caustic remarks of former insiders, Campbell replied, "I don't care what Cannon thinks. It is not the least bit slimy, as someone who knows the President and knows the First Lady well, to offer my insights to the American people. The money I've taken from those people was to help them get elected and re-elected. Now I'm trying to make a transition from having been a private adviser to now being a television pundit. I'm not an advocate for anybody at this point, except for myself and my own career."

While most of the coverage was reporters repeating reporters and anchors speculating without evidence, a few interesting details emerged that evening. Edna Merkin, the disgruntled former White House secretary, was at the center of the plot, just as she had involved herself in the Hal Goodall investigation and the Christine Putnam lawsuit. On the advice of her book agent, Mildred Gillars, Merkin had been taping telephone conversations with Daphne de Clerambault for several months and working in concert with Putnam's lawyers to lay a perjury trap for Cannon. Robert Bauman had been coaching Gillars and Merkin on what they'd need for a good story and, of course, a good book. Merkin had taken the tapes to Jeffreys, who was titillated but was unable to use recordings which might have been made illegally. On the day before Cannon's deposition, Merkin had then strapped on a tape recorder to snare Miss de Clerambault for Jeffreys, then his FBI agents drove her home to brief Putnam's lawyers that evening. Bauman, agreeing to hold the story until Jeffreys was ready to spring it, had the exclusive on what Jeffreys was calling Operation Trip Wire. This was what Mitch had been so excited about.

Gillars appeared to be Edna Merkin's publicist, as well as her book agent. Talking with reporters in New York and sounding as if she were speaking for George Jeffreys as much as for herself, Gillars said, "What I'm glad about is Cannon's getting caught. At something. If it took this to get him, fine. I'm a hero if this thing comes out the way my side would like to see it come out."

Why, one reporter asked, had Gillars encouraged Merkin to tape the phone conversations with Daphne de Clerambault? "We are just two middle-aged women who couldn't stand it anymore. We had no choice but to do this," Gillars replied. "I'm very, very proud of Edna Merkin. She was afraid she'd lose her job when she went public again, so she had to have proof. When you're tall, thin, blond and have big boobs, you can have any job you want, but Edna had blossomed to a size 16. After her comments about the Hal Goodall investigation and having told Robert Bauman about the incident between the president and Carrie Phillips, she had reason to be worried. She knew how Cannon's people had trashed her friend, Gary Ames, when he wrote his book."

Another asked whether Edna Merkin had any remorse about the way she betrayed a friend? "Oh, no," said Gillars. "The taping wasn't just for her book. It was also intended to benefit Daphne de Clerambault. If she ever decided to sell the story of an affair with Cannon, there would be proof she told a friend about it at the time."

When asked about the possibility that she and Robert Bauman might have criminal exposure for conspiracy with Merkin's illegal taping of the telephone conversations, Gillars said that was another reason Merkin had taken the tapes to Jeffreys. "Edna's former attorney had convinced her that she had done something illegal and awful, and she panicked, and she wanted immunity, and she had to have a lawyer who was connected to Jeffreys and knew how to get her immunity on the tapes," Gillars said. "Contacts were made to Tonya Vichy in Washington, then to Dudley Pelley here in New York, who referred her to John Trevor. Mr. Trevor, who had worked for President Stuart and had other connections to Judge Jeffreys, was able to arrange for the grant of immunity."

Someone asked whether Gillars or Merkin had been the ones who contacted the Ratched Institute and Putnam's lawyers to suggest that they subpoena Carrie Phillips and Daphne de Clerambault. Gillars denied that she had made the calls but said, "Even if Edna did, or if I did, so what? What's the problem? I don't see where it goes. They already had a lot on him."

One of the *Daily News* reporters at the news conference remembered that Gillars had been a campaign spy for Nixon in 1972, getting press credentials on McGovern's plane under the guise of working for the North American Newspaper Alliance. He asked her, rather pointedly, to explain her role then and what kind of materials had she gathered for Committee to Re-Elect the President. That question seemed to take Gillars by surprise. "This press conference is not about me, but I'll answer your question," she said. "They were looking for really dirty stuff. Who was sleeping with whom, what the Secret Service men were doing with the stewardesses, who was smoking pot on the plane—that sort of thing. I took the Nixon job because I wanted to get a book deal out of it. I'd do it again." Perhaps she just had.

Gillars was pretty straightforward about her participation in the scheme to get Cannon, but the real creep was Edna Merkin. As the evening progressed, the non-stop news shows filled in many of the blanks and answered many of the questions about her. Merkin had been hired as a secretary in the Stuart White House upon the recommendation of tobacco lobbyist Bill Hecht, and, for some unknown reason, Cannon's folks had kept her on the payroll. Even under Stuart, though, she had been a troublemaker. One former Stuart official was quoted as saying, "She always complained about her ex-husband. She had a chip on her shoulder. She always wanted to know where the dirt was, some controversial things. We all put her on the A-void list, don't tell her anything."

Merkin had been a problem in the Cannon White House as well. When her alimony payments ended, she tried to peddle a book about Hal Goodall, and she was working on another expose without much success. After she was suspected of leaking confidential information to a couple of right-wing authors and had been eager to disparage White House officials before Diletto's hearings, calling the White House lawyers "the three stooges," she was transferred to a position at the Pentagon, the traditional dumping ground for White House malcontents. The day she left the White House, said one co-worker, "She was very angry. Very bitter. She told me, 'I'm going to get you, and everyone else in this place, before this is all over.'" Arriving at the Pentagon, she implied that Cannon had to get rid of her because she "knew too much about Whirlpool."

On "Larry King Live" that night, Merkin was the main topic of conversation. Roy Black, a respected defense lawyer, offered his assessment. "I think that Edna Merkin is probably one of the most hated women in America today. I mean, to take advantage of this girl like this, so she can present the tapes to a special prosecutor, I think that's way beyond the pale," he said. "This is not whistle blowing. I can't think of anything worse than this. It's like your mother taping for you for God's sake."

John Kelly agreed, "I don't see her as a whistle-blower. I find her a very unsympathetic figure. I'm not sure what her motives were in the first place for making these recordings or why she went to Mr. Jeffreys with these tapes of personal conversations. There's no defense here for her."

"Yes," admitted one of Merkin's lawyers, "she clearly knows she's the most vilified person in the nation, but Edna is just the messenger. She doesn't want to be in the position of accuser. She still thinks of Daphne as a friend. Although they haven't talked since the sting operation, I'm sure in the long run they'll remain friends. By no means is this a betrayal, nor does she view this as a betrayal. I do look on her as a whistle-blower who is blowing the whistle on abuse of power and obstruction of justice."

Washington Post columnist Mary McGrory seemed to agree."Edna Merkin a whistle-blower? Calling Merkin a whistle-blower is like calling the tornado that flattened Florida a gust of wind. So far only one clear moral has emerged from the maelstrom -- Don't get on the wrong side of Edna Merkin. You cross up that lady and she will make you sorry you were born."

"Friends don't tape friends, so could we all quit calling Edna Merkin anything but the spy-provocateur she is? Nothing in this mess is more inexplicable than how anyone could record, day after day, the most intimate details, real or imagined, of another person's life. Evan Thomas, who heard the tapes, says she comes across as 'a somewhat manipulative woman,'" said a woman from *Time* magazine. "I'd say Edna Merkin comes across as a busybody with a large chip on her shoulder who'd had her first attempt at a White House book rejected. No one likes a snitch, especially one with so much to gain. Then, Merkin rails against "McCarthyistic" tactics, as if she were the one who had been taped and handed over to the FBI!"

Raising yet another question, a former Watergate prosecutor added, "Now we learn that her book agent, Ms. Gillars, has reportedly said that she was terrified because of the fact that her attorney told her what she had done in taping Daphne de Clerambault was both illegal and horrible, that she went out to try to get another attorney to get her immunity with George Jeffreys. But it's an interesting question as to why Edna Merkin got immunity. And I think that's one of the unanswered questions at this point. Usually, a witness gets immunity because the witness will refuse to testify or for some other reason. It's not here's your hat. Here's your coat. Here's immunity. So there are answers yet to come."

Following on the suggestion that Merkin was in this for profit, one of Cannon's attorneys said, "Gillars had downplayed the idea of doing a book with Merkin in her interview, but the conservative publishing house, Regency, said that Gillars had approached the company with a book proposal for Merkin about the Cannon White House for as much as $500,000. Whenever you see Edna Merkin involved in something like this, I think a responsible journalist should say, 'Well, wait a minute. What is going on here? I smell a rat in all this.'"

Robert Bauman attempted a defense of his source, if not of his role in the whole sordid affair. In discussing her role, Merkin told me, "I see myself as a victim." After a collective laugh, someone pointed out that being victimized seems to be a familiar theme in her life. According to police records, Merkin had been quick to ask the police to investigate petty incidents, things such as a torn screen door at her house. Police records since the 1992 campaign included 38 reports involving some member of Merkin's household as witness, victim, reporting party, or suspect.

Trying to defend his position but betraying his suspicious access to information about the investigation, Bauman claimed, "Daphne de Clerambault gave Edna Merkin a three-page document, which we will be publishing in next week's edition. It was titled 'points to make in an affidavit', and it appeared to encourage Merkin to perjure herself. The document, which Merkin immediately turned over to Independent Counsel George Jeffreys, is the single most tantalizing piece of evidence that someone engaged in obstruction of justice in the Christine Putnam case."

That was too much for Buck Etienne, who had been uncharacteristically silent thus far during the discussion. Buck squinted at Bauman and said, "Let me tell you something about this investigation. Jeffreys is a loser. He's wasted $40 or $50 million 'investigating the president,' and he's got nothing! Now he's off peeping through key holes looking for sex. That's all this is about! We've got an out-of-control, sex-crazed inquisitor prying into people's private lives. The American people are tired of this witch hunt. Enough is enough!"

Bauman returned fire. "Judge Jeffreys was authorized to conduct this investigation by Attorney General Otis after he presented credible evidence of serious federal crimes—perjury, subornation of perjury, and obstruction of justice. On the secret tapes, Daphne de Clerambault says that Vernon Montaigne got her a job to keep her quiet. It was a pattern, just like the hush money for Randolph Webster."

Buck Etienne rolled his eyes and shot back, "Oh, yeah, let's look at what happened. Edna Merkin brings him some illegal tapes and those so-called talking points you mentioned. He can't use the tapes as evidence, because they are illegal. Under Title 10, Subtitle 4 of the Maryland Annotated Code, it's a felony, punishable by up to five years in prison, to record a phone conversation without the consent of both parties. And nobody has any idea where your talking points came from. Maybe Merkin wrote them herself. Anyway," Etienne continued, "without even talking to the Attorney General, he has Merkin strap a tape recorder between her thighs and lure this young woman over to some hotel in Virginia and ask her a bunch of leading questions, trying to put words in her mouth. Now, that was pretty smart on Jeffreys' part, setting up the sting in Virginia, I'll give him that. If he's gonna try to frame Vernon Montaigne, he needed a jury that was a whiter shade of pale. So, then he finally goes to the Attorney General and says, 'Look at all this incriminating evidence I have. Please authorize me to investigate. And hurry, because Robert Bauman is about to print all this in *Newsweek*.' That's what happened, and you know it."

Bauman did not deny the chain of events, but he continued to stick to his story and his defense of Jeffreys and Merkin. "Judge Jeffreys had no choice but to pursue this investigation once he received the tapes," Bauman said without much conviction. "You act as if this is some conspiracy against the President, but Edna Merkin just wants to tell the truth, and Judge Jeffreys just wants the facts."

Etienne smiled. "Bauman, you don't know nothing about conspiracy. What would you say if I told you that this whole thing was just a

set-up to flush out all you sex-obsessed cooters? Did you ever stop to
think that maybe we sent Daphne de Clerambault over to the Pentagon,
put her in the same office with Edna Merkin to feed her a bunch of crap
because we knew she'd run to you and Jeffreys, and y'all wouldn't be
able to repress your own dark thoughts about sex? Think maybe you and
Jeffreys have been had? Think maybe Jeffreys and his Operation Trip
Wire fell for my little Operation Fly Trap? How 'bout that, Mr. Bauman?"

Bauman was stunned. "I stand by my story," he said.

"This is bottom fishing, as far as I'm concerned, and I have to hold
my nose to even talk about this thing," said a former judge who served
with Jeffreys on the Court of Appeals. "If an agent went into a federal
prosecutor anywhere in the country, and said, 'I want to wire a witness
for an investigation of possible perjury in a civil case,' the answer would
be, 'No.' Any prosecutor worth his salt wouldn't touch this with a 10-
foot pole. What kind of hard evidence does he have? He's got illegally
recorded tapes of two woman talking to each other, both of whom are
less than reliable. What Jeffreys has is garbage."

As far as I was concerned, that put Operation Trip Wire in the same
category with the rest of this investigation, but the judge was right. With
people like Jeffreys, Lecraw, Ellick, and Adolph—all experienced with
wiring witnesses in questionable cases—it was no surprise. Neither was
it much of a surprise the next morning when the *Washington Post* reprinted parts of the President's deposition in the Christine Putnam case,
the *New York Times* reprinted the infamous "talking points," and *ABC
News* had transcripts of several hours of the secretly taped conversations
between Edna Merkin and Daphne de Clerambault. Jeffreys had always
approved leaking tidbits to reporters who would do his bidding in the PR
battle against Cannon, but this was no longer bush league leaking. It
was hemorrhaging. And it was also a serious violation of the Federal
Rules of Criminal Procedure.

What I saw on "Headline News" that morning, though, was a surprise. A more amusing one, yet a surprise nonetheless. Almost as if to
emphasize the point for anyone who'd missed it, Jeffreys was on television, standing in his driveway and holding a bag of garbage while talking
to the assembled crowd of reporters. Quite a visual metaphor.

Kate was again back in Birmingham working on a story, and she
drove over that evening for bullshit and burgers at our house. I had
hoped we'd talk about something other than politics and its latest mani-
festation in Jeffreys' unseemly investigation, but that possibility faded
quickly. Just as I was bringing the burgers in from the grill, Kate and
Lindsey motioned me to come to the living room. President Cannon was
about to make his first public statement about the allegations on *The*

NewsHour. President Cannon gave a brief denial of any improper relationship with Daphne de Clerambault and said he had not asked anyone to do anything except tell the truth, but his lawyers had now instructed him to say nothing more.

I went back to the kitchen to get a beer and fix my burger, hoping I could move the group and the conversation but succeeding only on the first. Lindsey followed me and asked, "Do you think the president had sex with that woman?"

"Maybe. Probably. I dunno. I'd hate to think the president and the country have had to put up with this madness, if he didn't. Well, I still hate it, even if he did," I answered, trying to find an avenue to change the subject.

Kate wasn't going to let that happen, sounding exasperated as she asked, "Then why didn't he just say so in the deposition and be done with it?"

"Why would he? That's hardly the honorable thing. Gentlemen don't tell."

Still not letting it drop, Kate responded, "Well, according to the transcript in the *Post*, he admitted he'd had sex with another one of the women Putnam's lawyers asked about."

"Yeah," I replied, realizing that we were going to have this conversation after all, "but that was hardly betraying a confidence. She had sold her story to the tabloids, taken money from the Republicans, gone on national television, opened a 1-800 hotline to sell tapes, and written two books!"

"It was still perjury," Kate insisted. "which is far worse than being ungentlemanly."

I looked at Lindsey, hoping for some distraction. Sensing I was on my own here, I said, "I think not."

"How can you say that?"

I took a deep breath, feeling like I was talking with my first-year students. "Because Putnam's lawyers, in their religious zeal and missionary imagination, didn't ask the question in the right way. They presented Cannon with a precise definition of 'sexual relationship' that didn't include getting a blow job, then they demanded an answer. I think he probably answered their question truthfully."

"I think that's just a technicality," Kate said.

"Yes," I admitted, "but the law is always about technicalities, and the fault here lies with Putnam's lawyers who screwed up—they had the burden of pressing Cannon on any ambiguities in his answers—and George Jeffreys who has screwed the Constitution."

"Well," Kate replied, "it's still technically perjury."

I should have let it go, because that was an opportunity to change the subject, but I was now too much the professor. "I doubt it. For a statement to constitute perjury, even if he lied, it must relate to a material fact. Judge Hoffman never should have allowed that question to be asked, because it had nothing to do with Putnam's allegations. It was irrelevant. Except, of course, to Mrs. Putnam and her husband who were living high on the hog and to the right-wing cabal who engineered the whole charade. Hell, Hoffman should have dismissed the whole suit on day one. So, I can't see how it would ever be perjury, much less a high crime."

"But," Kate protested, "he had taken an oath to tell the truth, the whole truth, and nothing but the truth."

"Not voluntarily," I said, "so it hardly counts."

"Well, I disagree," Kate replied. "Truth is always the best policy."

I couldn't tell if she was serious or just being argumentative. "Do you really think that?"

"Yes," she said, "I do."

Okay, I smiled to myself, I'm game. So I asked, "Would you have printed the deposition if Jeffreys has leaked it to you instead of Danielle Leonard at the *Washington Post*?"

"Maybe," she answered. "It was news. And the public has a right to know."

Typical journalist's response and one I wasn't going to let her get away with. "A right? Where do you get that?"

"The First Amendment," Kate said, just as I knew she would.

"Well, have you read it recently? The First Amendment doesn't say anything about that. Nor," I said rather smugly, "can I find it anywhere else in the Constitution."

"You know what I mean," Kate said with a tinge of irritation.

"What I know," I said, "is that it was a deposition in a civil suit that was under seal by the court."

"Yes, but it was only illegal to leak it," Kate said defensively. "It wasn't against the law for the newspaper to report it."

Enough of this banter I thought. I winked at Lindsey, then turned back to Kate. "Okay, Ms Macauley, please state under oath all the men you've ever had sex with."

"Get real. You don't have time," she said with a nervous laugh.

"Just answer the question," I insisted.

"Fuck you! It's none of your damn business," she replied.

Doing my best imitation of Jeffreys, I said, "I just want the truth. Please answer the question, and we can be done with this much sooner."

"Forget it."

"Now, Ms Macauley, we already have enough evidence to put you away for 20 years, so you should make it easy on yourself."

"Oh," Kate asked, "how's that?"

"We have our ways. We've subpoenaed your phone records, your bank records, your medical records, your employment records, your credit card records, your e-mail records, your telephone answering machine, and your computer hard drive. We can get a search warrant for your apartment. We can subpoena your mother and your best friends. Now talk. Tell us, have you ever had a sexual relationship with a married man?"

"That's personal, and it's none of your business, Kate replied.

"Have you stopped having sex with married men? Just answer the question," I demanded with a smile, "yes or no?"

Knowing now that I was just playing, Kate said defiantly, "I take the Fifth."

"Oh, no," I continued, "We know you have dallied a bit, so don't make matters worse. We will give you immunity, though, if you'll tell us what we want to hear and wear a wire to help sting your boyfriend."

"I want to see my lawyer," Kate said with a laugh.

"No way, Ms Macauley. Tell us now, or the deal's off."

"No deal," she said.

"Okay. Fine," I said. "Lindsey, to the best of your knowledge has Kate Macauley ever been involved with a married man?"

"Lindsey!"

"Please hold your objections. Ms Armstrong has no rights with regard to that question, she's under subpoena, and you know the judge will grant a motion to compel. Besides, hearsay evidence is okay in a grand jury. You can answer the question, Lindsey."

"Okay, you've made your point," Kate conceded.

Wanting to make sure, I asked, "What point is that?"

"That you're an asshole."

"We already knew that, or I wouldn't have asked in the first place. So what's your point?"

"My point is," Kate replied, "it's none of your damn business."

"I just want the truth," I said, mocking Jeffreys.

"Yeah, well, sometimes the truth hurts other people who didn't ask to be involved," Kate said with some degree of seriousness.

"I just want the truth. The truth shall set ye free."

"That truth, Mr. Wilkes, is only between two people."

"Oh no! The public has a right to know," I taunted. "Putnam's lawyers have a right to know and to leak it. The independent counsel has a right to know. And leak it. Congressman Bardus has a right to know and edit your answers before leaking it."

"All right," she said, "so I was wrong. Would you lie under oath?"

"About that and under those circumstances? I think so. Wouldn't you?"

"Yeah, I guess," Kate admitted.

"You have to understand," I said, "I don't think it's always wrong to lie."

Lindsey jumped into the conversation and asked, "You mean little white lies?'

"Yeah. Say, for example, you asked me if I think that dress makes you look fat. I know the right answer. It's really immaterial to what I think about you as a person or to our relationship. Sometimes the consequences of fibbing are far less than the consequences of telling the truth. No one is harmed by answering that question in the negative, even if it were a lie. Or if some stranger called on the phone and asked you to describe your intimate thoughts, I don't think you'd be obligated to answer completely and truthfully. But I also think it's okay to lie about bigger issues, maybe especially about bigger issues. If I were being held hostage by someone who intended harm and they asked where my kids were, I would lie."

Kate sounded as if she were in reporter mode, asking, "So you don't think Cannon did anything wrong?"

"I didn't say that," I replied.

"You might as well have," Kate said, looking to Lindsey for affirmation.

"No. What I meant to say was that whatever happened between Cannon and that woman is none of Jeffreys' business nor of ours. The only person who had any right to know or even ask him about that and expect a truthful answer was his wife."

"So," Kate asked again, "are you saying you think it would be okay to lie about it in the deposition?"

I paused for a moment to ponder that before saying, "I guess I think that there are some questions that shouldn't be asked. If you have no right to ask them, then you shouldn't expect the truth. Putnam's lawyers were wrong to ask them, and the judge was wrong to allow it. And Jeffreys is wrong to ask them. If Cannon hedged or lied, I can forgive him under those circumstances."

Kate was trained to catch the nuances of language, and she asked, "What do you mean 'under those circumstances'? You sound as if maybe under other . . . ."

"Yeah, well, once it became clear that Daphne was telling the whole world, even Edna Merkin for God's sake, he was no longer under any moral obligation to protect her privacy. At that point, if something in fact happened, he could have fessed up. Just said, 'Yeah, she did. So what?' By continuing to deny it now, not under oath but just to protect himself politically, I don't think that would be right."

Kate was still pressing me and making me defend the position I was working through as we talked. "What about when he went on television tonight and denied it to the American people?"

"Well, even if he lied, that's not a crime. But it would be, in my opinion, much worse than hedging in a politically motivated civil suit or grand jury probe. I mean, it's not like it would be the first time a politician has ever lied to the people, but that doesn't excuse it. When you ask someone to trust you, whether it's in a personal relationship or a political one, you have an obligation to be honest with them. You have to realize that lying has consequences, that it hurts people, that it makes cynics of those who placed their faith in you and your words. It means you betrayed their trust, and it might be almost impossible to regain it. I think people will always doubt him, always be somewhat suspicious, even when he's telling the truth. It's going to be very hard for anyone to have much confidence in anything he says. But, like I said, Cannon should never have had to answer that question publicly. And that doesn't mean that what Jeffreys is doing is any less heinous, though. He's even worse. I'm afraid it's like James Burgh once told me, there aren't any heroes in this movie."

"So," Kate asked, "what do you think Jeffreys will do?"

"Burn in hell, I hope. He'd love to indict Cannon for perjury, but that won't happen. No one, except maybe Jeffreys, thinks a President can be indicted while in office. And furthermore, there's not a single case in the history of American law where someone in a civil case lied about having sex and was then indicted for perjury. Jeffreys will have to settle for making that allegation in a report to Congress."

Changing the subject, Kate asked, "What do you think about the suggestion by Senator Hatchet that Cannon should just publicly admit that he had some kind of relationship with Daphne de Clerambault and say he was sorry?"

"I don't know why he would," I replied. "Do you think there's anyone in America that doesn't think he did and that he wishes he hadn't?"

"Well, no," Kate said, "but Hatchet says if Cannon would just publicly confess, all would be forgiven, the investigation would be over, and everyone could get back to business."

"Oh, that's bullshit, and you know it, Kate. The Republicans would then complain that he didn't grovel enough, or they'd start a campaign for his resignation—or impeachment—saying he was morally unfit to lead the nation. They're just trying to trick him into publicly humiliating himself on national television. There's nothing they'd like more, since everything else they've tried has failed. No way he should get suckered into that game," I said.

Kate thought about that for a minute, then Lindsey asked me, "Do you think he'll be impeached?"

"Cannon or Jeffreys? Kidding. I think Cannon has already impeached himself with the American people, but he won't be impeached by Congress. He'll be re-elected because the public thinks he's doing a good job as president, and he will serve out a full eight years. Count on that, Darling."

She smiled but had a touch of concern in her voice as she asked, "Do you really think I do?"

"Huh? Do I think you count on it?"

"No," she said, "do you think I look fat in this dress?"

"Of course not, Dear. You look marvelous."

Chapter Thirty Nine

Southerners, like their Scottish ancestors, always look to the hills for their strength and support in times of crisis, and James Madison Cannon followed that example. You could almost hear the pipers playing and the sounds of Amazing Grace wafting across the Appalachians as the noted evangelist Graham MacWilliams talked with NBC's Katie Coerce. "I forgive him," MacWilliams declared. "Even if he is guilty, I would forgive him and love him just the same, because he's a remarkable man. I know the frailty of human nature, and I know how hard it is—and especially a strong, vigorous young man like he is. He has such a tremendous personality that I think the ladies just go wild over him, he's had a lot of temptations thrown his way and a lot of pressure on him."

While NBC seemed to revel in Cannon's difficulties, and the network's Tim Russert was always dealing in the latest rumors, Katie Coerce didn't always follow the corporate script. She was very good at her craft, having been trained by the Irish rhetorician John Sullivan at the University of Virginia, and she asked questions that allowed her guests to open up like a lobbyist's wallet. Coerce had interviewed Ira Dolor a few weeks ago, and it was there he had claimed that cigarettes were not addictive and did not cause cancer.

Now, though, Coerce was interviewing the preacher from North Carolina tobacco country, home of Helmut Duke and Reynolds Rantallion. The topic was the latest attack by the cigarette lawyer George Jeffreys, who claimed there was a cancer on the presidency. Responding to another question from his host, Reverend MacWilliams seemed more attuned to other aspects of the Cannons' situation when he spoke of the President's personal relationships. "He and Diane love each other, and I love them both," he said. "And I know and respect her, and I think she's a marvelous First Lady in that she's gone through all this and backed him and supported him. And I think that, in itself, is a testimony to people everywhere."

Back in Washington, though, some folks saw things in a different light. A "confidential" memo from GOP pollster Nelson Luntz advised the Republican leadership to go on the attack against Cannon. The talking points suggested asking, "What example is James Cannon setting for our children?" Another proposed that they should "forget the word 'scandals' and start using the word 'crimes' when talking about Cannon." And revealing the coordination between the politicians and the prosecutor, Luntz urged them to strongly support George Jeffreys and to always refer to him as "Judge Jeffreys."

The Luntz memo was embraced even more quickly than it had been leaked. Campaigning back in Indiana, Congressman Bardus called the President a "scumbag." His personal lawyers, Joe Desipio and Tonya Vichy, went on *Geraldo Live* to criticize Cannon, without disclosing that they represented Bardus or that they were being paid $25,000 a month as part-time sleuths for one of the GOP's numerous investigations. Nor did they reveal that they had been leaking information from Jeffreys to the *Dallas Morning News*. Desipio and Vichy were soon exposed, their credibility ranked right down there with Bardus, and they were forced to cancel their network pundit contracts.

The House Majority Leader, my fellow Texan Dick Denton, called Cannon "a shameless person," and asserted, "If it was me, I'd be so filled with shame that I would resign." Made me wish it were him. The best response came from another Texan, Paul Beluga, who laughed, "If goofy ideas ever go to $40 a barrel, I want drilling rights on Dick Denton's head. This is just further proof that the right wing of the Republican Party is trying to use the Jeffreys operation for partisan advantage."

Speaker Leroy Reichman took the floor of the House and declared, "We have never seen the level of complex, interlocking lawbreaking that we have here. A false statement under oath is a crime, and it should be prosecuted to the full extent of the law." One of his Democratic colleagues, making reference to the Speaker's ethics problems, which included a $300,000 fine but only a reprimand by the House, replied, "Mr. Reichman giving Congress lectures on moral authority is like Jerry Springer giving the country lectures on good taste."

Coming to Reichman's defense, Gerald Winrod of the Atlanta Legal Foundation published an op-ed piece in the *Washington Sun*. Explaining away the Speaker's false statements under oath, Winrod wrote in the passive voice, "Documents prepared by his attorney contained an inaccurate statement regarding the relationship. Mr. Reichman accepted responsibility for the characterization. We've seen Mr. Reichman admit a mistake, which amounts to little more than a clerical error, and take responsibility for that error. Conservatives across this nation should support him in that example of political responsibility."

Congress Bob Swill, a close associate of Winrod and a former president of the Atlanta Legal Foundation, renewed his call for impeachment in a speech before the John Birch Society, which picked up all his expenses for the event. During his 1994 campaign, Swill had pledged to uphold "the highest possible moral and ethical standards," but he was now in no position to throw any stones at Cannon.

A recent Federal Election Commission audit showed that Swill had accepted $50,000 in illegal campaign contributions, misstated his financial activity, failed to disclose political action committee donations, and did not make timely disclosures. Swill's attorney, former RNC Counsel Ben Ginsburg, said "Congressman Swill was not familiar with all those technicalities. As a result, some mistakes were made, all of which have been corrected now."

Even more embarrassing for Swill and his stance as judge of public morals, the *Atlanta Gazette* published photographs of him licking whipped cream off the chests of two women at a recent charity auction. While some thought he should have more sympathy for Cannon's predicament, Swill's record revealed a closer affinity with Jeffreys. As a United States Attorney under President Reeder, Swill had been investigated by the Justice Department for grand jury leaks and had been twice reprimanded by federal judges for his public statements.

In another flying wedge, noted Lone Star Loon and House Majority Whip Tom LeHay announced that he would lead a GOP Values Action Team and provide a GOP War Room to provide information about impeachment procedures. After a meeting that included Speaker Reichman, Majority Leader Dick Denton, and representatives from the Christian Coalition and Focus on the Family, LeHay held a rambling press conference to attack Cannon. "Here is a flower child with gray hair doing exactly what he did back in the '60s," LeHay said with a pious smirk much like the one Jeffreys displayed so often. "President Cannon seems to have no shame, no integrity, no dignity. When you have a president that in my opinion has cheated on his wife, he will cheat on the American people."

Reflecting both the partisan nature of the controversy and the deteriorating level of the conversation, the Democrats continued to reply in kind, giving as good as they were getting. On *Larry King Live* that night, a Democratic Committeeman from California promised to turn the tables and take a look at the GOP's credentials to chuck moral rocks. "I'm getting a little tired of these damn Republicans going after the President," said Bob Mulligan. "If the Republicans want to make attacks on family values and morals, then the public has a right to see their public record. Pretty simple. After all, these guys aren't from the Sisters of Charity convent. They have Leroy Reichman, they have Tom LeHay, they have Bob Swill, they have Dick Denton, John Ashcroft—they all go on TV attacking the president. They ought to just stop it and get back to the business of this country. And, you know, Bob Swill—I mean, if I see that guy on TV one more time attacking the president on this moral stuff, I think I'm going to puke."

The White House quickly denied any involvement with Mulligan's proposed counterattack, failing to provide air support for their infantry in the battle with Congressional critics. At least for now. The big guns were being aimed at George Jeffreys and his unending investigation of charges generated by paid political assassins. No White House denials followed the remarks made by Diane Cannon on the *Today* show the next morning.

As I tuned in, the First Lady was holding forth with gusto. "We've been through this so many times," she sighed with resignation. "I mean, James and I have been accused of everything, from drug-running to murder, by some of the very same people who are behind these allegations. So from my perspective, this is part of the continuing political smear campaign against my husband. You'd think that the media might catch on soon."

The guy conducting the interview seemed a bit unsettled by that last reflection. "But, but," he stammered as he asked, "you don't think it a bit unusual for the president to help an intern in the White House to get a job in the private sector?"

"No," she replied, "I have known my husband for more than 25 years, and we've been married for 22 years. If I don't have any problem with it, I hardly think it should be of any concern to you or George Jeffreys. The one thing I always kid James about is that he tries to help people who need help, who ask for help. That's why he chose to run for public office, to help people."

"Yes," he said defensively. "but I think what makes reporters uneasy is that a very dear friend of your husband, Vernon Montaigne, recommends this particular intern for two jobs in New York, and then drives her personally to a lawyer's office when she's subpoenaed by George Jeffreys."

The boy was out of his league now. Diane Cannon looked him in the eye and said, "First, you're wrong. Mr. Montaigne introduced her to an attorney when she was subpoenaed by lawyers for Christine Putnam, but that might well be a distinction without a difference. I don't know what makes you think that anyone besides you and George Jeffreys is even curious. I mean, Mr. Montaigne stood up and said what I believe to be the absolute truth—that he has helped literally hundreds of people—and it doesn't matter who they are. Is that a crime in this country now? Vernon Montaigne has survived a sniper's bullet, and he'll survive this attempt at character assassination by George Jeffreys and the members of his staff who resent Mr. Montaigne's leadership in the civil rights movement."

The host tried to regain control of the questioning, but he was clearly overmatched. The First Lady refused to yield any point, continuing, "The chattering news shows seem conveniently to omit the fact that Mr. Montaigne is a close friend of Daphne's mother's fiancé, Steven Strausberg; he delivered a eulogy at Strausberg's wife's funeral. Daphne's mother is also a friend of Walter Kaye, who has donated $350,000 to the Democratic party and who recommended Daphne for her White House internship. Mr. Kaye also contributed to Jessie Banaghan's legal defense fund, and, as you may remember, for that kindness he was hauled before the grand jury by Mr. Jeffreys. That's the only thing surprising in all this, that the press has ignored that abuse of the grand jury process, not that Vernon Montaigne would help a friend's daughter find a job."

Sounding as if he were convinced, or at least convinced to go with the flow, the guy asked, "Then you think that this is the worst and most damaging smear in the history of American politics?"

"Well, I don't know," Mrs. Cannon said with a smile and a history lesson. "Thomas Jefferson was accused of being an atheist and having a child by Sally Hemmings. Dolly Madison was rumored to have been unfaithful. Andrew Jackson's wife died of a heart attack shortly after reading vicious attacks on her character in a partisan pamphlet. Grover Cleveland was wrongly accused by Reverend Ball and the Republicans of fathering and abandoning an illegitimate child. Woodrow Wilson was accused of killing his wife. Then there were all the stories about Franklin Roosevelt, John Kennedy, and Lyndon Johnson. So, Democrats have been smeared by sex-obsessed conservative opponents since the country began. But this might well be the longest and best financed smear campaign of this century."

Trying to appear more empathetic than pathetic, he nodded and asked, "But this is pretty devastating?"

"Well, this is what concerns me," she explained. "We get a politically motivated prosecutor, who is allied with the right-wing opponents of my husband, who has literally spent several years and $40 million looking at every telephone call we've made, every check we've ever written, scratching for dirt, intimidating witnesses, doing everything possible to try to make some accusation against my husband. But, devastating? Only to the public's faith in the justice system and the political process."

Attempting now to appear to be directing the interview, the host said, "We're talking about George Jeffreys here, so let's use his name because he is the independent counsel."

"Well, we're talking about him," she replied, catching her breath, "but I wouldn't use the term independent. And it's the whole operation. It's not just one person. It's an entire operation."

"Did Judge Jeffreys go beyond his mandate, in your opinion, to expand this investigation? After all, he got permission to expand the investigation from a three-judge panel."

That was a standard defense from the Republicans, and the First Lady did not let it go unanswered. "Yeah," she said, "the same three-judge panel that removed Kenneth Burke and appointed Jeffreys. The same three-judge panel that is headed by a shill for Helmut Duke and Reynolds Rantallion. The same three-judge panel that has never said 'no' to any expansion he has requested. And I just think that this is deliberately designed to sensationalize partisan political accusations against my husband, because everything else they've tried has failed. And I also believe it is part of an effort, very frankly, to undo the results of two elections."

"But Attorney General Harriet Otis also approved," he interjected, hoping to deflect the First Lady's assignment of blame.

Diane Cannon's response gave me hope that perhaps, at last, the President finally realized what a disaster that appointment had been. "Well, of course," she said disdainfully. "What would you expect from her? Jeffreys got all excited when he heard some illegally taped phone conversations. He then conducted an unauthorized sting operation by getting Edna Merkin to wear a wire, manipulate the conversation, and entrap a young woman. Next he comes up with these bogus 'talking points' that are leaked to his friends in the press. Finally, he runs to the Attorney General and gleefully says, 'Oh, Robert Bauman's going to break this story in *Newsweek* if you don't approve it immediately.' So she approved it without even conducting any meaningful preliminary investigation as required by the statute."

Seeing the ground sink beneath his feet, the host moved back to his list of prepared questions. "Buck Etienne has said that this is 'war' between the President and George Jeffreys. You have said, I understand, to some close friends, that this is the last great battle and that one side or the other is going down here."

"Well I don't know if I've been that dramatic," she chuckled. "That would sound like a good line from a movie. But I do believe that this is a battle. I mean, look at the very people who are involved in this. They have popped up in other settings. The great story here for anybody willing to find it and write about it and explain it, is this vast right-wing conspiracy that has been working against my husband since the day he announced for President. A few journalists have kind of caught on to it and explained it, but it has not yet been fully revealed to the American public. And actually, you know, in a bizarre sort of way, this may do it."

"You've just made quite a charge," he gasped, "that there's a vast right-wing conspiracy to get the President. Can you back up that accusation?"

"Well, perhaps it's not exactly a conspiracy, because that would suggest that it's somehow secretive; whereas, the connection between George Jeffreys and Howard Mellonskoff is open and in fact," she said rather reasonably without raising her voice. "But, let's look at the very people who are involved in this coordinated smear campaign against the president. It doesn't take a rocket scientist to figure it out. It is a matter of public record that Howard Mellonskoff's foundations have funneled millions of dollars to such groups as the Independent Women's Forum, the Washington Legal Foundation, the Capital Legal Foundation, the Federalist Society, the Fund for a Living American Government, the Free Congress Foundation, the Lynch Legal Foundation, Executive Watch, the Atlanta Legal Foundation, and the American Speculator Educational Foundation."

"But," the young man asked, "what does that have to do with George Jeffreys? How does that make him a part of some right-wing conspiracy?"

"Let's look at these groups and what they do," she said. "George Jeffreys worked with the Independent Women's Forum when they wanted to file a legal brief for Christine Putnam. The Fund for a Living American Government funneled $50,000 in front money to Christine Putnam's legal fund. The Lynch Legal Foundation assisted in finding lawyers for Christine Putnam, and they represented the now discredited Ellende Varken who made the original Whirlpool charges. Executive Watch currently has 18 different lawsuits against the administration, though most recently they've been wasting their time trying to subpoena reporters' notes and harassing friends of the president. The Atlanta Legal Foundation is fronting a public relations campaign to defend Jeffreys. The *American Speculator*, which published the false and now-retracted story about the state troopers, has been using Mellonskoff money to hire private investigators who report to Mr. Gedney at the OIC and providing cash and other inducements to Roby Douglas, Mr. Jeffreys' star witness, both before and after his testimony in the Jefferson Savings case."

The guy was desperately fumbling with his notes, so the First Lady took advantage of the pause and continued her explanation. "Now, here's just one example of how these groups are all tied together. Barbara Stevens, former counsel to the House committee investigations of the Travel Office firings and the use of FBI files, is a founder of the Independent Women's Forum, an organization funded by Mellonskoff, which asked George Jeffreys to file a brief on behalf of Christine Putnam. Shows up all the time as a commentator on news programs without disclosing any of this. She is married to Thad Stevens, who sits on the board and is Treasurer of the *American Speculator*, another entity funded by Mellonskoff, which spent $2.4 million on the Alabama Project and other investigations of my husband. Mr. Stevens is a former law partner of George Jeffreys, also worked with him at Justice, and was one of the lawyers for Roby Douglas in the Whirlpool investigation. Got it now?"

"Okay," he conceded, "but just yesterday, four former Attorneys General released a statement defending Judge Jeffreys' investigation and asking the White House to call off the attack dogs. Now, one of those was Griffin Bell, who served under President Carter. He's not a Republican. Doesn't that blow your conspiracy out of the water?"

Not even blinking, she said, "No, actually, it makes my point. Bob Adams, George Jeffreys' personal lawyer, is Griffin Bell's law partner. Mr. Adams is married to Dot Holloway, a former Stuart staff member who tried to influence the investigation of Jefferson Savings during the 1992 election. None of that, of course, has been reported by your network."

Impatiently and somewhat testily, he asked, "That's a bit of a stretch, don't you think?"

"If you'll let me finish, I'll try to help you understand," she said, unintentionally showing her disdain for mediathink. "Griffin Bell, Jr. is chairman of the board of the Atlanta Legal Foundation, one of the groups funded by Howard Mellonskoff. In the past, that group distinguished itself by attacking affirmative action and food programs for the poor. Since taking the Mellonskoff money, they've launched a campaign to defend Jeffreys. The press release was only a part of this campaign. Congressman Swill, a former president of the Atlanta Legal Foundation, is the sponsor of the impeachment resolution in the House. The current president, Gerald Winrod, is an op-ed contributor to the *Washington Sun*, and he, along with Ike Parker, represented Gary Ames, the former FBI agent who wrote a fictitious scandal book that has since been exposed as a fraud. And the publicist for that book was the same GOP operative that handled the Christine Putnam press conference at the National Conservative Convention in Washington last year. And who was the publisher? Hank Regency, George Jeffreys' old friend and former Justice Department colleague, who was also considering Mildred Gillar's request that he publish Edna Merkin's book. Want more? I haven't even begun to discuss the ties that bind Dudley Pelley, John Trevor, Deborah Stone, Bob Swill, Mark Schine, Porter Andersen, Bob Benson, and George Jeffreys."

That was enough for the host. And it was enough to send George Jeffreys ballistic. He hastily called a 10 o'clock news conference at the Federal Courthouse and read a statement obviously written very carefully by Della Beckwith. "The First Lady today accused this office of being part of 'a vast right-wing conspiracy.' That is nonsense. I have had no direct conversations with Mr. Mellonskoff during this phase of our investigation."

Jeffreys should have stopped there, but, like Cannon, he always said more than he should. "Our current investigation began when we received evidence of serious federal crimes," he protested. "We promptly investigated by having the informant lure her friend to a hotel bar in the Northern District of Virginia and wear an electronic listening device to secretly record their conversation. Then we informed Attorney General Otis, and asked if we could pursue this matter. Our investigation is being carried out by highly-experienced federal prosecutors, such as Mr. Lecraw, Mr. Ellick, and Mr. Adolph."

President Cannon broke his silence during a photo opportunity that afternoon. Asked whether the First Lady's remarks on the *Today* show reflected his position on the Jeffreys investigation, Cannon replied, "It's obvious, I think, to the American people that this has been a hard, well-financed, vigorous effort over a long period of time by people who could not defeat me in the last election, who could not contest the ideas that I brought to the table, couldn't even contest the values behind the ideas that I brought to the table, and certainly can't quarrel with the consequences and the results of my service. Therefore, personal attack seems all they know and all they have left. All I can do is show up for work every day and do the very best I can. That's what I did today, and that's what I intend to do tomorrow."

I was having a cold beer and watching the controversy play out on *Inside Politics* when the phone rang. "John, this is Mitch. We're getting creamed. I've just received a copy of our latest poll results. Can I talk to you?"

"Sure," I said, paraphrasing Ross Perot, "I'm all ears."

"No, I mean can I come to Tuscaloosa. I don't want to talk on this phone."

I agreed, because Mitch was obviously worried about his future. "I'll throw on a couple of steaks, and they'll be ready by the time you get here."

When Mitch arrived he was still a bit shaken. He tried to make polite conversation with Lindsey, but his nervousness was all too obvious. I got him a beer and another for myself, and we went into my study. Handing me the poll results, Mitch plopped down in my favorite leather chair and sat silently while I surveyed the damage. It was worse than I had imagined.

Cannon's job approval rating was an astounding 73%, while 23% approved and 56% disapproved of the way Jeffreys was handling the investigation. A whopping 59% said Jeffreys should end his investigation now. Only 22% thought Jeffreys was interested in finding the truth, and 63% said he was primarily interested in hurting President Cannon politically. Even on the question of whether "Cannon's political enemies are conspiring to bring down his presidency," 59% said yes. The answer that must have hurt Jeffreys the most was a personal approval rating of only 11%, right down there with Edna Merkin at 10%.

I looked up with a somewhat pained expression, and Mitch said, "It gets worse," handing me a copy of a fax from Senator Hatchet to Jeffreys. It was an article from the *Desert News* in Salt Lake City. Even in Utah, the only state where Cannon had come in third in the last election, a Dan Jones poll showed that 59% thought it was time for Jeffreys to drop his pursuit of Cannon.

"Well, Mitch," I said, "if this were just a legal investigation, the polls wouldn't matter much, other than persuading witnesses and jurors to trust the prosecution. But it's not. It's a political investigation. And, if nothing else, Congress can read the polls. It's over. You can't indict a president for chasing nookie, and Congress isn't about to impeach Cannon for that. Not with those numbers this close to an election."

With a bewildered look, Mitch said, "Sometimes it seems like a nightmare that won't ever go away, and I always think to myself, 'It can't get worse than this.' But it does. Every day it seems to get worse and worse. What would you advise?"

"Well," I said, "if you move quickly and avoid the rush, you can probably get a Senate or House staff position. That's one of the options I considered when I resigned."

"No," Mitch replied, "I can't do that. I can't leave Judge Jeffreys now. I meant, what can we do to improve our public relations?"

Only then did it hit me what Mitch had been asking, because I had only been thinking of what was best for him. "Prosecutors work in the realm of facts and law, not public relations," I said, "and it's illegal to even discuss evidentiary matters publicly. Besides, Jeffreys' problem isn't public relations. The public knows very well what he's been doing, and no amount of spin can disguise that. The best thing y'all could do would be to stop peeping in keyholes, wrap this thing up, exonerate the innocent, and let people get on with what's left of their lives."

Mitch didn't want to hear that, and I hadn't intended to be so blunt. After a rather uncomfortable silence, we rejoined Lindsey for dinner and avoided the subject of politics for the rest of the evening. As Mitch left to drive back to Birmingham, I was still wondering what he might do. I knew he would stay on, that much was clear, and I doubted that he would have much influence on the course of the investigation, even if he considered my advice.

It didn't take long, though, to see the course chosen by George Jeffreys. Two days after Mitch's visit, Della Beckwith was aiding and abetting Jeffreys in a rather transparent exercise in public relations intended to rehabilitate his image and stop his free fall in the polls.

The opening volley was a hastily arranged self-promotional speech to the Christian Business Men's Committee. Trying to make himself sound like a regular guy, though revealing much more, Jeffreys told the group, "My favorite exercise is going on a morning jog to a little park called Pimmit Run. There's no one around, and I've got my favorite spot. And I sing a hymn. And then I offer a prayer. Then I begin my busy schedule for the workday, talking with the media in my driveway even before my driver takes me to the office. As I begin the third year of this investigation, I am working to complete this inquiry as thoroughly and as quickly as possible. When you think of the blessed life that Jesus led on earth, think of his time utilization. He didn't waste a lot of time. Three years, that's the length of time that this individual, human yet God, spent shaping the future history of the world."

The *Washington Sun* covered the speech and led with a page one paean to piety headlined, "Deeply Christian Jeffreys Starts Day Jogging, Singing Hymns." Buck Etienne wasn't about to let that one pass uncontested. "Yeah, Jeffreys plants a story, he jogs down to the Potomac and sings hymns as the cleansing water of the Potomac goes by, and we're going to wash all sodomites and fornicators out of town. Jeffreys publicly brags that he reads the Bible to guide his conduct in his little nickel-dime sex investigation. Well, it looks like to me that he must be reading 2 Peter 22," Etienne said on CNN. "People that pontificate, the Sunday morning talk show crowd, all of the people that don't drink brown whiskey or eat red meat, say, 'this is fine we're having this official investigation of somebody's sex life.' Well, I'm going to tell you, this is one shoe clerk in this poker game that says, I don't think this is a real good idea, folks."

It now seemed as if Etienne had been right when he said this was war. It was beginning to look like a Holy War.

Thomas Cromwell, chairman of the Christian Business Men's Committee, defended Jeffreys and asked, "Who are Diane Cannon and Buck Etienne to attack Judge Jeffreys' integrity? Would that they have one-tenth the moral fiber in his body." Similar praises came from the *Columbus Dispatch* in an article declaring, "Judge Jeffreys Is Carrying Out God's Commandments." I was almost expecting Reverend Marion

Rabbidson to lay hands on Jeffreys and issue a fatwah on Cannon. It was a fine line Jeffreys was walking, touting his religious devotion with such enthusiasm that he was in danger of being seen as a Puritanical zealot.

Instead, the planted stories continued in quick succession. Jill Abramson of the *New York Times* faithfully repeated the saga of the hymn-singing jogger who grew up admiring Richard Nixon. Even more brazen was a puff piece placed through Sue Anne Pressley in the *Washington Post*. Jeffreys arranged for sympathetic reporters to interview his 90-year-old mother, Fannie, to testify to what a fine man he was, and she readily obliged. "We started taking George to church when he was two weeks old, and he has never smoked or drunk or been heard to curse," she said proudly as scripted. "George was an indoor child, a straight-A student involved in everything but sports. He would play for hours, sitting on a stool next to his bed, moving wooden clothespins around. His main hobby was polishing his shoes. He was not a bit girl-crazy. He never did date girls to amount to anything."

When asked about the current criticism of her son for prying into President Cannon's private life, Mrs. Jeffreys had a ready answer. "Well, I don't think much of a man who would trifle on his wife. George was just not raised up to be familiar with anything like that. His daddy was not that kind of man either, as far as I know," she said. Then, as previously coached, she added, "I think it's awful that the country tolerates a President that has the reputation that he has. I think it's awful that he can't be satisfied with his wife."

Like his earlier attempts in public relations and political speech-making, Jeffreys' latest effort was another disaster. In one of his daily driveway news conferences, one that ended with an embarrassing babbling in Spanish, Jeffreys had compared himself to Dragnet's Joe Friday. That brought a scathing reply from the actor's widow, who wrote a letter to Jeffreys saying, "My God, my husband wouldn't want to have anything to do with you!"

Even old friends were dismayed. One GOP consultant told Larry King, "I think the reality is that he needs to disappear himself. He needs not to make anymore dumb PR mistakes. No more silly statements in front of his house in McLean, walking to the car. I mean, I think the reality is he doesn't give any information, maybe doesn't have anything. Every morning you watch him walking out late to work, and it doesn't make him look very serious."

A columnist in the *Baltimore Sun* was even less guarded, declaring, "George Jeffreys is a fool. They say he is highly intelligent, big IQ and all that. There is something wrong with the man. Only a fool would ramble on, disoriented, to a gang of hungry reporters in the driveway of his own home. What was he talking about? Stop! Go home! There is going to be no impeachment!"

Wired magazine had perhaps the best assessment that week, a nugget of wisdom from popular culture that made me smile. "In recent days, George Jeffreys, addicted to one of Washington politics' favorite drugs—seeing himself on the evening news—has come forward and revealed a bit of himself in interviews," observed the writer. "George Jeffreys is no Joe Friday. In fact, I'd argue that he's much more akin to Mr. Weatherbee of '60s comic-book fame, Archie's addle-brained high school principal."

"Mr. Weatherbee looks a lot like George Jeffreys," continued the article in making the point, "and has his more-or-less benign sense of outrage when even the most minor infractions are committed. Eyebrows popping right out of his head in fury, Weatherbee stalks Archie and Jughead relentlessly through the halls and playgrounds of Riverdale High. But he can never manage to catch them in any wrongdoing or prevail long enough to see them properly punished. Nor does he sense how out of touch with his own time and place he is. Unlike Joe Friday, this Weatherbee is doomed never to get his man. He is too clueless, oblivious, slow-footed, out-of-it. But like Weatherbee, it seems that Jeffreys will never quit trying."

Laughter is the pallbearer of fame, and Jeffreys could not stand the humiliation he had brought upon himself. He was further frustrated and infuriated by the success of Cannon's supporters in constructing a different picture of him and his endless investigation—the growing evidence of his questionable tactics and the abuse of power—causing even old friends to question his motives. "All these years I thought of my friend George Jeffreys as Mr. Nice Guy," said Bruce Flim. "Then I wake up one day, and he's the Anti-Christ."

Jeffreys seemed determined to prove his critics right. In a display of desperation fueled by paranoia, he issued a grand jury subpoena to Al Sidney, the White House Director of Communications, in an overreaching attempt to stop public criticism of him and his whole operation. "Our office in recent weeks has been subjected to an avalanche of lies," Jeffreys complained. "Misinformation and distorted information have come to us about career public servants, and we cannot tolerate this attempt to intimidate us. We intend to stop these lies about us. The First Amendment is interested only in the truth. We have a legitimate interest in inquiring into whether there is an effort to impede our investigation."

No one in the press corps seemed to know what Jeffreys was talking about, nor was it clear that he did either. Walt Lecraw, standing at his side, offered a further explanation for why they were targeting contacts between the White House and the press. "What you have here is a situation where somebody is peddling filth and lies about dedicated federal prosecutors, in what appears to be an attempt to intimidate us, and, based on what we have been told, we believe that the somebody is Al Sidney or someone else in the White House," he said. Then, sounding almost like one of Cannon's supporters, Lecraw added, "The sex smears are distortions and exaggerations of benign incidents."

Finally, Jo Gobles explained what had been behind the subpoena, what had caused Jeffreys to do something so dumb. "Our office is under siege by media queries regarding professional and personal misconduct by Judge Jeffreys, Mr. Ellick, Mr. Adolph, and other members of our staff," she said. "We have received more than 20 calls from news organizations seeking information on these matters."

The White House response was cleverly understated. When asked about the subpoena, Deputy Press Secretary Roy Gunter told reporters, "At one point Mr. Jeffreys promised the American people he would be investigating the leaks from his office. He's now apparently more interested in how we conduct press relations here at the White House. I think that speaks for itself."

Buck Etienne, however, was less subtle. Interviewed by CNN, he said, "Well, subpoena me! I'll tell Jeffreys right smack to his face, I'm spreading stuff every day. I'll be on the phone all day today talking to reporters about George Jeffreys. And if you don't like it, Mr. Jeffreys, too bad, because you ain't going to shut me up. George Jeffreys can go jump in a lake. If he wants by some kind of a fiat to declare himself above the constitution, I'm not going to pay any attention to it. He's a public figure, engaged in what I believe to be a slimy and scuzzy investigation. And I'm going to call it like I see it. The American people can't stand him. People know what he's up to. They're tired of him. You spend millions of dollars and end up investigating people's sex lives? You better believe people are going to criticize you. Now, this man has wasted $40 million, and he's complaining about having to answer the phone 20 times."

On another program that evening, Etienne proved that he was not just puffing and bluffing. He used the opportunity to show Jeffreys how ineffective his tactic had been, how the move had only reinforced public perceptions. "There was a stunning report on CBS last night," Etienne charged, "where Bart Gedney said that Jeffreys wanted to indict everybody for everything. They're harassing women all over the country. These people are obsessed with sex. He's a sex- obsessed pervert who's out to get the President. And everybody in the country knows that. He's concerned about three things—sex, sex, and more sex. That's all that man's about. This thing is totally out of control. We have a sick, out-of-control, sex-crazed prosecutor, who has spent $40 million of taxpayers' money investigating people's sex lives—and he's complaining because they got to answer the phone! Damnedest thing I've ever seen."

Perhaps Jeffreys had expected to further provoke Buck Etienne, but he could not have been prepared for the response from those who could usually be counted on to support anything he did. When I checked the online news services the next morning, even I was surprised at the uniformity of the reaction among his friends in the media. "I don't think it's good for the search for truth. It obviously has a chilling effect if people think they're going to be asked about talking to reporters," said *Washington Post* reporter Danielle Leonard. "A very disturbing development," confided one source at the *Wall Street Record*. "This just seems to be totally wacko," said NPR's Nina Totenberg, "We really are living in a police state." Alas, the *New York Times*, cheerleader of the investigation from the beginning, wrote, "On the tactical level, this move by the independent counsel is bone stupid. This latest blunder fits a pattern of chronic insensitivity to his public responsibilities."

Any vain hope Jeffreys might have had for friendly media support ended when William Streicher's column declared, "Jeffreys is abusing the power of a grand jury to suppress criticism of his methods and his aides. How easily he is manipulated. He lost his judicial temperament and went for the bait. But no matter what the provocation, George Jeffreys has no business going into court to go after the press, dismayingly unaware that the First Amendment's interest is not in truth but in freedom."

Not having classes that day, I stayed home to work on my book that morning. With Jeffreys now declaring that any public criticism of him was obstruction of justice, I wanted to be sure I included a conversation I recalled when he first tried to use that charge against the President and First Lady back when I still worked there and he had invented his theory about hush money. Or maybe it was the billing records. Couldn't remember for sure, but I did recall the conversation.

It was near the end of one of the Policy Committee meetings last year. "Excuse me for educating myself in public," I said, "but I don't know what you mean by 'obstruction of justice.'"

George Jeffreys smiled contemptuously. "Of course you don't—until I tell you. I meant there's a nice knock-down argument that we can use!"

"But 'obstruction of justice' doesn't mean a nice knock-down argument," I objected.

"When I use a word," he said in rather a scornful tone, "it means just what I choose it to mean—neither more nor less."

"The question is," I complained, "whether you can make words mean so many different things."

"The question is,'" said Jeffreys, "who is to be master—that's all."

I worked on the manuscript for a couple of hours, but, during the afternoon, I found myself spending considerable time watching the public relations meltdown on television. I flipped on CNN to see what Greta might have to say on *Burden of Proof.* Seems she'd had a bit of trouble finding one of the usual apologists for Jeffreys. Georgetown Law Professor Paul Rothstein surmised that the pursuit of Cannon's private behavior had caused Jeffreys "to lose all judgment." Neal Sonnett, a former federal prosecutor said, "Jeffreys has pushed the edge of the envelope all through this case, but this tears the envelope. This subpoena is totally inappropriate, and it just demonstrates his vindictiveness." Steven Shapiro, legal director of the American Civil Liberties Union was even more disdainful. "What George Jeffreys perceives as suspicious behavior, the framers of the Constitution saw in a very different light. They called it free speech," he said. Floyd Abrams, the noted First Amendment lawyer, agreed, "This is the stuff of the Sedition Act." There was no quarter offered.

Inside Politics was also devoted to the topic of the Sidney subpoena, and the commentary was equally critical of what Jeffreys had said and done. Trying to find some balance, Bernie Shaw directed the first question to Republican Senator Specter. Having been so ready to find perjury in Anita Hill's testimony and having advanced the infamous "single bullet" explanation in the Kennedy assassination, perhaps Specter would find a way to justify George Jeffreys' interpretation of the law now. But it was not to be. "George Jeffreys went too far in using the grand jury to counter criticism of him and his deputies. It is unwise to try and stretch the obstruction of justice statute as far as George Jeffreys did," the Senator conceded. "I think that's sort of a first-year law student's reading of the statute. The First Amendment is intended for freedom of speech. I think that George Jeffreys made a mistake on that."

Things only got worse as Judy Woodruff cut to a news conference on the House side. Congressman Conyers was less charitable to both Jeffreys and Attorney General Otis. "It's an obvious and blatant violation of Department of Justice rules as well as the United States Constitution," he said. "Prosecutors are not licensed to engage in arbitrary fishing expeditions, nor may they select targets of investigation out of malice or an intent to harass. Only the attorney general can curb Jeffrey, but, so far, I am sorry to report, she has said and done nothing since granting his request to allow him to get into this sordid mess."

Returning to one of the aspects of the Jeffreys investigation that Lindsey had recognized long ago, Representative Sheila Jackson Lee gave another perspective on what was happening. Without specifically mentioning the nebulous link Jeffreys had argued to implicate Vernon

Montaigne in his nefarious quest to get Cannon, she said, "I believe that the independent counsel is out of control. This is not the McCarthy era. This is not a time to take away the rights of our citizens. My fear, my apprehension, as someone who was in the civil rights movement when intimidation raged in this country, I would simply ask that we not go back to that era."

As the program was ending, I heard Lindsey's car pull into the driveway. Not wanting to appear the couch potato that I was, I rushed to my study to turn on the computer and appear busy. That, I thought, would also give me an excuse for not having started fixing dinner. A few minutes later I heard the television and figured it was safe to return to the living room, where I was also relieved to find that Lindsey had brought Chinese take out for us.

We were both engrossed in watching the news and following the developments regarding the grand jury testimony of Al Sidney and the outrage at Jeffreys for forcing him to appear and discuss his conversations with reporters. It was, of course, the lead story, and the first clip was Al Sidney on the courthouse steps after his testimony. "George Jeffreys' prosecutors demanded to know what I had told reporters and what reporters had said to me. If they think they have intimidated me, they have failed," he said defiantly.

Sidney's lawyers were even more antagonistic, though they were getting paid while he was having to spend not only his time but his money. Discussing his client's testimony, the first told reporters, "These people have this grandiose idea that there is a conspiracy afoot by the President and the First Lady to disseminate information about Jeffreys' office. That is absolutely false. They just made it up. It was a fantasy. They subpoenaed him to come testify about their fantasies."

Joining in immediately, his other lawyer had more to say about the ordeal. "Our conclusion after today is that George Jeffreys is out of control," she said. "He has total disregard for the rights of private citizens and for anyone other than himself. His whole manner in this has been unprofessional from the beginning. This kind of thing doesn't happen in America. It recalls the old Star Chamber or the Gestapo. Just outrageous. I find this total disregard for other people's livelihoods and rights and lives to be absolutely horrible."

Welcome to the Whirlpool World of George Jeffreys, I thought to myself as I fumbled with my chopsticks. These Washington types were just now learning what folks in Alabama had known for years. When Lindsey got up to go to the kitchen during a commercial, I grabbed the remote and flipped over to catch a bit of *Crossfire*. "I mean, this was absolutely stupid on George Jeffreys' part," Bob Novak was saying as I tuned in, leaving little with which Bill Press could quibble. Even former

Attorney General Thornberger, the evening's shill for Jeffreys, was without a plausible defense. "Well," he admitted lamely, "it may have been unwise to do."

I ambled off to my study for a while to prepare my lecture for the next day, but Lindsey called me to come back for a breaking news announcement. Bruce Adolph, one of the assistants who was allegedly intimidated by news reports documenting the $50,000 judgment against him for violating the civil rights of citizens when he was a District Attorney and whose public exposure had so angered Jeffreys, had announced that he was resigning from the OIC and returning to Florida.

The *Miami Herald* had interviewed Adolph concerning his sudden change of career plans, and his comments were very telling. "It's really not a personal thing at all," he said with reference to his reasons for leaving. More telling, though, was his acknowledgment regarding Jeffreys' recent obsession. "One of the worst mistakes a prosecutor—or any lawyer, for that matter—can make is to allow himself to demonize his opponent, meaning his target/defendant or opposing counsel," he said rather sorrowfully. "When you do that, you lose your objectivity, and that clouds your judgment."

This was too good. It had been a hell of a news day, but it was not over yet. I decided I could wing it in class by discussing the Code of Professional Conduct as it applied to Jeffreys, so I settled down to watch *Nightline*. The program consisted of Ted Koppel surveying the reactions of journalists to the latest developments. Such narcissistic fare, journalists asking other journalists what they thought, now passed as journalism, a fact sadly documented by a recent report from the Committe of Concerned Journalists analyzing media coverage of the latest "sex scandal."

Rich Cohen of the *Washington Post* was the first commentator, and his remarks must have disappointed his colleague, Danielle Leonard, the paper's chief Whirlpool reporter and Jeffreys loyalist. In response to Koppel's question about the effect of the Sidney subpoena, he responded, "If every time you open your mouth it's going to cost you a $1,000 or so, insolvency followed by silence will be the result." But Cohen didn't stop there. "George Jeffreys troubles me," he said. "For all his piety, he is insufferably arrogant. Because he himself is so sure of his moral and ethical purity, he thinks he need not prove it. If Jeffreys were Caesar's wife, he'd be wearing stiletto heels and dressing like a tart. The independent counsel has conducted himself in a manner that makes one wonder about either his judgment or his fairness—or both. He is unfit for the office he holds."

Indignation was not in short supply. A columnist for the *New York Daily News*, whose name had been given up to the grand jury by Sidney that day, offered a less than contrite confession. "I am guilty," he declared. "My only defense: To obstruct justice, there must first be justice. Jeffreys' operation fits no known definition of justice. This man is a threat to American liberties, a bully who whines when challenged and who uses the grand jury process for personal revenge when miffed. With the support of conservative attorneys, with the aid of right-wing politicians, political-hack judges and the *New York Times*, Jeffreys is setting precedents that jeopardize all of us. His abuse of the judicial process for partisan political motives and now out of his own personal pique is a far greater threat to American liberty than anything Cannon is accused of doing. If this be obstruction of justice, let us make the most of it. Come and get me, copper!"

A columnist for the *Chicago Tribune* charged Jeffreys with "astounding hubris" and said he "has gone from out of line to out of control." Nodding agreement, an editorial writer for the *St. Petersburg Times* said, "Yes, Cannon's spinmeisters have been saying George Jeffreys is out of control. Now he's using the power of his office to try to intimidate and harass his critics. That raises another question: Is he out of his legal mind?"

Frank Rich of the *New York Times* started off sounding as if he believed every unfounded rumor and improbable assertion the paper had seen fit to print since it first invented the Whirlpool investigation back in 1992. "Jeffreys is not a partisan zealot acting under orders from the right-wing moneybags Howard Mellonskoff. He is not the most fanatical foe of the First Amendment since Joseph McCarthy," Rich said with a dismissive tone. "No," he explained emphatically, "recent events give more credence to another possibility—that the guy is simply nuts. Only a madman would try to win over a hostile public by whining to TV cameras about how people are whispering such mean and rotten things about him. If there's anyone Americans despise as much as a snitch like Edna Merkin, it's a crybaby—especially a millionaire crybaby on the federal payroll."

Robert Scheer of the *Los Angeles Times* disagreed, "Let the record show that I don't think the man is nuts, just extremely dangerous to our liberty in a quite cold and calculating way."

That observation from Scheer was seconded by *Newsday*'s Michael Tomasky, who had the most insightful comment of the night. Giving perspective to the events of the last few days and closing the program better than Koppel's producers could have imagined, Tomasky said, "People understand liberty, and it turns out that they take it pretty seriously. Jeffreys is abusing his power in a more flagrant way than Cannon ever has. Everyone in America knows it, too. Except for Jeffreys and the media."

I resisted the impulse to call Mitch and say, "I told you so." Even Mitch must have known now what kind of man he was working for and the danger of what kind of man he himself could become if he stayed on much longer. A danger I knew all too well.

Chapter Forty

Jeffreys was not a quick study. Having learned nothing from his recent assault on the First Amendment, the following day he issued subpoenas to two bookstores, attempting to get records of every book purchased by Daphne de Clerambault during the last two years.

To most people, it almost seemed as if Jeffreys were trying to audition for *Dumb and Dumber*, but I knew him better than most and was not all that surprised. George Jeffreys didn't read books. He didn't think that there was a constitutional right to privacy. And he had already demonstrated that he had little understanding of the meaning of the First Amendment. As a noted constitutional scholar at Cornell Law School said, "A bookstore might as well be a fertilizer factory so far as George Jeffreys is concerned."

I still worried about Mitch and regretted that he felt trapped. Rather than calling, for fear that would only embarrass him further, I clipped an article from the *Chicago Tribune* by Mary Schmich and dropped it in the mail. It began playfully enough, but I circled her more thoughtful passages that explained, "Reading is a deeply private enterprise. It is your mind in intimate connection with itself. Through books, we take risks and dares we might not take in the flesh. We ought to be able to explore our own minds without embarrassment and intimidation, without fear of being stalked by a peeping prosecutor. Even if you're short on sympathy for the president, if you're a serious reader, you have to shudder at the thought of a government prosecutor leering at the books you buy."

Others were even less sanguine. Patricia Schroeder of the Association of American Publishers asked, "Where will this guy strike next? Is he going to go down to Victoria's Secret and see if she wore underwear?"

When a reporter asked about Schroeder's comments, Jeffreys was unrepentant, noting that his investigators had already seized books and underwear from de Clerambault's apartment. Revealing that he had now lost all perspective on the investigation, he asked, "What's the big deal about demanding to see a list of the books someone reads? We're following standard procedures. Prosecutors do it all the time, as in the World Trade Center bombing and the Unabomber and the like."

Senator Moynihan was unconvinced, taking the floor and asking, "What in the hell are federal prosecuting attorneys doing subpoenaing bookstores? You just don't do that. It is no crime to read, and what you have read has nothing to do in court. I don't like the taping. I don't like bringing critics before a grand jury. I don't like it. Did I make myself clear? I don't like it."

Neither, apparently did the courts. The Senior District Judge quashed the subpoenas and quoted Justice Douglas to the effect that "once the government can demand of a publisher the names of the purchasers of his publications, the free press as we know it disappears."

I hoped that would never happen, and I was encouraged in that belief both by the judge's decision and by Jon Katz's almost Madisonian article in *Wired* magazine. "More than anyone currently in public life, George Jeffreys helps us, a bit more every day, appreciate our freedoms and our struggle to keep them," Katz wrote. "Jeffreys reminds all Americans how valuable and endangered these liberties are. He makes it almost fashionable to be patriotic again, to resurrect musty words and ideas like privacy and freedom of speech. He provides us a reason to cherish these notions, even if the institutions responsible for protecting them seem too oblivious, distracted, or cowardly to respond."

Nonetheless, if the clear commands of the First Amendment were of no concern to George Jeffreys, any derivative right of privacy from the Fourth, Fifth, and Ninth Amendments were even less of an impediment to his personal will. The following day, ignoring as well the specific admonitions of the Department of Justice Manual, Jeffreys hauled Daphne de Clerambault's mother before his grand jury for a five hour psychological strip-search by four of his deputies. She left the courthouse trembling that afternoon, accompanied by her doctor. Brushing aside the intrusive media mob as he helped her into a car, her lawyer said, "No mother should be forced by federal prosecutors to testify against her own child. She has just been put through the same type of hell anybody in her situation would experience."

When I saw that scene on the evening news, it caused me pause to consider my relationship with my own children. I had always encouraged them to come to me with their problems, to feel free to tell me anything without fear of my judging them harshly or betraying their confidence. Jeffreys was dealing with the very fabric of society. There are relationships that we shouldn't interfere with, and this was another one that George Jeffreys had violated.

I was especially offended because the tactic appeared to be premeditated. When Jeffreys had interrogated Daphne de Clerambault for ten hours on the day of the sting, he had refused to allow her to talk with her lawyer, but he did let her talk with her mother. Was he so devious, knowing that Daphne's conversations with her lawyer would be protected but that no such privilege would stop them from interrogating her mother? Nah, he had already served a subpoena on her attorney and forced him to testify against his client and turn over his confidential files, something you only see in organized crime cases. Jeffreys no longer thought much of the attorney-client privilege, one he had thought so keen when he was hiding evidence of perjury for General Motors and trying to suppress damaging evidence about the big tobacco companies.

What would this madman do next? Subpoena the lawyers from the White House Counsel's office to disclose their conversations with the President? Subpoena Cassidy Cannon to circumvent the marital privilege and ask her about dinner table conversations between her parents? There was no law to stop him, and, in fact, he had tried to do just that in Alabama last spring, serving a subpoena on Joe Hill's son at his high school.

There was a short clip from a speech given by Senator Leahy that afternoon, confirming my reactions. "This is not the Spanish Inquisition," he declared. "For a mother being hauled before a grand jury to reveal her intimate conversations with her own daughter, for parents forced to be witnesses, this could mean having to spend all the money you have saved for your children's college education, or anything else, to pay for lawyers. Compelling a parent to betray a child's confidence is repugnant to fundamental notions of family, fidelity, and privacy. Indeed, I can think of nothing more destructive of the family and family values, nor more undermining of frank communication between parent and child, than the example of a zealous prosecutor who decides to take advantage of the trust between mother and daughter."

I thought the network producers might have had trouble finding anyone to argue otherwise for their usual charade of balanced coverage, but I should not have been so naive. The policy director of the Independent Women's Forum, laughed out loud at the suggestion that Jeffreys' actions violated the sanctity of the family. "This is standard prosecutorial conduct. It's too bad if they don't like it," she said in that smug tone used by all the bottle blond critics of Cannon that populated the news shows. A woman representing the Christian Coalition agreed and scornfully added, "Responsible parents would work in tandem with law enforcement to ensure that laws are upheld because no one in this nation is above the law. Parents should reinforce the law."

Turning off the television as the program ended, Lindsey looked at me with disbelief and asked, "You mean there's no legal privilege protecting confidential communication between parents and children?"

"Nope," I replied. "Private conversations, telephone calls, diaries, letters, e-mail, anything would have to be disclosed. Until Jeffreys' excessive zeal, though, such formal legal protection was widely considered unnecessary. Most prosecutors have more integrity, some sense of fairness, and better judgment than to try to set up family members against each other."

"But," she asked, "don't you think those communications should be protected?"

"Of course I do," I said without hesitation. "Evidentiary privileges are recognized or established to protect the relationships we hold most dear, to promote the essential values we consider even more important than the goal of fact-finding in legal proceedings—especially in ones like this, which has become the most obscene and expensive investigation of a quickie in American history. Mutual loyalty, candor, and trust in the sharing of confidences between parents and children—just like between husband and wife—these are important core family values. Without them, how can parents provide guidance and advice through the inevitable crises of life or effectively fulfill their lifelong role as counselor and mentor to their children?"

"So," she asked with a smile, "do you think we should get married, so I can't be forced to tell Jeffreys what you really think about him?"

"I think," I said after a short pause, "it's your bedtime, smartass."

That weekend, Lindsey and I flew up to Raleigh, where she was invited to present a lecture at North Carolina State, and I was enrolled for a Cajun cooking class at Chef Rameaux's Louisiana Market. While we were there, I saw an article in the Sunday News & Observer announcing that Jeffreys would be giving a speech to the Mecklenberg County Bar Association. I thought it would be a bit mischievous to show up in the audience, so I made a few calls, changed my return flight, and rented a car to drive up to Charlotte on Monday.

I arrived early and was able to get a seat at a table near the front of the room, hoping that Jeffreys would see me in the audience before he started speaking, but he was too busy schmoozing with the dignitaries to notice much of anything else. My prime reason for attending was not so much to hear Jeffreys but for him to know I was listening. I wanted him to be aware that not everyone in the audience would be taken in by his version of himself or his investigation.

As the tables were still being cleared, Jeffreys was introduced with the standard puffery and began his remarks. "I feel privileged to be here today in Judge Chase's home town and honored that he asked me to speak with you today," he began, paying homage to his patron. Then, looking up from his notes, he saw me, and that silly little grin disappeared from his face. There was a slight cutting motion in his eyes as he looked down and fumbled a bit with his notes.

Quickly recovering, Jeffreys continued with an awkward, somewhat strange transition to his main topic. "Let me also say that, thankfully, I'm about to celebrate my 28th wedding anniversary," he said, the grin returning now but his words were less forceful. "I was thinking about the dog. Not only do I have the same wife for the last 28 years; we've also had a number of dogs. And I am as faithful as a dog to my wife, though we now know that some men are not faithful, that they have defiled the sanctity of marriage. One can only wonder what lies behind this horror." I wondered what lay behind that comment conjoining his wife with a dog.

Then he returned to one of his familiar themes. "Some say it's the culture of the mass media, on television and our movies. Others say it's the breakdown of parental responsibility, permissiveness, secular humanism in the public schools, and the like." With an obvious dig at Cannon, he said, "Many believe that they should be able to act in a self-centered, egocentric, selfish way, and indeed, to act in whatever manner suits their interests, regardless of the effect that it may have on others."

I thought for a moment he might be describing the irresponsible way he had been issuing subpoenas, but then he explained, "This callous disregard for marriage vows, that sum of self-sacrifices, is threatening to this society. It threatens our very safety, but even more than that it threatens our moral foundations, our very way of life. The legal profession has likewise not been immune from this disease of selfishness. Think of the lawyers in public life today—President Cannon, Deputy White House Counsel Robert Bruce, Joey Welch, political fixer Vernon Montaigne, former Associate Attorney General Randolph Webster." Yeah, I thought, and George Jeffreys, Bart Gedney, Walt Lecraw, Nelson Grenier, Cliff Smegman.

The speech then turned from the unusual to the unbelievable. "The lawyer of yesteryear was a good person who upheld the law and who stood steadfast against reckless behavior. Some of us remember a movie, *To Kill a Mockingbird*, starring Gregory Peck as a lawyer named Atticus Finch. Atticus Finch strove relentlessly in the pursuit of truth. Atticus taught countless Americans, who have seen the movie, important lessons about truth."

That was a pretty audacious self-promotion, even for Jeffreys. Atticus Finch knew that "truth" was not the sole possession of the prosecutor, that the procedural protections of the Bill of Rights belong to every citizen, and that it was his duty to vigorously defend his client. Comparing himself to Inspector Jarvet would have been more appropriate, but claiming some affinity to Atticus Finch, in my mind, demanded an apology from Jeffreys to Harper Lee, back in Monroeville, Alabama. But Jeffreys never apologized for anything he did, and he didn't appear to know that the movie had been based on her book.

I would love to hear what Joey Welch, Cannon's attorney, might have to say about this speech. One can only imagine what would have happened if Jeffreys had been investigating Tom Robinson. Tom's old football buddy would have been recruited by the prosecutor to tape conversations with his friend. He would have been lured to a meeting by the same friend, where he would have been confronted by prosecutors and questioned for hours without a lawyer. His mother would have been hauled before the grand jury and grilled about private conversations with her son. Scout Finch would have been subpoenaed at her elementary school for criticizing the prosecutor on the playground. Records of Tom's purchase of a Bible at the dime store would have been subpoenaed. The local newspaper would have been full of prejudicial leaks from the prosecutors. And when Atticus interviewed possible defense witnesses, the prosecutor would have claimed he was obstructing justice and encouraging perjury. Then he would have denounced Atticus in a speech for blocking the "truth" by arguing for his client's constitutional rights.

No, Jeffreys had it all wrong. Today, Atticus Finch would be found defending someone against an over-zealous independent counsel. Atticus Finch would have told Jeffreys, in the words of Justice Brandeis, that "the greatest dangers to liberty lurk in insidious encroachment by men of zeal, well-meaning but without understanding." Yep, Joey Welch understood this better than I did.

I almost threw my napkin on the table in disgust, and pushed my chair back from the table. Jeffreys looked straight at me then. I don't know that my presence in the room actually affected him, but he clearly looked distressed about something.

"Now in contrast to Atticus Finch," Jeffreys said after slowly taking a drink of water, "today's popular culture portrays lawyers as greedy and unethical people who will cheerfully hawk their services—and, indeed, their very morals—to the highest bidder. Today's fictional lawyer will do anything for the client. The modern day image, if you will, of lawyers as hired guns, suggests that a good many lawyers have decided to pay less than scrupulous regard for the truth—the truth. We are in danger of becoming that which our ancestors vigorously resisted, indentured servants rather than professionals. As the educator and lawyer Robert Maynard Hutchins once put it very well, 'There are some things that a professional will not do for money.'"

What could have possessed Jeffreys and brought on that public confession? It was Jeffreys who had unsuccessfully asserted privileges in court to hide incriminating documents from Congress—documents that revealed a 35-year conspiracy by his tobacco clients to push their addictive carcinogens and destroy the health of Americans. It was Jeffreys who had asserted attorney-client privilege to hide incriminating documents from the court—documents that revealed a 14-year conspiracy to conceal evidence of perjury by General Motors and deny responsibility for fuel tank design that killed and maimed their customers. It was Jeffreys who had whored himself, moonlighting for such corporate clients and taking in $1 million a year while on the public payroll.

The crowd shifted nervously, realizing the obvious, but Jeffreys wasn't satisfied to stop there. He interpreted the nods as support rather than as acknowledgment of his sins.

"But now to speak personally," Jeffreys continued on yet another theme with even more irony, "none of these issues has been as baleful to our profession as its apparent loss of respect for truth. Truth indeed is the primary goal of our judicial system. After all, witnesses are sworn to tell, 'The truth, the whole truth, and nothing but the truth. So help me God.' I heard a hearty 'amen'—we must have an "amen" bench here."

"Chief Justice Burger, for whom I was privileged to clerk," Jeffreys boasted without shame or irony, "once said, 'An ethical lawyer simply cannot allow anyone to commit a fraud on the court. In no sense can a lawyer honorably be a party to presenting known perjury.' No longer, though, do government lawyers appear accountable to society as a whole for the authority, responsibility, and indeed power, that they wield through the justice system. Perhaps the more difficult question that we face is at what point does a lawyer's manipulation of the legal system to prevent the discovery of truth become an obstruction of justice?"

What was he doing? Was he out of his mind? Didn't he know that his audience was thinking about the perjured testimony he had allowed from Roby Douglas? Didn't he remember Jessie Banaghan's revelation that he had tried to get her to lie about the President? Didn't he realize that everyone knew about the tactics he had used against Daphne de Clerambault to get her to lie about the President and Vernon Montaigne? Had he forgotten about what he did to Bridget Bishop to get her to say things that were untrue and to prevent her from testifying truthfully? Hadn't he seen James Burgh on *60 Minutes* describing the false statement Jeffreys tried to make him read to the grand jury? Didn't he know the penalty for subornation of perjury?

Apparently not, and it only got worse. "This vision of the virtuous lawyer has particular resonance when we talk about a lawyer for the government," Jeffreys noted, removing any doubt that he was talking about himself. He was now looking directly at me as he continued, "The public servant lawyer owes a duty not to any individual, but to the people as a whole. In short, lawyers have a duty not to use their skills to impede the search for truth. The 8th Circuit, in fairly emphatic language, said, 'We believe that to allow any part of the federal government to use its in-house attorneys as a shield against the production of information relevant to litigation would represent a gross misuse of public assets.' Strong words. Surprisingly, that basic proposition, grounded in history, tradition and common morality, is the subject of controversy as we speak."

It certainly was. Jeffreys must have known that James Burgh had filed the complaints against him with the Office of Professional Responsibility and the Committee on Professional Conduct for misuse of government lawyers in fighting a private lawsuit, yet he seemed almost to be inviting sanctions for abuse of office. His hypocrisy about using his staff to represent him in a civil suit mocked both the court and the rule of law. Jeffreys was either oblivious to his own transgressions or secure that he was above the law. And either way, he was a fool.

After Jeffreys finished that strange speech, I waited around to talk with him, remembering the hostility in his last words to me as I had walked out of his office last summer. I didn't have to wait long, though. Unlike his campaign speeches to the faithful opposition back in Alabama, very few of the local attorneys had any interest in basking in his presence. Even the local media, lazy or compliant, seemed satisfied with the advance script and showed no interest in examining the source of the brooding self-flagellation we had just witnessed.

"Mr. Wilkes," Jeffreys said with that insincere tone and phony smile of a tent preacher, "it's a pleasure to see you."

"My privilege," I replied with a touch of irony that was lost on Jeffreys. "Speaking of which, your views on attorney-client privilege seems to have changed considerably since your recent brief in *Cameron v. General Motors.*"

That got him. He noticed at a couple of reporters still standing close enough to overhear my quip, and his eyes narrowed as he shot back, "It is well established that the attorney-client privilege is the oldest privilege protecting confidential communications, and it is also one of the most sacred and absolute. The public interest was served by honoring the public policies that underlie the fundamental protection offered litigants by the attorney-client privilege, Mr. Wilkes."

"Yeah, tell that to Frank Carter," I quipped. "It didn't seem to stop you from hauling him before your grand jury and forcing him to reveal confidential information about his representation of Daphne de Clerambault. Or is that privilege just reserved for the cigarette companies and your other corporate Johns?"

Jeffreys stammered a moment and glanced toward one of the reporters who appeared to be taking notes, before shifting the argument. "I was talking today about executive privilege, which has the same currency now as it did during Watergate," he said, making sure he got in that dig for the eavesdropping media. "The president and his lawyers cannot just make up claims of executive privilege whenever they want to frustrate my investigation. There is no such historical privilege for domestic affairs."

"They're not making it up," I replied. "Executive privilege has been around since 1792, and presidents since Washington have periodically withheld both documents and testimony from Congress. President Truman in 1948 refused to cooperate in any way with Nixon and the House committee investigating Alger Hiss. During the McCarthy hearings, President Eisenhower said Congress had absolutely no right to ask his staff to testify in any way, shape or form about the advice that they gave him at any time on any subject. It was a matter of principle with him, and he vowed never to permit it. Eisenhower, in fact, set the record by invoking executive privilege more than 40 times."

"Well," Jeffreys said, chapped by that rebuke, "requests from the courts—the judiciary—have been treated differently. Chief Justice Marshall's rulings established that a president is subject to a subpoena in the proper circumstances and that the final decision must be made by the courts, not unilaterally by the president and certainly not by his aides. No 20th century president tested executive privilege in court until President Nixon in Watergate. And if Cannon tries, we'll paint him with that brush."

"You seem to be so fond of Marshall, you might remember his opinion in *Marbury v. Madison*," I taunted. "He held that executive privilege could be invoked by a clerk and said that if the officer thought that anything had been communicated to him in confidence, he was not bound to disclose it. Perhaps more puzzling, your own opinion in *Friedman v. Bache Halsey Stuart Shields* acknowledged numerous privileges for domestic policy discussions, said subordinate employees could invoke the privilege, and complained about the unreasonableness of voluminous and expedited requests by subpoena, arguing that the information should be confidential."

"Yes, well, why won't Cannon cooperate and just tell us what we want to know? What's up with his specious claims of privilege? Executive privilege for his aides, marital privilege for his wife, and who knows what imaginary privilege they've invented for the Secret Service. That's as far-fetched as the assertion of a mother-daughter privilege or an attorney-client privilege for dead people," Jeffreys whined. "Why doesn't he just do what we ask?"

"Could be that he agrees with James Madison that the best security against a concentration of powers consists in the necessary constitutional means to resist encroachments of the other branches," I said with a smile that only further infuriated him. "Ambition must be made to counteract ambition. The words of Mr. Madison in *Federalist 51*."

Not denying that question about his motives, Jeffreys fell back to his script. "These evasions and exceptions to the demand for evidence are in derogation of our search for truth. Truth. The impediment that executive privilege would place in the way of Independent Counsel plainly conflicts with the function of the courts under Article III," he asserted with an air of authority.

"I don't recall reading anything about the Independent Counsel in Article III of the Constitution." Unable to pass up another shot, I added, "And you once said yourself, in *Bureau Of National Affairs v. United States Department of Justice*, 'Among the government's common law privileges is the executive privilege regarding the government's deliberative process. Advice, recommendations, and opinions that are part of the decision-making process of the government are protected from disclosure.' Remember that?"

"You'd dig up any old quote to defend Cannon," he said without answering.

"No," I replied, "and I'm not a big fan of executive privilege. The framers didn't include it in the Constitution, nor, I might add, did they ever imagine an unaccountable independent prosecutor. I do think, however, that it might be a separation of powers issue, to protect the executive from partisan investigations by special prosecutors."

Rational argument having failed him, Jeffreys lapse into the arrogance that was usually reserved for his driveway press conferences. "It seems clear to me then," he asserted without hesitation, "that no one in the United States government, speaking for the government, has standing to oppose the Independent Counsel in this proceeding, and, therefore, no court has jurisdiction over this case."

I was amazed by such hubris, even from Jeffreys. I saw one of the reporters scribbling furiously as I asked, "What do you mean by that?"

"I mean," he proclaimed, "that it is up to the Independent Counsel to decide whether the 'privilege' asserted by the White House as a government entity should be recognized. I can decide on my own whether people should be compelled to testify before my grand jury. The law gives me, and only me, the power to determine the appropriate balance between privileges and law enforcement interests in this particular case. Litigating against the Independent Counsel in this case is not among them. It is, in fact, flirting with obstruction of justice."

If that was his position, there was no need to continue the discussion. I turned and walked away, realizing that Jeffreys would not be stopped by conscience and doubting that he would be stopped by the Supreme Court. The effort to pursue this legal panty raid would not only get Cannon, it would do serious damage to the constitutional balance envisioned by the framers. Whatever else might come out of this, future presidents would be seriously impaired as a result of the scorched earth policies of George Jeffreys.

I was glad to return home to Tuscaloosa and the relative normalcy of my life teaching and writing. I was enjoying teaching the Professional Responsibility class, where I made references to Jeffreys' recent speech and often used examples drawing on the tactics being deployed by Bob Benson and the lawyers for Christine Putnam. The political maneuvering on both sides of that case were very evident, with the president's lawyers using press conferences as effectively as his opponents.

That Tuesday, I began the class making my point by showing a clip of one such effort, where the President's attorney said, "Putnam has no case. She has suffered no damages. Her filing is really not a serious legal document. It's a scurrilous paper which really proves that Christine Putnam and her political and her financial backers are pursuing this case as a vehicle to humiliate and embarrass the President and to interfere with his presidency. The Cannon-haters are trying to hound him out of office."

The class discussion that followed, concerning the use of the legal system for partisan purposes, was quite animated. We talked about the Jeffreys subpoena to Putnam's lawyers for all the depositions and investigative files related to rumors about Cannon's private life, a public charade to cover the fact that he already had copies. We discussed the propriety of the judge even allowing those depositions that were unrelated to the plaintiff's claims. We even examined the leaked copy of Cannon's deposition, following the Jeffreys strategy of going line by line in search of perjury. It seemed to be teaching the subject and holding their attention.

When class ended, I said we would continue our examination on Thursday, but, to paraphrase Harold Wilson, two days is a long time in politics. In an October Surprise of the first magnitude, Judge Hoffman agreed that Putnam had no case and granted Cannon's motion for summary judgment. Not only would that affect my next lecture, but it would shift the rhetorical ground and alter the national political landscape. Cannon would win the election in a walk, and Jeffreys would be out of business.

I missed *Burden of Proof* that day, but I got home in time to watch *Inside Politics*. The Democrats were gloating, and the usual suspects were rounded up for sound bytes. Congressman Conyers declared that the dismissal "should now be the final word on what has become an unprecedented partisan witch hunt. Ken Starr has been spending over $40 million to peek in peepholes." Representative Sheila Jackson Lee suggested, "Christine Putnam had no case, and now neither does George Jeffreys". Senator Torricelli followed, saying, "Clearly George Jeffreys is going to have to find an exit strategy. He has now established himself as a significant loser. He may try to salvage himself with a scathing report, but that can't change the conclusion."

There was little defense available for the Republicans. "This is not related to the Jeffreys matter," insisted Senator Hatchet. "Despite obvious appearances, Jeffreys is a completely different thing." Not even Hatchet believed that one.

The cable news programs were more interesting, though. I flipped around to gather a sampling of the public and pundit reactions to the dismissal and found it quite entertaining. Catherine MacKinnon, not surprisingly, blasted the ruling. "What the ruling means," she said, "is that women think they're going to have to put up with men exposing themselves at work." Some guy from the *Boston Globe* failed to see it that way. "Christine Putnam is a rather pathetic creature who was commandeered by Cannon's conservative enemies, paid, repackaged, and politically prostituted by right-wingers trying to undo the last national election. It was always about smearing Cannon." he said.

Robert Scheer, a columnist for the *Los Angeles Times*, also seemed unconvinced by Professor MacKinnon's considered analysis. "The clear implication of Judge Hoffman's ruling is that it is the president who has been the victim of harassment at the hands of political opponents bent on destroying him," he said. "Can Jeffreys honestly believe that a president should be impeached in a civil case that turned out to be a nuisance suit pushed forward by a well-financed movement of right-wing cranks? It is a fitting retribution that the so-called legal team of Christine Putnam will be stuck with the bills. And how about a bit of honesty from the media? They got the Putnam case wrong from the get-go and should now apologize. The justification for the past four years of dirt digging was to sell newspapers and increase television ratings."

The newspaper that had the most invested in getting Cannon, which had been seriously wrong and enthusiastically complicit on Whirlpool from the get-go, was the *New York Times*. While the suspect reporters were silent, one editorial writer admitted that the game was up. "While the relentless machinery of investigation may grind on for many months," he said, "it is now politically inconceivable that Congress will consider impeachment for alleged lies and obstruction in a case that no longer exists."

In response to that non-apologetic dodge from the *Times*, former Independent Counsel Lawrence Walsh was interviewed and moved on as he said, "Well, the real question is: why was George Jeffreys jumping into this case before it was even finished? There is no precedent that I know of for a federal prosecutor to come into an ongoing case, except when requested by the judge."

On the same program, Buck Etienne saw an opportunity to gig both Jeffreys and his lackeys in the media, especially Stuart Sellers, who had been negotiating a job with Jeffreys while continuing to write articles and appear on talk shows attacking Cannon and supporting Jeffreys. In unusual form even for Etienne, he ridiculed Jeffreys for a "form of prosecutorial premature ejaculation, causing him to get all tensed up and leak stories about the President's sex life since the day he was appointed."

"And Stuart Sellers, he staked his journalistic reputation on what a strong case Christine Putnam had," Etienne laughed. "That was just slightly off the mark. He's a fraud, and now everyone knows it. Mr. Sellers and Mr. Jeffreys are both utterly conflicted. But the facts of collusion in this case will pop the rivets in Jeffreys' fragile ship, regardless of whom he hires as a flack to write his final report."

That evening, as expected, Putnam's lawyers called a press conference, her press flack announced that they would appeal, and Christine Putnam refused to answer questions. That, too, was seen for exactly what it was. As the a columnist in the *New York Daily News* asked, "What does Putnam have to lose? She's not likely to win her claims against Cannon, but this case is about money and politics, not justice. An appeal lets Putnam continue the nationwide fund-raising drive that has financed her lavish lifestyle. It will keep her shrill publicist employed on the television talk shows. It will help George Jeffreys, allowing him to claim that the case is not moot."

"Yeah," I said to the television as much as to Lindsey, "and maybe Jeffreys can give Benson a little advice on how to generate scurrilous news stories and get Judge Hoffman removed from the case. It worked for him with Judge Cook."

The Putnam crowd was even more clever than that, though. They filed their appeal, attaching more than 3,000 pages of salacious depositions and affidavits from everyone willing to make unseemly allegations against Cannon. The Ratched Institute immediately posted the whole tawdry mess on their website, and sent out a fax alert to every news organization in the country and encouraging everyone to download the documents. By the time the 11th Circuit got to work the next morning and issued an order placing the appeal under seal, the damage had been done.

Neither Jeffreys nor Della Beckwith had commented on the decision, but there he was on CNN the next morning, holding yet another driveway press conference in front of his house. The first question should have been an easy one for Jeffreys, given his constant mantra about the rule of law. It was tossed with ease. "Do you support Judge Hoffman's decision?"

"Well," Jeffreys said nervously, "I'm not going to comment because I have not read the opinion, and if that sounds like a dodge, it's a fact; I have not read the opinion. But even more importantly, I am really not steeped in the law that she was dealing with, and I don't know the facts that she was dealing with. I do know it's a long opinion; I just haven't had a chance to read it. And now that process may continue. There will be an appeal, and I'm sure you all had a chance to read the pleadings on the internet. We feel good about that process."

The next reporter shouted one that would be a bit more painful to answer. "How important was the Christine Putnam case to your investigation?"

"Well, we have other aspects of our investigation, not just the Christine Putnam case," Jeffreys said, suppressing the standard comment about his case being at a critical juncture. "So losing that one case will not affect the other parts of our ongoing investigation."

"Do you believe the decision of the judge will affect the credibility of the investigation you are conducting?"

"Oh. well," Jeffreys hedged, "I would say let's don't have spin, let's don't have public relations, let's deal with the facts. Let's get every last one of those facts about adultery and sexual assault and improper sexual relations with an intern. The public has a right to know. My office has a need to know. And if that takes an indictment and putting the President and all these women on the witness stand under oath, then so be it."

"How unusual is it for a prosecutor to launch a criminal investigation of non-material statements in a civil case that didn't warrant going to trial?"

"Well, I haven't done research in terms of dispositions of civil cases and so forth," Jeffreys replied. "But I will say it's very important that people be honest. That's why we put people under oath. They're affirming or swearing, under God, so help me, God, that they will tell the truth. That's awfully important. It's in the Ten Commandments, just like adultery. There's no room for little white lies. There's no room for shading. There's only room for truth."

Then Jeffreys' eyes bulged a bit and he blurted emphatically, "You cannot defile the temple of justice. You can't engage in subornation of perjury, intimidation of witnesses, and obstruction of justice. Rather, you must play by the rules. We all must play by the rules. There are rules.

And just as in school there are rules, just as in most families there are rules, in court there are a lot of rules, and you'd better play by them. And if you don't play by those rules, if you lie under oath, if you intimidate a witness, if you seek to obstruct the process of justice, it doesn't matter who wins and who loses in the civil case."

Then came the final question, "Do you expect to complete your investigation any time soon?"

Jeffreys smiled, "Let me just say, the end is not in sight."

By Friday, the entire nation knew Jeffreys wasn't bluffing. He had secretly cut a deal with Daphne de Clerambault to give her full immunity, and she was appearing that day before one of his grand juries in Washington. The chase was on, and the media were in a feeding frenzy once again.

As the tension was building and the networks were speculating wildly while waiting for Daphne to emerge from the courthouse that afternoon, a breaking news announcement raised the ante. President Cannon was going to address the nation live from the White House at 4 o'clock that afternoon. Reporters were lunging for the cameras and babbling with unfounded excitement. They were so certain that Cannon planned to announce his resignation that several networks were showing file footage of Nixon's departure from the White House after his resignation.

In the rush to judgment, only one network carried the remarks of Daphne de Clerambault's attorney as she emerged from six hours of testimony. He said his client had testified that she had a sexual relationship with the President, and that was all the broadcast media wanted to hear. It would not be until I read a Reuters wire story in the paper the next morning that I would learn she also testified that the White House had no role in preparing the infamous "talking points" and that the filing of her affidavit in the Putnam case was in no way related to Vernon Montaigne's assistance in helping her find a job.

Cannon had a clear channel on every network as he began his solemn address from behind his desk in the Oval Office. The television news commentators and paid pundits suddenly appeared dejected when he announced that he had ordered a missile attack on a terrorist weapons facility. Not only did the media parasites and their invited doomsayers miss their anticipated opportunity to bag a president, they were singularly unequipped to provide any meaningful analysis on foreign affairs.

Cannon's remarks were appropriately measured and solemn, though I was slightly amused at one passage. Sounded as if he'd lifted a line from Michael Douglas in *The American President*, he told the nation, "Last night, before we took action against the terrorist operations in Iraq, I was up until 2:30 a.m. in the morning, trying to make absolutely sure that at that chemical plant there was no night shift. I believed I had to take the action I did, but I didn't want some person who was a nobody to me, but who may have a family to feed and a life to live, to die needlessly."

Then, demonstrating that the ongoing investigation had not knocked him off-message, he concluded, "It is always best to remember that we have to try to work for peace in the Middle East, for an end to terrorism, for protections against biological and chemical weapons being used in the first place. And we ought to pay our debt to the United Nations, because if we can work together, together we can find more peaceful solutions. I didn't just learn that when I became President. I learned it from Martin Luther King and the civil rights movement a long time ago."

Leaving the Oval Office and walking to the White House press room, Cannon made himself available to answer questions about the military action he had announced in the televised address. "Thank you very much for being here. I will be glad to give you as much information as I can about our military action last night. With me today to supply any additional details are the Secretary of State, the Secretary of Defense, and my National Security Advisor. Are there any questions?"

There were, but not about that topic. "Mr. President," shouted the first reporter, " do you think that George Jeffreys has gone beyond the call and is out to get you?"

"Well," replied the President, sounding slightly dismayed, "I think moderately observant people are fully capable of drawing their own conclusions about that question, but that is not the reason we are here today."

"Mr. President, Mr. President," came the next question, "whatever you may think about all of these ongoing investigations, they've pulled in a lot of your friends and employees and acquaintances, who have had to appear before the grand jury and built up large legal fees. And I wonder, do you still intend, once you're out of office, to help out with those legal fees?"

Cannon glanced at the Secretary of Defense then replied, "I feel terrible about all these people who have been put through this, who can never get their legal bills reimbursed. The independent counsel has an unlimited budget and can go on forever. So more and more people must spend money they don't have for legal fees that they can't afford. If I can think of something to do about it, I will. But, you know, if I even tried to talk with them to express my sympathy, Mr. Jeffreys would say that was tampering with witnesses. And any suggestion about my helping with their legal bills, he'd scream was hush money and drag them in again."

Trying to draw Cannon back into a trap the media had baited before, the next reporter asked, "Mr. President, how far along are you in your thinking about possible pardons for people who never would have come across any prosecutor's radar screen if you were not president?"

"No one has asked me for one, and there's been no discussion about it."

"Mr. President, the Republicans have been notching up questions about your moral authority. What effect do you think this whole wave of controversies has had on your moral authority?"

"I believe I have a good record of standing up for the things that will help us to raise our children better, make our families stronger, and keep our country strong. At least I have done my best."

The last question came from Lane Bryant of ABC News. With an insider's haughty sneer, she asked, "Mr. President, now that Judge Jeffreys has said that the end is not near, are you willing to live with these questions hanging over you for the rest of your administration?"

"I think when Mr. Jeffreys says there's no end in sight," the President replied, "I think he means there's no case in sight."

That, of course, remained to be seen, and I was beginning to fear the worst. On ABC News that evening, Jeffreys laughed when he was asked by his favorite television reporter whether he had heard the President's remarks. "I guess I shouldn't comment," he said disdainfully, "but you can tell him I've seen *Wag the Dog*. That's all I'm going to say."

That was vintage Jeffreys, still dogging the wag at every opportunity. The end of his investigation might not be in sight, but he certainly had the President in his sights now.

Chapter Forty One

George Jeffreys was now completely focused and deadly serious about getting the President. He took a leave of absence from Kirk & Polis, not to diminish his conflicts of interest but to devote full time to his pursuit of Cannon. The monthly Policy Committee meetings were replaced by daily strategy sessions at 5 p.m., involving all of the staff lawyers and investigators. In addition to the hundreds of people previously hauled before grand juries in Birmingham and Washington, Jeffreys had now subpoenaed more than 70 witnesses before three different grand juries to compel testimony in his sex investigation. No tactic and no strategy was beneath him, and no statute would stand in his way. He was determined to destroy the President, and it was beginning to look like he was going to succeed.

Even without any indictments and with potential evidence only of low crimes and misdemeanors to report to Congress, Jeffreys already had seriously damaged Cannon's ability to govern. He had almost succeeded in undoing the results of the last election, and now he wanted to help Dolor win this one. It was, he knew, his only chance for a seat on the Supreme Court.

Determined to stop the bleeding and save his campaign, Cannon took a serious risk, one not without potentially disastrous consequences. In fact, I thought it was a pretty dumb move, but, then, he didn't ask for my opinion. Cannon had always been able to talk his way out of political danger in the past, so I guess he thought he could do it again. This time, though, rather than denying responsibility for his foibles, he faced it squarely. The President waived his constitutional rights and testified before Jeffreys' grand jury, then he went on television to address the nation.

This whole melodrama was starting to take it's toll on me. I seemed unable to ignore it. Perhaps it was the guilt from having worked for Jeffreys, or maybe it was my anxiety about what he was doing to both the Constitution and the political fabric of our national life. Whatever the cause, I found myself spending far too much time reading about it in the papers and watching it on television. Not only did that contribute to the ratings and encourage the media in their soap opera approach to news, it was also distracting me from writing and from being a better teacher. And as for a social life, well, I couldn't remember the last time Lindsey and I had gone out in public together or done anything that resembled a normal date.

Despite my recognition of the problem, I could not resist. I did manage to ignore the spectacle of the afternoon television punditry speculating on Cannon's grand jury testimony and gleefully anticipating his demise, but I spent most of my class lecture that day discussing the ethical problems of Jeffreys' investigation and the legal folly of the President's decision to appear before a grand jury. I was beginning to bore even myself.

Lindsey, always cheerful, suggested that we record the President's address, go out for dinner that evening, and watch it later, but I made some weak excuse about not having time, realizing even as I said it that it would have been the sane thing to do. She was understanding, but I don't think this was the kind of relationship she'd signed on for when we moved to Tuscaloosa. Nonetheless, as I sat down to watch the President's televised speech later that night, Lindsey brought me a beer and snuggled up beside me on the couch.

"In recent months," the President began, "the Independent Counsel and certain members of the media have begun digging into my personal life. They have harassed innocent people in an effort to embarrass me. Friends, relatives and members of my staff have been probed with a variety of tasteless questions. The intense speculation about this matter has caused a lot of pain for some innocent people."

Then came the tough part, as Cannon looked straight into the camera and said, "I have misled people, even my wife. Indeed, I did have a relationship with Ms de Clerambault that was not appropriate. In fact, it was wrong. It constituted a critical lapse in judgment and a personal failure on my part for which I am solely and completely responsible."

At that point, I was having what I imagined was a collective national flashback with every man who had ever had the unfortunate experience of watching *Fatal Attraction*. At least I had the luxury of wincing in private, but Cannon was having to suffer before an audience of millions. Somehow, though, he continued and explained, "In an effort to protect the privacy of those involved, it was decided two years ago, among both parties involved, that this matter would remain private. One of the things that prompted me to go public now is the harassment this woman and her family have been subjected to by the media and by the Independent Counsel. Discussion of this matter has gone too far, and I hope that members of the media will accept my admission and allow people to continue their lives in peace."

Fat chance of that, I thought, then I looked to see Lindsey's reaction as the President said, "I have apologized to my wife and family, whom I love. I apologize now to the American people. I have certainly made some mistakes that are mine and mine alone. I acknowledge that I made a mistake. I deeply regret that, and I want to express my profound regret to all who were hurt and to all who were involved."

This speech was getting pretty painful, even for the audience, and I was hoping it was almost over. "We live in a society that rightfully depends upon people taking responsibility for their actions. I have done so in this matter," Cannon said. Then, at last, he closed in a somewhat differed tone, "I have never perjured myself. I have never committed obstruction of justice. I have been as straight as an arrow in my public duty. But this is private. I'm not going to talk any more about my personal life. Enough is enough."

It certainly was, yet I felt compelled to stay tuned for the post-game analysis. Lindsey and I agreed that he'd done about as well as could be expected under the circumstances, though we differed on one point. She said she thought the American people would accept his confession and be ready to put the whole deal behind them, but I argued, as I had before, that the political pundits and professional haters would never be satisfied and would turn even his confession against him. As it turned out, we were both right.

The instant polls and network focus groups revealed that 73% of the public was satisfied by the President's response, and 67% said that Jeffreys' should stop his investigation now. Lindsey had called that one right. She always had a good read on the public pulse and how average Americans would respond to political messages.

However, the gulf between the American public and those who regularly thrust themselves into the televised dialogue seemed more obvious than ever, and the self-important pundits dominated the discussion after the speech. The head of the Annenberg School for Communication parsed the President's words and sniffed, "He said he made *a mistake*, but he should have said *mistakes*." Someone from the Independent Women's Forum complained, "He did not specifically mention Christine Putnam in his expression of regret." Perhaps the most incredible reaction came from ABC's Corky Boggs, who whined, "He didn't seem contrite enough to satisfy me, and he never said, 'I'm sorry.'" It was all pretty sorry, I thought.

The Reverand Elmer Laud was holding forth on one of the shows, weighing in with his usual aplomb. "As a pastor, a man of the cloth, I am appalled. I think that I have a responsibility to speak out, as do 600,000 other pastors who have been very strangely silent, many of them. I've been hearing things and all this garbage! It's my first time to hear such outhouse talk on the news! Think of what this must be doing to the children watching television! The President must resign immediately," he said with a smug smile. No doubt he was already preparing another fundraising campaign or planning to market yet another outrageous "Cannon Chronicles" video to his flock. That sure reflected his concern for the children. And the truth.

The reaction on the Hill was even more ominous, as those who thought themselves without sin lined up to cast the first stone, and those without stones kept their mouths shut. "What a jerk! That was pathetic! That was the biggest mistake he's ever made," snarled the pious Senator Hatchet, whose cunning entreaties had encouraged Cannon's decision to make an apology to the nation. Congressman Bardus said Cannon was "a confessed adulterer" and should resign before he was impeached. Congresswoman Helen Palmer, a member of the board of the Ratched Institute, said, "Cannon's adulterous behavior has severely rocked this nation and damaged the office of the president. I believe that personal conduct and integrity does matter." At best, I guessed, this would present an opportunity for the Republicans in Congress to tout their own virtue, to give long and earnest speeches telling everyone just how faithful they had been to their husbands and wives, and to say they would never try to hide something like that if they hadn't been.

Democratic defenders were in short supply that night, for most were concerned about their own chances for reelection. Even more troubling, though, was that Cannon might not have strong party support even after the election. He had made the mistake of moving to the right and embracing many Republican policies during his presidency, sacrificing the Democratic heritage and Congressional majorities for short-term successes. Now he was reaping a bitter harvest. The Republicans still opposed him on every move, and the liberal Democrats were reluctant to fight for someone who had compromised their political agenda.

I was quickly reminded that my attempt to intellectualize political issues had little force when compared to the zealous crusaders of the airwaves. The Reverend Marion Rabbidson, erstwhile Republican presidential candidate and media mogul, was front and right on his own RBN Network News embracing an ecumenical denunciation of the President. "He has no moral authority to lead this nation," the preacher-politician proclaimed. "As the respected Taliban leader Mullah Mohammed Omar said, 'President Cannon is a sinner and a person of bad character who should be removed from office.' Under Islamic law, you know, he would be stoned to death for becoming involved with a woman who is not his wife."

Ignoring that screwball screed and showing some early symptoms of recovery from my political addiction, I turned to Lindsey and said,

"Hey, wanna go see a movie?" She did, and we spent the night happily ever after. It was a pleasant relapse into reality and a welcome relief from my current obsession.

Some degree of rationality returned to the public debate as well, and a kinder, gentler religious message was found in a "Pastoral Letter to the Nation" published in the paper the next morning. "As pastors and rabbis," the letter began, "we have found ourselves asking what is happening to our country. We want our country back! We urge a return to the real needs of the people. Urgent issues are before us. We want our presidents to be allowed to be president. We want religious leaders, the media, and public life to be guided by self-discipline, responsibility, and compassion. We want legal processes to be embraced by ethical considerations and by simple human decency. Presidents make mistakes; we are all sinners. But the God of love and justice does not judge us without the hand of grace and mercy. It is now time for forgiveness and healing."

George Jeffreys, though, was not about mercy and forgiveness. Nor, it appeared, was he about truth. Daphne de Clerambault's lawyer wrote an essay that week for *Time* that gave a picture of the events that led to her agreement to testify before the grand jury. "It was a continuing threat, a continuing squeeze to pressure her into statements that were not true. They wanted her wired to record telephone calls with the President, Vernon Montaigne and others. Jeffreys seemed to think it was okay to break the law to enforce the law. Only when they threatened to indict her mother did she finally give in to their demands."

Speaking from a federal prison where she was being held for refusing to testify, Jessie Banaghan confirmed such a pattern of pressure to lie. "I know exactly what they were saying to Daphne, either you tell our story or we prosecute you for perjury. There's no way you can go in and just tell the truth to these people. You have to understand that they're not interested in the truth. They asked me to lie. And I can't have anything to do with that. I will not speak to them no matter what they threaten me with. This is worse than McCarthyism. I don't think the people of America will stand for it. I think that Jeffreys is finished."

I doubted that Jeffreys was finished, but the American people seemed to be catching on to what he was doing. A poll released that week showed that 64% thought it was "inappropriate" for Jeffreys to call Daphne's mother before the grand jury. And 62% disapproved of the use of a hidden microphone to record a friend's conversations. More surprising, though, 48% thought that Jeffreys had "gone too far in the methods he is using to investigate the matter and should be removed from office."

While public opinion of the tactics Jeffreys was using would not be enough to remove him from office, he certainly faced some legal risk for those actions, and that gave me plenty of material to discuss in my class that week. His strategy of trial by leaks, unconscionable in itself, had inadvertently exposed his abusive investigative tactics. A *Washington Post* story, describing Ms de Clerambault's initial encounter with investigators and attributed to "sources close to Jeffreys," revealed that when told she was facing 20 years in prison, she had requested to call her lawyer and was told that would end any chances for immunity. Defending that action as standard prosecutorial procedure, Jeffreys said, "She was never actually barred from calling her attorney, and she was not entitled to a lawyer anyway."

"That doesn't matter," explained a spokesman for the District Bar Association. "Any attempt to plea bargain or discuss an immunity deal without a lawyer present violates the American Bar Association Code of Ethics as well as Rule 77.5 of the Justice Department's Rules of Conduct, which states that a Government lawyer 'shall not communicate about the subject of the representation with a person the lawyer knows to be represented by another lawyer in the matter, unless the lawyer has the consent of the other lawyer or is authorized by law to do so.' Are prosecutors entitled to ignore ethical prescriptions on the grounds that their pursuit of 'truth' justifies departure from professional standards? No, there's no defense for what he did."

Senate Democrats now showed a little courage, at least none that I saw on television. Durbin of Illinois told his colleagues, "This is a case where the Judiciary Committee should step in with an oversight hearing to see if Mr. Jeffreys is guilty of any breaches of ethics." Senator Levin, knowing that Hatchet would never hold Jeffreys accountable, suggested instead that "if George Jeffreys does not abide by the Justice Department guidelines, he would be violating the intent of the law, and this may constitute an abuse of discretion and grounds for a 'good cause' removal."

Jeffreys was stung by those who would question his sense of ethics, and he offered his own defense at one of his morning news conferences, "As Justice O'Connor has recognized—let me turn to her very modern voice—'Ethical'—what a wonderful word—'Ethical standards for lawyers are properly understood as a means of restraining lawyers in the exercise of the unique power that they inevitably wield in a system like ours.' However," he argued, "regulations of this type do not govern an independent counsel, who by design operates for the most part outside the Department of Justice."

Buck Etienne laughed at that one. "Well, I don't really want him fired anyway. I'm having too good a time, because the man's making a public fool of himself."

The federal judge overseeing the grand jury, however, was less amused, reinforcing what I had just covered in one of my lectures. She held a hearing on the allegation that a witness may have been questioned by prosecutors without a lawyer being present and advised that she would consider referring the matter to the Justice Department's Office of Professional Responsibility for further investigation.

As he was leaving the hearing, Jeffreys was confronted by reporters outside the courthouse. "Did you and your staff question Daphne de Clerambault in a hotel room without a lawyer present? Has the judge ordered the Justice Department to investigate that?"

Dismayed that the information had leaked quicker than he could put a spin on it, Jeffreys bristled, "Well, I just can't comment because these matters are under seal, and I can't comment again about the specifics of any court order. But, in fact, I would like to speak to that, because I feel very strongly that honorable career prosecutors, who conduct ourselves within the bounds of the controlling legal authority, should not have their reputations besmirched lightly, unfairly, and the like."

That response only brought another flippant question. "What about besmirching the reputation of a president?"

"Well," Jeffreys blustered, "you will never hear me besmirching anyone's reputation. Never in all of these years of activity have I ever said anything to besmirch anyone's reputation. Not once. Well, maybe once. I think from time to time one hears voices. And instead of engaging in name calling and so forth, let's refrain from engaging in scandal-mongering or rumor-mongering and the like."

The scandal-monger nearest to Jeffreys' heart, though, was in a bit of trouble herself. *Time* magazine somehow got access to some of Edna Merkin's illegal tapes and discovered they contained other information that Jeffreys had not leaked. These new tapes, said the article, "put the 'scandal' in a different light. Edna Merkin is heard repeatedly encouraging Daphne de Clerambault to ask the President get her a different job—two months before she was subpoenaed in the Christine Putnam case. That is significant, because Cannon's help in finding a job has been central to the investigation of whether he tried to obstruct justice. Furthermore, Merkin suggests that Daphne should send tapes and letters to Cannon via Speed Service Couriers, a company owned by a relative of Mildred Gillers, Merkin's book agent. At other times, Merkin seems to be raising subjects in order to have Daphne discuss them on tape, almost always failing in that effort."

Then another magazine reported that Merkin had once been arrested for stealing money and a watch from two men in a bar. Although she claimed that she had been "set up by a friend," a delicious irony, the stolen goods were found in the locked trunk of her car. That was a rather petty crime, but then it was revealed that Merkin had lied about the arrest when filling out a Pentagon form for a security clearance, a potential felony offense that could lead to both a substantial fine and imprisonment.

Rather than prosecuting Merkin for the false statement, Jeffreys granted her further immunity from federal prosecution. Instead, he began an investigation of the Pentagon officials who had discovered the problem, hauling them before his grand jury on the pretext that they were trying to intimidate his witness.

Jeffreys was big on granting immunity for witnesses who would give him damaging information about the President. He had earlier given Merkin immunity from prosecution under federal law for making the secret tapes. He had no authority to grant immunity from state law, however, and it was a felony to knowingly make those recordings in Maryland.

When the Maryland legislature and several local Democrats urged a state investigation of Merkin's actions, she complained, "I believe this is the latest in a series of attempts to intimidate me." Jeffreys must have thought so, too, because he issued a grand jury subpoena for one of the citizens who had urged appointing a special prosecutor for the investigation, raising a legitimate question about who was actually trying to intimidate witnesses and obstruct justice.

Emerging from the courthouse after questioning by Jeffreys and his prosecutors, the victim of that retaliatory subpoena spoke briefly to the media. With his wife by his side, he faced the cameras and said, "On that basis of personal phone calls, from our home, on our own nickel, on our own time, we get subpoenaed in front of the grand jury. And we feel that is an outrageous infringement of our First Amendment rights. We don't live in Nazi Germany or Stalinist Russia. This is the United States, and we have the right of free speech. This is an investigation that has gone haywire. It is a partisan witch hunt. And, we'd like to ask Mr. Jeffreys for an apology, because that might help restore public faith in the system."

If they expected an apology from George Jeffreys, they should have taken a number and been prepared to wait. Jeffreys still had not apologized for lying about James Burgh last year, and I doubted he'd ever apologize for anything.

Edna Merkin wasn't the only star witness to present problems undermining the legitimacy of Jeffreys' investigation. *Salon* magazine broke a story that Roby Douglas, while cooperating with Jeffreys and accompanied by his FBI investigators, had been hanging out at Lake Martin in the company of employees of the *American Speculator* and was being paid off with Mellonskoff money through the magazine's Alabama Project.

Jeffreys refused to comment, but Bart Gedney responded defensively to the story and told the press, "We're convinced that none of our people had any knowledge of the payments." Pretty funny, I thought, since Bart knew more about that operation than anyone other than Jeffreys and his pal Thad Stevens.

The FBI agents involved, however, weren't going to take the rap for that. One of the agents who felt used, was quoted as saying, "Because we now know those guys were being funded by Mellonskoff, there should have been an official record of every conversation. If Gedney had not been involved with him, that private detective from the *American Speculator* wouldn't have been allowed in the front door—or the back door for that matter."

A spokesman for the FBI, continuing to distance the agency from Jeffreys and Gedney, said, "The agent handling the Douglas probe followed procedures by the book, but this is worse than the phony investigation we were suckered into by William Russell. In that case we were only scammed out of $300,000. We had no reason to suspect any wrongdoing at the time. Thankfully, this is very unusual. No matter how much you prepare, there're still times when somebody goes bad and does the wrong thing. You just never think the prosecutor might be in on it."

On the Senate floor a few days later, Senator Robinson took the lead. "In my judgment," he told his colleagues, "the extensive conflicts of interest and illegalities by Mr. Jeffreys' office have violated the standards of conduct prescribed by the Department of Justice. Payments to Roby Douglas could be a federal crime, even if he was being induced to testify truthfully. The apparent failure to recognize, inquire into, or punish the tampering with a key witness is inexplicable and raises substantial questions about his ethics. Mr. Jeffreys cannot conduct an investigation where his own staff, his friends, and his financial benefactor are perhaps subjects and certainly key witnesses. I demand that Attorney General Otis conduct a formal inquiry to determine whether he should be removed or disciplined for repeated failures to report and avoid conflicts of interest."

As the story developed, it appeared that Attorney General Otis was finally going to be forced to investigate Jeffreys and his operation, but he was determined not to let that happen, at least not anytime soon. Jeffreys released a statement that afternoon claiming, "The Department of Justice is statutorily precluded from investigating the matters that my office is currently looking into and would itself be investigating the OIC. In brief, we are deeply concerned and believe it is impossible for the Department of Justice to conduct an unbiased investigation of any matters relating to my conduct or that of my staff."

That little public squabble between Jeffreys and Justice sent enough signals and delayed the investigation long enough for the key suspects to have time to coordinate their stories and misplace any incriminating records and documents. In the end, however, former Justice Department official James Angleton was appointed to look into the matter.

"Thank God we have an investigation of George Jeffreys now underway by the Department of Justice for payola, and people being paid off—his chief witness in Alabama being paid off with Mellonskoff money," shouted Buck Etienne on one of the talk shows. "But I think when we get to the bottom of this, we're gonna find out that Mr. Jeffreys has intimidated witnesses and asked a lot of people to lie under oath. I think he's out there defiling that temple of justice. He's just a little partisan right-wing cigarette lawyer, who's out to try to help the Republicans win this fall."

The trial balloon for Jeffreys' defense came from Chub Campbell, who was now on Jeffreys' payroll to do polling and media strategy and was appearing on the television circuit to counter Buck Etienne's broadsides. "Okay," Chub conceded to Etienne, "so what if Mellonskoff funded the whole scam? That wasn't public money, and they weren't the President of the United States. There is no moral equivalence between tax money and private money." That made me laugh as I pondered what might be the moral equivalent of paying Chub Campbell with tax money.

The appointment of someone to investigate his staff was only the start of a terrible week for Jeffreys. *Brill's Content* made it's debut with a "Pressgate" cover story on Jeffreys and the leaks from his office. Within the next two days, Jeffreys issued three rebuttal statements, including a 19-page letter to Brill. In none of those defensive actions, however, did he deny having given substantive, non-public information to supportive reporters from the *New York Times*, the *Washington Post*, *Newsweek*, and ABC News.

Compounding the disaster, a freelance writer produced tape recordings of conversations with Gedney and Lecraw, documenting the leaking process. "Jeffreys not only approves the leaks," the writer explained to reporters, "but who gets them. That's what was made clear to me—that Jeffreys controls the information, which runs contrary to the Office of Independent Counsel's public statements about its relationship with the news media. Bart Gedney told me he'd like to help me, but he said he'd need Jeffreys' approval. After a month's silence, my publisher Hank Regency phoned Jeffreys directly, and three days later, Walt Lecraw called me back and put me in touch with someone on their staff who provided substantive information. It's further proof that the OIC's investigation of the Cannon White House—regardless of merit—is political, partisan, and punitive, built on a series of well-timed leaks which have turned gossip into gasoline."

It wasn't the first time Jeffreys had been criticized for leaking grand jury material. "From the beginning," Jeffreys had said at a press conference last summer after being chastised for leaking information about the First Lady's billing records, "I have made the prohibition of leaks a principal priority of this office. It is a firing offense, as well as one that leads to criminal prosecution." He allegedly conducted an investigation of his own staff, but no one was ever fired, and no one was ever prosecuted.

"Months have passed," Cannon's attorney Joey Welch complained at a press conference on Monday, "and nothing has been heard about the results of Mr. Jeffreys' alleged 'investigation' of leaks by his staff. We are going to court this morning to seek judicial relief under Rule 6(e) of the Federal Rules of Criminal Procedure. The leaking of the past few weeks is intolerable. It violates the Rules of Professional Conduct of Alabama and the District of Columbia, the ABA Standards for Criminal Justice Relating to Prosecution Function and Fair Trials, the Prosecution Standards of the National District Attorneys Association, Department of Justice guidelines, and the Federal Rules of Criminal Procedure. It also violates the fundamental rules of fairness in an investigation like this. These leaks appear to be a cynical attempt to pressure and intimidate witnesses, to deceive the public, and to smear people involved in the investigation."

"We demand that you withdraw your motion by high noon today," Walt Lecraw replied in a hand-delivered letter to Welch. "Otherwise we will seek sanctions against you and the President, under whose name the motion was submitted."

"The request to withdraw is ridiculous," Welch replied directly to Jeffreys. "We look forward to a hearing on the independent counsel's illegal and unethical press offensive. The present public posturing on your part suggests to me a total loss of perspective. I don't believe that there's ever been a jugular here for you to go for, but in the last several months, you've demonstrated an unerring instinct for the capillary. The solution is to abandon your public relations campaign, get on with your investigation, and bring it to a speedy conclusion."

The motion was not withdrawn, and the judge seemed to share Welch's concerns. "The Court finds that the serious and repetitive nature of disclosures to the media of grand jury material strongly militates in favor of conducting a show-cause hearing," she announced. "The court also finds that movants have established *prima facie* violations of Rule 6(e)(2). Although the court finds that several articles establish *prima facie* violations, the court notes that a *prima facie* case may be established by only one article. The court further finds that the Fox News report regarding Mr. Jeffreys' comment to the press about the court's opinion on executive privilege establishes a *prima facie* violation of Rule 6(e)(2) and a violation of the court's order that the parties receiving the opinion not discuss it with the press."

The press? What was the press, I wondered, and what was I doing watching Geraldo Rivera? Maybe because what passed for news had become so hokey, Geraldo now seemed to be one of the more credible "news" commentertainers on television. He was, in fact, among the first to report the judge's order. "The independent counsel tonight is in real peril himself," Rivera announced, "profoundly threatened by a decision that he show cause why he should not be held in contempt for what the judge feels is a pattern of illegal leaks of secret grand jury information, in which Jeffreys could actually face possible disbarment or even imprisonment. And guess who's paying Jeffreys' legal tab for lawyers to defend himself. You and me, the taxpayers. It will be piled on to the tens of millions his panty raid has already chalked up."

Geraldo also noted that Jeffreys was appealing the judge's order, bringing a biting response from Robert Scheer of the *Los Angeles Times*. "The First Amendment was designed to protect against the official misuse of power, not to abet it. Leaks from Jeffreys never had anything to do with investigative reporting," he said with a touch of exasperation. "His responsibilities do not include convicting the president through leaks of innuendo and fragmented evidence, which involves the media as co-conspirators in suborning due process."

Ronald Noble, former official of the Stuart and Reeder Justice Departments, noted that Jeffreys might have additional legal exposure. "Moreover," Noble added, "Mr. Jeffreys and his staff members are also covered by the Privacy Act, which prohibits disclosing confidential information about individuals. This law covers all Federal employees, not just prosecutors. In short, there are few situations where substantive information on an investigation can be released. And if Jeffreys were permitted to say what he is saying and is prepared to be held accountable for it—why not do so on the record?"

Coming to the defense of his patron, Stuart Sellers tried to discount the seriousness of Jeffreys' transgressions, by saying, "My historical research so far has not turned up a single precedent in which a federal prosecutor was convicted for violating Rule 6(e) by leaking to the press. Those caught leaking have rarely been deemed culpable enough to warrant more than a reprimand."

"Oh, no," protested Harvard Law Professor Clausewitz, "I think George Jeffreys, because he's a former judge and because he set a high standard for himself, should be held to that standard. And he once said, 'The law is the law. And if somebody violates it, he ought to be brought to task.' Well, that same standard ought to be applied to George Jeffreys. He violated rule 6(e) and he ought to be brought to task."

Two days later, just as I had predicted to my students, the Court of Appeals agreed with Clausewitz. "As we have noted before in a case arising from this investigation, grand jurors, prosecutors, stenographers and others are forbidden from disclosing matters occurring before the grand jury—including not only what has occurred and what is occurring, but also what is likely to occur. Encompassed within the rule of secrecy are the identities of witnesses or jurors, the substance of testimony, the strategy or direction of the investigation, the deliberations or questions of jurors, and the like. Such violations of grand jury secrecy are not to be taken lightly, for as Justice Felix Frankfurter warned, 'To have the prosecutor himself feed the press with evidence is to make the State itself through the prosecutor, who wields its power, a conscious participant in trial by newspaper, instead of by those methods which centuries of experience have shown to be indispensable to the fair administration of justice.'"

And as if that weren't enough, that same morning, the District of Columbia Bar Association notified Jeffreys and his top deputies, Walt Lecraw and Bart Gedney, that they were subjects of an inquiry into possible ethics violations. I had found myself too embarrassed to mention in class that I had been watching Geraldo's program on Jeffreys' ethical problems, but it would be acceptable to discuss *Burden of Proof*. Besides, it would mean a legitimate chance to watch Greta in action while pretending to be preparing for a class lecture.

Greta opened the program that afternoon with the first public interview with George Chesterfield, the law professor who had filed the ethics complaint with the bar. "Professor Chesterfield," she asked, already knowing the answer, "what can you tell us about this complaint?"

"I filed it against George Jeffreys and all of the prosecutors, both here and in Alabama," Chesterfield explained. "It seemed to me the Bar of Disciplinary Committees, both in the District of Columbia and Alabama, is about the best we've got, in terms of somebody which could conduct the investigation quietly, without a lot of leaks, and would not be seen as being partisan or favoring one side."

Leading again, Greta asked, "What are you alleging was wrong?"

"I'm alleging very simply, Greta, if there were leaks, as we all know and admit, those leaks would then constitute a felony. So, it is a felony and an ethical violation. The only question is not whether it would be wrong, but rather who did it."

Turning to another guest, a former federal prosecutor, Greta asked, "Larry, is it redundant and piling on?"

"Well, Greta, as you know, lawyers have certain responsibilities, and prosecutors have different and additional responsibilities," he replied. "The Code of Professional Responsibility in the District of Columbia really limits what prosecutors can say about cases that are pending or investigations that are pending."

Greta quickly interjected, "For example?"

"To say, as Judge Jeffreys did, that you can interview a witness immediately before you put them into the grand jury and discuss with reporters what that witness said and that not be violative of 6(e), that's never the way I operated when I was a prosecutor," he explained. "I would have assumed, and most courts assume, that that's something that's covered by 6(e), particularly when the witness is there by subpoena. That's a pretty easy call—it's a clear violation in my view."

Turning to another guest, one of Cannon's polical defenders, Greta asked, "Kiki, what's your reaction to all this? Does this undermine George Jeffreys' moral authority to lead this investigation?"

The woman just smiled and said, "I keep waiting for George Jeffreys to address the nation and apologize for what he's done to the country—for the way he's handled this immoral investigation, the way he's drawn it out by asserting and appealing bogus privileges, the way he's abused his authority and wasted money, the way he stood up at a news conference and lied to the American people about his relationship with certain reporters, and now because it's clear his office illegally leaks like a sieve."

Yeah, right. Jeffreys would never apologize. He was oblivious to the conflicts that had dogged him since he took the job, and he was so sure of his own moral purity. The mote in his eye blinded him to his own transgressions, and he was a true believer on a mission—a mission was to humiliate the President, to do anything it took to get him, and to find something, anything, to hide the utter failure of his own perpetual and petulant investigation. These were things, however, that would have been more appropriate to discuss in a political science class, and I kept those observations to myself, discussing only the legal implications of prosecutors who conduct trials by newspaper and television.

Chapter Forty Two

As the election approached, news coverage of Jeffreys' legal and ethical problems disappeared from the media. The press and the Republicans were looking for something big from Jeffreys during these last few days, possibly a dramatic indictment or a titillating report that might be able to throw the election to Dolor. I knew Jeffreys would have done that by now if he could, but for the last month he'd been going on a bit too much about how it would be improper to announce any indictments before the election. That was a sure sign he didn't have the goods. He just kept saying that to encourage media speculation, to divert attention from his own deeds, and to reinforce the attacks coming from the Dolor camp.

Of course, I could be wrong. The whole idea of using a grand jury to find "truth" was ridiculous. Only one side of the story is presented, double-hearsay testimony is allowed, there is no cross-examination of witnesses, no testing of the veracity of favorable witnesses, no judge to hear objections, no restraints to prevent the prosecution from coaching or scripting witnesses to say things that are untrue, no obligation to present witnesses or evidence favorable to the defendants, and nothing to stop the prosecutors fromtelling whatever version of the story they find most damaging. And, coming up empty of anything approaching impeachable offenses, it wouldn't be beneath Jeffreys and his staff to load up a report full of salacious sexual details just to publicly humiliate and embarrass the President and try to drive him from office.

Kate Macauley was back in Birmingham, working on another "Women of Whirlpool" story, and she drove over to see us on Thursday. She and Lindsey decided they wanted to go to some Halloween party that night. Kate also said she wanted to pump Mitch for some inside information about the woman she was trying to interview, so I called him to invite him along.

"Mitch, Wilkes here. Hope you don't mind me calling you at the office. Would you have any interest in going to a Halloween party with us tonight? Kate's back in town, and she said she'd like to see you again."

"Oh, I was afraid I'd blown that," he mumbled. "I got a little drunk and passed out last time."

"That's not what I heard, you old dog. You must have made a real impression." Actually, Kate had laughed about him passing out and had said she had him figured for "a five hump and dump chump" anyway. But there was no need to share that now.

Of course, Mitch was free. And, of course, he wanted to go.

Driving over to Birmingham, I asked Kate to tell us about the story she was working on. I thought it might be Della Beckwith or Jo Gobles, since she had wanted to talk with Mitch. It wasn't that at all.

She leaned forward, resting her arms on the back of my seat, and asked, "Do you know anything about Jeffreys having a girlfriend in Birmingham?"

"What if he does? What's that got to do with anything? I thought you said you weren't in the scandal business," I said.

"Oh," she responded, somewhat surprised by my questions, "are you now defending Jeffreys?"

"No, and you damn well know what I think about him," I said. "My point was that questions about his personal life don't have anything to do with Whirlpool. It's nobody's damn business. That's all."

"Well, " Kate asked, "that didn't stop him from getting involved in the Christine Putnam lawsuit against Cannon, did it? And it didn't stopped him from sending the FBI out to try to dig up dirt on Cannon's personal life. And it certainly hasn't restrained him in his pursuit of the President for a relationship with Daphne de Clerambault. And I know what he's done, because I've interviewed some of the women he's harassed about that. And it just shows what a hypocrite he is, all that sanctimonious crap about his pristine reputation and family values."

"Still doesn't make it right," I replied, "and it still doesn't make a case that it would have anything to do with the Whirlpool investigation. There are plenty of other things he's done that you can write about without having to hurt a lot of innocent people. Don't ever forget what the press has done to Meredith Roberts and Daphne de Clerambault."

"It might be affecting the investigation if it explained why he's kept it going so long, and why he's still spending so much time in Birmingham," Kate said, undeterred by my pleading. "And it might be affecting the investigation if he were involved with the wife of . . . ."

"It might," I interrupted before she said the name, "but it's not something I'm going to discuss." We pulled into the parking lot at Mitch's apartment complex, and I was relieved that the discussion ended. But I knew Kate was right about one thing—Jeffreys was obsessed with sex. And if he ever got around to writing a final report, it would say more about his own psyche than any legal issues.

The Halloween party was pretty awful. I didn't know anyone else there, so Mitch and I stood around and got smashed, talking about whether anyone could beat Florida. Before too long, though, Mitch felt the need to justify why he was still with Jeffreys and to convince me they had a case against Cannon.

"We think we've got five possible obstruction of justice charges and two perjury charges to include in our report to the House," Mitch said, giving himself an opening to unburden his conscience.

I didn't say anything immediately. Instead, I reached in my coat pocket and pulled out two cigars, a Charles Parnell Double Corona for myself and a Robusto for Mitch. I clipped them both, lit mine, and handed the other to Mitch. Much to my surprise, he reached for my lighter and did the same. My intention was to avoid the topic of the investigation, but the fallback Plan B was to create enough smoke that no one would come near enough to overhear if Mitch insisted on talking about it.

"You know," Mitch began as he exhaled his first draw, "that 'talking points' memorandum is clear evidence of obstruction, or at least subornation of perjury."

"Mitch," I said dismissively, "I remember when that was supposed to be your smoking gun, and I know Jeffreys said it was the key to convincing Otis to let him investigate this deal, but you've got nothing. As I read it, there's nothing in it that Merkin and Daphne hadn't discussed a hundred times, and you've already given them both immunity. According to the leaks from the grand jury, Daphne even said she wrote the document. There's absolutely nothing to connect that to the White House."

"Well, okay," Mitch continued, "but you have to admit that trying to buy Daphne's silence or get her to lie by finding her a job in New York, that's pretty clear. Both Cannon and Montaigne could be guilty of obstruction."

"Three problems there, my friend. Edna Merkin is the one who urged Daphne to ask Cannon for help in getting a job, almost two months before the subpoena, even before she gave Daphne's name to Putnam's lawyers. It's a setup at best. Second, only leaks from Jeffreys to the gullible *New York Times* placed Montaigne's efforts after the subpoena," I said. "And finally, I think Cannon might have been eager to do almost anything to get her out of Washington and out of his life. She was a clutch that wouldn't leave him alone."

Mitch was not deterred. "What about the argument that it's an abuse of power by the President in using the White House's arsenal of lawyers and officials to maintain the deception that there was no improper relationship?"

"What about Jeffreys using OIC lawyers to defend himself in a private legal matter? Or what about him making that bogus 'informers privilege' to hide his illegal leaks of grand jury matters? No difference," I replied.

"Another thing that has not been in the press," Mitch then offered, "is Cannon's own testimony in the Vance-Banaghan trial that he requested a Mr. Ardee to ask Mr. Banaghan to stop talking to the press about Whirlpool. Judge Jeffreys and Gedney say that was part of a post-conspiracy act to conceal or frustrate the government's efforts, witness intimidation or an obstruction of justice."

"Hardly," I laughed. "It was a political move during the 1992 campaign. At the time, you have to remember, there was no government investigation of Whirlpool, Banaghan, or Jefferson Savings."

"What about the gifts," Mitch insisted, "and whether the president conspired with Daphne to conceal them?"

I took a long draw on my cigar, blew a little smoke, and asked, "What about them? What do they prove? Cannon admitted during his deposition that he might have given her gifts, and he even gave her a few more little trinkets after she'd been subpoenaed. Not much there. All you've got to report is an inappropriate relationship and two people who understandably tried to conceal it. If that becomes a crime in this country, Congress might have trouble getting a quorum."

"Yeah, well," Mitch went on, "there's witness tampering. He tried to coach his secretary on her testimony."

"What testiminoy would that have been? She wasn't a witness. Hadn't been subpoenaed in the Putnam case, and neither she nor Cannon had any idea that Jeffreys was looking to get into that in an official capacity," I said as I blew smoke toward the ceiling.

"We've still got a couple of perjury charges. You'll have to admit that. The President has admitted having at least some form of sexual contact, but he testified in his deposition that he couldn't remember having been alone with her. I'd sure remember that," Mitch argued.

I was incredulous. "So that's it? You've torn their life apart, examined every document of their public and professional careers, every aspect of their private lives, and that's all you have? Nothing on Whirlpool? Nothing on the Travel Office? No hush money to Webster? Nothing on the Bankhead billing records? Nothing on Hal Goodall's suicide? Nothing on the FBI files? Nothing on the pork belly contracts? Nothing on Jefferson Savings? So, you're gonna push a perjury charge based on his saying he might have been alone with her but couldn't recall, during an outrageous line of questioning, regarding non-material matters in a civil trial—one tainted, I might add, by collusion between Jeffreys and Putnam's lawyers—that has since been dismissed as having no valid cause of action? Come on, Mitch," I said. "You know there's not a single precedent for that even being a criminal charge in the entire history of American law, much less an impeachable offense!"

"Maybe not," Mitch replied, "but Judge Jeffreys says you can impeach a president for anything, even poisoning the neighbor's cat."

"Oh, get real, Mitch. Impeachment for a parking ticket? You know better than that, and so does Jeffreys" I told him. "The framers intended impeachment to be used only to prevent or stop a president from undermining the constitution or abuse of office in grave matters of state. 'High crimes and misdemeanors' was a term of art that, for the framers, had nothing to do with the kind of chickenshit allegations Jeffreys is trying to make. Read Madison and Mason in the Constitutional Convention, Hamilton in *Federalist 65*, or the early commentaries by James Wilson and Joseph Story."

"But you don't know everything he's got," Mitch replied. "There are also some inconsistencies in Cannon's grand jury testimony, too."

"I'll admit that I haven't seen his grand jury testimony," I conceded, "but I have some real problems with that. Looks like to me that Jeffreys manufactured a situation to try to create a crime. What was the point with that subpoena, anyway, other than trying to humiliate the President? Jeffreys had no constitutional power to compel the President's testimony, and the DOJ Manual clearly discourages subpoenas to any target. The President should have followed Jefferson's example, ignored the subpoena, and told Jeffreys to take a hike. Or, short of that, taken the Fifth on every question after his name. But, of course, Jeffreys would have leaked that and created a political firestorm."

"I think Judge Jeffreys was just trying to be thorough," Mitch said defensively. "He wants to leave no stone unturned."

"I'd say he wants to leave no stone uncast," I retorted.

"Doesn't matter," Mitch said, parroting what Jeffreys always said. "The law's the law, and no one is above the law."

"You think so, Mitch? How do you like that cigar?"

"It tastes good," he said with a satisfied smile.

"Well, sometimes a cigar is just a cigar, but that one you're smoking is a Cuban, substantial and credible evidence that you've violated the 'Trading with the Enemy Act,' a federal felony that carries a penalty of 10 years in prison and a $100,000 fine. You going to turn yourself in to Jeffreys?"

Mitch said nothing, and I took another puff on the contraband. Then, trying to offer more helpful advice, I said, "You know, when James McKay investigated Ed Meese, back in 1986, he found overwhelming evidence that Meese had accepted illegal gratuities from defense contractors. McKay was sure he could get a conviction, but he decided not to do it, said the political spectacle of indicting the Attorney General would be a greater harm than the original offense. He once told me that the decision not to prosecute is often the hardest decision a prosecutor has to make. I hope you'll remember that and give it some thought."

We left the party shortly after that, and the four of us went over to Mitch's place to watch a movie. As he opened the door to his apartment, Mitch flipped on the light and instinctively hit the message button on his answering machine. He was already in the kitchen getting the beer from the refrigerator when I heard that familiar voice.

Everyone seemed to freeze when they realized it was Jeffreys' voice on the recording. He sounded like he was either drunk or suicidal, and we all listened carefully as he said, "Mitch, this is George Jeffreys. Sorry to bother you, but I guess you've heard the news. I recognize now that I blew it. It hadn't crossed my mind that we needed to be accountable, but appearance-wise, it was all bad. Why did it take me so long to realize I'd done something wrong? I was angry and defiant and sometimes bull-headed, because I didn't think I'd done anything wrong. The whole mess is my fault. My best defense is that it was a bad mistake in judgment."

There was a short pause, then a slight sniffling. "I've been think-ing," Jeffreys continued, "with Cannon certain to win in a landslide and the Republicans being so weak, wouldn't it be better for the country to just check out? Seriously, because you see, I'm not at my best. I've got to be at my best. Hope I haven't let you down. Let me say you're a strong man, Mitch, and I love you like a son. I know this has to be a tough thing for you and Walt and Bart and the rest, so I didn't expect you to call right away. Interesting thing, you know, the only Senator who's called is Gastone Diletto, bless his soul. All the rest are waiting to see what the polls show. Really strong party, isn't it? Wish I'd never heard of Whirlpool, and I'm never going to discuss it again—never, never, never, never. When I make a mistake, it's really a butte. Anyway, just wanted to talk. I'm at the Sierra Tucson clinic. Please give me a call when you get in."

We rushed to turn on the television to see what had happened and why Jeffreys had sounded so distraught. The news was on every channel. Senator Robinson was on *Nightline* saying, "Only the Independent Counsel and those who care more about partisanship than justice should be disappointed by today's events. It's clear that George Jeffreys and his desperate henchmen would have stopped at nothing to validate their reckless $50 million inquisition, even if it meant twisting justice to fit their partisan schemes."

My first guess was that news had leaked that the Washington grand jury had refused to indict anyone in the White House or had adjourned without issue. We'd all been on our way to the party and missed the news. We soon discovered what was happening. Jeffreys was busted. At five o'clock that day, too late to make the network news programs, there had been several major announcements in both Washington and Birmingham about developments related to the Whirlpool investigation.

United States Attorney Mary Beech Gould had acted on the Office of Professional Responsibility's referral of James Burgh's complaint. She had secured felony grand jury indictments charging George Jeffreys, Bart Gedney, and John Hathorne with conspiracy to defraud the United States, mail fraud, wire fraud, and three related counts for aiding and abetting. Tim Pickering and Andy Volstead, the two staff attorneys who had represented Jeffreys in the lawsuit, had agreed to plead guilty to conspiracy charges and were cooperating with the investigation. The Alabama Bar Committee on Professional Conduct had temporarily suspended their law licenses, pending formal hearing, for those infractions as well as for leaks of grand jury matters to the media.

In Washington, the DC Bar had taken similar action on Chesterfield's complaint about the leaks, suspending Jeffreys, Gedney, and Lecraw and scheduling a hearing on revocation of their licenses. The district court had also ruled against Jeffreys and his staff on the illegal leaks and the questioning of Daphne de Clerambault without an attorney present. James Angleton had announced indictments of Bart Gedney and others for felonies related to the illegal cash payments to Roby Douglas.

Jeffreys had once proclaimed that you cannot defile the temple of justice, and now those words had come back to bite him on the butt. That was certainly an October Surprise for the media pundits.

Gastone Diletto's familiar face was on the tube. I didn't know what he might have said to Jeffreys, but it was obvious that he'd been reading the polls that showed Cannon close to 60 percent in New York while his own approval rating was less than 30 percent, the lowest for any member of the Senate. Mitch turned up the volume, as Diletto was saying, "It seems to me we should leave Whirlpool in the hands of the American people and not be attempting to substitute our own political judgment. Our job is to work in common toward our shared goals. I think I understand a little bit about holding hearings, but everyone has to make his or her decision. We do not need hearings on the Office of Independent Counsel. The courts are fully competent to handle any criminal charges against Judge Jeffreys and his staff."

Then, there was Jeffreys, blathering before the cameras. His face was puffed, and his eyes were red. "I am more personally humbled than I am anything else, I suppose, because some have suggested that I made a mistake in judgment. There will be those who argue that our investigation is now over. But it would be wrong—indeed, it would be dangerous—to draw any conclusions based upon my personal situation. This is also a difficult experience for my family, especially in light of, you know, we are blessed with children. We have to make plans now as to how we will face an uncertain future."

That was as close as Jeffreys would come to an apology to all the people whose lives he had ruined during his reign of terror. The only thing that surprised me was that the government had conducted the investigations of Jeffreys and his staff and secured the indictments without anything leaking to the press. I had almost concluded that was a lost art.

I looked over and saw that Mitch was crying. When he realized that I had noticed, he said, "I just feel so badly for Judge Jeffreys. Even if he's acquitted, he's finished politically. Now there's no chance he'll ever be nominated for the Court. He won't even be able to continue at Kirk & Polis. What's he going to do?"

"Well," I said, trying to think of something to comfort Mitch instead of mentioning the maximum sentence and the potential for prison ministry, "he can probably get a job at some second-rate law school. Maybe Hostus or one of those California correspondence schools? Or he could write books and go on the revival circuit with Chuck Colson. Maybe even get a radio show like Liddy and Ollie North. And then there's always the possibility of consulting fees from those wingnut foundations he's been helping. I wouldn't worry about Jeffreys. He's always been taken care of by friends in high places."

Lindsey and I left to drive back to Tuscaloosa. Kate went with us. We were all in shock and didn't say much on the way home, but I was somewhat relieved when Kate said she wasn't going to pursue the rumors about Jeffreys. Didn't really matter now. It made me realize, though, that wicked men like Joe McCarthy and George Jeffreys would always rise on hatred and eventually fall on their own sordid lies, but the press would endure—continuing to give credence to the inflamed charges of such legislative lunatics and political assassins, never learning, and never having to account for the damage done to private individuals and public institutions.

Dick Leech, Gastone Diletto, Helmut Duke, Reynolds Rantallion, Attorney General Harriet Otis, Circuit Judge Samuel Chase and his panel that aided and abetted George Jeffreys in his $50 million rampage were accessories-before-the-fact to this obscene governmental peepshow. Louie Fimus was a willing conspirator, and the FBI agents were enthusiastic pawns without the courage to balk. George Jeffreys' wet dream of ending up on the Supreme Court was now gone forever. The only good thing that might come from his investigation was the abolition of the independent counsel office that he so disgraced.

When Kate left the next day to go back to Atlanta, she had said she would see us in Montgomery on election night for the victory celebration. I wasn't so certain that anyone would have much to celebrate, regardless of who won. James Burgh's words kept haunting me, as I remembered him saying, "This movie's not gonna have a happy ending, and there are no heroes." I had been burned and burned out by the whole tawdry affair. I had been miserable working for Jeffreys, and I had seen him ruin people's lives without remorse. I had lost all faith in the role of the corporate media and all hope for the promise of the First Amendment. All that had taken quite a toll, I didn't know if I could ever unring the bell.

The last four years had been a bump and a blur, and I wanted to have a normal life again. I was through with politics. It was no longer a profession for decent people, and Madison's republic was in deep shit. Yet, there I was on election night, standing in the crowd on the capitol lawn in Montgomery, listening to James Madison Cannon making yet another speech and not having a clue as to why he was up there on the stage jabbering away before the polls had closed.

Old habits are hard to break, I suppose, and old times here would not be forgotten. Cannon knew how to summon the memories, sounding like some romantic character in a dusty novel as he said, "For every Southerner, not once but whenever they want it, there is the instant when the polls had not yet closed on that November day in 1992. It was going to begin, we all knew that. We had come too far with too much at stake, and for that moment one didn't even need to be a dedicated Democrat to think, 'This time! Maybe this time with all this much to lose and all this much to gain—New York, Pennsylvania, Illinois, Florida, Ohio, California, the nation, the big white dome of Washington itself—to crown with desperate and unbelievable victory, our desperate gamble, the cast we made four years ago, and the battle we have waged ever since that day.'"

"Four years ago, on these very steps," he intoned to his assembled friends, "we set forth on a journey to change the course of America for the better, to keep the American Dream alive for everyone willing to work for it, to come together as one American community. Diane and I thank the people of our beloved state, and we would not be anywhere else in the world tonight. In front of this wonderful old capitol that has seen so much of our own life and our state's history, I thank you for staying with us so long, for never giving up, for always believing in us. I would never have been elected president if we hadn't done the good things we did along the way. And, I might add, we were all working so hard we didn't have time to do all the things they've accused us of doing."

"I am very, very sorry for the price that too many people in this state have paid for the privilege I've had to serve this country," Cannon said, almost sounding sincere. "My election to the presidency has placed a special burden on the people of Alabama. I deeply regret this relentless, five-year personal-destruction attack that the Republican party and their financial patrons organized and executed. They caught up a lot of people who should never have been put through this ordeal and have hurt a lot of innocent people in our state. Ordinary, middle class people have had their lives wrecked by pure, naked politics. People who were never charged with anything, who have been dragooned and pulled up, who have had tens of thousands of dollars of legal expenses, who were completely innocent, have been subject to abject harassment and false charges. I know how hurt a lot of innocent people were. I know how a lot of Republican politicians and so-called reporters, who have never spent any time down here and don't have a lick of information about what our state's really like, took a lot of cheap shots at us."

"Progressively over the last however many years, we have tended to turn our political differences into legal battles in ways that have had enormous costs—human cost for the people involved in them and for our democracy," he continued, sounding a familiar complaint. "And the thing I really hate is that, when people that are completely innocent are basically confronted with a presumption of guilt and told to prove their innocence of charges, they're not quite sure what they're supposed to do. It's difficult. As far as I'm concerned, for me, it's just part of being in public life today, and I just swat away the bloodsucking Republican mosquitoes and go on with trying to do my job. Right now my heart's full of gratitude. But we should never be happy when innocent people suffer unnecessarily. No one can possibly be for that."

"When this whole process was just gearing up, enlisting all the institutions of the federal government, Congressman Leech said Whirlpool was about the 'arrogance of power.' And, without knowing it," Cannon noted, "he was right in a way. But a lot of people in both parties, I think, are now concerned about the cost as compared with any possible benefit from these abuses of power. So we need to try to seek out people's opinion about what should be done to make sure it does not continue and how we can prevent it from ever happening again."

"Regardless of the outcome of this election, I'm going to devote a lot of my time to trying to cut the cancer out of American politics, to put an end to the kind of systematic abuse so many people have suffered and that our beloved state has suffered. Some day very soon the truth will come out," he promised, just before getting to the point of his premature election speech. "I have just been informed by the Attorney General that, this afternoon in Washington, George Jeffreys submitted his resignation as Independent Counsel and surrendered his license to practice law. I have also accepted the resignation of the Attorney General for her failure to properly supervise the Independent Counsel."

The crowd broke into wild cheering, and some strange woman standing next to me threw her arms around me and kissed me. I missed part of what Cannon was saying, but when the noise subsided after a few minutes, he was telling the mass celebration, "I am reminded of the words of Leon Jaworski during another time in our history when Republican partisans were abusing the law and undermining the Constitution. 'First,' he said, 'our Constitution works. And second, no one—absolutely no one—is above the law.' That is as true today as it was during Watergate.

"I have to tell you that in these last days of the campaign, it has come home to me again, something I first learned as governor, but it wasn't burned in my bones. The anger, the resentment, the bitterness, the desire for recrimination against people you believe have wronged you, they harden the heart and deaden the spirit and lead to self-inflicted wounds. And so, it is important that we are able to forgive those we believe have wronged us even as we ask for forgiveness from people we have wronged.

"Let us now end this long political nightmare that has damaged private lives and delayed public business. Let us restore the Golden Rule to our political process. Let us have the courage and compassion to purge our hearts of suspicion and of hate. Let us begin the healing of our body politic. When I return to Washington tomorrow, I intend to issue a full, free, and absolute pardon to George Jeffreys for all offenses against the United States he has committed or may have committed during his tenure as Independent Counsel. However, a pardon cannot grant moral absolution. As the poet Shelley said, 'Those who inflict must suffer, for they see the work of their own hearts, and this must be our chastisement or recompense.'"

There were those in the media who would say Cannon had wimped out again, and there were many in Alabama who probably would have agreed. Ford and Stuart had issued pardons for their political friends and patrons; Cannon only issued them for his enemies. I'd heard that he had always been like that, though, rewarding those who opposed him and shafting those who stood by him. I wasn't really sure how I felt, except I knew I was too sober to be listening to his speech.

Then, I almost screamed, "Tally Ho!" when I saw Lindsey coming my way through the crowd. She put her arm through mine, and I gave her a big hug.

We turned back to listen as Cannon was finishing his speech, which would probably be the first of many that evening. As I held Lindsey's hand and realized how lucky I was, Cannon could have been reading my mind when he said, "On this beautiful night, it is hard for me to believe some of the things that have happened during the last four years. The most lasting and important thing that I have learned during the last four years is this: When we are divided, we defeat ourselves. But, when we join our hands and build our families and our communities and our country, America always wins. Our best days are still ahead."

Well, maybe. I certainly held high hopes for my personal life that night. And, at least, I didn't think the political future would be much worse than the past. And probably not much better until the people get tired of the politics of personal destruction, quit settling for that crap they now call news, and demanded better of the politicians. And of themselves.